Savarra and McLean wr_____ ____ dappled darkness. His finger_ _____ arms. She pulled away and with a last violent gesture she flung the pistol at him. It missed by a wide margin and fell with a thud on the leafy ground.

McLean was on her swiftly, his big body covering hers. Savarra, in a tumult of fury, stared up into the face above hers. Then without the slightest warning, he brought his mouth down and she turned to meet it.

Their lips came together with sweet and stunning force. An electric vitality opened up within Savarra. Passions burst like a tide in her. She was suddenly afraid and she didn't know why. No one had ever warned her where passion could lead.

"The author of the bestselling *Banner Bold and Beautiful* and, as Annabel Erwin, of *Liliane* is back with a longer, juicier, nicely plotted and far more readable historical romance."
—*Publishers Weekly*

FIREBRAND

Ann Forman Barron

A FAWCETT GOLD MEDAL BOOK

Fawcett Publications, Inc., Greenwich, Connecticut

For my four darlings
Barbara, Robin, Kim and Kirsten

FIREBRAND

© 1977 Ann Forman Barron

ISBN 0-449-13863-1

Printed in the United States of America

10 9 8 7 6 5 4 3 2 1

One

Savarra looked at her father, Lord Bainbridge, across the dinner table from beneath the black crescents of her thick lashes. The fever to reach Peter Haverley burned higher and hotter within her, but she quelled it firmly. She could wait. She *must* wait. The classical planes of her slim face were smooth, her brow serene.

This last of April, 1780, had been unseasonably cold in England, and a bright fire leaped and crackled cheerfully in a broad black fireplace at the end of the great dining hall of the Bainbridge town house.

Lord Bainbridge was speaking in his clipped British voice to old Lord Ashford, their single guest this evening. "Why they put a man like Germain in as Secretary of State for the colonies escapes me." Her father's voice was cold and level. "I was with my father at the battle of Minden in 'fifty-nine—near the Weser River in Germany. I saw and heard the order given him to charge, four times, and he ignored it. I was not quite seventeen at the time and I was enraged. The court-martial should have ended his career."

"A pity it didn't," Lord Ashford commented, smoothing back his white mustaches under his great beaked nose. He had fought with Clive in India years before. Savarra could remember his tales of it, when he had held her on his lap as a little girl. His booming voice would have ordinarily made her sleepy, *but not tonight!* His voice rumbled on, "And he's conducting the efforts to put down the American rebellion very poorly. Very poorly indeed. The whole bloody business should have been ended four years ago, yet we're into the sixth year of it. Any fool should know it's impossible to direct troops from three thousand miles away." Lord Ashford laughed dryly, adding, "I understand he writes to Clinton and Cornwallis and their letters cross en route. Germain's orders are always out of date."

"Lord Cornwallis should have authority to conduct the

war as he sees fit. He's the better man of the three. I know
Charles well," her father said curtly. His voice was deep,
appealing, and Savarra knew a sharp pang of guilt for she
loved her father dearly. Peter had been their first real disagreement. Now he was saying reflectively, "Germain's bone-
lazy and an arrant coward, and now that we are at war with
Spain and France once more, the drain on our armed forces
is tremendous."

Savarra only half listened. In her mind she was flying
down the dark street to where her lover waited.

Lord Ashford agreed. "I know, James. We're fighting from
the Spanish seas to the Bay of Bengal and in between. I had
hoped at the end of the Seven Years' War, we might know
many years of peace."

Savarra's father said dourly, "The French have in common
with the British the inability to accept defeat. And now, of
course, they have thrown their lot in with the Americans.
'Tis laughable—to witness a despotic government coming to
the aid of men who profess to be fighting for liberty." His
voice had grown faintly sarcastic and Savarra's foot tapped
impatiently under the table where the men could not see. Not
by look or movement of her smooth face did she betray her
restlessness.

"Politics and wars, my dear James, make strange bed-
fellows." Lord Ashford set down his empty goblet.

Sir James called, "Brim!"

The door to the kitchen opened and the tall, balding butler
stepped in. "Another round of brandy for us, Brim." Then
courteously to his daughter, "My dear, will you have another
glass of wine?" and Savarra shook her head, smiling.

She sat dutifully as they drank their brandy and listened
politely and with feigned interest to their conversation, which
went on interminably in discussion of the wretched American
colonies which had given Great Britain so much trouble for
so long a time. The war with them had dragged on until now
—over five years. Savarra had grown up listening to tales of
war, for her father was a soldier of the crown. He was a
brigadier now and just home from India, where he had been
fighting the French.

When Savarra's mother had died a year and a half ago of
the pox, it had struck her father with stunning force and he
had gone almost immediately to India to nurse the deep
wound her passing had dealt him. Now he had been home
nearly six months and had suddenly taken his duties as a

father greatly to heart, causing Savarra discomfiture, for she had become quite independent during his absence and had fallen deeply in love with Lord Haverley's only son, Peter.

It was not that Lord Bainbridge objected to her marrying, for she was nearly eighteen. He objected to Peter. He had said bluntly, "I do not believe the man intends to marry you, Savarra."

"Then what do you think he means when he says he loves me?" Savarra asked with cold pride.

"Peter Haverley is—" Lord Bainbridge hesitated, choosing his words carefully, "a handsome rake, who takes great pride in being the first with young maidens. He has seduced half the daughters of the gentry about London." His voice hardened. "And I'll not have him pursuing you."

It had meant meeting Peter slyly for the past six months, over which Savarra suffered qualms of conscience. Now she planned to elope with him to Bath. Tonight, if the eternal dinner with the windy Lord Ashford ever came to an end.

Now Lord Ashford downed the last of his brandy and said, "I understand it has been planned to invade the southern colonies at long last—a move I advocated four years ago in a chat with Lord North, but little attention he or Germain paid me. Anyway, the king is, for all purposes, his own prime minister and he does as he pleases."

Lord Bainbridge replied somewhat glumly, " 'Tis said we will take Charles Town at last, on the coast of the South Carolina colony."

"I am surprised, James, that you are not with them," Lord Ashford said, eyes a-twinkle, and Savarra gave her father a sharp glance. "If I were a young man of thirty-eight, I'd be with them, you may be sure. We *need* those colonies—the riches of America will dwarf those of India, mark my words."

Lord Bainbridge shot his daughter a quick look from vivid blue eyes and she met them with her own, so like his, despite her mother's olive skin and blue-black hair. "I would," he said slowly, "but I have left Savarra too much since her mother's death. I think she needs me more. Isabella's death has thrown her too much on her own as it is."

Savarra's mother had been Dona Isabella de Savarra y Cordoba. From her, Savarra had inherited the steel pride of her conquistador ancestors as well as a part of her family name. The aristocratic Isabella had brought her daughter up to maintain that pride under any circumstance. But Savarra had also inherited her mother's fierce passions and her father's inflexible will and, with his will, his daring, which had made him such an invaluable soldier of the crown.

They had been a beautiful pair, the black-eyed, black-haired Spanish beauty and the broad-shouldered, slim-hipped soldier with his shock of fair hair and blazing blue eyes. It had not occurred to Savarra to wonder how they came together until she was near fourteen. Then, in response to her questioning, her mother told her she and her duenna had been passengers on a Spanish galleon on their way to the islands where her father was a governor, when they had been captured by two ships of the British navy. As a Spanish noblewoman, she and her duenna had been guests of His Majesty, George II, until the cessation of hostilities between Great Britain and Spain. She had fallen in love with Lord Bainbridge when that event failed to take place within the year and married him.

Though the wars that went on continually kept him away much of the time, the love between Isabella and Lord Bainbridge had been deep and passionate. Savarra was, to their sorrow, the only offspring—not that they loved her the less, but they had wanted a large family. As a result, Savarra had been indulged somewhat. She wanted her way more often than not and she did not accede to discipline with grace.

Now she was in a fever of impatience for these two men to rise from the long mahogany table and eventually find their way to their beds. Then she would silently slip from the house with her small valise, long ago packed, to meet Peter at his home.

Lord Bainbridge was not only a brigadier general in the British army, he also possessed great lands and three manor houses in the countryside not too far from London, bestowed by a grateful king upon his great-grandfather, who, like his father before him, had also rendered great service to the crown. Now Savarra silently thanked God that her father had not decided to take her this early spring to one of the country manors. That would have made meeting Peter impossible.

Now Brim, tall, spare, impeccable of manner, who served not only as butler but as valet to Lord Bainbridge, came and cleared away the dinner things and the men rose. Savarra followed them obediently to the great, shadowy library, where they filled their pipes and sat down to further conversation beside a flickering fire.

"You may retire it you like, Savarra. Benjamin and I will

visit a while longer before he leaves." Lord Bainbridge smiled at his daughter. He was an extraordinarily handsome man and could have married again, for women pursued him shamelessly. Savarra had been grateful that he ignored their blandishments, for the memory of her mother was still vivid in her heart as was deep grief at her loss. Further, she did not fancy a stepmother, even though she realized it would take some of her father's surveillance off herself.

She made a polite and respectful farewell to Lord Ashford, bade her father goodnight and joyously took her leave. As she reached the stairs, lit by wall lamps, she caught up her full skirts and petticoats and pulled them high to take the steps at a run. In her room at last, she let excitement take her fully. Her heart beat hard and, by the light of the oil lamp that Cotty, her favorite among the maidservants, had lit for her, she peered into the mirror at brilliant eyes and flushed cheeks. Savarra's was a slender face, eyes extraordinarily wide apart. Her lower lip was full and the upper short and deeply curved, indicative of a tender heart, despite the temper and pride revealed in the cut of her features and the short straight nose.

Cotty had laid a small fire to take the spring chill off the room and Savarra shed her dinner dress swiftly, but not her petticoats. She forced herself to move more slowly. No need to be ready too far ahead of time. She would have to wait until the house was very still and sleep was on all its inhabitants, including her alert father. It would probably be as late as two-thirty in the morning. Peter had said he would expect her at any time after that and that he would be waiting. His father's London town house was but three squares over from the Bainbridge town house and his parents were away at their country estate for a fortnight. The two of them had decided it would be safer for Savarra to come to Peter than for Peter to risk meeting her father at two-thirty of a morning, surreptitiously approaching the imposing Bainbridge mansion.

Savarra lay down on the broad bed and allowed her thoughts free rein. She and Peter would be married immediately and possibly go to his father's second estate in Leicester after a honeymoon in Bath. Peter's family would be well pleased with the match—Peter had often said so. Now the prospect of being alone with him set her pulses pounding. Peter was tall and slender and handsome. In their stolen trysts over the last six months, they had kissed and caressed until Savarra found it hard not to succumb to him entirely. Ah, but now he was going to marry her and her strange and powerful new desires could at last be fulfilled.

Time dragged on. Savarra was wide-eyed. Tucking be-ruffled petticoats about her legs, she slipped between the covers in the event her father came in to bid her goodnight, as he often did since his return six months ago.

It was fortunate that she did so, for within the hour he rapped softly on her door and, receiving no answer, came in to sit upon the edge of the large testered bed and place his lighted candle upon the bedside table.

He sat silently for a moment while she feigned sleep and hoped fervently that he would leave.

"Don't play the game with me, Savarra," he said suddenly, laughter in his voice. "You are no better now at holding those long black lashes still than you were at five—and were not quite, but almost as naughty as you are now."

Her eyes flew open. Without volition, she said, "You don't really know Peter at all, father—only what jealous people have told you about him, just because he's handsome and women will scarce leave him alone!"

"Aye, and he meets them more than halfway. I know it well."

"He does not!"

"And think you to find happiness with such a one? The more fool you, Savarra. A man who says women will not leave him alone is one who *cannot* leave them alone."

"He doesn't—" she began, then broke off. She *was* a fool to argue with her father at this point. She had merely to allay any suspicions, for tomorrow she would be a married woman and free of all restraints. Only Cotty knew of her plan—for she had helped Savarra pack—and it was she who would lock the door behind her in the dark hours of the night. She repressed a shiver of excited fear. Her father was on familiar terms with violence and if he thought Peter Haverley were waiting for her in the darkness, he could well kill him. And get by with it too, for all that Peter was a lord's son.

She said coolly, "*You* don't need to fear. You have already forbade me to see him."

"And when would forbidding stop you, daughter?" He was smiling again, that endearing smile she loved so well. "Nay, I shall watch over you carefully until you recover from this fever, for I'll not have you wed a scoundrel."

"So you have said, father," she replied indifferently, "and you have convinced me. She hated dissembling with her father for she not only loved him but respected him deeply, and she knew he took enormous pride in her. He was proud of her graduating with honors from Miss Latour's School for Young Ladies, he was proud of her beauty and her resemblance to him and his beloved Isabella.

He said persuasively, "Now if you were to consider Colonel Scott Coyne, I'd settle a dowry on you that would see you in luxury for the rest of your life—and Scott's, too. And you'd fall heir to my estates as well through your son."

She bit her tongue to hold back a cry of rage. "I'll think about it, father."

"You sound suspiciously reasonable of a sudden," he said alertly.

"Well—you didn't say I *have* to marry Scott."

He pulled at his square, cleft chin thoughtfully. "That's true enough."

Lieutenant Colonel Scott Coyne was a nice enough young man in Lord Bainbridge's regiment when he was in India last year and had distinguished himself under her father's command there. His father was only a merchant, but a wealthy one. Handsome though Scott Coyne might be, she was indifferent to him when she compared his appearance with that of the tall, urbane Peter Haverley. She knew Scott would gladly court her, for his clear brown eyes had been openly admiring each time they met, months ago. But he was safely far away in America now, serving under Lord Cornwallis.

"Father, do go to bed and stop worrying about me. I shall do nothing to displease you." She again put down a fleeting guilt at the easy lie, as she stifled a yawn to accentuate her desire to sleep.

Sir James picked up his candle, brushed her cheek briefly and made his departure. Savarra took up her vigil eagerly. She could see the clock face on the mantel dimly by the light of the dying fire, but she could not discern the hour.

After a few minutes, she slipped warily from the covers and went to peer at it closely in the gloom. Only twelve-thirty! Her father would probably be another hour going to sleep. She scampered back to bed. She would not put it past him to return for another admonition, so fiercely and paternally suspicious had he become. She lay there with fast-beating heart as the moments dragged by, and when at last Cotty slipped silently into the room and stirred up the fire, she felt a great gust of relief. It would all go as she hoped! In just a little while she would meet with Peter in the gardens behind his town house.

Cotty whispered hoarsely, "Mistress?" Cotty Penderford was a pretty, plump dumpling of a girl and blonde as honey. "I brought yer valise—'tis precious little yer takin'."

Savarra threw back the covers. "Peter will buy a new wardrobe for me in Bath when we reach there, Cotty," she said, hastily pulling on the new pale-blue silk with flowered panniers from her tall armoire. Her father had chosen it for her only the week before, and again she knew a brief flash of regret over the lies she had told him.

"Ye'll never know how scairt I been, hidin' this valise in me bedroom," Cotty muttered, pushing back her fair, curling hair with a quick hand. "If the master ever finds out what I done to help ye, he'll kill me," then in a whisper, "an' I'll deserve it."

"What did you say?" Savarra demanded fiercely.

"Nothin'," the girl responded, lacing up her mistress's bodice hastily. "Yer want I should fix yer hair?"

"No," she replied, going to the commode table, above which hung a mahogany-framed mirror. It was a beautiful, flawless beveled mirror, oval in shape and taller than Savarra. It was tilted forward in order that she might see the whole of herself by candlelight. It had been her mother's, and Savarra knew a small catch of fresh grief, despite the eighteen months that had passed since Dona Isabella's unexpected death.

Cotty held a scarlet wool-lined cape over her rounded arm. " 'Tis cold for April, mistress." Her young voice grew worried. "I'm scairt for you to go out on the streets alone—ain't you?"

"Of course not," Savarra replied with rash courage. As a matter of fact, she did not look forward to the three long squares she must traverse to reach Peter's dark garden. She looked down at the valise with disfavor. She would hurry— she might even run the whole way. But the valise would slow her. Savarra stooped, opened it and swiftly crammed a fresh chemise and cologne into her large reticule. "I shan't take the valise after all, Cotty," she said quickly.

"But mistress! Yer chemises—yer nightdress an' toilette articles an'—"

"I shall buy all that in Bath," Savarra said. "Right now I can move much faster without them."

Cotty stood looking at her with a mixture of fear and admiration. There was something else in her round, dimpled face that was unsettling to Savarra. She noted then that Cotty still wore her maid's clothing instead of a nightdress.

Now the maid hesitated beside Savarra, adjusting the flowered silk panniers on either side of the full and luxurious skirt, then tightened the laces of the bodice and adjusted the draped stomacher.

"Give me the cape. I must be off," Savarra said impatiently, and Cotty flung the scarlet-lined garment about her shoulders.

"Seems a pity not to put yer beautiful hair up," Cotty said regretfully.

Savarra loathed the style now prevalent, powdering, rolling into elaborate curls, piling all over a piece of padding until she looked to be a tower of hair and all of it dull gray.

"Never mind." She brushed the long straight fall of thick black hair. "I shall tie it with a ribbon. I haven't time for all that great to-do," and she did so with a red velvet band that matched the flowers in her panniers and her heavy cape.

"Yer so pretty, mistress," Cotty said mistily, her blue eyes suspiciously bright. "I shall miss ye somethin' dretful."

"And I shall miss you, Cotty, dear," Savarra said, giving the maid a hug. Savarra's was a quick, warm heart and she could be exceptionally kind to those she loved, despite her hot temper. "I must fly now."

When they went into the chilly hall and took the dark stairs, neither of them whispered a word. The great house where Savarra had grown up was very still.

At the door, she glanced around to see that Cotty had thrown a cloak over her dress. The maid whispered with a sudden show of defiance, "I'm goin' to walk with ye, mistress. Far as 'is lordship's house."

"But you needn't, Cotty," she protested, whispering herself.

"Two be safer'n one, mistress," she said stubbornly.

"But I'm going straight to Peter Haverley!"

Cotty's voice, to Savarra's horror, rose slightly. "I'll just go so far as to see ye safe with him."

"Hush! You'll rouse my father and there'll be the devil to pay!"

"Oh, mistress—ye be talkin' so rough!" She followed Savarra out the door and closed it quietly behind her.

"Well, hurry on then," was the fierce reply. "It must be well past two by now." Then warningly, "As soon as I meet Peter, you must hurry back home and act as if you know nothing in the morning."

Cotty made no answer, panting a little as she kept pace

with Savarra's flying feet. The little narrow slippers Savarra
wore, with their curved wooden heels, threatened to turn her
ankle, but she was strong from an active life spent as much
in the country as in the city, and much of that on horseback.
Now she hastened on.

Halfway there, Cotty began to speak in a gasp, "Ah, 'tis
so afraid I am to meet the master in the mornin'. If he
suspects I had to do with this, he'll fair skin me!"

Savarra turned on her. "You swore you'd hold your
tongue," she said accusingly. "You *must* do so until Peter and
I have time to be married and get out of London. He has a
minister who will meet us within the hour to perform the
marriage. Cotty, if you tell too soon, I shall kill you if father
doesn't."

"But yer so young—ye just finished yer schoolin'," the
maid lamented, then fell silent as the two fled along the dark
street, past the silent, black-windowed houses. There was very
little light for there was no moon, only stars in the broad
arch of the sky above them. The great city of London was
wrapped in sleep, except for the beating heart of it, where
the younger rake-hells gambled and drank in the taverns and
clubs they frequented. And possibly there were the older,
more serious ones still up in Whitehall, where they plotted
and sweated over the miserable war between Britain and the
colonies now that France and Spain and even Holland had
taken up the colonists' quarrel.

Briefly Savarra thanked God that Peter, despite military
training, was not hotheaded enough to get his father to buy
him a commission and go off to fight in the wars. She felt
nothing but contempt for the Englishmen in the colonies,
calling themselves Americans, polyglot mixture that they
were, fighting the mother country which had saved them
during the French and Indian wars, which bought their
products and was even now prepared to protect them from
other enemies. Thankless crew they were, she thought, some
primal instinct rising out of her father's soldiering. They
deserved to be crushed and subdued.

Suddenly they were there. The Haverley town house loomed
up, dark and forbidding. Cotty and Savarra hastened along
the high wall surrounding the rear, where a gate stood open
into the gardens. Inside, Savarra discerned Peter sitting on
a marble bench near the fountain. She slammed the gate and
cried, "Peter, my darling—"

He rose swiftly and came to sweep her into his arms,

pushing back the hood of her cape. He kissed her deeply and tenderly, his mouth firm and warm against hers.

"Oh, Peter," she sighed, still clasped in his arms. "I thought the time would never pass. Let's leave at once for the minister's—or is he here? Have you our horses saddled?"

"My love, the minister came by but a few moments ago and told me one of his parishioners is dying and he must be with him. We must wait until morning to be married." His deep voice was distressed and he pulled her to him once more, kissing her again.

Cotty, beside them, said hesitantly, "Mistress Savarra, I'll go back now I know you're—here."

"Run, Cotty," Savarra told her, "so you'll be safe, too. And remember, you know nothing!"

When the maid had vanished, closing the gate behind her, Savarra said, "Shall we wait in the garden for daylight? I am so afraid, Peter, that if my father finds me gone in the morning, he will come looking for me here."

"We shall leave at dawn, Savarra, and find another minister if old Settle is still with his parishioner. I will have the servants saddle up our mounts and we shall leave at first light—on second thought, we shall take the carriage. No one can see and recognize us then."

He had taken her hand and was leading her toward the house. They mounted the stone steps and entered through the rear.

"Why not leave now, Peter?" Savarra asked uneasily. "I think 'twould be safer if we did."

"At this hour? All my servants are asleep, love, and we should rest as well, so that we will be fresh in the morning."

"You mean we should—go to bed and sleep until dawn?"

"I don't want my darling too exhausted to enjoy her honeymoon."

Savarra hesitated. "My father rises very early, Peter."

"Ah, don't worry about him. Cotty will hold her tongue and we shall be well on our way before His Lordship can put spur to horse."

He took up a candle in the darkness, struck flint and the flame flared up. He gave it to Savarra and lit another from it for himself. "Come, dear. I will show you to your room. You can rest there till dawn."

She followed him through the great hall and up the long staircase, her uneasiness increasing. Peter did not know her father as well as she did. His fury would be cold and quiet, but it would know no bounds if he were to discover she was running away with this man he held in such contempt.

At a loss, she followed Haverley into a bedroom. "You will sleep here, Savarra," he said, gesturing to a wide four-poster. "And I shall be in the next room, my dear."

"I brought no—nightdress, Peter. I left my valise so I would not have to carry it."

"Then sleep in your chemise—or better yet, without it." His grin in the light of the candle was mischievous. "Would you like me to help you unlace and get into bed?" His tone was low and intimate, and she quivered with sudden desire mingled with fear.

"No," she said, thinking of her proud mother and what she would say if she knew of the intimacy her daughter was sharing with Lord Haverley's son.

"Ah." He slipped the cape from her shoulders and bent to kiss the back of her neck lingeringly, brushing the long hair aside with a tender hand. "We will be married tomorrow, Savarra. Who's to know?"

A delicious languor crept over her as his firm, strong hands caressed her, fitted themselves about her waist and pulled her tightly against his hardening body. He kissed her slowly and expertly—an expertise Savarra was too young to recognize. She knew only that it was disturbing and she wanted more.

But he stopped and said, "I'll leave you now to undress, my love. Remember, I shall be in the next room if you need me."

After the door closed behind him she began slowly to disrobe. She could not lie down in the petticoats and full panniered skirts of her best dress. She wanted to look as lovely as possible on her wedding day. After the dress came the petticoats, one by one, until she stood in the chill room in her thin silk chemise. She went to the basin at the commode table, poured water from the pitcher into it and bathed her face and hands. She had neglected to put comb and brush into her large reticule, so she untied her hair and prepared to climb up the three wooden steps into the bed.

As she stood poised at the bedside, the door between the two rooms opened. The candle beside the bed guttered in the sudden wind. Peter stood there in his dressing gown. His handsome face was flushed and his dark hair in attractive disarray. The hazel eyes, almost gold now, were tender. He came toward her, hands outstretched appealingly

"How can I sleep, Savarra—knowing you are so near and I want you so desperately?"

"We must wait," she said confusedly. Her own passions were rising. It was the cold will of her father that made her protest. "It will not be long, Peter."

He continued approaching and she felt very vulnerable in the scanty underclothing she now wore. She tried to tell herself that it was all right for her future husband to see her so unclothed and she fought the urge to clutch up the bedding beside her and swathe it about her naked limbs.

"If you only knew how beautiful you are—with your hair so black, tumbling about your waist, and those astonishing blue eyes of yours gleaming." He reached for her and pulled her closely to him. "Let us not deny ourselves the sweetness of our love because of a few short hours."

He reached downward, catching one of her high, pointed breasts in his hand, lifting it from the chemise to bend his head and kiss it tenderly. His breath was hot and sweet against her flesh.

Still Savarra fought against the tide of desire that was sweeping her to him. "We shouldn't, Peter. Oh, Peter, don't kiss me like that—please!"

But he swung her up into his arms and was making his way to the bed with her. She had just begun to struggle, for he had pulled the chemise from her upper body and her breasts were bare under his warm lips.

It was at this moment the door from the hall to the bedchamber burst open. The young lovers halted, frozen at the edge of the bed, as Lord Bainbridge, sword drawn, stepped into the room.

"Put her down, Haverley." His voice was quiet and deadly cold. "Savarra, get your clothes on immediately."

Peter set her on her feet and she pulled the chemise up to cover her breasts. Her father strode forward, his swift, smooth passage scarcely fluttering the lone candle beside the bed. He lifted his sword and with one stroke cut the belt on Peter's dressing gown, and it fell apart, revealing his naked body.

Savarra stared in hypnotized astonishment at her first sight of a nude male body. Peter looked very white and vulnerable, and the passion she had known ebbed quickly under an avalanche of fear.

Pressing the point of his sword delicately into Peter's navel,

Lord Bainbridge said, "You planned this, did you not? With promises of marriage, you planned to seduce my daughter."

Peter stumbled over his words. "I—we—we *are* going to be married in the morning, Lord Bainbridge."

"That is a lie. I know your mode of operation well, Haverley, and I believe you had no intention of doing other than ravishing my daughter." His voice was heavy with contempt. "I have heard of your collection of maidenheads." He prodded with the sword and Peter Haverley shrank once more. Perspiration appeared on his forehead and he looked very undignified and rather pitiable standing there with his open dressing gown revealing his most private parts.

"Admit it," Lord Bainbridge spoke in the same quiet voice, "or I'll run you through here and now. There's not a jury in all England that would convict me—finding my seventeen-year-old daughter in imminent danger of rape. All that talk of the minister called to a dying parishioner was only to give you time for seduction, wasn't it?" He gave the sword a sudden thrust and Peter Haverley flinched and shrank further.

Cotty! Savarra thought with rage. She had run straight to Lord Bainbridge!

"I—for God's sake, Lord Bainbridge, don't kill me! I admit that it was a lie about the minister—but I *am* going to marry her. I *swear* it! I just didn't want to wait. Savarra's very beautiful and I love her devotedly. On my honor, sir!"

"Get those clothes on, Savarra," he spoke to his daughter again, "unless you want to witness my killing this blackguard."

Savarra flew into her petticoats and hastily let the dress down over her head, lacing the bodice with awkward fingers. Peter had lied to her, and in another five minutes he would have possessed her wholly. But he *loved* her and she loved him, argued her heart. Suddenly the affront to her pride, the awful indignity of the situation, took hold and her back grew ramrod straight. Her blue eyes blazed at her father.

"You're—you're not going to kill me, are you, Lord Bainbridge?" Peter asked. His pale face was resolute and there was a proud lift to his chin as he found his courage.

"That depends. Did he have his way with you, Savarra?"

"No!" she burst out.

"Then you live, Haverley. But I swear before God, if you come sniffing about my house or my daughter again, I shall call you out and kill you." He sheathed the sword slowly, his eyes narrow with fury in the candlelight.

"But I love Savarra, Lord Bainbridge," Peter protested, his jaw set.

"Love?" Sir James was contemptuous. "What do you know of love? You *lust* after my daughter! I'll kill you, I vow, if you come near her again."

Savarra looked into Peter Haverley's face as the color slowly returned to it. He caught up the sides of his robe to bring them over his nude body. She realized with sudden intuition that her father had spoken the truth, yet there was a subtle changing in Haverley's face, a stubborn kindling of the golden eyes as he glanced at Savarra. She responded to what she saw there.

"I love Peter, father," she said proudly, "and I will not give him up."

Lord Bainbridge turned on his daughter. "Knowing that he tricked you, lied to get you into his bed, you can still say that? By God, I've sired a damned fool!"

Pride and certainty fired Savarra's face and the ivory cheeks glowed. "He loves me—I *know* it. We shall be married today!"

Encouraged, Peter came from around Lord Bainbridge and moved toward her, but Lord Bainbridge stepped between them. "You'll not be married today or any other day. If I must save you from folly by force, so I will." The sword flew into his hand again and Peter Haverley stepped hastily back from Savarra.

"Get back into the other room, Haverley—at once." The sword swept menacingly near and Haverley, holding his robe with one hand, moved quickly to open the door and step through it. "As for you, you young chit, come with me." And her father caught up the candle, almost extinguishing it with the quickness of the movement.

She forgot her reticule and, to her mortification, Savarra felt tears gather as her father herded her before him to the door. With the candle guttering dangerously, he half-pushed, half-guided her down the dark stairs and out the door to the front of the house, where his horse stood at the hitching post.

He threw the candle aside and with quick violence sheathed his sword once more. He swung Savarra roughly up into the saddle before him and the two set off at a swift pace through the dark streets, the horse's hooves ringing against cobblestones.

"This will do no good," Savarra said between her teeth as they jolted along. "I will find a way to meet and marry him."

"The need to marry you, Savarra, would have vanished with the morning light," Lord Bainbridge said dryly. "I had hoped you could read a man's character better than this, your tender years notwithstanding. Your Haverley has done this before and he will do it again—now. His greatest joy—and his boast in enough taverns—is to be the first to deflower young virgins."

"I do not believe that lie! He loves me."

Lord Bainbridge swore softly under his breath, but he made no reply as they turned in the carriage drive of the Bainbridge house.

There were lights gleaming from two downstairs windows and Savarra said bitterly, "Cotty told you, didn't she?"

"She certainly did, when I caught her sneaking back into the house. Even Cotty knew the story about the minister was a lie. Your maid is smarter than you are."

"I'll never trust that girl again."

"No more shall I trust you, daughter."

In the days that followed, Peter Haverley attempted to smuggle a note to Savarra and it was promptly delivered by Cotty into Lord Bainbridge's hands. He proceeded to read it aloud to Savarra, who was confined to her room and kept there by the vigilant butler, Bartholomew Brim, and a bevy of housemaids. Savarra refused to speak to Cotty, which caused the maid to cry frequently.

The note was not very satisfactory anyway, for in it, Peter told her only that he loved her, over and over again, and that they would find a way to be married soon. This latter was far too vague to satisfy Savarra, who by now was in such a towering rage at her father she alternated between the desire to kill him and to beg him for sympathy.

Her love for his years of kindness to her fought with her fury at his obstinate rejection of Peter. Her feelings were a mixture, and pride was the iron rod that ran through the humbling knowledge that Peter *had*, after all, attempted to seduce her. Still, an instinct deeper than her own desires told her he was sincere in his wish to marry her *now*.

She had almost decided that she would try to slip past Brim and the maids and run away, though she had but a few sovereigns in her new reticule, when her father came home from Whitehall and told the servants to begin packing. He was going to America to help subdue the colonies. Hope Tennison, the second upstairs maid, told her this news.

At first, Savarra was overjoyed. This meant she would have the big house to herself, and she knew well enough that without Lord Bainbridge there she could bully the servants into doing what she wished. But her joy was short-lived, for her father came to her bedroom that very evening.

He looked exceptionally handsome in his scarlet-coated uniform as he stood before her and said coldly, "You will pack your things, Savarra, for you are coming with me to America, where I shall serve with Lord Cornwallis. You will travel there by freighter with Cotty and Brim. I shall go with my men in one of three ships of the line that are being sent to reinforce General Clinton."

"I won't go," Savarra said flatly.

"Yes, you will," her father said grimly. "I shall see to it."

At the implied threat, her back stiffened. "Would you beat me, father?" she asked sarcastically.

"I'm sure you won't make that necessary, Savarra." For a moment, he looked about to laugh, which was fuel to Savarra's anger.

"Suppose," she said with studied coolness, "I simply sit down and refuse to move?"

Cotty stood slightly back of Lord Bainbridge and her rosy face paled slightly. But Lord Bainbridge said indifferently, "Then we should have to put you in a litter and carry you aboard H.M.S. *Lion.*"

"Suppose I kick and scream?"

"That should be very interesting to the bystanders, who would all no doubt feel great sorrow for your poor father, saddled with a mad daughter." He turned and left the room.

Cotty Penderford said cautiously, "Yer want to start packing now, mistress?"

Savarra said scathingly, "You can send Hope up to help me, traitor. But for you, I should be safely married to Peter Haverley."

Cotty's blue eyes filled with tears and her mouth quivered. "Ye know I done it for your sake, mistress," she said pleadingly.

Her mistress gave her a stony glance and said, "Send Hope Tennison up here—and don't come back."

Cotty hesitated, then vanished into the hallway. Savarra looked after her mutinously, wishing with all her heart that Peter would come thundering up to the Bainbridge mansion accompanied by an army and demand that Lord Bainbridge give his daughter in marriage to the Haverley heir.

No such thing happened and May first, 1780, found Savarra on board His Majesty's Ship *Lion*, heading in a freshening wind toward a dark West as the sun rose slowly behind the ship. Its first destination was Charles Town in a colony called South Carolina.

Accompanying her were Bartholomew Brim, whose stern features exhibited no trace of emotion, and Cotty Penderford, who was a-tremble with excitement and terror. Cotty had told the silent Savarra that she was sure she would be drowned in mid-ocean and, if she were not, certainly the Indians who awaited their arrival just beyond Charles Town were bound to do away with her in some hideously painful manner. Too, the attitude of her mistress was such that it caused Cotty much distress.

As for Savarra, she retired immediately to her room aboard the ship, which carried munitions and other supplies to the British in America, and sulked. It took her three days to realize this course of action bothered no one but herself, for Cotty and Brim walked the decks of the freighter with the few other passengers, took hot chocolate and rum respectively with them in the small saloon and galley.

When she finally went above, she felt she looked pale and somewhat dispirited. She had tied her mane of thick black hair under a bonnet with a brim that caught the wind and forced her neck to hold stiff under a gale that had the sails bellied out and lines creaking with strain to hold them.

In fact, the wind was so strong that, as she rounded the forecastle, a gust caught her billowing skirts and would have swept her against the rail painfully if a very tall stranger had not been there to catch her waist and hold her until she steadied herself. She looked up into a disagreeable scowl above a pair of gray eyes as thickly lashed as her own. She had a flashing impression of great shoulders and overpowering strength.

"What the hell are you doing on deck in a wind like this?" he asked rudely. His hands were rough as he pulled her into the lee of the forecastle. His hat blew off and went sailing out over the rough water as she clutched at him to steady herself and his thick black hair whipped in the wind.

"Take your hands off me, sir," she said coldly, clinging now at the rim on the forecastle

He was gone before she could keep her bonnet from blowing backward, for she did not dare let go the ornamented side of the forecastle. Wind was whipping about her in a most distressing manner and she cautiously inched her way back to her stateroom, where she found Cotty mending a small rip in one of her neat gray dresses.

"Oh, mistress—I went out fer a cup o' chocolate an' come back to find ye gone! Brim told me there was such a gale I dassn't go above—oh, you *do* look blown about!" She paused and added queasily, "The ship's rockin' is terrible uncomfortable."

Savarra gave her a sullen glance and made no answer. But later that day, when the wind had lessened, she went up and took a bracing walk about the deck.

She did not see her unpleasant rescuer but she did meet the only other woman beside herself and Cotty on board. She was a Mistress Spencer Raintree. "But do call me Bonnie, my dear. How lovely you are—and what a pleasure it is to have another lady on board. I've just been visiting my parents in London—" and she launched into great detail about her visit, finishing, "and now, I am *so* homesick for my darling husband and children!"

She was about ten years Savarra's senior, dark-eyed, plump and pretty, merry with chatter. Her black hair was simply dressed with a large loop on the back of her neck and small tendrils about her smooth face. It developed that her husband, Spencer Raintree, was a very successful merchant in Charles Town and they were fiercely loyal to King George.

She was so sympathetic and maternal that in less than two days Savarra had confided the entire story of her frustrated love. Bonnie Raintree was marvelously comforting, and thereafter Savarra often walked the deck with her, finding the air bracing and her spirits much improved, despite her sorrow over the lengthening distance between herself and Peter. It served only to increase her longing and desire.

She met the other three passengers one by one. The first was a kindly giant of a man Bonnie introduced as Bowman Baltazar, a cooper from Charles Town. Savarra could be extremely winning when she chose and this big man who made barrels and casks for shipment of rice and tobacco from the colonies to Great Britain was charmed by her. Baltazar was about forty, with black hair graying at the temples and eyes as warm and loveable, as kind and understanding as her pet spaniel she had to leave at home. She liked him immediately.

Within the hour that eighth day, she had met Tyler Belion, a great rice planter, whose lands were some miles beyond Charles Town. He appeared a little distant after Bonnie told him Savarra was a lord's daughter—a lord who was also a brigadier general in the British army. Savarra assumed his attitude was compounded of awe and diffidence. He was tall, but not so tall as Baltazar, with darkly shining brown hair and hazel eyes. His smile confirmed his diffidence. It slanted upward at one corner and his eyes crinkled pleasantly. He looked to be between twenty-five and twenty-eight, and Bonnie whispered that he was very wealthy and most loyal to King George III. This latter warmed Savarra toward him, though her opinion of all the transplanted Englishmen in America was low.

The last passenger she met was her surly rescuer. His name was Cutler McLean and he was a rice broker. He was too big to be gentlemanly-appearing, like most Americans. He towered over all the men except Baltazar, whose height he equalled. He warehoused rice, indigo and lumber and shipped them all to London. Savarra felt that his effort to be courteous and friendly was as false as a crocodile's tears despite Bonnie's assurances that he, too, was a loyalist of impeccable repute. There was a certain reserve, touched by cynicism, in his sun-tanned face and she turned away from him indifferently.

In the following days, she became very friendly with Baltazar, and his singularly understanding brown eyes rested on her with gentle, indulgent affection. Savarra found herself wishing her own father would be so indulgent. Belion and McLean were not much in evidence as the placid days went by. They seemed to have much in common with officers of the ship.

She still had nothing to do with Cotty and often heard the little maid weeping almost silently in her bunk in the stateroom they shared. But Savarra was unforgiving and, after two weeks at sea, she was still taking her walks about the deck alone or with Bonnie Raintree.

Once, when Bonnie was kept in her stateroom with a headache, in the course of her walk alone, Savarra came unexpectedly upon McLean. He stood leaning against the rail, looking speculatively toward the endless horizon, lined now with a low fringe of dark clouds. She greeted him impartially,

The wind was almost nonexistent and sails flapped dispiritedly above them. Abruptly he swung about and fell in step beside her.

With sudden bluntness he asked, "What is your business in Charles Town, Mistress Bainbridge?"

Her eyes narrowed with surprise. She certainly was not going to tell this impertinent stranger she was being forcibly removed from her lover. "My father is going to serve in America with the British forces under Lord Cornwallis and he did not wish to leave me behind." She added, "I do dread going to such a primitive place and I am quite sure I shall dislike the country intensely."

He said curtly, "I'm sure you will dislike it, madame. It takes an open mind to find new pleasures." The gray eyes were cool but his white smile was friendly.

Automatically she widened her eyes, then let her lashes fall. "New pleasures in a wilderness—where our men are being slaughtered by a few rebels, who do not realize they owe their allegiance to their betters?"

"There are more than a few, madame, or there would be no slaughter."

"You sound as if you sympathize with them, sir."

His laugh was short. "Nay. I am as loyal to the crown as any man aboard the *Lion*. But I do not underestimate my enemies and I think you do."

"They were the scum from British prisons originally. I do not think it possible to underestimate them."

He laughed then, in genuine amusement. "How British you are, Mistress Savarra. You will be popular in Charles Town among those of us who are loyalists."

She looked beyond him toward the three ships of the line on one of which, H.M.S. *Drake*, her father sailed with two hundred picked men and their horses from his regiment. Then she looked forward at the long, low line of blue-black clouds on the rounding horizon.

McLean followed her glance. "Looks to be a blow coming up, mistress. This may be your last walk for a while."

"I'm not afraid of a little weather." she said pertly, wishing it would blow them all the way back to England and Peter. Darling Peter! She closed her eyes suddenly in a spasm of intense longing.

"In that case, I hope for your sake 'tis a lively storm," he said dryly and bade her good day.

She watched the big man walk away, his body responding

lithely to the increased roll of the ship. He was singularly graceful despite his irritating manners. As she looked, he was joined by his friend, Tyler Belion, who, after they spoke, glanced toward her and smiled. She nodded coolly. They were typical of the American breed of men, she was sure, too tall, too muscular, inferior and ill-mannered to a degree despite their obvious education and the apparent wealth of their impudent new country. She dismissed them from her mind and studied the rising clouds on the horizon with interest.

It developed that Cutler McLean was right, and it was three days before Savarra could take her walks with Bonnie once more. The storm had been a heavy one and Cotty had been pitifully seasick.

So devastating was her misery that Savarra, who had turned out to be an excellent sailor, put aside her anger with the young maid and nursed her through the worst of the storm.

The last day, when the seas began to quieten at last, Cotty looked up at her mistress and said brokenly, "I thought I was goin' to die, mistress—as punishment fer partin' you an' Mr. Haverley."

At this admission, Savarra's anger melted entirely. She said sympathetically, "My father would have found us out anyway, Cotty. Indeed, he would have pursued us all the way to Bath, had we left, and torn me from Peter's arms." Her voice hardened. "But Peter sent me a note before we left —and luckily for me, he gave it to Hope and she gave it to me. My father does not know of it. Peter has vowed he will not lose me—that he will find a way to come to America and get me."

Cotty's eyes rounded. "Mayhap he *does* love ye, mistress. An' I was wrong about him."

"You *were* wrong, Cotty. And so is my father." Her voice was cold and her young face set. She was finding it hard to forgive her father despite their long years of camaraderie.

"I feared the young master would take advantage o' ye, dearie," Cotty said, greatly relieved to be in Savarra's good graces once more. Savarra put a cool damp cloth to her forehead and she moaned then. "But little did I know the master would take it into his head to carry us away from England—an' to a wild place so far from home."

"Never mind, Cotty," Savarra soothed. "The storm is over and you will soon feel well again."

However, Cotty did not recover her spirits the balance of the voyage. Though Bonnie Raintree and Savarra brought her tidbits from the captain's table to tempt her appetite, she remained in their room. Not even Brim's insistence that she get out to take the air brought her forth.

Brim had thoroughly enjoyed the trip and he was intrigued by the tales told him by the other male passengers about the new land to which they were sailing. He punctiliously visited Savarra each day, inquiring after her health and offering to escort her about the decks, but she preferred to walk with Bonnie—or even alone, when she could brood to her heart's content about Peter. Brim was too taciturn, too correct to be good company for Savarra.

She and Bonnie became fast friends, and Savarra enjoyed the company of the sympathetic Bowman Baltazar. She spent the balance of the voyage in fairly good humor, but she tossed at night with fitful dreams of the hazel-eyed and handsome Peter Haverley.

It was mid-July when they reached Charles Town harbor and the freighter, sails flapping dispiritedly for the wind had fallen, moved majestically up the Cooper River to the wharf, where her sails were reefed and the gangplank put ashore.

Two

Savarra was miserable as she stood in the blazing sun before debarking. She had never felt such enervating heat in her life. It was high noon and there was scarcely a breath of air stirring the city so recently occupied by the victorious British. And what she could see of it from the ship was not too appetizing. There were many warehouses, merchants' houses, ropemakers' shops, shops of ships' stores.

Piles of merchandise stood on the docks, with barrels

stacked almost as high as the buildings. Great boxes of goods to be shipped were stacked near the barrels.

She squinted in the blinding glare at a long building that bore a sign, *Baltazar Cooperage.* There were unsavory-looking taverns farther down the long quay. The air was full of alien smells, tar, dry hemp, leather, fish and the pleasant pungence of what she was to learn was coffee beans. No one on shore seemed to let the wilting heat slow them down a whit as they went about their business.

Cutler McLean, Bowman Baltazar and Tyler Belion stood waiting for the ladies to step upon the gangplank, which they did. Bonnie Raintree following after Savarra said gaily, "The town is really beautiful beyond this rough harbor section, my dear—and when you are settled, I shall have you to tea as soon as ever you can come!"

Savarra clutching her skirts as she made the descent, was wishing devoutly that she had better protection from the scalding sun. Her bonnet was little use against it. Her clothing clung moistly to her body and she thought suddenly, *I hate this place and I shall find a way to leave it with Peter.* She *knew* Peter would come for her, despite her father's skepticism.

Bonnie was swept up in the arms of a tall, thin and somewhat sad-looking man. After their embrace, she immediately introduced him to Savarra as Spencer Raintree. Then she hugged each of her two children who stood beside him, presenting them to Savarra. Belle, thirteen, was brown-haired and hazel-eyed. Her ten-year-old son, Terrell, like his mother had dark brown eyes and black hair. They were very polite, but excited and happy to have their mother home once more. The family moved off together to where Spencer Raintree had a carriage waiting.

Savarra and the two servants stood looking about for Lord Bainbridge, for the ship of the line, H.M.S. *Drake*, had docked immediately after the *Lion*, the other two proceeding on up the coast destined to dock in New York. There was a great crowd of sailors about and merchants as well, but few women.

Savarra noted that Belion, McLean and Baltazar were met by two tall young men clad in the strangest clothing she had ever seen. They wore leather leggings with fringe down the sides, rough shirts, and carried long, slender guns. One had mischievous blue eyes under light hair and startlingly brunette eyebrows. The other, who appeared older, was also fair-haired, but his eyes had a drowsy amiable look about them

Both of these men carried a pack of animal skins on their backs and Savarra thought they might be hunters. As the five men talked, they glanced toward her.

Cotty said, "Cor! That young 'un with them innocent eyes —I bet he ain't half so innocent as he looks!" And it was true that the younger was looking at Cotty with appealingly guileless eyes.

Brim said stiffly, "Keep your eye out for Lord Bainbridge, ladies. He should come ashore at any minute."

But Savarra found her eyes drifting back to Baltazar and his companions. They appeared to be arguing good-naturedly. Then suddenly they approached the women and Brim.

McLean swept off his tricorne and said, "Ladies, two of the gentlemen with whom I do business would like to make your acquaintance. This is Gabe Sleep," he gestured to the tall, drowsy eyed man, "and this is Thad McHorry, who admires Miss Cotty tremendously."

"Indeed," Savarra said freezingly. That McLean should introduce her to such obviously low-class persons was intolerable. Her stare was icy, but Cotty giggled and turned quite pink.

"Mr. Sleep and Mr. McHorry are trappers—they are what we call overmountain men, for their homes are in the back-country mountains. They sell squirrel skins, bearskins, some beaver and deer—the better to line your cloaks against the winter winds, ladies," McLean went on conversationally.

"Indeed," Savarra reiterated coldly, and Brim was frowning like a thundercloud.

"Mistress Bainbridge's conversation is somewhat limited, gentlemen," McLean said with a malicious smile. "She is a lord's daughter and not accustomed to the likes of us." Then with specious warmth, "You see, Mistress Bainbridge, we haven't the class distinctions here that you have in England. I apologize, but my business associates would not take no for an answer."

Brim said haughtily, "Mistress Bainbridge, I see his lordship now. He is with his men."

Savarra glanced about at his gesture and saw that the redcoated soldiers were lined up on the quay at some distance, with her father before them. She recognized Colonel Scott Coyne at his side.

"If you gentlemen will excuse us," Brim said with a chill nod, "we will join Mistress Bainbridge's father."

"Glad to've met you, ma'am," Gabe Sleep drawled impudently.

"An' 'specially you, Miss Cotty," Thad McHorry said warmly, as Savarra swept past them, dragging the fascinated Cotty in her wake.

Between the broiling sun and her clothing clinging so moistly added to McLean's insolence, Savarra was in a temper when she drew up to her father, who had just dismissed his troops. The scarlet-coated men immediately dispersed to see that their mounts debarked safely.

"Ah, Mistress Savarra," Scott Coyne said with delight plainly written across his square, attractive face, "I am so happy to see you again."

"Thank you, Colonel Coyne," she replied shortly. Then, "Father, can we not get out of this sun? 'Tis enough to give us sunstroke."

"I have a carriage waiting, Mistress Savarra," Coyne said swiftly. "Come, I will see all of you to it."

Lord Bainbridge said briefly, "You look well, Savarra. I'm glad you weathered the voyage in good health." Then to Cotty, "You look peaked, Cotty. Have you been ill?"

"Dretful ill, sir," the maid said tremulously. " 'Twas the storm, but Mistress Savarra took good care o' me an' I'll be better now me feet are on somethin' that don't rock ever minute."

Lord Bainbridge's smile lit his handsome face. "So you are friends again, Savarra. I'm glad."

Savarra shrugged. "Cotty's telling didn't alter things too much, I suppose. You'd have chased me all the way to Bath and brought me back anyway." Coyne looked at them, his fine young face alert and curious.

Lord Bainbridge's voice hardened. "That's right. I would. You shall not ruin your life if I can help it. Now get in the carriage before you become too warm. You are not yet accustomed to this clime."

The three followed Colonel Coyne to a luxurious carriage, polished and gleaming black, pulled by two matched bays with coats like satin in the bright sun. Coyne held Savarra's arm as she mounted. His hand was tender, and she glanced down into the honest brown eyes and saw love reflected there. He was much too polite to question her about the previous enigmatic conversation with her father. But she was so hot and sticky that it merely added to her impatience and she was hard put to smile at him.

The black driver sat on the box, ready to transport them to their destination. Savarra was amazed at how many blacks there were in the crowds about them. They would have outnumbered the whites but for the newly arrived British troops.

Coyne took a seat beside her, his voice eager. "General Cornwallis has commissioned me to be your father's adjutant. 'Twill be like old times. And we have commandeered the home of Warren Pair for you. 'Tis one of the finest houses in Charles Town. I'm sure you will like it, Mistress Savarra."

When her father joined them and the carriage began to move, Coyne said to him, "The Pair house is next to the Brewton house on King Street, where General Cornwallis is headquartered, Lord Bainbridge. Warren Pair—an avid and unregenerate rebel—has been shipped off to the West Indies, but General Cornwallis said if 'twas agreeable to you, his wife and daughter will be permitted to continue to occupy a portion of the house. However, we think the ladies are reconciled to the circumstances."

"If they are not," her father smiled, "we shall have to inconvenience them somewhat."

Savarra, like her father and the two servants, was peering out at the sailors, civilians, traders, dockworkers and merchants who filled the quay along the Cooper River. The intense heat made Savarra more and more irritable, but she held her tongue.

Her father said, "Scott, tell me how things have gone for us since Charles Town surrendered."

The black driver on the box was having a difficult time driving the bays through the milling crowd and their progress was slow. Coyne said, "You know, Lord Bainbridge, the rebels expelled the royal governor long ago and they have a government in exile—a man named Rutledge is the head of it. President, they call him. But Sir Henry Clinton has left South Carolina under command of Lord Cornwallis, with orders to make it safe for the crown before taking on rebel forces in North Carolina and Virginia. These people are in a turmoil, especially in the backcountry, sir. We counted on more loyalists than we seem to have."

"From what I heard in England, a bit of leniency would secure all of South Carolina. What put them in a turmoil outside of Charles Town?"

"Lieutenant Colonel Banastre Tarleton and his loyalist dragoons indulged in an unnecessary massacre the last of May."

Savarra was looking at the people who passed the carriage and she only half-listened to the conversation between Coyne and her father.

"How?" Lord Bainbridge asked bluntly. "I know Tarleton —a headstrong and impulsive man."

"He is that, Lord Bainbridge," Coyne replied, lips tightening. "Late in May he drove his cavalry at a killing pace—his horse died under him—more than a hundred miles in two days to overtake Colonel Abraham Buford's regiment of three hundred and fifty Continentals at Waxhaws in the backcountry. Buford had evacuated Camden in the face of our advance and believed himself to be retreating in security toward North Carolina. But Tarleton and his dragoons all but surrounded Buford before he knew he was in danger. The rebels then undertook to negotiate, but the upshot was that Tarleton mounted a cavalry charge and, while the rebels were begging for quarter, his dragoons slaughtered nearly all of them—hacked them to pieces in cold blood."

Lord Bainbridge smothered an oath and Coyne wiped his face with a snowy handkerchief and added, "It's turned many a neutral and half-loyalist against us and hardened the determination to resist." He added bitterly, "And it has earned for Tarleton the sobriquet of Butcher—while the rebels now refer to no quarter as Tarleton's Quarter."

"A bloody fool thing to do," Lord Bainbridge swore angrily, and Savarra looked at him in surprise. She knew her father to be a man of honor and compassion and his self-control was such that he rarely lost his temper. Now he said, "Cornwallis should exercise more control over that young man." Then observing his daughter he said, " 'Twill not be long and we will be out of this heat, my dear. The houses in Charles Town are large and cool, they tell me."

"Indeed they are," Coyne said enthusiastically. Stimulated by the presence of Savarra and his obvious feeling for her, he began a running account of what they were passing, the great warehouses and taverns, the shops of wholesalers and brokers for rice, indigo and lumber. They passed a large shipyard, and the long building facing the river bore white painted letters, *Pair Shipbuilders*. "That was Warren Pair's business, but the court of sequestration has taken it over now."

Then continuing, "Charles Town is the fourth largest city in the colonies and has a harbor as fine as any in the world."

As they made their way into the heart of town, the houses

began to look exceptionally beautiful, as beautiful as many in England. Savarra was pleasantly surprised, but then she reminded herself that Englishmen had built this city and named it after their own King Charles, and she knew a swift dart of English pride.

The horses clopped down a cobblestoned street and turned onto King Street, where they passed an exceptionally fine house. Coyne said, "That's the Miles Brewton house. General Cornwallis has his headquarters there. 'Tis what they call here a double house—much like the Pair house next door, you see." Coyne gestured toward the big, cool-looking house.

Savarra eyed the two houses. Despite the devil's own heat, they appeared refreshingly shady under great spreading magnolia trees, whose green boughs were punctuated by white, velvety blossoms as big as a man's head. The heated air was impregnated by their rich perfume, combining with white blooms on bushes, which Coyne informed them were Cape Jasmine. It was a heady blend and, despite her discomfort, Savarra felt a stirring in her blood.

The Pair house was of white-painted handmade brick with four colonades supporting a lower and an upper bannistered porch. Two wings jutted east and west, while the house faced north. There was a porte-cochere on the left over a broad shell drive. The large fenced yard about the house was filled with flowers, a tropical riot of color and scent, flaunting themselves in well-tended beds.

Savarra realized that Warren Pair had given up more than his shipyards they had just left on the docks. Coyne had said he had been forced into exile in the West Indies a month before because of his violent sympathy for the rebellion. According to Coyne, there were many such men in the city who had been unceremoniously shipped off to islands of British possession. Those who remained were silent now, or openly loyal to the crown.

As they debouched from the carriage and walked up the brick path to the house, they were met at the door by a small, slender black man in well-fitted coat and breeches with a snowy linen shirt.

"Come in. I'll announce you to Mistress Pair," he said, inclining his head in cold courtesy as he stepped from the hall where the group stood to a door on the right. Savarra drank in the cool air of the house like the thirsty voyager she was.

As they waited in the spacious hall, they could hear the

black's voice dimly, and in a moment a tall woman, hand-some and coldly controlled, stepped out of a side door and greeted them. This was Anne Pair, and her dark eyes on Lord Bainbridge were implacable. Savarra felt an immediate hostility toward her. Beside her stood a young woman, who looked to be but a few years older than she, herself. This proved to be Anne Pair's daughter, Verity Pair, as Coyne introduced them. Verity Pair was not as tall as her mother, but her regal air, her thick, luxuriant brown hair and great dark eyes reminded Savarra of her own mother a little, but only a little. Verity had a firm, curved mouth, ripe in its fullness, an inviting mouth, and Savarra sensed something in the air immediately.

She looked sharply at her father to find his vivid blue eyes on Verity Pair in fascination. She knew a sudden uneasiness.

"Good day, madame," Lord Bainbridge said courteously to the mother. "I am Lord Bainbridge and this is my daughter, Savarra—our servants, Cotty Penderford and Bartholomew Brim. We are grateful to you for permitting us to share your home for the while we are here."

Savarra recognized command in these polite statements like a fine thread of steel. He would tolerate no rebellious activities and he was letting the ladies know in advance.

Anne Pair inclined her head slightly and the slender black man came forward. "Amos, you will take their luggage when it arrives to the two largest rooms on the south."

Amos murmured, "Yes, mistress," and vanished at the rear of the hall.

As Anne Pair turned back to Lord Bainbridge, her voice grew colder. "I shall not pretend that you are welcome, sir, for you are not. But we shall make every effort to be as unobtrusive as possible—knowing you might well exile us, even as you did my husband."

Coyne spoke up, his voice rough. "Madame, your husband was a troublemaker and made no effort to accommodate himself to the circumstances, as you well know. He was fortunate enough to have good loyalist friends to see he did not hang."

Verity spoke suddenly in quiet rage. "My father was a free man, as we shall all be free of you someday, colonel!" Her dark eyes flashed scornfully at Lord Bainbridge, a thick tangled fringe of black lashes framing their dilated pupils. Savarra calculated swiftly that she could be no more than twenty-three or -four.

Her eyes shifted to her father and saw his face as he looked into the upflung and flushed young features, and she sensed the stirring within him. Savarra knew her father well, and into her mind came an unexpected vision of Lord Bainbridge reaching out to crush the girl to him, covering that full mouth with his own. He was silent and Savarra felt a bud of real animosity toward Verity Pair swell within her.

Scott Coyne stepped into the breach. "Lord Bainbridge and his daughter and his servants will be more than welcome, I'll wager, before this is over, Mistress Pair. Good food on your table and safety from harassment—"

"There will be rooms for the servants on the third floor," Anne Pair interrupted coolly. "Where *is* your luggage, Lord Bainbridge?" she asked imperiously.

"It will be delivered shortly." Lord Bainbridge was brusque, his eyes still on Verity Pair. Verity had been staring into his eyes with something of shock in her own and now she tore them away, color high in each smooth cheek. Savarra's uneasiness increased. Her father was thirty-eight and that had seemed very old to her. Now she was dismayed by an electric current in the air about him and this rebel girl.

Coyne's face reddened with new anger and he said sharply, "Madame Pair, Lord Bainbridge and his daughter are not guests. They are residents. That you and your daughter remain in this house is a courtesy which I would not have accorded you."

"We are deeply grateful," Anne Pair replied in mock humility, but Verity turned on her heel and with a flare of pink skirts and white petticoats left them without a by-your-leave.

With her departure, Lord Bainbridge said coldly and flatly, "Unless you can accommodate to us, madame, I shall have to ask that you take up residence elsewhere."

"We shall accommodate, your 'lordship," Anne Pair replied distantly. "I want my husband to return to his home when this is over." She hesitated a moment, then added, "Indeed, I shall leave the entire house under your supervision. Verity and I will keep to our rooms in the west wing."

She turned to leave, but Lord Bainbridge spoke softly, iron lacing his voice once more. "Nay, madame. That will not be satisfactory. 'Tis your home and you will supervise it with my instructions. Nor will it be necessary to keep to your rooms. I shall expect both you and your daughter at table of evenings."

A slow, dark flush mounted Anne Pair's patrician features. She looked to Savarra to be near Lord Bainbridge in age. She was attractive, but not so attractive as that beautiful daughter. She said in a low voice, "Very well, your lordship. Now may I be excused?"

Savarra was suddenly aware of the presence of four more black faces peering from various points in the hall, one on the steps of the great turning staircase, one from a side door and two from under the edge of the stairs.

"First you will show us to our rooms," her father said quietly.

With sudden fire, Anne Pair retorted, " 'Tis *your* house now, sir. Find them yourselves."

There was a momentary silence before Colonel Coyne started to speak, but her father silenced him with a glance. Then he said in a chilled, measured voice, "Colonel Coyne, you will find other accommodations for Madame Pair immediately. Her daughter shall remain here and take up her duties."

Fear darkened Anne Pair's face, and Savarra looked at her father with quickened interest, her animosity forgotten in the sharp exchange. Before Coyne could speak up, Anne Pair said with real humility, "I beg your pardon, Lord Bainbridge. I have too quick a tongue. It moves before I think. Forgive me."

Lord Bainbridge looked at her, his handsome face without expression, and replied, "Quite." After a moment he added, "I shall invite General Cornwallis to dine with us tonight. We shall expect you and your daughter to join us. Now you may show us to our rooms."

As they followed the woman up the long, graceful stairs, Savarra was silent, reflecting on the unwelcome currents that had swept between them all. She wondered if Verity were affianced. She was quite old enough to have been married before now. If she were single, thought Savarra, it was by choice, for she was a singularly beautiful girl.

"This is our largest and best room on the south, your lordship. 'Tis cool as well, with the south breeze. I think you might like it." Anne Pair stood aside as he strode into the room.

Savarra, Brim and Cotty stood looking in. There was a row of tall windows and, though the July sun was oppressively bright, a cooling flood of air poured into the room. A broad, high bed centered the one wall with the usual three

wooden steps to mount it, while a tall armoire and chest of
drawers graced the west. A wide dressing table with a mirror
as fine as those Isabella had fancied hung above it on the
north. On the floor was a truly exquisite carpet, which Savarra
recognized immediately as having come from India. Her
father had brought home some like it for their manor house
in the country.

Her father said briefly, "This will do nicely, Madame Pair.
Now I will look at Savarra's."

Coyne, who had followed and stood somewhat back from
the others, said respectfully, "Lord Bainbridge, I will have
two of my men see your luggage is brought from the ships
immediately. And I must report to General Cornwallis that
you have arrived safely."

"I shall report to him myself as soon as we are settled,
Scott. Possibly less than an hour."

"I will tell him, Lord Bainbridge." His farewell look at
Savarra was a mixture of longing and frustration.

As Coyne departed, Savarra became aware once more of
the blacks who had come softly in behind Anne Pair. They
seemed to be everywhere and she knew she did not imagine
the hostility in their closed faces. It was obvious they felt
about the rebellion as the rebels did.

Now Anne turned and said to Savarra and her father,
"These girls will serve you in any way they may be of use
to you, Sir James. They are Tiqua, Monique and Frances.
You will meet Primrose, the cook, later." The three young
black women bowed impassively.

Her father regarded them, frowning. Savarra knew he did
not approve of the practice of slavery, but she shrewdly
concluded that their services were indispensable to their
owners. Father and daughter acknowledged their introduc-
tion and the three slipped silently away.

Savarra's room was found to be much like her father's.
There was the same arrangement as to furniture, and now
she and her father stood in the door and observed Brim
and Cotty mount the stairs to the third floor with Anne Pair
showing the way.

Lord Bainbridge turned to her. "Savarra, I hope you will
be comfortable here—despite the coolness of our hostesses."
He smiled at her briefly, adding, "I shall bathe my face and
make my way to Charles now."

Savarra looked after him with reluctant admiration, for
Lord Bainbridge, having served in India, had acclimated

himself to this kind of weather and he appeared cool and at ease in his bright red coat. She envied him. She was going to bathe as soon as she oriented herself in this house, even if it were midafternoon. But she leaned against the door and her mind darted back to the exchange between her father and that girl. That Verity Pair. Had she been attracted to him? His thick fair hair was cut short and he scorned wigs, as so many men did who had served in the hot climate of India. It curled along the back of his neck, fitting his well-shaped head neatly. He had found Verity attractive. She knew it, and dislike for the girl grew.

After bathing her own heated face in the bowl of cool water, she dried upon a hand-embroidered linen towel which was not very absorbent. Then she prepared to go downstairs. She wanted to ask the servants about a hipbath.

As she opened the door a fraction, she saw her father stride out and collide solidly with Verity, who had been on her way to the stairs. Savarra stood silently watching through the partially opened door.

They stepped slowly back from each other and Lord Bainbridge smiled into the young woman's wide, dark eyes. His was a singularly engaging smile and it made him appear much younger than his thirty-eight years. In an era of bad teeth, both Savarra's and her father's were remarkably white and even.

She heard him say gently, "I beg your pardon, Mistress Pair. I am on my way to meet with my commanding officer. I fear I have startled you." He was watching the girl's face closely. Savarra clearly saw Verity's desire to return his smile do hard battle with knowledge that he belonged to the enemy.

Turning from him, the girl said coolly, "You did not startle me, sir. I am on my way to see that your dinner is properly prepared. My mother has told me what you expect of us."

"I do not expect you to work in the kitchen, Mistress Pair," he said, laughing, hope to recapture her eyes plainly written on his face. He was successful, for she faced him as they reached the stairs. Savarra stood in the partially opened door, shamelessly watching. She did not like this new facet of her father's character.

"I do not plan to work in the kitchen, Lord Bainbridge. I shall merely tell the servants what to serve and how many will be at table."

He took her arm casually at the first step down, and Savarra saw its soft tremble. She stepped out of the room,

following surreptitiously to where she could hear them and
see them as they descended but was herself hidden by the
turn of the stairs.

Verity tried to pull her arm from his grasp and he tightened
it suddenly, his voice husky. "You are so fair to look on."
They stood still on the fourth step, and Savarra saw Verity's
dark eyes widen with a kind of fear at the passion that was
blazing in his blue ones.

Her arm under his hand went rigid. He released her
abruptly, and she would have fallen if he had not caught her
again, this time with both hands. They swayed together on
the stairs. She ducked her head as he drew her into his arms,
but her body appeared to be fluidly against his.

Savarra thought angrily, He took me away from Peter—
and here he is, doing the same thing! And who would have
thought it of the calm, controlled and reasonable Lord
Bainbridge?

As she listened, Verity's voice came muffled and distressed.
"You must think me cheap and tawdry booty of a captured
city, Lord Bainbridge, to treat me thus—but I am not!" She
pushed against him feebly.

Savarra thought disgustedly, She will yield to him in
another moment and he will kiss her, but she was wrong.
Instead, he released her tenderly. "Nay, I do not think that—
Verity. I think you are so lovely that for a moment I quite
forgot my manners. I beg your forgiveness."

Verity looked up into his face then and saw, as Savarra
saw, the iron control there and the urgency that was there
as well. Savarra thought her father was very shrewd, and
she had the feeling that it was as he planned when Verity's
eyes softened and she moved away from him reluctantly.
Her pink dress was low-cut and the thin lawn kerchief that
women affected then was almost transparent over her breasts,
which arched provocatively under it. He was looking at them
with undisguised admiration and desire.

He said, "Say you forgive me. It will not happen again."
And he smiled. Savarra, shrewd herself, thought this a lie,
and her lips curled upward with a newly found cynicism.
But her father's eyes were twinkling, and this time he was
rewarded by a tremulous movement of Verity's full and
passionate lips. "Ah, that's better," he murmured, "you are
smiling!"

The girl laughed then, with a little catch in her throat.
"You are a strange and winning man, Lord Bainbridge," she

said breathlessly as she moved on down the stairs. "'Tis hard to regard you as one of our oppressors," her young voice hardened, "which, of course, you are."

He stood still, as Savarra stood still, watching the lithe movement of the slender yet voluptuous body as Verity took each step. Savarra suddenly moved out onto the landing in full view. Her look at him was so intent, he turned his fair head and saw his daughter standing above him. Their brilliant blue eyes met and locked and Savarra smiled at him for the first time since he had drawn his sword on Peter Haverley, but she knew it was not the kind of smile he wanted. It was a knowing, cynical smile and she put a challenge into it.

For a fleeting moment he appeared bewildered before a knowing look of his own deepened and he called, "Come down, Savarra. You and Mistress Pair should become better acquainted. I'll wager she can show you all that's interesting in Charles Town."

Verity Pair halted at his words. She had reached the final step and she turned now to look up at Lord Bainbridge where he stood in the curve. She could not see Savarra from where she stood and her eyes were questioning.

"Come along, daughter," he said, a touch impatiently. "She can show you first the kitchen. Perhaps you will learn something of managing a household." His voice was brisk and authoritative. Savarra realized he did not mean to let her hold anything she might have witnessed over his head.

She came slowly down the stairs, and Verity waited for her at the foot. When she reached her father, he took her arm and escorted her to Verity, where he said cheerfully, "I hope you two will become friends. After all, Mistress Pair, despite what your rebel friends may have told you, the British are not savages. We are very like yourselves, as you will see." Then, as the two girls were about to leave, he said, "I noted from my window you have fine stables in the rear, but I saw no horses."

Verity spoke with sudden coldness, "Your Colonel Banastre Tarleton has preceded you, Lord Bainbridge. He took all our horses for his dragoons."

"No matter," he replied lightly. "I shall fill your stable with good British mounts when they are debarked from the *Drake*."

Savarra held back, watching him step out the front door and make his way down the brick pathway that ended at

King Street, where he turned briskly to walk the short distance to the Miles Brewton house.

She turned and the two girls regarded each other with a kind of hostile curiosity. "Do you really want to see the kitchen?" Verity asked.

Savarra shrugged. "What I really want is a bath, but I will look at the kitchen. I am interested to see all of the house where I shall be living—for a little while."

Verity made no reply, turning toward the back of the hall. Savara followed, her eyes taking in an enormous clock with a huge, ornate gold pendulum that swung slowly back and forth in the glass-covered base. Beside it was a glass cabinet filled with bric-a-brac from the Orient and strange statuary that Savarra could not identify as coming from any land she knew. Warren Pair must have traveled widely, she thought, following his daughter into the long hall that led to the kitchen.

It was terribly hot when they entered, because there was a fire in the great fireplace where the meals were cooked. The smell of fresh bread pervaded the air as a black woman clad in crisp white opened a great iron door in the side of the chimney where the oven was built into it.

"Primrose," Verity said in her soft, drawling voice, so different from the clipped accents to which Savarra was accustomed, "this is Mistress Savarra Bainbridge. Primrose is our cook."

The plump and attractive black woman nodded curtly, but she did not smile, and once again Savarra realized that the black community had little use for the British. Still, she smiled at the woman and remarked, "It smells very good in here."

" 'At's my bread," Primrose replied briefly. "I'll cut you ladies a slice in a minute if you likes, Mistress Verity."

A great polished wooden table centered the big kitchen and on it were several baskets containing fruit and vegetables. Wooden chairs were placed about the room and cupboards were built into the walls. The two young women, Tiqua and Monique, were cutting a pie crust and peeling apples respectively at the table. Frances was washing up dishes in a large pan in a dry sink. Their dark eyes on Savarra were expressionless.

"Primrose, there will be eight for dinner tonight. Tiqua, you may use the best china and silver." Then at Savarra's questioning gaze, she said, "Lord Bainbridge is going to ask

General Cornwallis to dine, and my mother has asked Mr. McLean, Mr. Baltazar and Mr. Belion to come also. We feel that your father will enjoy making their acquaintance, and they are already friends of General Cornwallis." A slightly bitter edge came into her voice as she added, "They are turncoats—ardent loyalists."

"I know them," Savarra replied coldly. Then, "I *like* Mr. Baltazar."

Verity's thick-lashed eyes widened with surprise. "Ah, then you all came from England on the same ship—I should have known. I am to assume you dislike Cutler McLean and Tyler Belion?"

"What difference does it make?" she shrugged. "Mr. Belion is all right, I suppose, but Mr. McLean is extremely— impudent."

Verity laughed shortly. "You should like him. He warehouses and ships enormous quantities of supplies to your country."

"How is it that you entertain—even for my father—what you call turncoats, Verity?"

"We have known these three men all their lives. Uncle Bowman has been like a second father to me. It was a great blow to us when the three of them remained loyal to the crown, but it did not entirely end so long a friendship. Though it is not as it used to be, of course."

"Hmmn," Savarra murmured, looking into the fireplace where two fat geese dripped juices that hissed on coals beneath the spit. As she looked, Primrose gave an iron handle a turn, which rotated the geese slightly. They were now a golden hue and by evening would be crispy brown. Savarra knew a sudden pang of hunger as Primrose reached into the oven, a tea towel in her hand, and lifted out a rack containing several brown-topped, fragrant loaves.

"Tiqua," Savarra said suddenly, "would you and Monique and Frances prepare a hipbath for me—I assume you have such in the house, Verity?" She spoke rather haughtily, for the subtle hostility in the room stung.

"Of course," Verity replied smoothly. "Monique, put the kettles on to heat. I'm sure Mistress Bainbridge would like a warm bath—'tis so much more cooling when one is finished."

By now Primrose had sliced the smoking bread and extended two hot and buttered slices on a thin plate toward the two young women. Both accepted it and went from the room savoring the crisp crust and soft centers. Savarra had not tasted anything so delicious in months, and she was still hungry when she finished the last bite.

"You'll want to rest after your bath, I expect, Savarra. Dinner will not be served before seven of the clock."

"I'm not tired," Savarra replied, "but I plan to have Cotty help me wash my hair during the bath—and she will also arrange my coiffure."

Verity smiled as they took the stairs. "We do not follow the European hair fashions here in Carolina. Most of us simply wash and roll it up in a soft manner. All that padding and powdering is such a trouble. Only a few ladies indulge in it." Verity's own hair was soft about her face and piled fetchingly atop her head.

"That's a relief," Savarra said with feeling. "I, myself, loathe it. I shall be only too glad to have Cotty simply curl and arrange it."

"You have beautiful hair," Verity said coolly.

" 'Tis very straight and coarse—hard to curl. I notice yours seems to be naturally curly. You are fortunate."

"It is still hard to manage," Verity replied, tucking a stray curl up behind her ear as they reached Savarra's room. She added, "The girls will be up with the tub and water soon," and the young woman went on down the hall.

In her room, Savarra took the pins out of her unruly mane and brushed it vigorously, wishing Cotty would come down. While she was thus engaged, Amos knocked at her door, and when she opened it she saw that he and a rawboned youth had brought all her luggage up.

"Your things done come in from the ship, mistress. Colonel Coyne an' some men brung 'em. Me an' Calhoon got all yours, an' we done put Lord Bainbridge's in his room, an' that Brim man is puttin' 'em away."

"Bring them in and set them down there," she gestured to the armoire. Then crisply, "Will you—or one of the maids— fetch Cotty down for me?"

"Yes'm." Then to the youth beside him, Amos said, "Calhoon, you go upstairs an' knock on Miss Cotty's door an' tell her Mistress Bainbridge wants her."

Thus Savarra luxuriated in the hipbath, brought by Monique and Tiqua. It was a very nice tub with flowers delicately painted on the sides and quite large enough to accommodate her entirely. Savarra was surprised at the civilized accouterments these colonists had acquired as she soaped herself liberally with French milled soap which had surely been imported. It smelled delicious and felt delightful on her smooth skin. She lathered her head twice and Cotty rinsed it for her.

"Brim likes this place," Cotty told her. "He likes his room an' he says the town looks to be most interestin'."

"I'm glad someone likes it," Savarra said somewhat grumpily. "Ouch, Cotty! You've got soapy water in my eye!"

The little maid hastily took a cloth and wiped Savarra's face, apologizing. When they were through, she fetched the maidservants, who took away the tub and water. After that, she helped dry her mistress's hair and rolled it up with strips of cotton cloth so it would curl softly when she piled it atop her head.

By the time the dinner hour arrived, Savarra was fragrant and beautifully coiffed. Her pale peach dress of finest lawn was cloudlike about her and she had never looked lovelier. She did not wear a kerchief, and the lowcut neck showed her well-formed and piquant breasts to great advantage. She picked up a small ivory fan and looped it about her wrist before going down.

Cotty said with deep satisfaction, "You look perfect, Mistress Savarra! I never saw a prettier girl in all my life."

Savarra knew a comforting warmth. She wanted very much to appear regal and lovely before these insolent colonists. She delayed her entrance until all the guests had arrived, and then she entered the drawing room to find the men drinking Madeira and smoking pipes.

Anne and her daughter were already there, but now the men rose at once as she drifted in. She noted idly that McLean was dressed in a beautiful velvet coat of ivory, with a design of brown and gold in it. His knee breeches matched and his well-shaped legs were encased in Hessian boots, polished to a high shine. The other men were equally turned out.

Lord Cornwallis, clad in his red coat and white doeskin breeches, greeted her with delight. "But you have become a grown lady since I saw you last, Savarra!" He was in his early forties, a fine figure of a man and a gentleman as well. He wore no wig, but his graying hair was curled up on each side of his ears and he wore it in a queue, neatly tied at the back with a black ribbon. His countenance was round, his nose rather humped and large, but his eyes were sharp and wise beneath level brows and his mouth was well curved and kindly. Savarra had always liked him.

"Indeed, your lordship, I have. I was eighteen just this month." She smiled winningly at the general.

"Ah, a lovely age—and a lovely young woman," he said gallantly.

Savarra was pleasantly aware of the scrutiny of the other men, as Lord Cornwallis said, "You must know how glad I am to have your father under my command, Savarra. He will set up headquarters for himself here—and he will be of invaluable help to me in subduing South Carolina." He took a deep draw on his pipe as she seated herself beside Verity on a small damask sofa. Cornwallis blew the smoke out lazily and added, "This is a rare treat, dining with good friends—even in a rebel home."

Baltazar, Belion and McLean sipped their wine with sympathetic expressions on their lean features as Cornwallis held forth. "Being in command of British troops in Georgia, east and west Florida, as well as the Carolinas, is very demanding," and Savarra had the feeling that he was taking up where he had left off at her entrance. "And you know, James, mounted troops are essential in a campaign to subdue a scattered civilian populace, so your picked two hundred are more than welcome." His voice grew somewhat acid as he added, "Sir Henry took forty-five hundred men back to New York with him, leaving me with, at most, three thousand men available for offensive operations. Except for Banastre Tarleton's legion, I have almost no cavalry. Another of my men, Patrick Ferguson, is a fine soldier, but cannot seem to be bothered with administrative duties—though he has enlisted and organized some fifteen hundred loyalist militia in the Ninety-Six area."

All the men listened intently to the general and he grew expansive under the Madeira. "Tarleton's my best man. The last few weeks, he's ranged the backcountry, capturing and killing a number of a troop of Continentals at Waxhaws, who were trying to escape after the fall of Charles Town."

"I heard about that," Lord Bainbridge put in dryly. "Out of three hundred and fifty Continentals, he took just fifty-three prisoners. Butcher Tarleton he's called now, I hear. A few more victories like that, Charles, and we will be facing a Carolina united against us as it never has been before."

Cornwallis reddened and his chin jutted. "I don't know who you've been listening to, James. Tarleton's a fine soldier

—absolutely fearless, and he's put some fear into these damned rebels. I would I had a hundred under my command as efficient as he."

"I know Banastre Tarleton," Lord Bainbridge said coldly. "I refused to let him serve with my regiment in Calcutta."

Cornwallis's eyebrows shot up and the other men leaned forward interestedly. "I didn't know that!"

"He's an ungovernable subordinate," Lord Bainbridge said flatly, "but my rejection of him is not on his record. I saw to that. He was a very young man at the time—only twenty—and I thought it possible he might outgrow his faults. I'm sorry to learn that he's created such bitter enmity in South Carolina."

Savarra was surprised as McLean spoke up, his voice a curious mixture of an Oxford accent and a Carolina drawl, "Lord Bainbridge, the thing that has really stirred up the rebels was Henry Clinton's final proclamation rescinding his offer of parole to all who laid down their arms. On June third, to be exact, he issued a new proclamation in which the paroles previously granted were pronounced void and those who refused to take up arms in settling and securing His Majesty's Government would be considered enemies. It means, of course, that the rebels must shoulder arms and fight their own countrymen. Those who do not are subject to imprisonment, or, in some cases, hanging."

"What moved Clinton to do that, Charles?" asked Lord Bainbridge.

Cornwallis shrugged. "He was anxious to get back to New York—he—ah—has a liaison there. And he had the authority of a conqueror. He thought it best, I suppose."

Amos came to the door and announced dinner and they all put down their glasses and filed into the dining room, where the two fat geese, beautifully browned, graced the table, which was set with the finest of sterling and bone china. During the meal, most of the conversation went on between Cornwallis and Lord Bainbridge, with an occasional sympathetic remark from the three civilian men.

As they talked, Savarra gathered that Carolina was far from subdued, that a number of men calling themselves partisans had sprung up in little bands and were harassing and even making off with British supply wagons as Cornwallis tried to set up his string of outposts throughout the state. She found herself interested despite her previous boredom. Listening, she learned that Charles Town and the land around it, far back into the interior, was filled with swamps, wet jungle-like areas, and it was here the partisans hid out. Furthermore, it was hard to tell friend from foe, because many of the partisans pretended to be loyalists when the occasion demanded. Baltazar was very outspoken against these rebels, and all three of the civilian men condemned the practice of playing both sides of the war.

She learned that the Ashley River to the south of Charles Town, and the Cooper River on the north, made a small peninsula of the city. The Edisto River was south of the Ashley—and the Santee, which began to the west as the Congaree, later becoming the Wateree River, then at last the Santee, was very confusing to her. This was indeed a strange and treacherous country. Belion spoke of the swamps, naming many of them. He spoke of Ox Swamp to the west, and beyond it Tearcoat Swamp, off the Pocotaligo River, and Halfway Swamp between that river and the Wateree. She gathered that the nearer the coast, the more innumerable the swamps.

As she relished the roast goose and delicious vegetables and bread, she concluded this was a very poor land in which to conduct a war, and she was very tired of the talk of it by the time dinner was over.

When they streamed back to the drawing room for an after-dinner brandy for the men, she found herself scrutinizing them. Baltazar and McLean were of an even height, a good two inches above her tall father. McLean's face was the stronger as well. Though Belion had a hawk-like nose, his jaw was not at the arrogant angle of McLean's. Her father was talking with these three men and it was obvious that he liked them, although he had been a bit brusque with Anne Pair when he discovered she had invited them without consulting him.

As they seated themselves, her father remarked to Baltazar dryly, "Your friendship with Madame Pair and her daughter must be deep indeed, to have survived your remaining loyal to the crown."

Verity spoke up suddenly, "I have grown up with Tyler and Cutler—and Uncle Bowman. We overlook their mistaken loyalties when we can."

"Then Baltazar is your uncle?" asked Sir James.

"No, but he and my father were in business together before I was born." Then coolly, "You will find that there are many tories"—she smiled faintly at Sir James—"in South Carolina,

Lord Bainbridge, and it is much brother against brother sadly enough."

"It need not have been, Verity," Belion said with sorrow. "God knows Cutler and Bowman and I tried hard enough to make Warren see that he should have remained loyal. Had he been a—more understanding man, he would have realized the rebels can never win. England is our mother country. 'Tis treason to defy her."

Anne Pair's face was very white, and Baltazar said to her tenderly, "My dear, if only Warren had listened to my arguments, seen the good sense in remaining loyal, he would be free and pursuing his business as I am today."

She whirled on him, her even features marred by fury. "Be a traitor to *his* country, you mean. Bowman, if you do not cease flaunting your freedom and my husband's imprisonment in my face, I shall never speak to you again, I swear it!"

Savarra saw that the big man's gentle face was stricken. "Oh, Anne—I did not mean to flaunt—"

"You *did*. You *do!* I'll have no more of it."

General Cornwallis had observed this exchange with dry amusement. Now he said, "Madame, it was only through the intervention of these good loyalist friends of yours that Warren Pair was not summarily hanged."

Savarra found herself wishing suddenly that Madame Pair was with her husband in the West Indies.

McLean said reasonably, "You know, Mistress Anne, that Warren was not amenable to anything. It was only by clever talking that Bowman and Tyler and I were able to persuade the authorities to take him to the Indies at the last moment, instead of placing him on a prison hulk in the bay—a sure sentence of slow death."

"I've not forgotten," Anne said, her face smooth again, "but it does not soften the pain."

"You surprise me, Madame Pair," Lord Bainbridge said with flat hostility, in which Savarra silently concurred, "being so discourteous to your guests—almost as much as your inviting them at all, considering their plainspoken and wise loyalty to King George III."

McLean's sudden laugh was easy, lessening the tension. "I can speak more plainly, Lord Bainbridge." His engaging smile was white in the tanned face. "I own three large warehouses along the Cooper River and I deal in rice, lumber and indigo, which I ship to Britain. My ties to Great Britain are fast—I am more than anxious to maintain the status quo. My fortunes depend upon it."

Belion laughed softly, his dark countenance brightening. "And I, your lordship, own twenty thousand acres of rice field and twenty thousand more of timberlands beyond Charles Town—and over a hundred slaves. I provide Bowman what he barrels and Cutler much of what he ships from his warehouses. It is not only our preference for the crown, but our innate acquisitiveness that assures you of our loyalty."

Lord Bainbridge laughed aloud and Cornwallis joined him. Even Savarra smiled at the impudence of the Americans' admission of avarice. "I admire your honesty, gentlemen," her father said.

"And I your astuteness," added Cornwallis with a chuckle.

"And I, Lord Bainbridge," Anne Pair inserted coldly, "invited them knowing you would do so—and thus enjoy the greater your duty in Charles Town."

"Then I congratulate you, Madame Pair, on your success," her father retorted, his voice hardening like the crack of a whip as he added, "but you will hereafter consult with me regarding your invitations to dinner. Your future choices might not be so welcome to me."

There was an awkward moment of silence as Anne Pair's dark, thick lashes rested on her pale cheeks, hiding her eyes. At that moment Amos entered carrying an exquisite and highly polished silver tray on which were replenishments of brandy and wine.

Savarra accepted a second glass of wine and noted once more how well the rebel Americans lived. The Pairs enjoyed sterling and silks, crystal and satins, imported rugs and finely wrought furniture. Yet Warren Pair had lost it all over the issue of independence. What a fool the man must have been, Savarra thought contemptuously.

Cutler McLean said regretfully, "We wanted to bear arms for His Majesty, Lord Bainbridge, but General Cornwallis himself refused—"

"Indeed I did. You three men are helping the crown much more in your businesses than you would in uniform." Cornwallis blew a thin stream of smoke into the still, warm air of the big room.

"Regrettable indeed," her father said now, scrutinizing the long length of the three men, their broad shoulders and the strength that was latent in their graceful bodies. "Trade must continue and our troops must be fed, of course."

"We shall," Cornwallis added tersely, "continue to expect your cooperation in keeping the rebels in line." His glance at the Pair women was significant.

"And you shall have it," McLean replied readily. "You will be glad to know, General, we strengthened our ties to England while we were there the last two weeks in April— saw most of our old classmates from Oxford, too." He frowned suddenly. "Tyler and I were somewhat—annoyed to find them complaining about the war and saying openly they wished to abandon America."

Cornwallis flushed. " 'Tis a prevalent emotion among some, now that we are fighting on so many fronts. They will be glad enough when we have secured our colonies."

Savarra was thinking, So the two younger men were educated in England. That would account for their faintly pleasant accents, not quite Carolinian, not quite British, but a blending of the two.

She noted that Baltazar was quiet for the most part of this conversation, his gentle brown eyes resting on Anne Pair frequently. With the heightened insight that had come to her since her arrival in this strange land, Savarra realized suddenly that Baltazar was in love with Anne Pair, had probably been in love with her for years. She felt a sharp sympathy for the big older man. For Anne Pair appeared totally unaware of him except as an irritant.

At the first lull in the conversation, she said to him warmly, "Mr. Baltazar, do tell us about your business. I know nothing of the manufacture of barrels."

He looked at her gratefully and in his slow, soft drawl said, "Mistress Bainbridge, there are other cooperages in Charles Town, but no better vessels are made than in mine. For a while, Warren Pair was in business with me, before he built his shipyard. We taught our boys, black and white, to put the hoops on hot, so their contraction on cooling binds the staves together more tightly. We do wet or tight cooperage too, for vessels that hold liquids—we are doing those now, so the hot summer sun will dry them tight." He glanced at Anne hopefully and added with a twinkle, "I'll wager what we're drinking at this moment came out of a Baltazar barrel."

Anne merely smiled, stifling a yawn, and Baltazar said hastily, "I invite you and General Cornwallis to come down to the cooperage, Lord Bainbridge—and Mistress Bainbridge to see how we make our barrels. Oak is best, but we also use elm, pine, gum, beech and bass, in that order. Much of it comes from Tyler's plantation forests—but I am boring the ladies." His glance at Anne was apologetic.

"And I thought rice was all you produced, Belion," Cornwallis said.

A smile creased Belion's ordinarily somber face. "Indeed no. But it still may come as a surprise to you, General, that since 1754 we planters have been sending Britain alone a hundred thousand barrels of unhusked rice each year, which comes to thirty million pounds of the finished product." He added quietly, "I'm very proud of my plantation, Belion House, which is upriver on the Ashley, where we plant the famous Carolina long grain rice." He halted, then at the intent interest on the face of Lord Bainbridge, he added further, "Mine are tidewater lands, above the meeting of fresh and salt water. Salt water is fatal to rice, Lord Bainbridge, but I have my fields dug so they may be flooded with water when the tide is high and drained when it is low. They are thoroughly protected by dikes against the salt water and from freshets above. Cutler brokers my rice for me."

McLean laughed, a pleasant sound rumbling out of his broad chest. "And I won't subject Mistress Bainbridge and the Pair ladies to details of *that*. Suffice it to say that we are an ardent trio working for the good of Great Britain and ourselves." His gray eyes with their black fringe rested on Savarra's father admiringly as he added, "And this is, frankly, what we had hoped to impress upon you, Lord Bainbridge, when we more or less invited ourselves to dinner."

"Ah, then your coming was *not* Madame Pair's idea," Lord Bainbridge replied, his sandy brows lifting.

"I was glad enough to have them," Anne said stiffly, her lower lip trembling slightly before her teeth caught it.

My father has thrown a proper scare into the woman, Savarra thought, glancing toward him. But he was looking at Verity Pair, who wore blue taffeta this evening, contrasting with the white silk on her mother. Without the eternal kerchief about her shoulders, they rose whitely, her breasts rounded full and satiny white. Savarra knew her own rose provocatively from the draped bosom of her dress, the bodice and stomacher of which outlined her slender shape exquisitely. Suddenly Lord Bainbridge's eyes swung around to meet his daughter's and the heat behind them cooled abruptly.

Cornwallis put down his empty brandy glass and rose to his feet, polished boots gleaming in the candle light. His slight bow to the ladies marked him for what he was, a peer of the realm. "It has been a most enjoyable evening, Madame Pair, regardless of whether the invitation came from you or Lord Bainbridge." His glance at Savarra's father was twinkling with amusement. "I must make my departure, James. I will see you early in the morning and we shall make plans together."

Savarra kept her seat as Anne Pair and Lord Bainbridge saw the general to the door, followed by the three men, Belion, McLean and Baltazar. They did not return, taking their leave along with Cornwallis.

Unbidden there rose behind Savarra's eyes the slim-hipped broad-shouldered form of Peter Haverley. He must find a way to rescue her from this wretched land, he *must!* She made her way to bed, only to lie there for a fevered time of fierce desires before sleep took her at last.

Three

At dawn, Verity Pair was roused from an uneasy slumber by the sound of horses on the shell drive below her window. As she came wide awake, she recognized the clink of bridles and bits and deep male laughter. There was the ring of horseshoes on cobblestones of King Street, and she knew suddenly that several horses were coming to the rear of the house— horses Lord Bainbridge had promised the day before.

She slipped from bed and in her long, white nightdress went to the window. She could see in the gray light horses streaming toward the stables far to the rear of the Pair gardens. The men were making an effort to muffle the sounds, but their exuberance was hard to contain and there were bursts of laughter as the animals trotted under the porte-cochere and down the wide drive to the stables.

Verity stood there a moment, seeking Lord Bainbridge's fair head, for she was sure she heard his deep baritone among the voices. But horses and men vanished behind a heavy stand of magnolias and crepe myrtle between the gardens and stables.

She went back to bed and lay down. It was too early to rise, but seeking sleep was fruitless. Verity was deeply troubled and confused. She had been stunned when she met Lord Bainbridge, for she had hated him violently until the moment of their meeting when their eyes first met. And she succeeded thereafter in hating what he stood for, but the man himself was another matter entirely.

He was tall, wide-shouldered, and with his high-bridged nose and vivid blue eyes was one of the handsomest men she had ever seen. Coupled with this was the fact that he had somehow remained unaware of, or indifferent to, his attractions. Curiously, this stirred her blood even more. She sensed he was a daring man—it was in those blazing eyes—with a strong will and a quiet pride. But more than that was the wholly unexpected magnetism that immediately sprang up between them. It was so strong, Verity knew well that she must constantly be on guard against it when near him.

Thus she lay in her bed, contemplating the madness that had rooted and bloomed within her since this man had taken up residence in her father's house. It *must* be curbed and wiped out, for suddenly all men paled beside this fair and intensely masculine man from England—*and she owed her affections to another.* Yet she was unable to stem her response to the English lord and she was torn by guilt and fear, for Verity was embarking on a dangerous and vitally necessary game.

When at last she descended the stairs for breakfast at the customary hour of eight, she saw Amos, Calhoon and two redcoated British soldiers carting chairs and sofas through the hall from the library.

"What are you doing?" she cried in consternation.

Lord Bainbridge emerged from the library and smiled at her, his eyes appreciative of her pale orchid muslin dress standing out from her tiny waist over the six ruffled petticoats she wore. She had taken special pains with her thick, fine brown hair, had even employed a delicate touch of rouge given to her months before by her indulgent father, it having been brought in from Paris by one of his vessels.

"I am taking the liberty of establishing my headquarters in your library, Mistress Verity," he said, and his smile seemed to melt her bones.

"But must you strip it of furnishings?" she asked, forcing a frown.

"I do not want the furniture in there to be too comfortable. I am replacing these fine chairs and sofas with straight-backed chairs more suitable to conducting military affairs."

"Then you *are* establishing a headquarters here," Verity said slowly. Her voice was unhappy, but this was the very thing they hoped for when it was first determined that Lord Bainbridge, brigadier general in the British Army, would occupy their home. It would make her and her mother's mission possible.

He bowed. "I must," he said quietly.

She turned away, then coolly, "Breakfast is served at eight, your lordship."

Breakfast, a little after eight because Lord Bainbridge was late, was an almost silent affair, for Verity and her mother pretended to be very upset by the rearranging of their home. Lord Bainbridge made no apologies. He said very little and he was brusque with her mother. Yet she found his eyes meeting hers often, and each time she experienced a shortness of breath as a warning bell rang in her mind.

Savarra was silent as well and Verity, scrutinizing her covertly, decided the young girl was brooding over something. Her eyes, so like her father's, were almost resentful.

It was an uncomfortable meal, for Anne Pair made no effort at easy conversation, and when it was over each of them went about his or her particular business. Lord Bainbridge took himself off to General Cornwallis's headquarters, leaving Scott Coyne and two aides ensconced in the library, where Warren Pair's huge teakwood desk had been completely usurped for Lord Bainbridge's use.

As the day wore on, Verity and her mother became more unsettled. Colonel Coyne and the two aides, Lieutenant Keith and Sergeant Queen, had been commissioned to handle the business of Lord Bainbridge's picked cavalry. The three men also set up files and hung maps on easels in the now severe library. It seemed to Verity there was a steady stream of British soldiers and disgruntled Charles Town residents who marched up the brick walk to the Pair house all morning. The sound of angry voices disturbed the usual quiet routine of the house.

At first, Verity had jumped each time the knocker sounded, but by twelve, she had become inured to it. The noon meal found only Verity, her mother and Savarra at table, Lord Bainbridge not having returned.

As they finished dining, Verity asked the quiet Savarra if she would like to go into town and look at the shops. "Now that we have horses once more, I can have Amos hitch up the carriage for us," she said.

Charles Town was a flourishing city of twelve thousand residents, and there were in the area scriveners, chaisemakers, sugar bakers, barbers, wigmakers, tailors, milliners and silk drapers. There were even three dressmakers' shops.

Savarra said indifferently, "Father has given me fifty pounds. I might as well spend some of it—if there is anything worth buying in this little town."

Verity restrained a frown. She had decided she did not like Savarra for reasons other than her nationality. The young woman appeared very nearly sullen, yet when their eyes chanced to meet, there was a curious challenge in those brilliantly blue eyes. *For little or nothing,* thought Verity, *we could scratch each other's eyes out.* And with the thought, she almost laughed aloud, knowing full well she was almost six years older than this English girl. Unexpectedly Savarra smiled, as if she knew Verity's thought and it was much like her own.

The smile changed her slender face, revealing teeth as even and white as Lord Bainbridge's, tilting the corners of her eyes upward and lifting the black, curved brows. Savarra was an astonishingly beautiful girl.

Startled, Verity said sincerely, "You are lovely!"

Her smile deepened and Savarra said, "I was thinking the same about you," and the challenge in her eyes was broader.

She knows, Verity thought with sudden terror. *She knows her father's effect on me.* She said quickly, "Then get your bonnet. And have you a parasol? 'Tis very hot today."

It developed that Savarra did not have a parasol and Anne, who refused to accompany them because of the heat, loaned her a pale blue silk one that almost matched her blue summer frock.

"I'll ask Cotty to come with us," Savarra said suddenly. "She would enjoy seeing the shops." Then to Tiqua who was standing near, "Tiqua, will you please tell Cotty to join us for a trip to town?" and the handsome, coffee-colored maid moved to do as she was asked. When she was out of hearing, Savarra asked curiously, "Why do Tiqua and Monique speak with a French accent?"

"They were born in Martinique and raised by the French. My father brought them home from one of his voyages. They speak French beautifully." On the heels of Verity's words, a flushed and pink Cotty hastened down the stairs, bubbling with thanks to her mistress.

Then as they made their way through the hall, Scott Coyne caught a glimpse of them from the newly established headquarters. He hurried after them. "Savarra—Mistress Pair, you are going out in this heat?" His eyes on Savarra were eager and it was easy to see that his heart lay in them. He stood before the door, holding it open for them.

" 'Twill be cool enough in the carriage," replied Verity, looking out the door to see that Amos had driven up under the porte-cochere. The spirited British horses that Lord Bainbridge had promised moved restlessly and Amos spoke soothingly to them.

"We're only going to see the shops, Scott," Savarra said casually, "and the carriage is waiting." Impatience touched her words.

"Of course," Scott said apologetically. Then with sudden hope, "Would you ladies like an escort? I can leave Lieutenant Keith in charge and accompany you. There are ruffians about who might take advantage of your lack of escort to accost you."

Verity gave him an icy glance. " 'Tis your countrymen, sir, who might accost us, and I assure you Amos will see they are sent on their way."

Coyne gave her a look of unconcealed animosity. "My countrymen, mistress, are gentlemen. The ruffians I refer to are those who *profess* to be loyal, but are in truth most vicious rebels in masquerade. They roam at will and call themselves loyalist militia."

Verity lifted her chin and said, "Come, Savarra—Cotty. Amos is waiting."

Savarra gave Scott Coyne a melting smile, as if to say she agreed with him wholeheartedly, and Verity's hostility toward her grew. Still, she remained civil and pleasant as the three toured the shops, where Savarra bought not one, but three parasols and Cotty took care that the shopkeepers knew the identity of the lady they served. She was especially voluble in the dress shop of Madame Jeanne Flammarion, a dressmaker who had made most of Verity's dresses.

Verity was sickened at the way all the merchants fawned over Savarra when they learned she was the daughter of Lord

Bainbridge. She herself had but a pound, though Lord Bainbridge had given her mother a goodly sum with which to buy food and other household items, such as candles, soap and oil for lamps. But the Continental money her father had left them was worthless and the income from the Pair Shipyards was impounded by the British. Verity could not afford to indulge her love of pretty clothes any longer.

Cotty was avidly interested in everything and she kept breaking into conversation about some item that "Mistress Savarra just *has* to have!" Savarra bought the little maid some small sachets to which she had taken a great fancy and Cotty was as pleased as if the gift had been a ball gown.

Savarra seemed to sense the Pair lack of money, for at one shop where Verity lingered over some fine lawn shoulder kerchiefs, Savarra said, "I shall take four of these," to the woman behind the counter. As the woman, who did not fawn when Cotty told her the importance of her customer, and whose hard black eyes were unreadable, went to package the purchase, Savarra said, "Verity, I would like to make you a present of two of them. You have been very kind to me."

Verity said freezingly, "I am not yet a charity case, Savarra."

The girl said imperturbably, "I did not mean to imply you were. It would pleasure me to give you the kerchiefs. And surely by now you have concluded I pleasure myself as often as I can."

Verity's big dark eyes began to twinkle. The irony was unmistakable. Savarra was telling her in so many words that she knew Verity considered her spoiled, selfish and inordinately indulged.

She burst into laughter and Savarra's full smile was once again wholly sincere in amusement. "Savarra, you are a very perceptive person," she said dryly, "and because it will pleasure you, I shall accept the gift."

Before returning home, they stopped at Mrs. Applegate's Bake Shop and were served coffee and pastry. "We do not drink tea, you know," Verity said, "that is, some of us do not."

"So Bonnie told me on the ship before we arrived. Our tea is no longer welcome here." Then with another ironic smile, "And no more are we."

"I will not pretend to you, Savarra. We are determined to be free of British rule."

" 'Tis nothing to me if you are," Savarra said surprisingly. "I did not come here willingly—'tis no desire on my part to see America remain part of England that brings me into your home." The blue eyes blazed with sudden fire before she dropped thick black lashes over them.

"Then what did bring you here?" Verity asked with sudden curiosity. There was more to this young girl than she had first determined. But at her question, the lashes lifted and blandness was behind them.

"My father," she shrugged. "He regards me as still a child." But there was something more that she withheld and Verity felt a faint stir of sympathy, not willingly, but because she could not help it at the dejection and unhappiness in the young British girl's voice.

When they arrived home, they were met in the hall once again by Lieutenant Colonel Coyne, who engaged them in brief conversation. This time he was determinedly pleasant and courteous to Verity. He remarked that he would soon close headquarters for the day and go to his lonely bachelor abode at the White Horse Inn. "I dread it," he grinned engagingly, "for the food they serve is abominable."

It was a blatant hint for an invitation to dine, but both Savarra and Verity expressed their sympathy and, with Cotty tagging after, coolly made their way upstairs. Verity glanced over her shoulder to see him look disconsolately after them for a moment before returning to the converted library.

Dinner that night was a somewhat strained affair. Lord Bainbridge was preoccupied with matters he had discussed with Cornwallis. Verity watched him surreptitiously from beneath her sooty lashes.

Toward the end of the meal he said abruptly, "I am leaving at dawn on a mission. I shall be gone some time."

That meant fighting, Verity knew, and her heart gave a sudden downward lurch. Already the man had come to mean so much to her. She tried valiantly to stem the tide of alarm. Anne Pair, not forgetting what they must do, asked innocently, "Where are you going, your lordship?"

"That I cannot tell you, madame. But I can assure you that the rebels will feel my saber. We mean to pacify this Carolina before many months have passed."

Anne's cheeks pinked up. "I'm sure it makes no difference whether you tell us where you are going to fight or not, Lord

Bainbridge. We have no recourse to any patriots. All we know are exiled or killed."

He gave her a cryptic smile. "That may be, but I'll not count on it."

"Then when will you return?" Anne persisted. "So we may have the house ready for you."

"I expect you to keep the house ready for me. And I shall return when my mission is accomplished. Since I am leaving so early, I do not expect you to serve breakfast to me."

"Very well," Anne replied, but Verity was shaken. The contradictory passions this man stirred in her breast were clashing. She wanted him safe, yet she knew they must inform the patriots of his going forth.

She went to bed that night, but she did not sleep as the hours went by. It was just as well, for shortly after midnight, Amos came rapping softly at her door. She rose at once, donning a voluminous wrapper, and admitted him.

He whispered, "Miss Verity, 'tis Mr. Belion—waitin' to talk to you in the gardens out back."

"Thank you, Amos—oh, do be careful not to be seen!"

"Don't I know that, Mistress Verity?" the slender little black man said aggrievedly.

"Of course, Amos. But now that we have some British in the house with us, 'twill be doubly hard for me to meet Mr. Belion and Mr. McLean." She followed Amos past Savarra's closed door and down the stairs.

In a moment she was out in the warm night air, and Tyler Belion loomed out of the darkness of a fully blooming crepe myrtle. Without a word, he gathered her to him and began kissing her temples, her cheeks, and at last his mouth fastened hungrily on hers. Verity was appalled at her reaction, for suddenly she was in Lord Bainbridge's arms and it was *his* mouth on hers, and fire leaped in her veins. His hands stroked the curve of her back, cupped themselves about her buttocks, and when at last he released her, Belion's breath was short as hers.

"If you only knew, Verity, those days in England without you were agony! My darling, let us secretly marry—I can come to the house and be with you in the night, leaving long before dawn!"

Verity, secretly affianced to Tyler Belion, felt her blood cool, for the tall, saturnine and dark-faced Tyler was not Lord Bainbridge and no amount of pretense on her part could make him so. The emotions Tyler evoked in her breast were embers compared to the fire that raged at the thought of Lord Bainbridge.

Still, in the hot night, with the murmur of nocturnal creatures in the trees and shrubs in her ears, her heart caught with fear as she thought of Tyler Belion and Cutler McLean, for they and Bowman Baltazar were partisans and their warm relations with the British were camouflage for patriot activities.

For every three barrels of rice or dried meat and fish they sent to Britain, one went contraband to the Continental Army by means of the secret network that had sprung up since the fall of Charles Town. Indeed, it had been in existence, only not so covertly, long before Charles Town had been taken. For the last five years, they had been shipping supplies by wagon over the long and torturous wagon trail that stretched from Georgia and the Carolinas through Virginia and on up into Philadelphia and New York.

Now they had to be devious, rarely taking the same route twice, but weaving through rough and virgin terrain to avoid British patrols and loyalist spies.

"I could arrange our marriage secretly—with our minister, Mr. McPhail," Belion urged, "and we could put an end to these brief moments—we could lie together for hours each night!"

"No, Tyler," she said breathlessly. "That would be too great a risk, and you and Cutler must remain friendly with the British at all costs." She went on rapidly, "Now that—he is—has established a headquarters here, we must do as we planned. Important decisions will be made, or sent from our house. Mother and I should be able to bring you information for the partisans that will help us immeasurably."

Belion took her again into his strong arms and his words were muffled in her thick, curling hair. "I know that, too. But Verity, you must realize how I long for you—not just a kiss or two." His voice roughened and she felt all his vigor and young manhood pressed against her. "I want you in my arms through the night. I want *all* of you."

"We must wait," she said uneasily, knowing a new and fiercer reason for waiting. "That man—Lord Bainbridge—is in the house even now. If he were to discover us—you must not stay long! He leaves on a mission tomorrow, but he will not say where nor how long."

Belion sighed. "We had heard about the mission—and I

suppose you're right. Are you able to listen at all to what goes on in headquarters here?"

"Not yet—but Amos will bring the baskets of waste out and mother and I shall go through them carefully. This mission he leaves on at dawn—"

"There are rumors we are giving them trouble in Georgetown. That's his probable destination."

She knew an instant uneasiness for Lord Bainbridge. "Will there be fighting?" Oh, God, she thought despairingly, how have I come to such a fool's pass?

"Probably not. There are too many of them—the British," he replied grimly. "There are at least two hundred men under Lord Bainbridge's command, all of them mounted, Cutler says."

"You know I shall send word the instant mother and I find anything of import, Tyler." She started to add *darling,* but something within forbade this hypocrisy. New despair shook her with the acknowledgement that it would be hypocrisy. She said swiftly, "I suppose mother and I could butter up that nasty Colonel Coyne—ask him to dine. He is so sick with love for Savarra, he might well be tricked into a revelation. Not that Savarra would be of any help," she added somberly. "She is far too shrewd for one so young." She paused, then, "In that way she is much like her father, I suppose."

Belion said shortly, "I care not for that man. He is truly dangerous to our cause, because there is the sweet scent of reasonableness about him."

Verity said fervently, "Would to God he had never come here!"

Belion swept her against himself once again. "What passionate sincerity. I'm glad you're on our side!" There was laughter in the soft, deep voice before his mouth closed once more on hers.

She clung to him determinedly, as if she could by force remove the desire Lord Bainbridge had stamped upon her, and was startled when Belion broke from her embrace. "Look!" he whispered and she turned and stared up at the house to see that pale light came from Savarra's room. The British girl had lighted a candle.

He pulled her further into the shadows of the giant myrtle between two jasmine bushes. Their fragrance in the still, hot night was a powerful aphrodisiac, but Verity drew away from her fiance.

She said uneasily, "I must go. I wouldn't put it past that one to go knocking on my door with some pretext and find me gone."

"It's been three months, Verity! And Belion House is so far from Charles Town. These few short caresses haven't made up for—"

"No, Tyler. You'll stay in Charles Town more than at your plantation." She pulled out of his arms. "And you yourself know the danger of these meetings. If the British get an inkling, if there is but a hint of your aid to the patriots, it would mean hanging for you and Cutler—and Uncle Bowman as well."

"Better that than the prison hulks in the bay," he said grimly.

"Don't speak of such," she shivered in the heat, for the hulks that lay far out in the bay were death traps. Since May, she had heard of numberless deaths—and they were slow and terrible ways in which to die. Tyler Belion spoke the truth when he said he preferred a quick death from the noose. "Go now. Mother will have you all to dinner again soon, darling." There! She had said it, but her heart beat hard with fresh guilt. "I will send word to you by Amos, if I learn anything worthwhile."

There was desperation in his last quick embrace, and determinedly Verity put the English lord from her mind, returning Belion's kiss with fervor. But when they parted and she turned toward the house, Lord Bainbridge was in her thoughts once more. She glanced up to see that Savarra's window was dark once more. Some innocent nighttime errand had got her up, no doubt, Verity reassured herself and silently closed the rear door. Her bare feet were damp from the night grass but noiseless as they crossed the planked kitchen floor, took the hall and found their way to the staircase. No sound came to her as she passed Savarra's room. The door to Lord Bainbridge's room stood open. At any minute now he might rise, she thought, visualizing the man.

She paused a moment there, looking into the darkness, observing the paler squares that were the windows opening on the back, and in her heart she cursed the chance that had brought this man into her life, even as she clung to the warm knowledge that he lay sleeping but a few feet from where she stood.

She went into her own room, leaving the door open behind her for better circulation of the still air. Suddenly the heat seemed stifling as she flung out of the wrapper.

She struck a flint to the candle on the wash stand and poured a pitcher of cool water into the bowl. Slipping from her nightdress, she dipped the cloth into water and bathed her flushed and beautiful face. She glanced up at her nude reflection in the mirror before her, at the ripe breasts and hips, the glowing eyes. Involuntarily she found herself disrobed before Lord Bainbridge, felt those brilliant blue eyes touch her caressingly, the curved mouth curl into a slow smile, saw him begin to remove his coat and shirt. Her wayward mind, having undressed them both, locked them in an embrace and watched him lift her high and carry her to the bed.

Suddenly she came to herself and her cheeks flamed as she stared at her bare white body and knew herself for a wanton. She would have prayed to God for strength to resist these thoughts, but she was too ashamed to put them before God. She was no better than the sluts who plied their trade on the streets of lower Charles Town!

But when she pinched out the candle and crept into bed, she was unable to stay a flood of passionate longing. Lord Bainbridge was likely dreaming of *her* this heated summer night. She knew it as surely as she knew her own thoughts leaped to meet his, and in the darkness she possessed and was possessed by Lord Bainbridge. It was a long time before sleep came to her.

Colonel Scott Coyne was extremely courteous as the days went by, asking only occasionally for a pitcher of water and that Amos take out the baskets of waste paper that accumulated beside Warren Pair's large teak desk.

And after Belion's visit to her, Verity began a campaign to win Coyne's friendship. Knowing that his aides went out for their noon meal to a tavern a mile away, bringing back a plate for the colonel, she cordially asked him to join Savarra, herself and Anne at noon. His surprise was tinctured faintly with suspicion, and Verity was brought up sharply by the realization she had been too friendly.

She said coolly, "I wouldn't offer, of course, but Savarra mentioned the other day that it was a shame you had to have your meal brought in to you, or do without. We certainly want to please Lord Bainbridge's daughter."

His face cleared instantly under the sandy gold hair and thick brows, and Verity hoped that Savarra would not discover so small a lie. After all, the British girl *had* mentioned the fact that Colonel Coyne must either go out, or have fetched for him his noonday meal, but she had laughed when she said it.

Nothing came of her small deception and Verity and her mother presided over a table that was more cheerful because of the open admiration of Scott Coyne for Savarra Bainbridge. However, Coyne revealed nothing that transpired in the library turned headquarters.

Neither did the waste baskets prove fruitful to Verity and Anne, as they carefully sifted the bits of clutter. All they found were innocuous orders to soldiers within the city, including leaves of absence, records of armaments taken from patriot forces. Some were rough drafts and either recopied by Sergeant Queen for the files or, in some cases, simply torn up. After being painfully pieced together they proved useless to the women.

This was explained when Verity herself took a pitcher of cool lemonade into the library as part of her effort to put the men there off guard. She found Coyne and his two aides absorbed in a small flare of bright flame that curled into the air of the dark, empty fireplace, then died, leaving the pale ashes to filter through the grate and settle upon the gray bricks that formed the hearth.

Later she reported to her mother, "I know why we find nothing in the waste that comes from the library. Colonel Coyne is a vigilant man. He burns anything of importance in our fireplace." She gave her mother an angry glance. "And little good it will do us to sift the ashes he leaves."

Still, day after day, the two went doggedly through the office litter as Amos brought it to the kitchen for them. Brim, who prowled the house almost at will, caught them at it once and Anne had to pretend she had lost a gold thimble.

"But madame, that is one of the baskets from headquarters," he said loftily. "Had you been sewing in there?"

"Dear me," Anne said coolly, "so it is. Amos, I thought you had given me our own basket. These are woven by people in the backcountry and they all look alike to me."

He had taken a cup of coffee from Primrose then and stalked out. Verity gave her mother a broad wink and said with hauteur, "But madame, you never know—Colonel Coyne could become careless," and the two women laughed as Primrose, near the hot fireplace, giggled at Verity's mocking imitation of the English butler-valet.

It was shortly after this Scott Coyne received his invitation to dine of an evening with the ladies and their other invited guests, which included Bonnie and Spencer Raintree, their two youngsters, Tyler Belion, Cutler McLean and Bowman Baltazar. It came about because Coyne informed Verity that he had received a letter from Lord Bainbridge, who had now been over a week. Verity and her mother were hopeful he could be persuaded to speak of it further.

Verity had continued through those days to be courteous and pleasant with Savarra, both of them taking tea at the voluble Bonnie Raintree's twice during the week. Afterward they had made another sortie into town where Savarra bought materials which Verity arranged for her dressmaker, Jeanne Flammarion, to make up for her. Still, there was constraint between the two and Verity could not bring herself to really like the young girl. Savarra met her halfway in this, with cool poise and little warmth or camaraderie. Now, when she told Savarra of their guests for the evening, Savarra's curved red lips went down as Verity added finally Colonel Coyne.

"He will relish *that*—dining with loyalist guests. Whatever made you and your mother include him—at a truly social dinner?"

Verity said bluntly, "He has a letter from your father. We thought you might like to hear of it." And she fought the glow that suffused her own heart as she thought of hearing of the man. Belion had made two other midnight visits to her, in which they had exchanged meager news, but there had been little time for lovemaking, for which Verity was grateful, an emotion that added to her guilt and apprehension.

Belion had told her the countryside was boiling now with new outrage as men were being forced into the British army or imprisoned. A great many were in hiding in the numberless swamps and the far backcountry of the Carolinas. Stories of British atrocities among the plantations and country homes of the Americans filtered to Anne's and Verity's ears through Monique, Tiqua and Frances. Amos brought his share from the market place. Even Calhoon, the rawboned black youth who worked as gardener, stablehand and handyman, came to them with stories told by other blacks brought in from the ravaged and burned countryside to be sold by the plundering British to planters in the West Indies and elsewhere.

That night, Verity and her mother sat with Savarra in the salon awaiting their guests. Cotty and Brim would dine in the kitchen. There was a certain amount of hostility between Brim and Amos, so Brim's offer to buttle the affair had been refused by Verity with great tact. She had softened the refusal by adding that she and her mother would appreciate his services for more important affairs when Lord Bainbridge returned.

Now Anne was embroidering a dainty bit of ruffling. Verity sat idly fanning herself with a gold silk fan.

Savarra looked down at her carefully buffed rosy fingernails and said, "I love Bonnie and that big, gentle Mr. Baltazar and I can stand Tyler Belion. But Mr. McLean is—well, I do not trust him."

"Why?" asked Verity, hiding her uneasiness. Savarra was far too observant to suit her.

Savarra's little smile was enigmatic. "Perhaps it is just because he does not like me—and because he's arrogant and insincere."

The guests began arriving then and Amos, with quiet dignity, announced them as they entered. There was a gay babble of voices as the Raintrees came in, with plump Bonnie fanning herself with a pink silk fan.

"My dear Savarra," she bubbled, "how simply wonderful to be with you again! I so enjoyed your and Verity's last visit. It's just lovely to have you staying with the Pairs. I adore them"—she looked roguishly at Anne and Verity—"even though their sentiments are—or were—contrary to mine. Perhaps when they see how charming the British can be, they will change their minds about this foolish independence squabble." Without stopping for breath she added, "Though I do think it is so dear of them to keep our friendship as it always was, even though Spencer and I are loyal to his gracious majesty, George the Third—"

"Perforce," the thin, worried-looking Spencer injected dryly.

His wife sent him a wounded glance and went on. "After all, my parents are in London, as you know—because they saw this dreadful thing coming on years ago. And though I was born American when my father was here on business, I shall always be a faithful British subject." Bonnie Raintree's smile was bright and beautiful. She was an engaging woman, despite her loquacity. When her eyes rested on Savarra, Verity thought Bonnie looked as though she knew more than she told, for all her chatter.

Anne spoke to the two youngsters who stood quietly in the background. As was the custom, both were dressed as adults in miniature, the boy in breeches and waistcoat with a tricorne on his head. The girl, Belle, a little older and taller, was clad in a full panniered skirt over myriad petticoats with a fetching bonnet tied beneath her rounded chin.

The two smiled shyly as Tiqua took hats and bonnets, murmuring that Amos would soon serve wine. The party gravitated from hall to salon with the artless Bonnie keeping up a running patter, so sunny and often interspersed with her rich chuckle that it was welcomed by all of them.

Belion and McLean arrived shortly, the same time as the freshly scrubbed and handsomely wigged Colonel Coyne. Amos showed them in and the conversation became more animated.

"We are sorry to be late," McLean smiled, "and I'm glad to see we aren't the last to arrive—but business kept me at the warehouse and Tyler waited for me. We have a large shipment of rice leaving tomorrow for Great Britain."

At that moment, Amos ushered in the towering, courtly Baltazar, whose weathered face wore his ingenuous smile. Bonnie said to him breezily, "You three are truly serving his majesty—barrels, rice and lumber and whatever." She finished vaguely.

McLean bowed over her plump little hand, kissing it lightly. "Indeed, we do all we can to crush this foolish rebellion."

"We are all good Englishmen," Spencer Raintree said with weary irony. "Now that so many American plantations have been confiscated and turned over to tories, everyone has money but the patriots. I sell our British friends everything from expensive silks and satins to imported goblets and silver, and I hear the wig shops and tailors are doing handsomely as well."

Bonnie said reprovingly, "Spencer darling, you are loyal I know, yet you make these—strange comments."

"Nonsense, Bonnie," McLean said with his cynical smile, "we all know that Spencer is melancholy by nature—doesn't mean a thing."

As the men took their seats, Verity noted that the three patriots were resplendent in the finest of clothes. Even Coyne was elegant in what looked to be a new uniform, the red coat setting off his snowy and perfectly coiffed wig and brown eyes, which were excited and joyful at being part of the social gathering. Hessian boots to the knee on each man were supple and gleamed in the lamplight, showing strong legs to great advantage. Altogether, the four men made a handsome appearance, but Verity could not include the mournful-eyed Spencer Raintree, who was built somewhat like a crane, his thin shanks showing to poor account by his slightly wrinkling breeches.

When everyone filed into the dining room, spirits seemed remarkably high, with laughter frequent and anecdotes more so. All seemed determined to ignore the war which raged over the country.

It was a meal that might have been unmarred by any un-pleasantness, but for Verity's taking measures to ensure the three partisans' cover. It came about as Bonnie chided her husband once more for his dolorous comments.

"Ah, my Bonnie," replied Spencer Raintree, his brown eyes sad, " 'tis ridiculous to ignore the fact that many of our wealthy patrons have come by that wealth through—seques-tering property belonging rightfully to their former friends and neighbors."

Verity cut in, "Now Spencer, you will offend Uncle Bow-man and our old friends Mr. McLean and Mr. Belion. After all, they are prospering under the rule of the British." Her voice was acid. "I'll wager they are three of your wealthiest patrons." Her eyes on the three men were bitter and her voice cutting. Savarra looked at her sharply.

Baltazar's expression was pained and Belion frowned, but McLean rose to her bait readily. "My dear Verity, do I detect a certain contempt in your reference to us?"

"And if you do, Cutler, isn't it well earned?"

McLean's gray eyes met hers and clashed. "May I remind you, my dear, that but for my legitimate connections, your father would be rotting in a prison ship in Charles Town bay?"

"Oh, yes," she retorted. "You remind me all too often. Be-ing exiled to the West Indies is a far better fate than the prison ships. But Papa should be *here,* looking after his own shipyard."

McLean shrugged. "Warren refused to take the oath—refused to cooperate in any way. Others who so violently opposed his majesty were hanged."

"I suppose we have you to thank that a British lord is pres-ently occupying our home as headquarters?" Verity's big dark eyes flashed and she deliberately ignored Savarra's drawn brows, as if too enraged to be conscious of the guests.

Scott Coyne was observing the contretemps with intent in-terest and Bonnie and Spencer Raintree looked curiously at their plates. The children were open-mouthed at the emotion boiling about the table. Anne Pair smiled grimly in the momentary silence, then rang the silver bell at her hand summoning Monique and Amos.

"We are through," she told them with icy composure. "You may serve dessert now."

As the servants filed out, bearing the empty plates, Savarra said slowly, "I wondered how you maintained friendly relations between rebel and loyalist in Charles Town. Now I perceive 'tis not so easily done." She gave McLean a level look. "*Are* you responsible for my father and me occupying the Pair house?"

"Unfortunately, no," drawled McLean. "When General Cornwallis and his aides chose the most suitable houses for his officers, I was in England, but I would have recommended this house. It would have been the kind thing to do." He shrugged. "If Mistress Anne and Verity but realized it, I would have then done them another favor by it. For one thing, your father's presence assures the plenty that graces this table. There are those of the Pair persuasion who are not faring so sumptuously this evening."

"A pity," Savarra said coolly, "that you cannot convince the Mistresses Pair of that." Her look at Verity was veiled.

Verity said composedly, "Forgive me, Savarra, but you must understand that I cannot help being a little bitter. I'm sure in my place you might feel the same."

"In your place," Savarra said evenly, "I would realize that England is a great country, wishing only the best for me and mine—and I would remain part of her empire gladly."

"Ah, there's a level-headed girl, Verity. Listen to her. She speaks wisely." McLean smiled pleasantly. "Thank you for coming to my aid, Mistress Savarra."

Savarra returned his smile with an inscrutable one of her own. "I thought you were doing very well by yourself, Mr. McLean, without my aid."

Spencer Raintree cleared his throat. "'Tis a regrettable thing, this division among us, Mistress Savarra, but alas, you will find it quite prevalent in our city—throughout the southern colonies as a matter of fact."

"And there's no need for it at all," Bonnie put in with a small distressed sigh. "Savarra is perfectly right when she says that England has only our best interests at heart."

"England has our riches at heart," Anne Pair said abruptly. "The English know the boundless commerce and produce and everything this land is capable of bringing to her narrow island kingdom—from tobacco and rice, to timber and manufactured goods—and eventually untold riches, no doubt, in silver and gold, all produced by Americans, ripe for England's taking."

"England has many dominions with all of those things for her taking," McLean said smoothly.

Bonnie said unhappily, "Please, my dears, do let's speak of other things. This talk makes me most uncomfortable." She unfolded the fan beside her plate and began fanning herself industriously, murmuring, "July is so warm in Charles Town."

Cutler McLean bent his smile on Savarra once more. " 'Tis said, Mistress Bainbridge, that Charles Town is a hell in summer, a hospital in winter, but a paradise in spring. I beg you to wait until spring to judge us."

"I do not expect to be—" Savarra caught herself. "That is to say, I do not mind the heat greatly, Mr. McLean." Then turning to Scott Coyne with a brilliant smile, she said, "Verity tells me you have heard from my father, Scott."

Pleased to be the recipient of such warmth, Coyne said hastily, "Indeed we did have a letter just yesterday. And he is well. I can tell you now he is in Georgetown, and when he first arrived there was smallpox in the town and many were afraid to enter, but it proved to be a few isolated cases, and he has been organizing loyalist militia with the help of Major Wemyss, Savarra."

"My father is very efficient," Savarra said coolly. "He probably has it all quite in order by now."

Coyne's brow under the sleek and fashionable wig furrowed. " 'Tis not so easy. He says that some of those who professed to be loyalists are, in truth, violent rebels—and even the loyalists are informing on each other, so ambiguous are feelings in Georgetown." He took a spoonful of the mousse that Primrose had prepared for dessert, savoring it fully before adding, "Indeed, he says the longer he stays there, the more aware he becomes of the disaffection of the people—though the gathering of a rebel force there appears to have been but a rumor. I expect him back any day now."

Silently Verity noted these facts. This was something the partisans would in turn inform their compatriots of, and they might well waylay and put an end to Lord Bainbridge on his way back. A cold little finger of fear touched her heart as she thought of the possibility.

Though dessert was eaten slowly and there was much more conversation, this was all that could be gotten out of Coyne, despite three glasses of Warren Pair's finest Madeira. The evening ended with Colonel Scott Coyne leaving the Pair house in a glow of good will, which seemed to extend even to his hostesses for all their rebel sympathies. As they bade him goodnight at the door, he was effusive in his thanks for the evening.

Anne Pair said, "We must do it again, soon, Colonel."

"Nothing would please me more, madame." He smiled at Savarra, who stood a little back from the others, and she gave him a faint smile in return.

As the ladies made their way upstairs, Verity said to Savarra calmly, "I could hate Cutler and Tyler—and even Uncle Bowman—were it not for the long years of friendship that lie between their families and ours."

"Their families?"

"Cutler's mother and father died only six months apart, he from a failure of the heart and she from some illness they could not name. She wasted away to skin and bones—and Tyler's died of the summer fevers about the same time, but it's over six years ago and they are quite over it."

"Where does McLean live?" Savarra asked curiously as they paused before her bedroom door.

"Over on Tradd Street in a very fine house, with his servants. Caleb and Corrie McLean are a legacy from his parents," Verity went on, trying to increase Savarra's sympathy for the man. "In fact, Caleb and Tyler's Abraham used to take the two boys out into the backcountry, hunting, when they were small—and later when they were growing up. They know the swamps like the palms of their hands." She caught herself suddenly. It would not do to point out their easy adaptability to partisan life! She regretted this last remark intensely, so she went on hastily, "Really, Savarra, Cutler is a very nice man despite his misguided loyalty to the crown. He has an office in his home as well as in his warehouses and he does do a great deal of good for your country."

Savarra lifted her shoulders and let them drop. "He does not talk like an Englishman, despite his loyalties. His accent is more American than English. And he *looks* American—too big and too rough for gentility, despite all those fine clothes."

Verity forced a light laugh. "That is true—he is big. But rough? I think not, and there are men like him in Tarleton's Legion, loyalist to their last drop of blood." Her voice hardened. "And they are laying waste to our land. At least Cutler is constructive in his loyalty to the crown."

"You mean by supplying your enemies?" Savarra's little smile was cryptic.

"Yes," Verity replied with a touch of violence. "Even that is better than laying waste, burning, plundering our plantations and farms—imprisoning his countrymen—or rather other Americans."

Savarra's little smile was skeptical as she said, "Goodnight, Verity."

Five days later, the third of August, brought a letter from England for Savarra Bainbridge. Verity received it from a British sailor at the door and took it to Savarra in her room.

"Mail from England," she said cheerfully. "Your friends are missing you." But she knew from the strong, dark script and seals that this was a letter from a man and a man of some importance.

Savarra said briefly, "Thank you," and tore into the envelope swiftly. She stood reading the contents and her olive cheeks flushed apricot.

Verity hesitated just inside the door, reluctant to leave without a hint of the letter's contents. There just might be something in it that would be of use to the partisans. She was aware, too, of the motionless Cotty, seated by a window mending a petticoat. Her needle was poised as she watched her mistress with a strained alertness.

Finally, Verity turned to leave and, as she did so, Savarra said tensely, "Wait, Verity—"

Controlling her eagerness, Verity paused a moment and turned back with a look of polite interest. Savarra's eyes were narrowed beneath the thick, feathery black lashes, but they were a hot, bright blue. Cotty was still waiting, still motionless, but Verity could not discern her expression because of the brilliant August day shining in the window behind her.

"You find my father attractive, I know," Savarra said quietly.

Caught off guard, Verity grasped and caught at the coat-tails of dignity. "Whatever do you mean?" Her astonishment failed to achieve the right note of outrage.

Savarra made a small gesture of impatience with the letter in her hand. "I'm not blind. I saw you on the stairs that first day."

"It meant nothing," Verity said roughly. "You and your

father—Cotty there and that nosy Brim who pokes through our kitchen—you are all our enemies."

Savarra smiled with grim satisfaction. "I take it then you would not be averse to seeing my father circumvented in at least one of his desires?"

"One?" Verity said with calculated intensity. "All!"

Cotty had risen, the petticoat fallen along with the needle as she hastened toward her mistress. "Mistress Savarra, what are ye speakin' of? Ye'll not be plannin' an' plottin' with a rebel?"

Savarra whirled on her. "Cotty, if you do one thing—just *one*—to prevent my marrying Peter again, I shall accuse you of theft and have you thrown into Newgate—or whatever Charles Town has that passes for a prison!" Her voice was low and passionately sincere.

"Do you wish to plot with me against your father?" Verity asked deliberately, her heart beating fast with anxiety.

"Yes," Savarra replied without hesitation. "But first I want you to give me your word of honor that you will reveal nothing of what I am about to tell you."

"That I cannot do. I am pledged heart and soul to the independence of our united states."

Savarra waved the letter, tossing the envelope on the dressing table. Cotty swooped upon it and cried, "It *is* from *him!* Miss Savarra, ye can't—"

"Hush your prattle," Savarra said with low violence. "You swore to me on that miserable voyage over here you would never again come between me and Peter Haverley." She turned back to Verity. "This has nothing to do with your damned rebellion—or your wretched colonies. And in the end, it might even send my father back to England in a rage."

By now, Verity had collected her wits and knew intuitively this was the source of the unhappiness she had sensed in Savarra from the first.

"If it in no way aids the British, I will promise you to say nothing," Verity said, smiling faintly.

Savarra said rapidly, "My father brought me to America to forestall my marrying the man I love, Lord Haverley's son, Peter. Now Peter writes that he has bought himself a commission and is to be an aide to Francis, Lord Rawdon, a British general here in South Carolina, and he could be here any day now." She paused, her face a mirror of grim determination, mixed with hope and joy. "I want you to help me elope with Peter when he comes for me."

"But if he is to be with Lord Rawdon—I have heard he is at Camden—you will be separated anyway," Verity said reasonably.

"Peter will find a way for us to be together—in Camden, until we can find a way to return to London," Savarra said with ruthless certainty. "But if my father returns before Peter can marry me, I will need your help in slipping away without father knowing."

Cotty spoke up with timorous courage. "Mistress, you got to promise to let me come with ye."

"With Peter and me?" Savarra's black brows drew together angrily. "I will not!"

Cotty's pink lower lip trembled. "Then I ain't promisin' nothin'."

Savarra's face grew stormy, "I'll tell Colonel Coyne you stole some of my jewels, I swear it—and they'll haul you off to prison!"

"Then do it," Cotty said defiantly. "I promised Lord Bainbridge I'd look after you an' I'll tell him all about this as soon as ever he gets here."

Savarra's face grew darker, "And you'd do it, too. What of your promise to *me*—that you wouldn't interfere between Peter and me? A fine one you are."

"I'll keep that promise if you'll let me come with you. I'd stay out of the way, keep yer clothes in order—dress yer hair. Ye'll need a maid in that—Camden place."

"Well," Savarra said in abrupt surrender, "I suppose I shall have to take you with us to that wilderness until he serves out his term of duty—or other arrangements can be made." Then to Verity, "Now have I your promise to help me leave here with Peter? It will likely be by night if my father has returned. And you and your servants can make that easy—give us horses, pack my things. I shan't take much." The girl's eyes were blazing now with hope and her vital, infectious joy communicated itself to Verity.

But a still inner voice told her, *If Lord Bainbridge disapproves of this man, there must be good reason, and Savarra is very young.* Still, she said firmly, "I will help you, Savarra. I will tell my mother and we will both help you." And if Lord Bainbridge mounted a towering rage, she would be cool and say she knew nothing of the whole affair.

When Verity told her mother of the situation, Anne Pair was quietly and vindictively pleased. "His *lordship*, she came down contemptuously on the title, "needs to be taken down a peg or two. I shall enjoy aiding his daughter in her escapade."

But Verity fought misgivings and she fought the strange melting tenderness that welled up, despite her efforts to stem it, each time she thought of Lord Bainbridge. With that tenderness there came the echo of Tyler Belion's deep voice and warm lips. I should love Tyler, she told herself. I *will* love Tyler, but even as she vowed it, her mind dwelled on thoughts of Lord Bainbridge.

That afternoon late, a heavy rainstorm blew in from the Atlantic. It was a near hurricane, and it was still a windy deluge after midnight, when Anne and Verity went through the waste from headquarters in the library. This time, they were rewarded.

When they were sure the British residents of the house slept deeply, they sent Amos out into the storm to the big McLean house on Tradd Street to inform Cutler McLean they had an important message.

Four

Verity and her mother sat tensely in the kitchen at first and Verity visualized the slight Amos walking against wind and hard rain to reach McLean's tall, imposing house. It was necessary for him to come to her. What she had found demanded explanations for it was a perfectly blank sheet of paper.

She wondered if Tyler were at Belion House up the Ashley. If he were, McLean would get word to him. Verity knew that McLean and Belion kept in close touch with the partisans who lurked in the swamps and Colonel Francis Marion of the South Carolina Militia.

Verity let her mind slide back. It was in those dark days when Charles Town fell and General Lincoln led his weary troops out to surrender, that Baltazar, McLean and Belion, officers in the South Carolina Militia, had hidden their worn uniforms and slipped back into town to vow they were ardently loyal to the king. Cornwallis and Clinton, glad to have influential men, men with good businesses and great lands, welcomed their oaths of allegiance. Immediately McLean, Belion and Baltazar had taken passage on a fast British sloop for London where they pointed up their strong ties to Britain.

Verity's anxious mind went back further, to the men she had known before the fall of Charles Town. She thought of Thad McHorry and his brother George and of Gabe Sleep, overmountain men who had left their homes in the great misty and cloud-hung mountains when news had come to them of the invasion of the British in February. These men had been in her home and, like McLean, Belion and Baltazar, they were American and ready to meet their enemies more than halfway.

Captain McLean, Lieutenant Belion and Lieutenant Baltazar had become fast friends with the McHorrys and Sleep and many like them when they had ranged the country together and fought their brief and bloody encounters. Belion had told her of those days before and during the siege of Charles Town. All of them had come together in the swamps, a taut little knot of men, and sought out Clinton's troops as those sturdy Britishers were crossing the Ashley River.

They had harried Clinton's outskirts, killed several soldiers, and had been pursued by several times their number into nearby Blackwater Swamp, where they finally drew rein and listened to their cursing enemies flounder back toward the Ashley in muddy darkness. Counting up that March night, they found that Thad's brother George as well as three other overmountain men were casualties, which increased Gabe's and Thad's hatred for the British.

All that Belion had told her boiled in her mind as she and her mother waited silently for McLean to come. She knew a warm flush of shame as her fears for the life of Lord Bainbridge flooded through her. Even as she said a brief prayer for his safety, she cursed herself for a traitor.

It seemed to her that it was taking an unconscionably long time for McLean to arrive. The wind and rain howled about the house, increasing her nervousness. But Verity told herself that all the rest of this household must surely be sleeping the more soundly for the drumbeat of rain.

"Mother, let us go into the drawing room and await him.

'Tis so much cooler there." The kitchen was stifling, with all openings closed to the storm and the cooking fires banked on the hearth. So the two women took their cups of coffee and made their way through the hall into the spacious drawing room, where Verity put down the low-burning lamp she carried.

She looked at her mother uneasily. What would she say if she knew of the fire that burned in her daughter at the mere thought of the English lord? Verity could imagine her icy contempt. Anne Pair and her husband, Warren, were puritan to their bones. They believed in thrift, prudence and, most of all, chastity. They had indulged Verity, for she was an only child. Even as Savarra Bainbridge, she thought briefly, recalling her disapproval of that spoiled young woman. Her ears burned with sudden heat. What nerve she had, condemning Savarra when her own faults were many and grievous!

That set off a train of thought regarding the English girl. She was so sure that her Peter Haverley would arrive at any moment. Please God, not at this moment! Verity drew a deep breath, assuring herself that no English lord's son would put himself to the trouble in the tail end of an August hurricane!

"Keep your hands still, Verity," Anne murmured calmly, putting her empty cup beside Verity's on a small mahogany table.

Verity looked down at her fingers twisting in her muslin skirt and stilled them. Perhaps Cutler had not been at home. Perhaps he had been off in the swamps somewhere with his compatriots. For a brief and selfish moment she wished this were the case.

Then suddenly a sound came to them from the hall and she looked up swiftly to see Amos standing there, looking half-drowned. Behind him came Cutler McLean, followed by Tyler Belion, Gabe Sleep and Thad McHorry. Verity's eyes flew wide. *Four* of them! Thank God they moved quietly. There was only the swishing sound of the removal of Belion's and McLean's oiled linen capes as Anne Pair murmured, "Amos, go change into something dry, before you catch a summer fever!" and the small black man vanished in the dark hall.

Anne turned to the men, "I'll fetch coffee for you—" and she turned to follow Amos.

"No," McLean's low baritone was commanding. "The message first!"

Anne reached into her frilly pocket of pearl gray muslin and handed it to him without a word and vanished into the foyer.

McLean smothered an oath. " 'Tis a blank sheet of paper! What foolish joke is this—"

"No," Verity gestured for his silence. " 'Tis not. Here, give it to me," and when he did so, she held it at a slant beside the lamp. When she did, lines could be seen, pressed into the paper.

McLean took it from her once more, eyes narrowed. "By God," he murmured. "Someone's borne so hard upon the quill on the sheet above—"

"True," Verity said low. "It impressed the message on the sheet below."

McLean's head lifted, scowl deepened. "I take it that little British snob and her maid—and that ubiquitous butler—are safely in bed and will not come nosing around?"

"Yes—no. I mean, mother and I didn't dare send Amos until all slept. Brim was last to go. Monique says he never snuffs his candle until near midnight."

McLean bent his head over the indentations on the sheet of paper, his damp black hair falling across his forehead. Thad McHorry crowded near to peer around his shoulder. Thad glanced from under his startlingly black brows at Verity, blue eyes mischievous under the light hair. She knew Thad was twenty and that he loved a good joke better than good liquor. His disposition was nearly always merry and he wore an undeserved look of innocence, she reflected, returning his smile.

"Read it out loud, cap'n," Gabe Sleep said. His name was singularly appropriate for he had deceptively drowsy blue eyes under tumbled fair hair. He was tall and rangy and Cutler had told her long ago that Sleep was one of the best marksmen in the Carolinas. He and Thad came in to Charles Town to sell pelts they trapped in the backcountry, but they were nearly full-time partisans and they were fiercely loyal to McLean.

McLean read slowly, "Tarleton—convalescent dragoons ordered out August third, to make a diversion for Wemyss— I can't make this out—Santee. Given permission to plunder rebel leaders' possessions as incentive to persuade men to join." McLean let out an explosive oath.

"Quiet," Belion hissed, his saturnine and aquiline features dark with anger. Gabe's eyes were drowsier and gleaming beneath the lowered lids.

McLean held the paper at a sharper slant. "I can't make out each word, but it looks like Cornwallis wants Wemyss to leave the organization of the loyalist militia in Georgetown to Colonels Ball, Mills and another I can't decipher. And Tarleton will carry new orders which will send Brigadier General Lord Bainbridge toward Camden. Something big is shaping up—and soon!"

Anne Pair came into the room, carrying pot, cups and saucers on a large silver tray. "You've deciphered the message?" she asked, low-voiced.

"Yes," McLean said, taking the cup she had poured for him. "We are grateful to you and Verity—Colonel Marion's ankle has healed enough for him to do some hard riding now. And we'll meet up with him halfway between here and Snow's Island. I believe we can intercept Tarleton."

"Reckon we might upset the Butcher's plans to aid ol' Wemyss, cap'n," Gabe Sleep drawled, his eyes going to Belion's. "Now there's the man *I'd* like to get a shot at— Bloody Banastre." Amos came into the room on the heels of his words, clad in dry clothing and bringing cream and sugar.

"Anne—Verity," McLean said, "You've done a great service. If we can intercept and do battle with Tarleton, we have a chance of knocking him out of action, which would be as great a blessing as any patriot could ask."

"We just come into town to tell the cap'n about Colonel Marion bein' back in action again," Gabe drawled. "This here is better'n we bargained for—a chance at the tories under Tarleton."

McLean's grin was white in his sun-darkened face. "I shall arrange to go to Philadelphia to check on a large shipment of rice to that city."

"And I'll go to New York to visit my British clients there on matters concerning my new crop—indigo," Belion said laconically.

"There *will* be fighting, then," Verity murmured, thinking of Lord Bainbridge's blue eyes and winning smile. What if the partisans were to fall upon *him* on his way to Camden? Two hundred men might outnumber them, but the partisans were expert in ambushing—killing—and leaving pursuit far behind them in the dim recesses of the swamps.

"We hope there'll be fightin', Miss Verity," Thad said, with the innocent look of a choirboy while his eyes on her bosom were admiring.

Gabe Sleep said, "Ol' Wemyss ain't makin' any progress in Georgetown, anyway, cap'n. Half of the town's pretendin' to be tory and mighty nigh all of 'em are patriots." He suddenly seated himself Indian fashion on the floor. Looking up, he said, "Wemyss has a knack they say, fer collectin' enemies. He ain't well thought of even among the diehard tories. But that Bainbridge—he's the one stayin' here, ain't he, Miss Anne?" And at her nod, he finished. "He's downright likeable. He grinned at Thad like he knew just what he was up to when he tried to sign up as a tory."

"Bainbridge is a dangerous man," Tyler Belion said suddenly. "For all that good humor, Gabe, he's a hard-line British soldier and he's been a soldier all his life. *He's* the one I hope to get a shot at one day." There was an unaccustomed touch of heat in Belion's ordinarily cool voice, and Verity lowered her eyes and her heart beat heavily.

Thad said, "I'm too wet to set on your couch, Miss Anne," and he took his seat on the floor beside Gabe Sleep. Both men took care to lay their rifles gently beside them. Verity knew they were a gift from McLean, who had a number of them smuggled into Charles Town from a gunsmith named Scout in Davisville, Pennsylvania. McLean and Belion each had one themselves and were excellent marksmen, which deepened her fears for Sir James.

"Will you try to intercept General Bainbridge on his way to Camden?" she asked casually, as they all sipped their hot coffee.

"We don't know when he'll be leaving," McLean said, "and we'll have all we can handle with Tarleton, if we can catch him." He and Belion stood, too restless to seat themselves. "If you and Anne succeed in securing further intelligence, get word to Caleb. He can find us anywhere in the countryside."

"We shall,"Anne said serenely. "Amos can take the message to him."

Amos standing by said quietly, "Don't nobody British pay much mind to us black folks. Reckon I can come an' go easylike. An' Caleb, he know the swamps like his own hand." Then with heat, "Them British ain't know we're anxious as white folks fer independence."

"*We* know, Amos," McLean said quietly.

Thad spoke up. "Colonel Marion has over half a dozen black soldiers, as trusted an' true as any partisan in the troop." And he winked broadly at Amos, who grinned in return.

Anne Pair laughed suddenly with a touch of sarcasm. "Lord Bainbridge being sent to Camden will make his daughter both happy and unhappy."

McLean looked at her sharply, "Why?"

"She had a letter only today from her English lover and he is due any moment—to marry her. He's to be an aide to Lord Rawdon in Camden—and her father brought Savarra over here for just the purpose of separating them." Anne's lip curled. "And you may be sure that Verity and I shall do all in our power to assist the young lady in frustrating her father."

McLean grinned, finishing his coffee. "Aren't you afraid of the general's wrath?"

Anne gave him a wide-eyed stare, which made her appear suddenly younger and much like her beautiful daughter. "Whatever do you mean, my dear boy? Verity and I shall be among the most astonished when her departure is discovered." She paused, then added, "And that little snip Cotty as well, for she has wrung a promise from the girl that she may accompany her and her lover."

"And when is this elopement to take place?" McLean asked.

"The moment the groom arrives," Anne said, smiling at her silent daughter, "and that could be any day now. With his lordship gone, we shall slip her out—as Amos says, slicker than a greased eel."

"You're a brave woman, Anne," McLean said admiringly. Then with curiosity, "Who is the bridegroom?"

Verity said slowly, "A Lord Haverley's son, Peter. And Savarra vows there is no reason on earth for her father's disapproval—which leads me to think there must be some very good reasons indeed."

"You sound as though you have misgivings," Tyler Belion said, hazel eyes narrowing, "or compunctions?"

Verity was silent and her mother said challengingly, "Have you, Verity?"

"Savarra seems uncommonly intelligent, but her judgment of men and bridegrooms is her problem—not mine," her daughter replied evasively.

Belion and McLean watched her closely. Belion said bluntly, "At dinner that first night, Lord Bainbridge seemed quite charmed by you, Verity. Both Cutler and I remarked on it afterward. Even Bowman noticed it. Is it his disapproval that worries you?"

Verity's cheeks pinked and she flared, "You think, Tyler, I would let the admiration of an *enemy* go to my head? How little you know me! I shall help Savarra and her maid with great pleasure and be happy indeed to have them out of our house." She looked at her fiance defiantly.

"That sounds better," her mother said with satisfaction. Then wishfully, "Now if we could only rid ourselves of that Brim and his lordship."

"Nay, Anne," McLean said quietly. "We agreed long ago 'tis well he and his headquarters are in the house and you and Verity are clever enough to make use of them. I have no doubt that this—" he held up the now folded paper, then slipped it into an inner pocket of his waistcoat, "is but the first of much you will be able to pass on to us." His voice was low as he added, "And I can give you ladies the news that Gabe and Thad brought me earlier. General Horatio Gates has taken over the southern army in North Carolina. That means there will soon be further and more decisive action."

"Gates! I've heard of Gates," Anne Pair said uneasily. "Warren told me at the time of Burgoyne's surrender at Saratoga in New York back in 'seventy-seven, that Gates was not the hero they made him out to be. A man named Daniel Morgan had more to do with that defeat of the British than Horatio Gates."

"That's true enough," Tyler Belion said, his eyes on Verity, "and the rumor is that Washington preferred Nathanael Green to head up the southern army, but we must do the best we can with what we are given—and Congress has made this decision."

Verity's eyes were lowered, the thick crescents of her lashes like fans against her fair cheeks. "This does not bring me the comfort it should," she murmured, "for father held General Gates in low esteem."

"At least it's put new heart into many, ladies," Thad McHorry said, blue eyes twinkling. "It has into Gabe an' me because now we can give the British somethin' more than hit an' run encounters."

"We must leave now—and hurriedly," McLean said, "for I want to be well on the way to Snow's Island before this night is over."

The men began to rise and ready themselves. Gabe and Thad took up their prized rifles and the four men stood ready to leave.

Upstairs in her bedroom, Savarra slept uneasily. She had been far too stimulated and excited about Peter's letter, having reread it several times before retiring. Her dreams were fitful and full of Peter and obscure danger. The sudden neigh of a horse above the heavy rain and rolling thunder roused her fully.

She sat up in the sticky heat of the night. Could it be that Peter Haverley had come? With the thought, she leaped from bed and went to the window, raising it to peer out. The rain was still heavy but the wind had diminished and it seemed to her she could discern four horses in the courtyard below. It *was* Peter! No doubt he was conferring with the Pair women this minute—why hadn't they come to waken her? Hastily, she struck flint to the candle and the room bloomed with warm, dim light.

She flew about, silent as a ghost, donning her most beautiful dress, a pale pink satin, with festoons of lace on the elbow-length sleeves and on the panniers that draped away from the stomacher.

Automatically, she thought of going up to rouse Cotty to help her, then realized with sudden relief that this was her chance to escape without the little maid. She struggled with the hooks herself. She had only hours ago packed a small portmanteau against this very moment. Congratulating herself on her foresight, she donned her silk hose and tied the pink satin ribbons of her matching satin shoes with their delicate and feminine curved heels. Oh, in only minutes she would see Peter!

She went to her door, which was open, and as she had hoped, dimly heard subdued voices from below. No doubt they would come for her at any minute. She hurried faster and her fingers trembled with haste as she attempted to twist up her hair, before she gave up and tied the long, coarse mane back with a pink satin ribbon. She went to the armoire and pulled out her elegant blue velvet cape with the satin-lined hood. After all, it was raining heavily. But surely Peter had a carriage out front. Oh, how fortunate that he had come before her father's return!

Seizing her reticule and the portmanteau, which was a little heavier than she had intended it to be, she ran into the hall. As she took the stairs swiftly, the sound of male voices, held low, came more insistently to her ears. As she reached the foot of the stairs, she discerned the sound as coming from the drawing room. She dashed across the intervening space, her excitement almost unbearable. Naturally Peter would have brought men to help make good their escape.

For a flashing instant she stood before their astonished eyes, clothed as if for a ball. Her exquisite pale pink satin dress, exposing much of her bosom, was barely covered at the shoulders with the long, dark-blue velvet cape and in her hand was the small portmanteau.

She gasped, "Peter—" Then the breath went out of her lungs as if she had been struck a stunning blow.

McLean said dryly, "Do come in, Mistress Bainbridge."

"Cutler McLean—Tyler Belion! And those savages I saw on the quay!" she whispered. Then with gathering awareness of the significance of the scene, her voice rose. "I *knew* you were rebels—I knew it! You liars! You traitors—I shall tell my father!" Her eyes flew wide as McLean was on her in an instant, jerking her into the room, sending her portmanteau and reticule flying from her hand.

"Keep your voice down, madame," he said in a low voice, "or I'll knock the wind out of you here and now." He did not loosen his grip, though Savarra struggled fiercely.

She opened her mouth and drew breath to scream, but with sudden brutality, he caught both her wrists in one iron hand and clamped the other over her mouth. A faint strangled sound issued behind his muscular fingers. She was frantic now and her rage ungovernable. She had begun with indifferent dislike of this man, but now she hated him with a violence that made her weak.

All the others in the room began whispering together, but McLean was silent in his struggle with her. Savarra was much stronger than she appeared and she was still trying to scream. Over his clamped hand she looked into the faces around her and saw the knowledge that, in this one fatal moment, Belion's and McLean's careful cover as loyalists was blown to bits. As she fought, Savarra savored their frustration.

McLean and Belion and probably that deceptively gentle Baltazar, though he was not with them this night, would now be driven to the swamps for refuge, instead of coming and going in Charles Town as men with power to aid the patriot cause—or better yet, imprisoned!

Into her rapidly working mind came the realization that

the court of sequestration would take over Belion House and its thousands of acres of rice, indigo and timber. It would take over McLean's warehouses, too—and no doubt they had been smuggling supplies to the rebels. All that would stop now! There would be no more camaraderie with British officers that had paid off so handsomely for these traitors in foreknowledge of wagons of supplies being sent to Ninety-Six, to Camden, to Monck's Corner and Kingstree, all those outposts of which her father had spoken. And all because she had assumed her lover had come for her! Unexpected exhilaration swept her.

Now she was making unintelligible noises against his hand, which he was careful to hold so tightly she could not use her teeth against him. Indeed, he was pinching her jaws with such great force, tears of pain filled her eyes.

That leather-clad savage she had met on the quay, McHorry, eased up beside her and drawled, "If you keep on tryin' to yell, ma'am, we'll have to gag you. Can't have you rousin' all Charlest'n."

Abruptly she ceased to struggle and McLean cautiously moved his hand from her mouth. She hissed, "It doesn't matter. I have found you out and my father will find and hang you. Every one of you!"

Gabe looked at her reflectively from under his sleepy lids. "I reckon not, ma'am. You're the only one who knows an' we ain't aimin' for you to tell."

"Then killing women is part of your barbarity!" Savarra said scornfully. She looked up, her eyes a blaze of blue fury at the man holding her.

For the first time he smiled. "I don't think we'll have to kill you, Mistress Bainbridge."

"Then you are undone, sir, for I shall certainly tell of this gathering in the night." Her eyes were scathing as they touched Verity and Anne. "And I shall tell of *your* collaboration as well, ladies." Then with sudden realization, "I suspected you from the moment you laid hands on me on board the Lion! I should have warned my father immediately we arrived."

"But you didn't," McLean said smoothly, "nor will you now."

"But I *will*," she replied with sudden cold certainty. "You cannot keep me from it without killing me." She lifted her chin and the long fall of black hair swung about her shoulders and waist.

Belion looked at her, annoyance plain on his dark, sardonic countenance. "But we shall not kill you, madame." He glanced at McLean, who still imprisoned her hands, and added, "We can keep her mouth shut but one way—by taking her with us into the swamps. After all, her father can be told by Verity and Anne she has eloped with this Peter fellow, and for a time her absence will be accepted—perhaps for months if her father doesn't run into the bridegroom. And you and I, Cutler, will have free access to Charles Town and our businesses."

Savarra's heart sank with sudden terror. She swallowed hard and her hands, in that iron grip, grew moist.

"I was thinking the same thing," McLean said softly. "A damned nuisance, but necessary."

"An' the sooner the better," Thad said uneasily. "We ought to be well away from Charlest'n before the hour's out."

Savarra's jaws ached from McLean's powerful grip and the skin about them felt bruised. She became aware of Verity's look of pity.

"Cutler, there should be some other way—" and she glanced at her mother for support.

"You think we could secure a promise of silence from her?" he asked with heavy sarcasm.

She flashed, "I'll tell—you may be sure!"

With finality, McLean said, "There is no other way. We must return to my house so Tyler and I can change clothes, pack our supplies and be on our way immediately if we hope to get word to Marion and stop Tarleton's slaughter of our people." He turned to Belion. "We can leave letters as to our supposed destinations—dealing with our businesses— with Caleb. You can leave instructions with him for Abraham at Belion House. Then Caleb can alert Baltazar by word of mouth. We can't risk a note to him." Still holding her wrists with one strong hand, McLean caught up his tricorne from a chair and slung his own cape on, pushing Savarra along in front of him.

"She ain't hardly got up for the swamps," Gabe drawled, observing Savarra's fine dress reflectively.

"Cutler, whatever will you do with her," Verity asked, "when you find Tarleton and engage him in battle? Shouldn't I get her one of my riding habits?"

"Nay, Verity. A riding habit would be no better than this ball gown in the swamps. She'll have to wear what we wear. I have that at home." Then with a somber look at the dismayed mother and daughter, "Will you be able to tell Lord Bainbridge of the letter from Haverley convincingly—make him believe she has slipped out of the house with him?"

"Of course," Anne Pair said coolly. "She will leave by stealth, and Verity and I woke to find her gone. Cotty will probably set up a howl when she discovers she's been left behind and will corroborate the story by telling him of the letter herself."

"Let's go," McLean said to the men, "and get out of here before others awaken. Move ahead, Mistress Bainbridge, and not a sound out of you."

Savarra began to struggle once more, her eyes enormous with disbelief. "But you can't take *me* into a—a wilderness. You can't!" This could not be happening to her, Lord James Bainbridge's daughter—but as she looked at the men about her, those two wild men clad in leather and carrying their deadly rifles, she realized that these men made their own rules and a lord's daughter was no more than a minor and disagreeable chore they must assume.

Her back stiffened and she drew on her innate courage. "You will not keep me. I shall escape eventually and I shall see you all hang for this. My father will see to it."

"Not likely," McLean said grimly as they marched down the hall. "You're going to lose this war, Mistress Bainbridge."

She laughed low and scornfully, "We will not. Look at you," she added with contempt. "You don't know soldiering or warfare. Those two—animals," her eyes raked Gabe Sleep and Thad McHorry ahead of them, "are typical of what you have to put up against crack British troops. And when you lose, thank God I can leave this miserable country and go home."

Verity, following after them with lamp held high, said coldly, "Savarra, you may hate our country and demean our men, but Cutler is right. We are going to win."

"You will not," Savarra repeated rudely. "You're a fool, Verity, in more ways than one. I've watched you. My father will never—"

McLean interrupted, "Verity, if you come across more intelligence, get word to Caleb—he can find us no matter where we are."

Verity said anxiously, "Do be careful. I fear for you, Tyler—Cutler—for all of you."

To Savarra's surprise, Tyler stooped, caught Verity in a brief, fierce embrace. After he kissed her swiftly, his husky voice was urgent. "My darling, I love you—" and they separated as the others entered the big kitchen.

So—thought Savarra, this girl is attracted to my father and she is likely promised to a rebel!

In McLean's hard, competent grip, she was perforce silent and she moved with reluctance, forcing him to jerk her along. She still could not believe that these men would actually take her prisoner with them into the steamy jungles that lurked beyond Charles Town. But as the reality bored in on her, her spirit rose to meet it. She was a hardy, healthy Engilsh girl, used to horses and country life. She would survive and flourish on the scanty fare and murky conditions in the South Carolina swamp country. She swore it to herself. The British were admittedly a tough lot and Savarra proposed to be as tough as she needed to be until the moment of escape came. And it *would* come. She would see to that.

When the door opened on the steady downpour, McLean turned her roughly about. "Here, put up the hood of that cape and wrap it about you. 'Tis a very wet night."

Savarra did as he bid when he released her arms. Then she reiterated in a chill, firm voice, "My father will penetrate your lies and he will come after you—kill you all."

"I wouldn't count on that, ma'am," Gabe Sleep drawled as they all trooped out the rear door into the rain, which struck them with force.

Without ceremony, McLean hoisted her into the saddle on his stallion and mounted behind her. It was awkward, for her billowing skirts hung over the saddle as she sat to the side. She clung to the pommel and they scarcely touched, so ramrod-straight was she during the wet and miserable ride to the house on Tradd Street.

Savarra was already dampened thoroughly when they entered the house from the rear, and she was left in the care of the uneasy Thad McHorry and Gabe Sleep in the kitchen while McLean and Belion went to don other clothing.

When the two returned, she noted they were dressed much like the overmountain men. They wore the fringed leather breeches and coarse white shirts, with leather coats, also fringed. The clothes were well worn and they fitted themselves to McLean's big body like a second skin, making him appear even taller than his six feet two inches.

While Thad kept close watch on Savarra, McLean, Belion and Gabe collaborated with a giant black man they called Caleb. His wife, Corrie, a coffee-colored and pretty woman of middle years, came in and helped with packing their knapsacks with food and utensils. McLean wore the little visored cap that marked him as a South Carolina militiaman officer.

The two partisans sat down at the kitchen table and, by candlelight, wrote a detailed letter to the men who would care for their businesses.

"Caleb, you give this to the foreman at my warehouses. I've told him I'm going to Philadelphia on business and shall return as soon as possible," McLean said and then gave him explicit directions on what to say to any British who came asking after him.

Belion then gave him a letter to deliver to his man, Abraham, at Belion House. "New York's my destination, Caleb," he said with his somber smile.

When they had completed their preparations, in a very short time, McLean looked at Savarra, who felt already bedraggled from her ride in the rain. He said flatly, "You're going to be extremely uncomfortable in those clothes for they will be soaked before the night is over. And I can assure you, if 'tis vanity that keeps you in them, the men you meet will have little use for you. In fact, I shall probably have a hell of a time posting guards over you." He scowled, gray eyes hard as agate. "My suggestion to you is to don men's clothing, preferably something of leather to protect you from the weather. I have some such here I purchased for some very young boys who worked in the warehouses. 'Twill be too large for you even so. Still, you'll be much more comfortable."

"I'll do no such thing," she replied icily. "I shall wear my own clothing and I shall not be your captive long enough to need other apparel."

He made no response, but to her annoyance he had Caleb and Corrie pack another knapsack with the male clothing as if it were inevitable she would eventually come to wear it. Her determination hardened further.

In less than thirty minutes the men were ready to leave. Caleb had saddled a large gelding, Tamar, for Savarra with a man's saddle. McLean told her he had no sidesaddles and she sat stiffly upright in growing anger, holding to the pommel, while McLean held the reins and led the horse along behind his. He was taking no chances on her bolting and making a run for it.

Savarra knew it must be near three of the morning and all Charles Town was deep in slumber. In fact, they saw no lights through the rain, no other person as they took the Cooper

River Road northward from the city, which would end at Monck's Corner. And they would turn off long before that town was reached, McLean had announced.

In an hour, under the heavily falling rain, Charles Town was well behind them and they were on their way to a place Gabe had called Wadboo Creek. Savarra gathered from the conversation among the four men that they must ride several hours to reach the safety of the swamps.

McLean remarked that he felt Tarleton and his dragoons were not far ahead of them and he did not mean to engage him with only four men and the added hazard of a woman with them, so he sent Thad McHorry ahead to contact Marion and his men wherever they might be—likely Britton's Neck, they agreed. Then the four of them could rendezvous at Dunnock's Glen, he told Thad. He said, "You'll probably find out Tarleton's whereabouts on your way, Thad, and by the time we are all assembled, we can plan an ambush of the Butcher."

Thad rode off in the darkness and Savarra heard his hoof-beats diminishing in the rainy night. She was acutely uncomfortable, for the rain had by now thoroughly drenched all her garments, but Gabe Sleep, Tylcr Belion and Cutler McLean kept up a steady pace and McLean would not give her the reins to Tamar.

He had said, "And have you bolt? Nay, mistress. You will have to accept being led until we are too far for you to try to escape."

"We will never be that far," she replied, voice hard.

The four of them clipped along at a good gait, despite the rain, which, to her great relief, was diminishing slightly. Such a deluge would surely turn the countryside into a bog and the swamps of which she had heard into moving lakes and the rivers into torrents. It was a respite, though, no matter how unpleasant, from the oppressive August heat. The ground beneath Tamar's hooves squelched spongily now as the Cooper River narrowed beside them. She noted the land grew more marshy as they approached Wadboo Creek, which she assumed emptied into the Cooper.

At last, in the pale light of the drenched dawn, Savarra saw that the river beside them was full and the water swift, so swift that the hushed rushing sound was audible above the cries of early morning birds and the burring of insects in thick trees beyond their narrow path. Rain stopped at last and there were little lakes of mist just above the ground in open spaces.

Savarra had maintained her silence and the men threw her a curious glance occasionally. Her cape was soaked through and so was the pale pink satin dress and the petticoats beneath it, all of which in the watery morning light appeared bedraggled indeed. They clung to her knees as she sat to the side on the bay, Tamar. Even her hair was wet and she could never remember being so uncomfortable. But under the curious eyes of the men, her back was ramrod-straight and the full lips were firm above a chin tipped at a determined angle. She would show these half-tamed rebels the rugged stuff of which English men and women were made, she thought grimly.

McLean still held the reins to Tamar as he and Tyler Belion were ahead and Gabe Sleep brought up the rear with Savarra beside him. Silently she cursed McLean's insight that made sure his captive did not suddenly seize the reins to order the bay about and flee. She cursed Belion and Sleep, too, who were only casually interested to see how her endurance held up.

They came at last to the confluence of the Wadboo and the Cooper, a great boiling and rushing of waters.

McLean turned to Belion. "Let's go on up a little further where the river narrows and we'll ford as usual on horseback. Then we'll take the bridge over Wadboo and make camp in Dunnock's Glen where Thad and the others will find us."

Accordingly they traversed the bank of the Cooper until they reached a fairly narrow spot. Even so, the water was swift and Savarra realized they would have to swim the horses across the better part of it.

McLean addressed her at last. "Do you think you can ford the river riding as you are, Mistress Bainbridge?"

"Certainly," she replied angrily. "Give me the reins and I can do very well." She did not sound the least tired or dispirited from the long hours she had spent on horseback. The steel pride that lay behind her deceptively soft face stood her in good stead.

"Nay, mistress," he replied dryly. "I am not in the mood for a gallop after you."

Savarra, who had thought to do just that, let her sooty lashes fan thickly around innocent eyes. "But I cannot ride without something to hold to—over so swift a river."

The men had reined up beside them now, preparatory to plunging into the river.

"Give 'er the reins, cap'n," Gabe Sleep drawled. "I'd enjoy the chase—an' the catch."

She gave him a contemptuous glance. "*You'd* never catch me."

"But I would," McLean said quietly. "Now you twist your hands into Tamar's mane and you'll have plenty to hold."

"If I fall off, neither of you could catch me," she said threateningly.

Tyler Belion's saturnine grin was wry. "Now *that* would solve all our problems. They'd fish you out in Charles Town Bay, which would end the mystery of your disappearance and our secret would be quite safe."

Savarra concealed her alarm. She felt sure it would be quite within character for them to allow her to flounder in that turgid water until she drowned before their very eyes. Then to her astonishment and immediate fury, McLean backed his great stallion, Jed, plucked her from the gelding and put her before him on his horse.

She stiffened, then began a brief but vigorous scuffle, which he ended by clamping his arm so tightly about her waist he cut off her breath. She felt the give of her slender rib cage under the muscles of his right arm, while he took his saber in its leather sheath and laid it, with his rifle, across the saddle with his left.

Almost fainting from lack of breath, she was quite still as McLean put his heels gently into Jed's flanks and they stepped into the Cooper River.

Trees and water swam before her eyes, then righted themselves as his grip loosened, permitting her to drag in a deep breath. The horse moved several feet forward before reaching water that came above his belly. Then with a sudden plunge he was swimming. Savarra made an effort to lift her feet and the mass of clothing that hung about them, but it was fruitless. Water swept over her to the knees and she felt the strong pull of the current on her skirts.

Under his heavy load, even so powerful a mount as Jed sank into the water with each stroke of his legs, which further soaked her already wet clothing. When the horse finally pulled into shallow water, she saw that McLean's breeches and boots were drenched to the thigh.

Gabe Sleep and Belion, leading Tamar, were already across by the time Jed pulled his riders up on the bank. Tamar stood, ears twitching, as he observed the two walk up to him. Without a word, McLean lifted the dripping Savarra unceremoniously and seated her once again at the side of the man's saddle on Tamar.

With sudden rage, Savarra caught the pommel and with a lightning-like and fluid movement, flung her right leg across and was astride in the blink of an eye. Her wet garments sagged over her limbs and with a minimum of movement, she had twitched them down and only her slender slippers and a few inches of narrow ankle could be seen dangling above the stirrups.

For an instant the men, who had been observing, were blank before Gabe Sleep broke into a roar of laughter. McLean restrained a smile and Belion wore amazement.

"Ma'am, I'd swear you been practicin' for that," Gabe said, still laughing.

Savarra's eyes were murderous. Her voice was chill. "A gentleman would never have seen that—let alone remark upon it."

Sleep's sun-burned face showed two spots of deep red on his cheeks and McLean said with cold sarcasm, "Surely, mistress, you do not labor under the delusion that we are gentlemen."

"I know what you are—descendants of the scum from England's jails."

"Here," McLean said roughly, tossing the reins to her. "We are too far now for you to hope to escape. But follow closely behind unless you want a swamp spider down your back, or a lizard up your skirt."

Savarra caught the reins and her olive face paled at his threat. She moved up to ride beside him, her eyes quick as they looked about her. The sun had come out now and the August air was steamy under the great cypresses, pines and oaks. The watery ground on either side of the riders kept them on a sandy ridge near the Wadboo, which was much smaller than the Cooper, but was very swift and full now.

She knew McLean was making for the rendezvous the men had spoken of, a small high place in the swamp they called Dunnock's Glen. Belion had spoken of it as being halfway to some ferry—Leneud's?—at the Santee River and she knew it must be in the deeps of the forest. They clattered suddenly over a bridge made of roughly sawn planks, riding at an angle away from the narrow road leading from the bridge. The trees rose about them once more, an impenetrable phalanx to one who did not know them.

She had been in the saddle nearly seven hours without pause for food or drink. Silently and bitterly, she regretted her headlong nature, her impatience and the sublime certainty that had driven her down to the drawing room last night. She knew well that her presence had slowed these men, put the burden of her welfare on them, though God knew they seemed to regard *that* lightly enough. For an instant, her shoulders drooped and she wondered if they would ever stop. Thirst was almost painful and she swallowed dryly.

McLean slanted a look at her and she lifted her chin, her brilliant eyes alert to every sight around her. Still, she could not hide the pale blue smudges beneath thick lashes. Savarra was tired for all her resolution not to show it. Without a word, McLean unhooked the canteen at his side, pulled out the cork and handed it to her. She drank thirstily, but returned it with equal silence.

McLean wound further and further away from the Wadboo and she directed Tamar quickly to follow each turn. She had learned to ride astride long ago in England. She was as strong as a girl bred in the country because of her father's manor houses in the rolling open lands and forests of Britain. Savarra's dexterity and stamina were considerable, and both were called on now.

The horses began splashing through swamp water, past high spots of black ooze. Great, feathery cypresses and pines were about them, but McLean and his companions were as easy as if they rode familiar streets. She recalled with renewed bitterness Verity's telling her McLean and Belion had been brought up with guns in their hands, shown pathways through this trackless maze by their black mentors, Caleb and Abraham. She should have realized then that Verity had very nearly given away their secret—that they were well equipped for partisan warfare.

Little brown and green lizards, discouraged by the heavy rain, were venturing forth again and could be seen on the broad rough trunks of the trees as they skittered, stopped, clung, eyes darting, then skittered again.

Suddenly she gave a gasping little cry and the men reined up to look at her. She pointed a trembling finger at a low hanging limb beyond. A monstrous spider hung still as death in a thick, dark web, a great sprawling black thing with long, terrifying legs spread out about it.

McLean laughed as Gabe Sleep drawled, "Ma'am, that's just an ol' swamp spider. The woods is full of 'em. We'll go 'round her."

McLean looked at the bagging black body in its ropey house and said, "It's a fairly harmless creature when undisturbed, mistress, despite its deadly aspect."

As they circled around it, Savarra repressed a shudder and asked, "Where are we?" and she looked about her with undisguised dismay.

"Well into Wadboo Swamp," was the short reply.

On either side of them were wallows and ooze and Savarra saw three huge, scaly bodies, long tailed and short legged, lying half on tussocks, half in the water, dozing. They were almost disguised by the terrain, so much like their muckled bodies that they blended into the surroundings easily.

"What—are they?" she asked, pointing and taking care that her finger did not tremble this time, even as she guided Tamar nearer to Jed. Her set face was even paler and she sat erect in the saddle.

"Alligators," McLean replied laconically as he looked down at the shallow water interspersed wtih tussocks. "But it's snakes we have to watch out for," he added, carefully approaching a series of tussocks.

Gabe volunteered, "Under them tufts of grass are sleepin' places for moccasins, an' their bite means almost certain death. Let Tamar have his head, ma'am, like I'm doin' with Whiskey. They know where to put their feet."

The other two men were as alert as he and all four riders let the horses pick their way daintily through the watery bog.

In less than an hour, they approached Dunnock's Glen. Higher ground was under the horses' hooves and, passing through a ring of giant cypresses, they stepped up onto a small, clear hillock of land. The sand beneath was dry from hot sunlight, which was unobscured over much of the mound of dry land. Rank grass covered some of it, but the men drew rein and Gabe let out a yell of pleasure as the horses bent to crop the thick grass edging the glen.

"By thunder, I'm thirsty and hungry," Gabe swore happily and unlashed the pans and knapsacks from the rear of his horse, adding, "Here, Whiskey, ol' boy, I'll take off your saddle an' then start some bacon an' hoecake."

"I've the coffee and a pot for it—rice for later, too," Tyler Belion said cheerfully.

Savarra sat Tamar, loking down at them with disdain. She

was utterly miserable in her wet, clinging clothing and wondered briefly if she would be able to endure it until it dried out. She reflected glumly that it would take hours for the petticoats to dry on her body.

McLean was watching her and he suddenly came to her and said shortly, "I'll help you down."

She looked at him with cold hauteur, but permitted him to reach up and lift her from the horse, a chore done without revealing too much ankle. The satin dress was wrinkled and dripping water still. Her expression was dour as she stood on the sandy turf, dress and petticoats so weighted with water they dragged the ground, picking up sand and dirt with each movement. She had long ago shed the soaked blue-velvet cape and it lay wetly across the back of her horse.

McLean reached up, pulled it off and attempted to wring it out, but it was too cumbersome. He said briefly, "I'll hang it over yonder limb." He turned, then added, "You know, Mistress Bainbridge, I have brought other clothing for you, more suited to riding—as you do," a little smile flickered, "and certainly it is dry."

"I know," she replied in sudden weary surrender. "I may as well put it on. This dress will be hours drying out, if ever it does."

"Days," he said succinctly, looking at the sodden mass that hung from her hips and stomacher. In the low-necked gown, much of her bosom was revealed, but she lifted her head under his cool appraisal and made no effort to cover herself. He added, "The shirt will cover you somewhat better, too," he smiled then, eyes twinkling, "leaving less exposed for the mosquitoes to feed on tonight. You will find they can be more than a nuisance."

She watched as he strode to a nearby stunted oak and flung the cape over a low limb. Then he went to his horse and unfastened the knapsack into which Corrie had packed a youth's breeches, stockings and shirt. He pulled out underclothing, which Corrie had thoughtfully added on her own, and said, "Wait here and I will find you a proper dressing room beyond the glen."

Savarra saw that he followed a slender strip of sandy land some distance from the glen and well hidden among trees and undergrowth. On his return, he examined the ground even more closely. Looking for snakes no doubt, she thought, and shivered. She waited dejectedly, reflecting she had never been so uncomfortable in her pampered life. She was exhausted, wet, hungry, thirsty and still suffering pangs of rage at having been so expertly carried off by these rebels.

McLean thrust the clothes at her. "They'll be too large of course, but there's a belt and they're dry." He took her by the arm and escorted her to the place he had found. There were a few palmettos, their spiky leaves thrust out like fans, and they formed a good screen. She eyed the ground and terrain warily and McLean smiled. Savarra was a quick study. Already she was alerted to many of the dangers in the swamps and she meant to survive this ordeal. There would come the moment when she could take Tamar in the dark of night and be gone, she told herself as McLean left her to the privacy of her palmetto-framed dressing room.

When she returned to the glen, the men had unsaddled their mounts, tethering them back near the trees where the grass was thick and green. Gabe Sleep had already kindled a fire and had the pewter pan with bacon in it over the flames. He was industriously mixing what he called hoecake in another deeper pan. Belion had put the coffee pot on and the first faint fragrance of cooking food and drink prodded Savarra's appetite.

She felt immeasurably better in the dry clothing and, though it was the first time she had ever worn breeches, she was not the least dismayed by them. In fact, though they were a little too large, she felt a freedom of movement that was enjoyable. Her breasts were pointedly visible beneath the linen shirt, but there was nothing she could do about it, having no undergarment for her upper portions. She carried her pink satin dress and petticoats, a soggy weight in her hands.

The only parts of her previous clothing that remained were the entirely useless little slippers on her feet. They were completely feminine, lacing up the ankle and covering only the forepart of her feet, the open backs being supported by absurd little curved wooden heels. They accentuated her incongruous male garb.

McLean, looking at them, smothered an oath. "Damn! I should have remembered boots for you."

"I'm going to throw away my gown and petticoats—they are ruined," Savarra told him.

McLean, squatting before the fire, said, "We'd better bury them. I'd be very unhappy if tories found them and tracked you down." He put a coal from the fire to his pipe.

"They will find me anyway," she said confidently, "and you will all receive your just deserts."

He said nothing but took the ruined garments from her and went to the edge of the bog. With a short spade, he dug a deep hole and poked the pink satin and ruffles into the yielding earth, then shoveled a heavy layer of it over the clothing.

Savarra noticed that the men glanced at her repeatedly and there was reluctant admiration in their eyes. She could not know it, but the boy's clothing accentuated her provocative figure and by sheer contrast added to her aristocratic beauty.

As they waited for the meal to cook, the men talked and Savarra listened. McLean seemed cognizant of the many facets of this semi-civil war, knowing that native Americans were fighting each other, tory and loyalist against whig and patriot, and they discussed the resultant bitterness in low, angry voices. As she listened, she became interested despite her disgust with the country and the men who inhabited it. She had taken another swallow from McLean's canteen, but her hunger was unabated.

She sniffed the air appreciatively but her question was arrogant. "When will the food be ready?"

Belion gave her a surly glance. "Soon enough."

Savarra felt an unwelcome pang of sympathy for him. He loved Verity deeply and her father had come between them. She *knew* it by a deep instinctual sense.

Shortly they were all seated back from the fire, eating hoecake and bacon, washed down with cups of delicious coffee. Savarra relished every bite of this strange fare, which surprised her considerably, the hoecake being a sort of cornmeal mixed with seasonings and water and cooked over the fire in a pan.

As they ate and drank, McLean said, "It's a long way to Britton's Neck and Thad may have to go that far to find Marion. We'll have plenty of time to rest and be ready when he comes—likely he'll have word of Tarleton's whereabouts as well."

"I hope Marion's gathered up enough men for us to take him on and whip him," Belion said. "If not, we can always fall back on ambush." Then contemplatively, "I sometimes think that's more effective than head-on conflict."

They talked on for some time, but Savarra was growing

extremely drowsy. Her lids drooped and she yawned prodigiously two or three times.

McLean bent his cold, slate gray eyes on her. "You'd better bed down for the day, Mistress Bainbridge. You've had a long day and night."

He went to the nearby trees, heavily bearded with curling gray moss, and ripped off an armful. He placed it like a mat under a great cypress and threw a blanket over it.

"It's hardly what you're used to, as a lord's daughter," he said mockingly, "but it will do for now."

Savarra was too weary to make a response, and when she stretched out on the makeshift bed she thought she had never felt anything so comfortingly welcome. No down mattress on which she ever slept felt better, and within five minutes she was deep in sleep.

It was late evening when she roused. The sun was setting, but all she could see through the thick verdure was the orange sky. As she looked about, she saw the men were stirring from their own substitute beds. In a little while they were up and about, preparing the last meal of the day. Supper was much like the noonday meal, but it was eaten with good appetite. Belion's sack of rice added to their menu. By the time they finished, they were well rested and darkness was coming on.

"It'll be at least tomorrow before Thad returns," McLean reflected. "He could have a hard time finding the colonel—they range the country."

Gabe drawled, "He'll be back by mornin', I'll bet. An' if he runs into the British—well. Thad can fool the sharpest redcoat with that innocent look of a countryman come to take up for the crown."

Belion's infrequent smile creased his lean cheeks. "That he could," and he sipped at a final cup of coffee.

Savarra looked at the three of them, thinking, *I hope he's been captured and they make him tell where we are!*

Gabe took the pans and the pewter dishes to the edge of the swamp where the water was clear and washed them thoroughly in the fading light. The rest of them prepared to retire to their moss beds for the night.

Just as the sun disappeared and the late evening heat was intense, a faint and unusual sound disturbed the stillness. The four of them heard it simultaneously, and in the act of lighting his pipe McLean halted, head up, eyes alert.

The sound grew and became recognizable as rapid movement through the watery terrain to the north. Savarra realized it was coming from the direction Thad had taken—where Leneud's Ferry and the Santee River lay.

Then all at once it was distinguishable—horses' hooves at a gallop and hoarse shouts. Instantly, the three men about her seized their rifles, polished stocks gleaming in the dimming light.

Savarra asked, "What is it?" A wild hope lifted her heart magically. Could it be British troops?

"Men—horses," Belion said shortly.

"You get behind those trees over there," McLean commanded her, "and don't make a sound." Then he added warningly, "If they're British, in this light you could be mistaken for a patriot and shot on sight."

But Savarra decided silently, if they were British, she would run screaming from the woods, shouting her name. Excitement filled her with fresh hope.

The splashing hooves grew nearer as the crashing sound of underbrush increased. All three men stood ready with their rifles, crouching behind trees, eyes fixed in the fading light toward the oncoming men. Suddenly, in the dying light of the day, Thad McHorry on his horse Rosy appeared.

He yelled, "Three men from Tarleton's Legion after me—" and he drew hard rein, forcing his mare to rear until she sank on her haunches as he slid from the saddle. Horse and man rose to their feet and Thad slapped the well-trained animal on her rump, saying, "Skedaddle, Rosy!" The horse cantered tiredly into the trees beyond the dying fire and Thad, gripping his rifle, ran to McLean.

Savarra, straining, could hear his hoarse young voice. "Tarleton's Legion was at Leneud's Ferry. I run onto 'em unexpectedly so I joined 'em. Told 'em I was a loyalist from Monck's Corner." His breath was short and the crashing sound of his pursuers came clearly on the still evening air.

Savarra crept nearer to where the two men were crouched behind the broad trunk of a cypress. Her small shoes sank into the marshy ground silently.

Thad's voice lowered. "I would'a got away with it an' gone on to the Colonel by dark, after I got all their plans, but fer that low scum from Charlest'n, Slayton Scurlock, spottin' me. Lucky I was still mounted—"

Three horsemen burst into the clearing and simultaneously four rifles spoke from the trees, the flash of fire bright in the evening dusk. One man toppled from his horse and the other two spun about, one lurching in his saddle, the other bawling, "Come on, Scurlock! There's a nest of 'em here!" and the thudding hooves went splashing back in the direction from when they had come.

Savarra straightened up, stunned. It had all happened so quickly—before she could run out and call to them, they were gone.

Gabe Sleep stepped out from his tree, swearing, "Hell, men—they'll get away!" and he whistled his gelding, Whiskey, out to mount him.

McLean called out, "No, Gabe! Let them go. Thad's horse is winded and Scurlock knows Tyler and me as well. By the time we get our wigs and daub our faces, they'll be too far to catch."

Savarra followed as the men came slowly into a circle about the glowing coals that were all that remained of the supper fire. McLean bent over the man lying sprawled beside it. He looked up at his companions and said bluntly, "Whichever of us nailed this one hit dead center. Right between the eyes. Anyone know him?"

The men looked at the dead man and each shook his head. Savarra felt a tremor run through her. She had never in her life seen a dead man and, even though the day was almost gone, the sky ranging from lemon yellow to darkest blue, she could see that the man was young, no more than eighteen—her own age. Regret and fear and rage welled up within her, blurring her vision.

"Let's form a burial detail," McLean said. "Gabe, you and I and Tyler will dig the grave near the edge of the glen—out of the water." He muttered under his breath, "He was too young to be toting a gun."

"We're all too young," Gabe drawled. "I ain't but twenty-four an' my grandpappy died at ninety-two—I ain't never going to make it that long."

They all laughed shortly and McLean said, "Thad, go through his pockets and see if he carries any orders or letters that might be of use to us." He looked about suddenly and shouted, "Mistress Bainbridge—"

"I'm still here, Mr. McLean, and a witness to your murdering an innocent loyalist."

Gabe Sleep's voice was hard as hers when he said roughly, "There ain't no such thing as an innocent loyalist, lady. He'd a'kilt us quicker'n a wink, could he get off the shots." He stooped and picked up the musket that lay beside the dead youth's body.

"An' they sure meant to kill me," Thad put in feelingly, "an' damn near did. They got off four shots at me on the way here. One of 'em knocked my hat off."

Gabe put out a big rough hand and rubbed up McHorry's hair, laughing.

"Go on an' laugh," McHorry said aggrievedly as he bent to go through the youth's pockets. "If it'd been you, Gabe, I reckon we'd a'heard you yell three miles away. An' meantime, you better round up this tory's horse. He looks to be a good 'un an' he'll come in handy later."

Savarra stood in the renewed firelight, watching them dig the grave with short spades they packed in their partisan gear. She felt her stomach twist afresh with impotent rage that she had walked right into their hands. *Peter!* she had cried, then found herself facing a roomful of enemies. What a little idiot she had been. She must take care not to give in to her tempestuous nature. She was learning a very hard way.

When they tamped the last spadeful of earth on the fresh grave, McLean came to her and said coldly, "Take your blanket and make your bed down near the fire now. Alligators have been known to crawl into the glen at night and wildcats are prevalent." As he spoke the last words, a faint scream, high-pitched and chilling, floated from the depths of the swamp and somewhere near a peculiar, hair-lifting cry suspended itself over them. Savarra felt gooseflesh rise along the backs of her arms. She did not like the swamps at night.

The tory's horse, tethered with the others, gave a quick neigh and Thad went to the gelding and stroked his neck, speaking soothingly.

"Screech owl," Belion said briefly, noting Savarra's wide startled eyes.

She squared her slender shoulders determinedly and took the blanket without reply. For a moment she stood insolently near McLean, aware of a powerful urge to strike at him, to hurt him for the indignities he had heaped upon her in the last twenty-four hours. He seemed to sense her emotion and, for a flashing instant, his muscles tensed and he looked at her mockingly.

With forced indifference, she turned away, saying, "I'm not afraid of this ugly land—and I'm not afraid of *you*."

But there was a timbre in these last words that belied them and McLean smiled slowly. She was afraid, and she sensed that it pleasured him. It was then she realized with a shock that the man's emotions were much like her own and for very little he would take hold of her, punish her for her hatred of him and all he stood for. He watched her alertly now, but she kept her eyes averted as she went to the edge of the clearing and picked up the moss he had gathered for her earlier in the day. He kept watching as she returned and spread it and then her blanket down not too far from the fire.

When she laid herself upon it, he turned away at last. The others gravitated toward the campfire as Thad motioned to them silently. Savarra laid very still and, as they came together, she closed her eyes, feigning sleep. She felt their eyes on her and this time she kept her lashes very still.

Thad spoke then, his voice low, and she strained to hear. "Men, while I was gettin' away with bein' a loyalist, I learned some things that'll have a bearin' on what we do now."

"Go on." Belion's deep voice was impatient.

"Reckon I oughta talk—with her so near?"

"Aw, she's asleep already," It was Gabe Sleep's deliberate drawl.

"It doesn't matter," McLean's voice was even. "She'll be in the swamps for the duration. We can't let her return and you all know that."

"That's true." Thad's voice was reflective, and Savarra lifted her thick lashes a fraction to see Belion leaning forward tensely as Thad took up a stick and made meaningless scrawls in the sand before him. McLean's broad shoulders and back were to her. She did not move a muscle. She wanted to hear what McHorry had to say and he began. "First of all, Tarleton was joined by twenty-five loyalist militia under Colonel John Coming Ball whilst I was there. An' they're gettin' ready to move on to Kingstree, plunderin' all the way. I heard Tarleton hisself, talkin' to Ball, an' they're goin' to Camden eventually. Somethin' big's in the wind an' there's a powerful concentration of redcoats at Camden already. Tarleton said Cornwallis hisself is there an' his man Lord Rawdon an' his regiment."

He fell silent and Belion asked, "Do you think they're getting ready to attack Gates?"

"I reckon," Gabe Sleep said laconically. "I told you when we come into Charlest'n, cap'n, that Gates has moved his army out of Hillsborough in North Carolina. My guess is Tarleton, Rawdon an' Cornwallis are massin' their men to meet Gates in combat."

McLean said nothing as the men conversed eagerly. Belion said, "By God, I'd like to meet up with Gates' army and join them. We could lick the British with an army to match theirs."

"Might be Colonel Marion an' his men have already joined Gates," Gabe said thoughtfully. "Bet Sumter's with him too, an' Pickens—most of the men in the backcountry will want to be in on it if there's a fight."

"And there will be a fight," Belion said quickly. "This could be the turning point." His voice deepened with excitement.

Gabe said hopefully, "We could strike out for Camden in the mornin' ourselves. We'd be bound to find some of our people who would know where Gates is, if he's marchin' on Camden."

Savarra felt an upsurge of hope. If they took her toward Camden—with all her countrymen massed there—

McLean said slowly, "I think we should go on to Britton's Neck to find Marion. There'll be some men gathering there, even if the colonel's gone with Gates. If he has, we can strike out for the army ourselves with the others who may have gathered there." He paused. "There should be more than four of us as we move through tory country."

"He's right," Belion said, deflated. Then with asperity, "What will we do with our British baggage?" Savarra could feel him looking at her as he added slowly, "If we do go into combat—"

"One of us will have to hide out with her," McLean said with an exasperation of his own. "I wouldn't put it past her to get into the thick of it on the King's side and bullets be damned."

"It ain't goin' to be me," Gabe said positively.

"Nor me," McHorry said with equal determination. "She's about the most beautiful woman I ever saw, but she's too thorny for me."

"We'll meet up with others as we make Britton's Neck. There'll be some older men, less eager to fight. We can put her in their care well back from the field," McLean said firmly.

Belion spoke through a yawn. "Think we should post guard in case Scurlock comes back? I know that bastard well and he's a tricky man in business as well as in war. He shortchanged Bowman on an order of barrels—claimed they were poor grade and wouldn't pay the full amount owed. Bowman wrote it off as a loss."

McLean said, "I think we winged him and he's not a man to take too many risks, being careful of his own neck. We'll strike out for Leneud's Ferry at dawn—Tarleton being gone—cross the Santee there and be well on our way to Britton's Neck by evening. I know some good patriots on the Black River who'll give us provisions."

There was silence then, but for the sound of movement among the men. Savarra lifted her lashes narrowly once more and saw they were dispersing to their own beds, not far from the fire.

As he bedded down, McHorry said, "We better sleep light. I wouldn't put it past that English wildcat to try to murder us in our sleep." General quiet laughter followed his remark.

But Gabe Sleep responded, "I've thought of that, Thad, an' I'll have one eye open and my gun and knife at hand."

Savarra, lying still on her bed of moss, thought grimly, *I'd do it too, if I could!* Instead, fatigue took her and, with it, sound sleep.

Five

Savarra roused before dawn when the men about her began stirring. She lay quiet while they built the fire and prepared the spare breakfast. Hunger drove her up when coffee began to boil. She had developed a preference for that beverage since her arrival in America, but she would not give her captors the satisfaction of knowing that.

She noted the dead tory's horse had adjusted to his new surroundings and was munching contentedly with the others on the luxuriant swamp grass that edged the glen.

"Breakfast, ma'am," Thad McHorry said, glimpsing her rising in the faint, pearly light. He eyed her warily, admiration and dislike mingling on his misleadingly innocent face. He held a steaming cup of coffee in his hand.

Sleeping in rough male clothing had made her feel unkempt, and her waist-length hair was hard to keep out of the way. Now she wrestled with it, trying to loop it up and tie it with the ineffectual pink satin ribbon, which was much the worse for wear.

McLean appeared suddenly and handed her a small wooden comb and two thin strips of rawhide. "Comb it and loop it. Tie it with the rawhide. It won't slip," he said curtly.

She took the comb and strips of leather without comment and he went to the fire to take up his plate and eat. It was a great relief to her to comb the long tangled mass of coarse black hair.

Breakfast was quickly eaten and, though it was much like their evening meal the night before, Savarra relished it. In less than an hour, with Gabe Sleep leading the extra horse by the bridle, they were leaving Dunnock's Glen. The sun was just about to rise over the horizon, barely glimpsed through thick tree trunks and undergrowth, as the small troop splashed into the swamp, avoiding gnarled cypress knees which thrust themselves up out of the water at every turn.

It was a long tedious ride to the thinly marked road leading to Leneud's Ferry, and all the time they moved forward Savarra was thinking furiously. From what the men said, she knew there were many loyalist farms and plantations not too far off their trail. If she could somehow find one, she felt sure she could escape. Her hatred of these men had reached such proportions, she was sure she could gladly pull the trigger on any of them—if only she could get her hands on a gun.

And now they were taking her farther and farther away from Charles Town and Peter. She wondered briefly if Peter had come to the Pair house after all and what excuse that calm-faced Verity and her chill mother had given him. Probably exactly what McLean had suggested to them! Even Cotty would tell him of the letter—likely show it to him. It had been in her reticule which had flown out of her hand when McLean had seized her. She came at last to the decision that, if she were to escape these men, she would have to do it on her own.

Thus she rode along, not speaking or being spoken to, until Leneud's Ferry was reached. There before her spread the Santee River, greatly swollen from the recent rains, and there was evidence on the trampled and littered turf that there had been a large encampment of men nearby. She wished with sudden violence that Tarleton and his helmeted legion would swoop down on McLean and his men now.

But the ferryman volunteered the information that Tarleton's Legion had been gone several hours. "He's on his way to Kingstree," he said, spitting tobacco juice over eight feet, "a-burnin' an' a-plunderin' all the way."

"Did you hear where they planned to go after that?" McLean asked casually.

"Nope. They're mighty tetchy an' prideful, them Britishers an' loyalists. A neutral has a hard time these days."

"I'll wager you do," Tyler Belion said sarcastically.

"I got no quarrel with the British," the man said defensively, "or the whigs. I just wanter live in peace an' ply my trade—it'll be 'alf a pound, no Continental money took—fer crossin' over."

By the time they reached the other side of the Santee, the defensive ferryman had given additional and meager information. He had overheard two men talking of Cornwallis's orders to lay punishment on the rebels without mercy.

Savarra was uneasy listening to these orders, for she could imagine the desolation that would lie in the wake of a man as impulsive and thorough as Banastre Tarleton—her father did not like the man. For the first time, she conceded in her mind that these rebels were not only fighting for their hard-won worldly goods but for their lives. But did they not deserve it, she asked herself stubbornly, for defying their mother country?

Three days slipped by and Savarra became inured to her days in the saddle. They passed farm houses and plantations, and always McLean knew which would welcome them. They were able to augment their provisions from time to time and Gabe Sleep nearly always brought in a brace of squirrels, or a young deer, both of which were delicious when roasted slowly over the fire.

When at last they reached Britton's Neck it was August tenth. There, Savarra was aghast at the sight of men in such a ragged melange of clothing they looked half-clad. But they also looked to be robust backwoodsmen bursting with health as they greeted the men about her.

The extra horse that had belonged to the dead tory youth was immediately spoken for by a man named Baldwin, who said his own mount had been shot from under him in a recent skirmish. Indeed, horses were at a premium and all the men who were afoot were hoping to secure horses eventually.

Most of them seemed to be long-time friends. They were deferential to McLean, knowing his rank of captain, but his clothing was but little less worn than theirs. The lanky woodsman, Baldwin, was in charge of the group, with the rank of sergeant, and her captors conversed with him at length.

In the hubbub of their arrival, it was learned that Marion and some of his men were already with Gates. A compact and competent man about thirty-five named Sam Kinley, who had his horse shot from under him by a British patrol, had a message for the men collecting here. He had hidden in the woods and slowly made his way back to Britton's Neck with word from Colonel Marion that patriots now collecting were to wait for word from him to make their next move. All of them seemed to accept Savarra's predicament with a kind of detached interest, which at first infuriated and then relieved her.

Late that evening, after she had eaten, Savarra unobtrusively sat in the shadows behind McLean and the others, where she could overhear.

"That Gen'ral Horatio Gates ain't too smart," Sam Kinley was saying over the last of his supper of venison and rice. "DeKalb wanted him to march through friendly country where provisions could be got on his way to meet the British. But he claimed that's too round-about to suit him." Kinley tossed a clean-picked bone off in the darkness. "So he's marchin' on Camden through the pine barrens an' ain't nobody but tories in there. I seen some of the men eatin' green corn an' peaches an' thickenin' their soup with hair powder. Honest to God, the men's bowels is in such shape they can't hardly march. But Gates—he's certain they'll meet and beat the British."

McLean said thoughtfully, "And even so, Colonel Marion is still with them?"

Kinley laughed shortly, "Not fer long, I reckon. The reg'lars look down on us militia—because of our ragged clothes." His voice was dry. There was a long silence as Kinley wiped his mouth on his sleeve. Then, "Fact is, I heard just before I left, that Gates just might—*might*, mind you—detach Marion an' his men to go down country and destroy all boats and crafts of any kind he can find on the Santee to keep Cornwallis an' the British from escapin' him."

Baldwin, big and burly with a full beard, his teeth gleaming in the firelight, laughed dourly. "Sure hope the gen'ral's as long on know-how an' success as he is on confidence. Sounds like a powerful know-it-all, to me."

"Then you think Marion will be coming back here to organize that mission?" Bellon asked.

"I reckon," Sam Kinley answered, "on his way anyhow. He's supposed to take over the Williamsburg Militia to help him carry out Gates' orders—*if* he ever gets his orders."

Savarra, sitting in the shadowy darkness, thought it was all very poorly organized. Gates sounded a fool, and so much the better for the British. Her father would surely be among those soldiers opposing Gates—and so might Peter. This last caused her some qualms, for Peter, despite his military training, seemed better suited to a social life. But she put her fears from her mind, reminding herself that Peter would excel at anything he chose.

McLean drawled, "We'll stay in camp with you until we know the colonel's plans and join in with him. Gates can obviously do without our disreputable appearance." The curious mixture of a British accent and the soft Carolina pronounciation was singularly attractive in his deep voice.

Gabe Sleep said flatly, "I'll stick with you, cap'n—me an' Thad, no matter what's planned at Camden."

Days went by and Savarra found she was not the only woman in camp on occasion. There were four wives and two daughters who appeared out of the woods to cook for their men and patch their fraying clothing, often. They brought meager food supplies and they came and went, but she did not strike up a conversation with any of them, nor did they approach her. Indeed, they looked at her resentfully and she knew they had been told her background and her sympathies, which added a kind of frustration to her already heavy heart. The men seemed to take her presence casually enough, though there were a few young bucks who watched her covertly.

They had remained on Britton's Neck for upwards of a week when word came that Marion had taken over the Williamsburg Militia and was seeking men to join him at Witherspoon's Ferry on Lynche's Creek, only ten miles southwest of them.

There was an immediate exodus and Savarra was unceremoniously roused from slumber that night of August seventeenth. Because of the shortage of horses among the men, she was given what they called a "tackey," while Tamar was given to Sam Kinley over her protests. The tackey was what the name implied, an insignificant-looking little animal, born and bred in the swamps, which it loved. It was a short, squat and placid horse and its large brown eyes wore an affectionate expression. Kinley had irreverently named the little beast King George III.

Savarra regarded the animal, which was without a saddle. Even the bridle looked worn. She said to McLean in outrage, "I will not mount such a beast!"

"You will or you'll walk," he said, as arrogant as she.

Savarra looked up at him in helpless fury. Above his head was the great vault of the sky, flowered with stars, and the night around them was filled with the carefully quiet movement of men and animals. The wives and daughters had vanished into the woods from which they had come and Savarra was once again the only woman among the partisans.

McLean pressed his heels into Jed's satin flanks. She could feel the eyes of Gabe Sleep and Thad McHorry, while Belion had moved on ahead with the other men.

Thad said warily, "Want me to help you mount, ma'am?" Short as the little horse was, she would have difficulty swinging a leg over him.

But she said disdainfully, "No," and, clenching her hands in the tangled, burry mane, she hoisted herself awkwardly on his back. The tackey moved obediently forward with the rest of the horses.

Savarra found herself mounted two or three feet below McLean and his men, who surrounded her now. The tackey took two steps to their one, which meant an uncomfortable jouncing gait for her. She burned with humiliation as they rode through the still August night toward Witherspoon's Ferry. Her clothing by now felt grimy upon her slender frame and her delicate nose was offended by the odor of leather, for she did not know how much of the smell came from her clothing and how much from her own person. Her only comfort was the fact that those about her were even more rank than she herself. She had performed superficial bathing in the dark swamp water and the rushing creeks, but none of it had seemed sufficient.

McLean had found a black felt hat for her with the brim pinned up on one side, a gift from a young partisan. Now she had her long, untidy hair pushed up under it, but the battered pink satin shoes still served her small feet. Altogether, Savarra Bainbridge was completely miserable.

The long ten-mile ride to Witherspoon's Ferry seemed interminable, but they arrived there long before dawn. Savarra was so tired, she lay down upon her blanket and slept soundly until morning, at which time she wakened and looked about her at the horde of big, quiet men that filled the camp.

She retied the rawhide strips and stuffed her hair under the hat once more and brushed ineffectually at her leather breeches. After smoothing her coarse linen shirt, she put on the little shoes, no longer pink, but a sort of dirty mauve. She had slept with the leather jacket rolled under her head and now she shook it out, laid it on the blanket and went to get her cup of coffee from the campfire that served McLean and his men.

It was then she got her first look at the man they had come so far to join. She had glimpsed him a moment before when Thad had murmured, "That's the colonel, ma'am."

He was now talking to McLean over a pewter cup of coffee and she almost laughed aloud at his appearance. She thought contemptuously, So this is the man they all think so highly of! A pack of fools led by a fool! He was old—at least in his forties—and he looked frail, with ankles and knees obviously malformed, and he had limped when approaching McLean. His face was hard, his forehead high, dominated by a jutting jaw and an aquiline nose, and he was dressed in a close, roundbodied scarlet jacket of rough texture. On his head was a scarred little leather helmet that bore a silver crescent and was inscribed *Liberty or Death*. Instead of an officer's sword, a short little dagger hung in a rusty scabbard at his side. It was then Savarra met his eyes and drew a swift, astounded breath.

Francis Marion's eyes were a polished black, gleaming and steady, and there was such a wealth of controlled power behind them that they caused her a sharp turn in opinion. Here was no fool, but a dangerous and powerful enemy.

He asked in a quiet voice, "And who is the young boy you have brought to join us, Captain McLean?"

McLean shrugged. "That is no boy, colonel, but a necessary evil. She is the daughter of General Bainbridge and I was forced to bring her to keep her quiet. She discovered our meeting in the Pair home. We must not lose our influence in Charles Town by having it known Baltazar, Belion and I are partisans. So," he spread his hands, "here she is."

Marion frowned. "She will be a hazard we cannot risk on our missions."

"I will see that some one of us will stay behind with her. She shall go on no missions. She is much like her father, I think, and wouldn't balk at killing any of us."

They talked on of the massed British and American armies. Savarra gathered that they would soon be facing each other with battle lines drawn. Marion confirmed that Gates had sent him to destroy all boats and crafts along the Santee to prevent British flight when defeated.

Savarra restrained a grim smile. General Gates' confidence was more than matched by her own in her father and Cornwallis.

Filling her plate with hoecakes, fried meat and baked yams, she took herself to a nearby fallen log to sit and eat it. Her mind dismissed the coming battle and fastened on her own escape. If they left her with but one man while they took themselves off on their nefarious missions, she would find a way to slip off. Tories were roaming the countryside as well as these rebels and she would find one of them who could lead her to the British army. As angry with her father as she had been, she conceded now that she would be overjoyed to see him riding up with his cavalry.

She sat devouring the surprisingly tasty breakfast and eyed Cutler McLean's long, hard body rebelliously. That he was a handsome man was undeniable, but she would love to see him captured—yes, and hanged! As she watched, the lean dark face grew intent, the slate-colored, thick-lashed eyes narrowed and his sharply defined lips tightened as Marion gestured to the north with expressive hands.

Her fury at McLean and his treatment of her was so strong she slowed in eating, almost losing her appetite. It wouldn't be much longer, she thought determinedly, looking at the abominable tackey tethered to a tree nearby. At least the animal could cover miles and it knew the dangers of the swamps. She would slip away on him at the first opportunity.

Her spirits rose and she finished her breakfast. She was almost cheerful when she took her empty pewter plate to the edge of Lynche's Creek where she washed it thoroughly along with her cup. She brought them back to Gabe Sleep, who was in charge of their implements.

It was still early when Marion formed his men into troops and set each one to the task of destroying craft up and down the Santee and its tributaries. Groups of men rode off in various directions. McLean and his band had grown in numbers since meeting with Marion. Now he directed them back toward the Santee and he ordered Savarra to mount the tackey and accompany them.

"There'll be no fighting on this mission—so come along," he said tersely.

Savarra, biding her time, made no demur and rode off with the men. She was dourly amused by the controversy between Gabe Sleep and Thad McHorry, for McLean had told them that one of them must stay with her when Marion needed them on a combat mission.

"I ain't goin' to stay with that wildcat," Thad said, his innocent face wearing an unaccustomed stubbornness, "an' miss out on all the action."

"Well, it sure ain't goin' to be me," Gabe Sleep replied, his drowsy eyes glittering. "No matter what the cap'n says. We'll just have to find some old man to stay with her in the backwoods if somethin' comes up. Maybe we could farm her out with a good patriot family on the way."

"They couldn't hold her," Thad said gloomily. "It'll take a man to keep that firebrand in tow."

Savarra hid her smile. *No one* would keep her in tow. She would escape. She felt it as surely as she drew breath, and the time was not too far distant now when she could make her move. She followed docilely as they went to crossings and fords, destroying boats and canoes and rafts, and observed their competent and thorough activity.

She was becoming familiar with the South Carolina country. She had a sharp mind, and in it she had kept track of all the places they had been, terrain they had covered, and she had listened intently as the men discussed various villages and towns. She knew their names well now—Monck's Corner, Kingstree, Camden, Waxhaws, Cheraws, Georgetown—and she had a surprisingly good map of them in her head. And she knew the directions by the sun, which by now spilled hotly through the trees and on the open spaces. She felt sure that, if she could get away, she would eventually make it to one or the other of these places, depending on which was nearest, where the British had a garrison.

An astonishing thing happened as they were destroying Elias Henderson's boats at the landing below his plantation house. A slave saw them and ran to get the old man, a patriot himself, who soon appeared with a musket in the crook of his arm and began to harangue the men for destroying his property.

McLean said, "General Gates wants to make sure the

British do not have means of retreat after the battle near Camden, which should take place any day now."

The old man looked at him dumbfounded, then burst out, "Haven't you heard? The British whipped the pants off Gates on August sixteenth. They say Cornwallis has so many prisoners and wounded, he's afraid the pox'll break out amongst 'em. The southern army's shattered and Gates has fled for his life."

Thad McHorry blurted, "You mean the battle is over an' we lost?"

"That's about the size of it, sonny," the old man said, "so you might as well leave me my boats."

McLean cursed low and Gabe Sleep's and Belion's faces tightened. There was muttering among the other men, Kinley and Baldwin among them.

Savarra's spirits soared and she could not stem her exuberance. "You see!" she cried. "You're whipped and you'd better seek out the nearest British detachment and surrender if you expect to live." Observing the stunned faces before her and Henderson's amazement to see a woman among them, she kicked the tackey into a fast trot, crying over her shoulder, "I'm going to find them! They'll still be up around Camden and my father will see that I get home."

But her euphoria was short-lived. McLean spurred Jed and was on her in an instant. "You're going nowhere, mistress," he said roughly. "We are not whipped as long as there's a man of us left abroad." He reached for her reins as the intimidated tackey slowed to a walk. "Besides, you'll get lost, you little fool. You know nothing of this country."

"I've heard you talk and I've learned—let me go!" There was a brief, violent struggle until McLean pulled the reins from her hands. She slid from the little horse and began to run, but his big stallion thundered up beside her and McLean caught her in his arms and with hard hands forced her to sullen acquiescence.

She said between her teeth, "You'll not keep me. I shall escape eventually and when I tell what I know, your life will not be worth a tuppence."

"So you say," he replied grimly.

Savarra made no reply. He was hurting her as he always did when forced to restrain her, but the pain around her ribs lent her strength. There was something in this rebel that roused emotions in her deeper than any she had ever known. She was in such a turmoil when she had contact with him, verbal or physical, she was almost uncontrollable. Even her mind refused to function reasonably, for she wanted to claw and beat upon him. It was inexplicable and so violent it defied analyzing.

Now he replaced her on the squat tackey, but he held the reins. She could tell the men were dazed by the news they had just received for they did not talk much.

McLean said harshly, "Come, men—we shall return to Snow's Island. I'm sure Marion will meet us there for he must know this turn of events by now."

It was a long day and the August heat burned them in the open spaces and was steaming in the bogs. When at last they stopped for the night, the men gathered around the campfires and talked so low Savarra could not hear them. She did not care, so elated was she that the British had laid a decisive defeat on the rebel army. They were but little bands of men now, in a sea of enemies, both British and loyalist. And she *knew*, if she could but find a loyalist group, she would be safe. As they ate their meager fare, she determined to escape in the midnight hours. She would be very quiet, but when they wakened she would be gone.

A great orange moon rose over the treetops beyond the little clearing in which they had made down for the night. They were some distance from a swamp, and she knew that north lay the town of Camden. Oh, if she could only reach Camden! Her father—and even Peter Haverley by now—must both be there, rounding up and marshalling the prisoners. Perhaps they were marching in this very direction!

She did not allow her lids to droop as the fires died and the men, one by one, reclined upon their beds of moss and ragged blankets. Her every sense was alert and quivering for action. She forced herself to remain still as the great August moon burned brighter, reaching its zenith above them, drowning stars in its brightness.

Sounds of deep night in the wilderness surged up around her, cicadas, owls, the distant scream of some small nocturnal beast caught by another and being devoured. Savarra shivered and thought of the peaceful, cultivated lands that surrounded her father's manor houses. Only deer, rabbits and coveys of game birds ranged those well-tended acres. There were beasts in these swamps she did not know of and she had the good sense to be apprehensive.

Could she possibly filch a gun from one of the men? She

could see Gabe Sleep's rifle lying beside him. It gleamed in the light of a probing finger of moonlight between leaves above. The gentle Carolina wind moved the treetops and light danced over the curly maple stock and Savarra rose cautiously.

Gabe moved restlessly, as if divining her thought, and she sank down. Her eager gaze went to McLean where he and Sam Kinley lay with no more than five feet between them. McLean had a pistol as well as a rifle, she knew. Would he sleep with it thrust in his belt? Surely not. That would be too uncomfortable. And she would be more expert with a pistol. Her father had taught her to shoot a pistol during the summers in the country. She knew how to load and fire rapidly. If she could just get her hands on his pistol and ammunition pouch— She moved forward, silent as a shadow.

She had taken off the ineffectual little heeled slippers that tied about her ankles, and her stocking-clad feet were sure of their hold in the soft, sandy soil. Her breath caught as she drew near. McLean was very still and his pistol lay on the blanket near his hand. The rifle was there too, and his sabre. Where was his powder horn—or the little leather pouch he carried at his waist?

Her eyes darted over his big frame and she could not discern it. Certainly he could not be sleeping on so awkward an object. She drew nearer, her caution increasing with the emotion that boiled up each time she approached McLean. She could not let her hatred get the upper hand of cold common sense. She crouched over him, searching for the bag of bullets and powder. Where had he hidden it?

He sighed deeply and shifted an arm beneath his head as she held her breath, for he had moved and a leather pouch could be seen near his shoulder.

With fingers light as thistle down, she plucked up the bag and the weapon. Then forcing herself to move slowly, she retreated. The horses were tethered among trees nearby and she went to them, sitting down long enough to put on the incongruous satin slippers. They were mud-spattered and ruined, but they were better than being unshod.

She looked at Tamar, sleek and powerful, who stood twitching his ears at her approach. The tackey—she found herself thinking of him as His Majesty George III—was nearby and Savarra hesitated. The tackey was far more at home in the swamps, far warier and more trustworthy in splashing through the snake-infested tussocks than the big fine horses. But he was so slow!

With sudden decision, Savarra began to loosen the tether on Tamar. Saddling him would be too risky, take too long, she thought, and she picked up the bridle and bit, carefully muffling the sounds. She was familiar with horses and her confidence was communicated to the horse, who blew softly through his velvety nostrils as if welcoming human companionship in these midnight hours. She soothed him by stroking his neck, running her hand over the softness of his nose. The camp behind her was still, though the noises of the woods around them were a steady hum, rising and falling. It was a soothing background of sounds that lulled the sleeper to deeper slumber.

Catching her hands in Tamar's long, coarse mane, she pulled herself lightly up on his back and with great care guided him into the trees slowly in a northwesterly direction. Camden lay that way and—please God—her father, Rawdon and his new aide, Peter Haverley. Oh, but she would tell them how she had suffered in the hands of the rebels, and they would track them down! And the sweet revenge she would know to see them punished!

When they had come far enough from camp, she put Tamar into a slow but steady canter. That way they would cover the miles without tiring the horse too much. She was faintly dismayed at the trackless woods through which she was traveling, but at least the ground was dry beneath Tamar's hooves. She did not know how many swamps she must cross or circle around before reaching Camden, but she was reconciled to the fact that she would have to cover more than one.

She had relaxed and was confident she had made good her escape when she suddenly stiffened. Behind her came a sound disturbingly like the thud of hooves. She tried to tell herself that it was some night animal and she attempted to load the pistol.

It was then she discovered the pouch contained parched and sweetened corn and a little dried meat. It contained nothing but food. Curse her luck! Now she was defenseless in the wilderness and something or someone was approaching from behind. She guided Tamar into the thickest of the trees, away from the open places where the lowering moon still lit the countryside, and she stepped up his pace. It was difficult in the thick woods, for small branches reached out to slap against her, to pluck at her garments, making her progress somewhat noisy. And ever, the sound of hooves behind her grew in volume. Someone was coming at a fast clip behind her. She was sure of it now. She told herself it was some night rider, a courier from one of the armed bands of men who roamed the backcountry now that the British had decisively defeated the southern army.

She determined to pull back in the trees and wait his passage. At the rate he was coming, he would soon be past her and she could safely resume her journey. But as she pulled farther into the woods, the hoofbeats slowed and suddenly she saw the horseman, tall in the saddle. In the bright moonlight that tall broad-shouldered figure could be but one man, Cutler McLean. Her departure had been discovered. Or had he known the moment she stooped over him?

She held her breath as he came on and then she saw him scrutinizing the ground in the bright moonlight. Tamar's hooves had left a trail of crushed grasses and indentations in the soft earth that led directly to her hiding place.

Panic took her and she kicked her heels hard against the flanks of the big gelding, wheeling him toward the deeper woods, and it seemed they made an unconscionable noise as she thrashed through the underbrush. Her pursuer heard it for, as she glanced over her shoulder, he turned his horse and rode directly toward her.

She looked up through the trees and cursed the brilliant moon. Though it had passed the zenith, still the cold, pure light filtered through the forest and revealed her moving horse. Speaking to Tamar with urgency she bade him gallop, and her little feet in their flimsy shoes beat a tattoo against his sides. He responded by lengthening his stride, but they were necessarily slowed by thick trees and scrub. Oh, if only she had filched the bag of bullets, she could have loaded the pistol and shot McLean as he kept drawing ever nearer! Now he could be no more than three yards behind her.

Suddenly he gave a shrill whistle and Tamar slowed immediately, though she beat ineffectually with her feet against his flanks and, by movement of her body, urged him on. He slowed to a trot, and in an instant McLean was beside her.

She wheeled about to face him, the pistol in her hand, and cried with feigned certainty, "If you touch me, I'll shoot you!"

He laughed low. "With an empty pistol? You took my food —you have no bullets," and he came abreast of her, reaching for the reins.

She jerked them from his hands, urging Tamar on, but the horse had long been a mount for McLean and he showed no sign of responding. They rode side by side and, in the fiery turmoil the man always stirred in her, she tried to strike him with the pistol. The two wrestled silently in the moon-dappled darkness. His fingers were like steel on her arms, and with a last despairing gesture she flung the pistol at him. It missed by a wide margin to fall with a thud on the leafy ground.

Still Savarra struggled. In her extremity, she felt imbued with enormous strength. Her disappointment at not escaping and her hatred of McLean were powerful stimulants in her blood. They grappled together, McLean trying to lift her from the horse, she resisting with extraordinary strength. Suddenly she wrenched free and slipped from Tamar's sleek back to the ground and began to run as hard as she could.

McLean was no less swift. He was off Jed and after her in a flash. She took no more than eight running steps when she tripped on a cypress knee and fell full-length on the thick layer of leaves and pine needles that carpeted the forest. McLean was on her swiftly, his big body covering hers, and they fought and rolled wildly among the leaves. Through an opening in the trees above there poured a flood of moonlight on the two entangled below.

McLean's breath was coming hard and Savarra was sobbing for breath. They did not speak, so fierce was the struggle between them. Now at last, she lay on her back and he pinned her arms to the ground, his long, hard-muscled legs forced her own to throbbing stillness.

Savarra, in a tumult of fury, stared up into the face above hers, mostly in shadow, and with unexpected abruptness she ceased to move. For a long minute they lay thus, his long length across her, their breaths mingling in a strange and irresistible impulse. Then without the slightest warning he brought his face down, and she turned to meet it.

Their lips came together with sweet and stunning force. An electric vitality opened up within Savarra. Passions burst like a tide in her. She clung to McLean and his lips were warm, as searching, as hungry as hers—for her mother, noblewoman to the end, had never cautioned her daughter nor warned her where passion could lead.

Cutler McLean's kiss slowed, became leisurely, thorough, drawing deeply from the deep and hot well of stimulation. His big, hard body over hers filled her with fluid weakness and she yearned to be absorbed in and with him. Her mind was in chaos for she hated this man, yet his power over her, his ability to stir her, was indescribably sweet and his caresses roused every sense to quivering response.

Her arms twined about his heavily muscled shoulders and pressed him to her. Under the sweeping flood of desire she was helpless in his arms, and there was a surprising tenderness suddenly in his hands, a light delicacy of touch on her clothing which left her naked and starving for more of him.

And he took her there on the forest floor, with a bed of leaves for their resting place and the hot night like a benediction about them, with the half-heard howls and cries from the nearby swamps a background for the ecstasy and delirium they shared without speaking. It was like the crashing together of rushing waters, inevitable and preordained.

She did not think of Peter Haverley, nor her father—nor of escape. Her mind was possessed by the man possessing her body, and for a little while Savarra was blindingly happy.

When he released her at last, they lay spent, languid and closely together, the cool, damp scent of fecund earth sifting up from their bed. The two horses standing nearby were still, and a nightbird in the tall cypress above them gave a timid, half-frightened cry and there was a flutter of wings as it vanished in the night.

Savarra came slowly to her senses, the delicious languor swiftly departing, and all at once she fought down a little sob. A desolation crept in upon her, a sickening sense of loss, and she drew a long, shuddering breath as she awkwardly drew up her clothing. Peter! She groaned. My God, she had forgotten Peter! This moment belonged to him and she had given it to McLean wtih both hands and a whole and turbulent heart.

McLean said tenderly, "Savarra, darling, don't regret. We'll be ma—"

"But I do!" she interrupted poignantly. "I regret this with all my heart. Oh, what have I done—"

He rose to a sitting position, careful not to touch her, and there was a long miserable silence between them. Then, "You can always cry rape," he said sardonically.

She did not speak for a moment and then she said quietly, "But it was not rape. It was not even seduction. I do not know what it was—insanity on my part, I suppose. Still, I cannot accuse you without accusing myself."

McLean bent his head in an attempt to look into her face,

but she turned away. He said, "I thought you hated me, but you—"

"I do! I despise you and this beastly land of yours and I cannot understand nor explain my terrible—indecent behavior. I have no excuse."

He laughed cynically, "I knew you were spoiled, over-prideful and selfish, Mistress Bainbridge. I did not expect to find you honest. I congratulate you on that one redeeming trait." His laughter deepened. "But I must confess, if this opportunity presents itself again, I shall take full and pleasurable advantage of it." He reached out suddenly, caught up his pistol where she had flung it and thrust it into his belt as he rose to his feet.

Savarra's face was hot. "It will never happen again."

"You mean you won't try to escape again?"

The moon was setting somewhere beyond the treetops and the black hours before dawn spread slowly over them. "I did not say that," Savarra replied. "Only that *this*—between us— shall never happen again."

He shrugged. "A disappointment indeed."

She rose, resentment washing through her at his cavalier tone. Pride alone kept her from weeping, from crying out that this was the first time for her, no matter how often he had experienced such a shattering upheaval of emotion.

All the stars had become visible now that the moon was down, and the sky was diamond-bright as she looked up through treetops. They were such a profusion of brilliance that she could dimly see the figure of the man looming up beside her. She turned away and his hand shot out to seize her arm.

"No, madame, you'll not be riding off alone again."

"I am only going to mount," she said wearily.

"Then I'll help you," he said and she put her foot into his cupped hands and mounted Tamar. "Those damned shoes," he spoke with asperity. "I've got to find some sturdy boots for you. These are no protection at all."

She made no reply, and in silence they cantered back to the camp near the Santee, to find it in turmoil.

Men were up and breakfast fires were burning brightly hours too soon. McLean, holding Tamar's reins, trotted swiftly to the huddle of men and dismounted, flinging questions at them as he helped Savarra dismount.

The newcomer among them, a young lad with tousled brown hair named Seth Barwell, had ridden hard from Marion's camp at Nelson's Ferry on the Santee a few miles above them. His big eyes were brown and brilliant with excitement. "I ain't been here but 'bout fifteen minutes, cap'n," he said quickly.

Savarra turned away, but McLean seized her shoulder, turning her about. He said quietly, "You make a move to escape again and I'll bind you—with wet rawhide. You will find that most uncomfortable." His voice was tough and angry, as if there had never been that tender, burning moment between them.

He released her but she halted, caught by young Barwell's voice as he said eagerly, "Cap'n McLean, the colonel wants you all to meet him at Sorel's Landing, just below Sumter's old burned-out house on Great Savannah. If we ride hard, we can be there 'fore dawn. An ensign in the loyalist militia deserted after the battle at Camden an' come into the colonel's camp 'fore midnight." The youth paused for breath and there was a soft murmur of voices as McLean's men continued their preparations to leave. Barwell added, "The ensign says there's a hundred and fifty American prisoners, all captured at Camden, camped out at Sumter's, an' the colonel aims to free them."

"We're ready to leave, captain," Sam Kinley said, shifting his musket to his right hand. "We've been waitin'—figured you was out chasin' down that English wildcat, when we saw my horse was missin'." His glance at Savarra was full of cynical humor in the light of the bright fire where she stood clearly visible.

But Seth Barwell's eyes touched her and clung. Wonder, admiration and surprise were in their dark brown depths as they lingered on her high, provocative breasts beneath the coarsely woven linen shirt. When his gaze lifted to her face, there was complete fascination in it. Seth Barwell was entranced by the young girl.

He looked away swiftly, but Savarra could see by the light of the fire the color on his lean cheeks.

"I can be ready in two minutes or less," McLean said, going to his blanket where he stooped to roll it up swiftly. Straightening, he strapped the saber about his waist and adjusted the pistol he had thrust into his belt earlier. Catching up his rifle, he wheeled about and said, "Let's go."

Fires were swiftly scattered, stamped out, and the night closed in on them, a black presence with only the stars to prick it in pinpoints.

Six

Once again Savarra was astride the tackey and King George III was trotting mightily to keep up with his larger cousins who were covering the miles swiftly indeed. It was miserable for Savarra, who clung to his mane to keep her balance. Thad McHorry, on McLean's instructions, was holding the reins of the tackey reluctantly while she rode between him and Gabe Sleep. She was weary from the long sleepless night, but she was alert. Turbulent regret kept her keenly aware. She held her head proudly, determined that by no look or word would she reveal a trace of her yielding to McLean, or the fact that even now it was hard not to seek out his tall form among the riders ahead.

McHorry and Sleep fell into a soft-voiced discussion of their destination. "You remember, Gabe, when Tarleton burned Sumter's last May, his dragoons brought Mistress Sumter out in a chair—she bein' an invalid. 'Tis said that Sumter had to watch it all from the woods while they fired his place. 'Twas what sent him to the swamps an' partisan warfare."

"What I didn't know was they was enough of his place left to shelter a hundred an' fifty men," Gabe drawled.

Seth Barwell had let his horse fall back until he rode beside Thad. He said, " 'Tis only half-burned, Mr. Sleep. I've seen it. Just bad enough can't nobody live there. They slaughtered his livestock, too—an' trampled his cornfields."

Sleep said grumpily, "I've heard the story." He looked down at Savarra in the dim light, "That's what your countrymen are about, ma'am. 'Tis a wonder Tarleton didn't run Mistress Sumter through with his saber."

Savarra scorned a reply and Thad glanced down at her uneasily. "What's the cap'n goin' to do with this British baggage?" he asked, making no effort to keep her from overhearing.

Gabe grinned drowsily in the starlight. "I figure he's goin'

123

to make you nursemaid, Thad. You ain't as good a shot as I am. Won't hurt you to miss this fracas."

"I ain't goin' to be no nursemaid to her! She's likely to claw me bloody!" He sounded faintly alarmed.

Well he might have been, because McLean did detail him to keep watch over Savarra, despite McHorry's angry protests, when they reached Sorel's Landing and Marion's men before dawn.

Thad sat his horse, holding the reins to King George impotently, while Marion sketched their coming raid to the men about them. His campfires had long ago been stamped out and his militia either sat or stood holding their mounts in readiness as he spoke. His voice was singularly musical, a soft drawl that was deceptively gentle and quiet, but it produced instant silence and intense attention.

"We'll ride hard to Sumter's. The house is on a little rise above Santee Swamp and there's a thick stand of cedars and live oaks, enough to provide concealment for an approach." He paused and his words, though low, came clearly to Savarra. "I'll circle and lead my men around to hit them from the rear. Captain McLean will lead his men up the lane that runs to the house. Understood?" There was a murmur of assent and a swift, silent mounting of men.

As they circled about to head out, Belion and McLean rode up beside McHorry. McLean said, "Thad, you two stay well back of us. We can't have a tory bullet hit Mistress Bainbridge." He laughed shortly. "Despite her opinion of us, we won't make war on women."

In the dim light, Savarra looked at him in astonishment. He and Belion wore elaborately powdered wigs. Their faces were so besmeared with mud from the swamps, they were unrecognizable. He and Belion wheeled their big horses and were gone in the darkness, and she realized that this was their disguise against recognition by any of the British officers and soldiers with whom they might have done business in Charles Town.

Bringing up the rear now, McHorry tried hard to keep a fairly short distance between himself and McLean's troop ahead, but King George III was tired and he would run a short distance, then droop to a walk. McHorry would then be forced to jerk at his reins. This made an erratic ride for Savarra, who clenched her teeth against complaint and remained upright on the insignificant animal's bare back.

One of the riders ahead dropped back slowly and was soon

beside the two of them. It was Seth Barwell and he said, "Mr. McHorry, I 'spect you're a better shot'n I am, though I been brung up with a musket in my hand. I'll keep watch over Mistress Bainbridge, do you want me to."

"By God, Seth, I'll sure appreciate that—" he paused then, doubt creeping into his voice. "She's made one attempt to escape an' the cap'n caught her. Reckon you can keep holt of such a wildcat?"

"I reckon," Seth replied. His young eyes on Savarra were kind but there was steel in his deep voice.

Without further words, McHorry handed the reins of King George to Seth and took off at a gallop. The two looked after him silently.

Then Barwell said, "You ain't thinkin' about tryin' to run off again, are you? I'd sure hate to have to tie you up."

"I'm too tired to try it again, Mr. Barwell," she said wearily.

The boy kept his eyes on her, however, and Savarra was not unaware of the admiration in them, nor the tenderness that lurked about the youngster's well-formed lips. They fell farther and farther behind the main troop under McLean's command, and every once in a while Barwell would give King George a mighty pull, resulting in a sudden spurt of speed.

Dawn was just breaking with a faintly rosy streak in the east when the crack of rifle and musket fire came dimly to them. Barwell's horse started at the sound and the boy gave a fierce tug at the tackey's reins. The little animal was too fatigued to respond and kept at his slow, steady pace. The gunfire beyond them was rapid now and unceasing, but by the time the two riders ambled from the woods and came upon the lane leading to the house, it had become sporadic and the men, as they approached, were milling about, for the actual fighting was all over. It had taken less than half an hour.

Savarra was to learn later that, as McLean led his men through the lane, a sentry had seen their shadows and fired wildly at them. McLean then dashed headlong up the lane while Marion drove in from the rear. A British captain, Johnathan Roberts, had allowed his men to stack their weapons, coats and accouterments in a careless fashion outside the front door, and McLean had seized them all as the loyalists rushed outside. They had put up a fight and some were killed, but it was over in short order. There were nearly a hundred and fifty prisoners released, not all of whom wished to join Marion.

Seth Barwell was solicitous of Savarra as the men came and went about them. In the spreading light of morning, he looked at her with renewed pleasure and he said, "Mistress Bainbridge, you are the prettiest woman I ever saw."

Savarra knew a bone-deep fatigue as the men set up camp on the grounds about the half-burned house. She said, "I do not see how that can possibly be," and she looked down at the soiled and wrinkled male clothing she wore. The odorous leather jacket hung limply across King George's burry neck, and in the light of day her slippers were incredible, the ribbons stained dirty brown, and a hole had been torn in the side of the right shoe, allowing a stockinged toe to peep out.

"Your clothes can't hide it, Mistress Bainbridge. You're beautiful," he finished reverently. His tumbled brown hair gleamed cleanly in the sunlight.

"Can we not rest awhile, Mr. Barwell? It has been a long night for me." She looked at him appealingly.

"Of course," he said swiftly. "I'll fix you a bed over there." He gestured to a large oak beyond the campfires and the men who were directing the loyalist and British prisoners to their places among the watchful captors.

Savarra observed the British officers scowling with chagrin, while the released Americans rejoiced. Her tired mind accepted the fact that there would be no overt escape from these alert partisans and she turned in her mind to a new and humbling plan. There *was* a way she might return to Charles Town—and, she hoped, to Peter—if she could but persuade McLean to it. She thought on it all the while the tall and eager young Barwell gathered moss from the nearby trees and began to put it thickly beneath her blanket.

The released prisoners were jubilant with talk and laughter as breakfast was prepared on the bright, hot campfires. And Marion gave out that he and his men would camp here for a time. As she stood observing them, she realized suddenly there were men lying still upon the ground and her eyes widened. Wounded or dead?

She went to Seth Barwell where he was arranging her blanket over the moss. She asked, "Were many—hurt?"

He looked up at her with guileless brown eyes from his stooped position in the early sun, not yet risen high enough for there to be shade beneath the tree. "You mean ours? Or yours, ma'am?"

"Both," she said, glancing back at the men upon the ground.

"Twenty-two of yours killed," he said and his face was compassionate. Then with relief he could not conceal, "An' we got one wounded. An' we got enough ammunition an' weapons to last us a long time." He added proudly, "They was only fifty-two in the colonel's troop all told." He rose to his full height and looked down at her. "Ma'am," he said softly, "your folks ain't goin' to win this war."

Her shoulders drooped and he asked gently, "You want some breakfast 'fore you sleep, Mistress Bainbridge?"

She shook her head and sank to her knees on the blanket. It was blessedly soft and inviting as she stretched full length upon it, turning her head so the young man above her could not see her face and the tears she was fighting to hold back.

"I could bring you a cup of coffee anyway, ma'am," he said hopefully.

She turned to him suddenly, eyes bright as sapphires in the thicket of black lashes curling out from them. "They won't leave without us?" It was very necessary that she see Cutler McLean and soon. Her plan would not wait.

"They ain't goin' to leave without me," he laughed, "an' I reckon that means you too, ma'am, since you're in my care."

"I mean Mr. McLean won't leave without us?" she said anxiously.

Seth Barwell smiled broadly, teeth white in his boyish brown face. His dark eyes crinkled at the corners like a mischievous child's. "Mistress Bainbridge, we ain't men to leave a poor defenseless little girl like you alone in the swamps. You can be sure of that."

Savarra gave him a faint smile and was almost instantly asleep. There was constant movement in the camp about her as the men came and went, but she did not hear it. Those reluctant soldiers who had been prisoners of the British and who wanted to return to their homes vanished one by one into the swamps and along the sandy trails beside the Santee River. Those seventy members of the freed Continentals who inexplicably demanded that they be allowed to continue into Charles Town as prisoners of war moved out with their own guides. The other eighty-five freed Continentals refused outright the invitation to join Marion's ragged troop, apparently believing that a militia unit was not up to their standards, and marched toward faraway Virginia. Of them all, only three men elected to remain with Marion, who put no pressure on them either way, preferring they do as their consciences demanded.

Thus when Savarra awakened, it was to a much smaller army of men. She saw the neat mounds of new graves beyond the trampled lawns of the half-burned Sumter house. Suddenly she was sure Seth Barwell had lied to her and gone with the vanished army during the day. It was very hot in the late afternoon when she got to her feet, mouth dusty and feeling perspiration spring out on her lip and forehead.

Her heart pounded heavily with the sudden fear that enveloped her. Her eyes searched frantically for Cutler McLean, who always towered two or three inches above most of the men. She did not see him and she ran toward a group of militia who lounged among the trees.

One man was engaged in trimming a fetlock on his horse. Another was cleaning his nails with a knife. Others were working with their guns, and three were talking together around a dying fire that had a pot of coffee on a metal rack over it.

She slowed as she approached them, licking dry lips. She recognized the slight figure of Marion, and he looked up as she neared them, his polished black eyes flicking her impersonally. Her eyes darted from one to another of the men and she saw the man she knew as Baldwin and Sam Kinley. But Seth Barwell, Thad McHorry, Gabe Sleep, Tyler Belion and McLean were not among them.

She was very thirsty and now a bitter taste pervaded her mouth. Barwell had said they would not leave her in the swamps alone. Well, she was not alone, that was true, but she knew she could never persuade Marion and his men to her plan for a return to Charles Town. With McLean, who knew her and had once remarked on her honesty, he might have been inclined to believe her when she presented her hope and her promise. Now he was gone.

Nearing the men drinking their coffee near the low fire, she said, "I'm very thirsty. Is there some water?"

Marion got to his feet courteously and handed her a small canteen from a hook at his waist, " 'Tis all we have at the moment, but you are welcome to it, Mistress Bainbridge."

She thanked him, uncorking the small metal jug and tilting the contents into her mouth. When the liquid struck her tongue and throat, it was all she could do to keep from spitting it out on the ground. It was warm, brackish and strongly flavored with vinegar. Swallowing, eyes watering, she replaced the cork and handed the vessel back to Marion with a thick, "Thank you."

He smiled imperceptibly. "I'm sorry 'tis so vinegary, but that is a protection against scurvy, ma'am. A lesson I learned as a boy when I went to sea."

She nodded, wiping her eyes and wishing she had endured her thirst silently. A bearded man got to his feet and said kindly, "Would ye like a little coffee, miss, to wash it down with?"

The men were courteous in their rough way and she gratefully accepted his offer. As usual, they did not seem to find her apparel surprising and they were not shocked by her presence among them. Savarra was to learn that most armies, British and American alike, had women camp followers. Too, she had the feeling that nothing much would shock these men. Their eyes were old and wise in their young faces, but they were razor-sharp.

Guns of all types, pistols, muskets, rifles, lay close at hand. She noted there were great stacks of them, like shocks of cornstalks in pyramids, under the trees where two other men sat, apparently in charge of the weapons. As she watched, she noticed two men emerge from a thick forest near the edge of what must surely be Santee Swamp. They were greeted quietly but warmly as they made their way to Marion.

Savarra sipped the scalding coffee, reflected bitterly on the defection of McLean and his three companions and surveyed her new set of captors. They moved with cat-like grace, a quality she had noted in all the rebels she had met, with the exception of the slight Marion—but even he moved with ease despite his lame ankle.

She knew a grudging respect for him, a man who would not become roaring drunk, who would not rob or plunder, a man who had valiantly pitted himself and his small band against the might of the British empire, who even now, behind that browned and expressionless face, was planning new raids to harass and hamstring her people. She knew she should hate him and all his men, but instead she knew an unwilling and reluctant emotion, almost but not quite admiration. She could not understand what it was in her character that made her victim to this weakness. She was certain that it was a weakness. She could not know that her own father, soldier of the crown though he was, respected and understood a valiant enemy.

She finished her cup and handed it to the bearded young

man who had given it to her. His smile was white in the brown well-trimmed beard. "Cap'n McLean an' some of his men has gone to Clear Spring down country apiece to fill our water barrels," he volunteered. " 'Tis the sweetest, clearest water in the Carolinas. Then you can have a good drink o' water. Swamp an' river water ain't much good, miss."

Relief and gladness flooded her. McLean and his men had not gone for good! Her eyes sparkled bluely and she turned a smile of such radiant warmth on her benefactor that he blushed red on his cheeks above the beard. She said, "Then they *will* be back?"

"Any minute, mistress. They been gone some hours."

She walked away and seated herself on a tree stump to watch for McLean and his men. She must approach him immediately—and in private. She had misgivings when she thought of what had transpired between them, but put that from her mind. Evidently it had meant nothing but a moment's pleasure to him. Probably he'd had many women, judging from his casual air afterward. The thought irritated her. She had forgotten his tenderness when he had said, "Savarra, darling, don't regret—" for she had cut him off, not waiting for him to finish. Now she was in a fever to present her request to him, to elaborate on her honor and her promises. She knew she could convince him! She *knew* it.

Faint pangs of hunger assailed her and she looked at the sky. It must be past four o'clock. It would be three hours before they ate. But her appetite had come back with the knowledge that McLean would also come back.

It was another hour before he and his companions returned. There looked to be several of them, and they had a pack horse with two large barrels holding water hanging across the saddle on the big animal. A number of smaller water vessels hung alongside as well, and the men had several each strapped to their waists.

They were raucously greeted, with much joking and laughter between those men who had remained and those who had accompanied McLean. Savarra watched narrowly as McLean cantered to the trees where the guns were stacked and began, with others, to unload the water they had fetched.

She was in a sweat to talk to him. When would be the best time? Tonight, she thought swiftly, when the others are retiring. After their supper, she would seek him out and lay her plan before him. All the men were clustered around him now, drinking the wild, clear spring water greedily, and she walked toward them. Her thirst was unquenched and one of the men handed her a large pewter cup filled with sweet, cold water. She drank deeply.

She found herself, as she had planned, near McLean and she spoke to him in a low voice. "Mr. McLean, I want very much to have a private discussion with you—when we can be alone."

"Alone?" His black brows shot up and a little smile touched the curved lips. "Am I to understand you have second thoughts about our—er—intimacy?"

"Kindly forget that episode," she said, straining to keep animosity out of her voice. "I have done so." This was a lie, but she could not let him know the turbulence the memory of his arms, his kisses brought to her. Even so, her face was hot and she was keenly aware of his quizzical and very personal stare.

"After supper," he said briefly, "we'll talk, though I can't imagine what we'll talk about since you detest me and loathe America. I hope you don't intend a diatribe on those two subjects."

"No," she said with restraint, shocked by her suddenly acute perception of his person, the definite line of his lips, the cool gray eyes and their thick bristling lashes under the tumble of black hair. She turned away quickly.

She left him to make her way to the creek, where she intended to wash dust and grime from every portion of her that could be reached with modesty. Seth Barwell had given her a little çake of soap made by a cousin, diffidently asking her to be as sparing of it as possible.

The creek was a good distance away and she could see the men only distantly when she reached it. Once there, she rolled up her breeches and washed her thighs as high as she could reach, then did the same with her arms. With sudden determination, she bent and washed her long, tangled mass of hair. It felt clean and cool when the water touched her head. She soaped it lavishly, ignoring Seth's request, and in a short time she felt much better.

Even her clothing felt cleaner, though she knew this to be imagination. Without towels to dry herself, she sat on the moist grass of the bank and let the late afternoon sun dry her. Though her hair was still damp, she made her way back to camp near sundown. She knew she had been under strict surveillance despite the careful casualness with which her return was greeted.

Refreshed and hungry, she smiled as Seth eagerly filled a plate for her. Even the monotonous fare of yams, crisp hoecake and rice looked good to her. Afterward, the young boy took her plate and cup to the creek and washed it with his. The old moon, lopsided and dusky, rose slowly above the treetops, and she grew restless. The plan to return to Charles Town was burning in her.

Marion had now decided to spend a few days at Sumter's to rest his hard-riding, hard-fighting men, but they would have to leave soon enough. Word of their exploit would reach the British quickly after this foray.

Savarra's eyes sought out McLean, and after a moment he felt her scrutiny. He looked up and shook his head imperceptibly while he continued his conversation with the men about him. She was forced to wait until nearly all of the men were bedded down for the night before he came seeking her.

Together and without speaking, they went some distance from the camp, into a little thicket of oaks and pines. The moon by now had lost its dusky orange cast and was white in the sky, giving the arch above them a washed look. There was a faint breeze, alleviating the sweltering August night.

Before she could speak, McLean said mockingly, "Are you going to tell me that, now you are a ruined woman, I must marry you?"

A sheet of fiery rage swept over her. "It would take more than you to ruin me! As for marriage to you, I can think of nothing more repulsive."

"For a girl who so willingly lost her—virtue, you are very haughty now." There was laughter in the words.

Savarra swallowed hard on her fury. It would not do to antagonize this insolent man, not when she wanted to impress him with her honor. She said coolly, "What I want to discuss with you is of great importance to me—and I am entirely in your power where it is concerned." It cost her dearly to make this humble acknowledgment, for in her heart she would gladly have taken a riding crop and slashed his smiling face had she the opportunity.

"What is of such importance to you that even your virtue should pale beside it?"

"Quit harping on my virtue!" she flared, unable to stay her anger. "Isn't it enough that I have been robbed of it? I suppose you are the sort of man who will brag about your conquest around the campfires—and my reputation be damned."

Stung, he retorted, "I never brag. And you weren't robbed of your virtue. You gave it—and eagerly, I might add."

She was silent. Then over her stiff pride, "That is true, to my eternal shame. But you have taught me something I shall never forget."

"And what is that?"

"To keep myself well controlled, and you may believe it has been a hard lesson. I shall never be so innocently caught up in desire again."

"You sound very objective." He was smiling again.

"I intend to be." But even as she said it, she recognized the contradictory attraction she felt for this man. She pushed it to the back of her mind as she said, "Mr. McLean, you once said I was honest—which implies honor. I think that you must know I am a woman of my word."

"We-e-ll, you may be. You're very young to have acquired such a firm and unyielding mind—and you're very impulsive."

"I know that, but I assure you my impulsiveness is bound by my honor."

"What has all this to do with me, Mistress Bainbridge?"

She said bluntly, "I want to go back to Charles Town and I propose to bargain with you."

He looked at her forbiddingly in the dim light. "I can't let you go back. I must remain in good standing among the tories in Charles Town to conduct my business. It would be the hangman for me if my activities were known."

Savarra drew a deep, trembling breath and she said levelly, "I will swear on my honor to say nothing of you or your rebel activities. And I will keep that promise." She meant it.

He was silent a long time, then he said slowly, "I cannot risk that. Knowing how you hate me and my men, I believe you would tell your father all."

She said desperately, "I wouldn't, I swear! I swear, Mr. McLean. I have even thought of a plausible story to explain my absence. I will say I left at midnight—no one saw me go—to Camden to find Peter, my fiance, for that is where his orders will take him. I can tell my father I went in the company of loyalists who were bound for that city." She was begging, pleading and she knew it, writhed under it. "Then, on our way, we were attacked and captured by rebels. When they found who I was, they held me for three weeks with the intention of exchanging me for rebel prisoners."

McLean's smile was wintry. "And how would you explain your return? With no demand for exchange."

"After the battle of Camden, my captors became hunted and discouraged. They disbanded after leaving me on the outskirts of Charles Town. Does that not sound reasonable to you?"

"All but the promise to hold your tongue about me and Belion and Baltazar." His look at her now was quizzical and faintly admiring, which gave her hope. "You have done nothing to make me trust you."

She looked down, heat flooding her face, and she was thankful for the silver concealment of moonlight. "You—you know something about me—what we have done together—" She hesitated, then finished in a rush, "In exchange for your silence, I give you mine."

His black brows drew together. "You have my silence in any event and I think you know it well."

Her chin went up. "You think I would repay that by revealing your rebel sympathies? You do not know me at all, Mr. McLean."

He grinned suddenly, "Not your mind, at any rate."

She said desperately, begging again, "I give you my solemn word—on my honor—I will reveal nothing of your activities if you will only let me return to Charles Town. My fiance may be there by now, and I will marry him immediately. There will be little converse between me and my father—for he hates Peter."

In the pale light his lean face looked chiseled in brown rock and her heart sank. She whispered pleadingly, *"Please—"*

Still he hesitated. Then abruptly, "No, madame. You will stay in the swamps until this war is resolved. If you think because you gave yourself to me so willingly that you can now return to Charles Town and divulge our activities, you are mistaken. I won't deny I enjoyed it—but it does not automatically confer trust. I think you're British to the bottom of your soul." He paused then brutally, "No. You stay."

Fury struck her and under the force of it, she drew back her hand to slap him with all her strength. But McLean was too swift for her. He caught her hand in a flash.

Laughing grimly, he said, "No, madame. I'll stand for no blows from that small British hand—nor treachery that would surely follow my releasing you."

Jerking free of him she turned on her heel and strode back to her bed beneath a tree. Frustration raged within her. *Now* when she escaped, and she surely would escape, she would tell every British officer of the secret activities of McLean, Belion and Baltazar. They would be caught and hanged if they set foot in Charles Town!

She had never known such consuming fury, and she felt half-sick with it as she laid down on the bed that emanated such richly living odors. The fragrance filling her nostrils brought up memory vividly when she was least expecting it. For even with her renewed hatred and rage, she knew a trembling desire to surrender each time she was near the man. Those frenzied and rapturous moments in McLean's arms had marred her indelibly, and she tossed with burning remorse, knowing that Peter's bride would not come to him untouched.

She must escape! She *must*. She fell asleep seeking a means, a plan that would work. And when McLean hung at the end of the gibbet, she would be free at last of his power to send this weakness of desire through her veins.

Seven

They stayed another day before striking camp and leaving for Snow's Island on Britton's Neck once more. Savarra was to learn that Marion's great success as a partisan lay in his ability to make a deadly and unexpected strike and melt into hiding, despite the many British patrols sent out in search of him.

Seth Barwell was more and more worshipful and helpful to Savarra, so much so that a seed took root in her mind before that day was out.

Seth was no more than sixteen and Savarra, from the vantage point of eighteen, felt worldly wise and seasoned when she dealt with him. She was smiling and warm when they conversed, openly grateful and admiring for the errands he performed for her, the sharing of his soap, the dozen little things he did to make her more comfortable. Before they left that day, he had fashioned a blanket into a sort of saddle for King George, which made riding him much easier.

During the following two days, Savarra saw to it that her

charms for him increased. She took pains to keep her hair and face clean and smooth. She adjusted her male clothing to show her figure to best advantage, causing McLean to lift his brows in an annoying way and the other men to watch her surreptitiously. But Seth Barwell, she knew, had reached the point where he would do nearly anything to please her.

And Savarra planned that he should please her by leading her back to Charles Town in the dark of night, and this time there would be no finding her out.

She began her campaign after they crossed Wiboo Creek and neared Cantey's Plantation. The two of them lagged slightly behind because of King George's gait and she talked low and sweetly to Seth. First, she would plant her promise of silence about the partisans. She had no intention of keeping it, but she would be earnest and eager when she told Seth of it.

Thus, when they were sitting at some distance from the main body of men, eating their noon meal together, she said to him, "You know, Seth, I would never, never tell about the partisans if they would only let me return to Charles Town." Her vivid eyes were sincere and guileless. "But I am not used to this kind of life—as you can see. If I were to—to get away, I swear I would never tell a soul. I would say to my father I had been kidnapped by an unknown band of rebels and held for exchange. Only, after the defeat at Camden they were discouraged and let me go."

She put her hand on his broad, tanned one, felt its tremor and looked into his eyes with young, hopeful anxiety. "Oh, Seth, if only you would lead me back to Charles Town, I would never tell *anyone*." Her voice broke, then trembled. "Dear Seth, could you—would you do that for me?" Then, at the discomfort on his youthful face, she hastened on. "McLean is so hard. He would never let me go, but I am so uncomfortable, so unhappy. And Marion's men come and go as they please. You could say you're going home to see about your family for a while and no one would know that you had taken me away—if you leave first in the day." Her eager voice carried only tenderness and distress as it fell to a murmur and the long, thick lashes swept her smooth cheeks. "Then, that night, I would mount King George and meet you in the dark. You could tell me where."

Seth swallowed hard and looked troubled, but his deep brown eyes on Savarra were melting and full of a boy's first love. He asked slowly, "You swear you wouldn't tell—about the captain an' all of us?"

"On my honor," she responded solemnly. "You would all be safe and I would be back where I belong. I'm only a nuisance to them, you know it well. I swear I'd never breathe a word about—any of you." And as she swore it, her rage at McLean rose up and her heart hardened.

And so she and the boy plotted, and the following morning Seth told his commander he would like to go home for a short time to see that his widowed mother and brothers and sisters were well. Savarra was quiet and subdued and carefully kept her distance from them all, including Seth.

Seth Barwell had been gone all day, but Savarra knew he was only a short distance away on the route to Leneud's Ferry. He had given her explicit directions to make finding him easy, and she plodded along, following the troop of patriots the balance of that day.

That night she did not try to secure weapons, and she did not take Tamar, for he was too obedient to his master. Instead, at the dead morning hour of three, she silently mounted King George III and slipped as silently away.

She followed the directions given her by Seth, and by four-thirty she had met him by an enormous old cypress, just off a well-worn trail. They did not stop, but traveled steadily toward Charles Town. By daylight, they were miles from the camp she had left.

On the way, they talked, low-voiced, and Seth told her of his close-knit and loving family. He had two younger brothers and two little sisters. So far, the British patrols had not come by their farm to wreak havoc on it, for which he was profoundly grateful.

As they munched cold hoecakes and parched, sweetened corn in the early morning sunlight, Seth told her, "They killed my pa durin' the siege of Charlest'n an' that's when I got ma to let me take our last musket an' pistol and join the colonel's men."

"I'm sorry, Seth," Savarra said, surprised to find that she meant it. There was something very endearing about this youth with his eyes, like brown velvet, and the deep respect he showed her.

They did not stop, but let the animals pursue a slow walk that ate up the miles without tiring them too greatly. They paused at the clear springs and rushing creeks they passed to let them drink and to assuage their own thirst.

It was midday, just before they were to stop for another meager meal, when there came to their ears the shouts of men and the sound of gunfire, which alarmed Savarra deeply, for the sounds came from the direction in which she and Seth were traveling. Had the partisans circled around, searching for them? No! It had to be a clash between the British and the American rebels! Hunger was forgotten as the firing and shouts grew in volume.

"Let's go 'round, Miss Savarra," Seth urged. "It's a fire fight—"

"No, Seth. Let's investigate. Look how thick the woods are hereabouts. We can approach without being seen." She tried to keep excitement and hope out of her voice.

Seth followed her reluctantly as she urged King George ahead. As the underbrush thickened, they dismounted and led the animals by their reins. Suddenly they halted in the protective foliage as they saw beyond a tilled field and a farmhouse. The house was encircled by men on horseback. Heavy gunfire was being exchanged with those inside the well-built and large log house.

A short, stocky young man, his uniform showing his trim muscled figure to great advantage, was leading a troop of green-jacketed dragoons and they were engaged in a fierce exchange of shouts as well as bullets with those beseiged inside.

"Tarleton!" Seth Barwell muttered. "Damn his butcherin' soul!"

Savarra was overjoyed and would have run immediately into the field beyond their hiding place. But Seth seized her arm desperately and whispered, "No, no, Miss Savarra— you're dressed like—you look like a partisan an' they'd shoot you on sight thinkin' you a boy!"

His hoarse command halted her. He was right and she knew it. But after the fight—when Tarleton was victorious—

So they crouched beside their mounts in the thicket before the small battlefield and watched. Savarra was in a state of high excitement for these were her people and they would escort her back to Charles Town. She would tell Seth to leave and get well away after the battle was over—for it could only end in a British triumph, with the people in the farmhouse taken prisoner. She did not want that fate for Seth Barwell. She had become much too fond of him.

Yet as she crouched there beside King George and peered through the leaves at the carnage taking place, slowly, slowly a sick sensation descended to the pit of her empty stomach. She counted seven guns answering from the windows of the log house.

The men inside the dwelling were grimly silent now, but the cries of triumph from their attackers carried clearly on the midday air, as two of the defenders abruptly pitched out of the windows to sprawl on the ground before the log house, plainly wounded or killed. The dragoons were circling ever faster now, firing at will, and they greatly outnumbered those within.

After approximately fifteen minutes, when two more guns at the windows were silenced, the dragoons flung themselves from their mounts and rushed the house. Two appeared superficially wounded, for they staggered and then rallied, and most of them burst in the door. The sound of musket fire within the house was silenced.

A lone man ran out carrying his gun, attempting to reload, and the man Seth called Tarleton, his reddish hair and helmet gleaming in the sunlight, rode him down. Lifting his saber, he delivering a killing blow on the man's neck and shoulder, felling him instantly in a scarlet gush of blood.

From the house came hoarse shouts of pleasure. To Savarra's horror, two young women rushed from the house, only to be pursued and caught by two dragoons, who dragged them back into the house. Their cries rang piteously in her ears.

"What are they doing to them?" she asked Seth frantically. She looked into his face and saw it set like granite, infinitely older than his years.

He said grimly, "Things I couldn't say to you, a lady, Miss Savarra. They'll kill them eventually."

Savarra was dumbfounded. "I can't believe it. No British man would do such!"

Seth laughed shortly, "They been doin' it ever since they set foot on our shores—an' don't forget, most of them dragoons are loyalists, people who are really *Americans,* but they take advantage of their British loyalties."

"Oh, can't we do something?" she whispered, her heart beating heavily, her previous feeling of joy at seeing the dragoons vanished like smoke.

"We could ride in there and be killed for our pains. Do you think when the bloodlust is on them they'd wait for you to explain you're a British subject—let alone believe you? Nay, Miss Savarra, 'tis certain death for me an' worse for you if we ride in there."

Suddenly, thinly, on the air floated a baby's wail, then a child's cry of terror, and Savarra knew another sickening plunge of heart, for the cries were broken off sharply. She wanted, with every fiber of her being, to run and rescue the little ones, and it was only Seth's hard young hand on her arm that held her back.

The sounds of conflict lessened swiftly and, but for the triumphant shouts of the dragoons and the fading screams of the young women as the men went about their rape and pillage, it was quiet. Soon, the men of Tarleton's Legion were coming out of the house, laden with goods looted from the home. The women who had screamed were silent now and not to be seen, and Savarra felt her flesh crawl imagining what they had been subjected to.

When all their plunder was safely out of the house, tied up in tablecloths, quilts and bedsheets, the dragoons systematically set fire to the house with all the dead and wounded in it—and the women, Savarra thought, her blood chilled, if they were not already dead.

She saw Tarleton mount his big horse, an electric vitality and command in his bearing. His face was patrician, even handsome, belying the bloody slaughter she had just witnessed.

Seth whispered bitterly, " 'Tis said Banastre Tarleton made the boast in Charlest'n's taverns that he'd kill more rebels and bed more pretty women in this war than any other man. He seems well on the way to it."

All at once, Savarra was washed with a savage repulsion and she was helpless to reason with it as she looked at the commander of this bloodthirsty troop. The rebels were right! He *was* a butcher. And she had been so sure she would be among friends! She had been so ready to tell all she knew of the partisans and their hiding places. Now she would be betraying them to the mercies of men like Tarleton and his followers.

Not even her father, with all his daring, all his courage and iron command could stay the hand of men like Banastre Tarleton and his like. Savarra knew it with a falling spirit and she drew a deep breath like a sob. One of those young women had long, shining brown hair, which had come undone as she fled the house with the men pursuing her. It had flung in wild disarray as the two tall men had seized her, dragged her screaming back to the house. She shivered violently and Seth Barwell looked at her compassionately.

The two knelt in the thicket and through the heavy leaves watched the dragoons mount, carrying their stolen goods behind them as they wheeled their mounts to the north at a fast clip.

As they dwindled in the distance, Seth muttered, "I live in fear they'll descend on ma an' the children, since pa was killed, even though our farm's far back in the woods."

Savarra made no answer for her mouth was dry and her emotions in a turmoil. There was a lack of reason, of even the barest restraint among these men. They were totally brutal, like animals, killing, raping, taking what they would. The vaunted honor of the British was not among them, and a hard kernel of doubt lodged deep within her. The fact that most of them might be Americans was no comfort at all, for they were led by a British officer who had, if he chose to exercise it, command over them. Tarleton could have prevented this bestial assault and the murders—he could have taken prisoners, could have respected the young women, pitied the children. Instead, he had joined the savagery, and now the patriots were all dead or being consumed in the flames that towered up from the house, an inferno felt even in the scrub where she and Seth crouched, waiting for the pillagers to lengthen the distance between them. The dead patriot, cut through the neck and shoulder, lay where Tarleton had felled him, with his blood seeping slowly into the ground he would have tilled.

"Ain't no use us tryin' to get in there an' save them," Seth remarked bitterly. "Likely they was all murdered before the fire was set—I didn't hear the children cry no more sudden-like. Did you?"

She shook her head, unable to reply. Her loyalties, her determination, her beliefs were in a crucible. What she had witnessed was burned into her brain and she could not erase it.

After a time, the two emerged from their hiding place. Seth took down his short spade from the pack on the rump of his big roan. "Miss Savarra, I'm gonna bury that planter," he said quietly.

"Yes," she replied simply, wishing they could do the same for those gallant and outnumbered men and women who were being consumed in the blazing house.

She helped Seth as he dragged the body further from the flaming timbers that were now crashing into the center of the house, averting her eyes from the raw and gaping wound. She stood quietly while he set to work with silent fierceness, and in a short while he had a long, shallow grave completed. It took but a few minutes to cover the body.

Afterward, the two of them traveled uneventfully and slowly because of King George and his short steps. They spent the night at the edge of Wadboo Swamp, and the next noon found them at the broad dirt road that led directly into Charles Town, only a few miles away. Here, Seth prepared to leave her.

"I can't go into Charlest'n. They's people who know me there for a partisan an' I can't risk it."

"Why do most of you from the backcountry call it Charleston?" Savarra asked abruptly.

His face hardened. "'Twas named for an English king— but it don't rightly belong to the English. We'd as soon forget it."

She smiled faintly. "I think you might have liked King Charles. He was a bit of rebel himself—and a rake, too, so my history books told me."

He shrugged. "You can easy find your way to the town from here." He hesitated, then added quickly, his face reddening, "Miss Savarra, I think the world of you. You ain't like the British. You're more like us—I hope to see you again someday."

Savarra said with totally unexpected heat, "You are the most courteous gentleman I ever met, Seth. I am deeply in your debt and perhaps someday I can repay you for your kindness." She reached up to him on his tall roan and he stooped so their lips brushed fleetingly as she caught his hand tightly. Tears filled her eyes, for she knew a sudden intuition that she might never see this clear-eyed boy again.

"Just knowin' you'll be comfortable an' easy again is pay enough, Miss Savarra," he said, releasing her small hand. He added, "Ride straight on in an' I'll go on to my folks now."

They parted there in the sandy road with tall pines and gums forming a wall along either side. The sun was still high when Savarra kicked King George III into an easy trot toward town. In two hours she reached the outskirts, and passersby eyed her without curiosity on her little mount.

Under her borrowed hat, she looked a country boy come to town, and she made straight for the Pair house.

Her spirits had lifted somewhat, despite the devastation and cruelty she had witnessed yesterday. She pushed it determinedly to the back of her mind as she trotted down King Street and saw the Pair house just beyond the Brewton house. A great feeling of relief washed over her. In a matter of minutes she was there and dismounted at the front, sliding from King George to leave him standing placidly munching the luxurious grass that covered the Pair lawns.

She ran up the broad porch steps and swung the door open without knocking, calling loudly, "Cotty! Cotty!"

Amos came into the hallway from the drawing room. His face was dolorous and his mien subdued, but his astonishment at the sight of the strangely attired Savarra was undisguised. Fear followed swiftly as he recognized her.

"Mistress Savarra," he whispered incredulously.

"Yes, Amos—where is Cotty? I need her dreadfully. And I need a bath and—what is the matter here?" she asked in swift alarm.

He replied mournfully, "We got turrible news today— an' Mistress Savarra, you do look powerful strange."

"I know that," she said, a new fear pushing into her mind. Had something happened to her father—to Peter? No, these people would rejoice if that were so. Yet the unmistakable sound of weeping came to her as she neared the drawing room door, and the deep rumble of a man's voice—familiar —was it Baltazar?—could be heard.

Amos seemed distraught and he turned in at the drawing room. Savarra, drawn by curiosity and dread, followed. All the servants were in the room, the women weeping unshamedly into their aprons. Anne and Verity looked up at her through tears, before their eyes widened with shock and fear.

Verity felt her face pale as she whispered, "Savarra—how come you're here? What has happened?"

The words had no more than left her trembling lips when a great banging of the front door sounded, then the quick firm steps of a man rang on the parqueted floor and Lord Bainbridge strode in the door, his coat dusty and his tricorne soiled, his eyes brilliant with triumph.

Verity's heart took a wild leap at the sight of this man about whom she had dreamed every night for the last five weeks. His eyes sought and found hers and his held a kiss, before they fell on his peculiarly attired daughter. They narrowed then as they took in her soiled and weary appearance. But Verity noted that Savarra's chin lifted and conflict was in her face.

Now, thought Verity with new terror, she will tell him about Tyler, Cutler and Uncle Bowman—and about *us*. The tears of grief that stood on her face slowly dried as she bit her full lower lip and sought control.

"What in God's name is going on here?" Lord Bainbridge asked, the triumph in his face fading. "Savarra, you look like a London street urchin."

Verity looked at Savarra beseechingly. Anne stood silent and white, her tears a steady stream down her face. Baltazar stood beside her, his hand on her arm. For a taut moment, the lives of Belion, McLean and all their compatriots hung in the balance.

"Didn't you know—" Savarra began slowly and under Verity's eyes, the English girl's face whitened, her lip trembled before she steadied it. "Didn't Verity and Mistress Pair tell you Peter was coming to America for me—that I ran away to Camden to meet him?"

Verity let her breath out in a gasp. Disbelief crowded close on the heels of astonishment. What was Savarra doing —why, she was *lying*!

"Camden? God's blood! I went from Georgetown to Camden. I thought you safely here with Verity and her mother. So that young blackguard is in town—"

Savarra broke in, "I just returned—not five minutes ago. I was running away to Camden with—with a merchant and his wife who were going there when I was kidnapped."

"Kidnapped!" Lord Bainbridge said explosively. "By Haverley?"

"I wish it had been Peter! He is to be an aide to Lord Rawdon and based in Camden—but a band of rebels set upon us, killed the merchant and his wife and took me prisoner long before we reached Camden. I was to be held for exchange of some high-ranked rebel captive. But it seems you and Cornwallis won the battle of Camden and my captors became discouraged and dispersed, sending me home on that small ugly beast you must have seen in the front when you entered."

"Then you've not been with your impetuous suitor, eh?" Lord Bainbridge's eyes went to his daughter's feet and

Verity's followed them. She had never seen a pair of shoes so filthy, so inadequate—the satin was scarcely recognizable, the ribbons that held them to the small feet were torn and discolored by swamp mud. Lord Bainbridge said irately, "You look like a bloody pickpocket from the slums." His eyes narrowed, "I'll kill young Haverley—" Then suddenly aware, "Is my daughter's appearance cause for all this weeping?"

"Nay," said Anne Pair bitterly, speaking out for the first time. "My husband has been killed by British soldiers as he attempted to escape the islands."

Verity looked up to find Savarra's eyes on her and there was a totally unexpected sympathy in them. Something had changed this girl in the past three weeks, a change that was deep and basic. There was something behind those vivid blue eyes that reached out to her with a new compassion. She had lied, Verity told herself once again, and it could only be to protect the patriots. *Why*?

Her mother had handed Lord Bainbridge the letter she held, and Bowman Baltazar said, "Lord Bainbridge, that letter arrived an hour ago—I had the sad task of bringing it to the Pair ladies and attempting to console them."

Lord Bainbridge scanned the letter swiftly. He said quietly, "Madame Pair, this letter from the British command in the islands says your husband killed three British soldiers in his effort to escape. His death was warranted."

"And you," Anne Pair flared, "would you not kill three patriots if you were their prisoner and had a chance to escape them?"

"Indeed I would, madame. And those are the fortunes of war. I extend to you my sympathies. And now, Savarra, tell me more of these rebels who captured *you*."

Verity put her handkerchief to her cheeks, blotting the last of her tears as Savarra launched into what Verity knew to be a convincing concoction of lies. She restrained an admiring glance by lowering her thick dark lashes as Savarra said she did not know any of her captors, but she had occasion once to see their leader, Colonel Francis Marion. The English girl concluded that one of them brought her to the edge of town and turned her loose, so dispirited were they over the defeat at Camden.

"Did you—suffer at their hands?" he asked in a cold implacable voice.

"Only the hardships of their lives," Savarra said evasively.

"Then I suggest we say nothing of these three weeks of captivity, my dear." He looked forbiddingly at the fascinated servants in the room. "And it is expected that you will all hold your tongues as well. I will have no gossip about my daughter while she was in the hands of the rebels." He appeared somewhat weary now.

Verity sensed he had come in flushed with the news of the sweeping British victory at Camden and had hoped to find his daughter neatly and cleanly dressed, ready to clap her hands over his news.

Anne Pair was still weeping silently and Baltazar had an arm about her shaking shoulders. Verity reached out and took her mother's hand tightly. Verity was one of those fortunate women who wept attractively, and her big eyes were white about their brown irises and her steady tears clung to her thick lashes like jewels.

Sir James turned compassionate eyes on the two Pair women. "Dear ladies, I regret your loss." He spread his hands. "I would comfort you if I could."

"How kind of you," Anne Pair's voice was choked and her sarcasm unconcealed.

His eyes went to Verity and they held a wealth of love and tenderness, before he turned his attention to Savarra once more. "You're sure they did you no—harm—took no advantage of you, Savarra?"

Verity, from under her dark lashes, saw Savarra avert her face and two spots of color appeared on the now-tanned cheeks, but Savarra said coolly, "I was forced to eat the strangest foods and I slept on moss from the trees. I haven't had a bath in all that time, so I will go with Tiqua and Monique now, father, if you don't mind." She looked once more at Verity and Anne and said gently, "I am so sorry about your father, Verity. You both have my sympathy—"

Cotty and Brim burst into the room, having been summoned by Frances with the news of the arrival of Lord Bainbridge and his daughter.

"Oh, mistress," Cotty wept. "You left me after promisin'—none of us knowin' where you were or why! I haven't hardly slept since you disappeared!" The young maid's face was thinner and there were faint circles beneath the light blue eyes attesting to the truth she spoke.

Brim was saying, "Welcome home—both of you! Ah, Lord Bainbridge, I have heard of the great victory in Camden. Congratulations!"

Lord Bainbridge turned to his valet with obvious pleasure. "Well, now, yours is the first cheerful voice I've heard. I came riding in as fast as I could to tell of it—only to be met by this avalanche of sadness. I fear my enthusiasm is gone, Brim." And he and Brim followed Savarra from the room, discussing the battle.

Verity stood looking after them thinking, *He believed her. He believed every word, thank God.*

But she was tensely anxious to talk with Savarra, actually to collaborate with her, since the English girl was obviously going to protect the partisans. Verity could not imagine why Savarra had determined to do this, but she was grateful to the depths of her soul.

Baltazar had led her mother back to the sofa and Verity followed, seating herself on the other side of her. He held one of Anne's hands in his big, hard one and he said firmly, "We cannot have a proper burial for Warren, my dear Anne —but I am going to take steps to see that you and Verity have what he would have left you."

"What do you mean?" Anne asked, wiping her eyes once more.

"I am going to ask Lord Bainbridge if he will not request that the court of sequestration turn over the Pair Shipyards to me, as your representative—and see that the proceeds after taxes come to you both."

"Oh, Bowman," Anne said, lifting freshly tear-filled eyes. "If only you could! We have nothing but what that man deigns to give me for supplies. I couldn't bear to take money from him for our clothing and personal needs."

"He seems a reasonable man, my dear, and if I present the case to him in a reasonable manner, I feel sure he will arrange it." His deep voice grew bitter. "He has the power. All he has to do is exercise it." His eyes went to Verity's and his voice dropped to a whisper. "Do you think she will keep silent?"

Verity's shoulders lifted, then fell. "We can only hope so," she murmured. She was restless. She wanted to talk to Savarra, to *conspire* with her, she admitted to herself. She found it difficult to believe they could trust the girl.

As Baltazar and her mother continued their low-voiced conversation, Verity concluded she must trust Savarra, for the girl had it in her power to betray them all. As much as she desired Sir James, she was not ready to accept British rule. Her heart cried out for freedom and the two emotions, love of the Englishman and love of her country, were at constant war within her. She knew a vast curiosity as to what had made Savarra determine to keep their secret.

After Baltazar had left, promising to make arrangements for a memorial service for Warren Pair and to talk to Lord Bainbridge about an allowance, Verity saw her heartbroken mother upstairs to her room.

The three crises had come almost simultaneously. News of the death of her father, Savarra's arrival like a strange apparition from the swamps, followed almost immediately by her father, Lord Bainbridge, had put the noon hour well behind them, and she persuaded her mother to lie down across her broad bed.

"Here, mother—I will put a damp cloth across your eyes. So—and now I will go see to the preparation of a light lunch for all of us." And she left the room, closing the door behind her.

In the kitchen, she proceeded to tell Primrose to slice the cold goose and prepare a salad of light greens. "You may serve Lord Bainbridge chilled Madeira and the rest of us will have coffee."

"What we do," Amos caught at her arm, "if she tells?"

"I'm going now to talk with her about it," Verity replied, her eyes compassionate on the dark faces turned anxiously to her. "And I'll let you know if we can trust her as soon as I do." Then she went upstairs to Savarra's room.

She knocked lightly on the door and Cotty, her face dimpled and smiling for the first time in three weeks, admitted her. Savarra, sitting by the window and working with her nails, looked up. Her hair gleamed black as a crow's wing, clean and shining as it fell moistly graceful about her shoulders, and she wore a light blue dimity dress over few petticoats. Her little slippers were of blue file and looked neat and fetching on the small feet.

"You look a different person," Verity said with a friendly smile, "and very lovely, too."

"Thank you," Savarra replied, and her enigmatic glance warned Verity to say nothing in the presence of the hovering Cotty.

Cotty was clutching up the discarded male clothing and she held the disreputable shoes as if they were two particularly obnoxious rodents. "I'm goin' down an' burn these, Mistress. They don't smell good—what is it that smells like—like an animal?"

"The breeches are made of leather, Cotty. Animal skin. Do burn them," was the cool reply, and the little maid stepped out into the hall with her unpleasant burden.

"Primrose will serve a late light meal in less than an hour, Savarra," Verity said.

Savarra asked abruptly, "Have you heard from Peter since I have been gone?"

"No. You still expect him to arrive at any minute?"

"Yes. After all, now Peter is a soldier, I think father will approve our marriage. He knows now, at last, that my mind is made up." A troubled frown appeared between her dark brows. "It didn't seem to before, but now I find that my father's approval is something I greatly desire. I feel sure if he comes to know Peter as I do—and Peter serves the crown —he should soften in his attitude toward him."

"Yes," Verity agreed, hiding her impatience. She did not want to talk of Peter Haverley. She wanted to know how Savarra came to be back in Charles Town and why she was lying for the partisans. She said, "Savarra, I can scarcely believe that you are willing to keep the secret of Cutler, Tyler and—"

"I can scarcely believe it myself," the girl cut in with asperity, "but something happened on the way back to Charles Town. In a way, I suppose I am trying to make up— make up for what I saw."

Verity's eyes were puzzled as she took a chair near Savarra's. "I don't understand—nor do I understand why Cutler would let you return—"

"He didn't let me return. I persuaded a youth to help me steal away." She laughed shortly. "I suppose the captain scoured the woods for me and is cursing me at this moment."

"Oh, Savarra—"

"And I witnessed Banastre Tarleton's butchery on my way back through the woods with Seth—" And Savarra launched into a description of the slaughter that had taken place in the opening before the two crouching in the thicket. She brought to vivid life the ravished women, the children in the burning house, the looting and plundering. The two young women were silent for a few moments after she finished. Then Savarra added, "I have decided that the safety of the captain and his men are fair exchange for those innocent murdered men, women and children."

Verity sensed there was more Savarra was not telling. It lay in her eyes, in her voice and in her demeanor, but she could not fathom it. She only knew that Savarra had lost much of her haughtiness and snobbery.

They talked on of the partisans, and Savarra told her of the raid on Sumter's house and the freeing of the hundred and fifty prisoners from the battle of Camden. Verity knew a warming toward this chill, aristocratic young woman who had suddenly become more human. A little longer and a little more understanding between them, she thought wryly, and she would find herself almost affectionate toward the British girl—a strange paradox considering they were poles apart in their beliefs.

"It cannot be much longer before Peter arrives, and I know he will come directly to me. Surely in uniform, with duties to perform, my father will treat him with respect," Savarra said, as Cotty returned and announced that the afternoon meal was served.

At table, Verity observed that Lord Bainbridge had bathed and shaved and appeared extraordinarily handsome. Despite her sorrows for her father, she could scarcely keep her eyes from him, and in this he met her more than halfway. When she lowered her eyes she could feel the intensity of his gaze, and it made her weak with longing for him.

He had touched her but the one time on the stairs, yet the memory of the feel of his body next to hers was indelibly imprinted in her mind. She had long ago faced up to the fact that she wanted nothing so much in the world as to lie in this man's arms, to have him take her, make passionate love to her. It could never be, she told herself angrily. An English earl and an American girl of rebel sympathies were an unlikely match. Still, the burning desire filled her and it had intruded a thousand times a day these past weeks.

Verity noted that her mother's eyes were still slightly swollen, but she had herself well controlled and Verity was struck by the beauty of her face. Grief seemed to have sharpened her attractiveness. She made a handsome widow.

That night, Verity's mind was a millrace as she lay in her great testered bed. Something had altered Savarra Bainbridge completely and, though the girl had told her much, she had not told her all. Verity's intuition was strong and incontrovertible.

And she would never again see her father, Warren Pair, with his boisterous laugh and black, unruly hair, his infectious sense of humor. Fresh tears stung her eyes and she fought them down, reminding herself they would at least have a memorial service for him.

The following morning, which was Sunday, found Verity clad in a snuff-brown dress she hated. She let Bowman Baltazar in the house shortly after breakfast. His tall figure was handsomely clad in black broadcloth and breeches. His buckled shoes looked new and gleaming below his black silk stockings and his white ruffled cravat peeped above an elegant white satin waistcoat. His rich felt hat was in his hand as soon as he set eyes on her.

"I have come to have my chat with General Bainbridge," he said in a low voice, as he entered. "Then, if you and Anne will permit me, I will escort you to church."

"That is very kind of you, Uncle Bowman—he is in the library, or headquarters as he calls it now. Since 'tis Sunday, Colonel Coyne and the aides will not be in, though I'm sure he has much correspondence to catch up on since his return."

He said, "His daughter has not divulged our secret?" And when she shook her head, "What made her—lie about her abduction?"

Hastily Verity told him the circumstance of Tarleton's raid on the farmhouse, and Baltazar nodded slowly, murmuring, "Thank God some of the English are tempered with mercy. I will get word to Belion and McLean that she is holding her tongue." He then added, "Now take me in to see the general. I have planned quite a campaign to convince him."

"May I stay and listen?"

"If his lordship permits it," the big man smiled genially, tucking his fine hat under his arm. His thick dark hair was graying at the temples and he affected no powder in it.

They approached the library headquarters and, looking in, saw Lord Bainbridge with his pipe in his mouth and Amos putting a coal from the kitchen to it. He drew deeply, then squinted through smoke at the two in the door.

Anne Pair, wearing a dull purple dress which still managed to set off her creamy skin, came from the kitchen at that moment. Seeing, she came to join them as they stepped into the room. Amos bowed to them and left.

"You are early visitors," Lord Bainbridge said, drawing again on his pipe, "and you look to be a serious delegation."

"My business is serious," Baltazar said, his friendly countenance stern, "and I would dispense with the worst of it first as 'tis more bad news for the ladies." He bent a compassionate glance on the two standing beside him.

"Come and seat yourselves," Lord Bainbridge said, rising and motioning to the hard, straight-backed chairs around the great teak desk.

"I cannot imagine worse news, Bowman, than that which we have already endured," Anne Pair said exhaustedly, and Verity knew a sudden tightening of nerves as they all seated themselves.

"'Tis no worse, but 'tis bad enough for your friends," Baltazar said. "Some of our most prominent citizens—old friends—have refused to exchange their paroles for oaths of allegiance to the crown, and Cornwallis has instructed Colonel Balfour to take up the most dangerous members of this cabal."

"I know of this," Lord Bainbridge said, eyes narrow. "You might tell the ladies of what they are accused."

"They are accused of corresponding with the enemy and are further charged with plotting, had Gates been successful at Camden, to fire Charles Town and, while the garrison was busy fighting the flames, to recapture the town for the rebels."

Lord Bainbridge surveyed them bleakly. "They deserve to be imprisoned. They cannot be trusted."

Baltazar looked at Anne steadily. "They are being deported today. Twenty-nine of them, including Lieutenant Governor Christopher Gadsden, are to be put aboard the *Lord Sandwich* and sent into exile at St. Augustine prison down on the Florida coast. The rumor is that some thirty more will be sent there later. Among them, Anne, are your and Warren's old friends, Thomas Barber and Frank Boothe. God knows how their families will fare during their absence."

"'Tis no rumor," Lord Bainbridge said shortly. "They will be deported—and you sound uncommonly distressed, Mr. Baltazar, for a man who is loyal to the crown."

"I *am* loyal to the crown, but these people are my old friends. I have known most of them all their lives and I tried hard to get them to take the oath of allegiance." Baltazar's kindly brown eyes were level. His mouth was firm and strong.

"Unfortunate that you did not succeed. But I believe Charles Town will be a safer place without these troublemakers." He sent out a cloud of blue smoke, adding, "Though I sympathize with the ladies, they can take heart that, when hostilities cease and America is safely under the crown, these men will be returned to their homes."

Baltazar cleared his throat and said soberly, "That is quite true, Lord Bainbridge. However, I came by expressly this morning to do a service for the Pair ladies—with your permission."

Verity and her mother lowered their lashes and the younger woman's heartbeat quickened. She felt Lord Bainbridge's eyes on her and she longed to raise hers and meet them, but she did not. She must *not* encourage this man who was her enemy. And it would be so good to have money of their own once more! Living on Lord Bainbridge's largesse sat poorly on both her and her mother. It made her feel beholden —not the same as having money from her father's business, which by rights belonged to them.

"And what is this service, Mr. Baltazar?" Lord Bainbridge asked warily. "I have the distinct feeling it concerns more than my permission."

"It does," replied Baltazar briefly, and Anne's face drew taut. Verity looked up at Lord Bainbridge then, her big dark eyes questioning and hopeful. His short-cropped fair hair was slightly tousled, and when he looked at her his eyes contained a young eagerness that set Verity's pulses pounding.

Baltazar said, "As you know, the Pair Shipyards have been turned over to the loyalist Jonathan Hatcher, who knows little of how to operate them." He paused, then in a calm, reasonable voice, "The Pair ladies are no danger to the crown, and I am willing to take over those yards myself in the name of Warren's widow and daughter. I have had much experience—indeed, Warren and I did much of our business together. Now the court of sequestration has left the ladies penniless, but for your generosity, which is great, we know. But I would formally request that you arrange to let me take over the shipyards—I am quite as good a citizen as Hatcher —and give a portion of the proceeds to Mistress Pair and her daughter, after duties, fees and taxes are duly paid."

Lord Bainbridge regarded him from beneath dark brows, his eyes sapphire bright. Verity was struck anew by the charm of the man when those eyes swung to her. They were questioning, and back of them lay desire to do for her that which would make her happy. She read it clearly. She held her delicately formed face, the beauty, the tenderness and the promise of passion in it, very still.

"I will write to Lord Cornwallis tomorrow. I think we

might well arrange it. As a firm loyalist, Mr. Baltazar, I know you would see that no rebel vessel was serviced or produced, and we can count on you to pay the fees and taxes due your king."

"Aye, you can count on me to do right by my king," Baltazar said calmly, "and the ladies would have money for their personal necessities, without your having to procure a stipend for them."

Lord Bainbridge's smile at Verity held an endearing touch of boyishness. "I shall attend to it, Mr. Baltazar."

Verity's eyes were starry, for she had chafed under their penurious mode of life since her father was deported. Now she looked directly into Lord Bainbridge's eyes, letting the well of genuine gratitude and respect shine forth in her own. The young eagerness was still in his vivid eyes and Verity's cheeks flushed suddenly.

Savarra spoke from the doorway. "A meeting? May I join you?"

"By all means, Mistress Bainbridge." Baltazar rose and bowed, his genuine fondness for the British girl obvious. "I was just about to tell the ladies and your father there are a number of balls and parties planned in the city to celebrate our great victory in Camden, in which Lord Bainbridge played such an admirable part. Bonnie Raintree is planning one the first of September, and she will probably come calling to invite you this very day."

"Verity and I will attend none of them," Anne said distantly, "with our grief so fresh and our mourning so deep."

"Well, I shall certainly go," Savarra said with quick firmness. "It has been months since I attended a ball—not since I left England, in fact."

Baltazar's clear eyes on her were faintly worried now. Verity saw that he was still wary of her silence. Indeed, as she looked into his rugged face, she realized that he was in dread that Savarra, so young, might yet divulge the sympathies of the three men.

But the English girl gave him an especially sweet smile, adding, "You will be there, Mr. Baltazar, will you not?"

"Indeed I shall, Mistress Bainbridge, All good loyalists will be there. You should have a splendid time."

"Peter will be coming in from England any day now, father. Perhaps he will escort me to the ball." She cast an appealing look at Lord Bainbridge, and Verity saw his face harden at the mention of Peter Haverley.

"He will have to distinguish himself as a soldier of the crown, daughter." His voice was cold.

"He will arrive any day now," Savarra said confidently, "and I have the feeling, father, now he is a military man you two will hit it off very well."

Lord Bainbridge drew on his pipe." I could wish you were a better judge of men."

Savarra bit her lip, but then her brow cleared and she said cheerfully, "I shall look forward to the balls and parties to celebrate our victory," and Verity wondered if Lord Bainbridge could feel the strong undercurrent in the room. It seemed palpable to her that not only was Savarra not telling all she knew, but that all of them were concealing the truth.

However, Lord Bainbridge was unaware, and in a short while they all made their way to St. Michael's Church, where the word had spread about Warren Pair's untimely death, and Verity and her mother were surrounded by old friends and neighbors. Even some of their loyalist friends offered condolences.

Returning home, they were served a sumptuous meal, and Baltazar stayed to dine with them, leaving at last with cheerful comments to Savarra regarding the coming festivities and reassuring Verity and Anne that he would see to the memorial services for Warren Pair.

Later, as Verity sat in her room, taking up and refurbishing a dull blue dress that would be suitable to wear, she had the strong feeling that Warren Pair, with his jovial laugh and high good humor, would scorn their ritual of grief and drab dresses, but custom was such that it could not be ignored. Further, she and her mother lacked money to buy proper black dresses for the coming days of mourning—for Baltazar had yet to take over the Pair Shipyards. *I shall look like an old crow in this,* she thought rebelliously.

Then she faced the fact that she was longing to attend the balls, despite her grief and loss. She longed to dance with Lord Bainbridge—flirt with him—tease him and stroll the gardens in the coming warm September nights on his arm. She tried sternly to keep from imagining his tender love-making and was only partially successful. Somehow her love for him intermingled with her love for her father and her aching loss to bring hot tears to her eyes.

Eight

In the days that followed, Savarra was aware that the loyalists were riding high and the heavy hand of the conqueror was laid on indiscriminately. Cornwallis had sent word to tighten up on all known patriot sympathizers, and Savarra knew her father enjoyed the warm feeling that victory was but a step away, when all of the colonists would be subdued, law-abiding, tax-paying subjects. She, herself, had no such comforting feelings. She remembered the implacable eyes, the set faces of the men in the swamps and she was uneasy.

This sensation was compounded two days after she had returned, when she went in the carriage with Verity on an errand for her mother, to pick up some materials at a warehouse on the quay. As they trotted down to the docks, it happened that they were witnesses to the departure of Charles Town's prominent citizens for St. Augustine prison in Florida.

There was a great crowd about these men, and many alert redcoated British soldiers, as they boarded the *Lord Sandwich*. It was a quiet multitude. The soldiers stood silently at attention, but there was something disquieting in the air. Savarra knew it should have been a triumphant moment for the British, but there was something menacing in the faces that were there to see the prisoners off—wives, children, uncles, aunts, brothers and sisters. The colonists' faces were set and their eyes burning, and as the carriage drove past Savarra knew a tightness in the pit of her flat little stomach. They looked like Englishmen—they *were* Englishmen, but no amount of rationalization could bring her to the comforting thought that they would eventually be one with Britain again. It added to the burden that Savarra already carried with her, recollections of those resolute and tough men who struck their telling blows from the secret reaches of the swamps.

As they neared the house once more, she said to Verity, "You know, we have a man in England who sympathizes

156

with the colonies, though he can do little to influence the king."

"I've been told there is more than one," Verity said as the carriage, with Amos on the box, took the turn on to King Street.

"But this one said something—" she hesitated, "that keeps coming back to me. I've thought of it often since—since I was with the rebels and Colonel Marion."

"And what is that?"

Savarra's brow under her ruffled lace cap furrowed and she repeated slowly, "He said, 'The temper and character which prevail in our Colonies are, I am afraid, unalterable by any human art. An Englishman is the unfittest person on earth to argue another Englishman into slavery.' His name is Edmund Burke."

There had been two teas and a dinner prior to the Raintree ball, all celebrating the great British victory at Camden. But Savarra had seen at those gatherings expressionless faces and knew they belonged to those whose sympathies were not with the British, though they would deny that. Some of these faces, wearing wintry smiles, would be seen at the Raintree ball, Savarra was sure. There would be patriots who paid only lip service to the king as well as ardent loyalists mingling during the festivities.

Still, her heart was light with the promise of Peter's arrival soon, and she bought a new dress for the occasion from the dress shop of Jeanne Flammarion in the heart of Charles Town. The Frenchwoman carried some ready-made frocks that came in ships from Paris, despite the hostilities, and this dress was a dream of misty white silk of such light texture it had the appearance of clouds about Savarra's slender waist. The neck was cut daringly low and there was a trim of black lace about the sleeves, with a large pouf, like an oversized sash in the back, also of black lace.

Cotty, arranging Savarra's black hair into a graceful creation of loops and curls in a fashionable pompadour on her head that evening, mourned, "Oh, mistress, if only you'd let me powder it—you would look so elegant."

"Powder is going out," Savarra said stubbornly. "Only the old people do it now. Especially over here in America."

When finally she stood before the mirror, she saw that the white dress with its black lace set off her dark beauty and cobalt eyes to perfect advantage. Cotty corroborated her satisfaction by saying admiringly, "Oh, Mistress Savarra, you do look perfectly beautiful. You should be the center of attraction this evenin'."

"Thank you, Cotty," she said, wishing vehemently that Peter could see her now. She knew he would be dazzled and she yearned to dazzle him.

She could not resist pirouetting to Verity's room to show her the dress, and she was most satisfactorily complimentary, which further pleased Savarra.

"I do wish you were going," she said impulsively to Verity, who sat beside the lamp with a book in hand, looking somewhat forlorn in her sedate snuff-brown. Her skirts did not stand out as Savarra's and it was a most unbecoming dress. But nothing could alter the beauty of Verity's face. Her white marble skin was smooth and exquisite, but the news of her father's death still haunted the great brown eyes.

"Have a good time for me, Savarra," she said, and Savarra sensed that the young woman's heart was longing to be part of the excitement and gaiety.

It was still suffocatingly hot despite the fact that it was the first of September, but Savarra looked cool as an iced drink in the black and white. And as she left the Pair house that evening in the company of her father and Scott Coyne in their scarlet coats and trim white breeches, they made a remarkably handsome trio when they entered the Pair carriage, with Amos driving them the several blocks to the Raintrees' enormous house.

The Raintree house was comparatively new and, as such, had the benefit of several additions not afforded to the older homes in Charles Town. The drawing room was of impressive size. There was a sitting room almost as large, as well as the hallway, called the great hall by Bonnie. It was, like those of the plantation houses along the Ashley and Cooper rivers, a tremendous room in itself.

This great hall was crowded with richly appareled guests. As the three of them moved through the crowd, Savarra's eyes were bright with anticipation and she thought, *Oh, if only Peter were here!* About to speak of Peter, she looked up at her father to find his gaze discontented. He glanced at the towering clock against the wall, which showed the hour to be forty-two minutes past eight of the evening, and Savarra knew that he was calculating how long he must stay. Already he was thinking of departure and she bit off her happy comment. Well, she would not leave until the end of this ball!

Not even if she had to contend with the lovesick Scott Coyne as escort back to the Pair residence.

"Oh, Savarra—Lord Bainbridge and Colonel Coyne!" trilled Bonnie, meeting them as they entered the drawing room. A servant took the men's hats and the fine white taffeta pelisse from Savarra's shoulders. Bonnie ran on. "How delightful to see you! Did you know Cutler McLean and Tyler Belion have returned from their trips to Philadelphia and New York? Happily they met each other in Georgetown three nights ago and came into Charles Town together."

Lord Bainbridge said heartily, "They're here?" and at Bonnie's affirmative, he added, "I should like to hear from Belion how it goes with Henry Clinton in New York."

"Oh, I've already talked to him and he says General Clinton is very busy, though heaven knows with what, for the war in New York is at a standstill. In fact, I do believe the rebels are conquered there." Bonnie followed them farther into the drawing room where a short, beaming black man with powerful shoulders under his black broadcloth coat served them spirits in a variety from a silver trayful.

As the men took whiskey, Bonnie and Savarra lifted glasses of Madeira to their lips. Bonnie did not miss a breath. "I heard General Gates ran away—from his whole army at Camden, Lord Bainbridge!" She laughed delightedly. "'Tis said he did not halt until he reached the capital of North Carolina at Hillsborough, three days after the battle—a dash of a hundred and eighty miles from the battlefield at Camden. Is that so, Lord Bainbridge?"

"So 'tis said," Lord Bainbridge replied dryly.

"And the American congress was so bullheaded about appointing him. I know for a fact—Spencer himself heard it from a patriot—that they talked of putting him over the whole of the American forces, to replace George Washington—after General Gates' triumph at Saratoga. Isn't that laughable? I wonder how they feel about him now." She paused for breath. "Oh, my goodness! Yonder comes Bowman Baltazar. I declare, I do wish I could get that man to take an interest in the widow Fairfield. She's very wealthy and quite attractive. Scott, do come with me, for I am reminded. I've a most eligible American girl you *must* meet—" And with the reluctant Coyne in tow, she left them, her light, merry voice fading as she made her way to greet Baltazar. And probably to find the promised American girl and the widow Fairfield, thought Savarra, smiling.

"She's better than any of our espionage agents and much more innocent," Lord Bainbridge said a touch grimly and lifted his glass, then turned to greet a fellow officer, leaving Savarra alone as she speculatively eyed the many finely clothed guests.

Her eyes caught on a very tall resplendent figure across the room, so resplendent in a rose-colored satin coat and breeches with a white lace ruffle at his brown throat she did not recognize him at first. Then he brought his glass up with a gesture of congratulation, gray eyes sparkling over the rim as he toasted her. It was Cutler McLean, and her blood suddenly tingled with anger even in her fingertips. She lifted her chin and looked away, but her eyes were unseeing and she was conscious only that he approached her directly.

"Mistress Bainbridge," he said softly at her shoulder. She turned and faced him coolly. "Bowman has told us that you have kept our secret after all."

"I have."

"May I ask why?" His voice like hers was very low, unnoticeable in the animated conversations about them, but he did not smile.

"Not because of you, captain, to be sure!"

"Nor because of anything that passed between us?"

"*Nothing* of any import has passed between us. And I have come to—loathe you, Mr. McLean," she spoke imperiously. "You are an undeserving recipient of my silence."

"Then tell me why," he persisted.

Her anger rose, partly because he stood so disturbingly near and partly because of what she was forced to admit. "I had the dubious opportunity of seeing Colonel Tarleton at work on my way back to Charles Town. I decided to trade with him—you, Belion and Baltazar for the men, women and children he slaughtered before my eyes."

"Ah," McLean said thoughtfully. Then with quiet anger of his own, "You are wise for your years. If there is any favor I can do you, you have only to ask."

"I have only one—let me see as little of you as possible!" She spoke heatedly, little dreaming of the dangerous future that would find her seeking this man's offered favor frantically.

His laughter was genuine. "That is one favor that will be hard to grant. The Pairs are dear friends—and co-conspirators—and I must add that your father looks on me with much favor."

"A distinct mistake on his part."

"But you will not enlighten him as to that?"

"No," she said positively, and McLean looked at her admiringly. The small orchestra at the end of the drawing room, couched among potted palms and consisting of three violins, a pianoforte and cello, began tuning up. McLean asked politely, "Will you dance with me, Mistress Bainbridge?"

But at that moment, a determined Scott Coyne bore down on them. "Mistress Savarra, will you share this first dance with me?" he asked, brown eyes bright with hope.

"Indeed I will, Scott," she replied with a brilliant smile of such warmth that the young colonel reddened with pleasure. McLean bowed deeply and moved away. With him went the stimulant of her anger, and Savarra was perplexed by a quick deflation.

As she and Scott swung out into the mass of dancers, she noted abstractedly that her father was dancing beautifully with Bonnie Raintree, who was chattering like a magpie. Lord Bainbridge looked bemused, which no doubt he was, for their plump and animated hostess was a well of all the latest news. Still, Savarra knew him well enough to be certain that in less than an hour he would leave this pleasant gathering. Was it the mass of papers on his desk that drew him—or was it that brown-haired, dark-eyed rebel girl, Verity Pair? She came back with a start.

". . . I said, Mistress Savarra, I love you deeply." Coyne's round face was pink and smooth. He had shaved very closely, she thought abstractedly, looking into those earnest and forthright brown eyes. "You must surely have known, my dear."

"Indeed no, sir," she lied quickly. "This scarcely seems the place to—"

He interrupted, "No, it isn't. I would have preferred the Raintree gardens and a full moon. But the moon is down and I fear I shall not be able to maneuver you into the gardens, for I see any number of Charles Town gallants looking at you." He paused, then asked, "May I speak to your father, Savarra, for permission to court you?" At her expression of dismay he added quickly, "Just to pay court to you. There is no need for an answer—I have not yet asked you to marry me."

"You know I like you well, Scott. And we are already together a great deal—you are so closely associated with father." She spoke with kindness, for Scott Coyne was a nice enough young man. Still it would be a great bother to have

him under foot when Peter came. "But you know I am affianced to Lord Haverley's son, Peter."

"You are not," Scott replied stubbornly. "Your father says
you are not."

Ire rising, she answered, "My father does not tell me whom
to marry!"

His jaw set. "You aren't married to Peter Haverley yet.
May I call on you until he arrives?"

The music stopped and Savarra shrugged. "Scott, I love
Peter Haverley. I'm telling you that now. If you want to call,
escort me to some of the parties, I may go—or I may not."
She thought surely this cavalier attitude would cool his ardor,
and for an instant his handsome young face darkened with
pain. Touched, she added softly, "I do like you, Scott, very
much. That is why I cannot be anything but honest with you."

His face brightened. "That is something to build on." He
spoke with forced cheerfulness. Then observing two young
British officers aproaching purposefully, he added swiftly, "I
shall ask Lord Bainbridge if—"

"And I can tell you he will say yes quickly enough," she
interrupted, laughing, her eyes on the redcoated officers as
they drew up beside them.

The taller began, "Colonel Coyne, would you introduce me
to the general's—"

"I saw her first," said the shorter, blue eyes twinkling and
grin engaging.

Both were cut short by another man who had approached
unseen. "Ah, Colonel Coyne, I see you have danced with
General Bainbridge's daughter once. Time to allow a change
of partners."

Savarra turned at the sound of the commanding voice and,
to her amazement, observed the newcomer to be familiar of
face and figure. There was a leashed violence in the man, and
as she stood looking up into his face she was both drawn to
and repelled by him. He was not tall. His compact figure,
clad now in a fresh and beautifully tailored green jacket
bearing the insignia of his rank, close-fitted white doeskin
breeches and polished knee boots, was impressive. His hair
was reddish-bronze and his eyes were thick-lashed and a
hazel-green, his features clean-cut and attractive.

All of her would-be partners fell back and Scott Coyne
said without expression, "Mistress Savarra Bainbridge, may
I present Colonel Banastre Tarleton."

The music began and Tarleton took her hand, and the two swung out in rhythm with the music.

"You are very beautiful," he said bluntly. "I didn't know Old Iron Jaw had such a daughter."

"But I know about you, Colonel Tarleton. People have much to say of you," she said coldly.

He was alert. "Not all of it good, I assume from your tone." At her silence he said shortly, "Your father has little use for me, I know."

"Indeed?"

"Indeed, mistress. Has he infected you with his dislike or is it the rebels you live with who have spoken ill of me?"

"You invite dislike, sir, referring to my father as Old Iron Jaw."

He laughed easily. "Have you never heard the general referred to by those terms before? I assure you, many of his subalterns have used it for years."

"And you have a sobriquet of your own, have you not?"

She looked up boldly and he looked down, their eyes locking. His hand on hers tightened cruelly. "To what do you refer, mistress?"

"Butcher," she said contemptuously.

He swung her about with restrained violence. "You sound like a rebel, mistress."

"I heard your sobriquet from an English officer, Colonel Tarleton, of impeccable repute."

"Who?" he demanded angrily.

"That I will not tell you. A man of your temper and character would surely call him out and kill him."

"I would."

For a moment they danced in silence, and Savarra knew an overwhelming urge to slap this man across his chiseled lips hard enough to cut them. The violence within her communicated itself to the man who held her.

He laughed suddenly and it was not a pleasant sound. "Mistress, you are far too lovely to quarrel with, and quarreling is the last thing I would do with you."

She made no answer and he said, "Are you not curious as to what I *would* do with you?"

"I would prefer not to know."

"Then," he replied audaciously, "you must know already." He leaned forward and whispered in her ear, "I am quartered at the Thorn and Thistle Inn. My rooms are very cozy and the wines there are excellent. Would you have supper with me there at—say, a little after midnight?"

Her eyes like rapiers met his and she said, "My father would kill you for that."

"My God—if you could see your eyes!" He spoke with genuine shock. Then laughing again, "But you will not tell him—look, he is leaving already." She followed his glance and saw that her father was indeed making his adieus. "Now you can leave with me anytime we like, Savarra. I have made discreet inquiries about you and I know, for example, that you await the arrival of a lord's son, Haverley, isn't it? And you are much sought after by the redoubtable Colonel Coyne. And you—I saw your face as he importuned you earlier— are not receptive to his overtures." He bent nearer. "Now I am a fine young buck and I promise you a rousing good time—at supper and later in bed." He paused and asked, "What time shall we leave, Savarra?"

The music stopped and Savarra was very pale. She was in such a towering rage, she was trembling. Tarleton did not release her hand, and the hot desire in the man was palpable about her. She turned away, not trusting herself to speak, but his hold on her hand tightened. She twisted it, giving a sharp jerk, but his hold did not lessen.

Suddenly Cutler McLean towered over the man. He bowed punctiliously and spoke in the most courteous of tones. "Ah, Colonel Tarleton, I have come to claim the next dance with Mistress Bainbridge. She promised me earlier."

Reluctantly Tarleton released her hand, his green hazel eyes hot upon her face. "Would you like to release yourself from that promise, mistress? I would have another dance with you myself."

Savarra simply stared through him. The man's conceit was monumental. "I think not, colonel." And as the music began again, she turned to McLean.

The two did not speak as they began the dance. In the turmoil of disgust and contempt Tarleton stirred in her, it came to her dimly that McLean, for such a tall and powerful man, was singularly graceful and light on his feet.

At last she said huskily, "I cannot understand why Scott or one of the officers did not come to me."

"Tarleton has evidently staked you out as his choice for the evening, Mistress Bainbridge. Only a civilian would have the temerity to claim a dance from you while in company with the Butcher. Unwelcome as it may be, I thought it possible you might prefer my company to his." His low laugh was cynical.

"I will not dance with him again," she said violently.

"I shall observe your refusal with interest. Butcher Tarleton is not accustomed to refusals from the ladies.

"The man is an animal—worse." The words were thick in her throat.

"You covered that very well as you danced, mistress. Your face was smooth—but I saw your eyes."

"I will not dance with Colonel Tarleton again," she repeated, still shaken by the man's open vulgarity.

And she did not. Two dances later, when Tarleton approached with his arrogant assumption of acceptance, she gave him an icy smile and said, "My dances are filled for the balance of the evening, Colonel Tarleton." Then as he reached for her in disbelief, she drew back and said low, but clearly, "If you touch me, I shall scream at the top of my lungs, manners be damned."

He looked into her eyes and saw the truth there and an ugly look crept over the handsome features.

McLean, standing near, coughed suddenly and hard and she knew he was hiding laughter. As Tarleton hesitated, she shot the partisan a savage glance and he sobered quickly, approaching her himself and saying, "This was promised me, was it not?"

Tarleton glared at him. "You're a presumptuous devil, McLean." Then to Savarra, "And mistress, you are not so cold as you pretend. You will accept my earlier invitation in the end." He smiled knowingly and strode away.

"Would you like a glass of Madeira?" McLean asked, not offering to take her arm though the music was lively now.

"That would be far better than dancing with you," she replied rudely. "Really, between you and that—that beast, my evening is ruined."

"Come with me then. Our friend, the Butcher, is predatory enough without the encouragement of finding you alone again."

Savarra followed him thinking mutinously of the gingerly manner in which the officers had regarded her after Tarleton's obvious interest. She wanted very much to tell her father of the man's indecent proposals, but she knew she would not. Her father would seek him out and in the duel that was sure to follow, he might well be killed. Tarleton was a young man, with all a young man's swift impetuosity and skill at arms.

McLean secured two glasses of Madeira from the laden table in the dining salon. As they stood sipping, she fumed, "I've never encountered such conceit in my life. If you but knew—"

"I know," he replied shortly, "and if it were not for my pretense at loyalty to George Third, I would kill him myself." Then with grim promise, "And the day may come when I meet him on my own grounds. They say he will be sent to search out Marion and when he does—" He broke off as another officer approached to request a dance with Savarra.

She saw no more of McLean that evening though she stayed until midnight. When Scott Coyne was taking her home in the carriage, she put down a contradictory urge to speak of the man.

And that night she dreamed of him, a strange dream in which Tarleton forced her to his rooms at the Thorn and Thistle. Yet when he took her into his arms, she looked up and saw that it was Cutler McLean who held her. She thought for a moment he had rescued her, but instead he flung her upon the bed, ripped her beautiful new gown from her shoulders, tearing the fine black lace. She saw it in shreds on the floor, and all the while a strange weakness was on her and she could not struggle.

At that moment she awakened, perspiring profusely, her heart pounding heavily. She was a long time going to sleep once more.

Nine

Much earlier that evening, Anne Pair had retired and Verity, restless as a cat and thinking longingly of the ball at Bonnie Raintree's, decided it was hopeless to go to bed for she knew she could not sleep.

The September night was hot and she told Amos and the servants she was going out to cool herself in the gardens.

She sat in the dark on a wrought-iron bench, thinking her unhappy thoughts and wishing with all her heart things were different. Tyler Belion would be at the ball, and for that she was grateful. Otherwise he might have come to the gardens, and Verity could scarcely bring herself to return his ardent kisses now.

Oh, she thought despairingly, *I have ruined my life by falling in love with an English lord!* For all her erotic imaginings Verity was morally strong, and she told herself she could never put her dreams into reality. Still, she dwelt now on Lord Bainbridge as he had appeared leaving for the ball tonight, his new uniform gleaming and handsome, his dark gold hair shining in lamplight, his face with strength and character stamped upon it—and those heart-stopping eyes when they looked into hers. Thus she leaned back and savored the man in darkness, with the final fragrances of departing summer floating about her.

Even so, she was startled when his voice came to her in the night. "Amos told me you were in the gardens—grieving, he said."

Her voice was breathy. "Lord Bainbridge, the ball isn't nearly over. What are you doing home so early?"

"Because I thought you might be lonely—might be grieving. You shouldn't be sitting alone, Verity, a beautiful woman sorrowing for what cannot be helped and is done."

There was no moon and the sky was thick with stars. Night air was heavy with rich perfumes. Magnolias were still blooming, and Cape Jasmine, combined with other flowers, made a fragrance of piercing sweetness.

Verity drew in a great lungful of it. "My father was a wonderful man," she said, somewhat guiltily for she had not been thinking of Warren Pair. "I missed him when he was deported. I shall miss him more, knowing I shall never see him again."

"I'm sure he was a fine man. Had he but acknowledged his king, he would have been a winner instead of a loser."

"He did what he felt was right." Her breath shortened as anger and desire mingled to make a potent fusion. "What *I* and my mother feel was right. His death cannot change that."

Bainbridge seated himself beside her and his voice was tender. "I wish to comfort you, Verity. You are so beautiful and you need comfort so greatly. You are too young for so much sadness. You should have been laughing and dancing at Bonnie's very successful ball tonight."

"Yet you left early."

" 'Twas the thought of you alone that brought me." His deep voice was full of compassion and desire. It was impossible to mistake it and Verity's breath grew more uneven.

"That is—kind of you," she said haltingly. "Mother has been inconsolable. We have not been able to comfort each other."

"Think then that your father died for what he believed in and take comfort from that. He was a brave man, I know. A man of high principle—even his enemies credit him with that." He paused, then added, "I have good news for you, Verity. Bowman Baltazar will take over the management of the Pair Shipyards next week and you and your mother will receive a very nice income."

"Oh," she said inadequately. His nearness was tantalizing, and her strict upbringing was in violent conflict with the surge of longing to touch him. It was so strong and so distressful, she felt tears gather in her eyes. They could be seen in the starlight, brilliant crystals on the lower lashes of her big, luminous eyes.

Sir James raised his hand and tenderly brushed them away. Then he took her gently into his arms and held her against his broad chest. She was helpless to resist as his hands touched the warmth of her slender body through the thin cambric of her dress and sent her blood coursing hotly along her veins.

His hands moved over her, drawing her nearer, caressing the flowing curves of her body, and as he did so one hand closed over a firm, uptilted breast. In the darkness her face stung, for she felt this was something he had done in his mind many times since he first saw her breasts beneath the lawn kerchief she often wore. But the reality was sharp and sweet and he murmured, "Ah, Verity, you affect me like a tumblerful of good brandy." With his other hand he tilted her face to his, whispering, "My darling Verity—" and his firm lips closed over hers. Suddenly, under their pressure, hers parted and she strained against him, their kiss deepening passionately.

It was as if some barrier within her had burst and a swift and burning urgency swept them both. Somewhere in the dim recesses of her mind Verity thought, *I am lost—lost.*

He rose, pulling her up with him, and his voice was thick with longing. "Come, darling Verity. Come with me."

Without a word she moved beside him and they entered through the darkened kitchen. The hearth was a bed of rose-red coals, covered thinly with ashes preparatory to starting the breakfast fires, but Primrose and the other servants were not to be seen. The house was still.

They made their way without candles to his room, where he struck flint to steel and lit but one. In the mellow gleam of it, Verity looked mistily beautiful, like a girl in a dream, and slowly he began to remove her clothing.

She made no demur, helping him with the buttons that ran from her breast to abdomen. In a matter of minutes they stood disrobed, and he lifted her nude body to his bed, slowly, deliberately, protracting each sensual moment. They laid together, face-to-face, the entire length of them pressed one against the other.

It is even more wonderful than I dreamed, Verity thought.

Lord Bainbridge at thirty-eight was a knowledgeable man, and he knew how to draw from each movement, every instant, the ultimate in sensation and pleasure.

Verity had one last fleeting instant of guilt, of shame, but it was lost as his hands on her body probed gently all those sensitive parts, and as they moved her excitement grew. She felt it rising to meet his, and their lovemaking grew more frenzied, wilder, sweeter. She pressed against him and in the final moments, they were fused, one to the other in a gust of passion that peaked and left them both spent and deeply satisfied. They lay so for an hour or more before she moved in his arms and said, "I must go to my room. Savarra will return soon—and my mother is a light sleeper."

He did not protest, seeming to realize they could not see the night through together. Verity sensed that he was grateful to her. She sensed too that there had been no other women since the death of his wife—and while he might be unaware of it, Verity had welded herself to him and she would never love another all her life long.

She slipped into her room and crept into her bed knowing she was guilty of fornication. She tried to condemn herself as she knew her mother would condemn her. But her full heart told her that it would happen again and again, for she loved Lord Bainbridge to the depths of her soul.

He had said nothing of marriage and Verity knew it was out of the question. Still she reveled in her love and fulfillment. And her conscience was drowned in desire.

The following days flew by and Savarra had several talks, surprisingly reasonable, with her father. She was persuasive and cheerful. In this she was met more than halfway by an unusually pleasant Lord Bainbridge. He seemed happier than she had seen him in months and, though he did not yield and give his ready consent to marriage with Peter Haverley, he was mellowing and promised Savarra that if the young man proved to be a good soldier, he would indeed give them his blessing.

This was a great comfort, to Savarra's astonishment. She had learned in a few short months that she loved her father deeply and respected his opinions. She convinced herself at last that she could wait. And, her lips firmed as she thought it, she would see that Peter *waited* as well. She often smiled to herself, thinking of his passionate eagerness, his impetuosity. Peter was a slender and elegant aristocrat who would do everything well, even soldiering.

The moments of fire and delight she had known in Cutler McLean's arms recurred more often than she cared to acknowledge, but each time she assured herself that it would be a thousandfold sweeter with Peter Haverley.

So she attended the balls and teas and afternoon socials either in the company of her father, Baltazar, or the quiet but steadily persistent Scott Coyne.

Shortly after the memorial services for Warren Pair, when the unseasonably warm month drew to a close, the city of Charles Town received astounding news. It infuriated the silent patriots and left the tories to a somewhat baffled triumph. The latter, like their British counterparts, were not sure whether they had received a victory or a distinct liability.

Savarra's father related the news first to her. He came in from Lord Cornwallis's headquarters next door to his own about midmorning. When Savarra brought him a pitcher of cold cider and glasses on a tray, he said, "Sit down, my dear, and I will tell you a startling piece of treason."

She placed the tray on the corner of the desk and seated herself in one of the straight-backed chairs, her heart beating swiftly. She was afraid for a fleeting instant that it was herself under discussion.

But his next words proved her fear groundless. "You have heard of an American general named Benedict Arnold?"

"Yes," she said hesitantly. "Verity said—I have heard he was responsible for taking Fort Ticonderoga from us and was instrumental in defeating our General Burgoyne, long before we arrived. A too-winning American hero—I think."

"Indeed," Lord Bainbridge replied, pouring himself a tall glass of cider from the pitcher and taking a long swallow. "It seems that General Arnold has, for a fee, become one of us. He was to turn over West Point to Henry Clinton this month, but due to some untimely interference by a pair of American backwoodsmen, who caught John André carrying papers detailing the operation, his treason has been uncovered and he will be serving with General Clinton in New York now."

"Good heavens," Savarra replied uneasily. "I suppose that is a frightful blow to the—patriots?"

"To the rebels—or to us?" Lord Bainbridge looked moodily out the window.

"What do you mean, father?" Savarra knew a deep discomfort. Her knowledge of the partisans in their midst sat heavily upon her at times and this was one of the times.

"I mean I think the rebels are well rid of a man who can be purchased in pounds—and that he is a liability to us. 'Tis said he is a very unpopular character in the British army now, nor can all the patronage he meets with from the Commander-in-Chief procure him respectability." The earl's voice hardened. "I personally would have such an aversion to the man that I would refuse to allow him to serve under my command."

"But father, he did it for Britain—"

"He did not do it for Britain," Lord Bainbridge said curtly. "He did it for money." His lip curled over the words. "His allegiance is not a matter of love of country, but love of money."

Savarra looked at the golden liquid in the pitcher unhappily. What would her father say if he knew what she was concealing—and all because she thought her fellow countrymen were unnecessarily brutal. Well, what she had seen *was* an atrocity. She lifted her chin and said practically, "I suppose that General Clinton will make the best use of him, father."

Lord Bainbridge gave her an amused glance. "Daughter, you are more astute than I thought, but I fear we have already received the most use we shall have of General Arnold. Actually, we lost our need for him when he was discovered for what he was—a traitor."

Scott Coyne, flanked by the two aides, Sergeant Queen and Lieutenant Keith, entered, his smooth young face flushed and his voice full of excitement. "Good morning, Mistress Savarra

—Lord Bainbridge, the whole town is agog with the news that the famous General Arnold has come over to our side!"

"Yes." She returned his smile. "Father has just told me. May I pour you gentlemen a glass of cider?"

As the three stood, hats in hands, Lord Bainbridge said, "Indeed, gentlemen, do have a chair and a glass and enjoy our—victory."

The young men seated themselves, and Lord Bainbridge asked ironically, "Would you care to serve under him, Scott?"

Coyne flushed, his mouth stiffened as Savarra handed him a crystal glass. "I would not care to serve any other commander than you, sir."

"Least of all the new British general, Benedict Arnold," Lord Bainbridge said sardonically, and Savarra quietly took her leave as the two aides sat uncomfortably, while Coyne and her father continued to discuss the illustrious background of the traitor to the American cause.

She glanced at the tall clock in the hall on her way to the stairs. Ten. There was just time to go into town to Jeanne Flammarion's dress shop and pick up the new dress for which she had been fitted the week before. She and Verity were invited to afternoon tea with Bonnie Raintree and she wanted to wear the dress. Her spirits rose. Bonnie was so amusing, so full of innocent gossip—yet she was able to keep a secret too, and she was always fun to visit.

Since Cotty was busily sewing new ruffles on Savarra's favorite outer petticoat, Tiqua accompanied her to town in the carriage driven by Amos. Verity was, with Frances' help, washing her thick long dark hair preparatory to being properly coiffed by Monique, who was as expert as Cotty with hair styling.

As they clopped down King Street to St. Stephen's and on into the city, they passed the town square and Savarra glanced idly toward it. Then her eyes riveted to the crowd of redcoated and green-jacketed soldiers and dragoons who swarmed about the raw wood of a freshly erected gallows.

She recognized Tarleton's green-jacketed men and her throat went dry at the memory of the carnage about the besieged planter's home as she and Seth Barwell made their way back toward Charles Town last month.

"Them's the Butcher's dragoons," Tiqua volunteered, in her faintly French accent. "Calhoon do say, mam'selle, they 'ave caught two patriot men who been pretending to be tories, and they are goin' to 'ang them *aujourd'hui.*"

Savarra's heart lurched downward and she asked in a muffled voice, "Who are they?"

"Calhoon says one named Peabody and one named Thomas. *Je ne sais pas*—we do not know them over to the Pair house."

Savarra let out her breath slowly, careful to keep her face smooth despite her distress. And she knew in that moment, no matter the provocation, she would never reveal the truth about McLean, Belion and Baltazar. This was the fate that awaited them. *I am no better than Benedict Arnold,* she thought, *except that my treason is for flesh and lives instead of money*.

Her spirits were still down over the sight they had now passed when the carriage rolled to a stop outside Jeanne Flammarion's shop. But Savarra was greeted effusively by the dark, bird-like little Frenchwoman, and as she tried on the new frock Madame Flammarion complimented her face and figure extravagantly.

"*Très belle, très très belle, mademoiselle.* Your figure— *magnifique.*"

The dress *was* lovely. It was made of light blue gauzy muslin over the breast. The elbow-length sleeves were shirred in three places along her arms, creating little puffs soft as summer clouds.

" 'Tis called the *gaulle,* or baby dress—or *à la creole.* The newest fashion, *cherie,* the design reaching Paris from America, of all things! See—the panniers are trimmed with grenadine flowers. Is it not beautiful?"

Savarra nodded as she turned slowly before the great gilt mirror. Jeanne Flammarion's smile made two deep creases in her soft, aging face. "It even has another name—the chemise dress. There are many versions of it now. All the rage!"

" 'Tis lovely, Madame Flammarion," Savarra agreed as Tiqua and two seamstresses stood by in open admiration.

"And I've just the *chapeau*—the hat to go with it." She clapped her hands and went to the rear of the shop, returning immediately with a pale-blue, wide and gracefully curved brimmed hat of delicate silk.

Yet later, when she mounted the carriage with Amos assisting, the raw gallows flashed into her mind. As they began the return trip to the Pair house, she determined to look toward the Cooper River this time. But she was unable to do so, for as they drew near the town square, Tiqua, who held the big white box containing the new dress and hat across her knees, cried out, "Oh, look! They 'ave 'ung them!"

Savarra found herself staring at the two bodies hanging lifelessly at the ends of the ropes. She could not tear her eyes away from those tragic figures as one rotated slowly in a light breeze. The crowd was still milling about the square, and there was a carnival atmosphere that repelled her further. The hanging men were tall and slim, and Savarra saw their dark, swollen features—and they were Belion and McLean. She gasped and cried out before realizing it was her own imagination that put them there.

Tiqua's inquiring glance at her was cold. "They'll leave them all day. And perhaps *demain,* tomorrow, to scare us up —who are not for King George."

That afternoon as she readied herself in the new dress under Cotty's admiring ministrations, Savarra could not put the hangings from her mind. Her vow to remain silent about the partisans took on strength and purpose. Marion's men had been kind to her in their rough way and she had listened to their grievances as they sat about the campfires, and those injustices had taken root in her mind.

Cotty, who had put the new ruffles on the white taffeta outer petticoat, stood back and admired her mistress, quite overcome by the new chemise dress and the matching hat. "Mistress, I do believe that's the prettiest day dress I ever saw—an' you won't have to wear a kerchief with it—all those ruffles." Her smooth cheeks were pink with pleasure over the dress.

"I'll have Madame Flammarion make up a Sunday dress for you, Cotty," she said. "A chemise dress, if you like, and silk too,"

"Oh, mistress—that would be so good of you! I could wear it to market, where I met those handsome men again—" She broke off suddenly, blushing furiously.

Savarra laughed aloud. "Ah, so you've met some men— *again*. Or is it *a man?*"

"It's two—I mean they are both very good-looking and—" Cotty broke off, her pretty pink face averted and the gold hair slipping slightly from the decorous loops behind her ears. She bent to adjust the new ruffles so that the blue dress stood out crisply.

Savarra's interest was piqued, and it was a good fifteen minutes before Amos would appear at the porte-cochere with the carriage. "Tell me, Cotty," she persisted. "Who are these men?" She added severely, "I'll not have you picking up with strangers at the market place. What were you doing there?"

"Oh, 'twas very proper," Cotty rose up, adjusting her own demure petticoats. She was flustered, but she looked at Savarra squarely. "I went with Madame Pair to market yesterday and we met up with Mr. McLean. He was dealing with those same overmountain men who had brought squirrel pelts in to peddle when we first come off the boat. You remember." She began to tidy up her hair self-consciously. "Mr. McLean was meanin' to have 'em made into the linin' of a winter cloak. He introduced us again."

"I'd forgotten meeting them," she lied. "Who were they?"

"Mr. Gabe Sleep an' Mr. Thad McHorry," Cotty replied, blushing afresh.

"Ah," Savarra said, her blue eyes narrowing. *Peddling squirrel pelts indeed.* She laughed silently and asked, "And you like these men?"

"Oh, mistress, they was so polite—an' so tall in their clothes made of skins." She shivered deliciously. "Nigh as handsome as Mr. McLean."

"And they had an eye for you, I'll wager."

Cotty giggled. "They seemed to, mistress. An' Mr. McHorry teased me so—said they'd be in town often and could he call on me. Of course, I told him no, properlike." There was a wistful note in this last. "Though Mr. McLean offered to ask you, but then Mr. McHorry and Mr. Sleep fell to quarreling over which could call." Her voice brightened. " 'Twas all very excitin', I can tell you." She looked down and Savarra was struck by the soft curve of her cheek and mouth. Cotty was really a very pretty girl, but no good could come of her attraction to Gabe Sleep and Thad McHorry.

Verity appeared in the door, wearing one of her subdued dresses, a navy-blue frock with an old-fashioned redingote and little ruffles in tiers below it. Savarra knew that Baltazar was seeing that some of the Pair Shipyard monies were flowing into the ladies' pockets, but during this mourning period there could be no new or lovely dresses for them.

"Ah, Savarra, you are delightful in the dress—and that luscious hat. So charming. Are you ready?"

"Yes, and thank you, Verity." With Cotty twitching last-minute folds in her full skirts, Savarra departed with Verity.

Bonnie did not disappoint the girls when they arrived at four. There were only the three of them, and Bonnie was bursting with news as she led them upstairs to her cozy sitting room and called for tea and pastries. Savarra soon discovered she had not escaped the Benedict Arnold melee, for Bonnie was full of it.

Bonnie admired Savarra's dress and hat with a running line of flattery, but when tea was served, she got down to her latest gossip enthusiastically. October was upon them but the weather was still fairly warm, though the nights were cool. Bonnie had glowing coals in the great fireplace of the upstairs sitting room. It made a very cozy atmosphere for exchanging tidbits of news.

Then at last Bonnie, over her cup of tea, said portentously, "My dears, I have the most amusing thing to tell you. I know you have already heard about General Arnold's joining the British. It's created quite a furor—but the best part isn't being talked about!"

Savarra was slightly bored. Benedict Arnold did not pique her curiosity, and her father's opinion of the man had flavored her own. But she could tell from Verity's smooth, still face that it pained her to think of Arnold's treason.

Bonnie sensed this as well, for she said, "Oh, I'm sure you consider him the blackest of villains—but what I have to tell, Verity, is most amusing. And I do admire the talents of Peggy Arnold, his wife!"

"Do tell," Savarra said, skillfully hiding a yawn.

"Well," Bonnie began importantly, "General Washington himself had ridden into West Point with his aides to see General Arnold that very morning. But General Arnold knew they were coming and that he had been discovered, so he hastily made his way to the river and was rowed out to the H.M.S. *Vulture* lying in the Hudson River. He had told his men—and they told General Washington in all good faith—that Arnold was on an inspection tour and would be back soon." She paused for a refreshing sip of tea, then continued, "Then the word of his treason meantime had been got to Washington. So the general went on and sent two men downstream to try and capture Arnold at a small fort, to no avail. He got clean away, thank goodness!" Her voice dropped and her big eyes rounded with shocked pleasure. "But all of a sudden, there came a piercing scream from Peggy Arnold's bedroom and it echoed through the upper hall. 'There's a hot iron on my head! No one else can take it off!' And Colonel Varick went down to ask the general if he would talk to the poor little thing, so distraught was she. Varick told Washington she had been raving mad for some time, racing half-naked through the house, sobbing and babbling incoherently. She now demanded to see General Washington. So Washington followed the colonel into Peggy's room."

Bonnie's voice lowered further to lend import to her story. "And there she was, hair dishevelled and flowing about her shoulders and wearing only a thin gown, my dears—too nearly nude to be seen even by gentlemen of the family, much less by strangers!"

Bonnie took time to sip her tea again and enjoy the rapt attention of her listeners and to let this shocking bit of information sink in. Savarra was no longer bored. She looked at her hostess intently as Bonnie took up her story. "Her face was contorted and tear-stained and, when Varick told her that General Washington had come, she looked at the general and cried, 'No! That's not General Washington. That's the man that was going to help Colonel Varick kill my child!' She refused to be quieted. Her husband could no longer protect her, she cried. 'General Arnold will never return,' she screamed. 'He's gone, he's gone forever!' and she pointed frantically to the ceiling. 'There, there, there!' "

Bonnie became so carried away with her story, she began acting the part of the apparently demented Peggy Arnold. She waved her plump white arms upward and cried, " 'The spirits have carried him up there. They have put hot irons on his head.' And my dears"—Bonnie whispered this— "she flounced in and out of bed and strode about the room with her child in her arms in uncontrollable despair."

She sipped her tea once more and said with great satisfaction, "General Washington left the room convinced that she was in a state of shock and innocent of treason." Bonnie smiled delightedly. "Which was just what she intended, of course. Oh, what a clever girl! I just wish I could have seen the performance—Peggy nearly nude and that great stick of a Washington looking at her with mouth agape."

Verity said quietly, "I think it was disgusting. And I doubt very much that General Washington watched with mouth agape. More likely he watched with pity and sorrow. He is a great gentleman to pretend to be taken in by Peggy Arnold's deceitful madness. She was always a tory, I have heard."

Bonnie looked pained. "Not tory, Verity, dear, *loyalist.*"

"Tory," responded Verity stubbornly. "And I heard that the general went on and dined with his officers there without a mention of Arnold's disappearance, and Varick was greatly impressed by his composure in the face of such a disaster. But it was a most melancholy meal. 'Tis said none of the officers with General Washington spoke. Gloom pervaded every mind."

Savarra, picking up a tea cake, asked, "Do you think they will catch Arnold?"

"Of course not," Bonnie said complacently, buttering a pastry and popping it into her pink mouth. "They have caught poor John André, though. He was the one taking Arnold's reports to General Clinton—and they'll hang him, for he was in civilian clothing."

Savarra watched her hostess covertly. Bonnie was as ingenuous and clear as spring water and Savarra was a touch annoyed, for she found herself siding with Verity in her reaction to this story of hysterics and false madness, to the villainy of a man in a high place who was trusted by his compatriots.

On the ride home, Savarra said abruptly, "My father has no use for this turncoat Arnold."

Verity's clear brown eyes on her were intense. "Your father is a remarkable man. It grieves me that he is our enemy, bound to keep us from securing our liberty."

"My father—and I—respect an able and valiant adversary."

"That is well, but I know you are both enemies of my country—despite your willingness to keep the secret of our three friends." The bitterness of her voice was laced with another emotion, one Savarra could not divine, but she knew a sharp stab of pity for the drably dressed but beautiful girl beside her.

"I shan't be in your home for much longer," Savarra said without animosity, "for Peter Haverley will soon come and take me away." *And my father, for all that he fancies you, will leave eventually—and alone.*

"I hope you will be very happy together," Verity said distantly, and the two girls rode in silence the rest of the way to the Pair house.

The following late afternoon Verity knocked on Savarra's door, to be met by Cotty, who said, "Mistress is takin' her afternoon bath. She'll be down soon—in time to dine."

Verity smiled and continued down the hall, taking the stairs to the lower hall. As she did so, there sounded an imperious knock at the door. Not waiting for Amos, she went to it and opened it herself.

Standing there was a tall, slim man who greeted her with

impeccable manners. "I am Lord Haverley and I have come to call on Mistress Savarra Bainbridge."

Verity was silent for a moment, so impressed by his appearance was she. She had expected to meet this man clad in uniform, but he was dressed superbly in a cut-velvet blue suit, fitted to him like a second skin, the coat skirt fashionably full in back. His white stock was ruffled lace and frothed beneath his patrician chin. His waistcoat was of the finest satin and his shoes, with their gleaming buckles, looked handmade. He was altogether the most impressive English nobleman she had ever seen. A fine English gelding was hitched to the post in the yard.

"She is here, I trust," he said after a silence. "I am her fiancé."

"I know," Verity replied, aware that his yellow gold eyes under light brown hair were admiring her. He was very tall, almost as tall as Cutler McLean. "She is—making her toilette. She will be overjoyed that you have come at last. I will send Tiqua to tell her you are here." Then ushering him into the drawing room, "May I serve you coffee while you wait?"

"That would be delightful, if you will keep me company as well," he replied, his eyes still clinging to her breasts. She knew a sudden discomfort, for this man had a predatory look about him, for all his aristocratic features. Indeed, he looked on the verge of seizing her, so voracious were his eyes.

"I will have Amos bring it to you," she replied with sudden coolness.

"Then you will not keep me company? I had been told the American women were beautiful, but now I think that an understatement." He smiled then, a slow, warm smile, and Verity suddenly realized why Savarra was so bent on marrying this man. He was extremely handsome.

"Yes. I will have a cup with you, Lord Haverley," she replied calmly. No use in letting the man know he made her uncomfortable.

So Amos brought the coffee and they sat and talked desultorily of his long voyage to America. Verity said, "I had thought you to be a soldier in uniform, Lord Haverley."

"I am, but I wanted to meet my affianced looking as well as possible. I shall don the uniform again this evening. Are you married, Mistress Pair?" His eyes were studying her intensely.

"No." She felt color in her face.

"Affianced?"

"I—was, but no longer."

"Then these rebels are truly backward. A woman so beautiful should be either of those." His slow smile was so intimate she flushed again and thought, *This is not a faithful man. I do not envy Savarra her choice.*

"I understand," she said distantly, "that you are to be an aide to Lord Rawdon in Camden."

"Those are my orders for now. I plan to change them as time goes on. I must have a command of my own to distinguish myself in order to partially placate Savarra's father—a stick if there ever was one."

Verity felt her dislike of the man grow. He was arrogant and a touch supercilious. But more than that, she sensed a—mercilessness in him, a disregard for others and an overriding ambition.

Another knock sounded on the door, and in a moment Amos ushered in Cutler McLean. He carried a box of bonbons as his excuse for calling on the Pairs, but Verity knew he was seeking information she might have filched from headquarters.

An incredible thing happened as she rose to greet him. Peter Haverley rose with her and, as she turned, he reached forward and gave her buttocks a hard pinch, then patted them familiarly.

Cutler McLean and Amos, standing in the doorway, were witness to this act. Verity gasped, turned white at the insult. McLean stared at the Englishman incredulously. What happened next was even more shocking.

McLean put the box of bonbons on a nearby table carefully, strode to Haverley, clutched the handful of lace and velvet at his throat and struck him a powerful blow as the Englishman stared at him in astonishment. Haverley went down, but scrambled to his feet immediately, his eyes burning almost yellow now in his patrician face. He lunged at McLean, who caught him again with one long arm and struck him another blow in the face which split his lip and sent him crashing to the floor.

Verity stood watching in white silence. Amos had also witnessed the entire contretemps with relish.

"Get up, you blackguard," McLean said between his teeth, "and apologize to this lady."

"Lady?" Haverley gritted, furious by now. "She's a low American wench and should be grateful for my noticing her!"

Suddenly the room was filled with such malignant hatred

that Verity felt smothered by it. It emanated from both men and she felt intuitively that they would be mortal enemies for the rest of their lives. Verity, knowing McLean so well, realized that he was on the verge of killing Savarra Bainbridge's fiancé.

McLean stooped, jerked the man to his feet. Haverley reeled and McLean's browned fist clenched his throat. "Apologize to Mistress Pair, or I shall kill you."

Haverley's face reddened under the pressure and he flailed ineffectually at the taller man, but McLean had moved with such rapidity he had the advantage of Haverley. His eyes were beginning to start from his head when he choked, "Madame—apologize for—liberty—meant no harm."

McLean released him and he gasped for breath, congestion fading slowly in the handsome face. Blood trickled down from his lip over his chin and dripped on the spotless cravat and the satin embroidered waistcoat.

"Sir," he said thickly, "you would not have laid hands upon me had I my sword."

"I rather think I would—" McLean began, but at that moment, Savarra Bainbridge entered the door, her face joyous with smiles.

"Oh, Peter! Tiqua told me you had come—" She broke off, bewildered. "Oh—what is the matter? You're bleeding, my darling!" She had meant to fly into his arms, but McLean was in the way and his face was darkly menacing.

He looked at her and said contemptuously, "So this is the man you are going to marry?"

"He certainly is." Savarra's quick temper rose as she took in the tableau. Amos was still an observer and Verity, her face pale, stood near the door. Savarra said accusingly, "How dare you, Mr. McLean? You have laid hands on Peter, you wretched man!"

"Wretched am I? Your high and mighty Haverley insulted Verity Pair and I'll stand that from no man."

Peter had taken out a handkerchief and was wiping his bleeding lip. His voice was muffled. "I meant no harm. It was in the nature of a compliment—to an American wench."

Savarra said coldly, "Fetch a bowl of water and a cloth, Amos. I will bathe Mr. Haverley's lip." She went to his side and looked up at him anxiously. "Your eye is swelling, darling —heaven knows, I had not expected to meet you under such circumstances! Mr. McLean is a ruffian—you must overlook his—rude behavior." She shot McLean a furious glance.

McLean said evenly, "Ask him to explain his 'compliment' to you," and turned on his heel as he and the white-faced Verity left the two alone.

As they crossed the hall, he exploded, "That fop—that sickly womanizer is the man Savarra Bainbridge intends to marry? I can scarce believe it!"

Verity began to laugh, her humor wry. "I don't know—I thought him rather charming until he paid me his 'compliment.' " Color was returning to her face.

McLean said, "I thought he was an *officer* in the British army. I had no idea who the overdressed fool was."

"He came dressed to impress Savarra."

They entered the sitting room across the hallway and McLean flung his long length into a chair. "I've never met a man in my life who stirred me to such—contempt in such short order as that poltroon. I pity Savarra. Her life will be a hell with that one."

"I shall serve you coffee, Cutler," Verity said, still standing. Amos, who had ignored Savarra's demand for water, had unobtrusively followed them.

Now he said, "No'm, Mistress Verity. I'll fetch it for you."

"Then tell Tiqua to fetch a bowl of water and a cloth for Mistress Savarra," she replied as Amos bowed and left.

The two of them discussed the grand Lord Haverley a little further until McLean said with sudden violence, "Let's speak no more of him. He disgusts me. I brought you some bonbons as an excuse to come. Tyler is kept at Belion House on business or he would have accompanied me—but I'll be damned if I go back to the drawing room to get the candy with that pusillanimous, overbred lecher in there."

Verity murmured, "I know you are hoping for more news from headquarters, but I have none at the moment, Cutler. Lord Bainbridge is out with his aides at General Cornwallis's headquarters, conferring with Banastre Tarleton and Patrick Ferguson—men he has no use for. He says they are both ruthless hotheads."

"I have a certain respect for Lord Bainbridge. He is an honorable man and I find myself liking him, while Tarleton is all I find despicable in the British character—and I have a strong suspicion that this fop Haverley is more of the same."

In the drawing room, Savarra said sympathetically, "Whatever set Mr. McLean off in such a manner? What compliment did you pay the chaste Verity?" She was thinking, I can't kiss him with that poor swollen and bleeding lip!

"McLean—I'll not forget that name. A pinch and a pat, which is a compliment to any low wench." Peter's voice was hard. "You know well, Savarra, all Americans are of the servant class, low and common, springing as they do from the dregs of Britain."

Savarra was somewhat taken aback at Peter's liberty with Verity and his evaluation of all Americans. His enmity toward McLean was more understandable, for she, herself, held much the same view of the man. Yet she restrained a desire to defend these people. Peter would learn that it was not so simple when he had been here a bit longer, she assured herself. Too, for some inexplicable reason she felt let down at the sight of this man she had loved for so long. His slim, elegant figure was broad through the shoulders and he was almost as tall as McLean. But the tropic summer sun had bronzed McLean, and Peter Haverley appeared pale and colorless beside him.

She looked around for Amos, but it was Tiqua who approached at last with a bowl of fresh water and a cloth. She stood holding them, a silent figure of disapproval.

"If you had been in uniform, he would never have dared strike you, darling," Savarra said, gently bathing the swollen and cut lip. Tiqua eyed him impassively.

"I doubt if the uniform would have deterred such a man." He reached out suddenly to stroke her slim, white arms. "But I wanted you to meet me looking my best—and now look at me." Blood flecked his lace cravat and spotted his blue velvet coat and breeches.

"You look very handsome to me despite this," she reassured him and dropped a light kiss on his cheek. Then reprovingly, "But you must remember that pinches and pats are frowned on by American men. Their women are much respected."

"Is he hoping to be her affianced?" Peter asked contemptuously.

"No, but he is a very old friend. They grew up together."

"Nevertheless, I shall kill him eventually." Haverley's voice was measured and deadly and Savarra knew an odd chill.

"Surely not, darling. You may even come to like him, when you know him better. He is a firm loyalist." As she added the lie, guilt crept through her like a chill wind. The burden of her secret knowledge still weighed heavily upon her.

Peter said with a touch of pride, "Well, my love, you will be marrying Lord Haverley now. It saddens me to tell you, my father died just before I left for America. That is what delayed my arrival."

"Oh, I am so sorry!" Savarra cried. Lord Haverley was always so jolly when she saw him and he had not been old, not even fifty. "What took him?"

"Apoplexy. He had suffered it several years, you know."

"And your mother?"

"She is well and looking after our estates while I finish this tour of duty." He drew her to him again, careful not to bruise his greatly swollen lip. Tiqua's eyes flicked them coldly and she took the bowl and made her departure.

Haverley whispered winningly, "Come with me now, darling! I have already located a minister at St. Michael's Church. We can be married and on our way to Camden before nightfall." Then with sudden urgency, "I took the precaution of finding out that your father is at Cornwallis's headquarters, conferring with Colonel Tarleton and others who are about to depart on a mission. If you hurry, we can be gone before he knows of my arrival."

"But—"

He hastened on, "I have a room at the Thorn and Thistle. Can you not pack a few things and come with me now?"

Savarra spoke with uncharacteristic caution. "But Peter, the knowledge that you have bought a commission in the army and will serve in subduing America has somewhat softened my father." She pulled gently from his arms, adding, "He has indicated that if you distinguish yourself, he will give his permission for us to marry."

Peter's golden hazel eyes narrowed. "I shall distinguish myself, you may be sure." He drew her near again, his strong, slender hands stroking the curve of her back from shoulder to waistline where her full skirts met the bodice. "But I think Lord Bainbridge would be quite reconciled if our marriage were an accomplished fact, my love."

She said hesitantly, "Peter—I had not realized how much my father's approval meant to me, but now I find it means a great deal. Are you not willing to wait for it?"

"But I must report to Lord Rawdon within three days after my arrival. That means I must leave here by tomorrow morning! It could be months before I see action—"

"I don't think it will be that long, Peter," she said dryly.

"I've lived among these Americans for some months now. Unfortunately, they are not yet a conquered people."

He looked at her quizzically. "You sound very different from the girl I knew in London, Savarra. What has changed you?"

She felt sudden heat in her face. "If I have changed, 'tis for the better, I hope—and this time I shall be wed to you before visiting your bedroom."

He laughed aloud, then winced and touched his lip. "Ah, my darling." He stooped and laid his cheek against hers. "Surely you have forgiven my foolish eagerness! You don't think I would travel over three thousand miles for *one* night with you? I want a lifetime of them!"

"*I* knew you were going to marry me—'twas my father who doubted it, and I do not wish to give him cause to doubt it again." But she laughed up at him as she said it, taking the sting from her sharp comment.

He seemed to realize then that his urgency would not move her and he said, "You have grown up overnight, Savarra. You have lost that beautiful wildness I loved so well."

"Indeed?" She drew herself up and her eyes glinted dangerously. "Then I am to infer you no longer love me?"

He caught her to him and with his swollen lip found hers as he held her fast against him. When he took his mouth from hers she felt his blood on her own lip. He took a handkerchief from his pocket and put it gently to her mouth and then to his.

"Let's hear no more of this not loving," he said roughly. "Since I must, I will wait. Surely I can get a furlough as time goes by and visit you occasionally." His voice grew bitter. "All these months of waiting, yearning, longing, and now I must wait still longer." His little smile was wry. "I do not think there is much possibility that Lord Bainbridge will ever come to like me tremendously. I hope only that he accepts me."

They talked at length then, seated on the large rosewood sofa by the south windows, making plans, discussing the long future ahead of them, and he recounted the news of friends and schoolmates she had left in London.

Thus Lord Bainbridge found them together in the drawing room. He entered unannounced and his face darkened as he saw the two on the sofa. Savarra looked at him coolly, without apprehension, for she had reconciled herself to await his approval.

"So you've arrived at last, Haverley," he said shortly.

Haverley rose to his feet at once and bowed gracefully. "Lord Bainbridge, though I realize you have cause to doubt my sincerity due to the reputation I have in London—and which I assure you is undeserved—I am completely sincere in my honest love for your daughter."

Savarra almost laughed at the pompous little speech. She had the feeling Peter had rehearsed it in his mind for some time and she was touched as well as amused. "And father, my love for Peter is equally sincere."

"Hmmmn." Lord Bainbridge observed them from under heavy sandy brows. "Haverley, you look as though you had already seen action—and out of uniform as well." His eyes touched the swollen lip, the darkening flesh about his right eye critically.

"I had—an altercation with one of these wild-eyed Americans." Peter flushed darkly. "I merely teased Mistress Pair and the man took exception to it."

"Ah—Verity or Anne?"

"I don't know which. An attractive young woman who bade me wait while she summoned Savarra. I—had just expressed my admiration of her when the man assaulted me like a barbarian."

" 'Twas Mr. McLean, father," Savarra put in, coming to Peter's aid. "Peter had no idea how strait-laced the American men are, and you know Cutler McLean has a nasty temper." Her father would never understand the insouciance of the uninhibited Peter, who meant nothing at all by his pinches and pats.

"Indeed?" Lord Bainbridge said skeptically. "It was Verity, then?"

"Yes," Savarra intervened once more. "You know how different the manners of the British are from the Americans. Peter meant only to show his admiration of her."

Lord Bainbridge said abruptly, "Now surely, Haverley, this undying love between you and my daughter can withstand the wait while you prove yourself militarily?"

"Yes, Lord Bainbridge," Peter said at once, glad to be relieved of further discussion regarding Verity. "Savarra has told me that it is the price of your permission to wed. I—hope to make you proud to have me as a son-in-law." He hesitated and then, "My father died two months ago, Lord Bainbridge, and I am heir to his title and his lands. Your daughter will be Lady Haverley."

"Sorry to learn of Henry's death. You will have a great deal of responsibility now. I hope you can handle it," Lord Bainbridge replied without smiling and without a great deal of conviction.

There was a moment of awkward silence, before Peter said, "Well—I shall try." Then regretfully, "I must leave for Camden at dawn tomorrow and report in to Lord Rawdon. I will take my leave of you now." His eyes on Savarra struck her as being somewhat forlorn. "I suppose I shall not see you again for some time, Savarra."

Relenting suddenly, Lord Bainbridge said, "Why not stay to dine with us? It will be served in less than an hour."

Peter regarded him with astonished gratitude. "That is most kind of your lordship. I shall be delighted."

When the earl left the room, the two young lovers held hands and talked more cheerfully of their future wedding. Peter was elated by Lord Bainbridge's unexpected courtesy, and Savarra spent some time with a fresh bowl of water and the wet cloth trying to remove bloodstains from his beautiful suit.

She said, "Father is already softening toward you. I can see it."

"It was deuced nice of him to ask me to dinner," Peter replied and his pleasant voice had a deep timbre of confidence.

But dinner was to be a rather strained affair, for it developed that Verity had invited Cutler McLean to dine with them as well. She had been shrewd enough to consult with Lord Bainbridge about it, when he peered into the sitting room after leaving his daughter and young Haverley.

Verity looked at him straightforwardly and said, "Good afternoon, Lord Bainbridge," as McLean rose and bowed.

"Good afternoon, Mistress Pair—McLean."

"Lord Bainbridge," Verity said, coming to the point immediately, "would you mind if my mother and I invited Mr. McLean to dine this evening?"

The earl smiled his boyish smile. "Indeed, I would enjoy his company." Then laughing outright, "It should be interesting for I have just invited young Haverley to dine with us and I understand you thrashed him, McLean, over a misunderstood compliment to Mistress Pair."

"Misunderstood—" McLean began angrily.

Verity cut in smoothly, "Actually, he mistook me for one of the servants and made a broad comment on my—charms." She sent McLean a warning glance. It would do no good to make things harder for Savarra, when the girl had done— nay, was *doing*—them the service of her silence. "I'm sorry Cutler took such exception to it."

McLean was silent, and Lord Bainbridge said, "Well, I see you look no worse for wear because of it, McLean. Didn't Haverley land a blow?"

"It didn't last long," McLean said shortly. "He apologized very courteously. As far as I'm concerned, the matter's forgotten."

But Verity, looking up at him, knew it was not. She was uneasy over the deadly enmity that had sprung up so swiftly between the two. A bone-deep intuition warned her that trouble lay ahead.

"I haven't had the chance to thank you, Lord Bainbridge," Verity said serenely, "but mother and I do appreciate the income from father's shipyards under Uncle Bowman's management. Though we haven't bought any new frocks because of our mourning, it is good to have money in our pockets again."

"Good British currency, too," Lord Bainbridge said dryly. "It will purchase what you need. I was glad to do it for you." He was very composed and cool and gave not the slightest inkling of the boiling river of passion that coursed between him and this beautiful dark-eyed girl. "Now I shall go upstairs and freshen up before dinner, If you will excuse me?" He bowed and left.

Thus dinner found the oddly assorted group at table together. It seemed to Verity that Savarra was the most uncomfortable of them, and she was at a loss as to the reason, for Savarra had her beloved by her side at last.

However, the gathering proved fruitful for Cutler McLean. Over the roast beef and rice, Lord Bainbridge announced, "I am going to Georgetown tomorrow to meet with Major Wemyss and Major Ganey and we are going to route that nuisance Marion and put an end to his depredations. Tarleton has been on his trail for some time, but he has managed to elude our estimable colonel." He sent a sardonic glance to Anne Pair, adding, "And incidentally, Brim has prevailed on me to take him along—vowing to keep my wardrobe in tiptop condition and see to my personal wants. So you ladies, Mistress Pair, must do without his services."

Anne replied imperturbably, "I'm sure Brim will be of great service—in catching Francis Marion."

"Marion is a plague," McLean put in agreeably, forestalling Anne's further comment. "I understand he has been disrupting and carrying off our wagons of supplies. 'Tis high time a stop was put to it."

Verity did not dare look at McLean, but she knew that he would relay the news of this renewed search to Marion immediately. She did glance at Savarra to see that she was toying with her food and her thick black lashes were carefully lowered.

"We will have a sufficient force to meet and defeat him, between the three commands," Lord Bainbridge said. Then, with a flicking glance at Savarra, "I have a score to settle with his men," but no word was spoken of Savarra's three-week captivity. To Verity's knowledge, no one ever mentioned it. It was as if the interlude had been erased from Savarra's life.

"We shall hang each and every man who has engaged in partisan warfare," Lord Bainbridge continued. Then with sudden asperity, " 'Tis incredible that such small bands of rebels —without any apparent organization—can make so much trouble."

"I would like to accompany you, Lord Bainbridge," Peter Haverley spoke up quietly. "Do you suppose you could arrange it? The sooner I see action, the better." He looked across the table at McLean and added calmly, "I shall enjoy killing Americans."

McLean stared him down. "I do not enjoy killing. I regret the necessity," he added in a cold, level voice. "It is just as well that my business precludes killing."

"You're very samaritan, McLean," Haverley said, speaking directly to him for the first time. "Or is it you haven't the courage to kill?"

McLean shrugged. "Who knows? If I am ever faced with it, I might stand up to it, or I might run."

Verity's eyes swung from Haverley's contemptuous smile to Savarra, who was looking fixedly at the silver in her hand. The English girl's face was rather pale. Her lashes lifted slowly and she met Verity's eyes. They clung and the girl's fear communicated itself to her. She felt a hard little knot of it in her own stomach as both girls looked away.

Why was Savarra frightened, she wondered? And then she glanced into McLean's closed features. His very lack of expression caused the knot to tighten, but it was the look in Peter Haverley's green-gold eyes that made her heart lurch. There was a look of savagery, an utter lack of mercy in those clear golden eyes. Verity knew a moment of shock. Lord Haverley was a *cruel* man! She wondered if Savarra knew it, then realized she could not or she would not contemplate marriage with the man.

"Ah, now, Peter." Lord Bainbridge's smile was wintry. "You sound very bloodthirsty for a man yet to have his baptism under fire."

"You forget, Lord Bainbridge—I killed two men in London for slurs upon my honor."

"I refer to the battlefield, Peter—not the so-called field of honor."

"I am not without instructions for that as well, Lord Bainbridge. Perhaps you have forgotten that my father insisted on five years' military training—from my fifteenth year through my twentieth?"

"I had forgotten," Lord Bainbridge's smile vanished, "since you have never before seen fit to utilize your knowledge."

Verity knew a sinking sensation as she looked at McLean's still face. Peter was not the useless fop McLean had called him. Verity surmised that he was a powerful and dangerous foe, and for the very good reason of the beating McLean had administered he was spoiling now for an excuse to kill the partisan. From the looks of the young lord, that excuse would be found eventually.

Now he said, "Lord Bainbridge, what of it? Can you arrange for me to ride with you in the morning in pursuit of this Marion?"

Lord Bainbridge's fierce blue eyes rested on the younger man and he said slowly, "You will see action soon enough if you can persuade Lord Rawdon you are fit for a command. I have a full complement of men."

Peter Haverley lifted his shoulders and let them fall. "I would have liked to see action under your command. I am anxious to improve your opinion of me, sir." His swollen lip was appreciably better, but the flesh about his eyes would be dark for some days to come.

When they retired from the table and made their way into the drawing room for after-dinner liqueurs, McLean said courteously, "I regret leaving such excellent company, but there are matters awaiting me on my desk at home. A large shipment of rice to our British troops in Philadelphia must go out in the morning."

There were brief goodbyes as Amost brought his cape, for the early October nights were cool.

Haverley left an hour later after enjoying a pipe and brandy with Lord Bainbridge. Verity noted once, when he bent to whisper something in Savarra's ear, that her lovely cheeks were apricot and her eyes bright with laughter. The girl gave him a twinkling smile and murmured a response.

But Verity was deeply uneasy for the girl's future with this man. She did not know why she should care, for Savarra had indicated only a reluctant liking for Verity. Now she told herself it was because the English girl was so much like her father—those eyes—that she could not help but feel an affection for her.

When Haverley had left and the four of them, Anne, Verity, Lord Bainbridge and his daughter, stood in the hallway together, Lord Bainbridge said slowly, "Savarra, I am not yet in favor of this marriage. There is something in Peter Haverley, for all the credentials he gives, that turns me from him."

"But father, he will prove himself! Just be patient."

" 'Tis you who must be patient, daughter. I love you and would see you happy in your marriage."

Amos appeared with an oil lamp to light them to their rooms and they followed him up the long, dark staircase. At the top, Anne and Savarra walked on to their chambers, but Verity and Lord Bainbridge paused to talk a moment at the top. Amos halted midway in the hall. Verity noted the troubled backward glance her mother gave them as Savarra went into her room.

When Anne had disappeared as well, Lord Bainbridge said quietly, "My darling, you will come to me tonight? I shall be gone for many days in pursuit of this Marion."

"You know I will," Verity responded with quiet passion. And two hours later, she sped swiftly down the corridor and let herself into her lover's room. They had decided some time ago it would be best for her to come to him, for if she were found in the halls late at night, it would be more easily explained than if Lord Bainbridge were found making his way from her room.

As she entered, he was waiting and swept her into his arms,

kissing her face, her lips, her throat, and she felt again the wild throb of emotion this man alone could evoke.

It had been more than a month since her last tryst with Tyler Belion and she wished fervently his ardor might be cooling. Still, she knew this was not to be, for Belion had loved her steadfastly for more than four years. But for the war, they would have been married long ago. Now she exulted that she was not bound by vows to him. She realized at last that her feeling for Belion was one of kinship, such as a sister might feel for a beloved older brother.

But now, as she and Lord Bainbridge began making love to each other, all thoughts flew from her mind. There was only the piercingly sweet and pleasurable sensations as they touched, caressed and kissed, aware only of the sensual delights that swung between them in achingly lovely gusts. His murmured endearments had the power to bring her to a pinnacle of sharp, almost painful ecstasy, and there was a bite in the October air which made their body warmth ever sweeter and more rewarding.

It was only when they lay spent and flooded with satisfaction that the troubling thoughts intruded again. As she lay there in the dark beside him, the fear for his life crept over her. He would be fighting with men who knew the jungle of the swamps as well as they knew their own bodies. They were deadly in those wet and marshy forests. Her lover would be in jeopardy in the days to come. The thought of his being killed brought a pain so cutting she smothered a groan.

"What is it, Verity?" he asked alertly.

"Only that I love you so dearly," she replied, thinking by now Cutler McLean had already sent a messenger in the night to warn Colonel Francis Marion and his men. He had told her earlier they were hiding out at Ami's Mill on Drowning Creek, far to the north, until they could assemble again. So many of his militia had gone back to their farms and plantations, for it was harvest time and their families must be cared for.

But they would rally now, when word reached them of this three-pronged attack. They would be watching, waiting, ready to strike the British and loyalists when they rode into their lairs. Masters at ambush, Verity knew well they could cut a much larger force to pieces, then disappear in the dense fastnesses of a dozen swamps.

Still Verity rejected the thought of warning Lord Bainbridge. Loyalty to her countrymen was too deeply embedded, too firmly rooted. She could only pray that her love would somehow survive this war, for her determination to be free of Britain's domination burned in her like a flame.

At last she rose softly, but he was awake and caught her hand, murmuring, "Not yet, beloved!"

"I must. 'Tis past three. I will be waiting when you return, my darling," and she made her way silently to her room.

She was awake in the dawn hours and heard Lord Bainbridge leave, the sound of his aides as they trotted down the shell drive to the rear, the low, husky voices and laughter that always seemed part of the start of a mission. When they dwindled in the dark, a bereftness swept her and she found herself crying hard into her pillow.

Though she was content to take his love as he gave it, knowing there could never be a love in her life to equal it, an English lord did not marry an untitled American girl and Verity had reconciled herself to that fact. Still, she could not stop her futile dreams of being with him for the rest of her life.

She could not sleep again, even when darkness settled silently about her. At last she rose and performed her toilette, then sat watching the sky slowly grow pink as she waited for the breakfast hour.

In the late afternoon of October fourth, Amos came to Savarra in the drawing room where she sat reading the Charles Town newspaper, which was published twice a week.

He appeared somewhat distressed and nervous as he said, "Mistress Savarra, two—uh—mans come here, they says, to call on Miss Cotty."

Surprised, she asked, "Where are they?"

"I—ah—done put 'em in the little sittin' room. You want me to fetch Miss Cotty?"

"Yes," she replied, putting aside her paper. She went into the hall and waited as Cotty descended the stairs. The little maid ran down the last three steps, her skirts and petticoats flying. She seized Savarra's hands, her own cold with excitement.

"Oh, Mistress Savarra, I just know 'tis Mr. Sleep and Mr. McHorry—the last time I saw them, they said they was comin' to call on me!"

"Together?" Savarra asked, smiling. She knew now the reason for Amos' hesitance.

"They're such good friends, they share everything—an' it looks like they're goin' to share callin' on me!" Cotty's eyes were starry and her curling blonde hair was attractively arranged about her pert little face. "Mistress, will you come with me—while we talk?"

Laughing, Savarra agreed. Gabe Sleep and Thad McHorry had been fairly polite, despite their reluctance to act as guardian over her those weeks in the swamps. And she felt Cotty did indeed need a chaperone.

When the two girls reached the sitting room beside the small drawing room, both tall young men rose immediately and bowed low. Their blue eyes were wary and they wore very respectable black broadcloth suits with waistcoats of satin. They looked a touch uncomfortable in these garments and so different from the backwoodsmen she had known that Savarra was taken aback. But they were superb in their pretense of not being fully acquainted with Savarra while Cotty performed flustered introductions.

She ended with, "You remember—we saw—met them with Mr. McLean when we first got off the ship from England," then flushed scarlet for revealing how much impressed she had been by that first glimpse and brief meeting.

After a few banal amenities, Gabe Sleep drawled, "Mistress Savarra, Thad an' me come a-courtin'. We figure Miss Cotty can take her choice."

Cotty tossed her curls and retorted, "*If* I make a choice! Mistress Savarra has need of me—I'm her only maid."

"Miss Savarra could get another one, couldn't you, mistress?"

"I'm sure I could, Mr. Sleep, if Cotty decides to leave me. But don't you gentlemen think this a bad time for courting—with war all about us?"

"Aw, Mistress Savarra." Thad turned his guileless gentian eyes on her. "We're in Charlest'n for just a day. We took the oath of allegiance 'way long time ago an' we ain't mixed up in no war."

Savarra's eyes held derision, but Gabe Sleep added, "No ma'am, we ain't in no war." His drowsy eyes were bland. "We're backcountry trappers—with a little piece of land to build on later."

"Ah," Savarra's smile twinkled with mischief, "you own the land together?"

"No, mistress," Thad said earnestly, "we own adjoinin' acreage. We come in town today to sell our squirrel pelts—"

"An' deerskins," volunteered Gabe. " 'Tis the time fer people to select linin's fer their winter cloaks—"

"An' throws for their beds," Thad cut in. "We do pretty well an' we could take good care of Miss Cotty."

"Together?" Savarra asked, laughing aloud.

They gave her a wounded look. " 'Course not," Thad replied with dignity. "But when she chooses—" he shot a swift look at Cotty and there was an endearing wickedness in the blue eyes, "we ain't tryin' to rush you, Miss Cotty—"

"Not at all," Gabe inserted. "We just want to get our bid in."

"With all these good-lookin' British soldiers hangin' 'round an' you bein' English—"

Gabe took it up, "We thought we better make our feelin's known to you, Miss Cotty."

They were quite a team, Savarra thought admiringly as Cotty blushed rosily. "I'm not ready—" she began haltingly, "to leave Mistress Savarra yet."

"We ain't askin' you to leave her yet," Gabe drawled comfortingly. "We just want you to know how we feel about you, Miss Cotty."

"We think you're the prettiest thing ever to hit Charlest'n an' we'd sure like to marry you—when the time's right, of course."

"Together?" Savarra asked interestedly.

Thad gave her a young, hurt glance. Then to Cotty, "We love you, Miss Cotty."

Silence fell, and Cotty twisted her pink fingers together in her lap and swallowed miserably. Savarra started to speak for her, but at that moment the little maidservant looked up, thick gold lashes fluttering, and murmured, " 'Tis a rare honor you pay me, gentlemen, but I beg you to give me more time to know you—both." She finished in a rush and Savarra resolved to compliment her later.

Now she rose and said, "I will have Tiqua bring you refreshments, tea and cakes, Cotty—and leave you to become better acquainted with your suitors." She added teasingly, "Now that I know their intentions are indeed honorable and it is not bigamy they propose."

Gabe shot her a grateful glance and Thad was audacious enough to give her a broad wink as she passed him.

When her callers left at last, Cotty rushed into the bedroom, where Savarra was drying her long thick hair. Monique had helped her wash it in a large bowl kept for that purpose. Toweling the tumbling mass of black hair, Savarra looked at Cotty warmly.

"Oh, mistress, ain't they handsome? How will I ever make up my mind between them!"

"That will be difficult, Cotty," Savarra agreed, realizing that she could not tell Cotty these were two patriots. Cotty was far too guileless, too open to keep such a secret. The maid's distress over Savarra's kidnapping and her days spent with the rebels had been enormous, and three times in the past weeks Savarra had to caution her anew not to speak of it. The ubiquitous Brim, however, had clamped his thin lips on the knowledge and never by word or flick of eyelash had he referred to the incident. Nor would he as he now rode with Lord Bainbridge.

"I only hope," Savarra said now, "that you will do nothing rash."

Cotty took the towel from her and gave her an oddly shrewd look. "You may be sure I'll not do that, mistress."

This caused Savarra a moment of acute remembrance. It had been Cotty who had divulged to Lord Bainbridge his daughter's plans that April night when she would have become Peter Haverley's in more ways than she cared to think about now, in a measure saving her from her own folly.

"They're goin' away today, anyway," Cotty added thoughtfully, " 'way back into the mountains they said. They have a lot of cousins back there an' that's where they trap for furs." She toweled Savarra's head vigorously, as Monique slipped silently from the room carrying the large bucketful of used water.

Cotty went on dreamily, "They say 'tis beautiful in the backcountry—no swamps—just mountains that rise up all smoky blue along their ridges, with valleys between, where rivers sparkle like silver—uh—fire, Thad said."

"My word—they are poets," Savarra laughed, but her fancy was caught by the description that Cotty quoted from her suitors. "Where is this land?"

"Beyond places they named, Rocky Mount—King's Mountain, and up into North Carolina."

Savarra was to have reason to recall these names in a few short days for the blood that would be shed there.

Ten

The fall days drifted by, the nights growing crisper, but the days were still warm. Twice Verity had been roused late at night to meet with Tyler Belion. Since the nights were cooling, they met in the kitchen in the still hours. She made it a point to keep him talking of the course of the war and her brief kisses were cool. On his second visit he remarked on this.

"Verity, I've a feeling we are growing apart," his voice was troubled. "You seem—what has changed you?"

Taking her courage in her hands, she said, "Tyler, I believe our love is that of old friends. I feel a great kinship with you. Indeed, I would lay down my life for you. But I do not feel we were meant for each other as man and wife."

There was a long silence. Then, "I know you are the one woman for me, Verity. Surely you do not want to break our engagement?"

"I—" she could not bring herself to say it. "No, but we must surely wait—until America is free." He was silent so long she was driven to speak again. "I must have time to think!"

He said slowly, "You are not the girl I loved before this Englishman and his daughter came to your house. Can you be wavering in your loyalty to America?"

"Never!" she replied with a fierceness that was irrefutable. "With this Lord Bainbridge gone, there is little transpiring in his headquarters. Thank God he has even taken his valet, Brim, with him—but I have been unable to find out anything of their whereabouts or even where they intend to strike next." This, at least, was true.

"They are striking throughout the land, my dear, leaving widows and orphans and burned homes in their wake," he said somberly. "Cornwallis is on the march again now, into North Carolina. And we know he is bent on conquering all the southern states. He seems in a fair way to achieve it, but for

197

our bands of partisans. Cutler and I have been twice with Marion's men, but for a few days only, so as not to arouse suspicion by our absences."

They talked a little longer of the war, and when they parted Verity's kiss was gentle and contained genuine affection. Belion did not try to take her in his arms. His look at her was veiled and there was strain between them. Verity was unable to ease it and no word was spoken as he opened the kitchen door, vanishing in the blowing darkness.

The following day, Baltazar came by with news that startled and distressed Savarra. She felt it as she stood midway on the stairs as he entered the hall to grasp Anne's hands in his, his dark eyes lit with inner fire. Verity, coming from the kitchen, joined them as Savarra descended and approached.

"There has been a great battle at King's Mountain, my dears, and the patriots have slain Major Patrick Ferguson and captured his entire regiment of loyalists!"

"Uncle Bowman," Verity cried, "Ferguson was almost as bad as Tarleton! When did it happen?"

Baltazar turned to her as Savarra drew up. She looked at him coolly. "This must necessarily be bad news for me—"

"Then he will tell it to us in the drawing room, over coffee," Anne said smoothly. "Amos," she said to the servant who had admitted Baltazar, "would you serve us in the drawing room?" And with queenly grace she led the way.

"I will tell you of it as it came to me," Baltazar said soberly.

"First, was my father—or my fiancé—wounded?" Savarra asked, bracing herself.

"Nay, my dear. They were nowhere near it. It happened thus—Cornwallis's march to North Carolina found his front screened by Tarleton's Legion, while well to the west Major Ferguson with some thousand tory riflemen from South Carolina flanked the British on the left. But Patrick Ferguson made the mistake of sending word some time back to the overmountain men that if they did not come in and swear allegiance to the king, he would personally come over there and hang them." He paused, his smile ironic. "This was a grave mistake and most unfortunate for Ferguson and his loyalists, for the overmountain men are a hotheaded lot, and they began to gather at Rocky Mount and to pursue Ferguson, who seemed oblivious to it. He took up a position atop King's Mountain and they overtook him there."

Amos entered, the silver coffeepot steaming, cups and

saucers on the tray. Baltazar halted in his story, to let Anne serve him a smoking cup. Then as the others were served, he took up his story.

"They say Ferguson was slack in posting outriders and was caught unawares. The long and short of it is that the mountain men, with their long rifles, were completely at home in those boulder-covered slopes that were covered with dense woods. Ferguson was killed—eight sharpshooter's bullets in him— almost at once, and white flags began to flutter." Baltazar's face grew graver. "But the overmountain men, with the memory of Tarleton's quarter at Waxhaws, were in no mood to parley and Ferguson's loyalists never had a chance. 'Tis said that before the firing could be stopped, a hundred and fifty-seven of Ferguson's troops were dead and a hundred and sixty-three others so badly wounded they could not be evacuated. I am told by a man who was there that they bagged six hundred and ninety-eight prisoners and over a thousand stands of arms."

"Butchery!" Savarra burst out, dimly realizing the import of this battle.

"On both sides, Mistress Savarra," Baltazar said gently. "And after all, Ferguson's troops were Americans—despite their disloyalty to their country."

"Fools!" Savarra said passionately. "How many Americans must die before they realize their loyalty belongs to Britain?"

In the little silence, Anne's voice was chill. "Possibly all of us."

"Did your informants happen to know where my father is?"

"He is to the east, still seeking the partisans."

Relief mingled with self-condemnation in her voice. "I should have known something like this was going to happen. Those two mountain savages, McHorry and Sleep, were here calling on Cotty over a week ago and they spoke to her of going west, to those places you mentioned. I'll wager they were in on the slaughter."

Baltazar looked at her quizzically. "They were my informants and they were indeed part of the army that besieged Ferguson."

Savarra looked suddenly young and distraught. "I should have told my father long ago—all that I know."

Verity said swiftly, "And be responsible for more death, Savarra? Have you forgotten Tarleton and his murders?"

"No."

Baltazar and Anne were staring fixedly at her, and he said slowly, "You know, Mistress Savarra, they would not ship Tyler, or me, or Cutler off to St. Augustine. For us it would be the gallows. As for Anne and Verity, I hate to think what would befall—"

"Don't," she said sharply. "I shall hold my tongue. Did your informants mention my—fiancé?" Her eyes glinted.

"Yes, they did," he replied grimly. "He is with Lord Rawdon, anchoring the British line at Camden, but he has already led a British patrol near Fishing Creek, where he killed a patriot and a lad of fourteen, who was fifer for the small troop of patriots, before they escaped in the swamps."

"An unarmed lad? I do not believe it," she said flatly.

"And I cannot prove it. 'Twas Gabe told me and he did not witness it, but the leader of the patriot troop, Lieutenant Tillman, said it was a Major Haverley who killed the lad and Stephen Desmesne and wounded two others with his saber."

"Major!" Savarra cried, "He's been promoted already!"

Anne gave her a contemptuous glance, her high-bridged nose flaring a fraction at the nostrils, but her voice was controlled and cold. "And all because he is an expert in slaughter."

The whole of October went by before Savarra's father returned late of a November evening. He was leaner, his face harder and darker, his hair with lighter gold streaks from the burning Carolina sun. The oil lamps in the hall sent a golden glow over the man in his dusty scarlet tunic and stained white breeches. It gleamed dully on his black leather boots.

Savarra embraced him joyfully, but her first question was about her fiancé. "Have you seen Peter?" she asked hopefully.

"No," he replied shortly, "but I have heard of his exploits. Rawdon has given him a command—the 5th Fusiliers."

Verity and her mother stood nearby. Anne was trying to appear pleasant and Verity was endeavoring to conceal her shining happiness. Brim was bustling in and out with Lord Bainbridge's baggage, his own clothing dusty and travelstained.

The excited Cotty came lightly downstairs. "Oh, sir!" she bubbled. "How good to see you! An' Brim, welcome back!"

Lord Bainbridge shook her hand, nodding to the Pair servants who peered solemnly through the doorways. Brim took his hat and cape, the valet's bald head agleam as he said importantly, "I shall prepare you a bath immediately—Tiqua! Monique! Heat water for his lordship at once—"

He followed after the two servants and Anne said pleasantly, "Will you have tea while awaiting your bath, Lord Bainbridge?"

"I'll have a brandy, madame," he replied briefly, leading the way into his darkened headquarters, the others following with Amos carrying a candle.

"You look very well, father," Savarra said. "Has there been much fighting?"

"Amos, will you light the candle and lamps in here for his lordship?" Anne cut in, and he did so with his candle.

Lord Bainbridge looked at his daughter and laughed sardonically. "My dear Savarra, there has been nothing but fighting, thanks to the bands of rebels who call themselves partisans. They infest the swamps and countryside like lice." His voice grew bitter. "And those who call themselves overmountain men are worse. They assemble like fog and strike like snakes. No doubt you have heard of the death of Patrick Ferguson at King's Mountain."

"Yes, Bowman Baltazar told us of it," Verity said. "He had heard it in town."

Lord Bainbridge sat down and looked at the neat, clean desk before him and murmured, "I had thought there would be much to do here—"

"There is, Lord Bainbridge," Anne said dryly, "but Sergeant Queen and Lieutenant Keith carefully take it with them when they leave."

He laughed again. "That's just as well, Mistress Pair. You ladies have sharp eyes." But he looked at Verity in the lampglow and there was expectancy in their brilliant flash.

He said, " 'Tis too late to call them back. Tomorrow will be plenty of time to take care of any work that has accumulated in my absence. I've sent Scott Coyne to his rooms at the Thorn and Thistle. It has been a long ride today."

Anne Pair poured a generous amount of brandy into a crystal brandy glass and handed it to him. "Can you tell us how the war goes?" she asked casually.

He looked at her from under his brows. "You probably know very well how the war goes, madame. But for your information—and it will be widely known shortly—Ferguson's defeat exposed General Cornwallis's left flank to possible attacks from the overmountain men of the west. And his invasion army has had to fall back from Charlotte to Wynnesborough. And there is word that your General Washington is sending a replacement for the inadequate General Gates. We shall have to subdue Carolina once more." His eyes swung to Savarra. "Lord Haverley is doing his part—raiding the countryside and burning out all rebel homes he comes upon in the Camden area."

"You do not approve of that?" Verity asked softly.

He took a long swallow of brandy. "I do not approve of that. War upon women and children is abhorrent to me. The issues should be settled between forces in the field," he replied curtly. "But we *must* eliminate this man Marion. His troops have disrupted our line of communication and supplies to Camden, to Kingstree—to every British-held post. I met with some of Marion's insurrectionists myself early this month beyond Georgetown. Indeed, he put Major Ganey to flight, one of his men driving a bayonet into his back so completely it protruded out the front. It twisted off in Ganey and he rode into Georgetown with it in his chest. They had surprised us on the road—by ambush—and put us to flight. But Marion could not take Georgetown. He came in, but we were behind the redoubts and there was an armed galley lying just off shore to come to our aid. Luckily, Major Thomason was driving on Georgetown and, rather than be caught between us, Marion retreated."

"Did Major Ganey die?" Savarra asked, appalled.

"No, he's a tough man. He will survive to fight again." He swallowed more of the brandy and his tight face began to relax. He added, "I'll not be here more than a week. Though I think Tarleton an impetuous and unthinking man, I must join him again in seeking out this Francis Marion. He is fast becoming a legend among the rebels and, as such, is a great danger to us. He and his men *must* be eliminated."

Brim appeared at the door in fresh clothing. "Your bath is ready, sir." The English lord got to his feet wearily. Though fatigue was heavy on him, there was in his eyes the sharp alertness that was part of his character and he moved with youthful grace.

"You will want supper after your bath?" Anne asked.

"Nay. I've eaten." His eyes were on Verity once more. A look of understanding passed between them which Anne Pair caught, and a shutter fell behind her fine dark eyes.

Lord Wolhuidge carried a candle into the hallway and up

the stairs. Verity knew that later, when all slumbered deeply, she would go to him. A great hunger to touch and be touched by him gnawed at her, and she was impatient with the hours that must pass before they could be together. That he would be waiting was tacit in the glances he sent her. That these glances troubled her mother, Verity was well aware.

Even Savarra had sent her a regretful and compassionate look, and Verity was sure the young girl must know something of the feelings between her father and herself. But she comforted herself that her mother would never conceive of their liaison and its depth. She might realize there was an attraction, but Anne Pair's own moral code was so strict and unyielding it would never occur to her that her daughter might engage in relations of utmost intimacy with any man, let alone an enemy of America.

Lord Bainbridge stayed until the early morning of November fourth. A cold, drenching rain was falling, blown in gray sheets by the wind sweeping inland from the Atlantic. Savarra, knowing he was to depart, had hastened to dress and reached the hall where she found Verity and Brim. The valet was vigorously brushing her father's black three-cornered hat. She was somewhat discouraged having Brim and Verity witness to her questions about her lover and their approaching wedding, but not enough to halt those questions.

Lord Bainbridge was once more brusque at the mention of Peter Haverley. "I have told you, daughter, if he continues to do the work of a soldier—despite a certain—despite what I feel in him, I will reluctantly give my consent. But I want you to wait until after the first of the year, my dear. Opinions and loves have a way of undergoing changes with time and the advent of other people."

At these last words, Verity's face darkened and the thick black lashes fell. Savarra noted this in the back of her mind and reflected briefly on the cause of it as Verity said slowly, "I will bid you farewell, Lord Bainbridge."

His eyes followed her hungrily as she left the room, but Savarra, bent on her own desires now, said, "I have told Peter it would likely be a January wedding, father." She tried to ignore Brim, who was now putting Lord Bainbridge's cloak about his shoulders before donning his own. "Would that be satisfactory?"

Lord Bainbridge swung the black cape about his broad shoulders and set the tricorne on his thick fair hair, his eyes still on the hall door where Verity had vanished. He said slowly, "Probably. But it is with grave misgivings that I would give you into that young man's care. And once you are married, it will be too late to change your mind. You will be his." He paused deliberately, then added, "And you will be subject to all his desires. A wife is very much at her husband's mercies and I cannot find comfort in that."

"Father, you do not understand Peter—"

"I understand that he is a handsome scoundrel and his appearance has entranced you—that and his glib tongue."

She was angered. "But you said yourself, he is leading troops in subduing the rebels!"

"So he is," he said with a touch of sarcasm. "Burning and pillaging farms and plantations of the insurrectionists. He is much like Tarleton and that I do not admire."

Brim gave one last vigorous brushing to the long folds of the rich, heavy wool material of the cape, then picked up their baggage and went out the front door.

As the door closed, Savarra said furiously, "I do not see how you can possibly compare him to Tarleton. I have met that man and he is crass and vulgar, as well as a bloody murderer."

He eyes narrowed, "Ah—you seem to have developed a rather detailed opion of Tarleton."

"I danced with Banastre Tarleton at Bonnie Raintree's ball and he was quite—odious."

He laughed shortly, "That is not his usual effect on women, and it surprises me that you have such clear judgment of Tarleton and such poor judgment when it comes to Haverley, for the two have much in common."

"They are nothing at all alike," she replied stubbornly. Then, knowing she would get no further in this argument with her father, she said, "I hope you are safe and successful in your mission. I shall miss you."

She leaned forward on tiptoes and kissed his hard, tanned cheek. Then there was a blast of chill, wet air and he was gone out the front door to the shell drive that curved beside the house, where his men and horses stood impatiently waiting under the inadequate shelter of the porte-cochere.

Savarra stood listening a moment to the sound of voices and restless horses that penetrated the heavy door. As they dwindled, she turned to make her way back to her bedroom. It was still dark outside. Things would go as she desired. She felt it deep within her as she took the stairs, and yet she was restless because of the fact that somehow it failed to satisfy her.

Early November slipped by with Baltazar, Belion and McLean coming to dine occasionally. Bonnie Raintree was a regular visitor as well, plump, pretty, her full red lips smiling, telling the latest gossip, expressing pleasure that Spencer's business was going so well, and her regret that it kept him away at night a good bit of the time. She wore lovely new clothes, beside which Verity and her mother, in their subdued mourning dress—they had purchased black frocks now that their income was restored—appeared as they intended, drab and sad.

Lord Bainbridge's headquarters ran on a skeleton staff, for Colonel Scott Coyne had once again gone with his commander on his mission. Activity in the big library was at a minimum. Anne and Verity could find no bits of information to pass on to the partisans. Finally, the few possessions of Warren Pair arrived by British freighter. Bowman Baltazar brought them to the Pair house. He pulled from an inner pocket in his fine wine wool greatcoat a gold watch, seals dangling, and a small leather pouch containing a miniature of Anne and Verity and two squares of paper folded many times to fit into the pouch.

Anne took them, tears flowing. " 'Tis our last letters to him, Verity."

Verity looked at the dark brown splotch across the page of her letter and caught her lip between her teeth in sudden pain.

"His blood, no doubt," Anne said harshly. She looked suddenly at Savarra, who had entered the room, drawn by the sound of weeping. Her face grew pale and her blue eyes misted, but Anne said in sudden spite, "You never knew him, how he could laugh away every hurt, how tender he was with Verity and me, how kind and thoughtful—"

Verity broke in, low-voiced. "You could be speaking to Savarra of her own father, mother, and she could lose him as we have lost father." She paused and added, "You know father himself would not be so unkind."

Anne put her hands to her face, her voice broke. "I know— I know. But I cannot forgive Savarra her country's crimes."

Baltazar took Anne suddenly into his arms. He was so tall her dark smooth head was pressed against his heart. His sad brown eyes looked into Savarra's. "Only time can heal her grief, Savarra. You understand, do you not?"

Savarra nodded silently and made her way from the room. At the door, she encountered Cotty, who had listened and was deeply annoyed.

"Come, mistress," she said gently, "I'll prepare tea for you meself. That woman's mean-mouthed, she is."

Savarra said reflectively, "I should likely speak much the same to her, if 'twas my father." Savarra was deeply disturbed and, despite her rationalization, her heart ached for the Pair women.

"Nothin' can happen to Lord Bainbridge." Cotty breathed the words like a prayer. "He's been a soldier all his life an' them in command, mistress, rarely gets killed or wounded."

Savarra regarded the little maid gratefully for, when she had looked into those two grief-ravaged faces, she had known a sudden start of terror as something akin to premonition seized her. War and death had seemed very far away during those years in the great brick mansion in London. It had been even farther away those halcyon days in the country manors surrounded by lawns and forests alive with deer and rabbits and game birds. But here in America she had witnessed it first-hand, and war had changed her for she was fully aware of it for the first time.

The Pair women retired to their rooms to grieve after Baltazar left. Thus Savarra found herself alone in the big salon.

She had been alone sipping the tea Cotty brought her but a half-hour when there came an imperious knocking at the front door. She stepped in to the hall to see Cotty open the front door on Peter Haverley. He was ruddy with cold and dashingly handsome in his bright uniform as he strode in on a gust of cold November air. She flew to him crying, "Peter, Peter!" The funereal atmosphere that had so depressed her lifted magically.

They clasped together in a fierce embrace. The damp, penetrating cold that came to American East Coastal cities in winter was dispelled. There were blazing fires on the hearths throughout the house and it was pleasantly warm inside.

Savarra held him away the better to admire him. He appeared taller, more muscular, and there was an air of command in him that she found quite stimulating. He laughed engagingly and said, "Darling Savarra, I have ridden half the night and all day to have some time with you."

They embraced again in the drawing room and, when they were seated on the sofa, Peter could not keep his hands from her. He caressed her arms, trailed a finger across the back of her neck, caught her hands and brought them to his lips, his breath warm and moist.

"You look positively wonderful, Peter," she told him breathlessly, warmed by his ardor.

His laugh was rollicking and infectious. "I find the military life is for me," he said, golden hazel eyes agleam. "I should have purchased my commission years ago. My friend Banastre Tarleton says that these people will never understand anything but fire and the sword and, by God, he's right. We're giving them a diet of it."

Savarra grew still, then slowly said, "I do not like Colonel Tarleton."

"But you must admit he is a superlative soldier. The whole country stands in awe and fear of him. And they shall of me before I am through. I will give no quarter to these perfidious traitors to Britain—they deserve none." Then he reached for her again, "Ah, come here, my little love." His strong arms held her closely. "I shall never get enough of you! How can I wait until January—such a cold month. But I will keep you warm in my bed!" He kissed her then, slowly, deeply, and together they savored the pleasure found in clinging lips.

Savarra thought, How I love him! How much more satisfying it will be than those wild moments in the forest with that terrible man—McLean. At the memory, she was so annoyed she pulled away from Haverley. Why should she think of that? Why couldn't she wipe her mind clean of the remembrance? and a touch of panic struck her at the question. Suddenly she leaned toward Haverley, catching the back of his dark head in her hands and bringing his lips down to hers with a wildness that caused his own desires to spring up violently. His hold on her tightened and he kissed her avidly until she herself broke away.

"We must wait," she said shaken. "Now—tell me of your triumphs. I am so delighted to see you are a major now."

"I will be a lieutenant colonel before we are married, Savarra," he said with a faintly cynical smile. "Lord Rawdon has said as much. I have led my Fusiliers on many patrols and routed out many rebels since last we met. I have become seasoned and expert at it."

"How do you know—the rebels?"

"We have a number of informants and we range the countryside cleaning out nests of traitors. I myself have set fire to seven rebel plantations."

"Do you kill them all?" she asked slowly, revulsion turning within.

"Sometimes we must. They breed more traitors, you know, and the children will only grow up to give Britain more trouble."

Repulsion grew. She drew back, her black winged brows drawn, blue eyes glinting dangerously. "Peter, I cannot condone the killing of children and women." Her voice was cold. "Have you killed any?"

Recognizing the danger, he said carefully, "Not I, dear. I feel for them, even as you do—but my men are hard to control for many of them have lost their homes and families to rebel raids. I have killed only men who would kill me, in a fair exchange of arms." He paused, then in a vibrant voice added, "Only two weeks ago, I trailed and killed a party of rebels who had burst in on Major Samuel Harrison's two brothers who lay ill with smallpox and slaughtered them in their beds. So you can see what cruelty we have to deal with in these insurrectionists. They recognize no mercy."

Savarra nodded, but in the back of her mind a small voice said, *No more do you, Peter. There is cruelty on both sides and so far,* she had to admit this unwillingly, *I have seen more of it on our side than theirs.*

The two continued to sit in the drawing room, caressing intermittently and discussing their wedding plans.

"Lord Rawdon has informed me that he's going to commandeer one of the finest homes in Camden for us, my love. 'Tis a two-story red brick with servants' quarters and much room. Beautifully decorated as well. I have been in it several times."

"What of the owners?"

"They will move in with relatives. While they have taken the oath of allegiance, their sympathies are still with the rebels and it is well known." He chuckled happily. "Nay, we shall have a fine house. There are several maids and a cook—and you will have the ubiquitous Cotty with you as well, I'm sure." Then suddenly, "You aren't listening," Haverley said, laughing. "Why do you watch the door so closely?"

She flushed, "I was thinking what a trial it is having to meet each other in this house—the servants—some of them could wander in here."

"What harm if they do, Savarra?" His smile was indulgent. "Still my little untouched girl, aren't you?"

Her color deepened and the thick tangle of black lashes dropped. He caught her to him with a quick possessiveness. "Do not blush, Savarra. Your purity is part of your charm for me. I want you all the more for it."

Panic flowered in her breast. As she returned his caress with timid gestures, she prayed hard that Lord Haverley would never discover her wanton moments in that moon-drenched August night with Cutler McLean.

"Will you have dinner with me tonight at the Thorn and Thistle, Savarra?"

She was reminded sharply of Banastre Tarleton's invitation the night of the Raintrees' ball. "Oh, I couldn't do that, Peter—"

"Darling Savarra, you carry your innocence too far, I think." His handsome face darkened.

"You must dine with us—here."

"With those two crows in black and probably that dreary old cooper, Baltazar? I'd rather sit through the dullest sermon in England!"

Savarra laughed to hide her alarm, for she remembered suddenly Belion, Baltazar and McLean were to dine with them tonight. She said teasingly, "I certainly cannot go to a public inn and dine with so handsome a man without a chaperone."

He smiled ruefully. "No one can make a refusal as flattering as you." He sighed, " 'Tis the influence of that Spanish mother who had a duenna in attendance right up to the bedroom door, I suppose." Then with a twinkle, "Do you think Cotty might be prevailed on to come with you?"

"Oh, Peter—that would be the answer! How kind of you to think of it."

"Well, as I must leave at dawn," he shrugged, "I will have to be satisfied with her presence during our last hours together."

Savarra was not surprised when Verity knocked at her door after darkness had fallen. At her call to come in, the American girl looked at her with astonished admiration. "You look lovely! The ball-gown you wore to the Raintrees' in September." Verity's eyes were admiring but somewhat shocked.

Cotty, in the new pink chemise-dress Savarra had promised, glowed over the prospect of acting as chaperone to her mistress. Now she began hooking up the long, tight bodice of white silk.

"You will add a touch of needed cheer in the gown tonight," Verity said, covering her astonishment with a smile. "Uncle Bowman, Tyler and Cutler will appreciate that at dinner, Savarra."

Savarra congratualted herself silently. Dinner with both Peter and McLean at the same table would have made for a terrible evening. "Verity, I am going out to dine with Lord Haverley." She spoke with more assurance than she felt. "I will need Amos and the carriage this evening."

"Oh?" There was still another question implicit in the small exclamation.

"I'm goin' with her," Cotty said pleasedly. "Mistress Savarra says I shall sit at table with them like gentry."

Tension went out of Verity's beautiful face and she said, "Of course. I shall have Amos bring the carriage around immediately—but I do wish you would come in and speak to our guests before you leave."

"I think not, Verity. You know how little use I have for Mr. McLean. However, do give my regards to Mr. Baltazar and Mr. Belion."

She was not to escape too easily, however, for when she and Cotty took the stairs, McLean stood in the doorway to the drawing room, clear gray eyes alert for her descent. When she reached the last step he came forward and took her arm solicitously.

"Ah—Mistress Bainbridge, I have been waiting to escort you and Mistress Penderford to the carriage." His smile was white in the sun-burned face. "Where will you dine tonight?" The question was ingenuous and, when Savarra did not answer, he bent his eyes to Cotty as he took her arm.

"We're goin' to the Thorn 'n Thistle, Mr. McLean," she said smugly.

"Ah. The Thorn and Thistle is known as a place of much—pleasure. The cuisine is very good, providing the company is also."

Savarra's fur-lined cloak fanned out as she walked swiftly toward the door, pulling against McLean's hand on her arm. Her reticule bumped his thigh and he added mildly, "You are in a tremendous hurry, Mistress Bainbridge," as they stepped out into the cold, blowing night. There was a single enclosed oil lantern flickering beside the door, and in the light of it she looked up to see his thick black hair toss in the wind.

They walked across the porch into the black shadows of the porte-cochere where Amos sat, muffled to the ears on the box of the carriage. The two lamps on it were lit, but they were pale and weak against the cold, dark night, and the horses stamped uneasily.

McLean opened the carriage door and handed Savarra in, saying lightly, "I am sure you will have a most enjoyable evening." Then as he handed Cotty in, he added, "I'm glad you are going with your mistress. Banastre Tarleton has given the inn somewhat of a reputation." And he closed the carriage door firmly.

Cotty pulled her squirrel-lined cape close about her, shivering. "I do believe this Charles Town place is colder'n London in November."

" 'Tis the dampness. We are so close to the sea."

"What kind of reputation do you s'pose Mr. McLean means?" Cotty asked innocently.

"Mr. McLean has a nasty mind," Savarra said heatedly. "He probably meant something horrible. But Peter will be there and we shall both be quite safe."

But she was taken aback when Amos assisted them from the carriage. The sound of revelry within was clear on the windy night and, when Amos opened the door, there were myriad colors and a throng of soldiers but few women within the inn. Some sat at table eating, others drinking, still others engaged in deep conversation. There was much laughter.

There was a long bar at the end of the room where a conglomeration of men stood drinking and talking among themselves. Men in fine satins, sober black broadcloth, and some in the fringed leather garb of backcountry were scattered about the tables. The overall impression was of warmth and merriment and a great lack of restraint.

Savarra looked anxiously about for Peter and was much relieved when she saw him rise from a table at the far end of the room. He was cleanly shaven with his uniform fresh and he looked exceedingly handsome. Good breeding was unmistakable on his even features.

Amos said, "I'll put the horses and carriage in the courtyard an' wait in the servants' room, mistress, till you're ready to leave." Savarra reached hastily into her reticule and drew out a crown. She handed it to him, saying, "Buy yourself a mug of hot rum, Amos. 'Tis such a blustery night and I know it must be miserable on that box in the weather."

He thanked her and left as Peter drew up to them. Cotty was round-eyed at the sights about her and her pretty pink mouth was slightly open as she scanned the room. "Lor'," she murmured under her breath, "so many kinds of different people."

Peter took Savarra's chilled hands into his strong, warm ones. "Come, my darling, I have a table for us at the back, away from all this noise." And he led her to the rear where a table of snowy linen was spread, with places set for three. There was a vase of camellias in the center, which surprised Savarra.

"I have ordered roast duckling for us, with dressing, and the Thorn and Thistle is famous for its side dishes and its wines. We will have wine before they serve the entree." His hands clung to hers as he seated first her, then Cotty, at the table.

The meal progressed, bringing great pleasure to Savarra. She had never seen Peter so gallant, so charming and utterly winning. Cotty was starry-eyed and she ate ravenously for the cuisine was, as McLean had said, excellent. Savarra drank enough wine to feel a rosy warmth, and her impatience for January and the wedding grew accordingly. Still, Peter Haverley was the essence of the courteous gentleman. He made no untoward overtures and, beyond expressing his disappointment over the month's waiting, he was the paragon of a well-bred suitor.

As they were finishing up dessert, a crusty and spiced apple tart, Peter looked toward the bar and his face darkened. "By God, that bastard—I beg your pardon, Savarra—that scum McLean is here."

Savarra turned her head, and there indeed was Cutler Mc-Lean, leaning negligently on the bar and sipping a pony of bourbon. He was looking toward them. Their eyes met and he lifted his glass to her, then tossed it down. At the bar with him were the leather-clad overmountain men, Gabe Sleep and Thad McHorry.

Peter's face was darkly congested. "I've not forgotten his attack on me when I first arrived—and I intend to kill him yet." He spoke between his teeth.

Gabe and Thad were looking admiringly at Cotty, who was

demurely finishing her tart. Her lids fluttered up and she smiled at them timidly.

For Savarra, the evening was ruined. That McLean would have the audacity to follow her to the inn and observe her tryst with her fiancé infuriated her. She did not finish her tart, pushing it way with a nervous gesture.

"I must return now, Peter," she said abruptly. "It will not do to stay out past eleven. Will you summon Amos for us?"

"Yes, and I will ride escort beside the carriage to see you safely home."

" 'Tis such a blustery night, Peter dear, and we shall be quite safe with Amos. You should not have to get out in it."

"I've been in worse," he said grimly, "and I intend to see you safely back to the Pair house." Then as an afterthought, "McLean is an impudent rascal—toasting you." His words held a wealth of venom.

They left under the curious glance of the habitués of the inn, and most especially was she aware of the close scrutiny of McLean and the overmountain men.

At the door of the Pair home, Peter took her into his arms and kissed her lingeringly. She clung to him, for suddenly she had the curious feeling that she stood on trembling ground that would give way at any moment.

"I may come back at Christmas, if I am not ordered out on a mission," he said huskily. "I will write you."

"If you come," Savarra said emotionally, "it would indeed make the season for me!"

"Only duty can keep me away."

The wind was colder and damper now. Rain was about to fall and Cotty drew her cloak about her, shivering a little.

"Goodbye for now, darling Peter," Savarra said, her own feet and ankles icy as the wind swirled about them. "I will pray for you every night."

He took her hands from her little fur muff and brought them to his warm lips, then took her in his arms and kissed her mouth once again. Savarra shivered with pleasure as well as with cold. How much more wonderful it would be with Peter, she thought for the hundredth time.

And when he was gone and she and Cotty were in the warm house, she thought of the future. Life with Peter would be exciting, every day holding an adventure, and her own eagerness rose up as her breath came faster.

Eleven

The Pair household had settled down after the fresh grief brought on by the return of Warren Pair's personal things. While Anne Pair continued to wear her doleful black dresses, Verity bought some new frocks of subdued color. Savarra heartily approved of this, for she felt Verity far too young to be decked in flowing black, and she admitted to herself that she had developed a reluctant affection for the American girl.

Peter Haverley wrote impassioned letters to her regularly and she responded with equally warm replies. Peter was never guilty of false modesty in detailing his missions, and always he made them sound as if he were protecting the helpless while slaying the perfidious rebels. Savarra's perturbation regarding his admiration for Banastre Tarleton was soothed.

Bonnie Raintree and a coterie of her loyalist friends invited Savarra and the Pair women to their holiday soirees. Savarra and Verity attended some of them, but Anne refused to go. Baltazar was a constant caller at the Pair house and he and the widow had long, low-voiced conversations in the drawing room.

One day a week before Christmas, when Verity and Savarra were in Mistress Applegate's bake shop having coffee and cake, Savarra said suddenly, "Verity, I believe Bowman Baltazar loves your mother—I have thought so from the beginning."

"I know it," Verity replied, "but my mother does not and she is, as you know, not the kind of woman you could blurt out that fact to and expect any reaction but shock and dismay."

" 'Tis a great pity, for Mr. Baltazar is a fine man."

Verity smiled. "Time is his ally. Mother may come to realize how much he has done for us and find herself returning his love."

"Perhaps," Savarra replied, but she had her doubts. She thought Anne Pair a hard and bitter woman and that no man could breach the walls of coldness she had built around herself. Her attitude toward Savarra was implacable and the girl felt it each time she was in her presence.

"I'm hoping that Peter will be able to come spend Christmas in Charles Town, Verity. He thinks he might." The blue eyes were vivid with excitement.

"That would be so nice for you," Verity said with restraint. She had heard from Belion and McLean of the atrocities that Haverley was wreaking on the country, but she did not comment on this to the British girl. Nor did she suggest that Savarra ask him to be a guest during the holidays. Her vehement hope was that the English girl would not suggest it herself.

Savarra, on the other hand, did not suggest it for she did not want to put herself in the position of refusing Peter's offers of physical proof of his love.

The problem was solved for both girls three days before Christmas, when Savarra received a letter from young Lord Haverley regretfully informing her he could not be spared for he was in pursuit of a rebel band under a man by the name of Andrew Pickens, who was almost as sore a trial to the British as Francis Marion and Thomas Sumter. He would probably spend Christmas in the field, eating army rations. But he concluded with tender words of love and reminded her that only days separated them from their union as man and wife.

On Christmas Eve, Savarra received yet another letter, this one from her father. She sat reading it in the drawing room, where Verity was putting the finishing touches on a red Christmas cloth over a mahogany table beside the sofa.

Verity took a very long time to do this, but Savarra was lost in the letter. The pall of grief was lifting in the Pair house and Cotty had assisted the servants and the three women to decorate the house for the season. There were pine boughs along the mantels and red candles in black wrought-iron holders, with other tall tapers thrust in among small limbs and put about the big house. A delicious spicy scent permeated the rooms, and there was cheerful secrecy among the servants and their mistresses as each prepared small gifts.

In the letter to Savarra, Lord Bainbridge wrote of his and Tarleton's pursuit through swamps, from one bog to another, through thickets, forests—and always the elusive Marion was just beyond them. He wrote that they had pursued him for seven hours and twenty-six miles one day. When they came at last to Ox Swamp on the Pocotaligo River, both the troopers and their mounts were too weary to attempt the foreboding waste before them. In disgust at last, Tarleton had drawn up his horse, hip-deep in murky water, and cursed Marion roundly, saying, "Come, my boys—and Lord Bainbridge—let us go back and find the gamecock, old Sumter. But as for this damned old swamp fox, the devil himself could not catch him," thus giving Marion a proper sobriquet. Now, her father continued, they were in pursuit of Sumter, who was, in his more fiery way, almost as great a thorn in the side of the British as Marion. Lord Bainbridge had added that Marion's exploits encouraged the rebels to renewed resistance. He finished by saying that it would be mid-January or a little later before he would return to the Pair house—at which time he would be ready to give his daughter in marriage at last to Lord Haverley.

"I do so reluctantly, Savarra," he concluded, "and I hope for your future happiness despite my misgivings."

"Good news, Savarra?" asked Verity, unable to restrain her eagerness to hear from her lover.

Savarra began, "He says—" when a loud and frenzied clatter sounded in the hallway. It was a bitter cold day, with a heavy sky threatening rain or sleet, and it was cozy beside the fire in the small sitting room. But she and Verity were so startled by the urgent banging of the brass knocker, they rose to their feet, Savarra dropping the letter on a small rosewood table.

Hurriedly they made their way into the hall, where Amos had opened the door. The other servants, drawn by obvious emergency in the forceful knocking, began to gather.

As they drew near, they saw it was Bonnie Raintree, her face almost unrecognizable, so blotchy and puffy was it from weeping. Her dark hair was disheveled and her cloak half-off, half-on. Even her dress appeared rumpled and awry.

Verity pushed her way to the woman and caught her in her arms, but Bonnie looked at Savarra and pulled away to clutch at the British girl. "Oh, my God, Savarra, they have arrested Spencer—and they say they are going to hang him! You *must* get word to your father. His high rank—oh, Lord Bainbridge could help us!"

"Arrest Spencer?" Savarra was stunned. "But why?"

"All these months I thought he was faithful to our—to the

king, he has been in secret correspondence with the rebels, spying—worse, he has been supplying them with needfuls—with all sorts of things—from our store!" She broke into wild sobs. "I never—never dreamed he would do such!"

Verity tried to soothe her, but she clung to Savarra's hands and wept. "He's been—shipping supplies to—to the Continental Army by wagon, secretly."

"How did they find that out?" Savarra asked, her eyes seeking Verity's.

"Soldiers commanded by Colonel Balfour—that man I thought so charming that General Cornwallis left in charge of Charles Town—broke into our house this morning and found what he calls—incriminating papers." Her voice broke into a wail. "Even letters from General Washington himself, thanking Spencer for his help and his reports."

"Dear Lord," murmured Verity, her face paling. "Did—were any others implicated, or did Spencer do this alone?"

Anne put her scented handkerchief into Bonnie's trembling hand and she blew her nose fiercely. "Others were implicated all right—the Boothes and the Barbers, but we all knew they were patriots all along and their men have been gone since the last of August, nearly five months now. At least the men—Tom and Frank are in prison in St. Augustine."

"Then our dear friends, Beth Barber and Doris Boothe are—have been helping Spencer?" Anne asked incredulously.

"I'm sure they have, but the colonel could find no proof of that—only that Frank and Tom had been hand-in-glove with Spencer. Oh, God—they are going to hang him!" She began to sob once more.

Savarra shook her. "Hush, Bonnie. They are not going to hang him *today*, are they?"

"I don't know. Can they?" Bonnie looked at her piteously.

"I'm sure they can," Anne said grimly, "but perhaps they will give him a trial—give us time to think of *something* or get help from someone."

"Where are Belle and Terrell?" Verity asked worriedly.

"They have spent the day with the Garrisons and their children."

"Thank God for that," Verity said relievedly. "They know nothing of their father's arrest?"

Bonnie shook her head and blew her tilted nose once more. "Savarra, if we can just get word to Lord Bainbridge, I know he would plead for leniency. I would rather he be sent to St. Augustine than be *hung*."

Anne turned to Amos. "Please fetch the brandy decanter and a glass, Amos. Mistress Raintree needs something to calm her." Amos vanished into the drawing room. "Come," Anne added calmly, "we might as well go into the small sitting room. 'Tis warmer there." And she led the way.

Because of the darkness of the day lamps and candles were lit, and the fire on the hearth leaped brightly, throwing out a rosy glow.

"Savarra," Bonnie said beseechingly, as she sank in a forlorn and rumpled little heap on the sofa, "can't one of the aides here at your father's headquarters get word to him of Spencer's plight?"

"Sergeant Queen and Lieutenant Keith have been given furlough for the holidays, Bonnie," Savarra replied, her heart full of pity for her distraught friend.

Amos drew up before Bonnie and poured a slender crystal glassful of brandy, handing it to her comfortingly. "There, Mistress Raintree. You feel better do you drink this."

Bonnie swallowed a mouthful of the burning liquid and coughed. "I must be home when the children return. I must tell them their father is—ah, God help me." She began to weep, silently now. "What can I tell them?"

Savarra spoke up with sudden harshness. "I will go to Colonel Balfour myself and ask him to wait until my father can return next month for a trial."

"Oh—" Bonnie looked at her with drowned dark eyes. "You are good, Savarra!"

"His headquarters are General Cornwallis's—next door, of course. Possibly he is there now. I will go at once and take my father's letter that informs me he'll be home sometime in January." She rose determinedly and, turning, saw that Cotty stood in the door to the sitting room wearing a long face of disapproval. "Cotty, fetch my cloak and gloves. I am going to the Brewton house immediately."

Cotty disappeared and returned in a few moments with Savarra's fur-lined cloak. She handed the delicate leather gloves to Savarra and draped the cloak about her shoulders.

"Wait here," she said confidently, drawing on the gloves, "I should return soon."

Amos opened the door for her and a gust of icy air swept about her. She hugged the cloak close, pulling the hood over her hair. A lock of it was caught in the wind and tumbled down, whipping along her cheek. The sweeping wind increased the chill of the day and she pulled against it on the brick walkway to the house next door.

She was admitted by a young lieutenant she had never seen before, but when she told him she was Lord Bainbridge's daughter come to confer with Colonel Balfour, he said respectfully, "Mistress Bainbridge, he is not yet here—business at the jail detains him."

"I know," she said coldly. "I will wait." And she followed him into a large room which she surmised had been the drawing room, for it was much larger than her father's library headquarters. A fire burned fiercely in the huge black fireplace and she took a seat near it, divesting herself of her cloak. The young lieutenant threw two more thick logs upon the blaze.

"Sorry you must wait," he said with an admiring glance at Savarra, whose cheeks were stung pink with cold, "but it being Christmas Eve, everyone is on furlough or pass except me. I shall have Christmas Day off, though. May I get you a cup of hot chocolate?"

"That would be pleasant, thank you."

So she sipped the scalding chocolate and waited for the return of Colonel Balfour, her father's letter tucked into her cloak pocket.

The colonel arrived in less than twenty minutes and looked at his visitor with great surprise. "Mistress Savarra! What brings you here on Christmas Eve—and such a raw day it is, too."

"I have come about my friend Bonnie Raintree's husband, colonel," she said directly, and was rewarded by the sight of his face setting like a rock.

His eyes were flint-hard. "Mistress, Spencer Raintree is a traitor. He took the oath of allegiance and he has been engaged in aiding and succoring the enemy since the capture of Charles Town. Worse, he is a *spy*."

"I know that," replied Savarra coolly. "Bonnie has told me. But you must remember that she is a fine and loyal subject of King George—and that should ameliorate the circumstances for Spencer."

"I'm sorry, but it does not. He will be hung after Christmas without a trial."

Savarra's back stiffened, her chin went up. "I think you would be very unwise to take such precipitous action, Colonel Balfour. My father will be here in mid-January. I have a letter from him here—see—to that effect. You could easily wait until then, less than four weeks, in order that he might review the case."

"There is nothing to review," Colonel Balfour said, his face reddening and his black eyes flashing. "Lord Bainbridge would be the first to say Spencer Raintree must hang. The man has been reporting on the movements of British troops and is responsible for any number of ambushes and deaths. He has been corresponding with the partisans that infest the swamps, as well as with no less a personage than the commander-in-chief of the rebel forces."

"Nevertheless, Bonnie is a good loyalist," Savarra said stubbornly, "and I do not see why Spencer Raintree should not be deported to prison, either in Florida or the West Indies, rather than summarily hanged."

"By heaven, these rebels need an example!" The Colonel's temper was rising. "And this man admits it all. He shall be hung."

"And you may regret your hasty action," Savarra said coldly.

"I think not, mistress. I am in charge here in the general's absence and I must enforce our laws as I see fit."

"There are two young children and Bonnie to think of, Colonel Balfour," Savarra's voice was steady. "It seems to me that justice must be tempered with mercy in this case." Then with a swift impatient gesture as he started to speak, "Yes, colonel, I know he is guilty, but this war will end with us victorious, and the man might be rehabilitated to one of the city's finest citizens."

The colonel's thin mouth went down at one corner and he lifted his heavy shoulders. "Mistress, these people will not be rehabilitated. Most of them will hate the king until the day they die. We can only make examples of the worst of them in order to keep the others in line."

Savarra knew he was right. The Americans would hate the king as long as they lived, but she felt the harsh justice her countrymen were meting out could only stiffen their resistance. She remembered Anne Pair's chill voice confirming that they might all well choose to die rather than live under the intolerable laws that made them slaves to Britain's whims. And she thought of the incriminating knowledge she had of partisan activities conducted secretly in the city, then turned from it quickly. This red-faced, intolerant and autocratic man who stood before her would hang all of them immediately.

"Then you do not plan to give Spencer Raintree the benefit of a trial?"

"He is guilty of treason," was the uncompromising reply, "and he will be hung."

"I see," she said slowly. "I shall tell my father of your summary decision when he returns. He will not like the fact that you ignored a trial for the man. My father adheres strictly to British rules of justice, and a fair trial for all is one of them."

For a instant Colonel Balfour looked uncertain. Then he said, "Lord Bainbridge will condone my actions when he learns of the circumstances. Certainly the rebel General Washington showed no mercy when he hung John André, who was guilty only of carrying Benedict Arnold's messages to General Clinton. And only because he was out of uniform, through no fault of his own."

"He had a trial, as I recall," Savarra said firmly.

"A very short one. A mere farce of a trial."

"But a trial nevertheless. If you will consider a suggestion, Colonel Balfour, you will let the law take its course and see that Spencer Raintree has a trial before he is hung, farce or not." She rose, gathering her cloak around her and pulling on the fine leather gloves. Her young face was forbidding.

The colonel's florid features were grim, but she saw in his eyes that she had influenced him. "I might do that—but it will be in very short order. No more than John André's trial. And Spencer Raintree will hang before the first of the year."

When Savarra reached the Pair sitting room, the others met her with simultaneous questions. She flung off the cloak and peeled off the gloves. Cotty picked them up and stood holding them while all listened.

"He is determined to hang Spencer," Savarra told Bonnie bluntly, "but I think he will wait—and he indicated that he might give him a trial. Perhaps I can get word to my father to come in sooner than he planned. He is in the Kingstree area—it would not take long for him to arrive. I shall write him immediately." Her eyes sought Verity's. "Do you know someone who might take the message to him?"

"I could ask Tyler—or Cutler. But it would be better if we had a man in uniform to take a message to him."

"Very well. I will ask Lieutenant Keith to do so, and I shall write my father this very night. I fear Colonel Balfour plans to hang Spencer before the year is out, and time is of utmost importance." Savarra turned to Bonnie, remembering her warmth and kindnesses and the fact she had kept Savarra's secret of Peter Haverley for weeks, a Herculean achievement for the voluble Bonnie. She took a plump little hand in hers and said soothingly, "Bonnie, take heart. I know my father will come posthaste and we may arrange for Spencer to be deported. Then he will return to you when we win this war."

Bonnie's voice was thick with gratitude. "Thank you, Savarra. I pray you are right." She gave a great shuddering sigh, her round face a mask of grief. "I must get home now and await my children."

"I shall go with you, Bonnie," Verity said compassionately. "You will need someone to help you explain—to reassure them that there is hope."

The Raintree tragedy colored Christmas for all of those in the Pair house and Savarra, for one, was glad when the holiday was over, for it meant that not only was it one day nearer her marriage to Peter, but also her father would soon be on his way to Charles Town. Lieutenant Keith had been sent to Kingstree with a short, urgent letter from Savarra, detailing the Raintree arrest and bearing down heavily on Colonel Balfour's merciless decision that Spencer Raintree be hung.

On December thirty-first of 1780, before Lord Bainbridge could arrive, a proceeding that was more mockery than trial was held for Spencer Raintree and he was sentenced to hang. The gallows in the city square had become weathered, but it still stood, gaunt and terrifying in the center of the square. Late in the afternoon of the last day of the year, Colonel Balfour and his redcoated soldiers marched the tall, thin and gentle Spencer to the scaffold and hung him.

Bonnie had taken to her bed, sick with grief and shock. The children were pale little ghosts that came to stay with the Pairs, and Savarra's heart went out to them. They were very quiet and read a great deal from books they found in the library.

Lord Bainbridge, when he arrived on January third of the new year, listened to Savarra's immediate and impassioned indictment of Colonel Balfour with a still face.

Then he said wearily, "My dear, I have already been to see Balfour. I have seen the written proof that Spencer caused the deaths of many soldiers of the crown. He was guilty of giving aid and comfort to our enemies. I could have done nothing but offer Bonnie my sympathy and agree with Balfour."

"But he *could* have been sent to St. Augustine—or the Indies!"

"His crimes were too great for that. If he had been guilty only of supplying the rebels, it might have been possible to imprison him with his townsmen in St. Augustine, but I saw the letters signed by the rebel general, Washington—saw that Spencer was guilty of revealing our troop movements. Does that not make you realize he should pay for it?"

Savarra bowed her head and made no answer. When she looked up, she saw that her father's eyes were on Verity's pale face, locked with her dark ones, and Anne Pair was observing the two of them narrowly. With suddenly sharpened insight, she knew there was *something*—a liaison between the rebel girl and her father. It displeased her deeply, but not so deeply as the execution of the kind, mild-spoken Spencer Raintree.

Lord Bainbridge stayed but three days at the Pair house before leaving for Camden upon the receipt of messages from Lord Rawdon. The day the dispatches arrived, he called Savarra into headquarters and looked at her with poorly concealed relief and satisfaction.

My dear, Francis writes that your fiancé's presence is needed by his command. The man the rebels have replaced General Gates with—a Nathanael Green—is proving to be more troublesome than we anticipated."

At Savarra's cry of disappointment, he shrugged. "I can do nothing about it. I must go myself to help put down these rebels. Your wedding will have to wait."

She said with sudden threatening intuition, her eyes brilliant with anger, "Lord Rawdon may be arranging to deprive me of my husband forever."

Her father's smile was wintry. "I doubt that. Your future husband will be in command of a number of men who will face the rebels before he will."

Savarra detected the deep undercurrent of contempt for Peter Haverley that underlay her father's words and she spoke cuttingly. "*You* should know, I suppose, having so conveniently survived so many battles."

But his face did not change and his smile was impervious as she turned on her heel and left the room, with Sergeant Queen and Lieutenant Keith observing her furious departure with shocked young faces.

That last night before Lord Bainbridge left, when Verity slipped into his room at two in the morning, he caught her to him with a touch of desperation.

"Verity, my darling, I miss you terribly when I am away. I would have you by my side every minute."

"And I would be there. I can think of no one but you." Yet she was thinking of Tyler as he had stood before her the night Spencer Raintree had been hung in the square. He had looked drawn and angry, but his eyes on her were tender. *"Cutler and I must leave tonight, supposedly for Norfolk where we meet with rice brokers from New York and Massachusetts. Bowman is to leave in two days. We'll meet, of course, with the old wagoner, Dan Morgan, toward Cheraws. I do not know when we can return."*

Now as she lay in James's arms, Verity thought of these things and the posibility that McLean, Belion and Baltazar might never return to Charles Town at all. She could tell her lover nothing of this, nor could she attempt to worm information from him—information that he knew and that might save the lives of her compatriots. Her heart ached unbearably, but she clung to her British lover, their bodies fused, and her stolen moments of love filled her with a blazing happiness.

At last there sounded, from beyond the closed bedroom door, the muffled chime of the great clock in the hall. One . . . two . . . three . . . four . . . then silence.

Verity moved in her lover's arms. " 'Tis four. I must go."

He caught her again, held her warmly against his powerful and muscular body. "Why?" he murmured into the thick fall of hair beside her throat.

"The whole house will be up in another two hours."

"I shall be gone in less than that. Stay—"

She laughed huskily, burying her face in his bare shoulder. "Why not bundle me into your knapsack and strap me across your horse? I could cook for you—mend your clothing—and comfort you of the long cold nights on your missions."

His voice was deep. "Very well. I shall arrange it immediately."

She pulled out of his arms. "Ah, my darling—if it were that easy."

He sat up, crossing strong arms over the covers across his drawn knees. "I shall return when that young scoundrel Haverley can get away long enough to marry my daughter— would to God she had never laid eyes on him." Verity struck a flint and lit the candle beside the bed and they looked at each other across the wavering golden flame. "What made McLean strike him?" Sir James asked abruptly. "You never told me of his insult to you."

She looked away, shrugging into her warm woolen wrapper. " 'Twas nothing—a tone of voice, the cut of his eye. American men are very sensitive to the treatment of their women."

"So are Englishmen. And you are lying. Ah, well, 'tis better I do not know what he said. It could be only one more black mark against him, and God knows there are enough already. I am swallowing every paternal instinct in giving my consent for Savarra to marry him."

It was not what he *said*, but what he *did*, Verity thought dryly, but she held her tongue. Savarra would have trouble enough when she married him without Verity feeding the fire now. She shivered slightly, thinking of Haverley's golden hazel eyes and their sudden lewdness when he greeted her on their first meeting. Now she leaned to Lord Bainbridge and kissed his mouth one last time, their lips lingering, but as he reached for her, she moved back.

"Nay, my love. This is goodbye for now. God be with you in the coming days." And she moved silently to the door, closing it noiselessly behind her.

She moved down the hall, lost in thought, when suddenly, as she approached her room, she drew up short. A dim blur of white stood in the hall. Her footsteps slowed. Could it be— Dear God, it *was*! Her mother! As conviction and dismay swept Verity, Anne Pair spoke in a whisper.

"Verity, come into my room."

A mixture of dread and guilt, shored up by defiance, filled her as she followed her mother into the room. Pale light flickered, and she saw that a candle had burned far down in its holder on the table beside her mother's bed. Verity's heart was beating heavily and her mouth was dry.

Her mother took her hand and led her to the broad sofa

before the fireplace where red coals glowed. The room was comfortably warm, but Verity shivered as with a chill. The two women seated themselves upon the sofa.

Anne looked at her daughter without speaking for a long time and Verity's will hardened. She would say nothing. Let her mother make the first overture.

Anne did so, saying with quiet fury, "You have betrayed your father and me, your upbringing—and now I suppose you are betraying your country."

"I will never betray my country," Verity said, sudden rage in her voice. How could she make this contained, self-controlled puritan understand what flamed in her heart at the very thought of Lord Bainbridge?

"You will eventually," Anne said evenly. "You have betrayed yourself and all things fine and good already. Do not try to tell me your tryst with Lord Bainbridge was innocent. I have been waiting two hours in the hall for you to come from his bed."

"I love Lord Bainbridge." Verity spoke in low tones, her voice husky and her breath short. "With a love you could never understand—being the kind of woman you are, you have never felt it."

Anne laughed shortly. "He will not marry you."

"Do you think I care?" she flared. "I would rather have his love than reject it, lose it for lack of courage."

"Courage!" The word was contemptuous. "Have you considered the possible consequences?"

"What consequences?" Verity looked at her mother's still face in the candlelight.

"My dear, you are twenty-four, and I know I lost my hold on you long ago." There was a touch of irony in her voice, but love as well. "You are old enogh to know what you are doing could lead to pregnancy. What will you do when you find yourself bearing Lord Bainbridge's illegitimate child?"

The breath went out of Verity. She had not permitted herself to think that far ahead. Her mother went on inexorably. "He will leave you with a bastard child one of these days and you will forfeit all respectability—all the honor in your father's fine name. It will not only be yourself that you would beyond repair, for I too shall bear the disgrace."

"Mother, you cannot understand," Verity said vehemently. "He is in my thoughts always. I *cannot* give him up."

"But he will give *you* up, Verity, when the time comes for him to return to his estates in England."

"I don't know—you can't know—"

"Do not tell me that again." Anne spoke with sudden anger. "I know more than you credit me. I am not unacquainted with passion—but I learned to control it. It breaks my heart that you have not that strength."

Verity's head drooped and her shoulders sagged. Her mother spoke the truth. For all her defiance of conventions, of rules, she feared the future even as Anne Pair. Yet she knew she could not deny Lord Bainbridge. He was in her blood, in her very bones. She repeated, "Mother, I cannot give him up. I have never known such a love. But I swear to you that we do not speak of the war. I have never, by implication, by look or word, revealed anything about our men. And I shall still seek all knowledge of British activities —though not from him—and relay it to them."

For a long moment, silence hung between them before her mother said heavily, "I believe you. What of Tyler Belion, who believes you will be his bride?"

"I will never be Tyler's bride. I shall—let Tyler go with as little hurt to him as possible."

Her mother's lips went down in a sardonic smile. "As little hurt as possible. How uncaring you are, Verity. You will break his heart." Then with sudden urgency, "I beg you to give up this—course of action. It is not too late. Please, my daughter, please promise me you will go no more to his room!"

"I cannot," Verity said in a low voice.

Anne's voice was suddenly venomous. "I despise the man! He is a murderer, an unprincipled blackguard, to seduce my daughter. I would kill him if I could do so, gladly."

Verity looked into the contorted face with shock. Nay, her mother was not unacquainted with passion, she was in the grip of it now. Anne drew a deep breath. "Fornication— committed by my own daughter and with a man who slaughters her countrymen, who seeks in the end to enslave us all. Verity, Verity, how can you do it?"

"I love him," she replied simply. "And now I am going to bed for one hour's sleep. He will be gone before we rise. He doesn't plan to return before his daughter's wedding to Lord Haverley, so you will be free of him for some weeks." Verity rose from the sofa and started to leave.

"Wait—" Anne said pleadingly. "I cannot prevail on you to avoid this liaison that can only lead to disaster for all of us?"

"Nay," Verity replied resolutely and she closed the door on her mother's white beseeching face.

Lord Bainbridge had been gone three days when Bonnie Raintree appeared at the Pair door. Amos admitted her just as Anne, Verity and Savarra, and the two children, Belle and Terrell, were finishing breakfast. Savarra saw her standing in the dining salon doorway first and her mouth fell open in shock.

"I have come for the children," Bonnie said, her voice as alien as her appearance. She was pale, her mouth almost bloodless, and Savarra could not believe she had lost so much weight within the short space of a week. Her face was no longer round and merry, but pointed of chin and big of eye.

All at the table rose hastily, and Anne Pair said to the staring Tiqua in the door to the kitchen, "You may serve coffee to us in the drawing room, Tiqua. Amos, please come and stir up the fire in there for us. Bonnie dear, you look half-frozen—" The older woman put a protective arm about the shorter Bonnie, guiding her toward the drawing room.

The children had come up beside her and Terrell asked anxiously, "Mama, have you been sick?"

Belle said, "Hush, Terrell!"

When they reached the drawing room, Anne said gently, "Here, dear, take off your cape," and she pulled the garment from Bonnie's shoulders, to fling it along the back of the sofa where she urged her to sit.

Amos had thrown two great pine logs on the fire and now he was adjusting them over the blaze with the brass poker fiercely, sending showers of sparks up the chimney.

"You are so good," Bonnie said brokenly. "None of my old friends have been to see me. Not Mary, nor Grace, nor Alicia—only you and Verity have sent word—have kept my children for me—"

"You did not expect them, did you?" Anne asked, her voice sharpening. "With them, especially Mary, the ringleader, so loyal to that tyrant, George Third?"

"That's not the worst of it," Bonnie said, and now her voice hardened wtih real anger. "Today they commandeered my house, my servants, and took all our horses for the military. A Colonel Hardwicke will live there. And they have given Spencer's store to those terrible Scurlocks. The children and I must live in the small house we shared before Spencer was successful as a merchant—that little wooden box on Trevel Street."

"Oh, Bonnie!" Verity stared aghast. Then with vigor, "You must come and live with us. You cannot manage without servants!"

Bonnie's dark eyes glittered. "I cannot do that, Verity. Lord Bainbridge would not stand for *two* families under this roof. Nay, we must walk where we go and accept the pittance we are allowed by the Scurlocks. Slayton Scurlock was always jealous of Spencer—now he and his Jane will enjoy seeing me struggle to get food and new clothing when the old wears out."

They were all silent under the enormity of the misfortunes that had befallen the cheerful Bonnie and her children. Savarra's heart ached for them. Now she said, "I shall ask my father again to intercede for you, Bonnie. You have always been loyal to the crown and *you* should not be made to pay for Spencer's mistakes."

Bonnie looked up at her, eyes glinting bitterly. "The king be damned. I am loyalist no more for they have shown me no mercy—and I have heard of the atrocities in the back-country. The British are laying waste to us and I shall never—" she paused and came down on the word, *"never* forgive them for the murder of Spencer."

"You have changed," Anne said calmly.

"I have," Bonnie replied grimly. "I changed the moment they brought my poor darling Spencer to me—his face all discolored and swollen, lying in the rough coffin they provided. I shall never forgive his murder."

Savarra looked at her with sorrow and Bonnie returned her gaze defiantly, adding, "I shall do everything in my power to frustrate the British now." Her little laugh was cutting. "No doubt they will find cause to hang me in the end—possibly my children will suffer their abuse as well. I must teach them to be strong and work silently and secretly for our independence."

Savarra thought, *How she has changed, is changing before our very eyes!*

Bonnie put her arms about her children where they sat on either side of her. "My little ones, you are no longer British subjects. You are Americans. Be proud of that."

It was with reluctance the three women bade the Raintrees farewell, with Verity still insisting that they come and live in the big Pair house—but Bonnie was adamant. However, she did allow them to arrange for Amos to drive them home to the small frame house on Trevel Street because the sky had darkened and a cold winter storm was building.

All three of them stood in the door, watching the carriage bowl down the street, each filled with pity for the small but gallant Bonnie. Savarra knew a strange new pity and grief for the bitterness, the alienation and the hammer blows of fate suffered by her formerly bright and gaily voluble friend.

And in her own heart there was a coalescing of diverse emotions, deeply unsettling, and she turned from it in unexpected panic.

Twelve

The weather was bitter as the month of January crept by. Skies were unrelievedly overcast with intermittent rain and some sleet. There was an atmosphere of apprehension and waiting in the big Pair house. All three of the women and even the servants knew that patriot and British troops were maneuvering and clashing violently somewhere beyond Charles Town. The library headquarters were idle, Scott Coyne and his aides having gone to join Lord Bainbridge, from whom no word came as to his whereabouts. There were no impassioned missives from Peter Haverley, which caused Savarra to suffer acute dissatisfaction.

Anne sent Amos to pick up Bonnie Raintree and the children and bring them to dine almost every evening, and it was on the occasion of January twenty-second that Bonnie entered, color in her face for once and a grim rejoicing in her voice as she and the children joined the Pair women in the drawing room that dark evening.

"There has been a great American victory, dear friends," she said, and her big dark eyes glowed with somber joy. She looked into the startled faces before her and added, "I was at the market today, seeking to buy staples for my kitchen," she lifted her shoulders eloquently and inserted, "—having no servants to do that for me now—and I overheard two tories talking of a great battle near Cheraws. Cowpens, they said, a place that has been used for drovers to rest and graze cattle being driven east to market. The Americans met and defeated Tarleton's Legion, Haverley's Fusiliers and hundreds more of the British. Put them completely to route," she finished triumphantly.

"Haverley's Fusiliers?" Savarra said, her throat constricting. "Did they say how many were killed—and if prisoners were taken?"

"They said merely that Cornwallis would avenge the defeat. Already he is in pursuit of Dan Morgan, the American commander." Bonnie's sober mien, so unlike her former sunny face, hardened. "He will never catch them."

"Did they say if Lord Haverley was taken prisoner, Bonnie?" Savarra asked huskily.

Driven, Verity cut in, "And did they mention if Lord Bainbridge was among them?"

"No, but I'll wager they were both in the thick of it," Bonnie replied.

Anne rose and said, "Come, Amos has said dinner is served."

It was a quiet meal, for Bonnie's customary bright chatter had vanished as completely as if it had never been. She talked on, but no longer of the American victory. Instead she spoke of Spencer, how good he had been, how kind to everyone, and a cry for vengeance was in every nuance of her subdued voice.

Afterward, when Amos and the carriage could be heard clattering into the porte-cochere and Bonnie was drawing on her gloves, she said, "Savarra, I hope your father survived, for I think he is a man of some compassion—but as for the rest, I hope the patriots put them all to the sword."

"But not Peter." Savarra spoke the name like a prayer, and silence fell on the others as Bonnie and the children made their quiet farewell.

It was not until two days later when Baltazar came to call that they heard details of the battle at Cowpens and received a stunning shock that lowered their spirits desperately, Verity's and Anne's at once, Savarra's more reluctantly, for she was less able to understand the emotions that shook her.

Baltazar came mid-afternoon of a Sunday. They had all been to church in the morning. Anne was still clad in her decorous black, Verity in dark blue, but Savarra wore scarlet velvet, so tired was she of the mourning clothes of the Pair women. Cotty, Brim and the servants had also attended services and the large noon meal had just been finished when Baltazar knocked at the door. Amos showed him to the drawing room where the ladies were drinking after-dinner coffee, Savarra having finally confessed she preferred it to tea.

The tall man looking at them from the doorway had dark circles beneath the kindly brown eyes and his face was drawn with worry and fatigue. Amos was openly listening as he held Baltazar's hat and great coat.

Baltazar came slowly into the room. " 'Tis a long story, dear ladies, and one not to Mistress Savarra's liking, I fear. Indeed, there is bad news in it for all of us despite the patriot victory."

"As long as Peter Haverley and my father are safe, I don't give a fig for the battle," Savarra said sharply. She had a peculiar sense of foreboding and her hands grew coldly moist with it.

"They escaped unharmed, Savarra," he said heavily, but that did not entirely relieve Savarra's uneasiness.

Anne said quietly, "Amos, see where Cotty Penderford and that Bartholomew Brim are. I do not want them eavesdropping to relay any of this to Lord Bainbridge. Savarra we must, of course, trust." But her eyes on the English girl were wary. "Would you like a brandy, Bowman? Or do you prefer coffee?"

"I think brandy is in order, Anne," he said wearily.

"I'll fetch it, Mistress Pair, then I go see about them Britishers."

Baltazar sighed deeply as he seated himself, stretching his long legs out in front of him as he eased his back into a comfortable position. "Where to begin?" he murmured. Then, "With the good news first, I suppose."

The women sat forward on the edge of their chairs, bodies tense and waiting. Amos poured the brandy immediately and handed the glass to the man, who sipped it gratefully, then the servant disappeared to seek the whereabouts of Brim and Cotty.

Baltazar looked into his brandy glass and said slowly and quietly, "I was in the battle, you know, but I must tell you first how the fight came about. General Greene meant to disturb Cornwallis, and he succeeded when he divided his forces. Cornwallis realized if he struck with his whole force at the Cheraws, Morgan could strike down at Ninety-Six, then east down the Saluda and the Congaree to the Santee, wrecking the chain of British supply posts. If he went after Morgan, Greene could drive down the coast toward Charles Town. So he did what Greene had hoped and ordered out Tarleton and his legion, backed by Haverley's Fusiliers, the 71st Highlanders and your father and his regiment, Savarra. When Cutler and I and Tyler arrived, Morgan had already been warned by Pickens of the British movements. Morgan —God, what a man—chose the spot where we would meet the British. We occupied a gently rising hill, with the unfordable Broad River about three miles to its rear and Thicketty Creek, easily fordable, skirting the woods to the front a mile away."

Baltazar's voice took on strength with the brandy and an excitement threaded it. "Morgan, though crippled with arthritis, hobbled about and gave us all instructions personally. Tarleton was but eight miles away that night—the sixteenth— and he would attack next day and we would await him. Then when the British assault was fifty yards away—not more—the first militia line would fire three volleys. 'Three shots only, boys,' Morgan said—then we would scamper back around the hill to shelter. The second line would repeat the procedure."

Baltazar laughed and continued, "He didn't tell us how far to run. The unfordable Broad River would take care of that. And it went just as he planned." He sipped the brandy reflectively. "Tarleton, his first line halted by Howard's Continentals and Virginia veterans, threw in the Highlanders on his left, along with Haverley's Fusiliers, and while this was going on, Morgan and Pickens, meeting the militia swarming back, rallied them, and Pickens started forward around the west side of the hill. Tarleton, seeing this, ordered a final charge, at the same time alerting his dragoons for the coup de grace. Then three things happened at the same time. Howard's troops, their line reformed, charged the British with bayonets, throwing them back. Pickens' rallied militia came around the hill on the British left to envelop the Highlanders. Washington's—you know of him, a cousin of the commander-in-chief—dragoons, returning from their original chase of the 17th Dragoons—and we three on horseback were with Washington's Legion—came slashing up from the British right rear into Tarleton's light infantry and legion foot soldiers."

Baltazar laughed drily. "I saw Tarleton's face, and his

shock and rage did my heart good as he ordered his legion cavalry into the melee. But they, too, saw what he was witnessing and they had enough. Turning tail, they galloped off the field. Tarleton and Haverley, with a handful of men, attempted to engage in a cut-and-slash personal encounter, then they both drew rein and followed their fleeing horsemen. And Morgan had won a complete double envelopment—" Baltazar's voice slowed, grew somber and reluctant. " 'Twas Belion and McLean who were engaging Tarleton and Haverley, and they were not ready to let them go. They pursued them beyond my line of vision."

"Surely—surely Cutler and Tyler are all right?" Anne asked tautly.

"That is the unfortunate news," Baltazar said heavily. "I got the word on what happened to them from a young Britisher I met when I was traveling back to Charles Town— as the loyal man of the crown I must appear."

"What has happened to them?" Anne's voice was thick.

"The lad said they followed Tarleton and Haverley so far McLean cut off the tip of Tarleton's finger as they fought, each with a sabre, but in moments they were enveloped and disarmed." Baltazar downed the last of his brandy and his voice was harsh. "The lad said that Haverley drew his saber on McLean after he was disarmed and would have severed his head from his body had not one of his officers intervened. As it was, McLean has suffered a cut on his left arm. Haverley was slashing at him like a madman."

Savarra's foreboding had prepared her for this news, but not the impact it had on her. She swallowed thickly, remembering Peter's vow to kill McLean. *Now McLean was his prisoner!*

"Oh," it was like a moan from Verity. "What will they do with them?"

"They have brought them back to Charles Town, where they will have a brief trial and then they will be hung—in the square." Baltazar's voice was filled with grief and frustration. "Already the court of sequestration has seized Belion House and the plantation, as well as Cutler's brokerage, his house and properties."

"Is there nothing we can do?" Anne asked brokenly.

"I dare not try to see them for I am known as a lifetime friend. I have had to let it out that I am aghast at their so called crimes and am totally unforgiving." He sighed deeply. "Lord Bainbridge arrives in Charles Town soon, 'tis said. Perhaps you ladies could prevail on him to intercede in their behalf." His hopeful eyes were on Savarra.

She said, "If they hung Spencer Raintree for merely writing of British troop movements—while Cutler McLean and Tyler Belion have not only posed as loyalists, but have engaged in battle and killed British soldiers—there is nothing my father can or will do." Savarra's eyes were very blue and unfathomable.

"I fear she is right," Baltazar replied slowly. "Our young friends will die on the gallows."

Verity put her face in her hands and her shoulders shook with silent weeping. Anne Pair's features were chiseled in marble, her great dark eyes stricken.

Savarra was thinking, *Peter will have his revenge. McLean will die.* And at the thought a thickness came into her throat. She did not like McLean. Indeed, she despised him. There was the humiliating episode in the forest that would at last be buried with him. Yet there was a strange rebellion taking place within her as she thought of his imminent death. It was her concern for the grief it would bring Verity and her mother, she told herself. She had let them become too dear to her.

Thus despite the American victory at Cowpens, tragedy blotted out that victory. Baltazar departed, his great shoulders sagging and his face grim.

Verity and Anne made every effort to see the two prisoners, but they were stiffly refused by the British guards. No patriots would be allowed to see the two men. Their crimes were unspeakable, parading as loyalists, relaying information to the rebels, actually fighting on the side of the criminal partisans, the captain of the guards told the two women sternly.

"You may see them—at the end of a rope," he finished coldly. "General Bainbridge and Colonel Haverley and others connected with the capture will be in town soon, and the trial awaits only their arrival."

Anne and Verity departed, holding back their tears until they entered the carriage. Savarra, when they related this to her, found herself preoccupied with the thought of the tall pair in the dismal jail she had passed often on her way to the dressmaker. It was hard to conceive of those powerful men hanging lifeless from the murderous gallows that hunched over the square.

She and Cotty drove by it a few days later on their way to Madame Flammarion's, where Savarra's trousseau was being created. She looked at the gaunt scaffolding, then turned her head quickly, the strange, unnameable emotion boiling up in her once more. She tried to fight it down, but there was swelling in her mind an impossible desire so fiercely that she could not wrestle it back into her subconscious. It rose irresistibly and it was warm as sunlight, as persuasive as music.

She was silent under the spell of it while Cotty chattered happily about the gowns that were taking shape under Madame Flammarion's talented fingers.

Savarra was barely eighteen now, young and in many ways untried, but she realized suddenly that she had reached a mature and irrevocable decision. She could not stand by and see Cutler McLean and Tyler Belion executed. With her acceptance of this fact, a plan began to form in her mind so easily that she felt it had been there since the moment Baltazar had told them of the capture of the two men.

When the two girls reached home, Cotty went up to Savarra's room to put away the number of lace and silk garments that had been ready for them at the dressmaker's. Savarra herself went directly to Verity where she was reading, in her own room near a cheerful fire. The American girl looked up in surprise, for Savarra in her haste had not knocked.

She came directly to the point. "Verity, we cannot stand by and allow Cutler McLean and Tyler Belion to hang."

Verity's dark eyes widened slowly. There was a touch of fear in them. "You—mean you think we can persuade your father to have them—shipped to St. Augustine?"

"I do not think my father will intervene at all for them." Savarra spoke with grim impatience. "Indeed, he cannot, for their crimes against the crown are too great. Neither tears nor tantrums would move him."

"Then there is nothing we can do," Verity said with quiet despair.

"Yes there is," Savarra replied firmly. "I am a brigadier's daughter and more. I enjoy the privileges of an Englishwoman of the nobility. They will let *me* in to see them—if I come to gloat! I will tell the guards that their prisoners had fooled me and I wish to throw their capture and certain death in their faces."

"What good would that do?"

"A great deal if I have two pistols secreted beneath the panniers of my skirts. We could put them in bags and I would tie them about my waist and beneath the panniers, one on each side. I could slip them to the men unseen—no one would suspect at all. Then we could arrange with Baltazar to have horses ready that night, handily ridden by some of McLean's warehouse workers. The two could seize the mounts and ride to safety in the swamps—only this time, there would be no return to Charles Town." Savarra bit her lip thoughtfully and added, "And we must do it soon or my father and Peter will be here and it will be too late."

Verity's lips had parted in astonished admiration, but she was silent so long that Savarra said irritably, "Well? Do you not think it would succeed?"

"I think it's a masterpiece of ingenuity, Savarra, but I am puzzled. Why are you willing to do it, when you dislike them so very much?"

Frustration and anger followed each other across Savarra's slender face and her straight nose wrinkled in displeasure as she shrugged. "I really do not know why I am doing it. For you and your mother, I guess." She frowned. "I know only that I cannot see them die—so horribly."

The following day found her dressing with care. On her bed lay two heavy cotton bags, drawn tight at the top. Inside each of them was a villainously large pistol and smaller bags of powder and bullets. They were quite heavy when Baltazar had handed them to her in the late evening of the day before.

He had not asked her why she was doing this, for which she was profoundly grateful. He had said merely, "If this escape is successful, my dear, I shall not be able to visit and tell you about it, for I fear I am becoming suspect myself. I must limit my visits to the Pair house, so it will be several days before I can call."

Savarra had nodded uneasily. She could not escape the feeling that she was betraying not only Great Britain, but her father and Peter as well, yet she could not stop herself.

After she had gone to bed, she tried to rationalize her desperate gamble for these two partisans by remembering how much blood had already been shed. After all, she was only preventing the shedding of more. But it went deeper than that and she knew it.

In the end, she came up against the iron fact that her

sympathies were with the Americans and she was helpless to argue against it. It had not come to her in a blinding flash, but rather like the inevitable progress of a glacier, slow but inexorable and not to be halted. These embattled people had touched some sensitive core deep within her and she no longer wanted Britain to win—even though she knew inevitably they would. She thought of Peter Haverley and her desire to see him come out of the service with honor. She reflected on her courageous father, but she had the suspicion that Lord Bainbridge was not entirely in sympathy with his country's course of action himself. She sensed that he admired these gallant Americans and understood their yearning to be free.

She remembered when he had bade her goodbye earlier this month, before he went to the ill-fated rendezvous at Cowpens, he said, "Savarra, I find myself recalling what Edmund Burke said nearly six years ago," and he had repeated the words she had spoken only weeks ago to Verity. He had laughed dryly then and kissed her cheek lightly and, with a swirl of his cape, was gone into the cold Carolina dawn. Her thoughts slowed at last and she slept, a dreamless and deep sleep.

Now, in the mid-morning sunlight from the tall south windows, she congratulated herself for having sent Cotty off in the curricle with Calhoon driving to fetch more finished lingerie from Madame Flammarion. Anne had arranged for Brim to go on horseback to the butcher shop on the outskirts of town to purchase meats and fowl. And now she was alone and wrestling with the lacings on her bodice when Verity knocked on her door.

At her response, the American girl came directly to her. "Here, let me help you, Savarra," and Verity finished the lacing and adjusted the thick folds of the skirts. It was a sweet dress made of light blue lute-string, with matching panniers, silky full and rich at each side. They stood firmly out over her many petticoats. She tucked a kerchief of delicate white gauze about her bare neck and the dress became demure. Then she looked speculatively at the draw-string bags containing the pistols and ammunition.

"I have brought stout cord," Verity said quietly, "and we will suspend the bags with it. It can be tied about your waist beneath the panniers and none will be the wiser."

For the first time, Savarra let a frightening thought creep into her mind. What if they caught her? What would be her punishment? Would they hang all three of them? After the first jolt of fear, she resisted the thought forcibly. She would *not* fail!

She and Verity took up the cord and tied the cotton sacks containing the weapons to it, so that one was at each side, with the cord about her waist and under the panniers. It was as if her clothing were designed for just such a secret. The cord was tied beneath her sash and the pistols and munitions nestled beneath the full panniers so smoothly it was impossible to tell they were there. Savarra drew a long breath of relief.

"You were so clever to think of this, Savarra," Verity said admiringly. "You are not afraid?"

"Of course I am—a little," she replied. But her fear was lost in a wild sort of elation that now filled her, an anxiety to get about the mission as she rehearsed in her mind the exact words she would say to the guards, the cruel and triumphant remarks she would hurl at McLean and Belion. She suddenly hoped with feverish intensity that the guards would leave them alone for a few moments while she taunted the two—giving her time to slip the bags to the prisoners. If they did not, she would have to do it in some surreptitious manner, she thought ruthlessly, for she did not mean to fail.

When she and Verity walked from the room, she could feel the weight of the heavy pistols swinging unseen beneath the elegant material of her dress at her hips.

"I wish I could accompany you," Verity said quietly. "You are very brave and I admire you greatly."

Savarra looked at the American girl with a touch of surprise at the passionate sincerity in her face. Verity added, in a low voice, "You will be one of us indeed when you have done this, you know. Your fiancé would never forgive you."

Savarra said calmly, "He shall never know. And in a short while, we will be back in England. I fear you Americans cannot win, Verity, but there has been death enough among you—I can bear no more."

Amos was waiting at the porte-cochere with the carriage. Verity and Anne threw shawls about their shoulders and accompanied her to it. Anne's face looked pinched and drawn, but her eyes, for the first time, held something of warmth and hope when she looked into Savarra's.

"God be with you and see to your success," she whispered as the girl, assisted by Amos, stepped into the carriage. The little black closed the door and climbed back on the box, calling to the horses, "Ho!" and they were out of the shell drive and clattering noisily on the cobblestones. It was very cold in the carriage, for the window curtains were rolled up at her request, but she drew her fur-lined cloak about her and tucked her gloved hands under it and watched the houses unroll beside her.

Soon they were at the square, and this time she looked defiantly at the gibbet standing there in the bleak and pale sunlight. *I will cheat you of your victims this time,* she thought determinedly as they swung by and on down toward the market place above the wharves.

The carriage rolled to a stop before the small and grim jail. Two British soldiers stood beside the door, leaning against a dull red-brick wall, their guns slack in their hands. They straightened up swiftly as the carriage drew to a halt and they viewed her with admiration mingling with deference. She was glad she had taken such pains with her appearance. But she gave them an arrogant and quelling glance as Amos assisted her from the carriage.

They appeared uncertain as she swept up narrow brick steps. Suddenly one of them swung forward and opened the door for her, his eyes full of questions at the sight of so obvious a lady at a jail, but she frowned forbiddingly as she entered into the ugly little hall where two more soldiers stood beside a door.

"Where is the captain of the guards?" she asked insolently.

"In there—in his office, mistress," one of the two replied quickly.

Without a word she stepped into the drab room, where a young man with a bulldog's jaw and narrow light eyes looked up from behind a desk and rose immediately.

Before he could say a word, Savarra spoke imperiously. "I am Mistress Bainbridge, daughter of Lord Bainbridge. You have the two traitors here—Belion and McLean?"

"Why—yes, Mistress Bainbridge. They await trial after your father—and others—arrive."

"Good," she said with satisfaction. "Captain, those two men came over on the same ship with me from England. They have dined at the Pair home with my father and me while masquerading as good loyalists. I was forced to be hospitable to them, the traitors!" She drew her dark tilted brows together, allowing bitter fury to take her voice, "I spoke with those—infamous men and accorded them my courtesy, when all the time they were lying, working against my father and our soldiers, the blackguards! Hanging will be much too good for them!"

"Indeed it will, Mistress Bainbridge," the captain said, smiling now, his eyes on her slender face appreciative.

"I have come here for the sole purpose of throwing my disgust and contempt into their faces. It will partly assuage having been duped by two such scoundrels." Her voice was scathing, "I cannot let them die without showing them my disrespect—telling them what wretched and vile creatures they are."

The young captain's smile broadened, his bulldog jaw relaxing. "A natural desire, Mistress Bainbridge, a natural desire! Come, I will escort you to their cell."

The jail consisted of several small rooms along a dank hall, each with a heavy door affixed with strong bolts. The air was rank with the odor of unwashed bodies. Those few doors that were open revealed a small high window in each cell, barred by iron rods. They were black, comfortless, with dirty pallets on the floor and nothing to sit on, no sign of facilities for washing up. At the stench about the place, her small nostrils flared in distaste. Most of the doors were closed with heavy iron bolts, and there was an oppressive silence in the dingy hall. She felt the heavy swing of the pistols and ammunition beneath her panniers as she followed the captain to the end of the hall. Her heart beat fast and heavily and her palms were moist, but she assured herself the pistols were completely hidden beneath her skirts and cloak.

The captain released the bolt on the end door and flung it wide. Belion and McLean were standing at the window, straining to peer out. When they turned, she saw how dirty and unkempt they were, their clothing soiled and ragged, several days' growth of beard dark on their lean faces. But there was nothing dispirited in those hawk-like faces. The life-fire in them blazed brightly as they rested on her. She noted the dirty and bloody bandage on McLean's upper left arm. The leather shirt he wore had been cut away around it, but he seemed to handle the arm easily.

He immediately gave her a low, ironic bow. "Mistress Bainbridge, what an honor!"

"Scum!" she spat. "I have come to tell you what I think of you—for all those lies you perpetrated on me and my father all these months. What scoundrels you are—what blackguards!"

The captain laughed softly behind her and she wondered

in brief panic what ruse she could employ to get rid of him. She decided swiftly that a forthright request might serve the purpose.

She turned and with a queenly tilt of her head, said, "Captain, you may leave us. I would rather you did not hear the unladylike things I plan to say to these—these poltroons."

The captain appeared taken aback. "But Mistress Bainbridge, these are desperate men—"

"They are unarmed, are they not?"

"Well, yes—but I can't leave you alone with them."

"I can scream very loudly, I assure you, captain, and if they make one untoward move while I am dressing them down, you may be sure I will scream at the top of my lungs." She whirled on the two and began, "The first night at the Pairs', when the two of you spoke so warmly of your relations with Britain, telling of all the things you were doing to serve the crown—I should have known those were lies! Hanging is far too easy a punishment for you!"

The capain backed away. "Mistress, you surely have a sharp tongue, but I must wait right down the hall where I can hear you—"

"*They* haven't heard the last of me yet, captain. Run along." And the officer moved reluctantly into the hall, saying over his shoulder, "Mistress Bainbridge, I don't think you should stay more than ten minutes in such company."

"I do not plan to stay that long," she replied sharply. "I can get it said in much less than ten minutes."

When he had stepped back into the corridor, she said vehemently, "When I think of the courtesies accorded you, and all the time you were planning our murder!" she cried loudly, and began swiftly untying the cord about her waist and pulled the bags containing the pistols and ammunition from beneath her panniers. She whispered urgently, "Here is a pistol and ammunition for both of you—Baltazar will see that two men will be passing by—loitering if they must—on horses at moondown outside the jail. You can seize the horses and escape into the swamps."

Her voice rose with fresh anger, "Oh, don't tell me you did not plan our murders! And I shall be at the square to see you dangle from the gallows—"

Neither man by so much as the blink of an eye registered surprise, but seized the weapons in the sacks and hurriedly secreted them beneath the filthy pallets. Then McLean said loudly, "Madame, I always thought you British were an arrogant race, overly impressed with your own importance, and you have proved it."

Savarra replied stridently, "And you low Americans are unable to recognize and be ruled by your betters. How common you are! And dishonest besides. I am greatly relieved to let you know there is one in Charles Town who knows you well for the wretches you are. 'Twill be good riddance when they hang you!" She heard the captain's footsteps returning and she added shrilly, "And they can't hang you soon enough for me. Remember, I shall be there, watching you kick to the end and return home rejoicing!"

McLean's voice was loud and harsh, "Others will take our our place, madame, and the British will leave our land a defeated army."

"Captain!" Savarra called, "I have had my say. You may come and lock these criminals up once more," and she drew her skirts fastidiously aside as the captain approached. As the two left the cell, the captain locked the door once more and Savarra added, "You have given me a great deal of satisfaction, sir. I could not let them die without knowing the low esteem, indeed the hatred, I have for them."

The captain was very respectful and saw her to her carriage, assuring her, "The trial will be very brief, Mistress Bainbridge. I'll wager they'll be stretched at the end of a rope before the week is out. A courier came in this morning with a dispatch informing us your father will be here no later than tomorrow evening."

She turned at the carriage step and gave him a warm, brilliant smile, her eyes vivid in the morning sunlight. She said throatily, "Captain, you *do* give me good news! It has been weeks since I saw my dear father."

Completely enchanted, the captain fumbled. "Well—ah—now, you have been good news to me, mistress." The guards against the faded brick walls stood very straight now, muskets held at their sides.

Savarra permitted her smile to fall upon them briefly, then fluttering her lashes, she added softly, "I really don't believe I shall sleep well until those rebels are hung, captain—but at least I have the satisfaction of remembering how they looked before they died, wretched and *conquered*."

"You may be sure you are safe from them, Mistress Bainbridge," the captain said earnestly, his jaw thrust out prominently. "We watch over them every moment."

Amos took her arm stiffly and, with the captain jousting

for position to assist, Savarra, with skirts aswirl, entered the sleekly polished carriage. Within minutes, they were swaying noisily down the street and Savarra leaned back against the slick leather cushions.

She felt a touch lightheaded and rather weak. Drawing a long breath, she went back over her actions carefully. The two men had been very dirty and they stank, she recalled, wrinkling her straight nose—or had that been the pervasive overall odor of the jail? She took a scented handkerchief from her reticule and put it to her nostrils. It seemed she could smell it still. Even the captain had carried it to the carriage in his clothing. Ugh. What a terrible place! She could not stem a rejoicing at the thought that the two bearded and unkempt men would be breathing fresh, crisp air in less than twelve hours if all went well. *If all went well.* It *must* go well, she told herself, and looked resolutely out the window at the Cooper River, sparkling coldly in the late morning air. Where were Francis Marion and his men? In the fastnesses of those towering cypress and pine forests that spread upcountry from this broad river, surely. McLean and Belion would find them, she thought comfortingly.

So swiftly had she accomplished her purpose that neither Cotty nor Brim had returned. Entering the house as Amos opened the door for her, she was met by a breathless Verity. Anne was just behind her and, before Savarra could speak, the coffee-tan faces of Monique, Tiqua and Frances were peering from the hall door. Primrose, shorter and fatter, was peeping frantically from behind them, first on one side, then the other.

"Did you—were you able to give them the pistols?" Verity asked as Amos helped her off with her cloak.

Savarra could hear Calhoon driving the carriage and horses to the stables at the rear. "Yes," she replied, her composure restored entirely by now. "And I must say they acted just as if they had been expecting me." She frowned slightly. "Do you suppose Bowman Baltazar got word to them I was coming?"

"Nay," Anne said. "Bowman has not dared go near the place. For little or nothing they would arrest him on the strength of his friendship with the two."

"Then they are cool heads," responded Savarra, "for they took the guns and hid them beneath their pallets—phew! it smelled dreadful in there—as if they had been rehearsing for it."

"Tiqua, bring hot coffee into the drawing room," Anne said as Savarra drew off her gloves and put them into her reticule. Anne added, "Amos, please take those up to Mistress Bainbridge's room so that Cotty will be none the wiser when she and Brim return."

Savarra handed Amos the embroidered wine-red velvet article and asked abruptly, "Do *all* the servants know what I have done?" She glanced at the dark faces that were now disappearing.

"All our people know what you have done," Anne replied with a little smile, "and their opinion of you has risen accordingly."

"You can imagine what my father's opinion would be, to say nothing of Lord Haverley and Lord Cornwallis," Savarra said tartly. "I hope they will hold their tongues."

Amos, on his way to the stairs, paused and turned surprised eyes on her. "You ain't need worry, miss," he said, outrage in his voice. "We are *Americans*." And he took the stairs two at a time.

The two younger women followed Anne into the drawing room and seated themselves together on the sofa before the glowing fire, where Savarra launched into a detailed account of her brief and sucessful visit to the jail.

"And Baltazar cannot come to tell us if the escape is accomplished," she finished regretfully, taking the coffee Tiqua served.

"I will send Calhoon down into the marketplace," Anne said. "That youngster appears so ingenuous—he is a gold mine of information on what happens in this city. Everyone confides in him, and that innocent look he wears is strictly sham. He can wheedle any information he chooses by employing it."

"It's the waiting that will be so hard," Verity said, impatience mingling with apprehension in her voice. "How can we endure it all night and tomorrow—for you know it will be noon before Calhoon can learn a thing."

"I'll send Amos, too," Anne said with sudden decision. "What one won't get, the other will while they are buying vegetables and staples for us."

"Mr. Baltazar said moondown, and that was what I told the men," Savarra said, her own impatience burgeoning.

"And the captain said your father will return tomorrow?" Verity asked, her face carefully smooth, but her dark eyes brilliant.

Savarra was conscious once more of the indefinable thread that existed between this girl and her father. Instinct told her what it was and she thought, poor Belion, poor Verity, for Lord Bainbridge would never marry again. Now she said shortly, "Yes, and Peter Haverley too, you know."

"Would you like to have Lord Haverley as a guest in our home while he is here?" Anne asked slowly, and it was obvious that it cost her something to make the offer.

"That would be very nice," Savarra replied. She was foolish to imagine that Peter would not behave—might come to her bedroom—in a house full of people, including her father, for whom he had a healthy respect. And with Peter in the Pair house, they could make plans for the wedding, which should be very soon now. Then she would be removed from temptations to help the rebels, her sympathies would not be stirred so deeply by being too close to the intrigues that filled the Pair home. She assuaged herself with the thought that she would then be able to put all of this out of her mind.

Tiqua returned, bearing a tray of fresh, steaming coffee fragrant on the air and the pitcher of thick, rich cream beside the sugar bowl.

After they had refilled their thin china cups, Anne Pair said slowly, "Before Cotty and Brim return, Savarra, I must tell you how grateful to you I am. To your father for having brought my beloved husband's body home for burial—and for your silence—and your aid in helping our lifetime friends escape."

"They haven't escaped yet," Savarra said cautiously.

"But they will," Anne replied a touch grimly. "I have a sixth sense about it. By this time tomorrow, they will be safe in the forests and swamps of the backcountry."

"I hope you are right," Savarra replied. Ah, well, she told herself silently, sipping the richly delicious brew, I shall be well out of it in a few weeks—married to Peter in Camden and then, in a few months, home to England. Why, she thought with fresh satisfaction, I will be Lady Haverley, mistress of mansions, both country and town. It would be a gay life of parties, balls and soirees, and she would float along on the tide of it like a brightly beautiful butterfly, with nothing more desperate to disturb her than the fitting of fine clothing. And Peter—dear Peter!—would be an attentive and tender lover. A thrill shot through her at the thought, and she was cheerful with the Pair women throughout the rest of the long day.

But when she retired that night, sleep would not come. Though she tried to put Belion and McLean from her mind determinedly, the sound of the great clock in the hall below struck the hours, leaving her no respite. When at last the sonorous chimes announced it was midnight, she sat up in bed, looking at the dying coals on the hearth. How would the two prisoners effect their escape? Would they call the guards and shoot them? She thought of the young soldiers who guarded the jail. They could be killed and their blood would be on her hands—ah, but if McLean and Belion were hanged, their blood would be on her hands as well.

She buried her head in the soft down pillow and squeezed her eyes tight. She lay tense and anxious until the clock struck one, then two and at last three.

Then at last relief crept through her—it must be over now. Either the two prisoners had been killed in their attempt to escape, a thought which made her heart fall sickeningly, or they were on their way to Francis Marion's brigade.

At last, she slept, but it was an uneasy, fitful sleep and, though she had determinedly visualized Peter's chiseled and beautiful features, it was of McLean she dreamed. In the dream, Peter was kissing her and it was their wedding night, but suddenly she pulled away and it was McLean who held her, drawing her back to him with that tender, yet cynical, smile upon his lips. When she fought harder to pull away, his arms drew her tightly against him and he was kissing her. Once more the wild excitement that had engulfed her in the forest that deep night was upon her and she abandoned herself to it.

She woke, sweating, heart racing wildly, and cursed the moments she had spent in the man's arms. She could not go back to sleep and rose in the dim dawn, feeling hollow-eyed and anxious.

The morning dragged interminably. Calhoon and Amos were both in the market place and all three of the women were in a fever waiting their return. Cotty helped Savarra wash her long, thick hair, tying it up in cotton strips while it was still damp, to make it curly. Cotty was determined to create a suitable upswept pompadour later in the day.

"You want to look your prettiest, mistress," she prattled, "with Lord Bainbridge and Lord Haverley comin' in sometime today." Then reprovingly, "I think 'tis so lovely when we put the padding in and powder it—gives you to be taller and such a lady."

"I hate that, Cotty," Savarra said impatiently. " 'Tis out of fashion, too, or is going out of fashion, and I mean to help it fall into disrepute."

Cotty sighed, "You're very set, mistress. Ah, well, you'll still be beautiful when they arrive! An' I must put out a washin' fer you. I've a batch of fine chemises an' petticoats."

By noon, Savarra, coiffed, bathed and dressed in her favorite apricot frock with a gauze kerchief tucked about the breast, went down to the noon meal with the Pair ladies.

It was a silent and somewhat tense meal, for neither Calhoon nor Amos had returned and all three of the women were on tenterhooks to know what happened in the night.

But shortly after they finished and all were in the small sitting room before the fire, the two black men returned. Unfortunately, Cotty entered just before Amos.

"Mistress Savarra, would you like me to get water heated fer to bathe tonight—before Lord Bainbridge an' your fiancé come in tomorrow?" Cotty was making an effort to curb her cockney accent since her arrival in America and doing very well at it, Savarra thought distractedly, seeing Amos just behind her.

Amos looked at the little maidservant and remarked, "Mistress Pair, do you come inter the kitchen, me an' Calhoon would show you what we picked out at the market."

Anne and Verity rose at one, and Savarra went to Cotty swiftly, saying "Yes, Cotty, and I want you to mend some of my favorite petticoats this morning." She caught the girl's arm, pulling her toward the stairs. "And where is Brim, Cotty?"

"He's in the kitchen, tellin' Primrose how to baste a goose," Cotty said plaintively, having no apparent desire to sew.

"Well, get him before you go upstairs," Savarra told her impatiently, "and tell him to get my father's wardrobe in good order for his arrival."

"But he's done that—"

"I'll wager he hasn't brushed them in over a week, Cotty. Get him." Savarra watched the girl follow after Anne, Verity and Amos. She was in a ferment to know the news the two men were so obviously bursting to tell them, but she could not until Brim and Cotty were safely upstairs.

Suddenly she went after the girl, following her to the kitchen, where Anne was pretending to make a careful examination of the meats and vegetables brought in by Amos and Calhoon. Savarra then elaborated on her instructions to Cotty and Brim. Brim was to air out two uniforms and press them, Cotty was to rearrange two of Savarra's bureau drawers, choosing some of the better garments that might be suitable to take with them to Camden.

When at last the two English servants were gone, Savarra turned to Amos, "Now tell us at once—"

"Wait!" Anne held up a warning hand. "Let us be sure they are out of hearing—"

Tiqua, like a dark shadow slipped down the hall and was gone but a moment. "They clear up zee stairs, madame," she said breathlessly.

Anne said low, "Tell us but one thing first—did they escape?"

"Yes'm," chorused Amos and Calhoon. Then Calhoon gave a small hoot of laughter, adding, "An' them British soldiers is in a terrible state, sendin' out patrols to try an' find 'em."

All the servants laughed softly and Anne's smile was grimly pressed. "Now, Amos, tell us the details." She looked directly at the older man.

Monique, Tiqua, Frances and Primrose abandoned any effort to attend their chores and drew near as Amos launched into his story. "Well'm, I heared two soldiers talkin' in the market place—"

"An' I went right up ter the bunch what was millin' around the jail—" Calhoon put in.

"You wait till I tell mine," Amos cut in angrily. "They was a big one with yeller hair an' a little squatty one what was doin' most of the talkin'. He say how Cap'n McLean an' Mist' Belion raise a big ruckus after midnight, hollerin' fer water an' sayin' they was big rats in their cells. When the English cap'n o' the guards come an' open the door, Cap'n McLean pulled his pistol on him an' Mist' Belion clamp a arm around his neck an' they helt him as a kind o' shield as they come out o' the jail."

Calhoon cut in excitedly, "But when they got ter the front door, two soldiers begun ter shoot—an' Cap'n McLean, he fire his pistol an' shoot one in the shoulder an' t'other in the laig. Then they run acrost the street, with Mist' Belion still hol'in' the English cap'n—"

"An' them two horsemen Mist' Baltazar arrange fer was happenin' by," Amos interrupted, giving Calhoon a fierce scowl. "An' Mist' Belion let go that cap'n who scuttle back ter the jail, hollerin' fer help. But by that time, Cap'n McLean an' Mist' Belion helt them riders at gunpoint and took their horses. Them two rid off down the street towards Camden like the devil was after 'em—an' the moon bein' down, it was so dark them British soldiers can't see nothin'!"

There was a little silence and Calhoon, with a deferential glance at the older Amos, said tentatively, "An' them soldiers around the jail say the cap'n o' the guards run to the garrison an' rouse up the mens an' they was half-asleep, but they got a troop mounted and took after the Cap'n an' Mist' Belion, but they was long gone. They say the troop come back about an hour after, mighty tard, an' say can't nobody find nothin' in them damned swamps."

Amos put in with a satisfied grin at Savarra, "It's created an' awful hooraw an' the rumor is that some patriot done smuggle them pistols inter them through the winders, 'cause the Cap'n an' Mist' Belion had been standin' by those winders, the English captain say, every day since they been caught, jes' like they was expectin' somebody."

Calhoon added, "All them redcoats is mighty uneasy now, 'cause Gen'l Bainbridge an' Colonel Haverley due in town any minute. They goin' to be fit to be tied."

Savarra's heart took a sudden plunge, but her relief at the escape of the two men was not to be denied. Her father and Peter would never know what she had done, she thought defiantly. She would be bland as butter with both of them and completely disinterested at the escape of the patriot prisoners.

Verity's heart on the other hand rose and beat fast with joy. Not only had her friends escaped the noose, but her lover would be home by evening. She could scarcely keep from singing aloud as the day wore on and evening drew near. The whole atmosphere of the house had lifted as if a murky cloud had blown away, and to add to the felicity the sun had come out from earlier clouds and the late January day was bright and cool. Fires in the house leaped and crackled, vividly orange and red in the great fireplaces. Anne Pair had made unaccustomed efforts to make the house warm and welcoming for the two British lords.

That night, Lord Bainbridge and Peter Haverley blew in on a strong easterly wind that had risen in the evening. They were late, for they had not come directly to the house but had stopped off at the jail and at Cornwallis's headquarters, where the men were still in a turmoil over the escape of the two patriots. Thus when they entered the door with the cold, clean air swirling about them, they were angry and solemn. Peter's handsome mouth was set in especially bitter lines.

Anne had arranged for a sumptuous meal, complete with the roast goose, and Amos stood by to take their heavy capes and black tricornes. Brim and Cotty were smiling in happy expectancy, while the three women met the two English officers in the hall.

Peter came directly to Savarra and, with his cape fanning out about him, caught her in a strong embrace. His clothing was cold against her and the smell of the out-of-doors was clean in her nostrils. He kissed her deeply, without attention to those about him, uncaring whether they approved or disapproved. She clung to him, hoping that what she had done for the patriots would in no way make things harder for him. His determination to kill McLean was truly abhorrent to her and she felt that, were he successful, it would leave a scar on their relationship that would never fade.

After embracing his daughter briefly, Lord Bainbridge spoke of what was uppermost in all their minds. "It seems we have returned to disaster. Did you ladies know that McLean and Belion are spies and traitors and they have by nefarious means escaped? 'Tis said they received pistols through the window in the dead of night and fought their way out of the jail."

"We heard. The servants picked it up at the market this morning, father," Savarra replied. "'Tis a dreadful thing—"

"They shall not escape," Haverley cut in with cold certainty. "I shall track them down in their hiding places." His eyes swung to Lord Bainbridge accusingly. "You should have let me finish off McLean at the moment of capture. Then we would have only Belion to contend with now."

Lord Bainbridge gave him a level and glacial stare. "No honorable British soldier slaughters an unarmed man. As a lieutenant colonel in His Majesty's service, you would have disgraced your commission and your country had I not stayed your arm."

Haverley's face reddened. "He was certainly trying to kill me right up to the moment he was seized, and in the melee about us none would have known he was unarmed. After all, he did have a pistol in his belt—"

"I would have known," Lord Bainbridge said, "and his pistol was removed as you swung your saber on him."

"Anyway, you are both home safely," Savarra put in

hastily, her eyes filled with love for the two men before her. They looked trim and clean, well-gotten-up after so long a ride as the one from Camden.

"I suppose," Lord Bainbridge remarked dryly to Anne and Verity as they made their way to the drawing room, "that you two ladies are rejoicing over the escape of your friends?"

"Indeed we are," Anne said serenely. "I shall not pretend otherwise. I have known those young men all their lives and I am devoted to them—though I must confess, I did not know of their patriot activities."

Entering the drawing room where the lamps were lit and the hearth threw out its red glow, Lord Bainbridge laughed with a touch of irony. "And now that you do?"

"I am proud of them," Anne replied steadfastly, taking up a polished silver bell from a gleaming table beside the sofa. She rang it and replaced it, saying, "Will you gentlemen have a brandy before dinner?"

"That would be more than satisfactory," Peter Haverley said, smiling at Savarra as Lord Bainbridge murmured assent.

"Knowing you would arrive this evening, we have prepared not only a roast goose for you," Verity said blithely, "but side dishes to make your mouth water."

He sighed audibly. "That sounds delightful—after weeks in the field on army rations, Mistress Verity. Colonel Haverley and I will do full justice to it, you may be sure."

Tiqua entered, and the gentle murmur of Anne's voice could be heard asking the young woman to serve brandy to the men and wine for the ladies.

Lord Bainbridge gave Verity a curiously piercing glance as he asked suddenly, "How did you know we would be here this evening?"

"Why—"

Savarra said swiftly, "I had to learn it from one of Colonel Balfour's aides, father." Her eyes on first Lord Bainbridge and then her fiancé were reproachful and faintly hurt. "Really, it seems to me that you or Peter could have written us."

Both men said defensively that they had meant to write, then Peter finished with a mischievous grin, "But actually, darling, I had looked forward to surprising you."

Tiqua returned and served brandy to the men and extended the slender crystal wine glasses to the ladies. In the interim, Verity noted that Peter Haverley sat very close to Savarra on the brocaded satin love seat. The young girl's face was ablaze with love for him, but Verity looked into that British face and, despite the undeniable look of good blood in it, she felt a quiver of repulsion. But it was his eyes, clear and golden hazel, that made Verity's heart sink when she caught them in passing.

They talked desultorily of the battle at Cowpens while they drank their liqueurs. Lord Bainbridge remarked, "It was a brilliantly executed maneuver on the part of Morgan, but not enough. We shall engage them again and in the end we will be victorious."

Verity and Anne kept bland faces during the conversation, but Lord Bainbridge appeared restive and somewhat pained. Later, the talk drifted inevitably back to the escape of the two patriots and they discussed it over the sumptuous meal that had been prepared.

Lord Bainbridge said abruptly, "The captain of the guard at the jail tells me that you came by to vent your spleen on Belion and McLean the morning of their escape, Savarra." He put his napkin to his lips and laid his fork and knife across the empty plate before him.

Savarra grimaced with obvious disgust. "When I found out they were traitors and liars, I couldn't resist throwing their capture in their faces. You know how I've always felt about them, father—I never liked them. They should have been hung long ago!"

Haverley smiled at her tenderly. "My little firebrand! I wish I could have heard you."

"You would have thought me no lady—I dressed them down properly!"

" 'Tis your fire and spirit—and the untouched innocence of you—that I love so dearly," Haverley said, his golden eyes admiring.

Again Savarra's heart thumped uncomfortably fast. *Her innocence!* The devil with it, she thought furiously, wondering if there would ever be an end to the reminders of those moments in McLean's arms.

Through her perturbation, it came to her that Peter was speaking to her father on a very important subject and she caught the last of it, "—can make firm plans for our wedding now, Lord Bainbridge?"

He held Savarra's soft hand in his hard one as they moved through the hallway. His was warm and sent tendrils of excitement through Savarra. *How I love him,* she thought fervently. There could be no one for her but Peter!

"I suppose so, Peter," Lord Bainbridge said slowly as they seated themselves about the fire. He pulled his pipe from a pocket in his tunic. He took forth a small sack of tobacco and began tamping it down in the bowl. "Though these are troublous times for a wedding, I can no longer stand between you." He paused, then added, "You realize, however, we came here only for the trial of Belion and McLean and must return immediately to Camden."

"I'll come to Camden for the ceremony," Savarra said eagerly, glad of the chance to leave this house of intrigue into which she had unwillingly been drawn. "My trousseau is well-nigh complete and Cotty and I could come as soon as the last of it is finished."

Her father looked at her obliquely. "I will arrange a military escort for you. 'Tis dangerous traveling the backcountry, for those pesky partisans can strike like lightning." He blew out a thin stream of fragrant smoke and added, "If you will decide the day, I shall arrange it with the military before I leave."

Haverley said with satisfaction, "I know you will want to bring Cotty with you—and perhaps Brim."

"Not Brim," Lord Bainbridge said shortly. "I plan to maintain my headquarters here and I shall have need of him when I am here. In fact, he is so indispensable to me I have considered taking him into the field with me."

Savarra laughed merrily, "And whatever would we do with broody old Brim in the house, Peter? He would be miserable if he couldn't take care of father's uniforms and fetch for him."

"I don't care if you come alone," Peter replied, eyes hot, "as long as you come to me. By the time you arrive, I will have arranged our wedding and have our house readied for us, my dear." He put a possessive hand over hers beside him. "We'll save our honeymoon trip for our return to England—which won't be too long now, I'll wager. We have this scarecrow army of rebels on the run now."

Lord Bainbridge looked at him from beneath dark slanted brows, his vivid eyes ironic. "I wouldn't be too sure of the time, Haverley. We've suffered two indisputable defeats at the hands of the rebels. The issues are far from settled."

"But in the end, we will subdue them," the younger man said confidently. "I'll wager the next time we can catch their slippery army, we will defeat it soundly,"

Anne smiled coldly. "You are very sure, Lord Haverley—and I fear you are in for a rude surprise."

He replied contemptuously, "I think not, Madame Pair. Superior soldiery and experience will inevitably win out."

Anne shrugged and made no reply, and the conversation continued, mostly regarding the coming wedding, for an hour longer before Lord Bainbridge knocked his pipe into the dish beside the sofa and said, "I am weary from the long ride today. I shall retire, with your permission, ladies." But his eyes belied the words. They were brilliant and alert and they rested compellingly on Verity with increasing frequency.

Anne had earlier extended the invitation to Peter Haverley to be a guest during the stay in Charles Town and he had eagerly accepted, sending Amos to the Thorn and Thistle for his light baggage.

Now Anne, Verity and Lord Bainbridge took their leave to retire, but Peter and Savarra remained, talking softly and intimately, unwilling to part from one another yet. Tiqua fetched fresh tapers, lighting them in their crystal chimneys so that a mellow and rich glow was cast about the two, mingling warmly with the replenished fire on the hearth.

Lord Bainbridge cast a frustrated glance at them as he left the room, but they were oblivious to his departure. He followed the ladies up the staircase, each carrying a candle, and went directly to his room. Verity's eyes followed him, and the warmth in her became tumultuous as desire to lie beside him welled up in her. After his door had closed, Anne caught her daughter's arm when she started to her own room.

"Verity," she said desperately, "I beg of you not to—do this thing! Think of your future—which will be without him. Think of the risk you take in going to him."

Verity's face closed against her importunate mother, her delicate jaw set. "Mother, I am a woman grown. I will live my life as I see fit."

"You care not how your actions may wound others—not just me—but others who are part of the fabric of decent society, your friends and companions!"

"You are right. I care not, for I love him."

"You will regret it," Anne said bitterly. Her eyes on Lord Bainbridge's closed door were filled with hatred mingling with sorrow. "He has seduced you—I hope with all my heart he is killed!"

Verity seized her mother's arms, superstition shaking her violently. "Take that back! Take it back! Or you may find yourself suffering for your viciousness. Can you not see that in your own way you are quite as obstinate as I?"

Anne pulled away from her, voice hard. "I will not take it back. I mean it from the depths of my soul—for he will never marry you."

Verity whirled away from her mother and darted into her room, where she flung herself across the bed and wept in frustration for her stolen love. *I shall never mention marriage to him,* she swore to herself. *Never!* Her pride was a powerful force in this decision. *Now* was sweeter than the promise of heaven.

Much later as they lay warmly entwined in the chill night, Lord Bainbridge spoke to Verity of the future.

"Charles—Lord Cornwallis—is even now maneuvering to get Greene's half-trained army to stand and fight. I must be with him for I am needed, my darling. But I shall return as often as I can to be with you. Meantime, I must operate out of Camden and help keep communications lines open between our outposts. The rebels disrupt them too often—too often." He talked to her as if she were a loyalist herself, and she said nothing to change it, but her heart ached. To be torn between love of country and love of a man was agonizing—and Verity was silent.

He continued, "I shall see to it, though, that I return at least once a month to be with you." He kissed her suddenly with fervent passion. "You cannot know how you have changed my life, Verity—I never knew such happiness could be, such fulfillment, such joy. I have come to look on each day as a gift, because I know you are here and that you love me. All the days I am away, I am thinking of the days when we can be together again." His arms closed about her so tightly they were bruising. "I love you," he said huskily and her heart soared.

This was worth any risk, any price she must pay.

When her father and Peter Haverley had left, Savarra became imbued with a fierce energy. She had Amos drive her and Cotty to Madame Flammarion's every day, urging that worthy seamstress to hurry, and the last of her trousseau took shape. By the end of the week it was finished at last, and Savarra had three large portmanteaus and a trunk full of clothing. Her father, as he promised, had arranged an escort for her and Cotty on the trip to Camden. He had told Bartholomew Brim he might come with Savarra and Cotty after all, to Brim's great relief, as Lord Bainbridge would have to remain in Camden for some time and he needed Brim's services. However, it was the middle of February before they were ready to depart.

The night before they were to leave a disturbing event took place. Cotty had taken down Savarra's hair and brushed it thoroughly before going to her own room, but Savarra had not yet disrobed for bed, when Verity knocked on her door.

Savarra admitted her, and her eyes went swiftly about the room before she let out her breath, saying, "Good! You're alone. Cutler McLean is here and he wants to talk to you, Savarra." She held a lighted candle in her hand.

Savarra's eyes flew wide. "He shouldn't—doesn't he realize the danger of being caught? And this time, I won't be here to—"

"He has come by stealth. But he says he must speak with you."

Savarra did not bother to tie back her thick fall of blue-black hair as she caught up her own lighted candle and accompanied Verity into the hall and down the stairs. As they entered the small sitting room, dark but for the low-burning fire, McLean rose and towered over them. He wore the strange leather clothing of overmountain men, fringed leggings and a soft leather shirt. His long rifle with the beautifully polished stock lay on the couch, and Savarra looked up into a face so darkly tanned she scarcely recognized him. The gray eyes were light and clear and his hair was cropped short, curling faintly and without a queue.

"What do you want?" she asked warily, heart thudding. He had not lost his talent to upset her by his mere presence.

"I have come to thank you for what you did for us."

"I did it in the hope that you would never return to Charles Town!"

"I know why you did it," he said bluntly. Inexplicably Savarra felt blood creep into her face as he added, "And I want to assure you of one thing. I will do anything, short of giving myself up, to repay you. This war is not over, Savarra, and things are not going well for the British. If you need my help in any way, you have but to let me know." There was a moment of silence and his sudden smile was white. "I had to express my thanks before you leave."

Then he had known she was leaving! How did these partisans secure their information? They seemed all-knowing, always. But she said coolly, "That is most kind of you, Mr. McLean, but I doubt there will ever be anything you can do for me half so satisfying as staying out of my life from now on."

His smile grew wintry and he gave her a short, courteous bow. "Nevertheless, the offer stands. Tyler and I are most beholden to you and we always pay our debts."

"This is one on which you owe nothing!" She spoke breathily now. A primitive appeal emanated from the man, intensifying her femininity and susceptibility. She squared her shoulders and said determinedly, "I shall be married in a few days and you can forget you ever knew me."

He laughed suddenly. "I'll never forget *that*, Savarra." His use of her name came easily, as though he had thought it many times. "You are a completely unforgettable woman—can you forget me?" It was an audacious question.

"I have already," her flashing eyes belied the statement, "except when you intrude into my life as you are doing now!"

He shrugged and picked up the rifle with one lean brown hand, pulling on a leather cap with the other. He said coldly, "But you *will* see me again, Savarra. I cover a great deal of territory."

"I certainly hope not," she replied with hauteur.

He laughed again, this time with a certain grimness. "I wish you happiness—but I do not think you will find it with Lord Haverley."

He had the power to infuriate her, and this flat statement brought an angry rush of words, "You *are* a fool—" but she spoke to his broad back and he did not turn again.

After he had disappeared on silent feet, Savarra wheeled to face Verity, who had not spoken once since they entered the room. She said defensively, "Well, he *is* a fool, if he thinks I shall ever need *him*, Verity!"

Verity's smile was inscrutable and there was something new in her wide brown eyes, tinctured faintly by surprise. But she said soothingly, "Of course you won't. You will be miles away in Camden and very happily married."

"He has a monumental conceit," Savarra fumed, unap-

"But he would have to be less than human to be ungrateful for your act of courage in making their escape possible."

"I'll give him credit for that," she said grudgingly.

"And you do have a very sharp tongue, my dear," Verity said mildly. "Now we had better retire, for I do want to rise in time to bid you farewell in the morning." Both girls started from the room, their candles fluttering with their movements. As they reached the stairs, Verity added, "I have really become very fond of you, Savarra. I shall miss you."

Savarra halted, her vivid eyes curious across the candle flame. "I thought it was my father of whom you had become fond."

Verity's face paled. Then with sudden decision, "I have become fond of him as well. But *you* should know that will avail me nothing. Your father is an English nobleman and I —as your fiancé pointed out—am a low American wench."

The candle in Savarra's hand shook suddenly. Her voice was very quiet. "There is nothing low about you, Verity, my fiancé notwithstanding. Peter was mistaken."

"I did not think your beloved could make a mistake," was the ironic reply.

Savarra was silent, then with a smile, "Your tongue is also very sharp, Verity."

The American girl began to smile, then, laughing together, they took the stairs. That there was mockery in their shared humor was known by both girls, but they said no more as they parted in the hall above.

Savarra could hear Cotty's teeth chattering, more from excitement than cold, for Frances had come in an hour before and built a roaring fire on the bedroom hearth. Even without the oil lamp, the room was bright enough for sewing a fine seam.

"H-here's your b-blue wool, mistress," and she draped the dress over the back of the sofa and handed a chemise to the nude Savarra, who slipped into it swiftly. "B-Brim's up long ago. I s-saw him when I went to fetch you a pitcher of hot water. He's s-so glad to be goin' to s-serve Sir James."

"Put a shawl on, Cotty. You're freezing."

"I ain't c-cold, mistress. Just excited," was the breathless reply. "D'you s'pose Thad McHorry an' Gabe Sleep'll ever find me way off in C-Camden?"

"I certainly do," she responded shortly. "Those two can

track down anything from a helpless little deer to a small English maid, no matter where they hide."

Cotty giggled. "I ain't a helpless little deer. I can handle them two easy."

Savarra began stepping into the petticoats that Cotty held, one by one. "I'm not so sure of that, Cotty," she said, restraining a smile at Cotty's assumption.

The maid briskly began tying the petticoats, fitting them snugly to Savarra's narrow waist, made narrower by her stays, which Cotty had laced very tightly indeed.

There was a light rap on the door and Tiqua stepped inside. "All zee soldiers is here, mademoiselle, an' Amos is hitchin' up zee carriage," she said in her peculiar mixture of accents.

"They're early," Cotty said in dismay. "Mistress hasn't even had her breakfast yet."

"*Je sais*—I knows. Amos tol' 'em zey have to wait. Mistress Pair an' Mademoiselle Verity is waitin' to breakfast with Mademoiselle Savarra. Primrose got it all ready. *Vous aussi,* Cotty."

"We'll be right down," Savarra said, hastily sliding into the hyacinth blue wool. "Cotty, get out my new capuchin and muff," and Cotty took the heavy velvet cape with fur-lined hood attached from the armoire. Opening a box in the bottom of the armoire, she took out the fox muff and laid the articles on the sofa.

Frances appeared behind the admiring Tiqua, asking, "Is zee fire all right?" and moved sinuously into the room to lay another log across the already blazing hearth. "You are very beautiful, mademoiselle," she said, frankly staring at Savarra. Then she added, " 'Tis near two hundred miles to Camden."

Tiqua added cheerfully, "Zey are many creeks an' rivers 'twixt Camden an' Charlest'n." Both young women were reluctant to leave, enchanted by the sight of Cotty now rapidly dressing Savarra's hair.

"An' dark, heavy woods, *aussi,*" Frances volunteered.

"So I've been told," Savarra said, smiling as her own heart beat faster at the prospect of the long ride with Peter Haverley waiting at the end of it. "And I know it will take us the better part of three days to get there, but I'm not afraid."

"Neither would I, wiz half zee British army alongside," grinned Tiqua, then hastily, "*C'est bon*—'tis good you have such escort, mademoiselle."

"So it is," responded Savarra as Cotty caught up the last strand of thick black hair, rolled it into a curl and pinned it deftly. Turning, she handed a bottle of cologne to Savarra, who splashed it liberally about her throat and wrists.

"Be sure to put that in my valise, Cotty. Peter is very fond of that particular fragrance—'tis carnation."

"I'll get it all—all your things, mistress," Cotty replied distractedly, going to the dressing table where she took up brush, comb, toilet articles and began placing them in the small valise.

"Let us go down to breakfast now, Cotty. You can get the last of these things afterward. But bring the capuchin and muff and my reticule, for I do not intend to return to my room."

"Yes'm," replied Cotty, and, surrounded by a retinue of respectful servants, Savarra descended happily to breakfast.

An hour later, after all her luggage had been safely stowed into the capacious Pair carriage, Savarra, Cotty and Brim prepared to embark. The Pair servants stood near Verity. Only Anne Pair was not there.

"We shall meet again," Verity said as Savarra entered, and for some reason the amenity sent a chill through Savarra. Goose flesh crept along her arms. It was as if she were suddenly gifted with precognition, but she made no reply as she sank down in her skirts and petticoats on the cold leather seat.

It was far too cold to raise the curtains at the windows, and the three of them sat in inky darkness as the carriage scattered shell from the drive and moved onto the harsher cobblestones with a jolting and creaking of the vehicle. Savarra could hear the hooves of the mounted soldiers' horses ringing against the smooth, hard stones.

She was on her way to Peter at last and with her father's blessing. This thought brought a measure of peace to her troubled mind, for Verity's words, *We shall meet again,* echoed like a bell tolling and she could not understand why they should carry such significance.

It was a long and tiring three days and nights before they reached the small city of Camden. There had been inns along the road twice, in which they had spent two nights, but on the final leg of the journey they had driven from dawn until this moment—past midnight. They had rolled the curtains up during the day at Savarra's insistence despite the chill wind that kept them tense with cold.

As the escort shouted, "We're in Camden, mistress!" Savarra said firmly that Brim must roll the curtains up once more, which he did reluctantly.

Now she could see the darkened town about her. There was a cold, brilliant moon which cast its light over the houses as the four horses pulled the carriage swiftly down the street.

The young captain of the escort had told her at the end of the first day that Lord Rawdon and Lord Haverley had arranged for the most elegant house the town boasted to be the Haverley abode, and now they made for that point. She saw it at last, looming up two-storied as they drew up the drive beside it. It appeared to be pink brick, but she could not be sure of the color in the pale wash of moonlight. Still, light shown from the downstairs windows, warm and welcoming. It did not boast a porte-cochere as the Pair house had, but the drivers halted in a drive that led to the rear of the house.

As they debarked, the door to the house opened wide, light spilling out. Peter Haverley and two black servants came forth, Peter at a run, to catch her in his arms and swing her about before putting her on her feet.

"I knew you would arrive today, but I had hoped it would be earlier! How beautiful you are in the moonlight—come, my darling." Then to the two who had accompanied her, "Welcome, Brim and Cotty. Brim, you will be billeted in the local inn, the Stag's Head. Lord Bainbridge has rooms there."

"Then I shall go there at once, if you will arrange with the drivers to take me, sir," Brim replied as the two blacks and two of the dismounted soldiers began taking up the portmanteaus and two small trunks.

"Gentlemen," Peter said to the two still on the box, "take Mr. Brim on into town to Lord Bainbridge's rooms at the Stag's Head." And Brim bade Cotty and Savarra a hasty farewell as he clambered back into the carriage, which rolled on past the house to the rear. There the driver turned and came back, passing before Cotty, Savarra and Peter had entered the house.

When Savarra stepped into the front hall, she was favorably impressed. Though it was not as large as the Pair house, it was exquisitely appointed, with fine small tables and big welcoming chairs. Two gold pedestals, one bearing the bust of Caesar and the other Shakespeare, were placed along the hall walls. There was the customary tall clock, which showed the hour to be near one, but Savarra was far too exhilarated to be aware of fatigue. Cotty's eyes were bright and eager as she took in her surroundings.

"Joab—Abel," Peter said to the tall, thin black man and his sturdy, square-shouldered companion, "take all of Mistress Bainbridge's luggage to the big bedroom upstairs. Mistress Penderford's will be in the smaller one adjoining it."

Without a word the two servants, one carrying a lantern, mounted the stairs which curved gracefully up from the end of the foyer. Savarra sensed a deep resentment in their silent, expressionless service.

Now Peter took her into his arms and kissed her with great tenderness. Cotty stood uncertainly, clutching the small valise which contained all of Savarra's personal toilet articles.

When Peter released her, Savarra said, "Cotty, you may take those things to my bedroom, and the servants will show you to yours, I'm sure." And the little maid, her golden hair somewhat untidy from the long day's journey, began climbing the stairs.

"Come, love," Peter said, his strong, handsome face wearing a broad smile. "I have had Pearl, our Negro cook, prepare a little midnight repast for us. Hot tea and pastries."

Savarra followed him into the small drawing room which, like the hall, was beautifully appointed. Looking about her appreciatively, she asked, "Whose house is—was this?"

"A Johnathan Barber's. He has rebel relatives in Charles Town but he took the oath and pretended to be loyal. Still, we have strong suspicions he secretly remains a rebel. We simply commandeered his house."

"Had he a wife and children?"

"To be sure. A wife and three children, but they are all cozily set up with his brother on the other side of town. It won't be too hard on him."

Savarra, with her newfound and unwilling sympathy for the rebels, suspected that the brother's house was smaller than this gracious home and that the inconvenience to all of them was great, but she said nothing. Seating herself on a satin couch glimmering in the firelight, she sighed. Despite her euphoria, fatigue was now making itself known. "I thought I would never arrive," she said as Peter sat beside her and took her hand.

"I, too," he said huskily, lifting her hand to his lips and

kissing the palm lingeringly as the cook, Pearl, came into the room bearing a large silver tray. On it was a steaming pot of tea and a plate of crisp pastries.

"Ah, Pearl," Peter said courteously, "thank you so much. Will you serve us, Savarra, darling?" And she did so, finding the hot tea sent a soothing warmth through her chilled limbs.

She had not removed her capuchin, so cold had she become in the long night drive, but now she divested herself of it and Peter Haverley regarded the hyacinth dress with appreciation.

He said with quiet intimacy, "You have the loveliest little body in the world, Savarra."

She felt a blush rising. "Peter, you are very forward—"

"I shall be your husband in less than twenty-four hours and I am an impatient young man!" Then with a wicked laugh, "But I shall spend the rest of this night in my old room at the Stag's Head out of deference to your innocence and your father's conventionality."

They talked at length and, over the second cup of tea, he told her of the arrangements he had made for their wedding. There was an Anglican church in midtown with a proper minister and they would be wed at four o'clock tomorrow afternoon.

"I have a perfectly beautiful wedding dress, Peter," Savarra said smiling. "You are going to be quite stunned by my elegance."

"I am already so in love with you I can scarce think of anything else."

"Even with all your military duties?" she teased.

He frowned. "That is the one bad thing. I must be at headquarters until near our wedding hour. We have captured two of Marion's men and we must dispose of them—by trial or by hanging, and I favor the latter." He added with something of relief, "Your father can stay only until you are wed. Then he and his men must leave immediately to join Cornwallis in North Carolina."

It was two-thirty before he took his reluctant departure with many kisses and caresses, vowing he would not sleep a wink in anticipation of the morrow.

When Savarra mounted the stairs and entered the strange room, the fire had been prepared for her and burned brightly. Cotty drooped on a chair, waiting to help her disrobe. In less than twenty minutes, both young women were in their respective beds and soundly sleeping.

Thirteen

Savarra's wedding day dawned bright and clear with a brilliant sun warming the February countryside. A hot fire leaped rosily in the broad fireplace. When she rose from the vast four-poster and stood looking out a tall, sparkling window at the gardens behind the house, it seemed to her that spring was already burgeoning with a luscious promise of velvety green in trees and shrubs. The many flowerbeds that flanked the area before the stables at the far end were meticulously kept, and she knew there must be a fleet of gardeners. She liked this house and was annoyed by the recurring and discomforting thought of the Barber family, who must have loved it dearly and who were now cramped into his brother's house.

Cotty's room adjoined the sumptuous bedroom she would share with Peter tonight. There was a door leading from one to the other, so Savarra could avail herself of Cotty's services in preparing herself tonight. She half-smiled at her eagerness to make a striking entrance to her and Peter's bedroom elegantly clad in the frothy nightdress Madame Flammarion had made for her first night.

She spent the entire morning and early afternoon happily readying herself for the moment of the nuptials. After Cotty brought her breakfast up to her on a tray, they began the elaborate operations. The little maid washed Savarra's long, luxuriant hair, then tied each curl fastidiously against the moment when she could arrange the thick polished mass in a coiffure of suitable elegance.

Later, Cotty, Pearl and another servant named Bessie brought up the hand-painted hip bath. Bessie had carried up two great steaming brass kettles of water which filled the air with smoky mist as she poured their contents into the tub.

The two black women were sullen and responded only briefly to Savarra's pleasant appreciation. She knew they resented their family's dispossession and she could not blame them.

Still, she luxuriated in the hot, scented water for nearly an hour, allowing Cotty to rub her down with fragrant lotion and delicate powder. Her nails were given careful attention with the buffer, making them rosy and smooth. The wedding gown was unpacked and hung up to permit the slight wrinkling of satin folds to fall out. Underclothing, foaming with the finest of laces, was laid out and Savarra saw to it that all of it was faintly perfumed with spicy, provocative carnation cologne.

By the time three-thirty was announced by a single chime of the tall, shining clock below, she was exquisitely turned out in gleaming satin, with small pearls encrusted along the breast and sleeves. Savarra permitted only a small, fleeting stab of guilt that it was so virginal and white.

As she and Cotty stood staring at the vision of purity reflected in the tall mirror, into her mind flashed Cutler McLean's dark, intense visage. There followed the customary knife-like remembrance of the touch of those hard brown hands, suddenly tender on her bare flesh, and brief panic shook her.

Thus it was that, when her father called to escort her to the church, she was disquieted. It flawed her joy and kept her from abandoning herself to the complete happiness that should now be hers.

As he handed her into the carriage, Lord Bainbridge said, "I have arranged a large wedding supper for you and Peter at the Stag's Head this evening, but I shall not be able to remain for it, my dear. Lord Cornwallis is planning a series of maneuvers to draw that wily Nathanael Greene into battle. His troops are only half-trained and, if we can meet them, we can end this war immediately."

"You think one final battle would end it?" she asked hopefully.

"All the organized rebellion at least—then we could take care of these partisan swamp fighters. Clean them out one by one." He turned to look at her squarely, where she sat beside him in the carriage. It was much more luxurious than the Pair carriage, which was rattling its way back to Charles Town even now. "Savarra, I hope to God that I am putting you in the hands of a man who will be kind and love you tenderly."

It was such a heartfelt speech and, combined with her own sudden uneasiness, she found her eyes filling with tears. She gulped down the lump in her throat and said huskily, "Father, I shall miss you."

Still his face was brooding. "I shall leave Scott Coyne in charge of my Charles Town headquarters and I shall return there first. But as for Camden, where you will be, I cannot say."

And she thought with a touch of cynicism, *Verity will see that you return to Charles Town, I'll wager.* She said quietly, "You will see how happy we are when you *do* return to Camden, father."

When they reached their destination, they found the large church filled with her father's regiment and her fiancé's fusiliers. There was a sprinkling of women, American women who had succumbed to the glamor of scarlet coats and white breeches of handsome British soldiers. The wedding which soon followed was impressive, sober and reverent and, when it was over, her father came to her and kissed her briefly.

"Take care of my daughter, Peter," he said, strapping on his saber.

"With my life," Peter said dramatically, "for I love her better than life!"

The crowd poured out of the church, and most of the men mounted horses that had stood patiently waiting in the late afternoon sunlight that spread long shadows across the churchyard. There were several carriages which filled rapidly, but Savarra's eyes watched only her father's erect figure as he and his men diminished in the distance.

The young fusiliers surged about her suddenly, shutting out her view as they joyfully offered their congratulations. As they did so, a curious vulnerability seeped into her. Always, Lord Bainbridge had stood like a rock between her and any possible disaster. Now she was Peter Haverley's and Lord Bainbridge had naught to say of her behavior or her lack of it.

As she and Peter were bowling down through town to the inn, she looked up into the clean-cut profile of her husband and was reassured. Peter was an English nobleman. Breeding and high birth were plainly etched on those patrician features. She did not see the lethal malice in that chiseled face, the deadly strength that lurked beneath its narrow, well-bred surface. *I love him dearly,* she told herself and smiled at him brilliantly.

Peter returned her smile with pleasure, full of good spirits, and he said, "You see, Savarra? I told you we would be married, despite all the obstacles your father put in our way!"

"Yes, Peter. You did and we are." Her spirits rose.

"You are Lady Haverley now," he said with cold, hard pride, "mistress of several estates in England. When we are finished with this sordid American uprising, we will lead a very pleasant life in England—when I am not called to serve the crown."

"I know. How I am looking forward to returning! How long is this tour of duty to last?"

"I can't be sure," he said evasively. Then with honesty, "Savarra, oddly enough, I find I like the soldier's life. There is a danger, an exhilaration and satisfaction in it that feeds something deep within me. I am accomplishing something for the first time in my life. I find meaning and gratification— even pleasure in fighting." Then he added quickly, "For my country, of course."

"I know you have become a fine soldier—my father has told me so." This was not entirely true. Lord Bainbridge had told Savarra that Peter showed courage, but that he was vicious in combat. "But I hate to think of you making the military your life. Father was away so much of the time."

"I shall be with you more often than you think. I will make it a point to be. After all, we must raise the next Lord Haverley and his brothers and sisters." His laugh was charming. "It was kind of your father to arrange our wedding supper before he left. All my fusiliers will be there, as well as Lord Rawdon and his officers. I am proud of you, Savarra. Have you any idea how beautiful you are?"

She hesitated, then said, "You are too kind, Peter. Will there be ladies present as well?"

"There will be women, you may be sure," he said carelessly, "for these American wenches are only too glad to be squired by his majesty's troops."

Savarra put down a rise of irritation. Though her relationship with the Pair women could not be called intimate, she had found them far from common.

They were slow reaching the inn and, when they arrived, there was an army of horses and carriages in the courtyard. Once inside, she thought she had never seen so many soldiers in a room. And it was a large room by British standards for inns, panelled in dark gleaming wood, warm with the scent of good food and strong spirits. A roaring fire crackled and leapt, scarlet and yellow on a black hearth. Somehow the innkeeper and his fleet of servants managed to serve them all at the long, smooth wooden tables, whose satin texture precluded the need for table linen.

Savarra smiled, nodded, was introduced to nearly all the guests either singly or in groups, accepted congratulations and good wishes over and over again. Peter drank every toast, and his patrician face was flushed.

When the festivities were over, a sudden wild excitement filled her as she and Peter left in a welter of toasts and light banter from the surging, brightly clad guests. She felt faintly tipsy from champagne, for in the hilarity and gaiety at the table she had eaten but little.

When she and Peter returned to the splendidly accoutered Barber house, she secretly observed her husband in the golden fall of lamplight as the servants ushered them inside. He had never appeared more aristocratic, handsome and desirable. Now her heart beat tumultuously as they lightly took the stairs and she contemplated the consummation of their love in the warm, dusky shadows of this lavish bedroom. She had waited so long!

But in that trembling instant, a still voice within said, *You did not wait. No matter how you seek to submerge it, the knowledge—the man—is there. Cutler McLean.* Impatiently she put the thought from her. By heaven, she *would* forget!

Kissing Peter lightly, she went into Cotty's room where she would undress and found the little maid full of superlatives about the wedding, which she had witnessed from the rear of the church.

"Oh, I never saw you look so lovely, mistress. Ah, but your dress was a vision an' what a handsome couple you make— perfickly matched, I do believe—after all me fears, too! Come, let me help you unhook yer bodice and put on your night-dress—oh, ain't it the most gorgeous thing?" She held up the diaphanous folds of fragile and thin silk, so thickly gathered the garment was a pearlescent cloud.

When it fell about her nude body, the sheer white gown appeared to float. There were narrow, shining white satin ribbons spilling from her pale shoulders and silk lace trimming the edges, the whole of it so transparent Savarra's slender, provocative figure, her pointed breasts and rounded thighs were faintly discernible.

She seated herself at the small dressing table and began pulling pins from her hair to let it fall richly, faintly curling to her waist. Cotty silently handed her the cologne and she

splashed herself liberally with the delicious, stirring fragrance.
She was ready at last.

As she stepped back into the big bedroom, closing the door
on the palpitating and excited Cotty, she saw Peter Haverley
seated in a great wing-backed chair before the hearth of snapping and leaping flames. He wore a green velvet dressing
gown tied about his lean waist, and the room was delightfully
warm with a suggestion of the scent of apples from the burning logs. When he looked up and saw her, he was speechless
for a moment.

Then drawing a deep breath he rose and said softly, "You
look to be an angel—so innocent, so immaculately beautiful."
Almost reverently, he took her into his arms. "Mmmn, you
are so sweet—even to breathe." Then with sudden fervor,
"My God, how I've *wanted* you!"

They stood together in the center of the spacious room,
clinging each to the other, with firelight gleaming redly upon
them, each anticipating the enchantment that was to come.

Then Peter laughed softly, triumphantly. He said, "I'm
glad I killed the beggar today! You are so virginal, so untouched." There was rising passion in his voice.

"You—*killed* a man today? On our wedding day?" She was
taken aback by the casual revelation. "But why, my darling?"

" 'Twas of little import," he replied negligently. "I told you
we captured two men belonging to the band of outlaws under
that devil, Marion. This morning one of them, when he
learned your father's identity, made a great hue and cry,
claiming that he had guided *you* back to Charles Town after
three weeks as a captive of Marion's men. A cock-and-bull
story to save his hide if I ever heard one." There was cold
cruelty in his meticulous English voice. Then with indifference,
"We were to hang them both tomorrow anyway."

"Who—was he?" she asked with a sudden clutch of terror.

"A Sam—no, Seth Barwell. The other was Sam Kinley, who
is still in jail awaiting execution."

A sickness spread through Savarra, a sinking and a revulsion all at once. "You *killed* Seth Barwell? A mere lad—"

"Of course I killed him." He held her back from him,
searching her face. "You cannot know him and I'll have no
canard bruited about my bride." Then alertly, "How do you
know him to be a mere lad?"

Savarra had gone rigid in his arms, her face pale and ill.
She was caught up in a turbulent emotion, and all caution left
her. In her mind rose up the face of Seth Barwell, thin, young,

eager—worshipful. His kindnesses to her, his thoughtfulness, his bringing her out of the hell of those swamps to the safety of the Pair house.

She blurted in shock and outrage, "How dared you kill a *boy,* an unarmed prisoner, I'll wager—for telling the truth? How brutal, how cruel and inhuman—" She broke off, unable to express her horror.

Peter's arms slacked about her and his own face drew taut. In the glow of the lamps the gold eyes became glacial. "You mean you *did* spend three weeks in the swamps—captive of those American rebels?"

"Yes, I did and, as you can see, I am none the worse for it. They were courteous and decent to me!" In her agitation and grief over the youth's senseless death, she let her face reveal her anger and disgust, the wild sorrow that flooded her.

His eyes narrowed and a muscle in his jaw quivered. Suspicion swept like menacing lightning across his narrow handsome face. "Ah," he breathed, thin nostrils pinched and flaring. "The very fact that you did not tell me of this three-week captivity bespeaks a certain guilt. You have been hiding something from me." His hands crept up her arms, bit slowly into her soft shoulders painfully. "And I can guess what it is," he said intuitively.

In the silence that gathered about them like a smothering murk, his voice rose, thick with fury and contempt. "Three weeks! A woman with those *savages*—you are no virgin! And you knew how much it meant to me to be the *first!*" He began to shake her violently and her hair flew about her face as she struggled to free herself. "Tell me." He spoke viciously between his teeth. "Tell me the truth. You have lain with one or more of those cursed foxes—I know it. I *feel* it."

Savarra could scarcely catch her breath in the frenzy of his assault. "Stop!" she gasped, clawing futilely at the iron fingers cutting cruelly into her flesh.

"Admit it," he gritted. *"That's* the change I've seen in you, felt in you and, fool that I was, I could not recognize it. Damn your soul to hell, Savarra—you have cuckolded *me* and long before our wedding day!"

Fury rose in her, hot and turgid. She regained her breath and spat, "Murderer! Murderer of children! That young boy was pure as a saint. He *respected* me—led me to safety and you have killed him!"

"Saint, eh?" His laugh was brutal. "I shall kill them all before I'm through with these Americans—every bastard that rides with Marion." He paused, a murderous scowl on his face. Under her widening eyes his face changed, grew cunning and knowing, the malice evident and evil. He said slowly, "I remember now you said—ah, so innocently—*you* went to the jail to throw your contempt in the faces of McLean and Belion the day of their escape—with pistols in their hands." Then with uncanny insight he said quietly, "I'll wager it was *you* who smuggled those pistols in to them. *You* gave them the guns. Don't bother to deny it—"

"I shall not deny it," she cut in with sudden and blazing fury, "for it is true. I *did* smuggle pistols to them. I would not stand by and see them hung. Enough blood has been shed in this bestial war as it is."

"Enough blood shed?" His eyes were crafty. Then with that unexpected and inexplicable second sight, he added slowly and deliberately, "What specious reasoning in a soldier's daughter. You delude yourself in your efforts to delude me. McLean is the man you lost your virtue to—I'd stake my life on it."

She drew a sharp hissing breath and said harshly, "You are mad—with jealousy and hatred." There was a fraught silence between them before she cried in a loud, startled voice, "You are *cruel*—a mean-minded creature. My God," her words fell to a whisper, "my father was right on all counts." She was appalled and sickened by the accuracy of Peter Haverley's suspicions, yet she no longer wanted to deny it all, to explain the strange, inevitable circumstances and how innocently she had fallen into the moonlit trap in the forest. She was far more distressed by the bitter knowledge that Peter Haverley was demonic in his lechery and she was, God help her, his bride.

The tenderness she had known on emerging from Cotty's room, clad in her cloud-like nightdress, had vanished with his cold, accurate accusations and the brutality that faced her now. They stood before each other, antagonists instead of lovers, each full of contempt—nay, hatred—for the other.

"So McLean has been your lover," there was almost triumph in the razor-edged voice, "and you don't deny it—or try to explain it, madame?" His eyes narrowed to glittering slits. "You're damaged goods, but I shall have my way with you. And you shall play Lady Haverley through all the years to come. You shall share *my* bed and my bed alone. I'll see to that."

Savarra felt the blood leave her face, but she said resolutely, "I shall *never* share your bed."

"But you shall, my faithless dear," and with one brutal sweep of his hand he caught the neck of her nightdress and ripped the translucent silk from her, leaving her nude in the warm, shadowy room.

He seized her then, catching her up into iron arms as she struggled violently. Her blood coursed through her like fire, lending her a furious strength, but he was too big, too sinewy and strong for her to break his hold. Revulsion filled her at his touch and she fought savagely, and with equal savagery he bent her to his will. There was no vestige of tenderness, just a hateful lasciviousness as he flung her on the bed and ripped away his robe. As he did so, she seized the opportunity to roll from the bed, but he was on her in an instant to throw her roughly back into the center of it.

So fierce was their struggle, their panting breaths came like that of animals engaged in life-or-death combat. She fought him with an instinct for battle she had never realized she possessed, clawing at the slim, patrician face, attempting to bite the hands that imprisoned her. She tore her arm from his grasp and brought it up to slap him across the mouth with a resounding crack, and blood flecked his lips where her blow had cut him against his own teeth.

He let out a string of unspeakable obscenities as he threw her down and straddled her. Still she did not give up, twisting, arching her back, lunging out with her legs. But slowly, inexorably, he pinned her flat, his muscular legs forcing hers apart.

There ensued the most painful experience of Savarra's life. She was forced to lie prone, even as she writhed beneath him, and endure the most brutal of all acts of animal lust. He was rough and sadistic, skilled in the artistry of pain. Once she screamed out in agony and he laughed, his breath hot and gusting across her face. He made no attempt to kiss her.

Instead he said, "That is nothing, madame. Before this night is over, you will be crying, Savarra, begging for mercy. You are my wife to do with as I wish—and I wish to do this with you and often. I advise you to relax. Your struggles only make it the worse for you and the more enjoyable for me—a little cooperation and it might pleasure you as it did with the rebel, McLean." His voice was ugly on the name, and suddenly he put his face to her throat and sank his teeth viciously into the tender place where it met her shoulder. She gasped and held back a scream as he chuckled richly with a sensual delight.

After that she lay flaccid and still, aware at last that her struggles were a satisfaction to him. After an interminable agony, he rolled off her with a grunt of temporary satiety.

"If you so much as move, I'll beat you within an inch of your life, Savarra," he said, his cultured voice all the more terrifying for the calm certainty in his words.

She said nothing, but lay rigid as he pulled the covers over both of them. A trembling seized her and she fought it down by sheer strength of will. The fire on the hearth was still bright, though the lamps burned low. All the furnishings in the beautiful room were clearly visible. Her wide eyes registered them all with loathing, and she knew she would never forget them and this degrading moment in her life.

She sensed that Peter would rest and then there would be the whole terrifying experience to endure once more. She felt she could not face it. *She would not!* He had much to drink at the inn, she remembered, for his face had been flushed and his breath heavy with strong spirits.

Thus she was motionless, muscles taut with effort, but by neither breath nor movement did she betray her terror of this man. Savarra had not known she was capable of such hatred, but she knew now that she would gladly kill Peter Haverley for the bestiality of his attack upon her. She was violated, debased and shamed, and escape was a fever in her brain. She felt she could not endure him to touch her again and she might well die from the horror of it.

Slowly, slowly the indomitable pride of her mother and the swift daring of her father crept into her veins, then surged through her bruised body, and she gathered strength as she listened tensely to his breathing beside her. As the moments ticked by, it became deeper and more rhythmic.

Cautiously she moved, and there was no answering movement from the broad bed beside her. Slowly she inched her way to the edge, and did not seek the three tall wooden steps beside it but slid sinuously from the covers to the cold floor.

The fire had sunk low and red in the fireplace now and the lamps had flickered and died, but the room was lit with a bloody light from the coals. Even her destroyed nightdress, where it lay in a silken pool, was bathed in the crimson glow as she stepped around it, shivering slightly.

She made her way silently to the door, opened it noiselessly and slipped into Colly's room, closing it softly behind her. She turned to see the little maid, her eyes wild, sitting bolt-upright in her bed, a candle guttering beside it, her mouth open in terror.

But Savarra put a hand to her own lips and in her nakedness approached Cotty, whose blonde curls were disordered and whose round, dimpled face was distraught. Tears gleamed on her plump cheeks and she could contain herself no longer.

She whisperedly hoarsely, "Oh, my God, mistress—I *heard* —I've been 'alf crazy with fear fer you. Oh, that terrible, terrible man!"

"Get up and get dressed," Savarra murmured with cold control. "We're going to leave."

"Leave for where?" Cotty was bewildered.

"The stable below is full of horses and you and I are going to ride back to Charles Town."

"But 'tis after midnight—alone? Oh, mistress, that's such a long way and we'd be *alone!*"

"I am not afraid," Savarra whispered huskily. "Hurry! He could rouse at any moment."

Cotty clambered down the steps beside her bed and began frantically getting out underclothing. Savarra said, "Get my black riding habit—would to God I had the boy's clothes I wore with the partisans!—and our fur-lined cloaks, Cotty. It is very cold and we have a long way to go. We shall not stop often—"

" 'Tis three days to Charles Town," Cotty whispered tearfully. "Oh, mistress, I am so afraid for us!"

But Savarra was donning her chemise and the petticoats that would lie beneath the riding habit, and Cotty was galvanized to speed. In a surprisingly short time they were fully clothed and slipped from the room. They dared light no candles and made their way by instinct through the darkened halls and down the stairs, out the rear door to the stables.

"Get the biggest and strongest of the geldings," Savarra said as they neared the black bulk of the building. "They will receive but little rest."

"Oh," Cotty moaned softly, "if only His Lordship was here—he'd save us!"

"Well, he isn't and we must save ourselves. Hurry— hurry!" Her eyes by now were well adjusted to the dark and she opened a stall to lead a great gelding from the enclosure. "Get the one next to this. He's as big as this one," she hissed.

Cotty did so, murmuring, "I don't know 'ow to put a bridle and saddle on a 'orse—I never done it before." In the extremity of their predicament, all Cotty's newfound pretenses at elegance had fallen away and her voice was all cockney.

"We're doing it now," Savarra said grimly, plucking a bridle and bit from a nail on a square post and tossing it to Cotty. She took another for herself and said with faint panic, "We'll not try to saddle them. I know I couldn't do that— it would take hours."

The two horses blew through their noses, and the one nuzzled Savarra's hand as she slipped the bit into his mouth. Cotty, fumbling miserably, failed entirely in her efforts and Savarra had to put the bridle on her horse as well.

It seemed an eternity before the two of them were able to mount, riding bareback, and Savarra was scarcely aware of her aching and bruised body as they walked the horses from the stables, through the yard and to the street.

She clutched the cloak about her throat, wincing as she brushed against the crusted and dried blood on the wound put there by Peter Haverley. "Keep off the cobblestones, Cotty," she said sharply. "They make such a racket."

"Which way is Charles Town, mistress?" Cotty whimpered. "I ain't got the least idea—have you?"

"I certainly have," Savarra responded forcefully. "I remember every foot of the way here. How could I forget?" *Oh, God, if I only could forget!* Instead, she felt that Peter Haverley had branded her with his evil ruttish brutality. She kept glancing behind her at the darkened house—no light flickered at the windows. *Let him sleep that drunken sleep,* she prayed silently as they moved alongside the road on the grassy turf, making their way out of the sleeping city of Camden.

Once beyond the outskirts on the well-traveled and sandy road to Charles Town, Savarra let the gelding out into an easy lope and Cotty followed, her plaintive little protests lost in the rising wind. They passed no fellow travelers throughout the long dark hours of the night. It was still dark when they passed through Monck's Corner without stopping in that little town.

When dawn broke at last, both girls were chilled and exhausted, but Savarra turned a deaf ear to Cotty's pleadings to stop and rest.

"But we can't go three days an' three nights like this, mistress! We'll starve, if we don't die o' the ride!"

"I've gold in my reticule. Plenty of it, thanks to my father and when we reach the proper inn, we'll stop and eat." She looked at her maid, frowning angrily. "And we shall make it to the Pair house long before three days. Traveling by carriage is much slower than two on horseback."

"Especially if them two don't stop fer nothin'," Cotty muttered. Then quickly, "But I'd keep right on, rather'n you get caught by *him*."

Savarra's mouth tightened. It was possible that Peter was even now on their trail, and with the thought she stepped up the gelding's pace. They were hungry and thirsty, both the animals and their riders. Fatigue lay on Savarra's aching muscles like a drug, but she did not stop until well past noon, when they reached a small settlement which boasted a run-down and grimy little inn. A stable adjoined it, Savarra noted swiftly.

Cotty moaned, "Oh, mistress, do let's stop an' at least get some water. These 'orses is tired an' thirsty, too."

Thus they drew up before the inn, looping their reins over a nearby railing, and went into the dark, stuffy interior. It was empty and Savarra concluded with relief that probably most of its clientele came in to quench their thirst at the end of the day. She was grateful for that. The fewer who saw them, the better their chances of eluding pursuit.

She adjured Cotty not to remove her cloak and hood and she drew her own closely about her. A plump young girl in a dirty mob cap came out of the gloom beyond the three rough tables and curtsied, her round dark eyes wide at the sight of Savarra's fine cloak and shining leather boots peeping beneath her black riding habit.

"Kin I serve you somethin', ma'am?" she asked, her smile revealing very bad teeth in one so young.

"Yes, you can," Savarra said crisply. "We will eat a meal here and I want you to prepare a basket of food to be taken with us when we leave. We have far to go and there may be no other inn for a long time."

"We ain't got no baskets. I kin put it in a sack—"

It was an unsatisfactory meal, cold sliced beef, cheese and dark heavy bread washed down with sour wine, but it revived then both. In the meantime, the young girl's father had come in and was inspecting them curiously. His hair hung untidily to his shoulders, thin and oily.

"You ladies travelin' alone? Them horses out there look wore out."

"My aunt is ill and my husband is a British colonel on a mission. My maid and I must travel alone to my aunt—have you fresh horses we can buy?" She was cold and peremptory and it had the desired effect.

The man bowed obsequiously, his voice meek and unctuous. "Them's mighty fine beasts you come in on, ma'am—even if they are tuckered out."

"Yes. I will let you have them and two gold sovereigns to boot, if you can furnish us with fresh ones. My aunt is very ill and haste is imperative." Then with imperious accusation, "Are you loyal to the crown?"

"Oh, yes, ma'am. Yes, yes!" the man affirmed hastily. "We ain't rebels—we don't even serve no rebels."

Savarra thought dourly that he very likely changed his allegiance with the patrons of his establishment. Now he went on with sudden anxiety, "I'll give you two fine mares—an' keep your geldings, ma'am. Nothing' to boot, either. Even trade an' glad to serve you. I notice you ain't got saddles. I'll sell you two from me stable, do you wish."

"We haven't time," Savarra replied coldly, wiping her lips with a handkerchief from her bulging reticule.

The daughter appeared in the dark and musky room, holding a half-filled coarse cloth sack, and Savarra accepted it coolly. "Did you put a bottle of the wine in with the food?"

"No ma'am, but I'll get you one." She bobbed the strange little curtsy once more and darted behind the bar to return with a long green bottle. She put it in the bag and handed it back to Savarra, showing all her bad teeth in another smile. " 'Tis all more of what you just had, ma'am," she said apologetically.

"That will be all right. We are too short of time—food is a secondary worry, with my dear aunt at death's door." She put a gold coin in the father's rough hand.

Their entire stay at the inn and stable had taken less than half an hour, and the afternoon sun was struggling against a rising overcast as the two girls swung briskly down the narrow, rutted road on two fat, sleek little mares. The tavern keeper had much the best of the bargain, two strong young geldings in their prime for the two smaller and stockier mares, but Savarra cared not a whit. *If I can just reach the Pair house— I will ask Verity to hide us, for I know Peter will come searching and soon.*

She found herself glancing back down the road behind them as the evening shadows lengthened, half-afraid she would hear the thunder of hooves and find a whole troop of the fusiliers descending upon them. But they met no one, other than an old man driving a wagonload of chopped wood and a carriage that bumped by, the occupants glimpsed briefly through the open windows. No one at all passed them coming from Camden.

It was midnight when they reached the outskirts of Charles Town, and the weather had turned bitterly cold once more with a fine misting rain and a cutting wind off the sea. But for the brief stop at the inn, Savarra and Cotty had not paused in their precipitate flight and the mares were drooping visibly as the dark houses and buildings began to take form about them. They had made the trip in less than twenty-four hours.

Savarra said firmly, "Cotty, we must dismount and turn these horses loose and walk the rest of the way to the Pair house. If we were to put them in the Pair stables, it would be proof enough to Peter that we are there."

"Oh," Cotty groaned afresh, "I'm so tired—an' whatever shall we do if he does come searchin' fer us? I'm so scared, mistress. He was so rough—so cruel—"

"Don't speak of him," Savarra said hotly. "We shall hide—until my father returns and I can tell him. Ah, but I *shall* tell him!"

There were no lights in the houses they passed. It was the dead hour of the night and Savarra peered closely at their surroundings as their gait slowed. "Here—this must be Tradd Street. We will walk from here." And clutching the mane of the weary mare, she slipped from her bare back as Cotty did likewise. Then she gave the mare a sharp slap across the rump and the animal whinnied and trotted off in the dark. "Send yours off, Cotty!" she ordered, and she heard Cotty give the horse a hard thwack on the hip.

The two girls paused in the cold wet wind for a moment, gathering their strength. Savarra knew she was weary beyond measure, but she was driven by a force more powerful than fatigue. She clenched her hands together and a sudden, horrifying realization came to her.

"My God!" she whispered.

"What is it? What is it?" Cotty asked shrilly.

"Hush! I've only just discovered, I'm still wearing his wedding ring!" She tore it from her finger, thinking to fling it into the black night about her, but she stopped.

"What are you doin'? Oh, mistress, whatever are ye doin'?"

"I'm burying it," Savarra said hoarsely as she grubbed about in the wet ground beside the cobbled street. The mud clung to her hands, but the hole grew and she pushed the beautiful diamonded circle into the wet dirt, hastily covering it with the soil she had removed. Carefully she placed a piece of turf over the disturbed ground and rose, wiping her muddy hands on a handkerchief from her reticule. A brief feeling of relief washed through her.

Her desire never to lay eyes on Peter Haverley again was like a raging fire within her. How this could be accomplished she did not know, but she would bend every effort to escape him and her wedding vows completely. She had heard of divorce and its attendant scandal. She had giggled and whispered about it with the girls in school back in England, it was so deliciously forbidden and shocking. Now she realized with icy determination that she would find a way to divorce Lord Haverley somehow, somewhere.

"Come along, Cotty," she said, her voice hard. "We have many blocks to go." And the two set off, Cotty faltering and Savarra pulling at her arm urging her on. Their small leather boots were silent on the cobbles, their clothing miserably damp and uncomfortable.

They covered two blocks, three, then five and six, and suddenly the Brewton house loomed in view, a darker bulk against the dark sky. The overcast was still heavy. There were no stars, no moon in the threatening sky, and Savarra was afraid a deluge would start pouring down upon them before they could reach the Pair house, only a few more steps away.

She started to run but Cotty gasped for breath and clung to her, holding her back. "Mistress, I can't—I can't move no faster—you—got to slow down—"

When at last they turned into the gateway and traversed the brick walk to the dark Pair house real hope rose in Savarra. She had no qualms about arousing the house at this midnight hour. She had not even thought of what she would tell them, so fevered to escape was she. But she thought of it now as they stepped upon the broad porch.

Lifting the knocker and banging loudly, she decided swiftly she would tell them part-truth and part-lie. After all, they knew of her captivity with the partisans, her smuggling pistols to McLean and Belion—she would tell them of the senseless killing of young Seth Barwell. She knew these two ardent patriots would be sympathetic. Cotty herself had asked no questions about the quarrel between Peter and her mistress, too intimidated by his rough and brutal treatment of Savarra.

It was a long time that the two girls stood shivering on the broad porch before the flicker of a candle appeared frailly in the window as the door beside it swung open slowly. Amos stood looking at them, his jaw dropped and eyes staring.

"Mistress Bainbridge—Miss Cotty— What's you two doin' here at this hour?"

"Let us in, Amos. I have run away from Lord Haverley."

Amos's eyes opened so wide the whites circled the pupils. Then he threw open the door and said, "Come in—come in! I'll go stir up the fire in the sittin' room. You ladies look like you might nigh froze."

"And hungry, too," Cotty put in exhaustedly as they followed him into the dim, warm house. Savarra began to divest herself of the damp cloak, which had taken on an animal odor from the moistened fur lining.

"I'll go git Primrose up to fix you somethin'—an' I spec' I better get Mistress Pair an' Mistress Verity down here—"

"Yes, you had," Savarra said urgently, "for Lord Haverley may well be right behind me—determined to force me to return to him, and I want you—all of you, to hide me."

"An' me, too," Cotty said tremulously. "I don't want that man to come nigh me an' Mistress Savarra."

Amos led them to the sitting room where he laid their cloaks across the sofa, took up a great oak log from a brass basket beside the hearth and flung it on the red coals, sending a shower of sparks up the black chimney.

"Set down an' warm up, ladies—I'll go fetch Primrose to the kitchen."

"No, Amos. Fetch the Mistresses Pair first, please," Savarra said, standing close to the hearth and rubbing her chilled fingers. She had not taken time to get her gloves in their flight and now the soft flesh of her hands was chafed raw by the wind and weather. She winced as she held them to the fire.

Cotty looked at her in the brighter light of the oil lamp Amos lit from his candle before leaving, her round blue eyes pinned back by gold lashes in distress. "Oh, mistress—your eye! 'Tis so bruised and the side of your throat—that terrible cut!"

Savarra put her hand to her slender neck and felt the blood still encrusted just below the collar line of her riding habit, where Peter's teeth had gone into her tender flesh. Her eyes narrowed to blazing blue slits. "That—beast!" she whispered, tugging at the collar, raising it higher to cover the spot.

Cotty murmured, "Mistress, you can't hide the bruise

around your eye and cheek without your cloak an' hood.
That's how come I ain't seen them till now."

"Well, I can't wear my cloak as long as it will take me to
heal," she said tiredly. "I plan to tell them most of the truth
of the matter anyway, as you will see, Cotty."

Tears welled up in Cotty's big gentian eyes and spilled over
on her cheeks, and she wiped them away with the back of
her hand. "Oh, mistress—had I been a bigger woman, I
would'a come help you—with that—awful man." Then with
a little wail, "I knew he was bad. I *knew* it back in London
the night you run off to him." Sobs shook her shoulders and
her voice grew muffled. "Could I got word to Mr. Sleep an'
Mr. McHorry, I'll wager they'd'a come help us! They told
me they's goin' up beyond Camden an' would see me there."

Savarra sighed. "Cotty, your Mr. McHorry and Mr. Sleep
are partisans and it's time you knew it. They ride and fight
with Colonel Marion—*and* Cutler McLean and Tyler Belion."

Cotty's gasp was loud and the sobs ceased abruptly as the
shocked blue eyes regarded Savarra accusingly, but before
she could speak, Anne and Verity Pair hastened into the
warmth of the sitting room. Rain could be heard now, drumming heavily in the gusts of wind from the sea.

Verity looked at the two pale faces before her and Anne,
and she caught one of Savarra's hands impulsively. It was
still cold and she felt the chafed condition before she looked
down at it. "Oh, my dear! When did you leave Camden—
your poor hands!"

"Yesterday before dawn, Verity—I forgot gloves and we
rode horseback. "

"Your mounts—where are—"

"We turned them loose in the city several squares away."

Anne Pair said calmly, "You have left Lord Haverley—
before your wedding, or after?"

"After," Savarra said bitterly, "unfortunately for me."

Verity pulled her to the sofa not too far from the fire, still
holding that cold, still hand. Savarra appeared controlled and
quiet, but in the light of the fire and the lamp the ugly
bruises about her face were obvious.

Verity, who had been lying sleepless and had heard the
knocker sound, sending a wild tremor of hope through her
that it might be Lord Bainbridge, now found her own newly
discovered problem receding in the light of Savarra's.

"You must hide me from Peter Haverley," Savarra said.
There was loathing and contempt in her voice. "Until my

father returns to extricate me from this hideous marriage."

Verity restrained an urge to hold the young girl to her breast and comfort those ravaged blue eyes and the sick heart that lay behind them. "You know we will help you," she said quietly. "Did you not risk your future to help us?"

Savarra's smile was a touch frightening. "I will tell you what has happened."

"You do not need to," Verity said swiftly, "if it gives you further pain. We will do all in our power to hide and protect you."

"I would like to know what has happened," Anne said bluntly, her long straight nose pinched and her mouth tight. "If we are to protect Savarra, we must know from what."

Verity looked at her mother with something close to anger. She had not revealed her own secret to Anne yet, and she dreaded it with the same dread she saw in Savarra's brilliant eyes.

But Savarra said, "Of course you must know, Mistress Pair. Sir Peter Haverley killed young Seth Barwell on our wedding day and, when he told me about it that night, I was —agitated—I let him discover my three weeks' captivity, for it was Seth who so kindly brought me home to Charles Town." Her voice lowered and the words were laced with hatred. "We quarrelled and he—struck me—more than once." She halted, and in the fraught silence the big clock in the foyer struck two. Savarra looked up, her glittering gaze like twin rapiers on Anne Pair. "He accused me of smuggling the guns to Mr. McLean and Belion and I flung my guilt in his face."

Verity caught her breath. "Oh, Savarra, you should have held your tongue! You have made it so hard on yourself."

"You think I care what Peter thinks?" She turned on Verity, her beautiful face a mirror for passionate hatred. "I am *glad* I helped them escape!"

Cotty, standing by the fire, seemed to be almost strangling, her hand at her throat, her eyes filling with fresh tears, and Savarra shot her a fiery glance. "You might as well reconcile yourself to it now, Cotty—with the exception of my father, I say my countrymen be damned in their efforts to reduce these people to slavery!"

"Oh. mistress—" Cotty's voice was smothered, but she said no more.

"He gave me to understand," Savarra's voice grew hard and cold as ice, "with a few blows for emphasis—that I would be Lady Haverley to the end of my days, and I shall not. So I expect him to come thundering down on Charles Town seeking me. That is why I ask for your help."

"You shall have it," Anne said decisively, her curved lips thinning as she drew her wrapper close about her. Anne's dark hair flowed about her shoulders, long and shining as her daughter's, and all four women looked very young and vulnerable in the firelight.

And they were vulnerable, Verity thought, to the onslaughts of such a man as Lord Haverley. She shuddered remembering those lewd pale eyes as he looked at her on their first meeting. She glimpsed the blood-crusted spot just below Savarra's collar and noted the English girl's hand reaching up to cover the wound. She had a brief instinctual knowledge of what Savarra had endured at the hands of such a man, and nausea twisted within her.

"You and Cotty will occupy my room. I shall sleep with Verity," Anne said with authority. "Thus when he arrives, no matter the hour, there will be only our two bedrooms used—and you were shrewd enough to dispose of your horses." Her voice quickened, "Being the man he is, he will no doubt search the house and you two will hide under my bed—oh, but we shall hear him long before he reaches my bedroom! And I shall pretend to to be dressing and be most indignant when he invades my bedroom!" She laughed harshly. "Ah, I shall give him a fair tongue-lashing as he or his men poke about my room—should they do so while I am but half-clothed."

Savarra looked at her speculatively. "Mistress Pair, are you not afraid Peter will have you thrown into jail if you upbraid him for seeking his wife here?"

Anne shrugged. "I am, in a way, under the protection of your father." Her eyes went fleetingly to Verity, who felt the blood rise hotly in her face, but Savarra, who was watching Anne closely, did not seem to notice.

"That is true," the English girl said slowly, "and we just may get away with it."

Amos returned with a large tray covered with smoking dishes and a silver pot of coffee. All the servants crowded in the door and Cotty and Savarra were greeted warmly by all of them. They stood silently and watched while the two girls ate hungrily of the roast chicken, heated biscuits and hot sweet potatoes. Anne refilled their cups as they emptied them. When at last Savarra and her maid tumbled into Anne's disordered bed, each clad only in a chemise, they slept immediately and heavily.

The following morning, Verity had trays brought up to the young women and they kept to Anne's room, for Colonel Scott Coyne and his aides had come into the headquarters and were busily conducting the meager military business that crossed Lord Bainbridge's desk in his absence.

True to Savarra's prediction, Peter Haverley and a picked handful of his fusiliers galloped noisily up to the Pair house shortly before noon. They heard his horses clattering down the cobblestone street and Anne flew to the bedroom, urging Cotty and Savarra to slide far back beneath the high bed, which was heavily draped with covers and included a thick ruffle tacked about the base of it.

As the knocker clanged imperiously through the house, Verity said quietly, "Slide clear to the back—'tis darker there, and make yourselves as small as possible. I will put mother's portmanteaus about you." And she pulled the bulky luggage about the crouching girls. "Here, mother, I'll help you take off that dress and pour the basin with water for your late toilette."

Then she took the stairs with a stately tread and reached the final step to be met by Amos, who was crying with all the outrage of the innocent, "Mistress Verity, this gentleman say his wife is here. He means Miss Savarra, I think, but I told him we ain't seen her."

Scott Coyne, hearing the hubbub as the fusiliers poured into the hallway, came to the door of the library headquarters. "What's going on—God's blood! 'Tis Lord Haverley! What are you doing here, colonel?"

Verity could see that Peter Haverley's patrician features were tightly controlled, his fine straight nose only slightly pinched at the nostrils, but the pale eyes betrayed his fury and frustration. "I have cause to believe Savarra has come to these rebels to pique me. We had a—small disagreement on our wedding night and she took it into her head to run away. That little chit, Cotty Penderford, is with her."

Scott Coyne's ruddy features paled slightly. Verity could see his dislike of Haverley struggling with respect for the man's title and commission. He said quietly, "I can assure you she isn't here, colonel. I have been here since very early morning—our horses are in the stables, which contain the usual number of beasts. No one has entered or left here since I arrived."

"Were you here all night?" Haverley's question was just short of a sneer and Coyne's face colored brightly.

"Of course not. But Savarra is an old friend. If she had come in, I would have been told."

"Not this time," was the venomous reply. "My wife is a tempestuous creature who needs a strong hand—she's half-Spanish, you know. She must be taught who is master in a marriage."

Revulsion and contempt filled Verity as she looked into the clean-cut, hard features. She spoke in her low voice. "Savarra is not here, colonel—nor is Cotty."

"Then you have no objection to our searching the house, have you, mistress?"

"Of course not, she replied coolly. "Will you begin on the first floor?"

He bowed shortly, "Unless you have a`basement."

"We have a wine cellar."

"Then we will start there."

Scott Coyne said, "And I will assist you in your search, colonel." His voice was cold. "I am familiar with the house and, in Lord Bainbridge's absence, responsible for it as well."

"As you like," retorted Haverley, striding after Verity as she led the way through the hall to the kitchen and thence to the dark steps leading down to the wine cellar. Three fusiliers accompanied their commander, while the other three remained in the hall.

Primrose hastily lighted a lantern and handed it to Verity, who murmured her thanks as they all took the steps carefully, reaching the dark cellar where the rows and rows of Warren Pair's fine Madeira, port, champagne and chablis lay in their multi-layered dusty racks.

From there they climbed back up to cover the first floor. Verity's heart thumped painfully as they took the stairs and began their search through the second-floor bedrooms. Scott Coyne followed closely after the three fusiliers who accompanied Haverley from room to room. He peered in closets and remarked on the fact that Savarra was not there.

"I know that fool maid of hers—Cotty—is with her, for two geldings were missing from the stables, and at an inn on the Camden road I found them. The innkeeper had traded them for the two." Peter's voice was icy with rage and a granite determination. "They rode away on two fresh mares not twenty-four hours ago, heading this way."

"There are no strange mares in the stables," Coyne said flatly.

"I'm sure of that," the pale eyes were calculating. "Savarra is not stupid."

They searched each bedroom meticulously, even opening the armoires and pawing among the clothes hung there. As they approached Anne's room, Verity remarked, "My mother is in her room. Will you knock, please?"

Haverley did so and Anne's muffled voice called, "Who is it?"

Haverley waited for Verity to speak but she did not. Then he said loudly, "It is I, Lord Haverley, madame. I must inspect your room."

Anne's voice rose an octave. "How dare you, sir! I am unclothed and in the midst of my toilette before we dine."

"Then clothe yourself, madame, and open this door. I am looking for Savarra and her maid."

"Savarra?" There was the perfect tone of shocked surprise in the words. "Why she is in Camden, sir."

"She is not in Camden, Mistress Pair," was the grim response. "Let us in or I shall force the door. It will not take long—"

Abruptly Anne flung open the door clad only in her petticoats and camisole. "British beasts!" she flung at them, her face livid with rage.

Verity came near crying out wtih surprise at her mother's audacity, and even Peter Haverley was taken aback. He averted his eyes and muttered, "You—I would have waited for you to don a wrapper, madame. I regret to disturb you but I must search your room."

"Search," responded her mother with cold fury. "You will find nothing but my clothing and toilet articles. I am concealing nothing, as you can plainly see."

Scott Coyne looked away from her, embarrassed. Truth to tell, Anne Pair was as well covered as any virtuous lady on the streets of Charles Town. But the simple fact that she was well covered with *underclothing* made all the difference. The young men were uncomfortable in her presence and hasty, which was what she had intended them to be.

While Haverley and the fusiliers went through the two tall armoires, Coyne, as he had done in the other rooms, picked up the covers about the bed and peered beneath them. He did not hesitate. "There is no one here, colonel," he said, straightening. "Are you determined to search the servants' quarters on the third floor and the attics?"

"I am" was the curt reply as Haverley himself stooped to lift the ruffle and peer under the darkness of the bed.

Verity held her breath, but he reached under and touched the portmanteaus, then withdrew and rose to his feet. Verity, her breath even shorter with the pounding of her heart, led the way from the room, with Scott Coyne bringing up the rear. Had Scott seen the two fugitives crouched behind the portmanteaus? she wondered feverishly. If he had, he spoke no word of it, made no visible sign as he doggedly accompanied them from room to room in their now-fruitless search of the third-story servants' quarters.

When they had invaded every room on the third floor, Haverley stood at the head of the stairs and paused, a finger stroking his strong chin in thought. Then without a word he moved lithely forward, taking the stairs down with a quick, light step. The others, with Verity bringing up the rear, followed. As he passed the second floor without stopping, she realized she had been holding her breath and she let it out silently.

Reaching the hall, he spoke shortly to his men. "The two of them have either been delayed along the way or are hiding somewhere in town. She had plenty of money—her father certainly saw to that. We'll have a look at the inns in the city."

Scott Coyne leaned an elbow against the wall; his clean brown eyes on Haverley were inscrutable, but Verity sensed the deep hostility in him.

One of the fusiliers who had accompanied them on the search, a thin, sharp-nosed young cornet who had been watching Verity with sly interest, said, "Sir, don't you think we should post a guard here—just in case?"

Haverley's pale eyes were almost green and his short laugh was ugly. "Good thinking, Morson. You and Goodmon and Jarrett will stay here in case she and Cotty try to slip in during our absence. Goodmon and Jarrett at the front and rear of the house respectively." He flashed a coldly amused glance at Verity. He had not missed Morson's interest in Verity and now he said, "And you will remain inside here with the ladies, Morson."

He was going to make it easier for that stringy snake to molest her! Verity's dark eyes burned with anger.

But Scott Coyne spoke up, his voice hard. "Colonel Haverley, you may post your guards outside General Bainbridge's headquarters, but I think he will take a dim view of your posting one *within* his headquarters."

Haverley turned his yellow gaze on Coyne with annoyance. "I think Lord Bainbridge will take a dim view of his daughter's precipitate and foolish behavior. If he were here, he would see to it personally that she abided by her marriage vows."

Coyne inclined his sandy head courteously. "I am sure that is so, but his military headquarters is something else again." There was iron lacing the words and Haverley shrugged indifferently. Verity shot Coyne a grateful glance.

"No matter. Morson, you will watch the front door and Goodmon will stand duty at the rear. Jarrett will return with us." He turned on Verity and his cold voice was lethal. "Mistress, if you or your mother harbor or help my wife in her willful disobedience, I will see that you pay dearly for it, your connection with Lord Bainbridge notwithstanding."

Verity replied icily, "My mother and I would never aid the *British*."

Haverley's smile was thin and cruel. "But my wife has aided the rebels, as you probably well know. Her father and I will see she suffers for *that*."

"I do not know what you are talking about," Verity said indifferently. "Savarra has never done anything to my knowledge but harm to the patriot cause."

"*Patriot* cause," Haverley said contemptuously. Then, "Coyne, you are in a nest of vipers."

"Yes," replied Coyne narrowly. "I know."

Morson observed the young colonel evilly before his attention again fixed on Verity's voluptuous figure. There was keen disappointment in his black eyes, followed swiftly by hopeful anticipation.

"Come on, my boys," Haverley said to the waiting redcoats. "Let us inspect Charles Town's inns. Morson, you and Goodmon keep a sharp eye on arrivals—*and* departures."

"Yes, sir," replied Goodmon, a thickset, small-eyed young man. "Come on, Morson. I'll take the back—you can take the front."

As the four men and their commander started out the door, Haverley turned to look back. Amos, Calhoon, Tiqua, Frances, Monique and even Primrose had come silently into the hallway and stood back of Verity. Coyne still leaned casually against the wall. Sergeant Queen and Lieutenant Keith stood in the library doorway, their curious eyes on Lord Haverley.

"I shall be back," Haverley said, his light eyes flicking those before him. "Savarra cannot escape me for long."

As he slammed the door, a gust of cold air rushed in. It was the first of March, 1781, and Verity thought irrelevantly, *It's spring.* They all stood there, a frozen tableau looking out the tall glass windows on either side of the door where Morson stood, hands on his upright gun. Verity could see Goodmon trotting around the front toward the rear. The others went to their horses, which had been tethered to the iron posts Warren Pair had placed there for that purpose so many years ago.

When they could be heard loping noisily down the cobbled street, Verity said bitterly, "That despicable man!"

Scott Coyne said vehemently, "Savarra deserved better than that! By God, he's a rotter." His face was congested with angry blood.

From the first landing on the stairs, Verity's fully clothed mother said, "Thank God they have gone."

"But they've posted a guard, front and back, mother," Verity told her, and Anne's dark winged brows drew together.

"You mean we are virtual prisoners?"

"So it appears," Verity replied, looking surreptitiously at Coyne. Had his inspection under the bed been so quick and casual he had not seen the two behind the portmanteaus in the darkness, or was he holding his tongue for love of Savarra? She concluded it was the latter.

"You two may come and go as you will," Coyne said. " 'Tis Savarra who will be a prisoner—*if* he finds her." His eyes met Verity's and there was an unspoken challenge in them as he added, "And I pray to God he does not find her."

Verity knew he had said all he could say then, and she was certain he had seen the two girls. As a British soldier and one who loved Savarra, he would say no more, but Verity's mind was a turbulent whirlpool. How could they continue to hide Savarra, if Haverley came back to make further searches? Where could they send her and Cotty, with guards at the doors? Her eyes sought her mother's desperately and saw in their depths a calm certainty. She sensed that her mother had already wrestled with this problem and solved it.

She began climbing the stairs toward Anne, aware that behind her the servants were dispersing silently as Scott

Coyne and his men went back into the library headquarters.

Reaching her mother's side, Verity said in a low voice, "How shall we keep her hidden? You know that man will return—for even a more thorough search."

"Do you think Colonel Coyne saw them when he looked so carefully beneath the bed?" her mother asked as the two women climbed the stairs to the second floor and walked down the hall.

"Of course he did, but he will say nothing for he loves Savarra—but he cannot allow himself as a soldier to become part of her escape."

"I know," replied Anne coolly. "Being a British soldier to the marrow of his bones, he will *do* nothing to help us either."

"Oh, if only Lord Bainbridge would come!"

Outside her bedroom door, Anne Pair stopped and looked into her daughter's eyes. Her voice was cold and pure. "My dear Verity, you had better count on nothing from that one. After all, British laws regarding marriage are what American laws are based on, and Lord Haverley has a right to demand the return of his wife to him." She paused and her eyes burned with a frightening light. "Lord Bainbridge has not that call on you—nor will he."

Verity looked away from her mother's accusing prophecy, her heart sinking heavily. How could she tell this woman of such strong moral beliefs that she, Verity, was now wholly bound to Lord Bainbridge and, though her mother could not know it, Anne Pair would eventually be bound to him by the tie of blood.

Anne said huskily, "Savarra, you and Cotty may come out now. They have gone to search the inns of the city."

There was a soft rustle beneath the bed, a pushing away of the protective luggage, and Cotty emerged first, her gold hair falling in disorderly curls about her face. Savarra followed, her long straight hair falling from its pins in a thick mass that formed a roll on her shoulders.

She got to her feet, pulling the rumpled petticoats down and silently thanking God that Peter and his men had failed to note the two still damp and soiled riding habits hanging in Verity's armoire. "He will return, you know," she said flatly. There were pale blue smudges of fatigue beneath her eyes. Cotty began to sob quietly, great glistening tears rolling down her already streaked face.

"Yes," replied Anne, "he will return, but he shall not find the two of you here."

Savarra's little smile was ironic. "I wish I could be so sure of that, Mistress Pair. Unless you turn me out, Cotty and I will not leave here."

"But you shall," Anne said impersonally, "and you will be —perhaps uncomfortable—but you will be safe from Peter Haverley."

Savarra viewed her benefactress skeptically, but Cotty's wide wet eyes held sudden hope. She gulped, "Oh, mistress, any place—away from *him*. He's a dretful beast—"

"Come," Anne said, beckoning the half-clad girls to the sofa before the hearth on which the fire still smouldered.

Verity took Savarra's cold hand in hers as the girl sat down beside her. "Do not look so despairing, Savarra," she said comfortingly, quelling her own fears. "Mother and I have devised a plan for your escape and we have already begun working to that end. Listen!—"

Fourteen

Verity stood peering nervously out the kitchen windows at the curving arch of the shell drive where it formed the courtyard. The British soldier, Goodmon, sat upon one of two wrought-iron benches edging the courtyard in the early afternoon sunlight, yawning deeply. He had a right to yawn, for the servants, in league with Anne and Verity, had served him a magnificent noonday meal, and Anne had been lavish with Warren Pair's Madeira. Goodmon was slightly stupefied as the warm Carolina spring sun beat down upon him.

Her mother had prevailed upon Verity herself to take Morson's meal to him in the front. She had smiled when she handed him the tray and spoke in a friendly manner of the beauty of the day after the wind and rain so shortly past. His eyes were hot upon her. Verity had thought coldly, *Ah, but I shall put you in your place quickly enough when Savarra and Cotty are safely away*. She had left a full bottle of Madeira with him.

Now as she watched, Amos rode into the courtyard beside

the kitchen, his skinny fourteen-year-old twin nephews upon a fat mule behind Amos, who rode one of the fine British bays from the Pair stables. The soldier, Goodmon, got lazily to his feet from the iron bench. Verity heard Primrose's sharply drawn breath behind her and Monique muttered a soft half-French, half-African epithet. But over the faint crackle of licking flames in the great cooking fireplace, they could hear the soldier plainly.

"Who have you there, man?"

"My two nephews from over to the Pearsons'. They does some spring yardwork for the Pairs. They gonna work fer Mistress Pair fer a little extry money an' they supper. This here's Rafe and this here's Lafe."

The soldier looked at the broad grins and shining black faces of the two slim young boys indifferently. "Well—get about it, then."

The two youngsters wore well-scarred but surprisingly good boots on their small feet and the usual rough handwoven breeches with coarse shirts under warm wool jackets. On their curly heads each wore a broad-brimmed heavy felt hat, somewhat soiled but effectively protecting them from the warm March sun. They slid nimbly from the mule, and Morson came around the side of the house to see what was occurring.

"We goin' in ter get a jug o' water," one said in a thin, reedy voice that was obviously changing.

"Get along with it," Goodmon said, and Amos took the two boys into the kitchen.

As they came in the door, they looked at Verity and the servants, their grins broad and mischievous.

"Here," Primrose said, grinning back, "set down and have a piece o' cake an' some milk 'fore you get to work. I'll fix a jug o' water fer you two rascals."

The boys seated themselves with bright anticipation at the long kitchen worktable. "Maw done let us wear our bes' boots," volunteered Lafe.

"An' our Sunday hats fer to keep the sun off," echoed Rafe, removing that item to the floor beside him and accepting a great feathery wedge of Primrose's chocolate cake, covered with thick white icing.

"You boys mind your tongues and don't talk to those soldiers guarding the house any more than you must," Verity said firmly, "and you know very well why you wear your best boots and hats."

"No'm—yes'm," they spoke hastily in unison. "Amos tol'

us he pinch our heads off do we make a slip," Rafe finished solemnly.

In a short while the two were out in the front yard, spading fork and hoe in hand, industriously working the many flowerbeds that bordered the fences and Pair house. It was a very long afternoon and it grew warmer as the day wore on. Verity had Tiqua take a pitcher of lemonade out to the boys and sent Monique out to Morson and Goodmon with a bottle of chilled but potent cider, and she observed from behind a curtained window as they drank thirstily. Several Charles Town citizens came and went, as well as some of the soldiers garrisoning Charles Town, keeping the headquarters fairly busy.

To Verity, the day dragged interminably. She and her mother sat in the kitchen before the evening meal and talked with Amos, while Savarra and Cotty remained hidden in Anne's bedroom upstairs.

Her mother said, "Amos, have Caleb and Corrie been very unhappy since the Scurlocks took over Cutler's property?"

"They sure have—they been miserable, mistress. They are happy to have this excuse to leave. Caleb say old Mr. Scurlock's been mean as sin since he got wounded in his shoulder by them patriots near Leneud's Ferry last August. Corrie say him an' ol' Mistress Scurlock got pitchers of ol' George Third hung all over the McLean house now."

Anne laughed dryly and said, "You needn't worry about your nephews. They will spend the night quite safely in the quarters upstairs—and your clothes ought to fit them well enough tomorrow morning. The trick will be to get another mule back here during the night so Rafe and Lafe can be working again very early and unobtrusively. Hopefully without being noticed by our—captors."

"I heard the one name Morson tell Goodmon they gonna be relieved after supper sometime an' two more o' Haverley's men'll take they places."

"We can't let the girls leave until near dark. It will have to be after the change is made. We mustn't stir the slightest suspicion." Anne spoke positively and Verity looked at her mother with admiration. "And it must be dark enough for us to get away with the deception."

"You're a very smart lady, mistress," Amos said respectfully. "I s'pect we'll get clean away with it an' Caleb and Corrie'll have 'em long gone by this time termorrow."

"If all goes as planned," Anne said cautiously.

"Mother, you are good to do this," Verity said quietly.

"Savarra has done us a great service in saving Cutler and Tyler. She deserves all the help we can give her." Anne shivered and added, "That man's eyes—that Lord Haverley— I never saw such rapacious eyes. She must have suffered greatly at his hands before she could escape him."

Verity had never told her mother of her meeting with Peter Haverley and his insultingly intimate pinch and pat. Anne had evidenced no surprise, no outrage, only disgust.

The day dragged on and the twins lazily spaded and pulled weeds, clipped overabundant shrubs and pruned among the crepe myrtles. They rested frequently and demanded a great deal of water and lemonade to quench their endless thirst. It was one of those rare days when spring and warmth came early and coats were not needed. The twins shed theirs and laid them on the porch, neatly folded.

Inside the house, Verity was in a ferment. She went often to Anne's room to discuss events as they took place with the two pale-faced girls who waited there. Once she said to Savarra, "My dear, you really should lie down on mother's bed and sleep, for this night will find you traveling far and as fast as the mule will take the two of you. Cotty, you should do so, too."

"I'm too nervous to sleep," Cotty said with a touch of hysteria. "I won't be able to rest until I'm fer away from Charles Town an' Lord Haverley. Are ye sure this Caleb an' his wife know the way to the rebel camp?"

"Patriot—partisan, not rebel!" Verity said coldly. Then with renewed sympathy, "Cotty, Caleb knows where many of the partisan camps are. Colonel Marion moves a great deal. No British soldiers have ever been able to surprise him. By this time tomorrow you should be near them and they will protect and conceal your presence." Verity thought of the restless and impatient McLean and felt a twinge of apprehension at the thought of sending him not two, but three women, counting Corrie, to follow their camp.

Then she reminded herself of his flat statement to Savarra —that he stood ready to repay her for her part in his and Belion's escape. She remembered too Savarra's imperious dismissal of his offer, certain she would never have to meet with him again. Ah, well, the sparks might fly, but at least Savarra would be beyond reach of her cruel and brutal husband.

At least Savarra had made no demur when Anne had told

her of her plan to slip them from the Pair house, clad in
boys' clothing, and send them into the swamps. Indeed, there
had been a brief flash of hope and relief lighting that weary
and beautiful countenance. She had said with bitter intensity,
"*Anywhere* away from Peter will be a relief, no matter the
hardship."

Now the household was suspended in the ordeal of
waiting for late evening when the twins, while supposedly
taking their supper, would remove their clothing in the
quarters upstairs and Savarra and Cotty would don it in
Anne's room. Primrose had garnered from the kitchen fireplace several chunks of soft charcoal and stood ready to
blacken the faces and hands of the two British girls.

If all went well, they would ride easily and slowly out of
the shell drive and down the streets of Charles Town
escorted by Amos, unnoticed until they could meet with
Caleb and Corrie on the outskirts beside the banks of the
full Cooper River. They would take the Camden road, but
they would turn off early and cross the Cooper to lose themselves in the vastness of the thick forests and swamps.

At last the supper lamps were lit. Colonel Coyne and his
men closed the headquarters and bade the Pair women good
evening. Coyne's eyes were bright, his mouth firm and his
manner imperviously British as they departed. The moment
for action had come.

Verity, bringing the young lads' clothing down from the
third floor where the twins were donning some of Amos's old
clothing, felt her nerves draw ever tighter with apprehension.
And she realized with something of wonder that not once
during the day had she thought of the hard and irrefutable
fact with which she must face her mother—and soon. She
put it from her mind now as she entered Anne's room where
Savarra and Cotty sat waiting tensely.

"First, we will charcoal their faces and hands," Anne said
briskly. "Then they will don the clothing and boots." She
and Primrose took the soft charcoal and went over each
weary face carefully, covering even their eyelids, until only
eyes and teeth were white. Cotty looked oddest, with her
gold hair clustered about the black face. The clothing was
a perfect fit on each girl, though the boots were a little large
on their small feet.

Primrose had brought their evening meal, a rich and
delicious one, to the room. They ate but little of it due to
excitement. The twins, in the kitchen below, did much better

by their portions, asking for seconds as they sat there clad in Amos's cast-offs and looking forward to sleeping the night in the big rooms on the third floor.

After supper, the moment came when Cotty and Savarra must go out and mount the mule. Amos would lead them, for he had planted the fact that he must watch over his young nephews' comings and goings in the late evening. They had not yet changed guards though near-darkness was on the city, with a faint crimson edge beyond town where the sun had set some time ago.

The two guards paid them scant attention as the two mounted the mule and moved off with Amos riding lead on the bay. From inside Anne and Verity watched them depart in the dim light, their hearts in their throats. Verity whispered a prayer, "God help them—watch over them in the coming times for it will be so hard on them."

Savarra was the pampered darling of an English lord and Cotty had been pampered by Savarra. Yet, Verity reminded herself, Savarra had survived three weeks in the swamps, traveling continually, and had flourished on it. She had looked glowing and healthy despite her trials last August. Verity restrained a smile. They were a tougher breed than they appeared. Lord Bainbridge, lean and hard, had taught her the streak of steel that ran through him.

The three, Amos, Savarra and Cotty, were lost in the shadows beyond the curving drive and Goodmon had scarcely noted them, so full of rich supper was he. Anne and Verity raced to the front and observed that the equally stuffed Morson paid them little heed, looking only briefly at them as they passed.

Then they were out on the cobbled street and Verity and her mother drew a deep sighing breath of relief. Half the scheme was complete. Now if only Amos could smuggle another mule in through the back, far behind the gardens in the dead of night. Then the two boys would work most of tomorrow and none would be the wiser.

Before they turned from the front windows they heard the brisk canter of several horses, and the two exchanged glances as the horsemen turned in on the shell drive.

"It's that Haverley—come back to change the guard and look again! He'll find Lafe and Rafe in the servants' quarters!" Verity said with sudden panic.

"No," Anne said smoothly. "Morson and Goodmon will

tell them there has been only the headquarters traffic and yardboys going and coming. Let me handle him."

But Verity stood beside her mother as they met him in the hallway. His face was murderous. "Well, madame, I understand you have had no visitors who did not leave at the appointed time. But I have decided to keep your house under observation for the next three days."

"Very well, colonel," Ane replied serenely. "You will find we harbor no one."

"But you would, if she came here," he said with his thin cruel smile.

"We would not," Anne replied blandly. "Your wife probably found refuge with country people long before she reached Charles Town."

"I doubt that. She is familiar with Charles Town, and I expect she is secreted in some house right here in the city." There was frustration in his clipped voice. Then firmly, "I will keep my guards posted about your house, madame."

"I should think your duties would call you—that you would have more urgent missions in which to employ yourself."

"Indeed I have, eventually," he replied, his voice cutting like a whip. "We plan to meet your stupid Nathanael Greene and slaughter him. Then we will wipe out the pockets of resistance with the greatest ease. By this time next year, the colonies will be completely subdued." His grim face was frightening and his voice disturbingly convincing.

"So you say," replied Anne, her smile chill. "Nevertheless, while you are out searching for Savarra, you can do no harm to the patriots. I hope you search for her for months."

"I shall find her shortly. I am doubling the guard about your house tonight. She will come here—I know it."

Anne's smile was inscrutable. "Perhaps you are right, but I can assure you we will give no British subject help."

"You are lying," he said flatly, turning on his heel without further elaboration and leaving the house.

Verity watched his departure thinking, *You are a liar, too. Savarra and I quarrelled,* he had said. What a masterpiece of dissembling. Verity remembered too well the bruises on Savarra's golden skin, the look of desperation and a new kind of terror that lay in those vivid eyes with tired smudges beneath them. She had a deep instinctual knowledge that Peter Haverley was a master of lies—and cruelty.

When the evening lengthened and the hour for retirement

came, the house grew quiet. Verity, full of thought and uneasiness, prepared for bed. She remembered her mother's remarkable sangfroid through the crisis, her cool solution and her apparent understanding of Savarra's desperation, and with that thought her own misery welled up in her until there was a great lump in her throat.

She looked at her nude body in the mirror before donning her nightdress and it was slim and perfect still, despite a curious feeling of fullness that plagued her these mornings. Her appetite had flagged and she knew the reason for it well enough. Could she confide in her mother—should she? At the thought, dry laughter mingled with tears. It didn't matter whether she told her now or later. The die was cast and there would be no concealing her condition as the weeks ahead unrolled.

The following morning found another mule standing in the stall munching straw in the Pair Stables, and the rising sun found the twin nephews busily pulling weeds and loosening the earth in the gardens behind the house. Verity, observing this from the kitchen with narrowed eyes, turned to Primrose.

"How did Amos pull it off, Primrose? That's Goodmon out there already."

Primrose shrugged as she pulled a pan of hot biscuits from the great brick oven built into the side of the fireplace. "Amos done slip that mule in 'fore daylight. He mighty quiet when he likes to be. An' Rafe an' Lafe slip out through the side winder whilst Goodmon an' that ol' Morson took over from them four night soldiers. They lookin' fer me to feed 'em now." She laughed suddenly, a chuckle deep in her massive bosom. "British soldiers sure likes our Carolina food."

"And drink," Anne said dryly from the hall door. Verity turned and saw that her mother was as always, perfectly groomed. It seemed to her she could smell the faint spicy scent of cologne across the kitchen. She added, "Savarra and Cotty should be well into the swamps with Caleb and Corrie by now."

"What will we tell Lord Bainbridge when he returns?" Verity asked, her heart beating faster at just the mention of his name.

Anne shrugged eloquently. "We shall know nothing of it." Then her dark eyes flashed to Verity's. "*Nothing.* Despite your rela—" She broke off, then finished. "Your father and

I have taught you to always speak the truth. This is one time we shall lie, Verity."

Verity's smile was bitter as she turned back to the window. Her mother had caught herself just in time. Primrose went about the business of beating up eggs as Monique and Tiqua, followed by a sleepy Frances, entered.

Calhoon, who had been out at the stables feeding the horses, clumped in through the back door, sniffing the air, which was filled with the fragrance of baked biscuits and frying bacon. His young face was split by a wide grin as he bowed to the Pair ladies. All the black people knew of the deception that had taken place the day before and last night, but by neither eye nor mouth did they betray an inkling of it. Indeed, their pride in outwitting the British colonel was almost tangible.

"You will feed the two British soldiers outside before you serve us, Primrose," Anne said with cool aplomb, adding, "Tiqua, you may take the tray to the one in the rear, and Monique, you may serve the one at the front." She exchanged a glance with her daughter. There would be no more meals served the soldiers personally by the Pair women. Verity's bitter smile grew.

Late that afternoon, Lord Haverley came again to the house. He entered without knocking and Verity, who was descending the stairs, paused in the shadows above to observe him. He strode to the headquarters door and stood looking in at Colonel Coyne and his men, who were readying to close down for the night. She heard Coyne speak but could not make out his words.

But Haverley's voice was nasty. "I know she will come here eventually, but I cannot wait any longer, nor can I spare my men to stay. I have just received word from Lord Rawdon and I must leave immediately for Camden."

Verity drew in a deep relieved breath. He was giving up then! At least for the time being, Savarra would have no pursuers and the Pair house would not be under such strict surveillance. Haverley's clean-cut profile turned and she saw it lined distinctly against the pale light from the two hall windows beside the door, handsome but without a trace of gentleness. Savarra had been an unthinking little fool, she thought.

Then as her stomach churned suddenly and nausea swept

her, she thought, *but no greater fool than I.* At least Savarra had had the promise of marriage, which was certainly more than Verity had or would have. She found herself hoping with sudden sadness that Savarra's brief and dreadful experience did not result in what Verity herself was now facing.

As if drawn, Peter Haverley looked upward and discerned her standing on the steps above him. He bowed and said, "Do come down, Mistress Pair. You will, I'm sure, be happy to know that I and my men are returning to Camden."

"I heard," she replied coldly without moving. "Goodbye, Colonel Haverley." When she saw Coyne and his two aides step into the hallway, she took the last of the stairs. She did not plan to allow Peter Haverley to be in a room alone with her again.

"Before I leave," Haverley said, eyeing her narrowly, "I shall go over this house once more and with a fine-toothed comb."

Anne, coming in from the hall, said, "This time you shall do so without my or my daughter's assistance." Her voice was icy. "Come, Verity. We will dine, for Primrose has said it is ready." Then contemptuously, "I presume you do not wish me to continue to feed your guards about this house."

"I thought that uncommonly gracious of you, madame," he said mockingly, "when Goodmon and Morson told me of it, for I had made no such request."

Colonel Coyne inserted smoothly, "We are closing down headquarters for the night, Mistress Pair. Good evening to you." And the three men moved swiftly through the hallway, closing the front door quietly behind them.

Without a word, Haverley went to the door himself, flung it open and called, "Morson! You and Goodmon and Lawrence come in—we're going to go through this house again. This time, you will open every chest, every cupboard, every closet and armoire." He turned on the two women who stared at him in dismay. "Yes, my dear ladies." His cultured voice was low and vicious. "You will have your hands full tidying up after *this* search, I assure you." Then, as his men entered, he smiled coldly. "Enjoy your evening meal, both of you." And he mounted the stairs, taking three steps at a time with his long, booted legs.

Anne and Verity looked after them as the four men reached the gloom at the first landing. Then Haverley leaned back and called, "Send your servants up here with four lamps, Madame Pair." Then as Anne made no reply, "You will do as I say, madame, or you will suffer. Your drapes and linens are not saber-proof, I assure you."

"I will send them up immediately, Colonel Haverley," Anne replied stiffly.

Amos and Tiqua took the lamps, one in each hand. In the dining salon, Amos paused. "You want we should stay by an' watch 'em, mistress?"

Anne hesitated, but Verity said, "You might offer to hold the lamps while they make—their search. Who knows? They might decide to fire the house." In the light of the candelabra of tall tapers, Verity saw her mother's pale throat work with fear.

Primrose's golden-brown fat hen might have been straw for all that Verity and her mother could taste. They listened tensely to the thumps and thuds above them as the British soldiers ransacked the house. Verity thought grimly of Savarra's and Cotty's riding habits and cloaks hanging sedately in her own armoire, their boots neatly side-by-side on the floor of the armoire. There was no way in the world Peter Haverley could tell they belonged to Savarra and her maid without a measuring tape. Even then, he could not be sure. He would find no trace of his quarry. The hunter would leave unsatisfied if she and her mother could only endure the waiting for him to go.

At last and long after Anne and Verity had finished their meal, boots could be heard clumping down stairs, and in a moment the four soldiers stood in the doorway to the drawing room. Haverley's beautiful and cruel face was stony.

"As you both probably know, I found nothing—no one. But I'd stake my life on her having been here at one time— probably before I arrived. I shall enlist Lord Bainbridge's aid in securing the return of my bride." His precise, clipped voice carried iron certainty.

Verity was unable to restrain her wayward tongue. "It was my understanding that Lord Bainbridge did not look with too much favor on your marriage to his daughter. Are you so sure his sympathies will be with you, Lord Haverley?"

His brows drew together darkly. "When I tell him how abominably Savarra behaved, he will certainly come to my aid."

"If she was so abominable," Verity could not stem the words, "why do you wish her to return?"

He laughed shortly. "I do not give up my possessions so

easily, mistress—and you are a forward wench to question your betters."

Anne shot her daughter a warning glance as rage mantled Verity's smooth brow and her pink lips parted. An unexpected wave of nausea struck her and she swallowed convulsively, saying nothing, her dark lashes lying like delicate fans against her cheeks.

"I bid you good evening," Haverley said curtly, and suddenly they were gone.

The two women stood motionless while the front door closed harshly. Rough male voices came to their ears as Haverley and his men mounted their horses. When at last came the rattle of hooves on cobblestones, Anne drew a deep breath.

"What a pity we cannot tell Lord Bainbridge of Savarra's —wounds at the hands of that brute," she said thoughtfully.

"Mother," Verity said passionately, "we *must* tell him. He must not be seeking his daughter for the purpose of placing her in Haverley's hands once more!"

Anne looked at her levelly in the warm glow of lamps upon the foyer tables. "Daughter, we cannot tell him. It would be very wrong to give him such a strong incentive for tracking down our partisans. He would be inexorable."

"I think—mother, I *know* Lord Bainbridge feels sympathy for us in our fight for liberty. He has gone so far as to tell me he understands fully our desire for it—"

"I've no doubt he said these things to you in the privacy— of his bedroom," her eyes on Verity held love and hurt and reproof, "in an effort to endear himself to you. It meant nothing, surely you know that. He is indeed already inexorable in his determination to conquer us. If he knew his daughter was with our partisans, he would spare no effort to retrieve her—even for that scoundrel Haverley."

"I don't believe it," Verity said stubbornly.

Her mother sighed deeply. "My dear, you must give me your word that you will tell him nothing of this. Other than the fact that Haverley ransacked our home seeking Savarra." Her dark eyes burned into Verity's as she added, "I can still trust you to keep your word—in spite of what the man has come to mean to you?"

Verity bowed her head. "Yes, mother. I will say nothing." *And I can say nothing to you of the burden I carry now. You would never understand, never forgive.*

The following morning, Verity rose to vomit quietly into the bowl on her washstand. She had missed two months and had concluded she was eight weeks along in her pregnancy. She remembered dimly that with Bonnie Raintree the nausea had lasted twelve weeks, but after that she had been rosy and delightfully comfortable right up to the day of her confinement. Though Verity had been a reedy adolescent, the events of the births of the Raintree children had been fascinating. She and her young girl friends had talked interminably of these things, learning but little from each other.

Bonnie was scarcely five years older than she, and with the thought of her round, amiable face and kind voice Verity felt a great pressure well up in her to confide. She had been genuinely fond of Lord Bainbridge, and he had in no way been responsible for Spencer's death.

Rinsing her mouth with cool water, she spat into the bowl and wiped her lips. A bitter taste was in her mouth and she could not dispel it. A resolution formed in her mind as she emptied the bowl into the porcelain container beneath her bed. She would have Amos drive her to Bonnie's small and humble home and ask her to accompany her to the shops in the city. Verity would buy their luncheon at Mrs. Applegate's Bake Shop, and over tea and cakes she would reveal her problem to Bonnie. Older and wiser, Bonnie might have a solution.

Oh, Verity thought as she slowly dressed, if only she could go away for seven or eight months—returning with a baby that could be adopted—a waif whose mother could not care for it! A thousand explanations and excuses flooded her mind. There must be a way out of this trap!

Lord Bainbridge would return one of these days and she did not know if she could conceal the truth from him. What would he say? It was hard not to imagine him shrugging his broad shoulders and remarking, *I'm sorry, my dear. It was a risk you took. Now you must solve your problem. I am a peer of the realm and I cannot marry below my station.* She was certain that would be his reaction and her heart beat heavily, a sinking depression upon her.

That afternoon found Bonnie exhilarated over the invitation. She sent Belle and Terrell to the Pearson house where they would spend the hours with their children and dressed herself quickly under Verity's haunted gaze.

Penury sat hard upon Bonnie for she had enjoyed the extravagance and spending she had indulged in while Spencer's merchandising business flourished. Still, she could not, she told Verity and Anne weeks ago, bring herself to write her affluent parents in London, so bitter were her feelings toward the British.

Now she chattered gaily to Verity as they entered shops, exclaiming over the delicate laces and the elegant dresses of silk, satin and velvet. She did not seem to notice Verity's quietness.

When at last they sat in the cozy confines of Mrs. Applegate's she looked at Verity with sudden sharpness. "My dear Verity, you look quite pale and you didn't eat your omelette. Are you not well?"

"No, Bonnie, I am not well. But 'tis something that will pass with time." Her low voice was so freighted with meaning that Bonnie's lifted brows drew together and she leaned toward her companion.

"What do you mean, Verity?" she asked alertly. Then intuitively, "Something *is* the matter!"

"Yes, Bonnie, and I must counsel with some one. My mother would never countenance what I am about to reveal to you."

Bonnie looked at her with complete absorption, her tea and cakes forgotten. Her small hands on the table were very still. "You can confide in me, Verity," she said quietly.

It was late and the patrons of the bake shop had dispersed, all but two elderly ladies in a far corner. Verity gave her friend the truth flatly and without preamble. "I am pregnant."

Bonnie's mouth made a small round O. Then, "You and Tyler have not been secretly married—you would not wait?"

"It is not Tyler's child. It is the child of Lord Bainbridge. I love him beyond measure."

Bonnie's mouth fell open and she stared in frank disbelief. Verity's voice grew lower, almost a whisper. "I know he will not—cannot marry me and I dread the moment he must learn of this! Oh, God, Bonnie, if I could go away to the country until it is born—if I could hide!" Then despairingly, "I *cannot* tell my mother!"

"No," Bonnie said reflectively. "You cannot tell Anne. It would break her heart."

"I know that," Verity said dully, unable to bring herself to reveal that Anne knew already of her liaison and was suffering from the knowledge. "What am I to do?"

Bonnie was silent for such a long time that Verity despaired of her advice at all. The she took up her fork and slowly and deliberately cut off part of a small cake and put it into her mouth. She chewed, took a sip of the cooling tea and looked at Verity with speculative sorrow.

Then she asked in a low voice, "Verity, do you want this —child of Lord Bainbridge?"

Verity, under pressure, burst out, "I want only to keep Lord Bainbridge happy. The baby means nothing to me but an obstacle—a formidable problem between me and my love. He has never mentioned marriage and I know he will not mention it." Her small fist clenched beside the teacup and plate. "He will never marry me and *I do not care*. I love him!"

There was a small silence, then Bonnie spoke in a voice thick with sorrow. "You did not know—no one knew, but two years ago I became pregnant." Her voice caught on a near-sob. "I did not even tell Spencer because I didn't want another child. I felt I had all I could handle and I—wanted to go to England to see my mother and father." There was a long silence, then, "I went to the midwife, old Mistress Marilla—"

"I've heard of her," Verity said slowly, the tales coming back to her. "Some say she's a witch, her cures are so miraculous—and she's delivered many babies—"

"She delivered me of my unwanted pregnancy," Bonnie said quietly. "For a large fee, she will deliver you of yours. But it must be early in the pregnancy—how far along are you?"

"No more than eight weeks, I think," Verity replied hesitantly. "What does she do? How can—you mean she *takes* the baby?"

"She has some metal implements and she can bring on the baby—" her voice trailed off and she added abruptly, "I wish I had kept it. It would be one more tie to Spencer."

"Were you very sick? Did it—was it painful?" Verity swallowed hard.

"Yes, it was painful but only for a short time. I simply took to my bed when I reached home, pleading a headache, and no one was the wiser." Her eyes on Verity were wide and tender. "I will take you to old Marilla, Verity, if that's what you want. You can go home to bed this afternoon, stay a few days complaining of an indisposition. You have plenty of money now that Bowman manages your affairs. And Marilla is one woman who can hold her tongue. I have it on good authority that she performs this service for many Charles Town ladies."

Verity's eyes were reflective. "I wouldn't have to tell mother

—anything. I should be well enough by the time Lord Bainbridge returns. It would solve—everything."

Bonnie said uneasily, "It must be done as soon as possible, Verity. There is danger to you when it is later and the baby is well formed." Her eyes went over Verity swiftly and she murmured, "Your stomacher still fits beautifully. You are slim as a reed."

A vast impatience swept Verity. "Could we go and have it done this afternoon?" she asked eagerly. "I could return home—with a headache and upset stomach. Mother would tend me and never suspect."

"Come then, we will go there. I will tell Amos I am going for some herbal medicines and advice while he waits for us. It takes a very short time."

But Amos looked disapproving when Bonnie told him of her errand. "Primrose says that ol' lady like a witch—she's bad."

"Nonsense," Bonnie said briskly, "she's delivered many healthy babies and I consult her for tonics for my children regularly, Amos."

But Amos drove with his lower lip thrust out and a scowl on his black face as they made their way to the outskirts of town on the Ashley River side. When they drew up before the small, dark dwelling, Verity looked at it with sudden misgivings. The yard was meticulously kept and the house was in good repair. It looked neat and there was a curious air of efficiency about it.

"I shall be in here some little time, Amos," Bonnie said carelessly. "Would you like to come in with me, Verity?"

"Yes. I'm curious to see the woman—she's a legend," replied Verity, stepping down from the carriage with Amos's hand under her elbow. He was still scowling and muttered his disaproval under his breath as he remounted the box.

The two women knocked and the door was opened by a tall, spare woman with masses of iron-gray hair looped at the back of her head. Her face was ageless and there was a sharp and shrewd look in her small, clear blue eyes. She was spotlessly clean, as was the dim room behind her.

She admitted the two with a curt, "How are you feeling, Madame Raintree? And what brings you here today?"

Verity had the feeling that nothing could surprise this statuesque woman with her immobile face. Bonnie removed her hat and Verity did likewise. Then Bonnie said slowly,

"I am well, Marilla, but I bring this young lady to you with the problem I had two years ago." She turned tender and troubled eyes on her friend and added, "She is eight weeks along and she wishes to terminate her pregnancy."

"Ain't you Warren Pair's daughter?" Marilla asked with a hawklike turn of her head, her cool eyes running over Verity's abdomen.

"Yes," replied Verity bravely, "and I am not married to this baby's father, nor is there any hope that I will be. Therefore, I do not wish to bear it."

Marilla nodded, her voice deliberate. "Then I'll fix it up for you right away. You have come early enough, though I could wish 'twas only four weeks past. Still, it's not too dangerous." Then coolly, "It will cost you, Mistress Pair."

"I will pay," Verity said.

Marilla ushered them to a back room of the house where a great wooden table centered the room, and she began spreading snow-white linen upon it. Then she began to assemble a series of long sharp metal probes and instruments. She lit two bright oil lamps.

As she watched, a strange disembodied feeling crept through Verity. All the time the woman went slowly and expertly about her preparations, Verity found herself suddenly preoccupied with the thought of the child she carried. Was it a little girl with blonde curls and those intensely blue eyes? Or was it a sturdy little boy who would grow up straight and tall like his dashing father? Those fleeting minutes drew out and Verity's emotions grew more turbulent.

All at once, she found herself thinking of the unfinished little one beneath her heart as a person. It was totally unexpected, and her heart began skipping beats so that she had to catch her breath with a gasp. She was going to put to death in this clean, sparely furnished room a person who had as much right to be born as she herself had when Anne Pair carried her nine months.

Then Marilla said, "Take off your clothing and drape this sheet about you, Mistress Pair. The operation will not take long, but you must lie quite still for an hour before you get up to return home."

Verity was seized by an unexpected terror and revulsion. In the flash of an instant she realized her baby had already come to be loved by her and, in her agitation over the problem its arrival would incur, she had refused to let that love surface. Now her maternal instincts rushed forward and she was in utter confusion and panic. Above that panic the stark truth towered up. She loved her unborn child and she could not give it up, no matter the cost.

She said harshly, "I have changed my mind, Marilla. I shall bear my baby."

Bonnie and Marilla stared at her in astonishment. Then Marilla shrugged. "I've had others come in like you and change their minds at the last minute," and with fatalistic certainty, "but they always came back—later, when it was harder on them."

"I will not return," Verity said, donning her cloak and hat and opening her reticule. "Here is a gold sovereign for your trouble, Marilla. Come, Bonnie, let us leave."

When they were out in the carriage once more, Bonnie's low voice was greatly disturbed. "Verity, darling, you have chosen a very hard road to follow. An unwed mother suffers —great contempt. Anne will suffer, too." Then suddenly her hand closed with hurtful tightness over Verity's and choked, "But I don't blame you!"

The most intensely protective instinct had loosed itself in Verity and it boiled out. "My baby—*my* little one. I must have been mad to think I could murder it—and *murder* it would be, for already it is becoming a person."

"People are such fools," Bonnie said bitterly. "They prattle of disgrace—"

"Disgrace be damned." Verity's voice was hard. "My baby has a right to life and I intend to see that she—or he—has it." In her mind she was facing Lord Bainbridge, flinging the fact of their baby in his face. Though she loved the man more than life, she found she loved her unborn child with equal fervor.

I will never give this baby up, she thought resolutely. *Never. If James turns away from me, I shall endure it alone. If mother turns against me, I shall survive it and my child shall grow up straight and strong and enjoy life to the fullest.*

In the silence that had fallen between her and Bonnie, she began marshalling her arguments and the revelation she would make to her mother. She did not plan to let it slowly become apparent that she was expecting. The fact would be honestly faced and Anne would adjust as best she could.

As they neared Bonnie's house, she took both Verity's cold hands in her own chilled ones. "My dear friend, if I can do anything—be of any help, you have but to call on me. You can—come to me at any time, for anything." She hesitated, then, "You are either very brave or very foolish."

"Perhaps I am a little of both, Bonnie, but I treasure your friendship and I will want you to be near me when my time comes—if you do not feel you will be disgraced by our friendship."

"I shall be there, Verity. You may count on it," she replied evenly.

The carriage clattered away and rattled down the streets to the better section of town. As they passed the fine houses, Verity made up her mind that she would tell her mother this very night. No more subterfuge, no living a lie—and her spirits lifted miraculously. She had not realized how deep into the miasma of guilt her thoughts had thrust her until this moment of decision.

As Amos assisted her from the carriage under the porte-cochere, he said, "Mistress Verity, I ain't gone tell your ma you an' Mistress Bonnie stopped by that ol' witch's house, an' I recommen' you ain't say nothin' either."

Verity gave him a lighthearted smile. "I shall tell her all about it, Amos. After all, we only stayed a minute." And she ran up the steps and across the porch to fling open the door.

In the hallway she removed her cloak and hat, which had not really protected her from the bright, windy March day for her hair was disordered. She looked into the hall mirror at her rosy face and brilliant eyes. A turning point had been reached and Verity was riding a high tide of euphoria.

I will call mother and tell her at once—get it over. Her conscience quivered slightly at the thought of the sorrow and sadness she would bring to the courageous and high-principled Anne Pair, but she stilled it. She had made her decision and she was still astonished at the sweep of love for the child she carried. It had become real, an individual—part herself and part her beloved James. Oh, she thought with a sudden catch in her heart, it will be a beautiful child!

She hummed beneath her breath as she mounted the stairs to her room, with cloak, hat, gloves and reticule in hand, and flung them on the bed. Without further preparations and while determination was on her, she went to her mother's room and rapped. There was no answer. She went to the stairs, encountering Tiqua on her way up.

"Where is my mother, Tiqua?"

"She in zee kitchen talkin' to Primrose an' Calhoon 'bout zee marketin' *demain*—termorrow.' "

"Would you go and ask her to come up to my room? I wish to talk with her."

"Oui," replied the slender maid and she turned to retrace her steps downward.

Verity sat tensely on the couch before the fire in her bedroom. It was a modest fire of low-burning logs, for the March day was almost warm.

It seemed a very long time before Anne stepped into the room through the open door, for Verity was in a fever to unburden her heart. Her eyes were so large and luminous, her erstwhile pale cheeks so rosy with excitement, that Anne looked at her in fond surprise.

"You look better than I've seen you look in weeks, my dear," she said softly.

"I feel better than I have in weeks, mother. Come and sit beside me. I have something of great importance to tell you."

Anne approached and seated herself gracefully, turning a smiling face to her daughter, and Verity stifled a flash of pain at the impending disaster that she would settle about her mother. And it was a disaster, she thought, suddenly chilled, no matter the transformation that had taken place in her heart in the grim confines of the midwife Marilla's small house of secrets.

"Mother—" she began, but her heart swelled up within her breast until she felt it near to bursting. "I—I must tell you—" she faltered and broke off.

Anne straightened to sit stiffly upright. In the light of the late afternoon through the north windows, she scrutinized her daughter's paling face. Her dark eyes widened slowly as Verity dropped her head and two shining tears slipped from beneath her lashes to roll down the smooth young cheeks.

Anne said slowly, "It is even as I feared. You carry Lord Bainbridge's child."

Verity looked up, two fresh tears glittering, poised at her lower lids, where wet lashes made black star points around them. "Yes, mother."

"How far—how long have you known?"

"It is eight weeks—I think."

Anne calculated swiftly. "That means it will be born in October." Her dark eyes were filled with pain for her daughter. "He will not marry you, you know."

Verity nodded silently. Then, "It does not matter. I love him still. I love his child and I shall bear it."

"Not without a name," Anne's voice was steel.

Verity smiled faintly. "I suppose a child can take its mother's name."

"Nay. This child shall have a father it can claim. I shall send for Bowman and he will get word to Tyler Belion, who loves you and will marry you—in spite of this."

"No!" Verity burst out violently. "Lord Bainbridge will return and I will have nothing stand between our love for one another."

Anne looked at her daughter in astonishment. Then she said, "Bowman came to visit while you were gone with Bonnie. He tells me the rumor is that Lord Bainbridge is with Lord Cornwallis in Hillsborough, North Carolina, from which they are maneuvering even now to get our men who are with General Greene to fight. And word is that our troops are almost ready to stand and face them. Lord Bainbridge will not return for months. Just an hour ago, Colonel Coyne and his men closed the headquarters and left to join him."

Verity's face fell and Anne went on inexorably. "Bowman says that Greene now has near four thousand troops, but some of them are unreliable militiamen. Though they say Colonel Henry Lee—the Virginian who is called Light Horse Harry—and his cavalry are with Greene as well, they do not number quite two hundred. So it will be touch and go, and you had better save your prayers and thoughts for your friends and your countrymen, my dear—instead of looking for Lord Bainbridge, an enemy, to return to you."

"I will not marry Tyler," Verity said in a whisper. Then firmly, "Besides, it would be far too dangerous for Tyler to risk coming to Charles Town, mother."

"I had in mind your meeting him beyond the city—with Paul McPhail, our minister."

"Nay. I will not do it," she replied determinedly.

Anne was silent. Then, "You mean to bear this baby—and the shame—alone?"

Verity looked at her mother bravely. "Unless you will stand by me, I shall have to do it alone." She longed to creep into her mother's arms and be comforted as if she were a child herself once more. Yet she knew she could not do this for she was a woman grown and this burden was of her own making.

Anne said nothing, but her fathomless dark eyes rested on her daughter bleakly. Then suddenly she put out a hand to her, and Verity took it to find it very cold. "I will stand by you, my darling," she said, the chill fingers closing about Verity's. "I will tell Bowman I cannot marry him after all," she finished woodenly.

Verity stared at her silently while tears dried. The stillness drew out between them as Verity realized that Anne was sacrificing her own hope for happiness for Verity's willfulness.

"I didn't know," she whispered. "You didn't tell me. When did you—when did Uncle Bowman—"

"Only last week," Anne said wearily. "He told me he has loved me for years—even before Warren and I were married. I didn't know. But he has been so kind, so good, and he said we would wait a full year. I found quite suddenly that I loved him. For that reason, I cannot bring this disgrace upon him."

"I should have stayed at old Marilla's," Verity murmured. "I should have let her take the baby this afternoon. I have no right to come between you and your happiness—"

"My God!" Anne burst out and suddenly clutched her daughter to her bosom. "You *didn't* go to Marilla! You couldn't!" Her fingers closed convulsively on Verity's shoulders as she held her away and searched her face. "Why— young women have died—doing that!" She pulled her daughter to her once more, half-moaning, "Oh, Verity my darling, give me your word you will never do that!"

"But how can I let my—child come between you and Uncle Bowman?" Verity's voice was muffled against her mother's shoulder.

"My love," Anne said fiercely, "you are *my* child. I feel about you—as you feel about the one you carry now. You must *promise* me you will never go to Marilla." Her voice grew pleading. "Please let us send for Tyler. He loves you so dearly. Please, Verity!"

Verity bowed her head. "I love Tyler, but not in the way I must to accept him as a husband." There was steel in the soft voice.

"Not even if you know it will make the life of your child —my grandchild—easier? Nay, it will make life bearable for your child."

Verity shook her head stubbornly. "Mother, I will go to father's aunt in Philadelphia. She is very old and she will believe me when I tell her I am a widow now. I can stay there."

Anne looked at her with agony in her eyes. "Not in these times—not carrying a child beneath your heart. It too dangerous, my darling. The roads are too rough. There are the outliers, who lurk among the forests. No, no! I cannot bear you to go!"

Verity herself shivered suddenly thinking of the outliers, those merciless men who pledged allegiance to both crown and patriot, robbing and killing in the name of either when bent upon their plunder. They hid out in the swamps and the backcountry, along roads, striking like snakes upon their prey, American and English alike, usually leaving no one alive to reveal their names or give even a partial description of them. They were hated by both loyalist and patriot with equal fury.

"Mother, if I promise you these things, you must promise me something in exchange."

"Anything," cried the distraught mother.

"You must let me tell Uncle Bowman about my coming child and let him make the decision about your marriage. And you must promise me to abide by that decision, for I know he will never give you up."

"But your baby will be born about the same time we had planned to be married," Anne said, aghast.

"No matter. You must promise me or I shall journey to Aunt Phoebe in Philadelphia."

"No, no! I promise," Anne said, and for the first time in her life Verity watched her mother cry for her. It was unbearably touching to watch tears fill those great black eyes and run slowly down the unlined ivory cheeks.

"Come, mother," she said tenderly, taking the trembling hands in her warm ones. Anne's were still waxen-cold. "You bore me at only fourteen and I am nearly ten years older than that. Surely I am old enough to know what I am—what I *have* done."

"I was near fifteen—and we married much younger in those days. Oh, Verity, I would do anything to spare you this shame."

Verity squared her slender shoulders. "Nevertheless, I shall bear the shame and my child as well. People have short memories. My baby shall grow up strong and splendid like his father."

Anne looked at her sorrowfully. "Nay, my daughter, people

have long memories where bastardy is concerned and they never let a bastard forget. Still, I promise I will abide by Bowman's decision."

Fifteen

As they made their way through Charles Town toward the Camden Road, Savarra sat very straight on the mule. Cotty, behind her, was inclined to droop as she held her arms about Savarra's narrow waist. When she did so, Savarra would hiss, "Sit up straight, Cotty—don't fall on me so!"

Supper lamps were lit in the houses they passed, but Amos on the big bay pulled the mule along by the bridle, which he held in his hand. The few passersby on the streets paid them little heed, for they looked to be two very young black boys in broad-brimmed black hats, following along behind an older black man, a common enough sight in and around Charles Town. The clothes of Rafe and Lafe fit the two girls very well, and the hand-woven heavy wool jackets were comforting as the night chill set in.

They had gone a mile beyond the outskirts of Charles Town when Amos drew up beneath a tall pine at the side of the road and sat looking about. It was very dark now and the woods behind them were impenetrable. Then suddenly from the shadows Caleb and Corrie McLean eased up beside them, each on a mule.

"Law me!" Amos ejaculated in a low voice, "you quieter'n a cat, Caleb. You an' Corrie done give me a start!"

"We got to hurry," Caleb replied. "Ol' Scurlock thinks Corrie an' me gone to see her sister to the Pearsons' a while. He likely to call out some British soldiers when we don't show up by ten."

"You got supplies?" Amos asked, peering at them in the gloom.

Caleb gestured at the saddlebags on the rump of his mule and Corrie's. "Mister Baltazar done give us these fine mules and he see to it we got plenty victuals packed in them bags.

Pistols, too. Even extry clothes—breeches an' shirts fer the young ladies."

"Best you all git started then," Amos said. "I got to git back 'cause sometime 'fore mornin' I got to slip another mule inter the Pair stables fer the twins to leave on termorrow night. They sleepin' at the Pairs an' gonna slip out an' be workin' the flower beds 'fore ol' Haverley's guards ketch sight o' 'em."

He turned his bay and Savarra said, "Amos, I am deeply grateful to you."

"Me, too," Cotty echoed tremulously.

"Glad ter do it, knowin' what you done fer us patriots, Mistress Savarra."

As Amos trotted back to the road and began his return to Charles Town, Caleb asked, "Kin you guide that mule, Mistress Savarra, or do you want me to pull him along by the bridle?"

"I think I can guide him," she replied firmly.

As they pulled out on the Camden road, Caleb said softly, "Mistress Savarra, you an' Miss Cotty is our two sons, do anyone pass us an' question us 'fore we gets off this here road and inter the swamps. Better leave me do the talkin' do we meet anybody 'twixt now an' then."

"D'you think we'll meet anybody?" Cotty asked timidly.

"Prob'ly not—no one that'll question us anyway. But we're on our way ter Camden, where our people, the Andersons, is. They done let us visit in Charles Town 'cause your grandpappy died. That's what I'll say ter 'em."

As they moved steadily up the Camden road, Savarra's mind went back to the wild night ride when she had first taken this route to the swamps, surrounded by McLean, Belion, Sleep and McHorry. How miserable she had been in the rain, clad in all that impossible finery she had donned to impress Peter. *Peter,* she thought and spat suddenly on the side of the road. God willing, she would never lay eyes on him again!

They traveled without talking and, though they passed two horsemen coming from Monck's Corner, the horsemen plodded stolidly by and no conversation was exchanged. In an hour more, they turned off toward the Cooper River, which ran near the road. Caleb followed the banks for some distance and, when they came to a low spot where the water ran more narrowly, he halted. It was very dark. The stars were hidden under a high, thin overcast.

But the river could be seen glimmering faintly as it swept along, and Caleb said, "I reckon we kin swim the mules acrost here. Here, Mistress Savarra, lemme hold the reins to that mule while we cross. Once beyond the river an' inter the woods, we ain't got to worry. We'll be safe 'til we reaches Cap'n Cutler an' the men."

Savarra obediently handed the reins to him and all three mules plunged into the slow-moving river. She and Cotty lifted their booted feet high, clinging to each other and the mule to keep from falling into the water. In a few moments, they were splashing from the river and clambering up the far bank. Then they were in thick pines and oaks where it was so dark Savarra could see nothing. They traveled silently, but for an occasional murmur of discomfort from Cotty, for another two hours, and Savarra knew it must be well past midnight.

Caleb drew up in an open glade and said, "Reckon we rest a while now, ladies. It'll take us two, maybe three days to get there."

So they made down for the night on the little rise of ground that stood above the marshy land about them. Despite blankets provided by Baltazar, Savarra was cold and uncomfortable, but she was so weary and so relieved to be beyond reach of Peter that her sleep was deep and healing.

Three days passed in this fashion as they approached Snow's Island, not too far from the border of North Carolina. About noon two horsemen thundered down upon them. There was a moment of panic before they recognized Gabe Sleep and Thad McHorry, who were riding scout for Marion. Caleb lowered his musket and Cotty gave a glad cry.

The two men greeted Caleb and Corrie and turned mystified eyes upon the two girls. Gabe drawled, "Caleb, who're these two boys you got with you and Corrie?"

"I'm no boy!" Cotty was outraged. "Me an' Mistress Savarra are disguised."

McHorry trotted up to her and stared in frank disbelief. Then, "God bless us! 'Tis Miss Cotty an' Mistress Savarra. What brings you ladies to this pass?"

Savarra, aware that she was going to have to make this explanation more than once, had been working on it during their long ride and her reply was curt and to the point. "I married hastily and my husband, Lord Haverley is—a brutal man. I have escaped from him and I seek protection—the protection Cutler McLean once implied he would give me."

Her bruises had not disappeared, but were well covered by the coating of charcoal.

"Well now," Gabe drawled, his voice grim, "we been hearin' about Peter Haverley. Seems he's been runnin' Banastre Tarleton a close second."

Thad bent his guileless smile on her. "You know we don't stay put in any one place too long, mistress."

"I know," Savarra replied, squaring her shoulders, "and I am ready to ride with you. Anything," she shivered slightly, "to keep from going back."

"An' we ain't goin' back to them Scurlocks, either," Caleb's voice held truculence and relief. "We done run away, me an' Corrie, to Cap'n Cutler. We be his cook an' body servant."

"Ol' Mistress Scurlock's a mean woman," Corrie put in. "She after me for somethin' all the time. I don't never do nothin' to please her."

"The cap'n'll be glad to see you," Thad said, his sunny, innocent smile embracing them all. "Gabe, you ride back an' tell the men they're comin' an' I'll stay an' escort 'em so's they won't get lost."

"You ride back an' tell 'em," Gabe retorted. "I'll show 'em the way." His sleepy eyes were on Cotty, who had taken off her hat so that her tumbling gold hair formed a ludicrous contrast to her blackened face.

Thad grinned engagingly. "We'll both ride with 'em then. No tellin' what might come out'n the swamps an' attack 'em." At this, all the men broke into laughter, for it was well known that Caleb was an experienced huntsman and quite capable of seeing the girls safely to Snow's Island.

The six of them rode at a good clip through thick forest, splashing through ever increasing swampy areas, circling towering cypress trees. Cotty kept surreptitiously trying to wipe the charcoal on her face off upon the sleeves of her jacket as she regarded her two suitors riding beside them.

Savarra finally said smiling, "Cotty, you'll have your jacket so dirty you can't wear it. Wait until we arrive and we'll take soap and water and get it all off."

Embarrassed, Cotty replied, "It's so *hard* to get off—just look at my hands."

"Soap an' water'll do it, Miss Cotty," Thad said cheerfully, "an' we're almost there."

It seemed to Savarra that trees increased, appearing larger, taller than ever, and underbrush was rampant with growth. It slowed them to a careful walk often, and there were many places where they splashed through shallow black water, so wet was the land. But where it was drier, pale blue wood violets were glimpsed among other strange, lily-like buds and tangled vines with pink blooms.

Gabe said, "You'll be safe fer sure at Snow's Island, Mistress Savarra."

"I shall be most grateful to reach it," Savarra replied. Then sharply, "Sit up straight, Cotty! You have leaned on me most of the way."

"I'm sorry, mistress, but I'm so tired." There was something in her complaint, for they had ridden steadily since dawn.

It was past four of the afternoon when they pulled up from the creek and onto Snow's Island. They could smell the campfires and food cooking, and Savarra drew a deep breath realizing that she was very hungry. Her heartbeat stepped up as they drew near and she glimpsed men moving about the fires. In the late afternoon light, she could see their ragged and irregular raiment. They were a familiar sight and one she greeted with relief, for they looked strong, reliant and competent despite their tattered clothing. Their faces were keen, alert and strongly individual, and she found herself seeking McLean's powerful figure among them. There appeared to be nearly a hundred men scattered about, some lying on sketchy beds on the ground, bandaged and obviously wounded. Some were grooming their horses, some working with saddles and harness; two appeared to be repairing their clothing.

She noted with surprise there were two buildings, one appearing to be a log house of sorts on a rise. The other, also of logs, was within a stockade.

Then she saw Francis Marion, short, almost squat, sipping from a battered mug. He stood with three of his men about a fire.

Thad called, "We've brought four refugees," and there was a sudden cessation of conversation and all the men looked up. They stared unblinkingly at Sleep and McHorry and their companions.

Colonel Marion rose and limped toward them, favoring his ankle, and Gabe said laconically, "You remember Mistress Savarra Bainbridge, the British general's daughter, Colonel Marion—the one who helped Cap'n McLean an' Lieutenant Belion escape. This here's her maid, Cotty Penderford, an' you know Caleb an' his wife, Corrie." He scanned the far edges of the clearing, his eyes roving among the men, and called, "Cap'n McLean?"

Marion stood looking at them speculatively and drinking slowly from the pewter mug as a tall, lean figure came from among the far trees. Gabe spoke directly to him as he approached. "Cap'n, we've brought Mistress Savarra an' her maid, an' Caleb says he's run away from the Scurlocks—"

"Cap'n," Caleb interjected fervently, sliding from his mule and hastening to meet McLean, "I come to be your body servant, an' my woman Corrie'll cook fer us. Them Scurlocks is mean people."

Savarra's eyes narrowed on McLean. He looked taller than she remembered, his face darker from the sun though clean-shaven still. He had given Savarra a lightning glance, but he greeted Caleb and Corrie warmly. Savarra sat upon the mule feeling Cotty's restless movements behind her.

"Let's get off o' this animal, mistress," she murmured.

But Colonel Marion still stood looking up at her, his polished black eyes piercing. He said in his deep, compelling voice, "I will admit I did not recognize you with your face so well covered, but I bid you welcome, Mistress Bainbridge. What brings you back among us?" He looked gravely into her blackened countenance and Savarra faced him bravely.

She made no apologies. She did not dissemble. "I am seeking a haven, Colonel Marion. My father is with Lord Cornwallis and cannot give me his protection."

"Protection from what?" Marion asked bluntly.

"The man I so foolishly married."

Cutler McLean was regarding her intently now, but Savarra avoided those cool gray eyes. She was aware that Gabe had dismounted and approached the mule, where he reached up for Cotty, shouldering Thad aside, who was attempting to do the same.

"You mean," McLean asked slowly, "that you are running away from your husband, madame?"

Colonel Marion was now regarding her with incredulity.

"My husband is a cruel and bestial man." The words were quiet and forthright, but there was a timbre of imperiousness in them. "It is possible that my bruises have faded in the last four days. If not, you will have visible proof of his cruelty when I wash the charcoal from myself."

She felt Cotty being lifted from behind her and heard her plaintive requests for water and soap. Now Savarra looked directly into McLean's slate eyes. "You once remarked you would repay me for my assistance in your escape. You can do so now."

His face was grave as he reached up to her, and she put her hands on his shoulders to slide from the mule. The feel of his hard flesh beneath the buckskin shirt increased her tumult and she stiffened under his hands.

"If you have been able to make a three-day ride from Charles Town, madame," Colonel Marion said dryly, "I assume your husband did not entirely disable you."

"Not because of any restraint on his part, sir," she replied shortly as McLean set her feet lightly upon the sandy, spongy soil. "After I discovered his true nature, Cotty and I escaped by night—riding all the way from Camden to Charles Town. Anne and Verity Pair hid us when he came—helped me to elude him there."

"You mean he pursued you from Camden to Charles Town?" Colonel Marion asked, still incredulous.

"He did," she replied briefly. "Will you accept our presence, sir, and give us shelter?" She looked at him, her blue eyes blazing in the late afternoon sun filtering through the great cypresses.

He bowed slightly. "We owe you a debt that cannot be repaid, mistress. I will remand you to the care of those you so ably assisted, Captain McLean and Lieutenant Belion." He turned and made his way back to the fire, where he squatted down on his short bowlegs and reached for the black pot on the rack over the fire to refill his cup.

Savarra looked up at McLean with some belligerence to find his gray eyes wary. His lashes, thick as her own, narrowed now, contrasting his clear eyes. "You are a—very impulsive girl, mistress. Are you sure you aren't just making a chase interesting for Lord Haverley?" There was distaste on the lean face as he spoke the name.

Her breath shortened. She said with quiet passion, "Given the chance, I will kill him."

He said with sudden coldness, "I will save you that trouble, Lady Haverley, when the opportunity presents itself."

"Don't ever refer to me as Lady Haverley again!" Her voice cut like a whip and Caleb, who had been approaching, fell back.

McLean smiled slowly. "Very well—Savarra. Would you like a towel and soap?"

She did not return his smile, her stormy brows still drawn,

and this time Caleb came forward saying, "Mistress, Mr. Baltazar give us soap an' towels and such-like in our packs."

"Thank you, Caleb, very much. Is there water near for bathing?" She looked about for Cotty, but the girl had disappeared in company with one admirer, probably to wash away her own disguise. She took the articles from Caleb.

"There is water on nearly every side of you," McLean said. "Come—I'll take you to the nearest creek." And he took her arm.

Savarra brought the bar of scented soap to her nostrils briefly, a feminine luxury that seemed strangely inappropriate in these rough surroundings, but she silently blessed Baltazar.

McLean steered her deftly past the men, who had now returned to their chores and gave her only a passing glance as the two made their way through camp and into the woods.

Savarra paused, glancing around. "I didn't know you— Colonel Marion ever took time to put up buildings in his camps."

He followed her eyes. "That's the old Goddard cabin in the stockade. We've a young British cornet in there since his rank keeps him out of the bullpen. In the other building we store munitions, as well as what food we forage for—but the stockade itself has twenty-three of your countrymen in it."

She looked up at him in amazement. "You take prisoners?"

"In some cases. A few days ago, Colonel Marion sent our young Postell to escort four prisoners from the stockade to Georgetown to be exchanged for some of our men. But your Colonel Watson recognized Postell as having captured De-Peyster—and proceeded to take him prisoner, though Postell was under a flag of truce. I might add, Colonel Marion is furious, and 'tis said Postell is in a cell where he can neither sit, nor lie, and is not even being given half-rations."

Savarra had stopped dead still, staring at the stockade. She drew a quick breath. "I would say I cannot believe such— but I know Peter Haverley and there must be others like him."

He smiled grimly. "You see why we find it necessary at times to take prisoners."

Savarra moved away and peered through the rough posts that formed the prison. She glimpsed several dejected redcoats seated on a fallen log in the enclosure. Others were grouped near the cabin.

Behind her, McLean asked sardonically, "I take it that you will not perform the service for them that you performed for Belion and me?"

She shook her head, then slowly said, "You know well that I have met Banastre Tarleton—and before I met him, I saw him in action. I know the brutality of—war."

"Then you are in sympathy with the American cause?"

"I love England," she retorted, moving away. "It is my home, and she cannot be held responsible for the actions of a few base men."

"A few, Savarra? I grant you a country cannot be judged by a few miscreants. Still, England must be held responsible for the Tarletons and Haverleys, for they are given authority by England."

"We will not quarrel about it," she said, lifting her head, "but I do not judge America by Benedict Arnold either. Both sides have their evil men."

"Nay, madame. *England* has Benedict Arnold now. Not America."

She made no answer as she hastened to keep up with his long strides. The sun was slanting downward through tree trunks now, casting long, dusky shadows through the heavy forest, and she was glad for Rafe's warm woolen jacket across her shoulders.

In a few minutes they came upon a swiftly running stream. The water was clear and looked cold. "This is Clark's Creek, Savarra. Good, clean water."

He turned to leave and she cried, "No—please, I am not familiar with this—place. Please stay. I will be quick!"

He seated himself on a gnarled tree root nearby. She stripped off the coat and rolled up her homespun shirt sleeves, shivering slightly with the evening chill. Swiftly she soaped the cloth and rubbed her face enthusiastically, wincing as the rough material moved abrasively across the wound at the side of her neck. She scrubbed more gently, removing the last traces of charcoal. She again dipped the cloth, rinsing off soap.

She turned, toweling her arms and face, hastily anxious to get into the warm jacket once more. McLean eyed her critically.

"You look yourself again," he said with amusement, "and very beautiful, as you well know." He scowled suddenly. "Even with the bruises—my God, did he take a knife to your neck?"

Savarra felt the blood leave her face. "No," she said huskily, pulling the coarse-spun shirt collar up to cover the dark, angry wound.

McLean's face was set, his eyes cold. "I should have killed him the day he first showed up in Anne Pair's drawing room."

"I wish to God you had," she said fervently. Her ankle turned suddenly on a half-buried cypress knee and McLean caught her in his arms, righting her swiftly. He held her only an instant but it sent her heart racing.

She said abruptly, "Did you know Peter killed Seth Barwell in cold blood on—our wedding day?"

"Yes. We heard he ran him through with his saber in head-quarters at Camden—and all because he appealed to your father for leniency."

"Seth told them he had guided me from the swamps. Peter did not know of my—kidnapping. It was the cause of our quarrel that night. He guessed what—I had done to help you escape the Charles Town prison—and what—happened during my captivity."

McLean turned inscrutable eyes on her. "And *that* provoked his beating you?"

"Partly—don't ask me any more." She averted her face.

"I don't need to ask. I *know* what happened."

"He never gave me the chance to tell him it all—meant nothing," she said flatly. "For that, I shall hate him forever!" They were approaching the body of the camp now and savory odors of stewing meat rose on the evening air.

"A pity. Since it meant *nothing*, had you explained, you might have saved your marriage." The words were biting.

"Nothing could have saved it," she said with finality. "Peter is a beast."

Cotty rushed up crying, "Oh, mistress, look! I'm clean again, too! Shall I do your hair up for you now? Ah, 'tis such a tangle. Come, sit upon this log. I have a comb and brush Mr. Baltazar so kindly provided—" Her face fell as she added, "But no pins at all."

"Then I shall cut you a leather thong again, Savarra, to tie it with," McLean said with a sardonic smile and left the two alone.

That night, Savarra and Cotty had their usual beds of thick moss, covered with the rough blankets Baltazar had provided. As they were preparing to bed down, Tyler Belion, tall and quiet, approached them. His dark eyes in the fading light of the fires were enigmatic.

"Mistress Savarra," he said quietly. "I would ask about Verity. Can you tell me how she is—if she is managing well and is reasonably happy?" His closed face hinted at despondency. Savarra knew her father was the reason for this and she felt an unexpected pang of sympathy for this tall, slender partisan, so soft-spoken and strong.

"She looked wonderfully well. And if it hadn't been for her and Anne, I should never have escaped Peter Haverley, you know. They hid Cotty and me. They planned and executed our escape very cleverly." And she proceeded to tell him of the twins and their masquerade in the late evening hour. "I only hope that everything went well after we got away."

"She knew you were coming to us. Did she send a message for me?"

"We left under such nerve-wracking circumstances, we thought of nothing, Mr. Belion, but escape. Peter had come searching for me, you see. Verity hadn't time to send you a message. I'm sure she would have written you a letter had there been an opportunity."

"Perhaps," he replied without conviction. "I am relieved that she and her mother are well."

"Very well. As long as my father's headquarters are there, they will be under his protection and quite safe."

Belion bowed his head. "I trust you are right."

"I don't think you need worry about Verity, Mr. Belion. She is very brave and clever and will do nothing rash."

"Thank you, mistress," he said quietly and disappeared in the shadows.

Cotty and Savarra reclined on their pungent beds and they slept soundly, so weary were they from their long journey. When they awakened, the sun was well up and Corrie was stirring about, preparing breakfast.

But glancing around, Savarra saw the camp was almost deserted. The only man she recognized was the Colonel Hugh Ervin to whom she had been introduced the night before. There were a number of guards around the stockade.

"Where are all the men?" Savarra asked, rubbing the sleep from her eyes.

Cotty replied, "They left before dawn—ain't they quiet as mice, though? Thad told me last night they just got word a British colonel named Watson from Georgetown is ravagin' the countryside. Gabe says they're goin' run him back to Georgetown."

The little maid was full of bright chatter as the March sun rose slowly in the sky. "Thad and Gabe says this here

Snow's Island ain't never been discovered an' it's been their hideout fer a long, long time," she volunteered as they gathered up soap and towels preparatory to going to bathe. "An' Thad and Gabe say this ain't a firm group, but men leave to see about their homefolks an' then come back. Gabe says that surprise an' cunning an' above all speed is Marion's best weapons."

Corrie looked up as they passed by and said, "Breakfas'll be ready in 'bout half an hour, ladies."

"We'll be back," Savarra said as they struck out toward the river. She noted Colonel Hugh Ervin was now beside a fire, eating breakfast with two black partisans. There looked to be a skeleton guard about the large camp, but the sick and wounded were being helped by others to their breakfast. She looked about, familiarizing herself with the terrain in the bright morning light. Shortly, they came to the nearby Peedee River, where Cotty's two suitors had taken her the night before.

Savarra remarked, "This place seems to be surrounded by rivers and creeks."

Cotty laughed joyously, her spirits high. "Not all the way, Thad says. Though there's a swamp on the side that has no river to perfect it. We're right next to the place called Britton's Neck, which lies between the Little Peedee River and the Peedee. They say ol' Watson's been burnin' and pillagin' the homes of patriots all along his way—while he's been lookin' for Marion's men. But Thad an' Gabe say they'll hide in trees all along the march of Watson an' keep him hoppin'. *He* won't be able to find 'em 'cause they're so good at meltin' into the swamps."

"Cotty, you sound like a rebel," Savarra remarked dourly.

"Well, ain't we, mistress?" the girl asked artlessly. "I thought that dretful Lord Haverley made a rebel out o' both of us."

"I don't know," Savarra replied broodingly as they seated themselves on the riverbank. She removed her boots and stockings and put her feet and legs into the clear, bitingly cold water. "My father would have killed Peter Haverley," she added as she soaped her feet and legs lavishly.

"His Lordship's a man who goes by the rules," Cotty replied cautiously, "an' by the rules you're married to Lord Haverley."

"I *will* not be—I *am* not married to him," Savarra burst out, thrusting feet and legs back into the river

"Well'm," Cotty said discreetly, " 'cordin' to the law an' the church an' all, you are."

"My father could have it annulled—we didn't spend even one full night together."

"Don't that take a heap of legal doin'—annullin'?"

"Oh, drat the whole business!" Savarra said furiously. Drying her feet, she put on stockings, then boots. "Let's go breakfast."

Corrie was frying meat and cooking a kind of mush over the fire when they returned. She handed the two girls a battered pewter plate each and gave them rough, handmade eating implements. Savarra remembered them from her last stay with the patriots, and now she looked at them with a contradictory mingling of relief and distaste. She was glad to be safe from Peter Haverley, but she had no real enthusiasm for the rough life they must lead until she could be reunited with her father.

Qualms assailed her as she thought of his reaction. He had tried in every way to keep her from marrying Haverley. Now with his fears confirmed, she thought dolefully, he might give her a hard time about it. But he loved her, she assured herself, and he would be enraged when she told him of what Haverley had—done to her. Vivid recollection swallowed her up, even as she put spoon to mouth, and she again saw the dark, firelit room, felt once more the man's lustful enjoyment in brutalizing her. She quivered, a sour taste rising in her throat, filling her mouth. Turning her head, she spat on the leaf-covered ground and took a deep swallow of the scalding coffee.

The next two days went by uneventfully. Savarra had no way of knowing that Cornwallis and the American general, Greene, were maneuvering to come together in a great battle to the west.

One dark, cloudy afternoon, Gabe Sleep came riding in bringing two bags of muskets, the British Brown Bess of which the redcoats were so proud. He was followed shortly by Thad McHorry, who pulled a mule behind his horse, laden heavily with bags of corn. Both Savarra and Cotty flew to these young men filled with questions, but Colonel Ervin was there before them.

"Well, colonel," drawled Gabe, his heavy lids giving him as always a look of secrecy as he replied to the colonel's question, "we ain't been nigh Charlest'n, but Gen'l Marion sent us to scout the Camden area, an' we discovered a boat-load o' corn at the mouth of Kershaw's Creek. We attacked the guard there and kilt two, wounded four an' captured eight British soldiers an' one stinkin' tory."

"Where is Marion—did you say *general*?"

"Yep. He's been made a general by Nathanael Greene his-self, as we can make out, an' high time, too. Sumter's been a general God knows how long—fancies hisself over Marion, too—but you know we ain't none of us ever took that too seriously."

"But where *is* he?" persisted Ervin who, Savarra knew, had been spoiling to leave Snow's Island and join his com-rades in battle.

"Last time we seen him, he was ridin' through the Williams-burg district, with men droppin' out like flies to go see their crops put in proper for spring plantin'. You know yourself most of the men is from the Williamsburg district right now. An' he's damn depressed over the way his troop's thinnin'."

"By God, I should take my men here and join him," Ervin exploded. The wounded men who could not walk had risen on elbows, and those who were able had hobbled to gather around the three men.

"No, sir, colonel. He wants you to man this here camp. Right now we been skirmishing with a British colonel named Welbore Doyle an' his New York Volunteers. Like ol' Watson, Doyle's tryin' to ketch us." Gabe chuckled, adding, "An' likely he will ketch us when Marion's ready to take him on."

Thad had slipped from his horse and turned to the mule where he began unloading the four bags of corn. The able soldiers who were part of Ervin's guard came up to shoulder them, but they stayed to hear the conversation between Ervin and Sleep.

"Suppose Doyle comes here first?" Ervin asked.

"If he should come this way you'll know it well ahead of time," Thad spoke up suddenly. "We don't aim to let Watson an' Doyle get together. Watson's damn near isolated now."

"We've destroyed most o' the bridges an' felled some pretty good-sized trees acrost what roads is through the swamp." Gabe added, "an' if he tries to skirt 'em, we'll pick 'em off like ducks in a row. I'd sure enjoy *that*."

Savarra was growing impatient. She wondered where Mc-Lean was at this moment and she wanted to ask if there had been any news of her father and Cornwallis. Now as the men continued to talk of British depredations, she bit her tongue.

Looking about, she saw that Corrie was also standing nearby, her even, ageless features betraying no emotion, yet she must be burning to know it Caleb were safely with General Marion and his men.

At last the soldier drifted off toward the storage house with the bags of corn, muskets and ammunition captured by the partisans, and Thad and Gabe were able to approach the two girls and Corrie.

Thad remarked solemnly, "Word is that ol' Colonel Watson's received orders to ketch a runaway maid named Penderford an' her mistress an' return 'em fer trial in Charlest'n immediately."

Savarra's heart gave a great bound before she looked into his twinkling blue eyes and realized his penchant for a joke. Cotty was not taken in. She tossed her head and shrugged her shoulders. "They'll never find us. In fact," she frowned, "even *we* don't know where we are, do we, mistress?"

"That's very true," Savarra replied. Then turning on Gabe, "Have you heard anything of the whereabouts of my father and Lord Cornwallis?"

Corrie, who had followed asked quietly, "An' my man, Caleb?"

Gabe turned to her, ignoring Savarra's drawn brows. "Corrie, Caleb's distinguished hisself. He shot two of them redcoats when he was patrolin' near Kershaw's Creek. He's been made a sergeant by Cap'n McLean."

Corrie glowed, then, "Reckon you an' Mr. Thad's hungry, ain't you?" At his nod, she trotted toward the storage house to secure supplies for their meal.

Savarra, angered, put on that certain arrogance which she knew to be extremely irritating to the Americans, who recognized no caste system. "You have not told me of my father, sir. Surely with scouts riding out each day, you have heard something of Lord Cornwallis and Lord Bainbridge!"

"Let me get some grain fer my horse, Mistress Bain—pardon me, Lady Haverley—"

"Mistress Bainbridge, if you please," she said curtly.

"Well now, mistress, I'll get around to all the news if you'll just calm down and let me tend my mount." He spoke with maddening deliberation, and she was boiling with frustration and anger as he took the beast and went toward the storage house with him, passing the bull pen where the redcoats peered out with cold hostility.

The sky overhead was becoming more threatening and the

distant growl of thunder could be heard as lightning forked
in brilliant slashes through the burgeoning clouds. Savarra
knew with a sinking heart it was going to rain again. It
seemed to her that it had rained every day since her arrival
in camp, and the ground would have been soggy but for the
thick carpet of leaves and pine needles that covered it. Everything felt damp. Savarra, Corrie and Cotty had washed their
extra clothing over twenty-four hours ago and it was still
moist. Corrie had it hanging inside the storage house even
now in order to dry it.

Later, when Thad had a blazing fire started, a few drops of
rain made spitting noises into it. Gabe was returning from
tending his horse and Savarra looked at him expectantly. If
it began to rain hard, they would have to rig a tarpaulin over
themselves as they had done in the past. Thad had rolled two
logs up before the fire and they seated themselves upon them
while Corrie busied herself with pans and the rack Thad had
put across the flames.

Gabe brought a pipe out of his buckskin pouch at his waist
and began tamping tobacco into it. Savarra observed him with
unconcealed disfavor.

"I suppose," she said acidly, "that you will tell me of my
father and Lord Cornwallis eventually."

"Right now, ma'am," he replied, putting the end of a
burning stick to the pipe and drawing deeply. When blue
smoke rose in the damp, cold air he turned to Savarra. "Cornwallis lost over two hundred men when he pursued Nathanael
Greene to the Dan River an' destroyed his supplies in an effort to overhaul him after the battle of Cowpens. Your pa
was with him when they reached the river just in time to see
the last of our men cross over—an' Greene destroyed all
boats, so Cornwallis was left high an' dry."

Gabe drew on his pipe deeply, enjoying his drawn-out
revelation. "Our scouts reported your pa and Cornwallis
was under the impression the countryside was teemin' with
loyalists, just waitin' to join his forces. But Marion, Sumter
an' Pickens have—ah—discouraged their enlistin', an' his
volunteers has slowed to a trickle. Fact is, we caught a British
courier an' intercepted a letter to Germain in England. In it
Cornwallis says he is 'amongst timid friends and enjoining to
inveterate rebels'—an' that's us, ma'am." He laughed deeply.
"Inveterate rebels." He drew on the pipe again and Savarra
noted that Thad was trying to capture Cotty's hand and she
was being very arch with him.

"Do you know if there's a chance my father will return to Charles Town where I can meet with him and he can legally extricate me from my—miserable alliance?"

"Not much chance, mistress. Greene's comin' back to South Carolina an' he's goin' to tangle with your pa an' his friends again."

Savarra's heart sank. Another battle was in the making and these elusive backwoodsmen maintained a network of spies— they knew every move the British made.

Gabe's deep, measured voice went on. "So your pa's either in Hillsborough, with Cornwallis, or he's on the march to meet Greene in another scrap. You wouldn't want us to take you to him in those circumstances, would you, Mistress Savarra?"

"No," she replied dispiritedly. "Besides, Peter may be with them and I know he will have painted me black as night to father." Her voice grew more despondent. "My father might even insist I return to Camden and remain there, where he would try to reconcile the two of us."

Thad asked curiously, "Think you could try again, mistress? Lots of brides are sorry a day after, they say, but come 'round after a while."

"No!" Savarra said violently. These men could not know— indeed, she did not know if she would be able to describe her wedding night and Peter's accusations and subsequent actions to her father.

"Then looks like you're still under our protection," Thad said amiably, "an' Cap'n McLean told us to send you his special greetin's an' to see to your care. You been treated all right since we been gone?"

"Oh, very," she retorted. "I've been living like a savage, with no comforts of civilization since I arrived."

"Well," Gabe said tactfully, " you knew that'd be the case when you came to us, mistress."

"Yes," she answered shortly, biting her tongue on further complaints. By now thunder was louder and intermittent rain drops fell more thickly.

"I better get a tarp," Gabe said. Then angrily, "Thad, you keep your hands to yourself! Miss Cotty's not made her mind up between us."

Thad, who had been vainly trying to circle Cotty's waist with his arm, grinned. "You get the tarp, Gabe, an' I'll help put 'er up."

Later, after they had eaten, the deluge came and the girls

and Corrie took refuge in the storage house, where many of the wounded men lay. It was close and had an evil odor, but they fell asleep to the drumming of rain on the roof and woke to find Thad and Gabe had slipped away in the early hours to rejoin their commander.

There followed a gloomy week for Savarra and Cotty. It rained incessantly and they were confined to the poorly ventilated and damp storage house. As she and Cotty went about the chores of keeping themselves clean between downpours, they spent a great deal of time talking to each other, and Savarra found that Cotty's fund of conversation was sorely limited. It consisted mostly of chatter about the food and clothing and the niceties they had left in London and the charms of Thad McHorry and Gabe Sleep.

One afternoon, when the sun had come out and was shining with unaccustomed warmth over the watery hideout, Cotty remarked for what Savarra felt must be the thousandth time, "I vow, mistress, Thad's so darlin' an lovable, but then Gabe's such a *man*, so tall an' quiet an' strong—"

A loud whoop cut her off in midsentence and both girls rose to their feet and strained their eyes toward the sound. The fire was hot, but Savarra knew a premonitory chill as the sound was repeated. Every man in the camp was still and alert. Only Colonel Ervin moved, strapping on his saber and catching up his gun to run toward the deep voice, which sounded once more.

Suddenly a horse bearing a tall figure emerged swiftly from heavy trees bordering the camp, and with unerring instinct Savarra recognized Captain Cutler McLean. Her heart leaped and she found herself, along with those about her, running toward him.

The big stallion reared slightly, sides heaving, as McLean slid to the ground before Colonel Ervin. "Doyle's already crossed Lynche's Creek at Witherspoon's Ferry and is striking for Snow's Island," he said tersely. "We've very little time to prepare. 'Tis said that turncoat tory, Ezra Brown, is guiding him."

Ervin swore lustily, "God damn Brown's cringing soul! Only last month he was swearing to serve General Marion faithfully."

A second horse plunged into the clearing and Thad McHorry slid from the saddle, "Cap'n, you an' Jed moved too fast fer me an' Rosy—"

"Doyle's driving his men hard," McLean interrupted, still speaking to Ervin, "because he knows Marion'll come after him—fact is, we've sent Gabe on to tell him now. But he's a good twenty-four hours' ride from Snow's Island and we've got to hold Doyle off until he can get here. Or at least give him a damn good fight."

Ervin said, "Captain, you know most of the men under me are wounded. The only able ones among us are those standing guard duty over our prisoners—but we'll make do."

"Let's get moving," McLean said shortly. He had not glanced at Savarra and Cotty, while the latter stood staring at McHorry with open-mouthed terror.

"Oh, Thad," she began hysterically, "Save me an' my mistress—"

"Shut up, Cotty," Savarra said quietly, "and come with me to the storage house."

"Whatever for, mistress—to hide?" Cotty whimpered.

"To get pistols, you fool," she replied, half-dragging the terrified girl along with her.

"But mistress, I don't know nothing about guns—"

"You'd better learn," was the grim response. "You're dressed as a boy—a rebel boy—and our countrymen will kill you on sight. If not then, later for being a spy and a rebel sympathizer."

"But I'll tell 'em we was prisoners! We couldn't help—"

"What a coward you are," Savarra said angrily. "I should have left you with Anne Pair."

"An' let that Lord Haverley get me?" was the terrified gasp as Savarra released her arm. The girl ran to catch up with her mistress but Thad was beside her by then.

"Now Cotty," he said soothingly, his voice deep and full of laughter as always, "I'll take care of you."

Savarra gave him a bitter glance as they drew near the weatherbeaten log house. "You'd better help get those wounded men to shelter, Mr. McHorry, instead of worrying about Cotty's fears."

"Now, Mistress Savarra, you can't blame Cotty," Thad said, taking full advantage of the girl's terrors and holding out his arms to her. She flung herself into them, weeping noisily, and Savarra moved off in disgust.

Inside the storage house, she found others there before her. Some of the wounded, those who were able to limp about, were taking up muskets and rifles, loading ammunition pouches and powder horns. There was a quiet air of determination among them and their voices were low and controlled.

She approached one of the men who were handing out guns and said, "I cannot fire a musket, but I can handle a pistol," and he reached into a shelf and took down a heavy pistol with a beautifully carved handle. It bore the initials J. M. C., and Savarra recognized it as a finely wrought British gun. The man filled a leather pouch for her with powder and bullets. She took them silently and made her way from the room.

As she stood upon the narrow porch of the roughly constructed building, she looked up beyond the trees at the darkly blue sky. The sun was still high. She thought with curious detachment that it was a fine day for a battle. Much better than if it were pouring rain. If she had to die, bright sunshine should make it easier.

The camp before her was boiling with activity as Colonel Ervin prepared to make a stand. She could hear orders being barked and surmised that those men fit for duty were being posted along Clarke's Creek. She saw Cotty, still clinging to McHorry, looking about her with wide, frightened blue eyes, and beyond her McLean was approaching.

Suddenly he loomed over her and said, "Are you prepared to take up arms against your countrymen?" He eyed the large pistol she had thrust into her belt with a touch of amusement.

"I am prepared to defend myself," she replied shortly, "against anyone who would force me to return to my husband."

"It will be well if you stand back from the front lines, Savarra, despite your pistol." He hesitated and added curtly, "I would hate to see you wounded."

"Thank you," she replied dryly. "I will do as I am commanded."

He entered the log house and she could hear his orders clearly. "Colonel Ervin has ordered all extra guns, ammunition and supplies dumped in Lynche's Creek."

There followed a spate of feverish activity as the supplies of food and munitions were hauled to the creek and thrown into the flooded stream. The men did this with anguish on their faces, and Savarra realized they were regretting the loss of these necessities, so hard to come by in this land ravaged by war and pillaged by foreigners to its shores. She realized too that this would leave Marion without a base of operations if Snow's Island fell, and from what she could gather, Lieutenant Colonel Welbore Doyle's New York Volunteers far outnumbered the pitiful few that now manned this place of refuge.

The British soldiers in the bull pen were in a state of high excitement, talking and shouting among themselves, calling out that they might as well release them now. One shouted, "We'll put in a good word for ye, mates, if ye let us out now!"

For the most part the patriots ignored them, but at last Colonel Ervin approached with the one British officer they had captured, Cornet Merritt. He had armed this young man and Savarra, standing back from them, heard him say, "Cornet Merritt, I place in your charge all the prisoners and the fifteen wounded we have who cannot move. You are paroled on your honor as a British officer, and it is your duty to see that they do not escape during the coming conflict." Then with sudden brutal truth, "And if you attempt to break that parole and release them during battle, we will shoot them down in cold blood."

Suddenly, the sound of musket fire cracked through the air, and Savarra went to the group of horses and mules that were tethered at the edge of the camp. As gunfire grew in volume, she prepared to bridle one of the horses, but a soldier ran past her and cried, "Not yet, mistress! Remain in camp until we turn them back—you are like to be shot by some careless rifleman!"

As the man dashed away, she paused uncertainly, looking about for Cotty. She had lost sight of the girl in the moil of hectic preparation, and now she could not find either McHorry or Cotty. Where were they? She ran toward the sound of conflict and, as she drew near Clarke's Creek, she saw that Colonel Ervin and his men were trying desperately to protect the boats at the stream's edge and were under heavy fire from Doyle's men, who outflanked the little band of partisans and were taking heavy toll among them.

As she stood back among the trees, she saw two of them fall, one with blood spurting from a head wound, the other clutching his chest, and Savarra knew they were dead before they struck the ground.

An angry, frustrated pity shook her as the others clung tenaciously to their posts behind tall trees, crouching back of fallen ones, lurking behind small mounds of earth. She could glimpse the scarlet coats among the trees across the creek, but they were wary and, as far as she could see, none received a wound.

They exchanged fire for some time, and Savarra felt a

faint hope stirring that they might stand them off as the sun began to sink in the west. But with the coming of darkness she surmised the British would forge ahead, cross the stream and be on the camp, and her hopes fell. She began to make her way from man to man, asking if they had seen Cotty or McHorry.

She came upon the two of them at last, far to the west, where Thad was regularly firing at the British across the stream, while Cotty, in a little miserable heap, crouched as near to him as she could.

Savarra slid down the slick pine needles to Cotty's side and said urgently, "Get up, Cotty! Let us return to camp and get horses ready—I fear we shall have to flee and we shall be unprepared!"

"Oh, mistress," Cotty moaned tragically, "I dassn't get up. I'll be shot!"

Thad turned on her, his face serious. "Cotty, she's right. Go back to camp—I can see five of our men have been killed already and we may have to make a run for it soon. 'Tis best you and Mistress Savarra be prepared." Then at her anguished little cry, he added with his irrepressible laugh, "Now Cotty, I'll come and get you first if we have to retreat. Don't be so scared."

A shot whistled overhead, uncomfortably close, and Savarra ducked automatically. "Hurry!" she whispered to Cotty.

McLean spoke suddenly from behind her. "I thought I told you to stay back of the firing line, Savarra," he said shortly.

"I'm going back," she retorted. "I only came to get Cotty."

"Cotty, get up from there," he said authoritatively, and the girl got quickly to her feet and shrank back against Savarra. "Now both of you get back to camp. I think there are enough horses for all of us to mount if we should have to fall back." As they stepped away, he added, "Don't come back here. We'll come for you if we must retreat before General Marion arrives."

As they made their way through the undergrowth, branches scraping against them and slapping at their faces, Savarra reflected that in all likelihood they would *have* to fall back. They were far outnumbered by Doyle, and his men were obviously in top condition.

When they reached the deserted camp, she saw Cornet Merritt standing beside the bull pen, where his fellow soldiers were urging him to let them out. "Men, I'm paroled on my honor, but I swear we will all be free of this accursed place in a matter of minutes. As soon as Colonel Doyle takes Snow's Island, I shall open the gates for you." Then glimpsing Savarra, he hastened to her and Cotty. "Mistress Bainbridge, I know who you are. Rumors have a way of permeating an entire encampment, and I urge you to stay with us. We will see that you and your maid are reunited with your father."

"I cannot go with you, Mr. Merritt," she said, "and I have good reasons which I cannot tell you at this time."

"Oh, mistress," Cotty quavered, "he could take us back to Charlest'n an' back to civilization."

"And into Peter's hands again," Savarra said flatly. "No, Cotty, I shall not return yet—you may, if you wish, stay with Cornet Merritt."

"Oh, no!" Cotty was torn. "I couldn't leave you—an' there's Thad an' Gabe—" her voice trailed off. Cotty wanted terribly to be safe and comfortable once more, but her loyalties lay with Savarra and her desires with Gabe and Thad.

Cornet Merritt said, "Mistress Bainbridge, I believe Colonel Doyle has crushed Marion and his men. You are endangering your lives unnecessarily. Summer is coming and these swamps are alive with mosquitoes and insects—yes, and wild animals. You could sicken and die of the summer fevers with no one to tend you. I beg of you to reconsider."

"Colonel Doyle has not crushed Marion. He is on his way here now." She looked into the young cornet's clear brown eyes. "And you may well find yourselves prisoners again instead of conquerors."

"I think not," he replied confidently, glancing at the eager faces in the bull pen.

She and Cotty left him and went to the area where the horses were tethered. She recognized McLean's great stallion, Jed, and McHorry's dainty little mare, Rosy. The mule, a stolid beast, strong but contrary, that she had ridden to Snow's Island stood nearby. She looked at him with disfavor, then at a gelding, a bay, clean-limbed beside the mule—and determined she would try to secure the gelding if they must flee camp.

Corrie came from the emptied storage house and joined them. "Ain't no cornmeal nor nothin' left to take with us, 'sides this here sack I got filled. I just hopes we get out o' here safe."

"We will," Savarra replied with a certainty that she did not feel.

The three women sat down near the restless horses, listening to the steady crack of rifle and musket fire from the direction of the creek, and waited. The evening lengthened and darkness began to fall. The firing from the creek became more sporadic. Finally silences began to stretch out, and one by one, in the deepening shadows, the partisans began to return to camp.

Savarra and the other two women rose and went to Colonel Ervin as he came up, barely discernible in the gloom. "Colonel," Savarra said, "have they gone?"

"Nay. We are going to retreat across the Little Peedee River in darkness. They have killed seven of my men and I do not think we have inflicted a single casualty on them. We must retreat."

"Now?" gulped Cotty.

"Yes, now," was the curt reply, and Cotty began to sniffle.

Savarra straightened her shoulders and said, "Colonel, I would very much like this gelding to ride—"

"Dickenson is dead. 'Tis his horse. You may have it, madame."

Thad McHorry came up at that moment and said with undaunted cheer, "Cotty, I'll put you on Rosy with me an' we'll make it out of here together."

By now, the small group of partisans that was left had trickled in. Silently they began gathering, bridling and saddling their mounts, preparing to make their escape in the night before Doyle could see they were dispersing. Savarra looked in vain for McLean.

She said to Ervin as he saddled his horse, "Captain McLean—he was not one of the—" she paused and swallowed at the dread that was filling her "—casualties?"

"No," Ervin replied shortly. Then to another partisan, "Here, James, saddle up Dickenson's gelding for Mistress Bainbridge," and the soldier fell to the task. "We must hurry, for we don't know how long it will be before Doyle realizes that we have pulled out. We will cross Lynche's Creek and lose ourselves in Ox Swamp."

Ervin approached Cornet Merritt and said, "Your countrymen will soon be here and you will be free, but you have given me your word to remain here until they come."

"I will, sir," Merritt replied, and Savarra felt a sudden warmth of pride. There were, after all, such men of courage and honor from her beloved England.

It was chaotic but quiet as they packed what they could on their horses and struck out for Lynche's Creek. An occasional burst of gunfire could be heard, and Savarra surmised that McLean and Gabe Sleep were among those remaining behind to cover their retreat. Even so it would be extremely dangerous crossing Lynche's Creek, for Doyle's experienced soldiers were very near it. Ervin had told them they would go far up the creek to cross and thereby circle around and away from Doyle's troops. It was well after ten o'clock when they trotted, a sadly decimated little band picking their way carefully, through the black forest beyond where Doyle was camping, ready to resume the unequal fight at daylight.

He would find an empty hideout but for the waiting redcoats, Savarra thought with a touch of grim satisfaction. Still, they had deprived Marion of his most secret hideout, and she realized that from now on they would have to travel constantly, making camp wherever they could find the safest spot.

After about an hour, during which they traveled in complete silence, a big horse moved up beside her, a knee brushing hers. McLean's husky voice, almost a whisper, came to her.

"You had a chance to go back with your own kind, Savarra. Why didn't you take it?"

She took a deep breath to slow her rapid heart and said, "You know well enough why. And what are my own kind? Certainly not Peter Haverley and his henchmen. I feel I am a woman without a country now." Her low voice was poignant and sorrowful. "I cannot return to England if I must live with Peter. And there is no place for such as me in this raw, new country."

"People make their places. You strike me as a woman who can make her place wherever she chooses. You are—to say the least—adaptable. I think you might make a very good American."

She made no reply, and he rode on ahead among the file of horses that strung out silently in the forest. True to his promise, Thad had Cotty upon his horse in front of him, his arms snugly about her as he held the reins. Cotty had subsided, comforted and secure in their circle.

Suddenly there was a murmur among the riders, and in the intermittent moonlight Savarra saw them looking back. She turned and saw a red glare where Snow's Island lay. So, she thought, Doyle had crossed over and discovered the deserted camp and set fire to everything in it. The orange light that was the burning buildings made a fiery glow in the sky, visible for many miles, and Savarra felt a pang of sorrow for Francis Marion, that sturdy, limping little man of iron, for Snow's Island was wiped out. She glanced upward to see a brilliant moon peering from behind scudding, ragged clouds, casting occasional silver light on the riders.

Suddenly from ahead McLean's voice could be heard. "We must increase our pace. They may decide to track us down."

"Aw, they won't know where to look, cap'n," Thad said encouragingly.

"Yes, and we didn't think they would break their habit of marching into battle in ranks. Yet they were shrewd enough to emulate partisan warfare of hit and run—Doyle did it." He was silent, then, "Don't underestimate the British, Thad."

Accordingly they stepped up their pace, trotting as fast as the thick undergrowth about them would permit, and at last reached a more narrow spot in Lynche's Creek and prepared to cross. Colonel Ervin urged them on and plunged into the rain-swollen creek first. The others followed, Cotty clinging to Thad in terror. The water was very swift and the horses had difficulty in swimming a straight course.

Savarra was last to enter the stream, and immediately her horse lost his equilibrium and was swept downstream. She did not call out as she fought to stay in the saddle while the animal threshed wildly in the swollen stream. She realized she was being swept away from the rest, but she thought she could right the horse and swim him across the stream a short few yards down from them. Instead, they were swept along swiftly, the horse fighting valiantly to ride the current.

She was suddenly under a great tree, with drooping boughs and a long tangle of vines hanging down to the water. The gelding was carried under this trap and Savarra was abruptly entangled in the vines. She had long ago lost her hat, and now her long hair became inextricably tangled in the vines and she was lifted from the saddle of the horse as he was swept on down the creek.

To her horror, she found herself suspended by her hair over the turgid and swollen stream. She called out loudly and the moon came from behind a dark cloud to cast brief, silvery light over the rapidly eddying currents about her. She looked up trying to see, but could not. Her long hair was becoming more tightly wound among the vines and, while she pulled at it frantically with both hands, she succeeded only in drawing the strands tighter.

She called out again and again, "Cutler McLean—Colonel

Ervin—help me!" but the night was silent except for the rushing water about her waist, for she was half-submerged, suspended by her tangled hair. It came to her then that the others were far across the creek by now and riding hard away from where she was held prisoner. Still, she did not give up. She called lustily, with all the strength in her lungs, time and time again, before it slowly began to dawn on her that she might well hang by her hair half in Lynche's Creek and half out until she died.

This lent impetus to her struggles, and she fought with renewed vigor the entangling mass about her head and shoulders. Sobbing now with her frantic efforts to escape, she suddenly went limp. She must conserve her strength, she thought, a semblance of calmness returning, but it was short-lived.

The rushing water about her hips swung her this way, then that, and the clutching vines were terribly painful to her neck and scalp. Drawing another lungful of air, she shrieked ever louder, "Help! Cutler—Thad—Cotty!" Then under her breath, "Oh, God let some of them miss me! Let some one hear me!" But the night air was still and cold and only the nocturnal sounds of the forests and river came to her ears.

Panic clamped its clammy fingers over her heart and squeezed it in a vise, making even breathing difficult. She put her hands up to the vines and held to them, easing the strain on her neck and shoulders. She was very cold and she tightened her jaw to keep her teeth from chattering.

Time dragged by and Savarra's arms ached from trying to hold the vines to prevent the swift flowing water from pulling too fiercely against her imprisoned body. Every few minutes, she would gather her strength and cry out as loudly as she could. The moon reappeared and she was able to see the broad stream and far shore.

If she were to achieve a release from the corded vines, she would never be able to swim that far distance in her clothing. The trees along the shore were black and thick, but moonlight on the creek was like flashing silver fire. She had never felt so desperately alone in her life, but her mind worked with appalling clarity.

She was going to die, she who had only begun to live. With this knowledge came the wholly unexpected thought of Cutler McLean and the realization that she would leave something vital, something beautiful unfinished there. She knew in that cold, clear instant that her only happy moments had been with McLean, despite the fury he never failed to stir in her. She was aware at last that she wanted him, no matter how she fought it—no matter that she had been merely one more easy conquest for him. He was, in fact, responsible for her present predicament, for she had been more than ready to rejoin the hunted partisans, share their precarious life like any of the women camp followers who trailed after Cornwallis's army, Burgoyne's army—and even the rebel armies. *And all because she wanted Cutler McLean.*

She let her hands fall and her neck ached unbearably, forcing her to reach up once more and seize the twisted vines to ease the strain. The water was bitterly cold and all the life force in her rushed up to fight against it.

She gave one last despairing cry. "I am caught—help me!"

She could not believe it when she heard the strong, deep voice from across the creek. "Hold on—I'm coming!"

Straining her eyes, she could discern nothing in the shadows that covered the far shore. She clutched the vines, pulling herself upward. She saw him! A dark figure on a horse. Midstream now, the flashing silvered water revealed him to her.

He called again, "Yell! I can't spot you!"

It sounded like McLean. God, please let it be McLean!

She sucked in a lungful of night air and shrieked, "I'm under this tree—the one low to the water—and I'm caught in vines!"

He was drawing nearer, guiding the powerful swimming horse toward her. In another moment he was there and she knew it was McLean when he spoke again.

"Good lord! You certainly know how to get into trouble—" and moonlight glittered on a long, sharp knife as he pulled it from the sheath at his waist. His great horse, Jed, was fighting the current as his master's knees guided him under Savarra's suspended body.

All at once she felt the horse and McLean solidly beneath her and she clamped her legs about the animal's muscled neck. She cried huskily, "I don't know if you can get me loose. My hair—my head—"

But McLean was slashing at the vines above her and suddenly she was free, his arm about her firmly, and the horse was swinging back out in midstream. Under her wet legs, she felt the hard outline of his rifle in his side holster, the hilt of his saber against her hip. In the wash of moonlight, she saw the far shore where the flooded stream had swept over the lower ground. It was lying in still pools of water even among the trees beyond. She was aware of bits and pieces of vine still in her hair and about her shoulders, hanging loosely now, but pulling still upon her. She put her hands up to it and made a violent effort to wrench them from about her.

"Here, now!" McLean said as Jed began clambering up the submerged bank of the creek and splashed noisily into shallower water beyond. "You'll be able to get loose of that when we stop—*don't*! You'll tear out your hair, Savarra!" And he caught her frantic arms and drew them down.

Sobbing for breath, she quelled her desperate desire to be free of this last reminder of her brush with death and leaned weakly against the man who held her.

He said gently, "You're trembling. I know how cold you are. I'll soon stop and make a fire for us—dry you out."

"Where are the others?" she asked hoarsely. Her throat was raw and she wondered how long screams had torn it before McLean had come.

"They are far ahead of us by now, I'm afraid. I've been searching for you ever since the bay loped up beside me, his back bare."

"Then I lost my saddle, too," she rasped. "I knew something had given way when the vines jerked me from him." She could not stop shaking, no matter how hard she clenched her teeth. The March air was chill and cutting on her wet clothing. The only source of comfort was along her back where it pressed against McLean's warm body. "I'm— fr-freezing," she chattered.

His arm pressed her tighter against him and he said, "Only a little farther. We don't want to risk a fire where Doyle's men can see it—though I expect they'll be heading for Camden soon enough, knowing that Marion will be looking for him."

"H-How will he know M-m-marion's got enough men to fight him?" she asked bitterly, wishing with all her heart that Doyle and his men were at the bottom of Lynche's Creek along with all the partisans' supplies.

"I expect Cornet Merritt and all those redcoats in the bull pen will have told him. Doyle won't risk an encounter with the general on his home territory with equal troops."

"I—I feel we're headed toward Camden," she said uneasily.

"No—Indian Town. Doyle and his men will head for

Witherspoon's Ferry again because the British don't like to swim our flooded creeks and rivers."

"That I can understand," she said dryly, putting a hand to her aching throat.

He added, "I figure Doyle will be on the same side of Lynche's Creek as we are by dawn, but far to the north."

"Do you think we can catch up with Colonel Ervin and the others soon?" she asked.

"Not before morning, and by then you'd be sick—if I don't stop and dry you out."

She was silent as he guided the swiftly cantering Jed. Trees were thick about them, and she could not discern that they were following any path. Then, as the moon was lowering in the sky, they came upon a small clearing and McLean halted his horse and slipped to the ground. He caught her about the waist and swung her lightly down. Her back felt the fresh night cold now and she fought against the trembling that seized her anew.

McLean moved swiftly, going out and returning with small sticks and some short, broader limbs. With one sweep of his long arm, he ripped moss from a nearby tree and began building his fire. His flint was wet as he was from thighs to boots and he struck it repeatedly, muttering an oath at last as the sparks flew but failed to catch. He took his foot and stamped upon a limb, crushing the rotten, dry wood, and caught up a short stick and began twirling it in the heart of the dry wood. Faster and faster he whirled it and Savarra, crouching near, saw smoke begin to rise from the point of contact.

"Oh," she cried huskily, "it's catching!"

Then in an instant a small red flame shot up and McLean snatched up the dried moss and laid it over the flame, which licked hungrily at the hairlike gray substance. The smaller sticks followed and the fire grew, until at last he laid the bigger limbs across it and it began to crackle with heat. Savarra stretched her hands to it gratefully, drawing as near as she could. Her boots squelched with water and her feet were numb with cold.

McLean said shortly, "Take off your boots, Savarra." She did so, upending them, and was astonished at the amount of water that poured from each one. She stripped off her long coarse stockings and wrung them out with shaking hands.

He frowned. "All of your clothing would dry faster off

you. A pity I lost my blanket. I fear you may come down with chills and fever while they are drying on you."

"I am, too," she replied faintly. She was filled with a weary heaviness and aching of limb and back.

"My buckskin shirt is dry. Would you consider donning it while we dry the rest of your garments?" In the brilliant firelight his sudden smile was slightly derisive.

She looked at him directly and his mockery died under her tired eyes. She was working slowly at pulling the last of the vines from her hair. He came to her swiftly and with big, tender fingers, began loosening the largest vine that was so knotted into the back of her long hair.

He said roughly, "You've had a hell of an experience—and I don't even have a comb to offer." He sounded frustrated and angry.

"It doesn't matter," she said tiredly. "If I can just get these vines out and tie it all back with something, I'll be glad to wear your shirt. I was never more miserable in my life." The fierce pride that was so deeply ingrained in her was crushed. She did not care if this man saw her humbled at this moment. Indeed, she was so weary that she did not even fight the foolish desire to creep into his arms where warmth and comfort lay.

His clear gray eyes were compassionate as he removed the long, fringed leather shirt, leaving his muscled torso and the thick mat of curling black hair on the broad chest bare in the red light from the fire. He left her then and went back into the dark woods nearby. When he returned with more firewood and several slender sticks, her clothing, which she had attempted to wring, was spread upon the ground and she sat hunched miserably in his shirt. She had pulled the leather garment down to cover her legs and feet and she was still shaking with cold, though she sat as near the fire as possible.

He took the sticks, notched them, drove them into the ground near the blazing fire, laying a third across the notches. Then he took her drenched garments, wringing them of more moisture with his stronger grip, and strung them carefully on the rack he had created from the slender limbs. He threw three more good-sized logs upon the fire and left her once more.

When he returned he carried a great armload of the feathery gray moss, which he spread upon the ground beside her. Her limbs were quivering now with an ague that made her ache all over, and her feet were icy.

McLean looked at her, brows drawn, and he said, "Savarra, you are suffering a severe chill. Lie down facing the fire. I will lie at your back."

Pride flickered faintly and her fevered eyes flashed, "Nay! I will sit facing the fire—"

"You will not, madame," he said curtly. "You saved my life once and I shall save yours now, whether you fight me or not." He pushed her down upon the thick moss and she struggled feebly. "You think I would take you by force—*now*?" His hands were rough upon her as he piled the moss about her feet and legs.

She ceased to struggle and said dully, "You did not take me forcibly before." It had been of her doing as much as his, and even now, sick as she was, she did not know how she should resist such close proximity.

He stirred up the fire, had it blazing merrily before he came to her where he rubbed her feet and legs briskly, stirring blood in them. Then he lay down at her back, pressing himself close to her, putting a strong arm about her waist and drawing her tightly against him.

Slowly, a feeling of euphoria penetrated her misery and she was suddenly excited. A floating sensation took her and she loosed every quivering muscle to flow against him. The warmth of his big hard body was so comforting, so heavenly to her chilled limbs, that relaxation spread through her like a powerful soporific.

His arm about her hardened as his hand sought hers and he encompassed both of her cold ones in his big grip. The feel of him, the clean man's smell of him, brought home to her more than those deadly moments suspended over Lynche's Creek had done the fact that this man had somehow become meshed with her. Her desire for him was bone-deep and irreparable and slowly, slowly, she began to warm. The blood in her veins coursed in an even pulse and her chilled feet and legs grew deliciously warm and relaxed. The shuddering cold left her and a heady warmth seeped through her.

Desire was riding the wave of heat that was reviving her. She fought a yearning to turn and face him, to take his face in her hands and kiss those firm, uncompromising lips once more. Memory was a powerful stimulant, and she remembered now with blinding clarity how those lips had felt against hers that hot August night months ago.

In the midst of her chaos of yearning and desire, her youthful but exhausted body, comfortable and easy at last, did what nature intended it should do. She fell soundly asleep.

Sixteen

Verity was brushing her long dark brown hair preparatory to retiring when her mother came into the room, an air of suppressed excitement about her. She put down the brush and looked at Anne questioningly. Her mother was panting slightly. Something had sent her up the stairs at a run.

"Oh, Verity, my dear—" she said breathlessly, "Tyler Belion is in the small sitting room. At great risk to himself he has come into town to see about us—mainly to see you, of course."

Verity frowned. "He should not risk his life like this. If they caught him again, he would surely hang!" Her heart sank as she voiced her fear.

Her mother approached and took her hands in her own and looked at her daughter searchingly. "Verity, my darling, Tyler will marry you, I *know*. Even if you choose to confide in him. I can send Amos for our minister and you can be married tonight!"

"Mother, there are patrols on the streets until near midnight! Tyler should leave at once." Verity felt her palms begin to sweat at the thought of what her mother was proposing as well as the prospect of her lifetime friend being caught once more.

"He is dressed as an overmountain man, his leather cap covers him very well and he has a beard. No one would recognize him."

"They might question him. Then—"

"Nay. He has come to town to sell pelts, and you know Tyler can ape the brogue of anyone." Her voice became pleading, "Oh, my dear, so much hinges on your marriage to Tyler—your baby's secure future—your own security—my possible remarriage—"

Verity looked up at her mother and their eyes held. She was very tired for she had been with Bonnie Raintree all day helping nurse a desperately ill Terrell. The ten-year-old boy had croup and his lungs had been so congested that he could scarcely draw breath. For ten hours Verity had tended a croup kettle on a brazier by the boy's bed while his mother tried vainly to spoon broth into his mouth. She had left only when Samantha Burbine had come to relieve her, and she had been looking forward to a hot bath as soon as Tiqua and Frances came up with it.

Now she began to slowly rehook her bodice and her mother bent swiftly to help, saying, "It does not so much matter about—Bowman and me—as it does the little one you carry. Think of her—or him—and how the world will look upon a bastard." She spoke the dreaded word without flinching, and Verity gave her mother a curious look before she went out the door and down the hall to the stairs.

When she entered the sitting room, a tall leather-clad figure rose from a chair beside the bright, firelit hearth. A single oil lamp burned dimly inside a frosted and flower-decorated globe and it glowed on the bundle of pelts Belion had placed beside the chair.

It was March eighteenth, and a suddenly cold Atlantic wind had blown into Charles Town from the Bay. It was whistling now with a forlorn cry where it met the eaves of the big house.

Verity went swiftly to Belion and his arms closed about her, pressing her against him, filling her nostrils with the strangely appealing fragrances of tanned leather and wood smoke, faintly mingling with tobacco in a pocket of the shirt under her cheek.

"Tyler, I'm so glad to see you looking so well."

His little laugh was husky with emotion. "How can you tell under this great bush I've grown?"

She looked up into the bearded face and smiled. "Your eyes are very bright and full of health."

"I'm well enough, Verity. I came to assure you and your mother that Savarra had made it safely to us with Caleb and Corrie and that little maid of hers, Cotty."

"We had heard through Bowman's contacts, but I'm glad to get first-hand information. Are they well?"

"The last time I saw them in camp at Snow's Island they were very well. But since then a British officer named

Welbore Doyle destroyed the camp there, captured the wounded and made off with our British prisoners."

Frightened, Verity said, "Oh, but Savarra—where is she?"

"We sent McLean and McHorry to warn them in plenty of time. Word is she's with them and Colonel Erwin and his men, on their way to join Marion once more. She knows well what an unsettled life we lead, but she seems of a tougher breed than I first thought."

He and Verity seated themselves side by side on the large damask sofa before the fire. He held her hand lightly, and she noted in the back of her mind that he made no attempt to kiss her.

"Verity, there has been another battle, this time at Guilford Court House, not far from Camden. Our men, under General Nathanael Greene, were driven from the field, but at great cost to the British—such cost that there are some who do not call it a victory. I imagine your temporary boarder is one of them."

"You mean Lord Bainbridge?" she asked in sudden terror. "Is he—was he wounded?"

Belion's eyes on her face were veiled. "Yes, but superficially, 'tis rumored. We heard from some stragglers that he'd been shot—merely grazed on the flesh of his arm."

She sighed with relief and Belion's dark eyes flickered away from her pale face. He said in a low voice, "Savarra's husband, Lord Haverley, fought in the battle as well. They said he killed two unarmed men who begged for quarter."

"He's a terrible man!" Verity flashed. "He *beat* Savarra, I saw her bruises."

"I'll wager her father knows nothing of that."

"No. And we cannot tell him, or he will know she is with you—our men, and we fear he would seek you out to recover her." Her voice was tense.

Belion continued to look at her in the warm, shadowy light, his eyes shuttered. Then in a hard voice, "I would welcome the chance to kill him, Verity, for he is that most dangerous of Britons, a reasonable and honorable man—one who would by persuasion and example keep us as part of the British empire."

Again she knew the chill of fear for Lord Bainbridge as Belion took his pipe from the pouch at his waist and tamped tobacco in it. All the while she thought, *Dear God, he has been wounded, my darling James, and now Tyler speaks of killing him!*

He rose, took a coal from the hearth with tongs and put it to the pipe. Blowing out a cloud of fragrant smoke, he asked slowly, "Would you like to be brought up to date on the war?"

"Oh, yes! We get only snatches and pieces from Calhoon and Amos who hear it at the market place—and occasionally some from Uncle Bowman."

Belion leaned back against the sofa and in his soft, drawling voice began. "After our victory at Cowpens, where Cutler and I were foolish enough to get ourselves captured, Cornwallis and his main army took out after Morgan and our troops. 'Tis said he burned most of his baggage wagons to speed the chase, but he's been slowed by thousands of slaves and women camp-followers. The British are great ones for liberating slaves—long enough to sell them profitably to the West Indies trade." He drew deeply on the pipe, then continued. "They told Cutler and me when we returned that the partisans had harried Cornwallis all the way to and through North Carolina—and he almost caught Greene, but was halted by the flooding Rapidan River, for Greene had prudently destroyed all boats. So Greene went on into Virginia to gather recruits and horses—and when his ranks had increased to about forty-five hundred men, he turned back southward and challenged Cornwallis in open battle at the Guilford Court House."

"What a terrible waste of life this war is!" Verity burst out. "And there seems to be no end to it—"

"Nathanael Greene says, 'We fight, get beat, rise up and fight again,' and he is close on the heels of Cornwallis even now." Belion's voice was somber, his eyes on Verity were brooding. "A courier arrived in Indian Town the day I left to come here and he said that Cornwallis is planning to march into eastern Virginia, where he will no doubt loot and burn tobacco and other stores, as Benedict Arnold has been and is still doing—in his service to the British."

"Arnold! Now there's the man you should wish to kill—"

"There are many whose loyalties are torn," he replied with an oblique smile. Then added, "The French have put ashore many troops to aid us. Their navy is in American waters as well. And 'tis rumored General Clinton in New York is much distressed over Cornwallis leaving South Carolina unprotected from our troops under Greene."

Verity said wearily, "I wish it was over—finished."

"Not yet, my dear," Belion said grimly. "There's a long

fight ahead of us—even with French reinforcements." He fell silent.

Verity hesitated, then driven, asked, "Will Lord Bainbridge continue on with Cornwallis—or have you heard if he will return to South Carolina—to Charles Town?"

"I do not know, Verity. We know only that the three earls are together, Cornwallis, Bainbridge and Haverley."

She did not speak, and at last Tyler said, a finality in his voice, "Verity, will you marry me tonight?"

Before she could stay her tongue, she blurted, "Tyler, I love you dearly, but I can never marry you!"

"Why?" he asked bluntly.

"I was—mistaken in my feelings when I promised so long ago to wed you. You are my dear, dear friend, but I *cannot* marry you."

"I know why," he spoke with sudden violence. "You have fallen in love with our enemy, Lord Bainbridge!" Then with a touch of dispair, "Verity, you must know the man will never marry you. There can be no life together for you and an English *lord*. He will return to England and you will be left alone. For God's sake, consider the consequences of your love for him!"

"I am suffering the consequences now," she said with painful slowness, yet glad that Tyler Belion knew, "but I cannot do otherwise." She put her hand on his with tenderness. "I did not want to hurt you, Tyler. God knows, I love you. You have been part of my life and I pray for you nightly. But it is not the love on which to build a marriage."

For a long moment he was silent and only the gentle slippage of the fireplace logs as they burned made any sound beyond the lonely cry of wind about the house. Then he rose slowly to his feet. "I must go—"

"Yes, yes!" She rose in a nervous rush. "You are in great danger here! I fear for you, Tyler—"

"One more thing. You must warn Bowman. I dare not go by his house for it is being watched. Word has come to us that the British are suspicious of him now. Tell him he must take every precaution when sending messages to us—or better yet, send none until he hears from us."

Verity's breath had caught. Bowman Baltazar was almost as dear to her as her father. He had taken her on many an afternoon jaunt to teashops, bought her dolls through her little-girlhood, and always his pockets had held treasures for her. Her hands were cold with new fear. "Mother and I will get word to him at once—but surely he must know they are watching him?"

"I fear not. He has moved freely about the city so long and has so many friends among the British officers." Tyler put the strange leather cap, still bearing the fur of the small animal it had been, on his dark head and he looked at Verity with an expression of sadness and longing. "Will you kiss me goodbye?"

"Of course," she replied automatically, thinking to brush his lips with her own. Instead, he caught her to him in a vise and his mouth came down on hers with all the pent-up loss he felt, all the passion that he would have to renounce. It was a long and fierce kiss and Verity did not struggle against it.

He released her slowly, his voice thick. "I will be standing by when you need me, Verity—and you *will* need me when your high and mighty lord is run out of America and returns to his estates in England."

Verity said quietly, "God be with you, Tyler. I shall pray for all of you."

He stooped, caught up the bundle of pelts and swung the strap over his shoulder. Verity followed him from the room. His pipe was clenched in his strong teeth, and she saw the controlled anger and disappointment on the sun-darkened features. In the hall they passed Tiqua and Frances, each carrying two steaming kettles containing water for her bath. The maids nodded silently and made their way toward the stairs.

At the kitchen door Belion reached for the heavy brass handle, then turned. "Verity, for God's sake, take care!" In the dim reflection from the banked kitchen hearth, his eyes were haunted, his mouth taut with yearning. "Do not give of yourself—wholly—to the man, lest you suffer in more ways than you should."

The faint scent of spices hung in the air, reminders of mince pies Primrose had baked earlier. Verity's little smile was twisted. "I will remember, Tyler."

He flung the door open with repressed fury and the strong March winds caught him, swept past to catch her in a chill embrace. Her eyes followed him as far as she could see his lithe form, swiftly taking the steps past the gardens to be lost in the black night that enveloped the far reaches of the Pair stables and lawns beyond.

She closed the heavy door slowly, silently, and in the

faint light turned to find her mother poised in the hall doorway, her dark eyes wide with hope. Verity's heart, already aching for Tyler Belion, knew fresh hurt as she looked at her mother and slowly shook her head.

"Ah—" Anne's breath left her in a great sigh. "You told him then—about Lord Bainbridge."

"I did not need to. He had surmised it long ago, I am sure."

Her mother's face grew paler in the half light. "He knows about the baby as well?"

Verity laughed dryly. "He warned me against giving myself wholly to James—lest I suffer more than I should." She put an arm about her mother's slender waist. "So it will come as no surprise to him when I give birth to Lord Bainbridge's child."

Anne Pair's shoulders sagged and she drew a deep, shaking breath. "Daughter," she said in a low voice, "I would have spared you this."

"You must not reproach yourself, mother," Verity said swiftly. "My problem is of my own making. Now I must tell you of all that Tyler said," and she launched into a low-voiced report of the battle of Guilford Court House and the whereabouts now of the British and American armies.

She finished by saying, "And now, mother, we must get word to Uncle Bowman that he is suspect. From what Tyler says, the British have suspected his patriot activities for some time and are waiting only for something tangible to incriminate him."

The two women halted at the stairs. Light from the sitting room spilled out into the darkened foyer and Anne's hand gripped her daughter's arm. "Then it will be doubly dangerous for him to come here at all! Oh, I must get word to him—I will send Calhoon immediately—"

"Nay, mother!" Verity caught her mother's arm as she started to take the stairs. "The British know Calhoon is a patriot—one of ours. We must wait until the next time Uncle Bowman comes. We must behave exactly as we have been behaving. Then you can warn him quietly, unobtrusively, and he can space his visits farther and farther apart."

"But he has complete control of the Pair Shipyards—"

"Then he must come only on business. After all, James—Lord Bainbridge arranged that himself. The British would not dare question Uncle Bowman for coming on shipyard business, or when he brings us our monthly stipend."

Anne wrung her hands and murmured, "Oh—I didn't know just how much I had—have all these years cared for Bowman until this awful moment." She began to cry silently and terribly and Verity was shaken.

She had never seen her mother cry in this fashion in all the years of their lives together and she did not know what to do. Anne had always been a source of strength, of comfort, of restraint and courage, even when her father was taken prisoner and during that dark day of the memorial service. To see her face twisted in pain and sorrow, in fear and love, was almost a desecration. Verity suddenly flung her arms about her tall, slim mother and murmured whispered words of encouragement, of soothing hope and tender love.

Under her daughter's arms Anne straightened suddenly, took a scented handkerchief from a pocket at the waist of her full skirt and wiped her eyes. With it she wiped away all sign of distress, and her smooth face was calm under Verity's anxious eyes. Even the traces of tears were dried.

Anne said, "Your water will be cooling my dear. You had better hurry to your bath. We will arrange to warn Bowman and he can curtail his activities on behalf of the partisans for whatever length of time it takes to allay British suspicions." She lifted her chin and added, "This, of course, is the exact excuse I need for the delay—and eventual end—of his desire to marry me." She added with a smile, "So you need not feel you are keeping us from marriage after all, darling. I should not have been able to marry him anyway. My patriot sympathies are too well known."

"But mother," Verity protested, following Anne up the stairs, "the war will end—one way or the other. *Then* you can marry! From what Tyler says, Cornwallis and all his men are marching into eventual disaster. Think of the power the French are providing us. Even their navy—"

"In any event, I cannot marry him now, and the war has gone on so long I fear it will last many years more." They reached the landing on the second floor, and a lamp in Verity's room dimly lit the long hall.

"I think you are wrong, mother," Verity said. "Tyler told me something Nathanael Greene said. *We fight, get beat and rise to fight again.* Men like that cannot be defeated. Even now Charles Town is isolated. How long do you think South Carolina can remain under British rule, when all the countryside is hostile to them?"

Anne shrugged and said wearily, "I only know that Bowman is in dreadful peril and you are facing the terrible ordeal of motherhood with a fatherless child. And the war is still a bloody one with Americans dying every day."

Verity had no reply. Her mother turned in the door to her own room and Verity entered hers to find Tiqua and Frances had prepared the tub of hot water and were waiting to help her disrobe.

The following day Terrell Raintree was much worse, and Bonnie sent for both Verity and her mother. She met them as Amos drove the carriage up to the small, stark house, her eyes frantic.

"Dr. Adams has been here and gone and he says there is nothing we can do but wait for the crisis." Bonnie's voice was anguished as she saw the two women into the close little room where Terrell lay, his eyes closed and his cheeks fiery pink. The croup kettle was still emitting steam, and Bonnie's light brown eyes had blue rings beneath them. Belle was a silent wraith at her mother's side.

Anne said compassionately, "Bonnie, dear, we will sit with him. You must get some rest."

"If Dr. Adams has given up, I'm going to send for old Marilla!" There was a touch of hysteria in Bonnie's voice.

"Oh, Bonnie, no. Her reputation is so bad," Anne remonstrated.

"But she cures more often than not," Bonnie replied stubbornly. "I know of too many cases that were given up— babies that couldn't be born and Marilla has brought them —she has cured the sick too many times."

"Her reputation is built on superstition and ignorance," Anne replied, removing her hat and cloak. Then, "Oh, dear, his fever is so high," she murmured placing a cool white hand to the child's forehead.

"I know, I know!" Bonnie wailed. "That's why I'm going to send for Marilla."

"You know that Dr. Adams will refuse to return when he finds that you have employed her, Bonnie," Anne said at last.

"He does nothing anyway! Please let me send Amos after her, Anne."

Anne hesitated, then in a rush of pity, "Very well, Bonnie dear. Go out and tell him to fetch her."

Verity was dipping a cloth into a basin of clean, cold water, and now she laid it across the fevered forehead of the boy, who rolled his head and muttered indistinctly. Bonnie raced through the house on her way to Amos, who sat on the box of the Pair carriage in front.

"Old Marilla is very tight about her fees, mother," Verity said, "and Bonnie has little money."

"We will pay her," Anne replied grimly, "*if* she does the boy any good at all."

Verity looked into her mother's composed face with sudden appreciation and love. Anne was strait-laced, puritanical, but in a crisis she could be counted on to be steadfast and generous.

Amos returned with Marilla in less than an hour. She carried a large basket filled with pots of medicine and jars containing the essence of herbs. There were bottles of dark, evil-looking liquid which she set upon the commode table preparatory to treating the boy. In a matter of minutes she had a pungent medicine in the croup kettle, filling the room with clean, sharp odor, and she had ordered hot water to mix with poultices to be placed on the boy's chest. She immediately administered two teaspoonsful of the black liquid to the half-conscious child, and her grim face was determined and dedicated.

Three hours later, when Bonnie was safely in bed and sleeping from a potion Marilla had given the exhausted woman, Terrell Raintree was breathing almost freely and his fever had abated miraculously. Before she and Verity left, Anne had sent for Tiqua and Frances to stay while Bonnie slept and to do Marilla's bidding.

In the carriage Anne sighed. " 'Tis like doing business with the devil, dealing with Marilla."

"Nay, mother. Marilla gives the people only what they ask for, insofar as she can. You saw how much improved Terrell is now."

"I'll give the devil his due," Anne said grudgingly. "I told Marilla we would pay her handsomely if she saves the boy."

Three days later Marilla appeared at the Pair rear door, and Verity watched her mother pay the spare, expressionless woman five gold sovereigns. Anne even said, "We are grateful to you, Marilla," but the basilisk eyes did not blink.

"When you need me, madame, I'll always come—for a

fee." She turned and mounted a fine bay horse and trotted back up the drive, disappearing from sight.

Anne looked at her daughter. "I never saw such a quick turn for the better," she said thoughtfully. "Only this morning Bonnie sent word by Tiqua that he was eating a hearty breakfast and his chest is clear." Then with a quiver of fear, "Yet she would have risked your life for a fee to abort your baby."

Verity said hastily, "I don't like to think of that. Better to think of Terrell and the wonder of saving his life."

"I am thinking of the time when your baby will be born," Anne said slowly, "next September. We shall have Dr. Adams, if he is willing to deliver a nameless child."

"My child *will* have a name," Verity said heatedly, "and it will be Pair. And I shall hold my head up in Charles Town, too! My child will be accepted!"

Anne's eyes were sorrowful on her young, embattled daughter as she said, "Your child will be marked for life, my darling, and you must reconcile yourself to it."

It was April, and green, tender fledgling things of the earth were bursting forth under warm and frequent showers. April roses were blooming, perfuming the air about the Pair house with their heady fragrance, and lilacs were a profusion of purple, adding deliciously to the scents of the air. It was on this luscious spring morning that Lord Bainbridge rode into Charles Town with a handful of seasoned warriors.

He came directly to the Pair house with Colonel Coyne and his two aides, Sergeant Queen and Lieutenant Keith. Verity saw them arrive, for she was out clipping roses to put in the house, and they nodded coolly, but their eyes met brilliantly, each starved for the sight of the other. He looked leaner, browner to her, and his hair as he swept off his tricorne was sun-streaked to golden fairness.

He spent the day opening headquarters, conducting affairs of his office with Coyne and the two young aides. Anne, by adroitly moving about and seeing that Verity accompanied her, managed to avoid their conversing together until the dinner hour.

When the three finally met in the dining salon after he had bathed and shaved for the evening meal, Anne was icily polite. His glance at her was slightly puzzled before he turned his attention to the glowing Verity.

She asked, "How came you to return to Charles Town, Lord Bainbridge? We had heard you and General Cornwallis were far to the north."

"So we are—but military business brings me back to Charles Town very briefly."

Over dinner, the conversation was courteous and banal, dealing with the weather, the social life of the British in Charles Town, the news of the neighbors about them. Verity was in a fever to get it over with so she could be with him alone in the later hours.

But as they were finishing up dessert, he said abruptly, "Lord Haverley tells me that Savarra has left him and he thinks you ladies helped her in eluding him."

"Yes," Anne replied coldly. "He came and disrupted our household searching for her, even posted guards about the house. She was not here, of course."

"He tells me she turned on him immediately after the wedding and for no apparent reason, unless she was frightened and unprepared for the responsibilities of marriage. I am very disturbed over her irrational actions. Have you no idea where she may be—possibly with that Bonnie Raintree?"

Anne gave him a level, icy stare. "Of course she isn't with Bonnie. We should have known of it long ago. My guess is that your daughter has taken refuge with country people. We have heard ugly rumors—that Lord Haverley is a harsh and cruel man."

Verity flashed her mother a glance of admiration. She had not expected Anne to stand up for Savarra. Now she added, "Yes, mother and I have heard through the servants' gossip that Lord Haverley has killed several unarmed men in cold blood."

"He has," Lord Bainbridge said curtly, "and I think the less of him for it, but he is a soldier of the crown and conducts himself well in battle." His voice softened and he continued, "I am very concerned for Savarra and Cotty, but I have not the time to search the countryside between here and Camden—duty demands my presence with my commander, General Cornwallis." Then even more slowly, "She has married Lord Haverley and she owes him her loyalty. I had not thought her so flighty and unreliable."

"She probably had her reasons," Anne said even more coldly. There was a finality in her voice that annoyed Lord Bainbridge and Verity saw the blood in his cheeks.

"I should have to speak with her about them," he said stiffly. "Haverley tells me he was tender and gentle with her —argued with her for half the night. But she fled as soon as he slept."

What a liar was Lord Haverley, Verity thought contemptuously. She could visualize his charming smile, those polished manners as he blackened Savarra's character to her own father. Oh, if she could but tell him the truth of the matter! She did not know if she could hold her tongue on Haverley's calumny.

The meal was over at last and there was a brief, uncomfortable time in the salon during which she and her mother sat trying to make inconsequential talk while Lord Bainbridge had an after-dinner brandy with his pipe. Verity was growing more and more anxious to be with him alone, and each time their eyes touched it sent a quiver of anticipation and desire through her veins.

At last, the three of them were lighted upstairs by Amos, holding high a chimneyed candle. Verity undressed hurriedly, having refused Tiqua's offer to unhook her bodice. She wanted to be alone until she could go to Lord Bainbridge.

She had a new nightdress, made by Madame Flammarion, a gauzy, lacy white garment, and madame had teased her about having it made for a trousseau. She took it from the bed of tissue and slipped into it slowly. Then she seated herself before the great mirrored dressing table and took the pins from her long, dark hair, letting it tumble over her shoulders and down her back while she brushed and brushed until it glimmered like brown satin.

She took her time now, for she wanted the house to be deep in slumber before she made her way to his room. As a final touch, she took a vial of perfume, also purchased from Madame Flammarion, who told her in a whisper that it had been smuggled in from Paris. She put it to her wrists, her temples, her throat. The delicious and delicate fragrance stirred her senses and she was suddenly fluid with yearning for his touch. She looked at the small clock on the dressing table—only eleven thirty! She must wait until after twelve.

She went to the north windows, which were open to the warm spring air. It carried a thousand scents, each as seductive as the French perfume at her throat. The curtains stirred faintly, and she leaned her hot face against cool wood that framed the window. Nothing should spoil this night for her, nothing! She thought of her mother and with the thought came a sudden fear. What if Anne stood waiting in the hall with arguments and recrimination? Worse, what if her mother confronted Lord Bainbridge with her pregnancy?

Verity flung away from the window and almost ran from the room. As she sped along the corridor, her thin white nightdress streaming out from her slender shape, she did not see her mother. Nor was there light coming from the open door to her room. Verity slowed, breath short, and slipped like a ghost down to Lord Bainbridge's room. She did not knock, but opened it silently and stepped into the dark room to close it as quietly behind her.

Against the windows to the south a shape rose up to meet her, and in the shadows they melted together and clung wordlessly for a long moment. She could smell the faint fragrance of the pipe he had smoked while waiting for her, mingling with the warm, sweet breeze from the gardens and the clean scent of his flesh as she buried her face against his throat and chest.

"Verity, Verity," he murmured into her silky hair, "if you knew how I have longed for this moment—"

"I do know," she whispered, letting her hands slip across his bare shoulders. He still wore his white breeches and boots.

"I must have the sight of you," he said huskily and turned to the bedside table where he took up a tinderbox. In a moment he had lighted the candle there.

They stared at each other beside the great four-posted bed beneath the pleated white tester, and Verity thought for the hundredth time she had never seen eyes so blue, so tender with longing, nor a face so strong and handsome. She moved to him, hands outstretched, and he took them in his, pulled her to the bed where they sat side by side.

"Did you guess," he asked, drawing off his boots, "that all my military duties here are trumped up? On excuse that I must close up my headquarters permanently, I came solely to be with you. I have ridden near five hundred miles and will ride more than that to return—all for the love of Verity Pair." He laughed softly as he removed his breeches and took her once again into his arms. He said, "That is a beautiful garment you wear. Do you retire each night looking so deliciously desirable?" and he helped her remove it.

Her husky laughter mingled with his as they came together

in the big soft bed. "Ordinarily I look like a summer nun when I go to bed."

"Thank God you are not one," he said, kissing her with rising passion.

When at last they lay side by side, their love once more fully consummated, Lord Bainbridge reached out and put a thumb over the candle, snuffing it. Darkness settled about them and Verity lay in the curve of his arm, her thoughts drifting idly, sleep nearly upon her.

"Until I met you, I had loved but one woman in my life," he said. "Now I give you all the devotion that was hers. 'Tis yours in your own right."

"Do I remind you of her?" she asked with sudden jealousy, wide awake now.

"At first you did. Now you seem very different from Isabella."

"I am not a—noblewoman—not of your station," she said in a smothered voice. "Savarra told me her mother was related to the King of Spain."

"A second cousin only." Then with tired anger, "Savarra is a great disappointment to me. Running away from the man she married, like any flighty tavern wench."

Suddenly Verity was boiling with rage. "I am surprised, James, that you would take the word of a man you so recently despised." Her voice shook slightly.

In the sudden taut silence between them, Lord Bainbridge said nothing, but rose to a sitting position and reached unerringly for the flint, relighting the candle he had just snuffed. She turned on her side, away from him, but she could feel his eyes upon her. "My dear," he said quietly, "look at me."

She turned and faced him, the sheet still covering her naked bosom. " 'Tis very late," she said defiantly. "Why have you lit the candle again?" Her feelings were in such a tumult she could not extricate the strands of emotion that formed them. Partly it was the coldness of his voice when he spoke of his hotheaded young daughter, partly it was jealousy of the dead Isabella, and most of all it was because she carried his child and could not tell him. How many things she could not tell him! To her horror, she began to weep silently.

He reached out to pull her against him, but she twisted away, all at once unwilling that he should see her nakedness, though she had gloried in it but moments before. She reached for her nightdress at the foot of the bed and he watched silently as she pulled it over her head, tears slipping unheeded down her ivory cheeks.

He did not try to touch her again. He only watched while she fumbled with ribbons and lace. Then she suddenly clasped her knees beneath the sheet and laid her face upon them, her long dark hair falling about her like a veil, shielding her from that unwavering blue stare. At last, unable to endure the silence any longer, she struggled from the sheet and said thickly, "I will leave you now."

"Nay." He reached out and caught her arm. She winced at the iron grip. "I did not ride five hundred miles to have you leave my bed like this. I have given a whole heart to you—yet you give me nothing but your body. What do you hide from me, Verity?"

The truth of his accusation struck her such a blow her breath went out in a gasp. Her low laugh held a touch of hysteria which she forcibly quelled. "Better to ask me what I do *not* hide from you, James—such as the fact that I love you with all my soul."

"With all your flesh, at any rate," he replied dryly. Then with a tender curiosity, "Are you so afraid of me that you cannot confide what it is that makes you weep?"

All the characteristics she admired in him, his gentleness, his strength and courage, his calm reasonableness, rose up to rebuke her. "I am torn by too many loyalties," she said hopelessly. "I cannot confide in you, James."

"You think you are the only one torn in loyalties?" His voice was low and bitter. "I know and respect—nay, I *like* the rebels I have met, though I am sworn to subdue or kill them. I love my daughter, yet a peer of the realm tells me that she cursed and left him on her wedding night. I love you, yet I know you will not have me because your love of country forbids it."

She relaxed under his grip, turning back to stare at him with wide dark eyes and trembling lips, two starry tears glittering on her thick lashes. "*I*—will not—have *you*?"

"Aye. You have made it plain enough many times."

"In what way?" she asked, obscurely frightened.

"Do you think when I hold you I do not know when your mind slips away from me? Do you think me such a dullard I could love you as I do and not know of inner secrets held from me?"

She shook her head wordlessly. She could not tell him of

the coming child. She must not tell him of Savarra's whereabouts. She *must* not.

"You see?" he asked ironically. Then to her complete astonishment, "I will show you how much you love America. Will you marry me then and, when this is over, return to England with me?"

Her tears dried in the long silence that followed his question as disbelief struggled with the import of his question. She whispered, "You mean you would *marry* me? A rebel. A—a *commoner?*"

"My dear, I am not royalty," he said with a droll smile. "You see? Your subterfuge is to answer a question with a question, which is no answer at all."

"Oh, James," she cried and with sudden stormy violence, flung herself into his arms. "I will marry you. I *will*." She pulled back suddenly, examining his face with brilliant eyes and flushed cheeks. "I haven't tricked you into asking? You haven't guessed—"

"Guessed?" he asked alertly. "That you loved me enough?" He held her against his warm broad chest, stroking her hair gently.

"Ah," she murmured, relief and love and happiness flooding her, "I can tell you—all—now."

"All what?" he asked with a smile, "Your secrets, Verity? Just because I want to marry you? Surely you must have known that for months. I wanted to marry you the moment I set eyes on you."

"But I didn't, James. Truly I didn't. I thought I was only amusing—entertaining to you for a brief time and you would tire of me."

"I do not amuse myself in this fashion, Verity." Then with something of wonderment, "How little we know each other after all."

"James, I will bear you a child in September."

There was a moment of utter silence before he crushed her in an embrace that took her breath away. "My darling! I cannot believe it! My God—so that's what has been troubling you. Did you not know our marriage would make me the happiest of men?" He began to kiss her face, her temples, her chin, even the tip of her straight little nose. "We will be married tomorrow—no, *today*. I'll not return to Virginia until you are my wife."

Verity began to laugh, a low, rollicking laugh that grew until she shook with laughter. Her heart was feather-light and her astonishment still so real that it swelled within like a spring bud bursting to flower.

"What is it that makes you laugh so, Verity?" he asked tenderly.

"My mother—she will be overcome with surprise—"

"She knows of our love for each other?" he asked quickly.

"And she is certain that you, an English lord, would never marry a rebel girl."

He chuckled. "We will have her as a witness. I shall ride out and secure a minister and arrange it for one in the afternoon." His voice grew heavy. "I must leave again day after tomorrow, love, for Charles Cornwallis needs me and my men. That is why I shall close down the headquarters permanently, for Colonel Coyne and Lieutenant Keith and Sergeant Queen must return with me." Then with rising joy, "Perhaps 'twill be a fine son—something I have always longed for—an heir to my title and estates. Savarra is so feckless," his voice grew saddened, "and she cares nothing for me or my wishes. She is headstrong and willful, over-prideful—and I love her deeply."

"I cannot let you think those things about your daughter, James." The words boiled out of Verity in a flood. "She *did* come to us in the night—Lord Haverley had beaten her, *brutally,* and I think he took her by force as well. My mother and I saw the bruises and a dreadful *bite* on her neck, crusted with blood. She was frantic with fear of him—"

"God's blood! That liar—that blackguard—"

"He turned on her when he found that she had been a captive of the partisans, accusing her of—unspeakable things." Verity stopped, hesitated a long moment before she said in a low voice, " 'Twas Savarra who had the courage to smuggle pistols to Tyler Belion and Cutler McLean for their escape from the Charles Town jail—and Lord Haverley somehow guessed it. In the course of their quarrel she admitted it and he treated her—utterly without mercy."

There was a long silence before Lord Bainbridge laughed dryly. "By God, she's thrown her lot in with you rebels! I suppose she's with them now—and Savarra gives her whole heart to her decisions." He paused, then musing, "I believe I'm proud of her. Where is she now?"

"With the partisans. That's why I could not tell you—for fear you would seek them out to rescue your daughter and kill them all in the doing."

"Which partisans? There are so many." There was wry

humor in the question. "There is Pickens—and Sumter and Marion and God knows how many others on their own. Besides, Charles and I are after bigger game than these small, harassing rebels."

"She is wtih Marion—for Tyler and Cutler are with him and 'twas Cutler who slipped back into Charles Town to thank Savarra. He told her if he could ever in any way help her, he would do so."

"Ah. There's a man of his word. A clever, strong and honorable man."

"You can say that, when he broke bread with you in the guise of a loyalist?"

"I would have done the same had our roles been reversed. I would fight to the death to preserve Britain. These Americans are British in their reaction to the foreign threat to their country. Nay, I have only admiration and respect for Cutler McLean—and even that surly Belion." He laughed once again with regretful amusement.

They had talked for more than an hour longer when at last Verity murmured, "I must leave. Mother must not find me in your room this morning, though she knows—all. We must observe the conventions for her. She will be so happy—stunned, I expect—when we tell her of our plans to marry."

"Now I know why she was so cold and inimical to me when I arrived," he chuckled. "Dear Anne. She will make a fine mother-in-law and an even better grandmother."

Verity kissed him lightly, and as the candle guttered out she left him, her happiness unalloyed.

Verity was correct in her surmise. Her mother was dumbfounded when her daughter informed her of Lord Bainbridge's determination to marry her at one o'clock that afternoon. Verity had waited until he was gone to make arrangements to inform her mother.

Anne sank down into a chair in the sitting room as if her legs were suddenly unable to support her. "I cannot believe it —and you say he asked you before you told him about the baby?"

"Yes, mother. *That* is what makes it quite wonderful. He thought *I* would not have *him*."

"And you told him all about Savarra?" Her big dark eyes were very wide and they gave her the ingenuous look that made her appear so young at times.

Verity took her mother into her arms exultantly. "Yes—all,

and he has no desire to track our patriots down. He knows Savarra is safer with them than with that—terrible Lord Haverley." She laughed gaily. "Now you and Uncle Bowman can marry—whenever he is free of suspicion. And perhaps the war will soon be settled. James is so understanding and reasonable, I know if he were negotiating for the British we would soon have our independence. His heart is not in fighting our patriots."

"I can scarce believe it," Anne said. Then with sudden perturbation, "You did not tell him of Bowman's partisan activities?"

"No, there was no point in it. I feel sure he has guessed as much, but he will say nothing. He must set out for Virginia tomorrow to rejoin General Cornwallis." Her voice fell at this last and a shadow of fear crossed her face.

"Oh," Anne said, her voice breaking slightly, "I am so *glad*—so grateful that you will be spared the shame—the loneliness and sorrow." Then with a touch of sadness, "But I shall lose you to England, Verity—I shall not see my grandchild grow up. I feel it in my bones."

"Mother, you and Uncle Bowman can come to England to visit. Every year, if you like!" Verity's euphoria, her sparkling joy, was so infectious that Anne herself began smiling at the rosy prospects her daughter painted.

The wedding was performed with British dispatch. All of the men, some fifteen, attended their commander's nuptials, and the couple left the church under a shower of congratulations.

Anne, with the help of Primrose, Tiqua, Frances and the two men, Amos and Calhoon, had decorated the house with flowers and prepared a wedding feast for the evening. Lord Bainbridge invited his four officers to dine with them, and many toasts were proposed with Warren Pair's fine Madeira. There were more after dinner with the stronger brandy.

Lord Bainbridge took occasion to remark, "I am surprised that your loyalist friend, Bowman Baltazar, is not here. He is so fond of you, Verity."

"I asked him," Anne replied, carefully noncommittal, "but he had business to which he must attend. After all, he is responsible for the Pair Shipyards as well as his own business." Then cautiously planting a seed, "We do not see him often often. As a firm loyalist he has much to do for the British as well."

Lord Bainbridge merely smiled and said no more about the absent Baltazar. Verity knew a fleeting moment of anxiety, remembering Baltazar's haunted eyes when he and her mother discussed his precarious place in Charles Town.

That night, for the first time, Verity and her lover went openly to his bedroom to spend the long, sweet spring night in each other's arms. She had no presentiment of disaster then, no thought of the future, nothing beyond the pure joy of those moments with Lord Bainbridge.

But in the morning when the time came for him to make the return journey to Cornwallis and his army in faraway Virginia, her throat filled with sudden thickness as she stood beside his horse. His men were milling about the rear courtyard, but Verity was oblivious to them. She saw only the tall, fair man she had married and loved to distraction. And she clung to him with a touch of desperation before he mounted.

"You will return—soon?" Her eyes searched his.

"As soon as possible," he said briefly, as if he did not trust himself to speak of the uncertain future.

"Before—September, or by then?" she asked urgently, aware now that Colonel Coyne was looking at her with compassion and a faintly bitter sympathy.

"I will leave no effort untried to return by September, my darling." With a final brief kiss, he mounted and the troop trotted out to the shell drive, past the porte-cochere and out upon the cobblestoned street. Verity, her mother and the servants followed and stood watching from the front as they clattered down the long street to turn and disappear around a corner.

They walked slowly back to the house and Verity wondered at the darkness that descended upon her spirit. She felt suddenly bereft and saddened. She knew Lord Bainbridge lived with danger, had lived with it most of his thirty-nine years and had come through unscathed. There was no reason for her uneasiness.

The silent and empty headquarters was once again Warren Pair's library. There would be no more soldiers or strangers entering the Pair house uninvited. Perhaps that was the source of this strange and fearful depression.

She put her mind on the baby and was cheered and, when the two of them were alone, she and her mother fell to discussing a layette for the little one.

Still, her premonitory sense of approaching disaster clung and colored the balance of the day no matter how she argued with herself as the hours passed. And she had never felt so lonely in her life as when she climbed up into the big bed in Lord Bainbridge's room without him that night.

Seventeen

Savarra awakened slowly to find the fire still burning warmly, and she herself was wrapped in dry moss. McLean was nowhere to be seen. She sat up, pulling the gray, hair-like growth from about herself. She was clad still in McLean's deerskin shirt, which came almost to her bare knees. A warm sun shone above the trees which cast a lacy shadow about the small clearing.

She moved stiffly for she was very sore, her tangled hair still filled with bits and pieces of vine. Putting a hand to her neck, she rubbed the muscles that ran to her shoulders and winced at the movement of her arms. Where was McLean? Even his horse, Jed, was gone.

Her eyes, which also seemed to move reluctantly, scanned the forest nearby on both sides of her. A slow crawling fear began in the base of her brain and crept to her heart, and it began to race. Her breath shortened and she bit her lip upon an urge to cry out at the top of her lungs.

Fighting down the urge, she looked at her hands and was horrified to find them scratched and covered with dried blood. Her nails were broken but washed clean by the flooding creek the night before. She put fingertips to her face to find it smooth, seemingly untouched by the danger and terror that had claimed her so short a time ago.

My hair, she thought, *my dreadful hair. It will likely never be untangled again,* and she ran her fingers through it ineffectually, stopping to work at knots and twigs, telling herself McLean would surely not ride away and leave her in the forest.

She spoke aloud, "He's only gone to find the others," but the sound of her hoarse, crackling voice only added to her fears. Her throat was raw and sore. How long had she screamed in that dark prison of vines last night, with the flooding waters whipping her body from the waist down? It had seemed an eternity before she had heard McLean's voice, had felt his strong, competent grip, heard him slash and sever the vines.

Her eyes fell upon her clothing hanging from the poles. It looked to be dry. She got to her feet, wincing once more, and walked gingerly to it, her feet tender to the rough ground, stooping to run her scratched hands into the boots. The tops were stiff, almost dry, but inside the foot was still damp and gave off an evil smell. The coarsely spun shirt and stockings were very dry, the breeches also warm and dry, but the heavy woolen coat felt still faintly damp. Her delicate underwear, the only thing that was actually hers, was very dry but discolored by the creek waters.

The fire before her was blazing quite high, and she told her fast-beating heart that the man who had replenished it must not be far away. Then her eyes fell upon his saber on the ground beside her bed of moss. She expelled her breath in relief. He would not leave that! She sank weakly to the ground, a slight dizziness enveloping her. Putting her head down in her hands she waited for it to pass and realized that she was sick with hunger. Unexpectedly she found herself possessed of a violent wish to return to that moment the night before when McLean had eased his big body down beside her and taken her into his warm embrace. Her shivering had ceased and she had gone to sleep so quickly—too quickly. That had been a moment to savor and she had slept it away!

She took the underwear from the branch between the two poles and slipped it slowly up her bare thighs, covering her nakedness. It gave her a small touch of security and she sat back down, angered by her feebleness.

She would not yell for him. She would *not*. He could not hear her anyway, she scolded her fears. Probably he was far off in the woods, searching for Colonel Ervin's camp. But he should have awakened her! He should have told her he was leaving. She reached out and caught the dry breeches to pull them over her short pantalets trimmed with their incongruous and dirty lace trimming. Then she took up the stockings. They were rough, warm, and they felt good for the morning air was chill. She sat close to the fire debating whether to put on the coarse shirt, and decided against it.

The coat was still too wet to don, and McLean's deerskin shirt was much warmer than the shirt alone would be.

After that, she crept back to the bed of moss and sat down once more. Her throat was parched along with being sore, and she wished heartily for a cup of Primrose's scalding sweet coffee. Even a drink of creek water would taste good. She would even settle for a swallow of Francis Marion's vinegary canteen, she thought forlornly.

Then, so silently that she was startled to hear his voice, McLean rode into the clearing. "Ah! You're awake. How do you feel?"

"Terrible," she croaked, looking up at him with great relief, which she tried to keep out of her voice. This was easy, for her voice was not hers at all but that of a raspy stranger. McLean's torso was still bare but he did not appear cold, which seemed strange for she was shivering again. He smiled, and the sunlight striking his dark hair gleamed briefly. She felt blood burning in her face and was both annoyed and frustrated, but she kept her eyes on the two plump rabbits slung across his saddle.

He said matter-of-factly, "I'm sure you must be hungry, but game is all I can give you, Savarra—we have no utensils. I have a little coffee in my pack, but we have nothing to brew it in." She looked at him wordlessly, reluctant to speak in her hoarse abrasive voice. He smiled again and added, "I'll clean the rabbits and we'll have a late breakfast."

He went to the edge of the woods, and with the long, bright blade he had used to free her from the tangled vines, he skinned and prepared the two small animals. She sat watching silently as he returned and constructed a spit over the fire, knocking the burning brands apart until he had a low, hot bed of coals, and strung the rabbits over it.

"Glad your clothes are drying," he said conversationally. He did not seem aware of his bare chest but she found it difficult to look away from it.

"My coat is still damp," she croaked. "Your leather shirt is warmer than my cloth one—I thought you'd gone to find the others."

"My God," he said, looking at her intently, "your voice sounds like the foghorn in Charles Town bay."

"I screamed for at least five hours before you found me."

He laughed, "It wasn't that long—no more than two, though it must have seemed forever." He went to the small leather pack that had been strapped to his saddle and took out a little vial of precious salt, sprinkling the rabbits generously and turning them.

"Where are the others?" she asked.

"Somewhere to the south and west of us. They're headed for Indian Town, for that is where Marion is now."

The dizziness was on her again and she lay down abruptly on the moss bed. He looked at her speculatively. "First you're red as fire, then pale as a ghost." He came to put a big, rough-textured hand to her forehead. "I think you have a fever."

"I guess so," she replied, looking up into his hard dark face. The moment of revelation in the creek surged back to her. In those black moments with death at her side, she had seen this man for what he was, a powerful force in her life. He had been so from the moment they had collided on board the *Lion*. Now Savarra felt a thousand years older and wiser looking back on the fool she had been. Little good that did her now, with those cool gray eyes scrutinizing her without expression. She had ruined her chances with Cutler McLean long ago, and he thought of her only as a spoiled baggage, a selfish and headstrong British girl. *And so I am*, she thought glumly. Experience was a harsh teacher, but it had not yet completely killed her pride, which now rose to support her in this moment of self-condemnation.

"You're not well enough to travel," he said with slow decision. "We'll camp here until you recover before moving onto join Marion."

"What if they all leave Indian Town?" she rasped. "How will we find them?"

He smiled aagin. "We have a network among patriot farmers and planters. Finding him will be simple—for me."

She sighed tiredly, the gnawing in her stomach growing. "I'm so thirsty," she murmured.

He took his canteen from beside the saddle on Jed and unstoppered and handed it to her. She took a long cool swallow. "Mmnn, that's good—doesn't taste like the creek—"

"It isn't. There's a clear spring about a mile from here. I just filled it." He replaced the stopper, adding, "I wish to God I had carried more equipment with me when we left Snow's Island."

"You didn't know you'd have to go back and find me," she said wearily. "By all rights, you should be with the others now."

"Are you feeling sorry for yourself?"

"No!" She flared, eyes flashing. "I'm merely stating a fact."

"After all, I owed it to you," he said lightly. "You saved my hide for me, and turn about's fair play."

She made no response. He had the power to make her furious even in her weakened condition, and it frustrated her unreasoningly that he should merely be repaying a favor in saving her life.

They said no more as the rabbits slowly browned. She ached in her bones and she knew it was fever from the cold she had caught in the swollen creek last night.

When at last the rabbits were golden brown and emanating savory odors, her previous hunger had disappeared and she ate with little appetite. McLean watched her closely, urging her to eat as much as she could to build up her strength. Her coat and shirt were thoroughly dry by mid-afternoon, and she gave McLean back his shirt after a brief and rather comic scene in which she made him go into the woods while she changed.

That night she slept poorly and fitfully, though McLean once again put his long warm body back of hers and held her in the crook of his arm. He gave her water from the canteen regularly and so they passed the second night.

They spent four days and nights in the small clearing with McLean bringing in fresh game for their meals, squirrels once, quail another, and then rabbits once more. With each passing day Savarra's strength returned. Each night he held her in his arms, keeping the chill March nights from touching her, and each night as she grew better she found herself more and more taking a tantalizing and sensuous delight in the feel of that long, muscular body against hers. It became a sort of delicious torment.

By the fourth day, she was fretting for a comb and brush and had worked with her hair until all the twigs and knots were out of it and McLean pronounced her ready to travel.

She sat behind him on Jed and, when he cantered, she put her arms around his lean hard waist, pressed herself against the broad back and felt a security she had not known since she was a child. As they rode along, it occurred to her that it was an astonishing fact that she had been alone with this man who stirred her passions to white-hot depths for nearly a week. Yet, but for warming her at night, he never attempted to touch her. Each night she had been tense, fearing her own reactions as much as his, but she had encountered an iron control in the man. Thus, as they sought Marion, she realized that to Cutler McLean she was now a married woman, and he would make no move to satisfy the longing that more and more heated her as each day passed.

Savarra was not sure she loved him. She only knew she needed him, wanted him, that her body cried out for his and, had he made the slightest overture to her, she would very likely respond passionately. The thought was frightening as well as sobering, and each night she told herself grimly that she would never, *never* by the slightest move let him know his effect on her.

On their way through the country, McLean avoided the residences of those he knew to be tories and stopped only at plantations and farm houses where they were welcomed by their inhabitants. He introduced Savarra as a refugee from British cruelty, which surprised no one. Women camp followers, for whatever reason, were common enough. But the two of them ate fairly well and often of whatever their hosts had to share, and it was April before they reached Marion in a wooded glade beyond Indian Town.

The camp was alive with excitement, but Savarra did not note it as she was reunited with Cotty, who wept copiously at the safe return of her mistress. The maid had been given a comb by the enterprising Gabe Sleep, and she proceeded to help Savarra wash her hair and braid it neatly. It was the first time in days that Savarra had felt even a small touch of tidiness. She was most unhappy with her clothing, but nothing could be done about it, for in the escape from Snow's Island they had left their extra clothing from Baltazar behind.

McLean vanished in the mass of men that surged about the camp, and Cotty proceeded to tell Savarra the source of the excitement. While braiding her hair, she said, "Oh, mistress, a patriot colonel is coming to join us. His name is Henry Lee and they call him Light Horse Harry and he has a whole legion with him. Him an' General Marion is goin' to work together under General Greene's orders. Thad says he's a real gentleman soldier from Virginia."

Cotty proved to be right, for when Lee's Legion came riding in they were an impressive sight. Clad in green jackets and white breeches, with flashing helmets, they looked to be the epitome of seasoned, disciplined and competent warriors.

Savarra saw Henry Lee himself and observed that he was a handsome and personable young man, sitting his horse with easy authority. He was a dashing figure, and the camp was full of tales of his daring. When he and Marion met, they made a strange couple, Marion with his melange of clothing and charred leather cap and Lee with his impeccable uniform and dapper appearance.

Still, as the next few days passed, the two men seemed to respect and collaborate with each other as they made their plans to harass the British. There were other women in camp with their men, some wearing full cotton skirts, but they came and went and Savarra and Cotty made only fleeting acquaintance with them. It still seemed odd to Savarra, brought up on stories of British discipline, that Marion's command was so fluid—even the men left to attend chores at home, only to return when they were finished. And Henry Lee, Virginia gentleman that he was, seemed to bear great respect for the shabby little militia general, putting his men at his disposal willingly.

After a few days, they moved northward, a ride Savarra and Cotty made on another mule, horses being in short supply. Caleb took Corrie up behind him on the fine roan he had been given out of respect for his prowess in battle. They made camp at last in a stand of trees near the Peedee River.

She saw little of McLean now as he came and went on partisan missions. But once he returned with a set of deerskin clothing for Savarra that, to her astonishment, fit perfectly. She was very grateful and was hard put not to give her joyful exuberance free rein.

As he gave the clothing to her, he said, "There is a comb in the packet there," he pointed to the leather pouch with the suit, "and soap. But I didn't—I couldn't find—buy under-clothing for you, Savarra. I did not know where to seek such." His eyes were twinkling and her cheeks pinked.

"I'll manage, captain." Her smile was quick and warm, half at him and half at the new raiment.

"We will soon have to move," he said, grinning at her obvious pleasure. "Camping here on Wahee Neck, we are not too far from where Watson has bivouacked on Catfish Creek. And word is that we are to attack Fort Watson soon, for if we take that post, we will not only break the chain of British-held posts, but capture a quantity of badly needed ammunition and supplies."

Savarra grew very still. "You plan to—leave us behind?" She had not realized last August just how much Marion and his troops moved about. She had thought their moves during that three-week period were the exception. Now she realized they were the rule. These men were nomads, moving constantly, and she had little mind to be left behind.

McLean looked at her with a touch of pity which made her lift her chin at once, her eyes stormy, and he smiled again. "We've built a good brush arbor here. Caleb and Corrie could look after you—but I don't know when we'd return."

"No," she said with quiet determination, "I will not be left behind. Have I slowed you? Have I been in your way?"

"Well, there was the episode in Lynche's Creek," he laughed. Then sobering swiftly, "I meant only to make you comfortable. The spring rains are constant now and I thought to spare you the discomfort of a mule ride with Cotty hanging about your waist."

"I can manage the mule *and* Cotty—for if I fall into the hands of my countrymen, I know it means they would send me posthaste to—Peter Haverley."

McLean looked at her, his jaw hardening. "After all, you *did* marry him. And willingly. If I recall correctly, he was the source of much loving regret the night you and I shared our brief moments—together."

She flashed, "You'll never let me forget that mistake!"

"I'm not convinced it was a mistake," he said with male bluntness. "And didn't it precipitate your major quarrel with the bridegroom?" His eyes were wintry and the curved mouth was taut.

She was silent, then said thickly, "I don't want to think about that—night." But she knew she lied. She had relived it a hundred times over the months.

"You'll have to think about it one day and come to terms with in one way or another. You can't run away from it forever."

"I can try," she replied fiercely. "And I will follow Marion's brigade wherever it goes."

His lips tightened and he said, "Then I shall have to make the decision for you. You and Cotty must remain here. I had hoped you would have the wit to realize it."

Looking up into his hard face, Savarra was reminded sharply of the moonlit night she had begged him to release her, to let her return to Charles Town. Her pleas had been useless then and they were useless now.

"Damn you!" she whispered furiously. As she flung away from him, she heard his low laugh, which increased her anger tenfold.

She sat on the ground, that blue April morning, with her

back to the men as they readied themselves and moved out. Caleb was unhappy at being left behind to protect the three women and, after a word to Corrie, went off in the woods, ostentatiously to hunt game for them that night, but mainly to vent his spleen. Savarra wished she could do the same, but she eyed the two stolid mules McLean had left for their use with disfavor. She could scarcely run off her anger on a mule.

Thus the four of them—herself, her maid, Corrie and Caleb—spent the whole of April and half of May together in the thick woods, with the sinuous creatures of the wilderness for company at night and the irrepressible song of the birds chorusing about them during the long, sweet spring days. Savarra realized now why McLean had told her Charles Town was a paradise in the spring. Each day she discovered new wildflowers, and Cotty was entranced by the brilliant cardinals and bluejays in the trees about them.

Twice during those long weeks, Thad and Gabe rode in to bring them news of the brigade. With the aid of Light Horse Harry Lee they had taken Fort Watson after a few days' siege, they informed the girls and Caleb. The second time they arrived, they were in high spirits.

"We took Fort Motte, ladies!" Thad grinned, over the venison Corrie had roasted. "Mistress Motte, who was livin' in her overseer's cottage some distance from the Motte plantation—"

"Which," Gabe put in, "the British had commandeered from her—a little widder—and called Fort Motte—"

"And she give the cap'n a bow an' arrows her husband had brung back from India. He rubbed 'em with resin, set 'em afire an—" Gabe tried to cut in.

"Thunk! The cap'n landed it right on the roof o' Fort Motte!" Thad gestured widely with a well-gnawed bone in his hand.

"Mistress Motte declared if 'twere a palace it should go," Gabe inserted.

"But each time the British would scramble up to put out the fire in the shingles—thunk! the cap'n would shoot another," Thad said with satisfaction. "I didn't know he was such a handy man with a bow."

" 'Twas me an' Abraham what made bows an' arrers fer him an' Mister Tyler when they's just little tads an' taught 'em," Caleb said quietly.

They finished the meal, and as the two men were about to

leave Thad turned to them, his eyes on Cotty. "We'll soon be returnin' for you all. Ol' Rawdon's comin' out o' Camden, the last we heard. Abandonin' it—burned the jail an' half o' town —and he an' his men are after us now, since we took both Fort Watson an' Fort Motte."

Savarra could not help herself as she stood nearby. "Where is—Captain McLean? You said he was the bowman who shot the arrows—"

"Cap'n's been sent by General Marion to route out a bunch o' redcoats on the Georgetown road. I 'spect he'll be along about the time we come to git you all—no more'n two days, I promise you, Miss Savarra."

Two days! Savarra groaned silently as the men rode off. It would seem like forever, she thought—and it did, as the four members of the waiting group moved restlessly about, slept restlessly and talked very little. Even the voluble Cotty was depressingly silent.

At last Thad and Gabe came alone again, on tired horses in the early morning of the third day.

"We've come to get you, ladies. We're goin' to a new hide-out—Peyre's plantation," Gabe said, sliding from his mount to let him graze on the thick grass at the edge of the clearing.

"Get your stuff together—here, Miss Cotty, I'll help you," Thad said, going to the little maid's side.

In a few moments, they had packed up their few belongings and were on their way to join the rest of the brigade. Savarra's heart quickened and her cheeks grew pink under their golden tan. She wanted to ask about McLean, and she was grateful to Thad that he saved her that revealing moment.

"The cap'n ain't come back yet, ladies." His voice was faintly troubled and he added hastily, "But that don't mean anything's happened to him. He had over thirty men with him."

"The General's hopin' to take Rawdon's baggage wagons on our way," Gabe volunteered, "an' if we come acrost 'em, you ladies stick with Caleb. He'll keep you out o' the line of fire."

"Dear me," Cotty said in a small voice, "I didn't think there'd be fightin'—"

"You thought ol' Rawdon would just give 'em to us, didn't you, Miss Cotty?" Thad grinned at her.

They were proceeding slowly, Gabe having said that they must rest their mounts. Corrie was mounted behind her husband on one mule and Cotty, as was her custom, was leaning against Savarra on the other.

"Sit up, Cotty," Savarra said. "I'm not going to ride all the way with you drooping so."

The girl straightened and Thad said, "I'm sure sorry Rosy's too tired to take on two, Miss Cotty—Miss Savarra. But after she's rested awhile—"

"It ain't far, ladies," Gabe put in. "No more'n a mile now."

The women were uncomplaining as they rode beside the men, each one glad that her lonely vigil in the woods was over. When they came upon Marion's men they were greeted somberly, and Savarra's heart sank. Thad and Gabe urged their horses forward and vanished among the men, some of whom were on horseback, many afoot. Even so, they moved along at a brisk pace.

Soon Savarra saw they had good reason for their grim faces. As they rode through thickets and swamps, she observed with alarm that men were dropping out of the militia. As was the custom with Marion's men, they were leaving to care for their spring crops.

She was not surprised when Thad rode back with word that there were too few of them now to try to capture Rawdon's baggage wagons and Marion had wheeled about. They were now riding directly to his new hideout.

Peyre's Plantation, like Snow's Island, proved to be on higher ground surrounded by swiftly flowing streams and impenetrable marshes. It wasn't long before the men had created brush arbors and lean-tos that gave the new hideout much the appearance of the old.

It was late afternoon and Savarra, with Cotty and Corrie, had settled down under a brush arbor when a young lad she had never seen before galloped into camp. His horse, a thin, scrawny animal, was breathing heavily and there was foam about the bit in his mouth. The boy slid off his bare back, his own breath short, and he snatched off a battered old tricorne as he approached Francis Marion. Savarra, who had been assisting Corrie, dropped sweet potatoes she had just cleaned and ran quickly toward the congregating men.

"—an' they's gettin' the worst of it, gen'l, sir. Cap'n McLean's been wounded an' that British colonel's got 'em pinned down not too fur from the Sampit River on the Georgetown road." The boy's thin reedy voice faded in the hubbub that sprang up over it.

Savarra moved frantically around the tight knot of men

until she came upon Gabe Sleep and gripped his arm. "What is it? What's happening?" she asked, her heart pounding. McLean wounded!

"Go back, Mistress Savarra," Sleep said, "an' when I get all the news, I'll come tell you."

"Before you go?" she asked, eyeing his polished rifle, already clenched in big brown hands.

"Yes'm," he responded grimly.

She turned to see Cotty poised, twenty feet from her, eyes wide with fear. Corrie had not left the fire under the brush arbor, but her big dark eyes were searching among the men hopefully. The boy's voice had been so desperate! She glanced back—already men were leaving the group at a run, making for their mounts. But Gabe Sleep had shouldered his way to the middle of those left and was conversing with the general himself.

Savarra waited halfway between the melting knot of men and the brush arbor where Corrie now went resolutely about her tasks. Cotty crept up to her and asked, "Mistress, whatever has happened?"

"Hush," Savarra said sharply, straining to hear what the men were shouting to one another as they seized guns and moved to mount their horses.

"—eighty regulars an' five tory militiamen garrisoning it—"

"The general'll take it—"

"Worse'n bloody Ban, the scoundrel—"

"Mistress," Cotty ventured timidly, "please tell me—Thad's in the thick o' them men around Gen'l Marion."

"You can thank God he's here yet," Savarra said distractedly. "Cutler McLean's been wounded and I don't know if they are going to his aid or not." She stood there hoping Gabe Sleep would soon come, but he was still talking earnestly with Marion.

Cotty moved restively, "Let's go get Thad—"

"No, no! We must wait. Gabe has promised to come tell us as soon as he gets all the news."

"Then come on back," Cotty said practically, pulling at her shirt and wiping her moist face with the back of her hand. The late evening was humid and oppressive. Clouds were gathering to the east, indicating a storm approaching. Savarra fell into step with the little maid and in a few moments was seated disconsolately on a fallen log, back from the fire.

As she watched the men, they parted and the limping general led them toward the remaining horses. The others, who had already mounted, sat waiting, some saddled, some bareback.

Gabe, following, turned and looked back where Savarra had half-risen, intending to run after him. Thad was beside him and Gabe spoke to the younger man shortly, then turned back toward Marion. Savarra leapt to her feet, but before she could move Thad came at a lope to the brush arbor. Corrie set her pan of cornbread over the rack above the fire and rose to meet him. The three women and Caleb converged on him.

"McLean an' his troops are penned down by a British brigade under Colonel Peter Haverley about twenty miles from here. We aim to go get 'em out o' there."

"Peter!" Savarra gasped, swallowing hard. "He's that—near?"

McHorry gave her a keen glance. "He was sent back to aid Rawdon an' he's been raisin' hell along the south coast instead. McLean intercepted him on his way inland from Georgetown. They—he's got two captured British fusiliers, which is one reason Haverley's stickin' to 'em. Usually, he operates hit-an'-run like his counterpart, Tarleton."

"But I heard them say Captain McLean was wounded?" Savarra's voice shook.

"Yes'm," Thad responded. "Haverley spotted him in the thick o' the fight and come up on his rear, slashed him through the side o' his chest with his saber—from the back—"

She blanched. "Dear God," she breathed, "through the breast—"

"No," Thad cut in. "Through the fleshy side of his *chest*. Didn't strike a bone. The wound's a flesh wound, but so bad he's lost a lot of blood."

"Then I'm goin' with you all," Caleb said, mounting one of the mules.

Corrie let her breath out in a sigh. "Then he'll be all right."

"Good man, Caleb! Word is there's only eighty men mannin' Georgetown garrison now, an' the gen'l wants to take it after we relieve Cap'n McLean. He's sent couriers out to round up his militia at their farms. When we get enough men we'll attack."

"But you are going to the captain's aid right now, aren't you?" Savarra's blue eyes were huge and stark.

"Yes, ma'am! *Right now*. But you ladies will be safe here, for the men'll be driftin' in all night from the countryside."

As he and Caleb turned to leave, Savarra spoke one last time. "You'll bring the—captain back here?" She glanced up at the rise just back of them where Peyre's Plantation stood, a blackened hulk, victim of Banastre Tarleton's wrath.

"Yes, Mistress Savarra. It oughtn't take us long. We got night onto a hundred men an' word is that's as many as Haverley's got—an' we're a hell of a lot better marksmen than his." He and Caleb left, and Savarra half-stretched out a hand toward their departing figures, then let it fall.

Cotty burst into tears and both Savarra and Corrie looked at her somberly. "Ain't no good to cry, Miss Cotty," Corrie said calmly.

"They could both be killed," Cotty wailed, "by that terrible Lord Haverley. Oh, Gabe," she sobbed, then, "Thad!"

Savarra said morosely, "If only the militia hadn't kept dropping out—then there'd be plenty of men to face Peter." She sat down abruptly on the fallen log back from the hot fire. Her mouth felt dry and sour. "Have we any fresh water?"

Corrie turned the potatoes that were roasting in the ashes. "In that bucket yonder—what Caleb brung up from Peyre's well two hours ago."

"That'll do," Savarra replied and going to the bucket, took up the wooden dipper beside it and drank deeply. *Twenty miles,* she thought. Cutler McLean could die from loss of blood before they returned to this encampment.

All night long campfires burned brightly as the militia straggled in from the fields and forests along the Santee. Nearly a hundred had come quietly in during the night and most of them lay sleeping in their ragged quilts and blankets.

Savarra had lain sleepless through the long dark hours, listening to the growing rumble of thunder, watching the sharp flash of lightning as it knifed the rolling darkness above her. It was a bleak dawn though no rain had yet fallen. Still, the ominous growl of thunder was drawing ever nearer as the first faint gray light showed itself. Looking up at the brush arbor, Savarra could not see the sky, but she was aware that darkness was not so thick about her.

It was morning at last before the main body of Marion's men returned. She had rolled on her side and saw the riders as they emerged from the thick forest into the open space of the campsite.

Sitting bolt upright, she observed them come in on tired horses, a sadly depleted troop under Captain Cutler McLean, who reeled in the saddle and was helped down by the tall, strong black man who had ridden close to his side.

Corrie was up swiftly and half-running toward them in her deerskin clothing, which she had not removed in the night. Savarra, who had also slept fully clothed, followed more slowly, her heart beating in slow, labored thumps as she saw McLean lurch heavily against Caleb. One sleeve dangled emptily from his shirt and her heart fell sickeningly as she thought, *They have severed his arm!*

But drawing nearer, she saw that it was bandaged tightly against his side, and his shirt under the arm and across the back was stiff with dried blood. She remembered with fresh terror Peter's deadly voice. *I will kill McLean.*

Corrie reached the two men first and drew them toward the arbor. As Savarra came up in the humid gray light, McLean gave her a faint smile.

"How good a nurse are you?" 'he asked briefly.

"I don't know," she replied, trying to return his smile, but her anxiety made it a small grimace. "But I'm willing to try —Oh, Cutler—I'm so sorry."

He said bleakly, "First time I've ever been cut from the back."

"Peter probably thought it was safer to do it from the back," she said bitterly.

"It was," he replied as they reached the fire, which Corrie began stirring up, throwing on fresh limbs as she hurriedly put a pot of coffee on to boil.

"Cap'n, you better bed down. You plenty weak an' you're still bleedin'," Caleb rumbled.

Savarra's anxiety increased. "He's still losing blood?"

"Yes'm. Can't seem to get it stopped."

"I'll get it stopped," Corrie said firmly, "when I can get some hazel leaves t'make a poultice. 'At look like a mighty dirty bandage. We don't want no blood poison settin' in."

"Are you hungry?" Savarra asked McLean.

Cotty sat up quickly, rubbing her light blue eyes and looking bewilderedly at the four around the fire.

"Not very," McLean replied to Savarra, his face pale under the heavy tan. There were dark circles under the gray eyes. "But I know I must eat something—I'm so damned weak."

Caleb led him to Savarra's vacated bed, which was only a blanket thrown over the inevitable moss. His sigh as he

stretched out wrung Savarra's heart and she restrained her
desire to go to him, to cradle that dark head in her arms, to
stroke the strong cheek. He had lost the thong on his short
queue and his dark faintly curling hair tumbled about his
face, giving him a singularly young and vulnerable look as
he closed his eyes and lay very still. She could see now that
there was fresh, red blood over the old on his shirt.

"We need clean bandages to bind the wound tightly," she
said suddenly, remembering talking in England with her father
and his friends about wounds and their care.

"Yes'm," Caleb said. "We got some good cloth—make
good bandages. I seen it—it come from Fort Motte when the
men took them provisions. Corrie's mighty good at tendin'
wounds. We'll fix him up, Mistress Savarra."

Later, McLean drank a cup of the black coffee, sweetened
with sugar also captured with Fort Motte. But he seemed exhausted and lay back down immediately.

Shortly after breakfast, when Caleb had gone to secure the
bandages, with a cracking roar of thunder the rain began to
fall in a deluge. The brush arbor was poor cover, for rain
dripped through the thick brush in great drops about them
and they were soon damp. It worried Savarra that McLean
was getting wet.

Cotty, who had been unnaturally silent, said, "This rain
ain't goin' to help Cap'n McLean," and Savarra noted with
surprise that the little maid had been crying silently and
steadily.

Further, the rain prevented Corrie from going into the
woods to secure the hazel leaves to make her poultice. She
was muttering unhappily about this when Caleb returned with
thick folds of cotton material wrapped in an oiled leather
cover. Corrie said they would wait until the rain stopped to
change the bandage. By then, she could surely make her
poultice.

In the meantime, the newly returned militiamen had eaten
their hasty breakfast and ridden off with a courier to make
contact with Marion for the attack on Georgetown. The camp
was deserted but for the five beneath the brush arbor.

Cotty was comforted, for Caleb was able to tell her that
Thad and Gabe had helped send Colonel Haverley's men back
in a strategic retreat. "Them two British soldiers we took, tol'
the cap'n that Haverley had received orders to return to
Charlest'n to meet with Gen'l Rawdon," he concluded.

Savarra knew a fleeting relief with the knowledge there would soon be further miles between her and her husband.

The rain continued heavily, and Corrie decided to put a fresh bandage on McLean without her poultice. In a very short time it became red with fresh blood once more. Toward evening, McLean's face grew flushed, his eyes very bright.

Corrie shook her head and murmured to Savarra, "I'm worried, mistress. He look like that wound goin' to fester—like he's gettin' a fever."

"I know," Savarra said, anguished. "Oh, if only we had a proper shelter for him."

"If Thad and Gabe were here, they'd see we had a proper shelter," Cotty said, quietly lachrymose again.

Caleb said softly, "Ol' man Jethune's cabin ain't no more'n five mile from here. He an' his family been run out by raidin' tories an' there ain't nobody there. It's a good, solid buildin' an' it's back in the woods. We'd be safe there till the cap'n gets well."

The rain was a steady downpour, and Savarra thought with dread of a five-mile ride in it. Cotty was first to complain of the prospect. "Our clothes—the cap'n—we'll all be soaked," she said tearfully.

"We must do it," Savarra said decisively. "Cutler must be given shelter until he can recover."

They set off, Cotty and Savarra on the mule in their leather breeches and cotton shirts. Caleb was riding double to hold McLean in the saddle on his big stallion, Jed, and Corrie was astride Caleb's newly acquired roan. On the roan's rump were packed all their utensils and supplies in leather sacks. Over the saddle horn Corrie had slung two other leather bags containing their meager extra clothing and the material for bandages.

Savarra and Cotty rode beside Caleb and McLean, and it seemed to Savarra she could see fresh blood seeping into the bandages as they rode through the woods. It was a long five miles, and the cabin was in the heart of a dense forest, with little cleared land about it. It looked forlorn and dismal under the gray sky and steady rain.

But when they entered, Caleb built a roaring fire and they spread their clothing to dry before it. The two young women went into the second of the two rooms and donned the extra breeches and shirts, which Corrie had carried in her leather bags. Their moccasins were damp and they removed them to go barefoot. When they returned to the main room, Corrie had cut McLean's bloodied bandages and the remains of his shirt off him and was in the act of putting another fresh bandage on the angry, scarlet slash than ran down McLean's left side.

There were three beds in the two-room cabin with corn-shuck mattresses, all in the second room, and now Caleb and Corrie lifted the captain to his feet and helped him stumble to the first of the beds. He was very silent now and his eyes were fever-bright. Corrie muttered her determination to go into the forest, rain or no rain, and seek out her leaves and herbs to treat the wound.

Savarra, who had followed, looked down at McLean where he lay, his broad hairy chest bare and the bandages ever reddening along his left side. Now she sat down beside him as Caleb and Corrie left the cabin on their errand, while Cotty crouched miserably on a corner bed in the close room.

McLean's eyes opened a slit, glittering as he looked up at Savarra. He laughed suddenly and muttered, "Beautiful, beautiful Savarra—so proud and so stubborn."

She took his hand in hers, then laid it against her cheek. She was powerless to stem the tide of emotion that flooded her with his words, with his eyes, the color of rain now, touching her. His hand was hot to her cool face, and she put her own hand to his forehead and found it burning with fever.

"Lady Haverley," he said distinctly. "British nobility, by God—what are you doing with the rag-tag-bobtailed patriots?" She shook her head, words sticking in her throat, and he laughed again. "He's going back to Charles Town, your fine English lord—"

She shivered and murmured, "Not mine, Cutler. Never mine. I was such a fool—"

He rolled his head back and forth, and she knew the fever was mounting. "But he won't stay there," he muttered. "He'll see Rawdon safe and go back to Cornwallis. Haverley loves to kill, 'tis meat and drink to him—and I never even knew he was behind me—"

"Don't think about it now," Savarra urged. "Try to sleep. Corrie will soon fix a poultice for your wound and you will be much better in just a few days." But there was a thick lump in her throat and fear laid a heavy hand on her heart.

She went to the bowl of water on top of a cupboard and took a cloth, wringing it dry of the cool water, and laid it upon his forehead. She did this silently and repeatedly until Cotty rose and came to her.

"Let me spell you, mistress. You been at that over a hour."

"No," Savarra replied. "I will do it."

Cotty subsided, going back to a roughly constructed chair and sitting in silent misery. The rain was slackening at last and thunder trailed off in the distance. The fire in the next room made the cabin very close, and the myriad odors were all unpleasant.

In her intense concentration on McLean, Savarra was unaware of these things about her. It comforted her when she took the big, competent hands of McLean into hers and bathed them with the cool water. Her feelings were too chaotic to analyze. She knew only that she could not leave this man who had infuriated her, had kidnapped and held her prisoner, had taken her on the forest floor with sweet wild passion, and who had saved her from death in Lynche's Creek.

When at last Corrie returned with Caleb, they carried two wooden bowls filled with various leaves and herbs. Corrie went immediately to the broad fireplace which took up the whole of one wall. She hung two black pots full of leaves and water over the glowing coals.

Savarra did not know it then, but she was to remain in the cabin for nearly two months while Cutler McLean came within an inch of losing his life.

Eighteen

Her pregnancy had not gone well with Verity Bainbridge. Her feet and ankles, even her hands, were often swollen. They were swollen now in the quivering July heat, and she lay upon her bed with her feet propped up, looking at the still lawn curtains in Lord Bainbridge's bedroom, untouched by any relieving breeze from the south. In her hands she held a letter from her husband, which had arrived by a British courier only that morning.

It was tender with love and anxiety for her, full of hope

that he would be able to return to Charles Town, if only for
a short week when the baby came. "We have had some success against the rebels in Virginia," he had written. "There
is a young Frenchman, Marquis de Lafayette, who faces us
here, but we have had two skirmishes with him and beaten
him both times. Once on June twenty-sixth, when we collided
with his pickets outside Williamsburg. 'Twas then we realized
he had been following closely on our heels. It set him back
a bit, but then on July sixth we set an ambush for him and
his American counterpart, Anthony Wayne—whom the Americans call Mad Anthony. We waited until this impetuous man
led the head of the American column into our trap, then
opened fire with masked cannon. Wayne withdrew his troops
and we were able to cross the James River unmolested. I
think we taught them a costly lesson, for it is reported they
lost a hundred and forty men. Lafayette had two horses shot
from under him. But unfortunately, we had no more than
reached the south bank of the James than Cornwallis had
an urgent message from Clinton, asking for reinforcements
for his New York garrison in the face of threatening moves
by the American General Washington and his French ally,
Rochambeau. We were forced to do it, which I fear invites
disaster, for we both know our army could be penned up in
some acres of an unhealthy swamp—liable to become a prey
to the French, who have temporary superiority at sea."

He went on at some length, recounting their misadventures
on the invasion of Virginia and the fact that both he and
Charles Cornwallis were of the opinion that, if they could
conquer that province, they would cut the south in two and
there would be a cessation, they hoped, of the conflict, with
the rebels accepting their defeat.

Verity lay thinking of all these things, and the hard kernel
of fear in her breast for her beloved told her that it was not
to be so handily done. She knew from the servants' gossip
and what Bowman Baltazar had told her that South Carolina
was about to throw off the British. He had further said that
Lord Francis Rawdon was still suffering from the summer
fevers and this summer they had come back upon him with
renewed force. He was a sick man, sick of fighting in Carolina, sick in body and heart. It was rumored that he was
going to turn his command over to a Colonel Stewart and
take his foot in his hand and leave for England. Her love for
Lord Bainbridge clashed with the irrepressible joy that the

British were being slowly but methodically defeated in the Carolinas.

Her mother came into the room, bringing a pitcher of cold lemonade. "Here, my dear," she said cheerfully, "let me pour you a glass. I have never seen a hotter July." She poured the crisp beverage into a tall, crystal glass, and the sound of the splashing liquid was pleasant to Verity. She sat up slowly and took the glass from her mother's hand, drinking thirstily.

"How are you feeling now?" Anne asked anxiously, looking at her daughter's slightly swollen little hands.

"Better, since I heard from James. He is going to do everything he can to come in September after the baby is born." Then forlornly, "But he is so far away—in Virginia."

"That is not so far away," Anne said briskly. "On a good horse, he can make it in a few days."

"Calhoon said today he heard two soldiers laughing at the market place about the Virginia legislature declaring a good dragoon horse was bringing a hundred and fifty thousand. Imagine! Our Continental money is worth so little."

"Don't worry, dear. We get our allowance from the shipyards in pounds, and they are very solid." Anne took the empty glass. "Would you like another?"

"Yes," she said thirstily and took the fresh glass to drink it more slowly.

"I'm going to have Dr. Adams come by and look at your ankles and hands, Verity. There must be some remedy for this swelling and your—listlessness."

"I have never had so little energy, mother," Verity said wearily. "I feel so terribly heavy—it must be twins." Her little smile was wan.

"Bowman comes tonight with our allowance. I declare, I have missed his frequent visits, but I believe he has allayed British suspicions. Amos says he's heard no rumors about him in his trips about town and through the markets—and you know Amos. He can insinuate himself into a group of soldiers without their notice at all."

"I am worried about Savarra and Cutler—and Tyler. We have had no word from them in weeks," Verity murmured, lying back down and raising her feet to the two pillows beneath them.

"I wouldn't be surprised if Tyler didn't pay us another midnight visit soon," Anne said cheerfully. "He's like a fox, slipping in and out of Charles Town at will."

"And risking his life each time he does so," Verity said gloomily.

"Now don't be despondent, darling. It isn't good for the baby."

Verity looked at her mother with affection. Anne had been so happy since the marriage of her daughter. She and Baltazar were looking to the day when the war would end and they could be married. "It *has* to end someday," she had said the last time he visited them on shipyard business. But he had laughed and reminded them of the Hundred Years' War in Europe, which dampened their spirits considerably.

With Charles Town so filled with British now, they had few visitors, with the exception of Bonnie Raintree who came often, bringing her children with her. Verity was afraid Bonnie had little to eat in her house, for the three of them appeared quite thin. Verity knew also that she was given but a pittance from Spencer's store, now in the hands of Slayton Scurlock, who enjoyed a reputation for being a sharp man with a dollar and who also had charge of McLean's property.

So they rejoiced when the Raintrees came to dine, and the three of them ate heartily each time. Anne had offered Bonnie money as a loan, but Bonnie had seemed almost offended, replying stiffly that they would get by until the British were beaten. Bonnie never seemed to entertain the slightest doubt that the patriots might be defeated now.

Now Anne said, "Dear, why not remove your dress and lie in a loose garment?"

"Because that makes me feel I'm ill," Verity said irritably. "I like to stay dressed. After all, I'm *not* ill."

Anne's eyes concealed pity as she said, "Then let me loosen your bodice."

"No," Verity said stubbornly, "I shall come down for dinner this evening and I don't want Tiqua fussing about, hooking me up again." She looked down at the mound of her stomach, which looked very large to her from the angle at which she held her head. Two more months, she thought wearily. It seemed an eternity.

Still, the July days dragged by, steaming hot, and they heard rumors that Lord Rawdon had fifty men drop dead of sunstroke as they marched from post to post in an effort to hold the British lines of communication. They were troops that had come in from Ireland only a few weeks before—two thousand of them had landed at Charles Town. From the cool, green clime of Ireland they were ill-prepared for the searing summer of the Carolinas.

Even Amos had complained this summer, mopping his wet brow. "This here's the worstest summer I can remember in all my forty years here." Verity agreed, for she herself could remember no more enervating heat than this July of 1781.

August came at last, bringing even hotter winds, a more scorching sun. The gardens wilted under it and Anne kept the twins, Rafe and Lafe, busy hauling casks of water in an attempt to save the flowering beds of color. Even so, they drooped in the intense heat.

Then in mid-August Tyler Belion made one of his unexpected trips to visit the Pair house. He came in the dead of night and was admitted by an anxious Amos, who rapped on Verity's door, rousing her and sending her hurriedly into the loose, voluminous wrapper Madame Flammarion had made for her pregnancy.

She slipped into her night slippers, thinking this was the first time she had seen Belion since that visit months before, when he had warned her against Lord Bainbridge and offered her marriage. She was sure he had heard of her union with Lord Bainbridge. She caught up the candle she had lit on Amos's rap at the door.

In the hall she met her mother coming from her room, tying a wrapper about her slender waist. Anne's eyes were big as saucers and she whispered excitedly, "Mayhap he has news of Cutler—and Savarra and the others." Then comfortingly, "Your marriage will come as no surprise to him, since you told him months ago that you and Lord Bainbridge were in love with each other."

Verity said nothing as the two women made their way down the turning staircase, the candle fluttering with their movements. In the hallway they could see light spilling out from the small sitting room door and they hastened toward it.

When they entered, the tall, bearded Tyler rose. His clothing was astonishingly good. His Hessian boots were polished and gleaming below well-cut breeches. His stock was plain, but fresh and clean. A comparatively new tricorne was in his hand. He looked to be a well-to-do farmer on a trip to the market place.

Anne reached him first, embracing him and kissing him warmly on his hard brown cheek. "Tyler," she said with joy, "you look so fine. Those clothes "

"Were part of our booty when we captured Georgetown the end of May," he smiled, his teeth white in the black beard. "How are you both?" He held Anne's hands in his big ones, but his dark eyes were on Verity's white face.

"I'm fine," Anne said quietly, "but Verity's not been feeling too well."

Verity came to him then, lifting her face as Tyler bent his head to brush her cheek briefly with cool lips.

"You are pale," he said carefully.

"I am married to Lord Bainbridge and I am expecting his child in September," she said bluntly, aware of her mother's slight wince.

"I know," he replied, "but are you well?"

She smiled evasively. "How did you know?"

His laugh was short. "Amos told my man Abraham when he was in town from Belion House, who told Caleb McLean when he was last in town. Caleb told me the last time I was at the Jethune cabin, where Cutler, Savarra, Cotty and Corrie are."

"Tell us of them," Anne cut in swiftly. "Are they well? Do sit down, Tyler." Then to Amos who was hovering in the door, anxious to hear the news as well, "Amos, do fix a pot of coffee. We will tell you all the news when you serve us." And the slender black man vanished.

As they seated themselves, Tyler sighed tiredly. "I have ridden for over sixteen hours to get here—at night—and I must leave before dawn. I cannot risk being seen on the streets of Charles Town, you know, but I had to see you— it's been so long. Are you aware that Haverley is here?"

"Oh, yes," Anne said with contempt. "He has already paid us a call, to accuse us again of assisting Savarra to escape him. He was ungentlemanly enough to inform Verity that he would eventually repay her for having told Lord Bainbridge the truth about his treatment of Savarra. It seems Lord Bainbridge threatened him with death if he tries to force Savarra to return to him."

"And James never mentioned it in his letters," Verity said. "I knew nothing of it until Peter Haverley paid us his call in June."

"Yet he still seeks Savarra?" Belion asked.

"Very much so. For vengeance, not for love. He seems to have become a very bloodthirsty man, declaring he will kill Lord Bainbridge himself if it comes to that, removing the last obstacle to the marriage," Anne said dryly.

Belion said slowly, "Did he tell you that he struck Cutler from behind, nearly killing him in May?"

Both women gasped. Anne's hand went to her throat. "Oh. no! Where is—how is Cutler now?"

"He has spent the last two months at Jethune's cabin. Jethune was a man who was killed by tories and his family dispersed. 'Tis deep in the woods about five miles from Peyre's Plantation on the Santee. He nearly died from an infection of the wound. Had it not been for Caleb and Corrie, he would have. He is recovered now and is slowly regaining his strength. He will soon be able to ride with us again."

"And Savarra and Cotty are with them?"

"Have been, since May. Savarra has become almost as adept a nurse as Corrie. She feels she owes her life to McLean, for he saved her from drowning in Lynche's Creek in March." He laughed suddenly. "And that little maidservant, the blue-eyed Cotty of the gold curls, has Gabe Sleep and Thad McHorry almost ready to fight each other instead of the British. Every moment between battles, they ride to Jethune's to see her, but she won't leave her mistress."

"Tell us of the battles—are we winning?" Anne asked tensely.

"We took Georgetown on May 28th—securing much plunder and a great deal of salt. I brought you ladies a bag of it, knowing what short supply there is in Charles Town." He took a drawstring bag of coarse cloth from the floor beside the sofa and handed it to Anne, who thanked him profusely, then asked that he continue.

"We couldn't leave Georgetown as soon as we liked, for the garrison had made it away in a schooner and two gunboats which hung about in Winyah Bay. We were concerned they were waiting with reinforcements to retake the town." He smiled again, adding, "We were all outfitted with new clothing in Georgetown. Even General Marion fitted himself with a new suit of regimentals and acquired two mules to transport his baggage. Though he threw away his old half-burned blanket, he still wears that little charred leather hat of his."

Amos appeared with the steaming coffee and cups on a tray. After serving them, Anne said to him, "Sit down, Amos —and listen to what Lieutenant Belion has to tell us now. I will tell you what you have missed later," and Amos perched eagerly on a nearly straight-backed chair.

"Anyway," continued Belion, after sipping at his cup, "we captured many stores and much ammunition, which we have stored in magazines scattered about the country. You knew about the two thousand Irish troops Rawdon received in June?"

"Yes, Verity and I were in town the day the ships came in. We saw them arrive. They looked so young and fresh it depressed us for days."

"Don't fear from them any longer," Belion said with a smile. "They are tired and ill men. This climate is deadly to most who have not grown up with it. Those men have been dying like flies of sunstroke, and 'tis said some are about to mutiny as a result of their long, forced marches. Even Rawdon himself could take no more of it."

"We know. Calhoon brought us a vivid description of his departure for England." Verity smiled in real amusement.

"Nathanael Greene wants Marion to work with Pickens and Sumter, but they will never do it. Sumter is jealous of his seniority in command, and you may have heard of Sumter's Law—the payment of his men out of plunder, and General Marion is repelled by such practices—and Pickens is a lone and morose man."

Amos stepped up to Belion as he finished tamping in tobacco and held a lighted candle until he fired the pipe. Then he continued, "I cannot tell you on how many missions we have ridden, nor how many battles we have found since I saw you last." His eyes on Verity were suddenly pleading and full of love.

"I'm so glad that you have come through unscathed, Tyler," she said. Her big dark eyes with faint blue circles beneath them were full of genuine affection.

He said, "We hear your—husband is with Cornwallis in Virginia, maneuvering to take the state. They have laid waste to the plantations and tobacco warehouses, every prospering business that Benedict Arnold and Phillips did not destroy before him." His voice had grown bitter.

Verity looked down at her clasped hands. "I know," she whispered. "We must each do what we believe is right. James has great sympathy for us—Americans."

Tyler laughed sarcastically. "I'm sure he has. He can hardly bear to kill us—to see our country devastated."

"I won't try to defend him," she said in a barely audible voice. "I only know he told me that he *liked* you, admired your courage."

"Sporting of him, I'm sure," Tyler said coldly. "And when it's all over—win, lose or draw—you'll be sailing off with him to England, won't you?" Then with quick rage, "*If* he survives this war."

All at once fear made her legs weak as Belion asked Anne, "How do you like having a British general who is your own age for a son-in-law, Mistress Anne?"

Anne murmured, "He has been kind to us, Tyler—and Verity—loves him very much."

He got to his feet suddenly, picking up his long rifle with a touch of violence from the edge of the sofa where he had leaned it. "I must be going." Then with torment in his eyes, "I have dearly loved you both all my life. Your welfare is of utmost importance to me—still."

"Thank you, Tyler," Anne said swiftly, rising with him. Verity sat quite still, fear a black hand clutching her heart. *If he survives this war.* The words rang like a knell in her brain. He must survive this war, he *must*—or she would herself die.

Anne followed him to the doorway, saying, "We both pray for you, Tyler—each night." Verity sat where she was, feeling too heavy, too frightened to move, but her eyes followed him.

He turned and looked back at her. "I hope all goes well with you, Verity. You must take good care of yourself."

"We plan to have Dr. Adams attend her," Anne said. "She should be quite all right after the baby is born."

"I will be back, my dears," he said, standing tall and young and handsome for an instant. Then he vanished in the dark hall and they heard his footsteps die away as he went to the kitchen.

"Do you suppose he has a horse—to get out of town upon?" Verity asked dully.

"Yes, Mistress Verity," Amos spoke up for the first time. "I was bankin' the kitchen hearth when he rode up. I seen his hoss in the moonlight."

Anne then told Amos briefly of Cutler McLean and those who had cared for him, and Amos showed his relief in a broad smile. He said admiringly, "Can't nobody beat that Cap'n McLean. He's some *man*. You ladies like one more cup o' coffee?"

"No, thank you, Amos," Verity said, getting awkwardly to her feet. Her mother took her arm and the two women went into the hallway, where the candle Anne carried cast flickering light.

When they reached Verity's bedroom, Anne asked sympathetically, "Would you like me to rub your back, darling?"

Verity had suffered backaches from the time she began to grow bigger with Lord Bainbridge's child. Her back was aching now. She looked at Anne gratefully. "That always eases it, mother. You are so kind."

The two climbed into the great bed. In the still, August heat, Anne began slowly and methodically to massage her daughter's back.

Two days later, Bowman Baltazar presented himself at the door to the Pair home, and Verity admitted him. He had come with their monthly allowance from the Pair Shipyards. When Anne joined them in the drawing room, Tiqua had already served tall, chilled glasses of tea with a sprig of mint in each.

The late morning was stiflingly hot, but Bowman was tastefully outfitted in blue broadcloth breeches above his polished boots, and his stock was frilly with lace at his strong throat. He had placed his new tricorne on a table, and his brown hair, with the sprinkling of gray, shone cleanly.

Anne, who had been expecting him, wore a pale blue lutestring frock with a very low-cut bodice, but her gauze kerchief was tucked demurely about her throat and breast. Her eyes met Baltazar's and clung. Verity, despite the discomfort of her increasing bulk, knew a warm flush of pleasure and a feeling of well-being as she observed the two.

Baltazar's brown eyes twinkled as he said, "We received a letter from Lord Bainbridge yesterday, and he has arranged for us to increase your allowance by fifty pounds a month to take care of additional expenses for the baby—"

"Oh, how good of him! Did he say anything else?" Verity asked eagerly.

"Let me finish, my dear. The fifty pounds is from Lord Bainbridge himself, and he plans to increase that when his child is born. And he further said he planned to move heaven and earth to be in Charles Town in the latter part of September."

"Less than a month—" Verity murmured happily.

"But you, Bowman," Anne said, low-voiced, "I know you have been careful of *sending* messages—have you had to receive—meet with any partisans lately?"

"Yes, I have, Anne, but I did it by stealth at night, when

all of Charles Town slept." His eyes were warm upon her. "You must not worry so, my love."

"But I do worry," she said, her low voice shaking slightly. "I've lost Warren. I do not think I should survive losing you."

Verity looked at her mother with compassion. She knew the emotions that boiled in her breast only too well. They beset her own heart constantly.

They talked of what news there was in Charles Town, mentioning Tyler Belion's visit two nights ago. Then Baltazar said, "Anne, Bonnie is so outspoken now—more so than ever, and she has alienated every tory friend she had. I fear for her. She and the children look so thin."

"We've noticed that," Anne said quickly. "We feel there is little in her cupboard, and we have them to dinner as often as they will come. They eat as if starved, and Bonnie is always after them about their manners."

"I have offered to lend her money—or to write to her parents in London," he said thoughtfully, "but she is very proud."

"I know," Anne said sorrowfully. "I have met with refusals on that score as well. I feel that possibly—" She broke off as suddenly there came to their ears the sound of boots, many of them, heavy of tread on the porch.

It was followed by the sound of the door flung aside so heavily that glass shattered somewhere. Anne half-rose in alarm, for the sounds were authoritative and carried approaching disaster like a hot wind.

Amos, in the process of taking away the empty tea glasses, looked at his mistress in consternation and hastily put the tray down, hurrying to the hallway. Before he could reach it a troop of redcoats barred his way, and he fell back into the drawing room. Their leader was tall and handsome in a cruel way reminiscent of Lord Haverley. In his hand was a cocked pistol.

Anne stood erectly. She spoke with icy dignity. "What is the meaning of this, gentlemen?"

"Your guest, madame, is a traitor and a spy. He is guilty of treason to the crown," said the young lieutenant arrogantly.

"You are mistaken," Anne said coolly. "Bowman Baltazar is a loyalist and a fine one. He has done much for the crown."

There was coarse laughter among the men crowding behind the lieutenant. "You are lying, madame. We have intercepted several messages—the last being less than half an hour ago—

from Bowman Baltazar to the rebel Francis Marion. Further, he has been secretly shipping provisions to him. We will thank you to step aside while we take him in. His is a hanging offense."

Anne's face went paper-white. "You are mistaken," she reiterated bravely. "This is the home of my son-in-law, General Bainbridge of His Majesty's service, and you are insulting his guest."

"We know General Bainbridge is married to your daughter," the young lieutenant said with a touch of uneasiness, "but you are harboring a traitor. General Bainbridge would be the first to turn him over to us, were he here."

"That is a lie," Verity said, rising slowly to her feet. "Mr. Baltazar is a good friend of my husband."

The lieutenant smiled thinly. "No doubt. He was a good friend to every Englishman, waiting only to stab him in the back. Colonel Balfour has proof this man is a rebel and has issued orders for his arrest. Step aside, madame."

"I will not," Anne said resolutely. "Leave this house at once, sir!"

Suddenly the lieutenant raised his pistol threateningly and the soldiers behind him surged forward. Verity, watching in wide-eyed terror, saw Baltazar pull a pistol from under his coat, and there was a sudden crack of gunfire in the room from both the officer and Baltazar. Verity glimpsed her mother between the two men, holding out her hands to shield her betrothed.

Another pistol cracked behind the lieutenant and, under Verity's horrified eyes, her mother's pale blue lute-string bodice flowered with red as she put her hands to her chest and sank slowly to the floor.

For an instant, silence and immobility froze the tableau, the British soldiers stunned by what had happened, and Baltazar's face blanched as he stared down at his beloved.

Verity wrenched herself forward, rushing to her mother and crying wildly, "You have shot my mother! Oh, mother—mother—" and she and Baltazar knelt beside Anne's limp form.

The dark eyes were open wide, pupils dilated blackly. "I am killed," she whispered breathily, and Verity pulled her into her arms, rocking her back and forth in a frenzy of fear and grief.

"No, no, mother—no!" She strained her mother to her

breast, attempting to pull her into a sitting position, turning terrified eyes on Baltazar. "Uncle Bowman, help me—we must put her on the sofa."

By now, all the servants were crowding into the room behind the British soldiers. A high keening burst from the lips of Tiqua, followed shortly by cries from Frances and Monique. Amos and Calhoon stared in shock and disbelief, while Primrose put her apron to her face.

Verity and Baltazar together lifted Anne to the sofa. Her bright blood now stained her daughter's blue muslin-covered breast, where Verity had held her tightly. Verity whispered, "Mother—" Then frantically over her shoulder, "Amos, Calhoon! Ride for Dr. Adams at once—hurry!"

But Anne was looking up at her daughter with clouding eyes. "I'm sorry—" Her breath was shallow, so light Verity could scarcely hear the words. "I always—feared—I'd not see my grandchild. Take care—darling Verity." Then she was gone.

Tears streaming down her face, Verity turned on the soldiers. "You have killed my mother! You shall suffer for this—I shall write my husband immediately, and when he comes he'll see you hang for the murder of an innocent civilian!"

"We'll see Baltazar hang first," the lieutenant said grimly. "If your mother had not put herself in the way of Atkins' bullet, it would never have happened. It was an accident, and your husband will be told the full facts." Then with cold authority, "Stephens, Merritt—Atkins—bind that man immediately and let's get out of here."

Baltazar was seized where he stood, immobilized by the tragedy that had befallen them. His stricken eyes were fastened to Anne, lying on the sofa with the widening stain of scarlet on her left breast. He submitted to his captors in a daze.

Then for an instant he looked as though he would fight with his bare fists, for the soldiers had torn the gun from his hand as Anne had fallen.

Verity cried, "No, no, Uncle Bowman—go with them! I shall write James. He will save you." Her long wet lashes were clinging together in star points and her mouth trembled.

The lieutenant eyed her. "Don't worry, Lady Bainbridge. We shall see that your husband is sent a full report of this *accident*. Your mother was a foolhardy woman."

"Get out," Verity said in a low, violent voice. "Get out of my house!"

"Immediately," the lieutenant replied coolly. "Have you tied his hands tightly enough, Atkins? Ah, yes, a good job," he added as he turned Baltazar roughly in order to examine his hands. Already, blood was darkening in them from tightness of the cords.

The servants fell back as the little band of soldiers marched Bowman Baltazar through the door. Their heavy, booted footfalls could be heard in the silent room as they stamped through the hall, followed by a shattering slam of the front door.

Verity remained on her knees beside her mother's body on the sofa, her tears unceasing. Tiqua came to put her hands on the girl's shoulders. "Mistress, we must prepare her—lay her out. Let's send Amos to make arrangements fer a coffin."

Verity got to her feet slowly, heavily, and as she did so, she felt something deep within her rupture with a searing pain, and she bent double with a gasp.

"What is it, Mistress Verity?" Tiqua cried in alarm. "What eez the matter?"

Verity was silent, feeling the warm trickle of fluid between her thighs as pain subsided. She put a hand to her distended stomach and felt it rock-hard. "Tiqua," she said faintly, "I think my baby is coming."

"*Bon Dieu!*" cried Frances standing near. "*Mais non!* Eet eez not time, Mistress Verity—you weel lose eet. What we do, Monique?"

"I'll send fer Mistress Raintree—she's had two leetle ones. She'll know what to do," Monique replied.

Amos said fiercely, "Mistress Anne wanted Mistress Verity to have Dr. Adams. I'm goin' to send Calhoon after him right now." And he left them, pulling Calhoon with him.

Verity looked down at Anne. A strange calm had descended upon her in the midst of disaster. "But first we must do something for mother—yes, send for Bonnie, Monique. She will help us."

Monique was on one side of her, Tiqua on the other, and Frances hovered near saying, "We fix her in a minute, I promise. Now can you climb them stairs, Mistress Verity?"

Verity murmured, "Yes." Then distractedly, "I must prop my feet up. James's baby must be full term. I cannot lose it. I *cannot*," but she was aware of the two maids exchanging glances, and she looked down to see the rug beneath her feet was wet in a dark circle.

"Your water done broke, Mistress Verity," Tiqua said gently. "I'm 'fraid this baby on the way."

Climbing the stairs was more of an ordeal than Verity had anticipated, and at the first landing another pain tore at her abdomen and, under the force of it, she sank to her knees between the two maids. Her back felt like it was breaking into two pieces and a great pressure was on her stomach, pushing at her loins, agonizing in its severity. They stood silently until it passed and she was helped upright once more.

"You go turn down her bed," Tiqua told the hovering Frances. "An' start gettin' out linens—an' Primrose, you go get water boilin'," she added to the distraught cook who had followed them. Frances sped up the rest of the stairs to run into Verity's room.

The three young women walked slowly down the hall, and in a matter of moments the maids had disrobed Verity and laid her upon the bed. Tiqua bathed her face with a cool wet cloth, and she began to feel that possibly the baby would not be premature after all. Her mind turned to her mother with aching grief, realizing how much she had depended on her being near when the baby came.

"You must prepare my mother, Tiqua," she said huskily. "Bathe her and put on her best white muslin—bind up her wound so it will not soil the dress. We will bury her tomorrow." Her voice choked over the words.

Monique muttered something softly in French, then. "Do not to mind, Mistress Verity. We take care o' all that fer you. Amos know what to do. Don't you worry, miss."

"Oh, Tiqua, how can I not worry? Dear Uncle Bowman— to be hanged. Oh, I cannot bear it—" and with the words the pain struck her again, taking her breath. Her stomach under her clutching hands was constricting once more, and she bit her lip on a cry.

But Tiqua had seen it and she muttered, "Calhoon better get that doctor here quick. This baby comin' fast."

"But it's more than a month before it's due!" Verity gasped as the pain subsided. "I can't have it yet. I *can't.*"

"Mistress Verity, we all do what we has to do. I've heard tell o' babies at even seven months born healthy an' fine, an' your baby's almost eight months along. My sister back in Haiti had one at seven months, a fine healthy little mite," but there was no conviction in her voice, and Verity knew the girl was lying to ease her.

Her limbs and body felt sticky, for the pain made sweat

burst from her. There was no faint breeze from the south windows. Looking through the white lawn curtains at the brilliant white light cast by the sun made her eyes ache, and she turned her head from the windows.

Tiqua reached down and began taking pins from her hair, loosening it about the pillow, and she muttered, "That Calhoon—he better hurry."

Verity felt another pain gathering itself to bear down agonizingly upon her. She bit her lip until the salty taste of blood filled her mouth, restraining the urge to scream. Each pain had been deeper, sharper than the last. "My arms—I feel so sticky—"

"I fix that," Tiqua said, dipping her cloth and wringing it to wipe down Verity's perspiring limbs. She took up a palm-leaf fan and began to fan the girl's moist face. The cooling breeze brought a sweet relief to her and Tiqua muttered again, "That Calhoon—maybe that fat old doctor is treatin' somebody else. He better get on over here." Her voice was truculent.

There was the sound of voices in the hall and Bonnie Raintree rushed into the room. "Oh, Verity, my dear—Amos has told me all. Our dear Anne—no wonder you have been thrown into premature labor! But don't be afraid. You and the baby will both be fine. I just know it." She sounded like the old, voluble Bonnie, full of talk and all of it cheerful. "Dr. Adams should be here soon. The old bag of wind—he delivered both my children and both of them were hale and hearty. I do wish we had another doctor in town, though, someone younger and not so set in his ways."

"My mother," Verity said through stiff dry lips. "My darling mother. We must bury her tomorrow and I must be there."

"Now Verity, Frances and Monique are taking good care of her. They will see that she is laid out beautifully. And my darling, remember, she is with your dear father now. You must take comfort from that and concentrate on having this baby as easily and quickly as possible."

But it was not done easily—or quickly. Dr. Adams was at the hospital tending wounded British soldiers, and he had sent a distracted Calhoon back with word that the women could well attend Verity until he could leave the wounded men, many of whom were deathly ill of the summer fevers.

Thus the burden fell upon Bonnie and the three maidservants, but as the day wore on and Verity's pains sharpened, she sweated so profusely they changed the bed linen and her nightdress three times. Her suffering was so agonizing that Bonnie turned desperately to Tiqua.

"We must send Amos after old Marilla," and when Tiqua and Monique expostulated at the woman's reputation, Bonnie said fiercely, "Old Marilla knows more about birthing babies than Dr. Adams, and Verity must have *help*. She could die—as well as lose the baby."

Amos, with his lip stuck out in reproval, was prevailed upon to mount the carriage and fetch the woman. When they returned, Marilla was a one-woman army, commandeering the others, readying her implements, calling for stacks of fresh bed linen. She took from her basket vials of black medicine, jars of ointment and crushed leaves from which she demanded that Tiqua brew a tea. "Makes the pain easier," she said tersely. Verity's torment was such that all of them were frantic to do anything that might ease her.

Marilla and the other women hung about the bed in a state of tense anxiety and spent the long night with Verity as she labored. After three o'clock in the morning, it grew so terrible that she drifted in and out—half-nightmare, half-reality, conscious only of the exquisite pain that wracked her body unceasingly.

At last, toward dawn, when the pains were almost continuous and the bearing-down agony in her hips and stomach were unbearable, she was dimly aware of Marilla's hands upon her, of their probing and shifting within her as the pain reached a crescendo. Then suddenly the excruciating pressure was released.

There was a long moment of silence as ease slid like oil through her torn and aching body, even as she felt the warm gush of blood that came from her. She half-heard Marilla say, "Ah, a boy—a little on the skinny side, and breech at that, but that's because he's near two months early. He seems to be in fine shape—at least six pounds." And a thin wail emanated from the frail little form Verity could see through swollen and slitted eyes.

She whispered, "He'll live?"

Marilla said flatly, "He'll live. It's you I've got to fight for."

There was much flurried activity about the bed and in the room, but Verity lay very still, a vast weakness flowing through her even as her life's blood was flowing rapidly out of her. When Marilla discovered this, she flew into action as Bonnie and the maidservants took over with the baby.

"She's hemorrhaging," Marilla said, and her fingers now

about Verity's body with the ointments and packing of fresh linen in an effort to stay the gushing flow of blood. Marilla swiftly took up the two bottles of black, evil-looking medicine and poured a teaspoon of each, forcing Verity to swallow even as she gagged over both of them. Then she propped two pillows under Verity's hips, lifting her lower parts from their flat angle.

Verity was dimly conscious of Bonnie weeping. "Oh, she'll bleed to death—Marilla, save her!"

But Marilla was grimly silent, and Verity, in the euphoric state of painlessness, knew only that her condition was critical —but she no longer cared. The baby was all right. James's son was going to live and that was all that mattered. That death was at her elbow did not disturb her as she drifted into oblivion.

As time slipped by, she drifted in and out of consciousness, aware of snatches and pieces of conversation. Bonnie was weeping. She could hear her sobbing voice, "She is bleeding to death." Then a long time later, she heard Bonnie again. "Marilla," she asked desperately, "is there nothing we can do?"

"We can wait," was the calm reply. "I've given her good medicine for hemorrhaging. We got to wait for it to work. I've saved others this far gone."

Verity's head felt very light. Her whole body felt light, as if it might float out of the bed and up to the ceiling. She smiled at the thought as Marilla pulled bloodsoaked cloths from between her legs and packed her with fresh ones. If this were dying, it was very pleasant, a lightness, a freedom from pain that had lasted so interminably. She thought of the baby suddenly and pulled herself back from the blackness that was so alluring. She tried to speak, but her voice was so weak and her breath so short she could only whisper.

"Is—little James—all right?"

Bonnie bent her worried face down to hers and asked her what she had said, and she repeated her words with great effort. Then Bonnie replied strongly, "He is small and thin, but has a lusty pair of lungs—and there are little gold ringlets on his head." Then with sudden desperation, "Verity, hold on—don't let go. He needs you so!" But the blackness had swallowed her again and she was floating, floating.

It was a long time before she opened her eyes once more. This time she saw old Marilla, her expressionless, long face peering at her from the foot of the bed. She was saying to Bonnie, "Well, we've got enough of my medicines down her and I've packed her afresh—and I think the hemorrhaging is lessening. 'Tis a matter of time now—and much depends on whether we can get some food down her." She shook her head, with the gray hair pulled into the thick loop on her thin neck, and added, "I never seen anyone so near gone."

Their voices faded to a buzz in Verity's ears before she focused again on Marilla's dry voice. "I got a good girl in mind to wet-nurse the baby—God knows, Verity can't. Name's Clarissa Morse—a British soldier's easy lay, and her baby girl was stillborn. Common but good-hearted. She'll be glad of the job. Her pa's told her she's not welcome at home now. I'll send Amos after her now and you get some of that beef broth Primrose's made—" The woman's voice faded in her ears and she slept.

Then Bonnie was saying, "Open your eyes, dear. Come, Verity, look up! I've some good broth here with bits of beef in it—"

Verity would have shaken her head in a negative if she could have moved it, but she had not the strength. She was not hungry. She wanted only to sink back into that sweet darkness she had risen from, but Bonnie was going on. "Your little son is doing well—Marilla has found a fine wet nurse for him, and he eats like a little pig even if he is an early baby."

James's son. *Her* son, and he was all right. A great flood of thanksgiving filled her and she tried valiantly to sip the broth from a spoon. Much of it spilled, but the persistent Bonnie got most of it down her. She knew a faint stirring of strength, but she still could not speak. She wanted to look at her baby, but she could not form the words.

Marilla said instinctively, "Bring the baby in here and put him beside her. That will give her as much strength as the broth."

In a moment the baby, full and sleepy, was laid beside her. With great difficulty, Verity moved her head and looked down at him. He was very pink, and the flat gold ringlets on his well shaped head were beautiful. *He* was beautiful and he looked strong and healthy. How long, she wondered hazily, had she been unconscious?

She looked up at Marilla. "My mother," she whispered, fresh pain tearing at her heart. "What has been done for her?"

Bonnie came to the bed and took one of Verity's thin white hands in hers, "Darling, you have been very ill for five days. We thought so many times we had lost you. Your mother was buried four days ago." She paused and added kindly, "All your friends and even your old tory friends came. She was greatly respected."

Verity sank abruptly into the deep dreamless sleep once more. She slept for a long time, and it was evening when dim consciousness returned to her. She first became aware of muted voices about her, but they were familiar voices and their soft indistinctness was soothing. Slowly they began to separate themselves and she recognized Tiqua's liquid drawl.

"—since four this mornin', Mistress Bonnie. *Vraiment,* that eez too long. You go sleep now in Mistress Savarra's room next door. Now Mistress Marilla, she got a bed in here an' she catch catnaps."

"You're right, Tiqua, but I do want to be here when she awakens again, to tell her about Bowman Baltazar," Bonnie replied.

Verity struggled to speak, but her lids felt weighted. They would open only far enough to let her see fading light from the south windows and her breath was too light for speech. She lifted a hand feebly. *Uncle Bowman.* She heard again the soldier's harsh voice, *And that's a hanging offense, madame.* Had they hung him already? She remembered her last glimpse of him, his tortured eyes on her mother's still features, so beautiful, so youthful in that last sleep. He had looked back until one of the soldiers had shoved him brutally forward. Then, with head bowed in silent grief, he was gone.

Perhaps even now he lay in the Charles Town cemetery only a few feet from his beloved Anne.

She felt the slow burn of tears under her heavy lids and a little groan escaped her. Instantly there was a presence beside her and she heard the distinctive, husky voice of Marilla, then the cool feathery touch of her fingers as she brushed the tumbling hair back.

Her lashes lifted slowly. "Uncle Bowman?"

"She's wantin' to know about Baltazar," Marilla said matter-of-factly. The statement was followed by a light cry of hope from Bonnie and a crisp rustling of her skirts as she came to lean over Verity.

"Oh, Verity," she said joyously, "Bowman is still in the Charles Town jail, but they daren't hang him!"

Hope surged up in Verity, lending her strength. "Then James—must be here—"

"No, dear." Bonnie was slightly crestfallen. "I have written to Lord Bainbridge for you, but he's not had time to receive it. It's only been five days."

Verity gathered herself for another effort, "You—said—tell me about Uncle Bowman—"

Bonnie said rapidly, "Verity, Francis Marion and his men have captured a British colonel—Lieutenant Colonel Marchand, and they came to the very gates of Charles Town to take him. Now they have sent word that they will hang Marchand if the British hang Bowman." Bonnie's little laugh was triumphant. "Indeed, my dear, they are said to be negotiating an exchange."

Verity smiled faintly. "So—glad," and fell silent.

"We must get more of that beef broth down her now, while she's awake," Marilla said brusquely, and shortly Frances spoke in her high young voice. "*Ici*—here 'tis, Mistress Marilla."

Then Marilla was urging, "Open your mouth, miss. We must replace all that blood you lost."

Verity opened her mouth obediently and her lashes lifted. The broth was hot, and this time it tasted exquisitely delicious. Someone had lighted two candles, and they fluttered now in a blessedly cool breeze from the south. It blew across Verity's body, clad only in a light lawn nightdress. It caressed her bare legs where they extended from the gown. When she finished the broth, she sighed. A tiny bud of strength was burgeoning once more, and she gave Marilla a grateful glance.

That expressionless woman gave a wry smile. "You'd not have been near so close to death if you'd stayed that day last winter at my house—" Then with a dry laugh, "But then you'd not have had Lord Bainbridge's fine son. Skinny but very hardy."

Verity repressed a shiver and she whispered, "I'd rather have died than give up little James."

Marilla gave her an inscrutable glance. "I hope your English lord deserves such love."

"He is wonderful," Verity said breathily. She was suddenly very tired again. "How long before I regain my strength, Marilla?"

"Long time," was the flat reply. "You come within a whisker of leaving us. Now go to sleep—that'll do you more good than anything. Give your body a chance to build back itself."

Her phrase brought back the tragic memory of her mother's body in the drawing room below and the blood on her pretty blue lute-string dress. She *must* not think of that now. She must get well for James and his son.

Lord Haverley paid the Pair residence one more abrasive visit, but Verity was still too weak to receive him. Bonnie told her about it later over a cold glass of tea, spiced with mint. It was the last of August, and the light wind from the south windows was steamy with heat.

"Oh, he came stalking through the front door when Amos admitted him—you know we keep it locked since it was fixed after your mother—well, he wore that icy authority of his, for all the world as if he owned all of us, lock, stock and barrel. Handsome to be sure, but those funny yellow eyes of his look *so mean*. When he saw me standing in the salon door —you know Amos won't talk to him and he just walked off— well, Haverley strode up to me like a big cat—" and Bonnie launched into the scene with all the verve of an accomplished actress.

"Madame Raintree, I will speak with Lady Bainbridge, if you please."

"You can't," Bonnie had said firmly. "Lady Bainbridge is still ill."

"She will see me."

"She will not see you. She sees no one but her nurses—"

"Nurses, pah! You mean those three black wenches and that old charlatan, Marilla? Yes, madame, I heard in town that old witch delivered Lord Bainbridge's son. He will be furious when he hears *that*—and I shall see that he hears of it, for I am leaving within the hour for Virginia and Cornwallis."

Bonnie had laughed tauntingly. "You think he will believe you—after the way you lied to him about his daughter and her reasons for leaving you?"

Haverley flushed dull red. "What do you know of that?" His voice was dangerous and low.

"Enough," Bonnie replied, unabashed.

"Lady Bainbridge has a loose tongue. 'Twas she who filled Lord Bainbridge full of lies about my conduct with his daughter."

"Lies?" Bonnie's little laugh was shrill. "She got it straight from Savarra, who showed her unspeakable bruises."

For a moment he was speechless with rage, his face nearly the color of his beautifully fitted coat. Then suddenly his face paled. "Then I have been right all along, and you too, madame, must know the whereabouts of my wife."

"I do not," Bonnie replied, dimly alarmed.

"Ah, but you do," he said smoothly, taking a step toward her. She fell back.

"If you touch me, I shall scream for Calhoon and Amos."

Amos said from the doorway, "You called me, ma'am?"

Haverley whirled and said, "She did not. Leave us alone."

"On the contrary," Bonnie replied bravely, "you may serve Colonel Haverley some Madeira, Amos."

"I haven't time for that, madame."

"You will bring it at once, Amos."

"It's right here, mistress," Amos replied, courageously entering the drawing room and going to the decanter which was surrounded by thin-stemmed glasses.

"Get out of here," Haverley said viciously.

Amos gave him a baleful glance and calmly poured a glass of wine. "Your wine, sir," he said, extending the glass to Haverley, who ignored it as he turned again to Bonnie.

"I interviewed that old hypocrite Baltazar yesterday evening in the jail. He spent most of the time cursing our men for accidentally killing Madame Pair, and then he boasted I had not quite succeeded in killing McLean—"

"By a sneak attack from the back!" Bonnie flashed.

He smiled coldly. "How else would you kill a mad dog? Be assured I shall finish the job eventually. I plan to scour the countryside on my way back to Virginia." He gave her a heavy-lidded look of pure venom. "For I have the curious feeling that my wife and McLean will be found together."

"Never in the way you think!" Bonnie interrupted furiously. "You filthy-minded scum."

His pale eyes glittered. "Ah. Then they *are* together. *That's* what I came to find out."

Bonnie put her hand to her wayward mouth. "I did not say that!"

He laughed mockingly. "But I am satisfied she is with McLean—and I shall smell them out. I have one of your former partisans who was wise enough to return his services to the crown in my troop now. He knows their hideouts. The swamp fox, they call that fool who leads them," he said, laughing contemptuously. "They are half-trained savages, stupid and sly. We shall wipe them out." He ignored Amos, still holding the Madeira, and he made her a graceful bow. Still smiling, he strode out of the house.

Now Bonnie turned her ingenuous blue eyes on Verity.

"And Verity—when he heard the door slam, Amos pulled from under his waistcoat the most horrific knife I ever saw. A foot long and honed sharp enough to shave his face of every whisker. His eyes were so black and shiny and he said, 'He ain't know how clost he come to gettin' his heart cut out.' I just gulped a couple of times and came right up here to tell you all about it." She sighed and took a big swallow of tea.

Verity's face was very pale and her dark eyes enormous. Her heart beat heavily with dread. "I fear for all of them— James, Tyler, Cutler and Savarra—as long as Peter Haverley is loose on our land."

"I, too," Bonnie said, her round face hardening. "The man has changed since we saw him last, Verity. He has become— he appears to be—"

"He is what he accuses us of being—savage."

"That is it," Bonnie burst out, "without any restraints any longer—without mercy or decency. He is truly evil."

There was a soft rap on the door, and the two women looked up to see Tiqua standing there, her even, beige features wreathed in a smile. She came into the room, bringing with her the fragrance of fresh starched linen and the hot, sunny out-of-doors. Clarissa, holding the baby, was behind her, and her blunt features were pleased as well. Clarissa was about eighteen and her cheeks were always red, her disposition good. Her full bosom was putting weight on little James.

"Guess what?" Tiqua said, like a mischievous child, glowing with her secret. Clarissa evidently shared it for her smile was broad, revealing good but slightly crooked teeth.

"What?" Bonnie and Verity chorused.

"Calhoon just come in an' he say Mister Baltazar been exchanged for that ol' British colonel name Marchand—just outside Charlest'n. Calhoon say them soldiers down to the market been talkin' 'bout it. They say our men just melt inter the woods with Mister Baltazar this mornin'."

Verity and Bonnie let their breath out in unison, and Verity asked, "Did they say who—which of our men came to bring Marchand and take Uncle Bowman?"

"No'm, only they was more'n a dozen, and Calhoon say the soldiers say, 'Gawd knows how many more was lurkin' in 'mongst the trees.'" She laughed delightedly. "Calhoon say they got a mighty respect for the aim o' our men and their rifles. One redcoat say, 'Them guns o' these rebels ain't like our Brown Bess. They don't miss nothin' that moves.'"

There was a moment of silence and Clarissa said timidly, "I thought you might like to see little James fer a while, ma'am."

"Yes, Clarissa, do bring him to me!" And she held out her arms for the handsome infant.

Tiqua said, "Primrose an' Marilla down in the kitchen an' they fixin' you roas' beef an' rice an' gravy. You hungry?"

"Yes, I am," she replied, cradling her small son in her arms.

At the door, Tiqua turned back. "On his way back from market, Calhoon see that ol' devil Haverley ridin' out with his fusiliers on his way ter join Gen'l Cornwallis. Calhoon say he was clost enough to spit on him an' he look mean an' ugly enough to break daylight with his fist—them yellow eyes an' that ol' iron helmet an' stiff brush a-stickin' up like a cattail." Then, "I bring your dinner in 'bout half hour." And she and Clarissa stepped into the hall.

Verity's eyes went to Bonnie, and fresh dread spread through her at the thought of Haverley with murder in his heart as he sought the partisans. She put her cheek down on the baby's soft curls and wished desperately that Lord Bainbridge would soon arrive.

Nineteen

August was drawing to a blistering close and Savarra, sitting on the edge of the Jethune cabin's narrow porch with a disconsolate Gabe Sleep beside her, looked down the narrow trail leading into the forest beyond which lay the Black River.

Down that trail the fickle Cotty was riding with Thad McHorry, which accounted for Gabe's lugubrious countenance. And earlier this evening, McLean and Caleb had ridden down it to hunt game, a leaner, paler McLean, but a man growing stronger every day.

"And Bowman Baltazar told you Peter left Charles Town the same day he was exchanged?" she asked morosely.

"That's right," drawled Tulie, stretching his long deerskin-clad legs out straight. He wore moccasins like Savarra's, but his shirt was of some coarse light hand-woven material. She was wearing a pair of the leather breeches she had been given and one of her two cotton shirts, miserably worse from the wear and many launderings.

"He could be anywhere in the woods around us," Savarra remarked uneasily.

"We got a lot o' scouts out, Mistress Savarra. Ain't likely he'll get far without us knowin' where he's at."

"He is a man with little or no principle," she said shortly, "and no mercy at all." She put her finger surreptitiously to the little scar at the base of her neck.

"Reckon you don't need to worry, ma'am. Cap'n McLean's going' to be ridin' with us termorrer. With him an' Baltazar an' Belion, it's goin' to be like old times. Lots o' the militia has come back to Gen'l Marion, too. If we run into ol' Haverley, I 'spect he'll turn tail an' run."

She laughed shortly, "Whatever he is, Peter is not a coward—"

"A man'll run to save his skin, Miss Savarra. Make no mistake. Even though he may call it a strategic retreat." And silence fell about them once more, enhancing the sound of the cicadas in the tall trees, the flutter of wings as birds flew from one limb to another and their cheerful little cries. A mockingbird at some distance was trilling a melody with the soft, tender background of a mourning dove calling from the depths of the woods. The slow hot breeze carried the scent of wild honeysuckle and a pungent tang of wild mint.

Savarra let her mind drift back over the past weeks when McLean, with his infected wound, had rolled and tossed in a delirium. She thought of the long hours she, Cotty and Corrie kept vigil over him. He had muttered of battles, refought them in his fevered illness, and he had called her name—always with mockery, with a defensive cynicism and a kind of anger. Twice she had despaired of his life, and they had been the darkest moments she had ever known.

But Corrie, with dogged perseverance and her miraculous medicines and poultices, had pulled him through. When Savarra sat beside his bed on long hot nights, with a burning sycamore ball in a dish of fat for light, she had looked at the strong face, the straight and prominent nose, the uncompromising and clean-cut lips, the tumbled sweat-damp hair, and contradictory emotions had swept her, defying analysis. She owed him so much.

When he had come out of his delirium and weakly taken food, he had been scrupulously polite and grateful to her for aiding Corrie in his care. But there was an insurmountable barrier between them and she could find no words to breach it. She was vaguely aware that much of it stemmed from the fact that she was married to the man who had sworn to kill McLean. Now she struggled against a fatal sense of approaching tragedy. It was as if a miasma hung over her and, no matter where she turned, it shrouded her thoughts, colored her outlook. And through it all was a hunger for McLean, an inner burning she had never known before. And, as always, she yearned to touch him. She had to fight against it constantly.

Now Gabe beside her gave a mournful sigh. "I reckon Mistress Cotty ain't never comin' back. Yet I swear she looks at me like she loves me. You reckon she loves us both, Mistress Savarra?"

Savarra smiled, "I think it's possible, Gabe. I know she speaks very highly of you."

He brightened, then lapsed again into discouragement. "But she wanted to go off with Thad alone—I offered to go with 'em, but that Thad," there was affection and exasperation in his voice, "he made it plain enough I wasn't welcome."

"She'll ride with you alone tomorrow, I'll wager."

"She won't have the chance. You know we're all leavin' tomorrow mornin' to join the gen'l an' the militia."

"That's right. I better go pack my few things. I hate the prospect of riding that mule with Cotty hanging about my waist."

"Horses are very scarce now, Mistress Savarra—but Thad and I captured three extrys on a raid 'mongst the tories down the Sampit River the other day. I'll see if I can't get the gen'l to give you one." He laughed lightly. "An' then Miss Cotty can ride the mule by herself. Do her good."

They rose together and entered the cabin, with Gabe saying appreciatively, "Lord, Corrie, that smells good!"

Corrie, tending the food over the fireplace, replied, " 'Tis good—roast rabbit an' fresh greens I gathered this mornin'—with hoecake an' honey."

Savarra stepped into the small room they had all shared together these weeks past and began gathering together her meager belongings and packing them into a leather bag, leaving out the breeches and shirt she would wear tomorrow.

But her mind now was on Verity, her mother cruelly shot to death, her own narrow escape from death at the birth of the baby. Gabe and Thad had brought all this news only this morning, along with word of Baltazar's escape and his presence now among Francis Marion's men.

With a renewal of wonderment, Savarra thought, *I have a little brother,* and with the thought came an unbearable longing to see him, for Baltazar had said he was told the baby was a replica of Lord Bainbridge, with gold curls and eyes of brilliant blue. A warm suffusion of love for this unseen half brother filled her now that she knew of his existence. It had been a shock and surprise when she had learned of her father's marriage some time ago, but from the perspective of the last months it had come to Savarra that she bore a deep affection for Verity.

She had been afraid to return to Charles Town because of Haverley's restless travels—and those fears had been justified by various couriers who came in with news of his forays. If she had been in Charles Town, he could have taken her by force many times in the past few weeks. Even now, there was no way of knowing how often he and his troops would return there. No, she could not risk going to Verity.

She finished packing before the others returned, Thad and Cotty first, faces pink from the August heat and eyes starry. Thad looked at Gabe mischievously as they entered the cabin, and Savarra found herself smiling.

He slapped Gabe on his cotton-shirted shoulder and said, "Well, Gabe, congratulate me. Cotty's goin' to marry me when we can find a preacher!"

Cotty's face grew scarlet, and she sputtered, "Thad McHorry, what a lie! Gabe, I said no such thing either—" Her small fists beat a tattoo on Thad's broad chest, and he collapsed with laughter.

"Always ready with a joke." Gabe's smile was dour. "Too bad he ain't as handy with that rifle."

"Better'n you'd like me to be—with the rifle *and* with Cotty," Thad said with imperturbable good humor.

"He's conceited too, Miss Cotty, as you can plainly see." Gabe was grinning now.

"I know it." Cotty's chin lifted so her fair, tumbled hair swung across her shoulders.

The sound of male voices floated into the too warm cabin, which was rich with the smells of savory food cooking. Caleb and McLean, Savarra thought, her heart beating swiftly as her eyes flew to the open door where the late evening sun slanted through the opening. McLean strode in, followed by the equally tall Caleb, and dropped a brace of squirrels on the hearth.

He grinned at Corrie. "We'll have those for breakfast before we leave to join General Marion, Corrie."

"I'll clean 'em after supper, honey," Caleb told his wife.

"Sure are nice fat ones," Corrie remarked, lifting the plump little animals. "Looks like they mought be two pounds apiece."

"Them's ever' one shot by the cap'n." Caleb took off his battered tricorne and wiped his forehead on his sleeve. "He ain't lost his tetch with that rifle o' his."

McLean laughed ruefully. "And I can lift it now without shaking like a wet dog. High time."

Gabe looked at him thoughtfully as they pulled the three chairs around the small rough table. "Reckon the gen'l will be plumb surprised to see you termorrow," he said, "fer you been a mighty sick man."

"He been up an' about fer two weeks now," Corrie said almost truculently. "He got back his strength. He's a young man an' he's tough." She began serving portions of the tender greens and rabbit. Savarra bent to serve hoecakes, picking them out of the pan and laying two each on the rough wooden plates Caleb had made weeks ago. The three women sat in the chairs at the table and the men squatted cross-legged to eat from their plates on the floor.

When they had finished, Cotty gathered up the utensils and took them down to the creek to wash. She took with her a bar of the crude soap Corrie had made from ashes and animal fats, and she was followed in the dim twilight by both Gabe and Thad, quarrelling good-humoredly with each other as they carried part of her burdens.

Caleb lit a corncob pipe and sprawled tiredly on one of the chairs, while Corrie seated herself in the one beside him, and they began a low-voiced conversation. Savarra went out the door into the cool hush of evening. She took the rough steps down and walked out where a faint, rising wind could ruffle her long, heavy hair, which was tied back from her face with the inevitable thong. Dear lord, she thought for the hundredth time, to see satin ribbons and lace again!

She looked back and saw that one of the cabin's occupants had lit a candle, and in the square of the door the tall, broad-shouldered figure of the captain leaned negligently against the framing. Was he going to follow her? Her pulse quickened. She went only to the edge of the clearing, where the cooling wind was strongest, and seated herself on a tangle of fallen limbs, a favorite spot with her. The wind was too strong for mosquitoes to light upon her, for which she was grateful. They had not been too bad this last week because of the heat and dry weather. Too, Corrie had an evil-smelling concoction brewed up of what looked to be weeds, seasoned with deer-fat, which could be rubbed on exposed portions. All insects gave those so anointed a wide berth. Cotty had remarked of it, "No wonder skeeters won't come nigh—even people wouldn't come nigh, 'tis so dretful a smell."

She glanced again at the cabin and saw the man in the doorway step out into darkness. He was coming out! She looked up at the deepening blue of the sky, where three or four pale stars gave forth tentative twinkles. Over the eastern trees a lush, smoky moon was lifting with majestic deliberation, seeming twice as large as normal.

McLean came straight to her and seated himself on the bare tangle of limbs. From somewhere deep in the woods came a dove's threnody, sweetly mournful, evocative of all that was tender and lost.

He was smoking one of the rough pipes Caleb had fashioned from corncobs. "Would you like to go back to Charles Town now?"

"I would love to go back to Charles Town to help Verity, who is so weak and ailing—to look after my little brother. But I dare not, as long as Peter Haverley comes and goes as he will."

"Are you so afraid of him?"

"Of course I am! The man is a monster. I would rather be dead than to fall into his hands again." Her voice shook. "Bowman Baltazar told Gabe that Peter had vowed to him no less than a month ago to scour the countryside on his way back to Virginia, looking for me—for you—for Marion's men, to kill you all."

McLean drawled, "Well, with him looking for us—and us looking for him, we're bound to meet and settle your problem. I do not plan to be caught from behind again." There was a chilling conviction in his voice, and Savarra felt goose flesh rise along the backs of her bare arms, yet her heart sank and a thrill of fear coursed through her.

She murmured, "Then again, he may turn back to Charles Town—or wait until he *can* take you unawares. Oh, if only some of the rebels could come upon him and his men and kill each of them!"

He laughed softly. "You sound positively deadly—a wife eager to become a widow."

The moonlight, turning faintly silver now, crept across the little meadow to touch them with gentle fingers. Savarra averted her flushed face though she knew he could not see the color. Her words were muffled, "I tell you I am no wife to him—"

"You are *married* to him."

"I know, I know!" There was desperation in her voice now, a touch of panic as well. If only McLean would reach out, gather her into his arms where she could lose her fears in his nearness. He did not smell of Corrie's abrasive soap, but of the woods, tobacco smoke and fresh, growing things.

"I had thought of sending you back to Verity, with Gabe and Thad as escort for you and Cotty." He spoke dispassionately.

"I cannot go back," she answered. "You do not know my husb—Peter's ways. He will get word of my presence there and I might not—escape a second time."

"Then we won't take the chance," he said reassuringly. "You will stay with us until we know his whereabouts." His voice was deep and comforting.

Yet she found anger rising as silence drew out between them, and she realized abruptly that it was because he did *not* take her into his arms. Oh, she *was* a fool. This man, this rebel *American*, meant nothing to her. Just because he spoke like an Englishman—was born of English parents—did not make him an Englishman. And she belonged to England, even as Lord Bainbridge belonged to England, for all that both of them could sympathize with these people of their blood and bone. Oh, if only she had not yielded to him! He had branded her—

"What is it?" he asked, sensing her stiffening, her rage at herself.

Before she thought, she replied, "I was remembering—" Then she broke off, her face on fire, for she was filled with that moment a year ago—a whole year ago, when he had held her in his arms, had put his mouth to hers, had pinned her to the forest floor after her wild struggle against him, against herself. And the instant of sweet yielding—

"Remembering?" he asked alertly, as if he knew the swift currents of recalled passion that were flooding her now.

"Remembering—how much Verity needs me," she replied, her throat dry.

"You were not," he said flatly.

"Then what, pray, was I remembering?" she asked furiously.

He put down his pipe and faced her in the moonlight. She could see his eyes glinting under their thick stiff lashes.

"This," he said, and before she could move he caught her to him, pulled her upright and pressed her body to his as he brought his lips down upon hers. The feel of them and his hardening loins was shockingly sweet.

For a fleeting instant she clung to him, but in that instant pride slashed at her. She had been begging him for this with every move of her slender young body, with every vibrant nerve within her, and what had he said a year ago? *But I must confess, if this opportunity presents itself again, I shall take full and pleasurable advantage of it*, and she had handed the opportunity to him with beseeching hands.

Burning with shame she pulled from his arms and her hand flew away and up to slap his face with stunning force. His cheek was hard and smooth under it and her palm stung as they faced each other, moonlight a veil of living light about them. He did not move or speak.

Turning, she fled blindly back to the wavering light in the old Jethune cabin. At the door she paused, breathing hard, trying to put a semblance of calm upon her. But her heart was racing and her lips were moist and trembling with frustrated desire.

In the dark dawn of September first, Savarra was glad that she was not alone with McLean while they readied themselves for the long ride to Marion's camp. Gabe generously offered to let Cotty ride behind him. "So's you won't be crowded, Mistress Savarra," he said gallantly.

Thad grumbled so loudly that Cotty said, "I'll ride behind you tomorrow, Thad," in a melting voice.

Savarra, clad in leather breeches and cotton shirt, looked at her somewhat dourly. A little more attention from those two, she thought, and Cotty will become well-nigh insufferable. Still, she was glad she did not have the complaints in her ear and Cotty's tendency to lean on her during the ride.

They strung out single file through the thick forests toward the west. Gabe and Thad had told McLean that Marion received word from Nathanael Greene some time ago that he was to support him in a possible attack on the man who had taken the ailing and fevered Rawdon's place, Lieutenant Colonel Alexander Stewart. Greene was seeking to close with Stewart, for he felt he had a good chance to defeat him, which would wipe out a major British force in South Carolina. For two days McLean, leading his little band, sought Marion's elusive forces.

When they reached the camp site where Gabe and Thad had left them a scant four days before, it was deserted. All traces of fires and signs of men had been wiped clean by the careful partisans.

Gabe said philosophically, "Well, cap'n, they've moved again. But we're bound to run inter a scout soon. We'll just keep movin' west because that's where Stewart's army lies—somewheres around Eutaw Springs. Leastways, that's the direction our scouts said he's headed."

So they continued to ride, Savarra looking like a slim boy with an old tricorne on her braided hair. She was, by now, quite inured to the lazy mule's plodding gait and the fact that he kept falling behind the others despite her moccasined feet often beating a tattoo on his sleek, well-fed flanks. She was glad to bring up the rear, for she did not want to face McLean. He had paid her no attention since they began their journey. Indeed, he had been curt with her, short in his advice as to where they were headed and how long it might take them to connect with Marion.

It was near dusk when it happened. The others were strung out far ahead of her, and then suddenly they were lost to sight as they curved off into the heavy trees. Tiredly she urged the mule forward, but he kept up his stolid gait.

All at once from the thick trees beside her there erupted three men, their coats scarlet in the twilight, their helmets glinting.

One of them, pressing his thigh tightly against hers, growled, "If you yell, I'll knock you senseless, boy."

Her mouth flew open in horror, for she recognized these outriders as fusiliers from their insignia. One of them seized the mule's reins from her hand, nearly pulling her from his bare back. She started to slide off the animal, with the intention of running into the forbidding woods to lose herself. Her heart was beating wildly, but the threatening faces about her cut off her screams before they began.

As she started to slip from the mule, one of the men cried,

"Look out! He's going to run for it!" and another one rode up beside her and plucked her off as if she were a child.

She kicked and fought in silent, frenzied terror, and the man holding her struck her on the side of her head, knocking the tricorne to the ground, loosening her braids.

"Blimey!" he said low. "It's a female! By God, we've caught a rebel female!"

One of the others said, "Let's get out of here before they miss her up ahead—quick, now!" and dragging the mule after them by the bridle, they rode into the darkening woods. They headed south and Savarra winced at the cruel grip about her middle.

She spoke through her teeth, "I am Lord Bainbridge's daughter. Take your hands off me!"

The second man laughed coarsely. "And I'm George the Third," he mocked. His accent was American. A tory, she thought contemptuously, an American turncoat. She had come to loathe those people who professed loyalty to the crown. It was all to save their own skins.

"There will be a fortune in gold if you will take me to my father in Virginia," she said, grasping at straws.

"Well now. She does know Lord Bainbridge is in Virginia. But that's a long way, mistress," he said judiciously, as if considering her offer.

"She does speak like an English noblewoman, Campbell. The accent is British—not American."

"Pah! Anyone can mimic an English voice. Sit still, you little rebel bitch!" He jerked her roughly, twisting an arm behind her to force her to cease her struggles. It was painful but she did not cry out. By now they were too far away for the others to hear even if she screamed like a banshee. She said no more.

She rode silently before the man on his big bay, listening to their banter. They had been sent out on a scouting mission and had been trailing McLean's party for some time. Apparently they thought she could be induced to give them information as to the whereabouts of Francis Marion and his men when they reached camp.

When they reached camp! A sickening terror crept through her at the thought. She did not have the heart to ask the name of their commander, but some sixth sense told her who it was. Her greatest fear had come upon her: she was on her way to the camp of Lord Haverley's fusiliers.

They rode for a long time and it was fully dark by the

time they approached an open space with a few tents thrown up about campfires. The moonlight was brilliant, and by its light she saw baggage wagons and mules for carrying extra supplies. There were two field pieces on the perimeter of the camp.

"Go tell the colonel we've captured a rebel wench," Campbell said to the man called Norris, and he trotted to the larger tent in the center of the encampment.

Campbell slid from the bay and reached up to pull her roughly from the animal's back. She was aching from sitting stiffly for so long a time, repelled by the touch of the man's body against her back. In firelight and under the brilliant moon his face looked fat, with a strangely bulbous nose and little close-set eyes. He pulled off his helmet, tucking it under an arm, and ran a hand through his bristly hair, but he kept one hand clamped about her arm.

They waited a long time before Lord Haverley strolled out of his tent, immaculate in a white shirt and white doeskin breeches, his thick dark hair in a becoming queue. It was fully dark now, but the blazing fires and the moonlight enabled her to see him clearly. He had not recognized her yet.

"Ah, Campbell, I see you brought back a prisoner from your mission. Did you locate Marion's men?"

"No sir. But we came across a party of seven strung out in the woods. The four men at the head were heavily armed, so we did not risk a skirmish. We followed and were able to capture this prisoner when she fell behind, and the wench can likely tell you of Marion if we apply the proper pressures." He shoved Savarra toward the man.

Her hair by now had come loose and hung half-braided, half-flowing freely to her waist, black as a crow's wing with the light of the fires redly upon it.

Suddenly Haverley's narrow head struck forward, his jaw clenching, and he reached a hand to her face, catching her chin and tilting it upward. For a long instant their eyes locked.

"God's blood!" He spoke with deep feeling. " 'Tis you, Savarra!"

"Yes, and you would do well to send me to my father immediately." She held her voice steady, her eyes unwaveringly on his pale amber ones. "I understand he means to kill you if you abuse me further."

"Abuse you?" he said softly. "Abuse my darling wife? Nay, I am overjoyed to be reunited with you."

"Your wife!" ejaculated Campbell. "Then she wasn't lying! She *is* Lord Bainbridge's daughter—"

"Of course she is," Haverley's voice was smooth. "We must make her welcome in camp. Come, darling, our tent is that large one yonder. I'm sure you would like to freshen up."

"I am not your wife," Savarra jerked out of his hand.

"But you are. Campbell was one of those who attended our wedding, weren't you, Campbell?"

"Yes, sir," Campbell said fervently, "and a beautiful wedding it was, too, sir."

"What terrible clothes you are wearing, my dear, but, as a captive of the rebels, I suppose *any* clothes are better than none. We will secure you some dresses from the homes we will take on our way to join Colonel Alexander Stewart's forces." He laughed lightly. "We are to join him at Eutaw Springs shortly—it seems I am to help Stewart before I go to Yorktown in Virginia, that is, if I don't find Marion and his men in the meantime. You *do* know where they are, don't you, darling?"

She shrugged, "How should I know where they are?"

"Ah, too bad. But I shall find them. Come, Savarra, I have water—soap—all the amenities in my tent." As he took her arm, he whispered intimately, "You will want to be fresh and lovely for our first time together since our wedding night."

Then in a hard voice as they entered the tent, "You shall not escape me again, my sweet." His lips thinned in the lamplight and his yellow eyes narrowed on her with malevolence and desire mingling in them. She stood stiffly, unmoving. He said with a malicious laugh, "You know, Savarra, I have had over a hundred virgins in England—noblewomen as well as tavern wenches—but I must confess I got more pleasure out of you—knowing you were already despoiled by McLean—than any of them. I look forward to a repetition tonight."

In the pale glow of the oil lamp Savarra's wide cornflower eyes searched frantically for a weapon, anything to lay hand to, and he observed her with feline pleasure.

" 'Twill do you no good, Lady Haverley, to seek a weapon or to scream your pretty head off. It would only attest to my virility, and my men will admire my prowess. 'Twill afford them a titillating diversion from army life to imagine what is going on in this tent tonight."

He went to a narrow wooden box serving as a commode table at the side of the tent and poured water from a pitcher into a bowl on top. "Now bathe yourself well, my dear. My tastes are fastidious, as you well know, and you look like a rebel street urchin. I must go congratulate my men—break out a case of brandy—for the recapture of my bride." Then laughing, "No need to worry about a nightdress. I'll take you bare."

He opened the tent flap and went out into the moonlit night. Savarra began frantically searching the close confines for something with which to fight the man off. There was nothing but his saber, but it was so awkward and heavy in her hand she knew she could not lift it for a blow before he would be on her.

She did not bathe nor did she touch her disheveled hair as she sat down upon the narrow bed that was Peter Haverley's. Her legs trembled and weakness shook her.

It came to her that her struggles against him were what afforded Peter such pleasure. He reveled in hurting her, in seeing her suffer. It had increased the intensity of his passion on their wedding night. Yet she could not bring herself to lie supine while he had his way with her, even though she knew it would decrease that pleasure. Pure panic struck her, and it was all she could do to keep from running from the tent, screaming hysterically.

In less than a quarter of an hour, Peter returned. His face darkened with anger. "Still unready? It has just occurred to me that you probably have been living with McLean—are you pregnant?"

"No one has touched me since your bestial attack!" Her voice was high and terrified.

"Ah, good. Then I shall surely impregnate you, and that will cut down on your flights about the country. You are, after all, of noble blood and we must have an heir—or heirs, no matter the stormy relationship between us."

Her eyes were filled with loathing. "I will carry no child of yours!"

"Ah, but you will, my dear, and often. Cornwallis with my help will decisively beat the Americans in Virginia—cut the colonies in two—and we can all go home triumphantly to England, where you shall reign over the Haverley estates." His eyes glittered light and colorless. "And I shall enjoy our battles in bed. Indeed, I relish the prospect extremely.

Now will you unclothe yourself, or shall I resort to the methods I used on our first night together?"

Slowly she backed away from him. He followed inexorably, drawing nearer and nearer. Suddenly, she ducked her head and darted past his reaching arms, parted the tent flap and was outside and running hard. But Peter Haverley was a big man, a lithe man, and he was on her in an instant, his hands deliberately hurtful as he forced her back into the tent.

"Fight me," he said mockingly. "I like it when you fight. You are quite a fighter, little Savarra."

And she fought him, pitting her lesser strength against his greater. He was not even breathing hard when he caught the throat of her woven shirt and ripped it from her body. "Ah," he breathed, "you have the most delicious breasts, my dear Savarra—a pity to bruise them," and he jerked her forward, putting his face down against them, his breath hot against her skin.

Her breath came in sobs now as she pulled at his hair, shrinking and drawing away with all her strength. But he put a booted foot behind her, pushing her off balance, and she fell heavily on the bed at the side of the tent.

As he came down upon her, there sounded a wild cry in the night, followed by the clash of arms and the rattle of musket fire. The camp beyond the tent was in a totally unexpected uproar. Shouts of men mingled with gunfire and Peter Haverley raised himself from Savarra, seized his saber and strapped it about his waist. Picking up his Brown Bess he ran to the tent flap and disappeared into the night.

Savarra got slowly to her feet, sharp relief bringing tears to her eyes. She pulled the torn shirt over her breasts and pushed the tent flap open to look out upon a boiling mass of men engaged in fierce hand-to-hand combat. She saw Peter dash into the thick of it, whirling his saber about his head with deadly expertise.

The tattered and patched clothing of the attackers identified them immediately. Partisans from the swamps. Marion's men? Her heart leaped with hope. There appeared to be hundreds of them, more than Haverley's brigade of fusiliers.

Then suddenly she saw Haverley being driven back by a tall and powerful man with saber in hand. The two were swinging viciously at each other. Peter had dropped his musket in the shadowy light. She had seen it fall, and she could not tell if the other man possessed one.

Both were expert with the saber, and the two weapons

whistled through the cooling night air with adroit deadliness, each man escaping blows by a hair, parrying and thrusting anew. Screams and groans rose from the vicious combat in every corner of the swamp. There was little gunfire now as most of the fighting was hand-to-hand.

Peter began to circle the man in a sudden flare of firelight, and Savarra drew in an anguished breath when she saw that the man fighting her husband was McLean. She stood immobile, wondering feverishly what she could do to aid McLean.

Then she realized that the British and tory soldiers were disengaging in the thick of the fight. Some running for their horses were cut down in flight. There was a grim and deadly inexorability in the experienced movements of the partisans.

She glimpsed Baltazar, an avenging fury as he laid about him with his saber, his eyes wild in the light of the fires. Belion was at his side, recklessly careless of his life as he drove a fusilier to his knees and killed him with one swift blow. This surprise attack was part of the partisan way of life, and they knew every angle that would wreak the most devastation and death. Some of the fusiliers, seeing their compatriots falling on every side, began asking for quarter and fighting slowed.

But McLean and Haverley, crouching before each other, showed no sign of slowing. She heard the rumble of McLean's voice, then Haverley's violent reply. "I'll kill you this time, McLean—face to face!" and with lightning swiftness he slashed at the man and the tip of his saber ran from shoulder to mid-arm before McLean's saber met it midair and, with a dextrous twist, flipped the weapon from Haverley's hand, sending it flying into a nearby bed of coals. Blood appeared black on McLean's shirt sleeve.

Haverley did not pause a second. Before McLean could anticipate his move, Haverley closed in on him, and the two fell to the ground, rolling in the sandy earth beside the fire. Savarra's scream rang over the sounds of battle. "Cutler, he has a knife—watch out—watch out!"

But even as she cried the warning, she saw McLean's brown fingers move with lightning speed to drag his long, bright knife from his waist and the two rolled, slashing viciously at each other, over and over in the trampled soil. Blood was covering McLean's shoulder and darkening the whole of his shirt where it was slit to the wrist.

But in that instant he rolled atop the struggling Haverley,

and for one brief moment Savarra saw the long, sharp knife raised high and glittering in the light of the moon and the dying fires, before it plunged downward to the hilt in Lord Haverley's chest. Haverley made one last desperate slash at McLean's throat above him, but his arm fell before he could finish the blow and his long body sprawled still and limp on the ground beside the fire, his fine white shirt darkening slowly over his breast.

Savarra stood quite still. Her eyes were fastened on the lifeless body of her husband, and she could not stem the sweeping tide of relief and freedom that shook her soul. She moved toward McLean.

Their eyes met as he rose, deliberately wiping the blood from his long knife and thrusting it into his waist. He asked quietly, "Was I in time?"

She nodded wordlessly and his lips twisted in a strangely cold smile. "So you have your wish. You are free—a widow now."

She moved closer to him in the rapidly clearing camp. Many of the partisans had ridden after the escaping British, but bodies lay all about the clearing, dim and pathetic in the last wavering light from the campfires and the brilliant moon. At a far side, the partisans had rounded up a number of prisoners.

Looking down at her husband, Savarra said haltingly, "Death is so terrible—for anyone young—but I must thank you for saving me once again. Another ten minutes and you would have been too late—for me."

He nodded curtly, glancing at the blood that stained his arm. "We must gather up what supplies we have captured here and get on the road to meet Nathanael Greene near Eutaw Springs. We will face Stewart's army there, and Greene has great need of us."

Savarra said humbly, "First let me cleanse and bandage your arm, Cutler."

" 'Tis not deep—a long shallow slice—" but he followed her into Haverley's tent where the lantern was still shining serenely. She ripped up a sheet from the bed, bathed McLean's long, thin wound from the bowl of water and bound it neatly. The blood from it had lessened fast, and soon the bandage would halt it entirely.

"How did you find me—this camp?"

He smiled grimly. "When you didn't come 'round the bend, I halted the others and tracked your captors long enough to see their direction." Then dryly, "Fortunately for you, we came upon General Marion within the hour, and we all struck out for Haverley's camp. Marion's scouts had already located it anyway."

"I owe my life to you once again," she said wearily, "for I would have died rather than live with him." She sank down on the narrow bed.

He replied dryly, "I think not, but it might have been unpleasant for a while." Then as he turned to leave, "You may as well rest here while we attend to the business at hand. I'll send Cotty to you."

She made no reply, but she did not lie down upon the bed. *The business at hand.* The partisans would, with their short-handled narrow spades, dig graves and bury the dead from both sides. They would bandage the wounded. Those who were not disabled would ride to meet Nathanael Greene, while those who could not would be left in the care of two or three men to recover as best they could. Everything that could be of use to the partisans would be taken, and what could not be carried with them would soon find its way into the deep, swift Santee or be hidden in the fastnesses of Ox Swamp.

But Savarra, free at last, sat upon the long narrow bed of the man she had begun by loving and had, in the end, loathed. She no longer need fear him, yet she felt a curious uneasiness, as if some part of her life were over and grief was only a breath away. Not for Peter, she thought, never for Peter. But heavy on her spirit lay the sense that she had not finished with sorrow.

She thought of Baltazar fleetingly, his ravaged face grim, his reckless fighting indicative that he no longer cared if he lived or died since his beloved Anne was gone. Tyler Belion wore much the same expression, and depression settled more heavily upon her.

I'm ill, she thought feverishly, looking down at the ripped shirt which she had succeeded in tying about her. This feeling of gloom was part of a fantasy that would swiftly pass. It was the aftermath of shock that came from seeing men die. Still, she felt it deep within, a wounding vacuum.

Cotty burst in through the tent flap, bringing cool, early September air with her. "Oh, mistress," she cried, clasping her arms about Savarra and hugging her close to her heavy cotton shirt. Her curling hair hung loose, a foible she had developed despite its getting tangled in limbs and brush, because Gabe and Thad admired it. Beside Savarra's cheek it smelled pungently clean from sessions with Corrie's strong soap.

Cotty bubbled on, "I'm so glad ter see you—I feart for you somethin' terrible, but now Cap'n McLean says that dretful man is dead— Blimey! What's happened to your shirt?" She looked scandalized as she took in the rags that were tied about Savarra's breast.

"Peter—he ripped it off me," she said, the words dredged up from the recesses of her thoughts. "Thank God they came when they did. I'm free at last."

"An' we can go back to Charlest'n an' live like ladies again! Lor' lumme, I'm so tired of breeches!"

Savarra looked at her with a touch of surprise. "I hadn't realized that—yet. But it's true. I can go to Verity and my little brother." With the words, a small glow lit the void that filled her. "Likely my father will be returning to see his new son, too." She spoke with rising hope. "I'd—I'd like to tell him he was right all along."

"I 'spect he knows that, mistress, by now."

"Still, I owe him an acknowledgment—an apology."

"A courier come in just before we left for this place, an' he said your pa an' Lord Cornwallis are in a little place called Yorktown near the James River in Virginia, an' they are fortifyin' it to make a stand against that Frenchman, Lafayette. An' they heard that General Washington is marchin' to meet him an' there'll be a terrible bloody battle."

Fear, that old familiar, seeped into Savarra. "But my father must go back to Charles Town—to see his son."

"Oh, there was a big hubbub about the battle that would be fought—but you can't believe everything you hear. After all, the British navy will come to your father's aid, an' likely they'll beat the rebels an' end the war right there."

"If only it *would* end," Savarra sighed.

Cotty was now brushing and braiding Savarra's hair once more and she said hesitantly, "Mistress Savarra, when we win, I don't want ter go back to England. I—I have lost my heart to Thad and Gabe."

"We may not win," Savarra said cynically. "We may be run out of America whether you will or no."

Cotty looked shocked. "Oh, no'm. We always wins—then I can settle down with Thad or—Gabe—I do declare I can't make up my mind between those two—in the colonies and live my life here. Our navy will back up your father an' Lord Cornwallis. You'll see, an' that'll be the end of it."

The flap lifted and Cutler McLean entered. "Ladies, we cannot spare an escort to see you back to Charles Town yet. You will have to wait to return until we have met with the British. It should be no longer than a week. And I regret to ask you to come and mount up again, but we must travel to Eutaw Springs."

Savarra was exhausted, but she looked at McLean and said coolly, "Can you find another shirt for me?" as she held the shreds of her torn garment around her.

"Come, Cotty," he said, "I will give your mistress one of mine." He turned to leave, then halted with the tent flap half-open. "By the way, we've captured more fine British horses than we know what to do with, so you both shall be mounted in the best style."

In the lamplight Cotty looked crestfallen as he went out. "I shan't be able to ride with Thad—or Gabe," she murmured.

Savarra merely looked at her. She had pulled the shirt around to the front to cover her breasts and now her back was bare. And after the night's events, the fact that Cotty grieved because she could no longer ride snuggled against one or the other of her suitors struck her as being the height of idiocy.

Cotty seemed to realize it as well and she said timidly, "Mistress, you weren't—he didn't?"

"Rape me again?" Savarra finished brutally. "No, but 'twas only because he hadn't time, thank God."

"Thank Mr. McLean, too," Cotty said, sinking to a seat beside Savarra now that she had finished her hair. "He was like a crazy man when he come back from trackin' those three men an' you through the woods, an' he didn't 'low any time wasted after we got to Gen'l Marion."

Savarra looked up, her eyes ablaze, heart pounding, but Cotty's high, cockney little voice went on, "He told Gen'l Marion we had a chance to wipe out strong rein—reinforcements for Colonel Stewart ahead of time. I heard him sayin' Nathanael Greene would likely cite all the partisans an' they'd get an—an—well, it was somethin' bettern'n a medal from the Continental Congress itself."

Savarra's eyes fell. Then it had not been for *her* that McLean had hastened the partisans. It had been for America, of course. For the future nation for which he fought. Well— she squared her shoulders—he had been right. The fusiliers were dead or prisoners now and Stewart was that much less prepared.

When McLean said from outside, "May I come in, Savarra?" she replied with a cold affirmative. He entered carrying a white shirt, clean but very wrinkled from a long sojourn in his pack. He handed it to her and said curtly, "Get ready as quickly as you can for we must leave here immediately."

Less than ten minutes later, the men set fire to the tents and British gear that was not wanted and they were on their way through the moonlit countryside. Savarra, clad in McLean's voluminous shirt, looked back over her shoulder at the flames that shot up above the trees. The tents were highly combustible and their blaze was short-lived. In only minutes the sky behind them was dark but for the sinking moon that peered curiously over the treetops at her. Cotty had taken strips from her torn shirt and bound them about Savarra's narrow waist, giving her new garment some semblance of shape. She had bound the cuffs as well so that the sleeves did not fall down over her slender wrists as she held the reins to the spirited gelding she rode. Strength had flowed back into her tired limbs as they set out, but Cotty, beside her on a big roan, drooped.

Thad, dropping back, looked at her in the pale moonlight. "Just hang on, Miss Cotty. We're swinging wide away from the Santee right now, to bypass Stewart an' his troops—but we'll soon be at Henry Lauren's plantation, where we'll stop an' wait for Gen'l Greene to meet us."

Savarra asked skeptically, "And where is this Lauren's place?"

" 'Bout seventeen mile above Eutaw Springs, mistress," he said in his pleasant drawl. "We're only 'bout sixty mile from Charlest'n an' I heard the cap'n and the gen'l talkin'. Reckon you'll get to go back to Mistress Verity's after this little scrap."

Savarra made no reply and Thad fell to teasing Cotty, offering to take her up on his horse before him if she grew too tired. "You could sleep in my arms, Miss Cotty, an' not be afeared to fall off," he said audaciously, and Cotty made a coy answer. Savarra restrained a sarcastic comment. She was miserable, but that was no reason to make Cotty so.

A string of excellent horses, following behind Marion's brigade, were roped together and under the care and surveillance of Caleb and two other black soldiers. They had taken no prisoners, but a few tories had escaped and were no doubt on their way to Charles Town by now. Savarra reflected on the number of her countrymen and tories who were afoot in the swamps and bogs of South Carolina, but she could not dredge up any sympathy for them. She found herself thinking more and more of the partisans as "our men," and she was struggling to come to terms with it. Probably she would return to England, but her heart would be in this semi-tropic land forever. And the tall powerful McLean would be a vivid ghost in her life, though why this was so she did not know, for the man never failed to infuriate her.

The hours dragged by, and dawn sent its first pale light into the eastern sky. Gabe Sleep rode up beside the girls and said, "We're almost there, an' soon you'll be able to rest a while."

Savarra, who was numb by now with fatigue, merely looked at him, but Cotty, voluble with her aches and pains, said, "Lor', 'tis high time. Gabe, you must make us a bed and let us sleep for a day an' night."

It was full daylight before they reached Lauren's Plantation and the hundred or more men fell to making camp. It was a hot and sultry day, the kind only September could bring, with its mixture that promised fall but held the last searing touch of summer. When Gabe and Thad made down a bed, the two girls fell into instant slumber. They slept throughout that day and through the cooler night.

And while they slept, Nathanael Greene's ill-clad and scrawny army marched into camp. Henry Lee's legion was the only group with a real look of the military about them. The total strength of the garnered troops amounted to about twenty-three hundred and they were a melange of oddly assorted warriors.

When Savarra and Cotty roused the next morning, they were ravenously hungry, a state Corrie assuaged with what provisions she had at hand. Then they looked about them to see that there was the South Carolina militia under the Marquis Francis de Malmedy, there were Andrew Pickens's men and three Continental brigades, along with the North Carolinians and Brigadier General Jethro Sumter. There were Virginians under Campbell as well, and there was Colonel Washington, cousin to George, with his dragoons. There was even a troop of Delaware Continentals who were to act as reserves.

Savarra observed them all with a jaundiced eye. They

looked, for the most part, bearded and tattered and scarcely deserving of the term soldier, despite those among them who had managed to secure respectable uniforms.

For a day they were drilled briefly, forming their battle lines to teach the raw recruits to form with coolness and recollection. Savarra and Cotty, along with Corrie, watched the maneuvers that day, and each was filled with her own particular apprehensions. Savarra thought hopefully, *After this one last battle, I will go back to Charles Town where there is a semblance of civilization*, and she found herself looking forward to it with a sort of starving desire.

"Cap'n McLean an' Gabe an' Thad look almost like our nobility—real gentry to me now," Cotty said thoughtfully.

"What do you mean, *our?*" Savarra said waspishly. "It appears to me that you long ago became one with the rebels, what with your peculiar ability to love *two* of them."

Cotty was tactfully silent, for she had secured a curry comb from Gabe with which he had curried his horse. Having cleaned it thoroughly, she was now combing Savarra's hair with it, albeit very gingerly. Still it performed well, removing tangles and leaving her hair smooth and manageable.

After that Cotty combed her own, and still later the two girls and Corrie went to a nearby creek and performed their baths. Though Savarra loathed Corrie's pungent soap, she was forced to concede it was better than nothing, and she felt refreshed and much cleaner after the use of it.

There were other women at the creek who had trailed after the men in arms. Savarra, Cotty and Corrie made their acquaintance in the brief hours before fighting began. They were hardy souls, these women, some following husbands, others lovers, and some could not be described as anything but drabs. They were all to wait in the grove of trees below the burned remains of the Lauren house until combat with Stewart's forces was joined at Eutaw Springs and settled one way or the other.

Later they learned that they were on the periphery of the last great battle of the two main opposing armies in the south.

At four o'clock in the morning of September eighth, 1781, Nathanael Greene set his oddly assorted troops in motion to attack Stewart's at Eutaw Springs. The patriots had been so careful of their movements that Stewart had no inkling they were about to attack. Savarra and her two companions wakened in the dark to hear the whispered voices and clink of bridles as the men made ready to go.

Savarra sat up, looking at the dampening fires, and she knew that the clash of men in arms was imminent. She got to her feet and, while seeking McLean, she found Thad McHorry.

"Will you keep us informed on how it goes?" she asked in a tense whisper.

"I reckon," he murmured laconically, "if I can get away. This battle's goin' to decide whether the British can roam and pillage our countryside at will, or whether we can bottle 'em up in Charlest'n."

In a short while they were gone, but she could not go back to sleep. She had seen enough of war's bloody casualties to know now that every man, British and American, was laying his life on the line. She thought of McLean and ached for him. He had had two narrow escapes. Would this third time be the end? She put the thought from her and lay awake until dawn broke in the east and the sultry day of waiting began.

Savarra loathed these times of limbo, when waiting was all she could do. At her urging a reluctant Cotty was dragged to the creek, and they washed their hair with Corrie's strong soap and dried it in the burning September sun. The day dragged on and on interminably. They could dimly hear the faint sounds from the battle raging in the far distance, and Thad did not return to tell them how it was going.

When at last the men carrying their wounded began to straggle into camp, Savarra's heart sank. They looked defeated and exhausted. The women who had been cooking, tending fires, washing clothes in the nearby creek, rose and ran toward their men, begging to know of the battle.

Cotty and Corrie were among them, but Savarra sat on the moist turf, her back against a tree, and bit her lower lip. She did not see McLean among those returning, but Belion rode into the group, his horse foam-flecked and exhausted. It was the first time she had seen the tall rice planter in several days, and his face was gray wtih fatigue in the late afternoon. Bowman Baltazar, his face set like a stone, rode beside him, and Savarra knew a sharp pang of pity for the man. He kept to himself the days she had ridden near him, his eyes far away, and his answers to her well-meant efforts at conversation were remote. She had at last left him in his grief.

Now she glanced to the east and saw the sky was filling

with clouds. It was going to rain again, she thought with crawling dread. And the men had not thrown up a single brush arbor around the entire encampment among the oaks and pines.

As she sat watching Corrie and Cotty go from man to man and finally fasten on Belion and Baltazar, she noted that some of the men were gathering themselves into troops and marching out, followed by their women as they struck off through the woods. Still Savarra did not move. She had known so much of terror and anguish, of hope and regret in the short days past, that a blessed numbness crept upon her.

From the direction of the head of Eutaw Springs a number of Continentals emerged herding before them a good-sized troop of redcoats who looked thoroughly dejected. It was then she saw McLean sitting tall and straight in the saddle on Jed, and both horse and man appeared weary beyond measure. Sleep and McHorry were mounted near him.

Savarra rose to her feet as Cotty glimpsed them, and both men slipped from their saddles to embrace the indecisive object of their affection. She saw McLean's gray eyes searching the tangle of humanity about her. His eyes found hers and clung briefly, as he dismounted. Leading the horse by his bridle, he approached. The numbness left her and an old familiar hurt took its place.

She lifted her head and asked briefly, "You won?" and he shook his head. Another one of Greene's defeats, she thought and asked again, "You lost?" and he shook his head, a faint smile tilting his lips.

"We won and then we lost," he said. "Stewart's men are doubtless destroying the last of their supplies preparatory to marching toward Charles Town."

"Then how did you lose?"

"It was touch and go for a long time. We crowded them clear to the creek, though Colonel Washington's mount fell on him and he was taken prisoner—and Colonel Campbell of the Virginia Continentals was killed. The sharpshooters in Patrick Roche's fine brick house near the head of the springs kept us from reaching the body of troops behind it."

As she stood listening to his low, quiet drawl, she could picture the battle, horses rearing and plunging to the ground as they were shot. She could see them with manes and tails flying as they coursed through the human wreckage sprawled upon the dusty ground, upon the lawns and gardens of the

Roche three-story house built at the head of the crystal-cool springs. She envisioned the ragged patriots and her red-coated countrymen with bayonets at the ready, charging at each other in bloody conflict.

"The remaining British troops had retreated through their own camp, and there was much booty in that camp," his voice grew bitter, "for our thirsty, near-naked men. A number of us rushed through the camp in pursuit of the British, only to look back and see our hungry men stopping to loot the tents. And God knows, it was enough to tempt them—liquors, meats, bread—even sugar and salt, all in plenteous supply. And that's when the British took proper advantage of our confusion." He sighed. "The fighting seesawed back and forth. Nearly all the gunners manning Greene's two field pieces were either killed or wounded, so Greene retreated to the protection of the trees, where we all took stock of ourselves and what remained. And those we had taken prisoners."

"What of the—British?"

"Stewart and his men, after four hours of bitter fighting, were too exhausted to follow. Now Marion is planning to besiege him as he marches to Charles Town. After we catch our breath, of course."

By now the two had reached the campfire where Cotty and Corrie were preparing food, each of them falling over the other's questions to Thad and Gabe. Belion and Baltazar had unsaddled their weary mounts and were themselves sprawled out before the cook fire Cotty had prepared.

Belion said, "Caleb came through, all right, I can assure you, Corrie. He'll be along with the extra horses in a little while. We came out of this thing with a goodly number of horses."

The sky was growing darker swiftly and the low grumble of thunder reached their ears. The ruined Lauren house offered no protection to the swarms of men and the few women, so the weary patriots began to erect brush arbors, felling trees and limbs and stacking them upon a network of limbs lashed together above four poles. Some they attached to trees, and by the time the first drops began to strike most of Marion's tired men were under cover of sorts.

Marion himself came to the campfire where McLean and his men were sitting under the arbor they had erected. The stocky little general with his misshapen knees and his limp surveyed them with gleaming black eyes.

He said, "You performed most creditably, captain—and you as well, Lieutenants Baltazar and Belion. Couriers are out scouting now to ascertain the movements of the British, but we will rest here—as they will have to rest—before we pursue them." His eyes went to Savarra. "Madame, a courier came in with news of Cornwallis and his army, just now. I understand your father is with them."

"Yes," Savarra replied alertly. "What is the news of my father?"

"The French fleet is engaged in battle with the British navy in the Chesapeake, and they are winning. Your father and Cornwallis and all their men will be bottled up in Yorktown, where they have dug in. His escape route by sea will be cut off and Lafayette, Rochambeau and Washington are proposing to lay siege to Yorktown."

Savarra swallowed down a surge of fear and said calmly, "My father is a seasoned soldier. He has been known to fight his way out of many military traps."

Marion smiled and it was surprising how it lightened his stern visage. "I give the British credit for great bravery, madame. I include you in that compliment," and he fell to discussing his plans with McLean, Belion and Baltazar.

They were to rest here overnight and take up pursuit of the battle-weary British at dawn tomorrow. The nut-brown little man said, "I've had to let some of my men go to see to their fall crops—and there may be others who'll join them—my troop strength will be down, but I think we can harass and ambush Stewart's men."

"I'd like to make it into Charles Town myself," Belion said grimly. "I would like to check on my—friends there."

Marion surveyed him silently and compassionately, and Savarra wondered how much of his thwarted love for Verity was known by the general. Belion's again fully bearded face was a good disguise. She would never recognize the smoothly shaved young man she had met on shipboard in this hairy, leather-clothed man.

The redcoats, who had no brush arbor, were sitting miserably huddled in the downpour, their sodden clothing clinging to their limbs, and some of them looked to have a fever glitter in their eyes, which Savarra could see by the sputtering campfires. It was damp enough under the arbors. She was relieved to see that the tired partisans were sharing their food with their captives.

Caleb had come riding in with two other men, each with a

string of horses behind them, and now Corrie was seeing to his wants. She served him hoecake and sweet potatoes with some of the greens for which she had foraged in the forest.

At last all were bedded down for the night under the steady downpour. Savarra had surreptitiously noted where McLean prepared his bed long before he retired to it and put her own down as closely to it as she dared, all the while cursing herself for a weakling, Marion's compliment notwithstanding. She knew only that she felt safer, less apprehensive when near him—even though his brusque conversation and short answers reduced her to helpless and silent rage.

As she was dozing off, she was startled to hear him speak her name.

"Savarra," and at her response, he said, "the general says Belion and I may escort you and Cotty back to Charles Town at an early date. Perhaps as we trail Stewart there. And we've a mind to go to Virginia and join Washington's troops. Yorktown could be the end of this war."

Trailing Stewart was a harrowing experience. Savarra and the other two women rode far behind the men. Stewart's soldiers had felled trees and piled brush over the road to make it more difficult for the partisans to catch up with him, and circling these obstacles was exceedingly tiresome. Besides, by the time Marion had detailed a squad to guard the British prisoners, his troops were decimated and they could only sting Stewart en route. Once they captured twenty-four British soldiers and four tories as they straggled along behind the main army, and the partisans herded them all the way back to the camp above Eutaw Springs.

Then Marion's outriders returned with the news that Stewart had received four hundred fresh troops under an officer named McArthur from Monck's Corner to cover his withdrawal. It was then the partisans concluded that discretion was the better part of valor under the circumstances.

Thus it was the middle of September when McLean approached Savarra. "Tyler, Gabe, Thad and I will see you safely back to the Pair house. We've been given indefinite leave and we plan to journey to Yorktown after we deposit you. They'll have need of us there," he told her. Caleb and Corrie, as well as Bowman Baltazar, had chosen to stay with Marion's small band. Baltazar bade them a somber goodbye with a message of love to Verity.

Savarra's heart was high at the prospect of seeing her little half-brother and the kind and gracious Verity. She would miss Anne's stern but understanding presence, for she had been good and basically kind. Savarra hoped the baby would fill Verity's loss in some measure.

They traveled slowly through the mornings and the hot afternoons, for McLean was in no mood to hurry. All of them were still tired from the ordeal just past, and it took them three days to reach the outskirts of Charles Town, where McLean stopped. They sat their horses in a small copse of woods, looking at the churned road over which Stewart's forces, with their fresh troops along, had just entered the city.

McLean opened the leather bag at the back of his saddle and took out a rather meager-looking soiled white wig, which did cover his dark hair satisfactorily. He perched a pair of spectacles on the bridge of his high, straight nose, further changing his appearance. Belion, behind his heavy beard, was unrecognizable as the immaculate planter, while Gabe Sleep and Thad McHorry in their raccoon-skin caps above innocent faces looked to be hunters who were enduring a rather bad hunting season.

McLean grinned, "We're all good tories, and I'll wager with the turmoil in Charles Town now with Stewart's exhausted army milling about, not many will question us."

He was correct. Only one surly redcoat in arms did so as they neared the town square. McLean lied cheerfully, giving them all an impeccable slate. But the more convincing argument came from Savarra who, despite her disreputable raiment, put on her imperial British dignity and confirmed McLean's statement they were loyalists and had given her safe harbor from vicious rebels.

The soldier became effusive in his apologies and offered to escort them to the Pair house, an offer that was rejected.

"I know the way perfectly well, sir," Savarra said coldly. "These good men who have given me safety will be most welcome there."

Bowing and stepping aside, the soldier let them pass, and they proceeded to the Pair house without further incident. It was near noon and the mid-September sun was burning, the air humid, and all of them were perspiring freely by the time they turned on King Street and passed the Brewton house.

Then, as all the grimy riders halted before the big, welcoming Pair house, there was a sudden clatter of hooves and the rattle of a vehicle. The carriage appeared under the portecochere. Amos was on the box and beside him sat Tiqua. Their dark faces were grim and disapproving, but when their eyes fell upon the disguised McLean and Belion, then Savarra, their relief was monumental.

Drawing rein on the two bays, both servants scrambled down from the box and hastened to the newcomers. "Before God, cap'n, I was never so glad ter see anyone in my life!" Amos cried.

"Meestress Stvarra, *vous parlez*—you mus' talk to Meestress Verity—" Tiqua was so distressed she could scarcely speak English. "She done take it eento 'er 'ead to go to Lord Bainbridge, clear to Virginia!" Tiqua caught her hand as Savarra dismounted and squeezed it until she winced.

"Cap'n, she's got that wet nurse, Clarissa, an' all our clothes packed, and we was gettin' ready to leave this minute—" Amos glanced back at the house and his jaw firmed. "An' I got ter tell you Mistress Verity near died havin' that little boy ahead o' time like she done. She ain't up to no near-six-hundred-mile trip—"

The door slammed behind him, and Verity's voice cracked like a whip. "I certainly am, Amos Pair, and if I have to go to Colonel Stewart myself—oh, Cutler—Tyler! Dear lord, it's Savarra and Cotty, too!" Tears filled her big brown eyes.

In the door behind her there appeared a plump, brunette girl with a ruddy but pretty face, full of good humor. In her arms was a small bundle with just the crown of a golden curly head showing.

Savarra felt her throat swell with a lump and tears pricked her eyes as she and Verity ran into each other's arms. After a single fierce embrace, each young woman pulled back to survey the other.

Savarra, too close to tears to speak, heard Verity saying in a thick, husky voice, "You're brown as a berry, my dear!"

The English girl looked into a face too pale, brown eyes too large with blue smudges beneath them. Verity was smiling, but her smile trembled and she blinked at glistening tears. Savarra, still unable to trust her voice, put her arms about the older girl once more.

Tyler Belion said grimly, "Do the rest of us get such a

greeting?" and there ensued a general show of emotional joy among them all, with Cotty weeping copiously as everyone embraced.

Thad McHorry took shameless advantage and kissed Cotty soundly before she realized it was her traveling partner and his kiss was hardly one of greeting.

"You!" she cried and drew her hand back. He caught it easily and laughed, his blue eyes innocent as a spring sky. "Why, I declare, Miss Cotty—I thought you were Mistress Verity!"

Both Verity and Savarra burst into laughter at the blatant lie. Cotty, looking confused and frustrated, turned to Gabe, who reached an arm out, drawling, "Come here, Cotty, I'll protect you from that skunk!"

She flounced away, "I want ter see Lord Bainbridge's little lad—" but Savarra was before her in a flash. Clarissa beamed at them and pushed aside the light lawn from around the baby's face.

Strong emotion swept Savarra and she knew a curious lightness of head as she looked into the pink features under pale gold hair. It was amazing how much he resembled her father! She was nineteen years old and, besides her mother and father, this was the first really close relative she had ever had. "May I—hold him, Verity?" She glanced at the others, who were observing her narrowly.

"Of course." Verity had come onto the porch, her pale forehead beaded with perspiration as Savarra reverently took the baby from the grinning Clarissa. She restrained an urge to hug him to her breast and weep with joy.

Verity sank weakly into one of the weathered woven chairs that had been all summer on the porch. "It's very hot—this time of year," she said breathily, and Savarra knew a prick of fear.

"Are you—well, Verity?"

"Quite," was the reply, the big dark-circled eyes going accusingly to the now silent Amos. "And certainly well enough to go to my husband." She fumbled at the reticule in her lap and pulled out a white square of paper. "Here, Savarra, read this."

The others were coming up the porch steps now, crowding around and exclaiming over the baby. Then McLean said courteously, "Verity, we are very thirsty and hungry—and tired."

"Do go in, Cutler—all of you. Amos, tell Primrose to prepare a large meal, please."

Savarra handed the baby back to the wet nurse and took the letter her father had written his wife. Those about her moved after McLean, and suddenly she and Verity were alone on the porch together.

She was suddenly aware of two redcoated soldiers looking at them curiously from their mounts in the street. Calhoon was leading the riderless horses around to the stables where they could be watered and fed.

Verity said under her breath, "The town is positively crawling with them since Colonel Stewart's battle at Eutaw Springs. They say they won," she laughed shortly, "but if they did, I should indeed like to see them defeated—they look so sorely whipped now." Under her stare of annoyance, the two moved on down King Street, the hooves of their horses striking the cobblestones with a ringing sound, but Savarra was lost in her father's letter.

My darling,

I have just received news that we have a fine, healthy son! How can I tell you the joy in my heart to know such? However, it alarms me that he has arrived beforehand—and the fact that I have had no letter from *you*. Only a note from Bonnie Raintree by way of the courier who arrived today from Charles Town. She also tells me of the untimely and wrongful death of your mother at the hands of British soldiers. You can imagine how this distresses me. Bonnie says you are recovering but slowly—I am sorely tempted to desert my post with General Cornwallis and hasten to you, but you and I both know that is contrary to my character. No matter the anguish that shakes me, I must honor my duty and my commission. General Cornwallis has told me that under any other circumstance and at any other time, he would gladly release me, but we are entrenched in Yorktown—a town where the York River of Virginia meets with the Chesapeake Bay. We are fortifying the town heavily, and I urge you not to fear for me, for our fleet will soon be in the bay behind us and we will have their support. Our position will be well-nigh impregnable. So much so that I could wish you and young James—how kind of you to name him that!—were with me. I am established in a very nice little home here. It is of brick and while of modest size, is very well accoutered.

There was a long stroke of the quill, then—

God, Verity, I love you and miss you and long to see our son.

There was a final postscript after his signature.

If by chance you should again see my daughter, Savarra, assure her of my love and continuing concern for her.

Savarra felt the pull of the letter, the longing in it—and he had remembered *her*. Even after hearing of her experience with Haverley he had not condemned her nor closed his mind and heart to her. Her throat ached with love for him. He represented security from years gone by and wisdom and kindness and humor. Two tears gathered at the tips of her long, lowered lashes.

Verity said tenderly, "That is the way I felt. And that is why I shall let nothing stand in the way of my going to him."

Savarra's eyes were very blue as she said slowly, "I must tell you that I heard the French fleet is in the Chesapeake and is now doing battle with our English ships. My father is in greater danger than he knows."

Verity's eyes widened with fear and she said in a rush, "All the more reason that I must reach him as soon as possible. Surely you see that, Savarra?"

"But Verity, you are so pale and thin—"

"I lost a great deal of blood," she said impatiently, "but old Marilla has given me a tonic. I feel stronger every day and my appetite is tremendous."

"I fear my father would take a different view of your long journey, dear. He would want you first to take care of yourself—for he loves you very much."

Verity's pale face set implacably and she said quietly, "I am well enough and I am going to him."

Savarra observed her silently as she folded the letter and handed it back to her. Then she said, "I feel much as you do, in that I long to see him—to tell him he was right and I was wrong. I owe him that for I bear him a great love, too." Savarra stood looking down at the girl before her, white, resolute and courageous.

Verity was much too young to be looked on as a stepmother, but she was mother to her half-brother, and Savarra realized that she had become very dear to her. She could not stand by and let the American girl go off in the flimsy carriage over the long rough roads, beset by outliers, partisans, enraged tories and a few ungarnished desperadoes.

Not without *her*. It was too dangerous, despite the musket she had seen in the box beside Amos.

"Verity, would you wait—a day or two and give me a chance to ready myself to accompany you?" She did not know if McLean, Belion, Sleep or McHorry would agree to their mad flight along the coasts to faraway Virginia, but she determined in an instant to persuade them to act as escort. After all, they themselves were planning to join Washington and Lafayette there. Savarra could not bear the thought of her tiny brother and his mother subjected to the perils of such a journey with only Amos, Tiqua and the wet nurse to protect them.

Verity's slender jaw set. "Only if it is no more than a day and night. 'Tis mid-September now. The rains will soon set in and it will take us more than two weeks to make the journey. I will wait no more than today and tonight, Savarra. *I will go if I must walk every step of the way*." Her leaf-brown eyes were filled with a new fire.

Savarra took both the cool, thin, long-fingered hands into her warm tanned ones. "Just one day—to rest our mounts and refit ourselves, I promise." And the two young women entered the house, arm in arm.

Twenty

But the following morning brought more dissension, and Savarra had a difficult time in persuading Verity to remain while she tried to talk the men into allowing them to accompany them.

She had slept heavily that first night in her old bed, but she woke well before dawn and lay tossing, unable to return to sleep, her mind a-boil. By the time the sun rose at last, Savarra had gone over the whole of the year and two months she had spent in South Carolina and had come to the bitter conclusion that she was to find no rest on these shores—and her heart was heavy with the old uneasy, quaking sensation that heartbreak lay in wait.

After cajoling Verity into giving her the morning to put the question of escort to McLean, she left her stepmother in her room with little James and Clarissa and sought the captain.

She found him in the kitchen, where he had wheedled an extra biscuit and cup of coffee out of Primrose and was preparing to go out to the stables and curry Jed. His scanty wig was awry and the glasses reposed in the pocket of his white shirt. He put down his cup and Savarra said doggedly, "Cutler, I *must* talk with you about it—"

"Come along then." He gave her a cynical smile. "You know how little while we have to stay—with the town full of Stewart's men." He listened to her plea as they made their way to the stables and smiled skeptically when she paused, inserting, "I agree Verity should not attempt such travels with only Amos and the two women—especially where there promises to be heavy fighting." He paused, then added with sudden coldness, "No. She must remain here." Anger surged through her and, in that instant, she determined that she would do everything she could to help Verity reach Lord Bainbridge—and nothing should stop her from accompanying her stepmother.

"She will not remain here. If you do not give us escort, we will go accompanied by the servants."

McLean paused, holding the rough comb in his hand where it rested on Jed's flank, and the big horse looked around questioningly. "You know damned well that the main British army is dug in at Yorktown now! If I could persuade Belion, McHorry and Sleep to allow you women to go with us, we would leave you at the outskirts. There is no way you could get through the battle lines."

"I have heard my father speak often of a flag of truce to permit entry and exit of people during battles!"

"That is not always possible, Savarra, and you know it."

"I have persuaded Verity to wait two days. After that, we shall leave, with or without you." Savarra's chin was up and her eyes were a furious blue. "She has given me a rather enormous bag of gold to defray our expenses."

He began to laugh and turned to curry the horse once more. "What a hothead you are, Savarra—between your headlong nature and Verity's iron will, we have no choice." He looked back over his shoulder at her and his gray eyes were hard. "But I make no promises to get you into Yorktown—you will be on your own once we reach the battle lines.

And the road is a rough and dangerous one. I've made the trip often on business. You won't find it easy."

She exulted silently, but her voice was steady. "We can leave Wednesday morning."

When she parted with McLean in the early sunlight, surrounded by the fading Pair gardens, Savarra knew the die was cast, but she felt strangely discomforted by her triumph. McLean was right, she thought, a touch forlornly. She brightened thinking of Belion. He would be only too willing to accompany Verity anywhere—and Gabe and Thad would be all too pleased if she took Cotty along!

Thus it was that they left early that Wednesday morning with the rising sun promising a heated September ride. At the edge of town, they suffered a brief interrogation by two of Colonel Stewart's aides, but on learning the identity of their titled passenger and her stepdaughter, they became exceedingly polite. Indeed, the two even admonished those ardent but false loyalists, Belion, McHorry, Sleep and McLean, against the partisans who infested the forests of South Carolina. The patriots solemnly agreed to be alert to such dangers, and the carriage, carrying the two girls, Clarissa holding the baby, and Cotty inside, with Amos and Tiqua occupying the box, clattered off down the pot-holed road.

After they were out of town and well on the northern road, the men removed their disguises and took their long rifles out of hiding beneath the women's feet in the carriage.

Now, Savarra thought, as she jolted along beside her slender and determined stepmother, McLean had underestimated just how terrible this road actually was. The wet nurse, however, sat placidly across from them, cushioning the baby easily in her plump arms. Cotty, who had reservations about another long journey, but had refused to be left, looked out the window a touch resentfully at Gabe and Thad.

Clarissa Morse was woefully ignorant and her language a scandal, but Savarra appreciated her sunny temper and the fact that her milk was plenteous and she was more than willing to travel. Indeed, she looked out the window with avid interest in the small, twinkling black eyes.

Savarra's eyes followed the nurse's and saw she was regarding McLean, who rode his sleek stallion alongside. Clarissa's face innocently mirrored her admiration, and her wide mouth was ajar. The man did look uncommonly attractive this morning, without the mangy wig he affected in

Charles Town and wearing his recently acquired linen shirt which sported a small frill at the throat. His legs were shown to fine and muscled advantage by the tight doeskin tan breeches. Feeling her gaze, he turned and looked at her, the gray eyes clear and cool in the late morning light. She looked away.

"How far do you think we have come?" Verity asked impatiently.

"I'll ask Captain McLean," Savarra replied, secretly glad of the chance to speak to him. She leaned from the window and called out the question.

"About ten miles," he replied, giving her the cynical smile which always ruffled her. It was as if he did not believe her capable of a genuine emotion—as if he considered her an immature, emotional fool. And with good reason, she told herself with painful honesty.

She leaned her head back against the jouncing carriage, but the motion was such that she raised it again immediately. There would be no dozing as long as they traveled, she thought, and looked up to see Verity's luminous brown eyes bright with sympathy.

" 'Twill be a long and rough ride, Savarra—but your father is at the end of it." She breathed a sigh. "And we will both be safe with him. He is so wise and so kind."

Savarra looked at the small, heart-shaped face so filled with love and tenderness, and she said bitterly, "Yes, he is all of that. If I had only listened to him, how much pain and sorrow I could have saved myself."

Verity put a pale hand over Savarra's warm, golden-tanned one. "Do not blame yourself for your marriage. Lord Haverley was a handsome man."

"Indeed he was," Savarra replied scornfully, "and he used his handsomeness extensively among the ladies of London, but idiot that I was, I thought the stories of his conquests and exploits all lies. I thought him *ill-used* by gossips." She laughed shortly.

"You are free now," Verity said tranquilly, "and you will not mistake charm for character again, I am sure."

"I don't know," was the moody reply as she glanced at the strong, aquiline profile of McLean. Certainly there was charm there, but his character seemed so overpowering, his beliefs so strong and ingrained, his mocking assessment of her own character so derogatory, she could not understand his attraction for her. And she had long ago faced the fact that she was attracted to him. Oh, yes, Savarra Bainbridge was a fool, no doubt about it, she thought glumly.

They rattled down the rutted and winding road through virgin forests until darkness fell, crossing Wambaw Creek over a rickety bridge. In twilight they drew up before an inn near the Sampit River bridge, which they would have to cross in the morning, and McLean halted the carriage.

As Amos took Verity's arm, she looked even paler and her lips were firmly held against discomfort, but Savarra could see she was exhausted. At least she would have Tiqua and Clarissa in her room to tend her wants, Savarra thought.

Cotty had been unusually quiet, and when they were in their room at the inn Savarra questioned her about it.

"Well, mistress," she said frowning, "I been thinkin' an' I'm about to decide it's Thad I want. It just ain't possible to be in love with both. Do you think?"

"I don't know anything at all about love, Cotty," Savarra said brusquely. "I only thought I did."

"Well'm," Cotty said tentatively, "you did make a dretful mistake in thinkin' you loved Lord Haverley. Still, it seems foolish to have two like I have."

Savarra had, with Cotty's preoccupied help, divested herself of clothing and slipped into a warm, pale-pink nightdress. The September night was cool as they were not too far from the Atlantic coast, and she slipped under blankets on what proved to be a surprisingly comfortable bed.

"Come to bed, Cotty," she said tiredly. "You'll know which one to choose when the right time comes."

In the following days they crossed rivers and circled estuaries, following the winding trace along the coast to the north. Amos, with the coffee-tan and hardy Tiqua beside him, drove the two bays carefully. McLean seemed able to gauge their speed to bed them down at an inn of some sort each night.

They ate many times along the road, with Gabe shooting pheasant, quail, rabbits and doves. Past Wilmington, North Carolina, they went over Moore's Creek bridge, and Savarra thought silently that she had never seen a land with so many inlets, rivers, creeks and estuaries. There were more even than in her own island home.

The carriage, due to the uneven and rutted roads, became more rattly with each passing day. North Carolina was more sparsely settled than South Carolina, and they passed but few spots where civilization had encroached on the thickly forested countryside.

By the fifth day, Verity's color looked better to Savarra, and she herself had become inured to the tooth-jarring ride in the backwoods from the coast. But on the sixth day, disaster overtook them.

They had passed Cape Fear, and it was near noon when there burst out of the woods beside the road a band of men, shouting and waving their sabers, firing their guns. Amos drew rein on the bays, who were rearing wildly in fear.

"Lay down your weapons, or we'll shoot to kill!" cried one of the men, brandishing a pistol.

Savarra, frozen with shock, was still able to count five, all mounted on fine horses. Verity reached out to Clarissa and clutched her son to her breast, her face white. Even her lips were bloodless.

"Who are you?" McLean asked calmly, his rifle lying across his arm with deceptive casualness.

"We're the king's own loyalists and we want your rebel horses an' your goods."

"Then you are mistaken, for we are loyalists and this carriage holds the daughter and the wife of Lord Bainbridge. We are on our way to join him." McLean spoke firmly.

Then a second man spoke up. "Well, Tate was mistook. We're really patriots an' we plan to plunder your dirty loyalist carriage an' all your belongin's."

"Outliers," McLean spit out the word with contempt, "preying on both sides."

Two of the men laughed heartily. One, apparently well-educated, said, "It's a wise man who takes advantage of more than one opportunity. Whatever you choose to call us, we will take your horses, your supplies and your carriage, and you can proceed on foot. And you can be thankful that we don't kill you. All we want is your supplies—and the devil with your Lord Bainbridge's daughter and wife."

"Get out of that carriage," bellowed another, a big, bull-necked man with coarse features and a guttural voice.

Savarra's heart was beating wildly, and she noted that all five marauders were bearded, their clothing dirty. One had no tie for a queue and his hair fell about his face in wild disarray. Her eyes went to McLean and the three men about him who had dismounted on loudly barked orders from the apparent leader of the bandits. All the outliers kept their guns trained on the carriage and its escorts. At the leader's reiterated demand, McLean and his men put their rifles on the ground. There was no sound from Amos and Tiqua on the box.

Slowly the occupants debarked the carriage. Verity holding her baby came first, followed by Savarra, Cotty and finally Clarissa. They stood uncertainly on the edge of the rutted trail, and Cotty burst into sudden tears. Clarissa, casting frightened eyes about her, gave a low wail.

"Here! We'll have none o' that caterwaulin'!" shouted the guttural-voiced man. The leader, a slender man with eyes that almost met at the bridge of his flat nose, made a fierce gesture at his rough companion.

"Now," he said soothingly, "we aren't going to hurt you, ladies." Then forcefully, "Tate, you and Kelly get that baggage and those horses—"

Savarra looked angrily at McLean and his men, who stood silent and alert beside their horses. She knew that thrust deep at their waists were pistols, scarcely visible.

The first outlier said admiringly, "Well now, it looks like we've captured us a clutch o' pretty women. We'll take you ladies with us, by God." His companions, with guns at the ready, were swarming over the carriage, throwing baggage to the ground as they readied themselves to plunder everything in it.

Amos and Tiqua sat stiffly upon the box and were suddenly pushed unceremoniously aside and forced to scramble down by the thick-necked man. At this show of brutality, Cotty gave forth a freshet of tears and Clarissa followed suit. McLean and his men were still silent and unmoving. Savarra looked into their expressionless, smoothly tanned faces as the renegades went systematically about their depredations.

The bull-necked man said with a coarse laugh, "We won't be needin' this rickety carriage, will we, Lute?" He looked inquiringly at the leader who directed them.

"No, we will not" was the curt reply. "Burn it."

Immediately, the foremost two of the men unhitched the bays and the other two, with thick, strong arms, overturned the carriage, and it fell with a crunching sound of splintering wood upon its side like a big, awkward beetle. Savarra was becoming more and more angry and frightened. Her pointed little chin lifted and whiteness apeared around her fine nostrils.

One man knelt with flint in hand, while another pushed twigs and dried grass beneath the carriage. The man struck his flint and there was a yellowish flare as the materials caught fire and smoke spiraled upward in the still noon air. The man called Lute bent over the largest portmanteau, flung it open and pulled out a pale blue silk chemise belonging to Savarra. There was a burst of raw laughter as the others saw it. So intent were the outlaws upon their plunder and so convinced they had intimidated and cowed McLean and his men that they paid them little attention.

"You wimmen git back from the fire!" bawled one of the men. "Git on inter the woods."

"Not too far," interruped Lute, his little eyes fastened on Savarra lewdly. "We don't want to have to chase you down." He stepped forward and caught Savarra about the waist. "Here, my pretty, I'll help you on your way—but first a little kiss on account." He pulled her to him and she went rigid. Drawing her hand up with amazing swiftness, her nails raked his bearded face, bringing the blood as she shoved him violently.

The other outliers stared in silent fascination at the struggle between the two, and at that moment gunfire exploded. With the keen skill of years spent in action and split-second decisions, McLean and every man who appeared so cowed erupted with guns blazing. They had taken full advantage of the outliers' moment of inattention to draw their pistols, and the marauders were hit before they knew what had happened —and with deadly accuracy. Three of them sprawled dead in the dusty road, and the other two—Lute was one of them— leaped on their horses and fled as the men stooped to seize their rifles and began to fire. But the escaping two vanished into the thick trees beside the road where the carriage was now blazing brightly. The horses of the three fallen men and the two unhitched bays reared wildly and galloped after the departing outliers.

It was over so quickly Savarra scarcely had time to draw her breath. She looked down at her small hand to see the outlaw's blood still bright red upon her fingertips. With sudden and instinctive revulsion she wiped them on her fine, wine-colored file dress.

Verity was clutching her baby to her breast so tightly that the child gave forth with a healthy squall, and both Clarissa and Cotty were giving full vent to their fears with sobs that shook them. Gabe and Thad approached and began to comfort the girls, while Belion spoke a tender word to Verity before he mounted and took out after the stampeding horses.

Amos had a thin arm about Tiqua, whose shoulders were trembling with fright.

McLean thrust his pistol into his waistband once more and said dryly, "Thank you, Savarra, for giving us the opportunity we needed." He laughed silently, adding, "I think your would-be suitor will carry your favor for years to come. You looked to strike an inch or more deep."

"I meant it to take half his ugly face off," she said, her bosom heaving.

Still laughing, he turned away, saying, "Thad—Gabe, Cotty and Clarissa will survive. Let's pull that baggage back from the fire."

The three men fell to moving the pile of baggage, Tiqua and Amos joining in. Amos's voice was shrill with excitement, "They ain't got away with nothin'—'tis all here."

"And we're three saddled horses to the good," McLean drawled as Belion rode out of the forest holding the reins on both bays and the three outlaws' mounts.

"Ain't no use tryin' to save that carriage," Gabe said reflectively, the flames rising ever higher as the vehicle was consumed.

"I know Savarra and Cotty can ride and well, upon a horse. Can you, Verity—at this time?" McLean asked.

"You know I've ridden sidesaddle about town, Cutler," Verity replied doubtfully. "But holding the baby and the reins—"

"Never ye mind, missus," Clarissa spoke up, surprisingly calm now that danger was past. "I'll carry the wee'un on horseback. I done it many times afore fer my maw, God rest her soul."

"We'll put the baggage on the two bays—and these horses of the outliers look to be good mounts. All three geldings. At that some of us must ride double."

Savarra groaned. "That means Cotty will have to ride with me, no doubt."

The little maidservant's lip quivered with hurt. "Mistress, am I such a bother?"

"You wouldn't be if only you sat up and didn't lean on me," Savarra replied heartlessly. "See if you can do that."

Thad bent his innocent blue eyes upon Savarra and said helpfully, "Reckon I could take her off your hands, Mistress Savarra. She can ride behind o' me on Rosy."

"Good," Savarra responded, smiling for the first time. Both

Thad and Cotty would enjoy her falling upon him and Savarra would be free upon her own horse.

Belion and McLean were examining the outliers who lay upon the ground. They turned them over and Thad and Gabe bent to look at them as well.

Thad remarked laconically, "Looks like three of us are dead-center shots. All three in the head. How come you missed, Gabe?" He looked mischievously at his friend, who did not rise to the good-natured insult.

Savarra shivered and turned her head away. She saw that Amos was closely observing the woods into which the remaining two outliers had escaped, his long Brown Bess lying across one arm, with Tiqua close beside him. Then she looked at Verity, still holding her baby close, her pale face whiter than ever under the sultry late September sun. Clarissa Morse was gabbling relievedly with Cotty and making little sheep's eyes at Gabe, who ignored her.

"Hate to waste time doing it, but I guess we'd better bury this trio of cutthroats. I doubt if their companions will return to perform that duty after we leave." McLean rose to his feet and looked critically at his rifle, then carefully rubbed the curly maple stock on his sleeve until it gleamed.

Gabe and Thad went to their horses, holstered their guns and took their short-handled spades from the pack behind each saddle.

"We'll dig 'em just inside the woods, cap'n," Gabe said, "Kinda marshy in there. Oughtn't to be hard to do."

Without further ado, Belion, McLean and Thad each jerked an inert body to their shoulders and followed Gabe into the woods. Savarra wanted to cry out, *Don't go too far!* but at that moment Verity murmured weakly, "Savarra, take little James—"

Savarra turned just in time to catch the baby from her as she sank to the ground where she lay in a pool of gleaming and finely tucked beige silk that was almost the color of the dusty road. Her dark hair had come loose and it, too, was flung like a brown satin banner beside her head. *My God,* Savarra thought in a panic, *she's dead!*

"Clarissa—Cotty—Tiqua—get over here this instant!" she cried as little James let out a lusty cry at his rough handling.

The three women, seeing what had happened, flew to her and Clarissa took the baby in her arms, while Cotty and Tiqua bent with Savarra over the unconscious Verity.

"Get some water—a wet cloth for her head. I must bathe

her face," Savarra said distractedly and Cotty looked at her blankly.

"Where eez there water, meestress?" Tiqua asked anxiously.

"Look in the men's packs. There must be some canteens." And she and Cotty hastened to do her bidding. Savarra began to rub Verity's pale, cold hands, and she spoke to her urgently. "Verity—Verity, darling—open your eyes and look at me. 'Tis all over. We are safe." But the still face was carved in marble. There was no flutter of the lids. Savarra felt fresh fear rise in her. "Hurry, Cotty—Tiqua!" she called.

"I am," the two chorused, and in a moment Cotty returned with a canteen and her handkerchief, which looked none too clean. Savarra poured water on the cloth and began bathing Verity's still face. Though Verity's hands were cold, there was a fine beading of perspiration on her forehead and upper lip. The gentle rise and fall of her bosom allayed Savarra's fears that death was imminent. The sun was beating hotly down upon the girls, and Savarra told Cotty to shade Verity's face, which she did with her outstretched skirts.

After what seemed an interminable time, the long black lashes fluttered and Verity looked up at them. "I—I fainted," she murmured and began to struggle to rise.

"No, lie still a bit longer," Savarra said instinctively. "You're so pale, darling."

Verity frowned, "I have never fainted in my life—I must be weaker than I thought." She turned her head and saw the smoking embers of the carriage. "Oh, we have no carriage!" And she let her head fall back dispiritedly.

"But we have three fresh horses—all saddled, remember? We can ride in comfort as soon as you are feeling better."

"Little James?"

"Clarissa is nursing him. He is just fine." Savarra glanced over where the wet nurse was feeding the baby under a large tree at the edge of the woods.

"I feel so—queer," Verity murmured. "Hot and cold and sticky all at once."

"It's just the shock of our experience," Savarra said soothingly, but she thought with a sinking heart that it sounded like Verity was coming down with a fever. "You'll be much better if you lie still until the men come back. They have gone to bury the outliers."

Verity shuddered. "Those terrible men. I know they meant to kill our men and take us captive—God knows what would have happened to us."

"Well, they didn't," Savarra said grimly, her eyes seeking the woods where the men had disappeared. "And we shall take their horses and ride right on into Yorktown." She continued to bathe Verity's white face until the men emerged from the woods.

They were very concerned over Verity when they saw her lying in the rough road, but her strength had returned sufficiently for her to make light of her faint. She was helped to her feet and swayed slightly until she righted herself.

After that, the men divided all the baggage on the two horses that had pulled the carriage, and Tiqua mounted one while Amos mounted the other. Clarissa and the baby had one of the captured horses to themselves. Cotty rode happily behind Thad, while Savarra and Verity mounted the last two horses of the bandits. Verity drooped and her face began to show two brightly pink spots in each cheek. Her eyes were abnormally bright, and Savarra realized with increased apprehension that Verity was a sick woman. So sick that they would not be able to ride to Yorktown. She approached McLean as they plodded down the rutted trace.

"Cutler, Verity is ill. I know it. You can look at her and see it. We must find a place along the road where she can rest and recover. Is there such a one—an inn we will reach soon?"

"There is one on Albemarle Sound, a body of water we must cross by ferry." He looked at the swaying, slender figure of Verity and added roughly, "She should never have undertaken this trip so soon after the birth of her child."

"I canot blame her," Savarra retorted. "She belongs with my father and we must see that she reaches him."

At the inn on Albemarle Sound they secured rooms, and none too soon, for Verity's fever rose higher and hotter with each passing hour, until she rambled incoherently in her speech.

Savarra arranged to be in the room with her, for her anxiety was great. Cotty, Tiqua and Clarissa with the baby were in an adjoining room. Surely Verity would rally in a few days—they must stay there until she recovered and could resume her journey.

Belion was very concerned, his love for Verity still all too apparent. He haunted Savarra with questions as she, Cotty and Tiqua bathed and worked over Verity.

There was a fat, jolly woman with red cheeks and bright black eyes who was the innkeeper's wife, and she proved to

be a fund of medical information. Her name was Esme
Duncan, and she examined Verity carefully, then cheerily
pronounced, " 'Tis only the last of the summer fevers. She
is thin but wiry and she will weather this."

Savarra was not so sure during the days she sat at the
bedside, bathing Verity's burning face. But time crept by,
and Esme Duncan brewed beef broth and was able to spoon
a good bit of it into Verity. Still, the hours dragged and
Verity's recovery seemed painfully slow to Savarra. Cotty and
Clarissa had become fast friends and they alternated caring
for the baby, but the men were restless and anxious to be
moving again.

They had been at the inn over a week when Savarra left
Verity to the ministrations of Cotty, Tiqua and Clarissa and
came down late to dine. It was dark outside and stormy.
Rain beat against the shutters of the inn, but there was a
blazing fire on the hearth and candles gleamed on the long,
polished table.

Kitty, Esme and Joe Duncan's daughter, came in and set
the table for her, remarking languidly that the men had
already dined and were gone to their rooms, as well as the
women. But the girl was mistaken.

McLean came stomping in the door, shaking rain from his
cape and hat and saying brusquely, "Kitty, I'm hungry as a
wolf. I'll dine with Mistress Savarra—set a place for me."

He strode to the fire and stood there, letting the heat dry
the dampness in his leather breeches and coat. He said shortly,
"Thank God they've a good stable here for the horses." His
finely woven white shirt was open and the strong column of
his throat was dark against it, his hair tumbled and curling
from the wet night air. His penetrating gray eyes fastened on
Savarra from under black brows. "How is Verity?"

"Much better. She is anxious to get up and leave, but
Esme says she should wait two more days to regain her
strength."

He said broodingly, "We have come too far to take her
back to Charles Town—though God knows that's where she
needs to be. 'Tis but a short journey to Yorktown now."

"I know," Savarra said. She wore a butter-yellow woolen
dress which she had donned this morning, thinking of Mc-
Lean as she did so. She did not have a kerchief tucked about
her breast and now she was glad, knowing that the yellow
set off her ivory cleavage and heightened her brilliant azure
eyes. She had not done up her hair and it spilled in an ebony

tide about her shoulders and down her back, vividly contrasting with the sunny yellow dress. She noted that McLean was still looking at her, desire and hostility mingling in the slate eyes.

He said acrimoniously, "You know on reaching the vicinity of Yorktown, we men will join the American and French forces there. It seems a fool's errand—you ladies trying to join Lord Bainbridge in a beleaguered city. I was a fool to agree to take you this far!"

"We must all do what our conscience dictates," Savarra said slowly, remembering how her father had *liked* McLean, admired him. Soon they would face each other over a blaze of gunfire, and her heart lurched downward at the thought.

"A very trite but astute observation," he said with that light mocking note in his voice, "from such an impetuous young lady."

She looked at him levelly. "You must know that, since my arrival in Carolina, my conscience has altered irreparably. I think this war is bloody and useless, brother against brother, Englishmen against other Englishmen. America should be given her freedom and all of us who are British should go home."

"You will," he said calmly. "A rider was by here this morning and he informed us that General Washington and our French allies are marching from Williamsburg, Virginia, on Yorktown to face the British." He laughed dryly, adding, "He said that Washington had issued flour to powder the American troops' hair and ordered them to look as neat and respectable as possible—clean-shaven as well, so the impeccable French soldiers would not put us to shame." He paused. "It will be impossible to get you and the ladies into Yorktown if heavy fighting is going on there when we arrive."

"Surely they will let us go under a flag of truce—four women, a tiny baby and two black servants!"

"Your certainty always amazes me, Savarra. In your riding with Marion, did you not see how battles go? Truces are rare and not always honored. Marion has sent men out to parley with the British under a flag of truce and they have never returned."

"From what I have seen of the patriots, they would certainly allow women and a baby to cross the lines. Once with my father, we shall be safe."

Kitty had brought meat and bread, stewed dried vegetables and a tankard of ale for McLean, before she disappeared into the kitchen once more. They ate, sitting across from each other, and Savarra was sharply aware of the powerful pull McLean had for her. She wondered angrily if he knew it.

She said, "It is hard for me, owing my life to you and being British—to think of my father exposing himself to your gun. Would you shoot him if he came within range of your rifle?"

McLean frowned, the dark winged brows coming together in a way that sent a sharp thrill through her. "I trust that event will not happen."

"But would you?" she persisted.

He took a deep draft of ale and set the tankard down. "What would you have me do, Savarra, if your father was bent on killing me?"

She paled slightly and her voice shook. "The thought frightens me, for I do not know. I only know I love him dearly—"

"And you have little use for me," he put in shortly. "That should answer your question."

Tension between them drew tighter, and Savarra was conscious of his big body, his fine drawn lips, the lean browned face. She knew well enough what she wanted of him. Her body ached with it and she was edgy and furious with herself. But he had made a woman of her more than a year ago now, a full-blooded passionate woman. It was his fault, not hers, she told herself.

The dining room of the inn was dark and warm from the blazing logs on the huge hearth. Between the flames and the candles on the table, the food-scented room was intimate and cozy. Inexplicably, Savarra felt a lump form in her throat, and she blinked rapidly at the hot prickle behind her eyes. Over the cheerful snap of the fire, cold wind and rain could be heard buffeting the inn.

The two continued to eat in silence, but for the howl of wind in the eaves. It was October sixth, and Savarra did not see how troops could do battle in such weather. This was the night that General George Washington was to make his first move, marching out a column of forty-three hundred men in the midst of this cold rainstorm, to where they would halt in the darkness only eight hundred yards from the British trenches. Then fifteen hundred patriots would begin digging a new trench some two thousand yards long, running from the head of Yorktown Creek near the center of the British position in a long arc to the right and ending on the bluff overlooking the York River. The siege of Yorktown had already begun.

Kitty came from the kitchen slowly, straightening to thrust her bosom out as she looked at McLean. "Here's yer pastry, ma'am—sir," she said, putting down a thick plate with two tarts upon it. She eyed McLean and licked her lips, adding, " 'Tis ma's best—apples were dried, but they plump up mighty fine fer ma."

"Thank you, Kitty," he said, his smile white, eyes twinkling at the obvious flirtation directed at him.

When the girl had swayed from the room, he looked at Savarra with a touch of mischief and slowly winked at her. But Savarra was wrestling with her conscience. She was no better than this tavern wench in her reaction to the man across from her. She thought of him too often. Her eyes had strayed to him as they had journeyed along, while he had never given her any encouragement beyond his astonishing tenderness on that burning August night. If only she could forget that!

A wry smile touched her lips faintly at the thought. She knew only too well that was impossible. McLean had marked her, made her his—and yet no word of love had been spoken between them. It was this that rankled, made her heart-sore. *Like animals,* she thought. *Oh, but when my father and I return to England, I will forget him fast enough!* Verity and her little brother would be with them then, but the knowledge did not cheer her. She looked at McLean somberly as they finished the tarts and rose from the table.

"I will light you to your room," he said courteously, and there was hard restraint in the dark face as he took up one of the candles. There was a distant rumble of thunder, and occasionally a sharp thrust of light flickered through the closed shutters as lightning slashed the sky.

McLean took her arm, and it seemed to her that every nerve in her body concentrated where his flesh pressed hers. She swayed involuntarily against him and they stood transfixed, so near and yet so far apart. There was a weakness in her thighs and a warmness between them, a desperate hunger that was both frightening and triumphant filled her. The man looked in her shining eyes with surprise, and neither of them moved for a long moment.

Then slowly, slowly, as if he were afraid of breaking the magic of the moment, he set the candle down on the table and put his hands on her shoulders first, then slipped them warmly, gently over the open, scooped neck of her dress. When he moved them down about her waist and pulled her to him, her very bones were fluid. She flowed against him, her breasts pressing his broad chest, her head tipped back over his arm as she looked, heavy-lidded, into his clear gray eyes.

It seemed an eternity to her before his warm, smooth lips came down upon hers, and when they did, a flash of such joy filled her that it was almost pain. They clung together for a lifetime—and all in the brief moment of that kiss. His mouth grew more demanding and her lips parted. Passion filled her as he swept her up into his arms, forgetting the candle on the table, and carried her to the stairs.

"We will go to my room, Savarra—God, how sweet you are to kiss!" He took the stairs, and her heart beat wildly. She wanted him more than she had ever wanted anything in her life, but as he took the stairs in great steps, a semblance of restraint crept into her. She began to struggle feebly. He had not said he loved her—he offered her nothing but a night of wild delight, and that was suddenly not enough.

"Put me down," she said huskily. "I cannot go to your room and do—what you wish."

"What *you* wish, as well," he said, his low laughter slightly jeering. "You may be an imperious English noblewoman and much too good for a common American, my dear, but you are flesh and blood and you want me as much as I want you."

She struggled harder as he reached the top of the stairs, panic seizing her, for there was none of the tenderness he had shown the first time. His arms were like iron and they tightened as her struggles increased. He meant to take her by force if necessary, and fear and resentment flooded her.

"You put me down," she spoke between her teeth, "or I shall scream to wake the dead!"

"Why this sudden modest retreat? Savarra, you have been luring me since the moment we came together again," he said angrily. "And you know it well."

He spoke the truth, but the pride that was so deeply ingrained in her refused to let her succumb like a wanton. Cutler McLean offered her nothing, not marriage, not love—and in that instant, sudden, blinding revelation swept her. She loved him, had loved him from the moment he first took her. She was limp in his arms from the shock of it.

"That's better," he murmured, opening the door to his room as he held her pliant body in his arms. It was black and lightless in the room, and he bumped against a chair as he felt his way to the bed and laid her upon it. In an instant he had struck flint to the candle, and giant shadows leaped about the room.

The lashing rain and wind were suddenly forlorn in her ears, comfortless and chilling, and Savarra sat up, her limbs shaking with the fury of her emotions. She looked at the tall, powerful man before her as he began to unbutton his white shirt. Putting her feet on the steps that led up to the high bed, she rose.

She said quietly, "I cannot do this, Cutler. Your accusation is quite correct and honor demands that I confess it. But I am not a woman to be taken lightly and you have taken me—lightly—once before."

"I did not take you lightly, madame. While we are confessing, I will say my enjoyment of you was deep. I have never known a woman like you—as desirable as you, for all your high and mighty bloodlines. And since we are such poles apart, why not take our pleasure in each other while we can?"

Still he had not said what she wanted so desperately to hear, and she would not abase herself to ask for it. She stood straight and tall, swallowing back tears of disappointment. "I cannot stay with you," she said, her voice trembling, "and I do not think you cruel enough to rape me."

He stood before her, his broad chest with the curling black hair upon it, his muscled shoulders strong and beautifully symmetrical. She had never wanted him so greatly in her life, but she moved toward the door and he did not stop her.

As she reached it, she turned to look back and found his eyes flat and cold. "Damn your pride and your noble blood that fancies you better than me. Go on to your empty bed —and sleep well." His voice was harsh and bitter, and Savarra fled, tears burning her eyes.

She stood for a long time outside the door to the room she shared with the women, fighting to control herself. When at last she opened the door, she found a single candle burning, and Clarissa was nursing her small brother. Verity, having been served a full meal followed by peppermint tea, was fast asleep.

Spent, Savarra disrobed immediately and got into bed beside Verity, but sleep was not so easy to come by. She lay wakeful until the rain stopped and only the cry of the wind came cold and wailing to her ears. She had made a soul-shaking discovery in the knowledge that she loved Cutler

McLean with a passion that would last a lifetime, would have kept her in America as long as she lived, but he did not return that love.

The future stretched out before her, barren and sear, and she felt she would live her lifetime unfulfilled. She had never known such loneliness.

Two days later the little entourage was on its way once more. Verity was even paler, thinner, but the indomitable eyes were unchanged. She would go to her husband or die in the effort. The rain and clouds had cleared away, but the wind was bitter cold and all of them were uncomfortable as they followed the rutted trace toward Norfolk, where they would have to circle a wide bay into which the James River ran. Verity knew vaguely that, once they reached Williamsburg, the way to Yorktown should be clear.

She silently cursed her weakness as she rode beside Savarra. Her will was iron, but her limbs were trembling by the time the first day was drawing to a close. She clamped her lips on complaints and rode stoically with the others. She would not become ill again, she would *not!* McLean and Belion stopped frequently for her to rest, which was all that made it possible for her to stay in the saddle the entire day.

Toward evening, as they neared an inn McLean and Belion had set for their goal, a flock of geese were flushed from a marshy area nearby. Like a flash, Thad and Gabe fired as rapidly as they could reload. The result was six fat geese, which they roasted over an open fire before dark, and everyone ate hungrily.

This was just as well, for the inn Belion and McLean took them to was small and food was scarce. The owners grumbled about being caught in the middle, having been raided by both tories and patriots. Their rooms were cramped and boasted only the barest minimum for sleeping. The mattresses were stuffed with dried corn shucks which afforded little comfort and smelled abominably despite rough, clean linen. All the women were in one large room containing three hand-hewn beds, and the shutters on the two high windows banged dismally. Clarissa and the baby were in one bed, Verity and Savarra were to occupy the second, Cotty and Tiqua the third.

Shivering in her petticoat, Cotty said plaintively, "These blankets are turrible thin."

"They are indeed," Savarra agreed, picking up one of the

offending blankets. "We shall all have to put our cloaks over them."

Verity looked at her in the dim light of the single candle and smiled. "You are hardy as any patriot, Savarra," she said admiringly, "and use your head as well." The candle flickered wildly in the drafty room.

Savarra laughed shortly as the two of them, wearing long flannel nightdresses over petticoats to keep out the cold, climbed into the pungent bed and pulled their fur-lined cloaks over them. "I have learned a great deal since coming to America," she replied, putting a thumb over the candle.

Verity lay beside her, warming rapidly and thinking of the bitterness in the voice of the girl who had become her stepdaughter. Something was troubling Savarra. She had not been sleeping well, for there was a faint darkness beneath the brilliant blue eyes. Too, the young girl had become fiercely protective of Verity and had insisted on sleeping beside her each night. Verity, who slept lightly, had been aware of the turning and tossing beside her. She had first feared it was herself and her baby son that worried the suddenly maternal girl, for she knew well that Savarra had come to love them both dearly.

But then Verity had watched Savarra's eyes seek the hard profile of Cutler McLean, and there was rebellion and despair in the black-lashed blueness when they found him.

Verity lay quite still. She was remembering all those weeks Savarra had been gone. How she had worried about the girl —until she remembered that Tyler Belion and Cutler McLean were with her. How many weeks had she spent in McLean's company? McLean and Savarra—was it possible?

"Savarra—"

"What?" the girl asked alertly.

Verity was silent. She realized suddenly that she could not ask Savarra if she loved McLean. If the young girl wanted anyone to know, it would surely have been Verity in whom she confided. "I—I—" she sought substitute words.

"Are you thinking of Charlest'n?"

How the girl's clipped, British voice had altered in the seventeen months since she debarked from her English frigate! "I—yes. It has been a long—journey."

"Are you homesick, Verity?" The whisper was full of concern now.

"No. I am only glad to be so much nearer your father—" She was interrupted by a whimper from her baby son in the bed next to hers. Then silence came as Clarissa popped a fat nipple into the baby's mouth. Thank you, Lord, thought Verity, for Clarissa. Little James had comforted that plump little mother whose daughter had been stillborn, even as she comforted him with her abundant and nourishing milk. "I am sorry if I wakened you, dear," Verity whispered. "It is only that I find it difficult to sleep at times."

"Take heart, darling," was the sturdy response. "Cutler—Tyler says 'tis but a few more hours' ride to Williamsburg. He—they say we shall circle round Jamestown and take a ferry across the James River, then ride to Williamsburg." Savarra's whisper surged with hope and comfort. "We shall soon be with my father."

But Verity was remembering the ferry across Albemarle Sound, a dreadful, rough raftlike thing of logs lashed together and covered with rough planking. The patriots who manned it looked very much like the outliers to Verity, bearded and ragged and spitting tobacco downwind with hearty regularity. Three of them there had been, and they were full of news which they shouted to Cutler and his men.

". . . hundreds o' gabions filled with earth—an' within a hour the ditch was already three foot deep, protected by the mound o' fresh dug dirt," shouted one, as he plied his paddle. He had an eye that was slightly cocked, which made Verity feel a little odd when she looked into his face. "An' th' British gunners fired a few rounds, 'tis said, an' a huge white English bulldog come a lopin' out, chasin' the cannonballs. This sojer said th' American officers ordered some o' their men to catch the dog so's they could send a message inter Yorktown." All three of the ferrymen broke into roaring laughter as the one finished, "But them sojers was scarder o' that big mean-lookin' beast, his jaw all slung out under teeth like knives, than they was o' the British. They just let 'im run back!"

"So the siege is under way already," McLean said loudly, for the wind across the broad sound carried it away.

"Sure," yelled a second ferryman. "On October ninth, our last passenger told us all the French an' American guns were in line. He said a deserter come out from Yorktown an' told our boys that Cornwallis had told his troops they'd naught ter fear since the Americans had brung up no heavy guns an' the French fleet was afeared ter attack. He said ol' Henry Knox an' his gunners sure enjoyed that story, because our front was full o' huge guns, half-a-dozen heavy mortars, two eight-inch howitzers and six other siege guns, three of 'em twenty-four-pounders."

They had talked on, yelling back and forth among themselves, and the tenor of their comments had disturbed Verity deeply. Lord Bainbridge was in extreme danger, and she knew frustration because none of them spoke of how she and those with her could pass through the siege lines and into Yorktown.

Now she felt in the bedclothes for Savarra's hand and found it, firm and warm beneath the blankets and their fur-lined cloaks. "I am so afraid for James," she whispered. "Those ferrymen on Albemarle Sound talked as if there were no escape for the British army."

"My father has been a soldier since he was scarcely seventeen," Savarra said reassuringly. "He will come out of this and we shall all go home to England, where you shall be Lady Bainbridge and preside over two country manors and a town house—and raise my little brother to be the next Lord Bainbridge."

Warm at last, Verity took heart from the young and certain voice. There was a strength and determination in Savarra equal to her own and each strengthened the other.

Twenty-One

To Verity's relief, crossing the James River in a cold, crisp wind proved much simpler than crossing Albemarle Sound, for the distance was not nearly so great and the two ferrymen were taciturn and silent. They had acquired another horse, a plodding beast, from a farmer before reaching the river, and now Amos, with Tiqua behind him, was mounted upon it and the two bays were carrying only baggage, which was considerable. McLean paid the ferrymen in gold from the pouch Savarra had turned over to him on Verity's request, and they directed him on the shortest route to Williamsburg.

"There's heavy fightin' at Yorktown, captain, sir," one of

them said after learning their destination. "You'd be wise to leave the ladies in Williamsburg—'tis in our hands, y'know."

Verity spoke up firmly, "I will not be left in Williamsburg, Cutler—Tyler. I have not traveled so far to be frustrated at the end of my journey."

The men said nothing, but when they set out for Williamsburg she noted McLean's jaw was grimly set, and she could not stem the perturbation that welled up in her at the thought of being denied entry to Yorktown.

On arriving at Williamsburg in Virginia, they found a bee-hive of activity. There were government officials, meetings being held in a great red-brick building, soldiers and civilians coming and going, and everyone was in a state of high excitement. The news from Yorktown was all good for the patriot cause. Verity found her reaction profoundly disturbing. She was American to the last drop of blood, yet unwillingly, secretly, she yearned to hear that Lord Bainbridge was triumphing.

They stopped and ate at Christina Campbell's tavern and had the best meal they had enjoyed since their stay at Esme and Joe Duncan's inn. There was roast duckling and dressing, with fresh autumn greens grown in back of the tavern and plucked only that morning. There were light, hot breads and country butter, and Verity ate with a building appetite. Even the custard pie was superlative and she had two slices.

Savarra looked at her approvingly. "You will soon gain back your lost weight, Verity dear, if you eat like this."

Verity smiled, her eyes warm on her stepdaughter. She felt so close to Savarra, and the nagging instinctual knowledge that the girl had lost her heart to McLean worried her, for the man was all business now and had little to say to Savarra. Indeed, he seemed to avoid her company when he could.

They stayed a day and a night in Williamsburg and arranged for Amos and Tiqua to stay at the Campbell Tavern with other servants. Both seemed relieved to remain, but Amos looked at them apprehensively as they prepared to leave.

"You goin' to come back an' get us, cap'n?"

"To be sure, Amos," he replied reassuringly, pressing his heels against Jed's flanks as they began the short journey to Yorktown.

Verity's impatience rose with every mile they covered. The air was bracing and cool, but the early morning sunlight was a golden flood over the countryside. All were singularly silent, each somewhat preoccupied as they traversed the broad and even road to Yorktown. It had been pounded by thousands of soldiers and very heavy artillery as they beat their way down it to the battle that was now in progress. Verity's impatience rose. She might well be in Lord Bainbridge's arms tonight, and the thought made her a little lightheaded. She traveled the miles in a dream of the moment she would run into his arms.

Toward late afternoon they drew near their destination, and there came to their ears the thunder of guns, which struck fresh fear to Verity's heart. She had known the battle was in progress, but somehow that she would hear the actual sound of it had not impressed itself upon her. Now her mouth went dry with apprehension and she swallowed repeatedly, finally asking Tyler Belion for a sip of his canteen, which did no good—for her mouth was dry immediately after.

As they entered a thick stand of pines on the turning road, they came face-to-face with a small troop of mounted French soldiers, impressive in their white uniforms trimmed with blue and gold. They looked dapper and were extremely courteous. One of them spoke English fluently. McLean introduced himself and engaged him in conversation.

"*Oui, capitain,* you are but two miles from Yorktown. We cannot allow you to come much nearer."

"But I have Brigadier General Lord Bainbridge's daughter and wife and son. They have come to be with him—at great effort and distress. They must be allowed to enter the British lines under a flag of truce."

The French lieutenant's brows soared. "*Mon Dieu, capitain,* you do not know what you ask! We have very nearly destroyed the city already. Just on October tenth, we permitted an old man to come from Yorktown—his house was destroyed —he had nowhere to go. He hobbled to our lines led by servants, and was reputed to be the uncle of Virginia's Governor, Thomas Nelson."

"Then both sides are honoring flags of truce?" McLean said quickly.

The lieutenant shook his head doubtfully. "The old man barely escaped with his life—he is the only one who—it was a lull—a small lull in the fighting. He brought word the British headquarters have now been driven into a cave in the marl bluff at the riverside. Though a British relief fleet is expected, the shelling has battered the town to pieces. Thousands of horses have been slaughtered, and casualties among the troops and camp followers are rising." Then cheerfully, "He said that the British are a good deal dispirited."

"I must get to my husband," Verity put in, her soft voice laced with iron and her eyes darkly determined.

"You should turn back, madame," the French lieutenant said politely. "Your life will be sorely endangered, and that of your servants and your small son."

"I do not care. I will be with Lord Bainbridge. *I will!*" Her delicate brows drew together and there was such strength in her voice that the young lieutenant was at a loss for words.

McLean cut in. "Lieutenant Auvergne, let us take her to the American lines and see if we can arrange her entry by a flag of truce. There are only four women—the wet nurse, Lord Bainbridge's wife and daughter, her maid—and, of course, the baby—who need safe passage. Then we four men," he nodded at Gabe, Thad and Belion, "will join the American and French troops to fight alongside them."

The lieutenant again shook his head, the snapping black eyes skeptical. "We will welcome your aid, *capitain*, but you cannot know what a holocaust Yorktown is at present." He pulled thoughtfully at his little mustache, then said decisively, "I will escort you to our commander—we have been scouting this area for deserters, spies and runaways."

Thus they moved along, escorted by the clean and sharp French soldiers, and as they drew nearer to the siege lines the sound of battle grew. It was like a constant rolling thunder with the staccato sound of musketry intermingling its deadly accompaniment.

Nearer and nearer they cantered, and Verity's fears increased. What if they refused to let her go into the city under a flag of truce? She put the thought determinedly from her mind. Surely the commander, whoever he might be, would allow them to enter. They would go straight to the caves since the city was demolished, and British ships would come and take them away by way of the bay.

They could sail to England where it was peaceable and life could take up a happy rhythm. With the thought, she looked across to Savarra with a tremulous smile. But the English girl's face was grim, her cobalt eyes narrowed in the late sunlight as she peered at the smoke of battle, which was plainly visible now.

McLean and Belion rode forward at an increased pace and the French soldiers, who had an eye for the women, nudged their horses closer to them, speaking in their courteous manner. A slim handsome one with a drooping black mustache murmured, "Madame, *pas à vite. Lentement, lentement—vous*—you 'ave zee great impatience."

Verity smiled at him briefly, "I am anxious to reach my husband."

His white smile widened, but it was plain that he did not understand.

Now they were among the tents and camps of the followers of the French and American forces. Cooks, boy drummers and bootblacks, black women and menservants, white women —some in fine clothing, others obvious drabs—stared at them briefly, then went about their chores of tending the wounded who lay upon the ground.

Verity looked desperately above the trees—that smoke was still a mile away. Dear God, how many wounded there were here! And these men were supposed to be winning. How much worse must it be beyond them in Yorktown! She glanced at Savarra once more, and now the English girl met her eyes, her own naked with worry. They passed a large tent with harassed orderlies moving in and out. Groans rose about them as they moved forward. There was not enough room in the makeshift hospital and the wounded spilled out and lay on the ground about it.

"We have not suffered so many wounded as the British, they tell us," the French lieutenant said encouragingly, smiling at the women. "But your papa—your husband, madame, he is a general, you say. He will not be one of the wounded. They stay to the rear—"

"My father is first a soldier," Savarra said briefly. "He will not remain to the rear."

"Don't say that!" Verity said sharply, and Savarra looked at her with compassion and love and shook her head. Verity, aware that the girl knew her father better than she, quailed within herself at the sudden vision of Lord Bainbridge riding his horse into the steady roar of the gunfire beyond them.

"Wait here, ladies—*capitain*," Lieutenant Auvergne said as they halted on the trampled turf and offal beneath the last outposts of towering pines. Far ahead of them lay a plain and beyond that the long trenches filled with men, firing, reloading and firing once more. Great mortars were mounted upon platforms hastily thrown up, and they shook the earth as they roared forth their message of destruction while the Continentals, mingling with the dapper French soldiers, swarmed about them. Even as they watched, Verity saw two men spin about, struck by fire from the British. The lieutenant concluded, "I will bring *mon colonel,* Alexander Hamilton, to speak of madame's proceeding under a flag of truce. He is in charge of French troops." And he galloped off.

McLean urged his horse toward the women and spoke loudly to be heard over the din of gunfire. "Ladies, please ride further back among the trees. I fear a stray shot might find a mark among you."

The baby began to cry as they moved back among the trees, followed by the four tall riflemen on their well-trained horses. The nurse said cautiously, " 'Tis all them guns, mistress! They got him feared." Her plump face screwed up as a distant cannon roared.

"Give him the breast," Verity said forcefully. "That will quiet him."

"With all them French sojers lookin'?" Clarissa glanced furtively at the young men who were looking interestedly at her.

"Do it beneath your cloak. No one will see," Verity replied, and the girl did as she was bid, shifting her cloak about her in such a way that it covered both her breast and the baby.

After that, there was a tense silence. Gabe and Thad sat their horses negligently, their rifles lying across their thighs with careful carelessness. Belion moved restlessly, his eyes swinging from Verity to the distant trenches. McLean spoke to him, but Verity could not hear what they were saying as they sat their horses side by side in front of her. There was excitement in the lines of the four big bodies, alertness in the swing of their broad shoulders, tautness in the muscled thighs.

Her eyes met Savarra's bitter glance and there was unspoken agreement between them. *She knows,* Verity thought, *she knows all four of them can hardly wait to join their comrades facing the hell of fire beyond!*

She and Savarra had heard them as they rode through the woods, discussing Francis Marion and their exploits in South Carolina with Lieutenant Auvergne. He had been impressed, ejaculating *"Mais oui*—we know of Francis Marion, the swamp fox—even in Massachusetts we heard of him." Then proudly, "He is French, *capitan.*"

McLean had grinned, drawling, "Yes, we know."

The sun was sinking lower in the west behind them now. Shadows were lengthening darkly beneath the trees and the men about them grew more restless. Some of the French scouting party cantered back into the trees, then returned, and Verity heard their impatient voices conversing in rapid-fire French. From admiring them as four pretty women, they were now regarding them as four nuisances. Verity's schoolgirl French informed her of the gist of their remarks. They had been interrupted in the performance of their duty, there was no guessing now how many spies, deserters or informants had escaped during this long wait among the trees. These ladies were not ordinary camp followers like the Colonel Sacherie's mistress, or the women who did laundry just to be near the men. They belonged to the enemy, though one was supposedly *Americaine*. What a bother they were—even though two of them could no doubt become a colonel's mistress if they so desired. Verity felt blood mount her cheeks and was thankful for the lowering shadows.

Then before them, they saw between the great rough trunks of the pines two horsemen riding at breakneck speed across the plain that lay before the trenches. As they drew near, they recognized Lieutenant Auvergne. The other rider was a much smaller man, diminutive in fact, but as he drew up in the fading light of day, it could be seen that he was young and his eyes were blazing with anger.

As they drew to a halt, McLean moved his horse up before him smoothly and said, "Colonel Hamilton, our apologies for calling you from your duties—"

"Sir, we are preparing to storm the British redoubts between here and Yorktown. What is this idiocy about Lord Bainbridge's wife and son?"

"And his daughter and her maid and the baby's nurse, Colonel."

"Four women," he said disgustedly, his eyes falling upon them at that moment. "And Lieutenant Auvergne says you are a captain in Francis Marion's brigade—and that you are Lieutenant Belion of the same." The piercing eyes went to the other men. "And these are two of your men."

"That is right, sir" was the easy reply.

"Then what in God's name could persuade you on a fool's errand from Charles Town to Yorktown with four women and a baby in tow?"

McLean's even drawl broke in. "The desire to join you, Colonel Hamilton, once we have made an effort to reunite our lifetime friend, Verity Pair Bainbridge, with her husband." Then after a pause, "And of course, Lord Bainbridge's daughter, Savarra, and the two maidservants."

Hamilton's eyes softened as they rested on the baby in

Clarissa's arms. He was a head shorter than Belion and at least twelve inches below the tall McLean, but there was such command in his mien and power in his voice that he seemed to ride as high as they. "Madame, I cannot send you to the British lines under a flag of truce. You have come at a most unpropitious time. Fighting is continuous and we are on the eve of an assault of such proportions that any contact with the enemy is out of the question."

"Even if that enemy were to send forth a white flag?" Verity asked pleadingly.

Hamilton's smile was wintry. "You fancy your husband and Cornwallis are ready to surrender, Lady Bainbridge? If you could guarantee that, we could cease fire immediately."

"She did not say that!" Savarra's clipped voice became very British and sharp as a sword. Then with cold hauteur, "My father would never surrender—but he would send forth a white flag to permit me, my stepmother, my brother and our servants to come to him." Her words were punctuated by the thunder of cannon followed immediately by the dull boom of mortars. Now that darkness was falling, the red flashes of the shot were clearly to be seen, thick and hot.

Hamilton's flashing eyes were admiring, but his reply was blunt. "I think your father would be the last one to permit such danger to any of you ladies. No one could guarantee your safety under present circumstances—why, madame, you have but to look at our lines to see that!"

Verity's shoulders drooped and her small, white face was despondent. She was heartsick to be so near and yet be unable to go to her beloved. "If there should come a lull—" she began haltingly, "if word could be got to Lord Bainbridge—"

"I cannot give you such hope, Lady Bainbridge. We Americans and French have waited too long for his moment."

"I am American—" Verity began, but Alexander Hamilton cut her off.

"I think not. You have married yourself out of us. You and your servants—and you, mistress," his eyes flicked the enraged Savarra, "will wait behind the lines. You will return to the tents and I will have Lieutenant Auvergne arrange for you to share one with the other—women and camp followers."

"But if there should come a moment," Verity begged, "if the firing should cease—"

"Verity, do not lower yourself to beg this man," Savarra said icily. "He has no—compassion."

Hamilton bowed courteously in the saddle. "I am most compassionate, madame. But since you are unable to realize your danger I must decide for you, and I have decided that you will remain behind the lines until we have received a British surrender. Then you will be reunited with your father."

"You will never receive *that*, sir." Savarra's blue eyes were narrow and sparkling in the last of the twilight.

"But we shall, madame," Hamilton replied with equal arrogance. Then turning to Lieutenant Auvergne he said, "You will escort the ladies back to camp and you—" he looked at the four Carolina riflemen in their plain leather breeches and coats, the worn tricornes on their dark heads, "you will come with me."

Belion turned to Verity. "Do not despair, Verity," he said quickly. "Stay in camp, where we can find you—and I swear the moment there is a change, I will come for you and your son."

McLean drawled laconically, "And try not to do anything rash, Savarra—curb your natural instincts for once and stay with Verity. She needs you."

The young girl gave him one scathing glance, but Verity saw the quivering lip held fast by small white teeth as they turned back. Colonel Alexander Hamilton and the four Carolinians rode off at a gallop into the fast-closing darkness, and Lieutenant Auvergne spoke briskly in French to his men. They all retraced their path to camp.

Supper fires were burning brightly, and Verity realized suddenly that she was very hungry. It was growing quite cold now that darkness had fallen. Auvergne introduced them to a full-breasted, blowzy young woman with a bucktoothed but ready smile. "Lady Bainbridge, this is Justine Danielle, and she will see that you ladies are properly housed—ah—during your stay with the armies."

Justine had a bright red kerchief tied over her dark head and she spoke with a marked French accent. *"Soyez le bienvenue!* But welcome, *mesdames*. I 'ave 'eard about you. So sad, zee leetle one cannot see his papa," she went on volubly, "but eet weel soon be ovair, you shall see! Come— you may share my tent wiz me and I weel see you get some food. Not so good maybe as you are used to, but eet weel nourish you, you shall see."

Lieutenant Auvergne wheeled his big gelding and with his men was gone in the dusk. Looking about her at the scraps and dregs of humanity that followed the French and American armies, Verity drew her cloak closer. She felt cold, and a pulse throbbed in the pit of her empty stomach. The hard regular strokes were like a hammer, and her eyes again sought Savarra, who was dismounting.

The English girl said curtly, "Justine, we do not wish to lose our mounts. We will want someone to look after them while we remain here."

"Blenchie!" Justine yelled, her big square teeth gleaming in the firelight as she smiled. A young black lad sprinted up to them." "Blenchie, take care of zeze four 'orses for ze ladies." Justine bent her ready smile on all of them with equal warmth, and Blenchie took the reins to Savarra's mount first.

"You will see he is fed, Blenchie?" Savarra said anxiously, and Verity knew that the girl had no wish to be afoot among this rag-tag-bobtailed mixture of humanity. No more did she.

"Yes'm, I sure will. We ain't got nothin' to feed horses, but there's a pasture 'bout half a mile away with good grass. I'll stake 'em out there."

Verity got stiffly down from her horse. Her body ached slightly, but she felt so much stronger than she had when they embarked on this journey that she made no complaint. Clarissa and Cotty, silent for once, dismounted, and Blenchie took all the horses by the bridles and led them away in the darkness.

The fragance of cooking meat and bread and some sort of spice floated in the still, cold air. Justine kept up a running chatter as she showed the girls into the large tent in which there were but two cots. "We can make ze pallets wiz canvas on ze ground. But you weel have to keep warm wiz your cloaks," she gave a Gallic shrug, "for we have no blankets, *mes amies*. Keeping warm is hard to do—especial when eet rains."

She chattered on as Verity and the others put their small packets of luggage down on the dirt floor of the tent. They had cut down their belongings to the utmost, leaving the balance with Amos and Tiqua at the Campbell Tavern in Williamsburg. It developed that Justine was in love with a French soldier, a Lieutenant Etienne Doumet, and had followed him all the way to America. She had performed the staggering feat of marching behind the French Army all the way from Connecticut, following her lover. She cared for his uniforms, doing all his cleaning and mending, and cooked for him when he was off duty. Now she was preparing dried beans in a large black pot over the fire. "I 'ave cook them all day. Tender!" she rolled her eyes. "Juicy. You shall see!"

Later, the girls were greatly relieved to find that the food, which sounded so drab, was delicious. Justine had seasoned the beans and stewed dried fruit in another pot, and there was crusty French bread baked in a queer little oven right over the fire. When at last they all bedded down in the confines of the tent, their fatigue was so great, sleep overtook them at once.

However, at two in the morning they were rudely awakened by a great racket outside the tent, people bellowing raucously and running toward the front. Verity immediately assumed the British had attacked—and Lord Bainbridge would be with them. She sat bolt upright to find that Justine was hastily donning her thick cotton dress and heavy jacket. The others roused one by one, Clarissa and Cotty making frightened cries, only to be shushed by Savarra. Little James, jostled rudely by the excited Clarissa, began wailing, but that young woman immediately thrust a nipple in his mouth and he was silent.

"What is happening?" Verity asked Justine. "Are we under attack?"

"I'll go see, madame. You—all of you wait 'ere," and she darted from the tent. The others began to dress quickly for, whatever was happening, it demanded action of some kind.

Justine returned in a state of wild excitement. *"Vite, vite!* Come and see—the sky is afire!"

Galvanized to speed, the girls dashed out of the tent and saw to the northeast great flames leaping into the sky, their orange fury brilliant against the night sky. All the camp followers were out, some still in night clothes, staring fascinated at the holocaust.

"What is it?" Savarra asked.

Justine replied excitedly, "One of Lieutenant Auvergne's men came in and told us that Cornwallis is burning a dozen or more of his own vessels in Yorktown harbor. And our French gunners have heated red-hot shot and fired into the remaining fleet—they are going up like tinder and the bombardment of Yorktown eeze weethout stop. Zee town is leveled, they say!"

"But surely the British fleet will come to their rescue!" Verity blurted.

Justine looked at her with mingled pity and satisfaction. "*Non, madame*. Our French fleet has the whole of Chesapeake Bay bottled up. *Bien*—they are giving aid to our men—zee French and *Américaine*—by shelling zee British from zee bay."

Verity watched transfixed. Somewhere in that hell of mortars, howitzers and cannon fire, Lord Bainbridge was rallying his men with Lord Cornwallis. The sound was a distant roar, and from the encampment they could actually see the torrent of fire which spread with vivid brightness among the combustible rigging of the tall-masted ships. Cornwallis must be desperate to burn his own ships for fear of them falling into the hands of the Americans and being turned against him. Verity stood observing the fiery sky, her heart aching and her anxiety for Lord Bainbridge growing insidiously. It was easy to see now that no flag of truce could be seen or honored in the hell of fire that was constantly exchanged between the beleaguered British and the attacking allies.

The women stood a long time watching flames consume ships as they licked up tall masts, observing the brilliant flash of heavy gunfire and smaller flares as muskets were fired. It was near dawn before they returned to the tent to sleep for two more hours.

All four women and the baby spent two more days in the company of Justine Danielle, whose unfailing good humor was but a faint antidote for their gloom. It was October fifteenth, but two miles from the girls, when Cornwallis finally confessed for the first time that his plight was hopeless. But Verity's wait was not to be so easily finished.

In the early and misty morning of the sixteenth, Justine's Etienne Doumet rode into camp, rousing his faithful Justine and bidding her fix him something to eat. Waking also and hastily donning their clothing, Savarra and Verity joined the two at the campfire, leaving the deeply slumbering Clarissa, the baby and the drowsy Cotty in their pallets.

When they approached, Justine looked up and said, "*Alors, mesdames*, there has been a beeg fight in our own trenches. *Parlez anglais*, Etienne, zee ladies weel want to know of thees."

The girls looked into the powder-blackened face of the

young French lieutenant. He was a tall, thin young man, handsome in a cold aristocratic fashion, and Verity thought fleetingly that he was the kind who would use Justine, then marry a duke's daughter. But he smiled charmingly at the two of them, revealing teeth that gleamed whitely in his blackened face.

"Ah, madame—et madame, I 'ave been telling Justine that *au nuit*—that is, by night, the British sent over three hundred men to fall upon us and spike our guns, and they were very nearly successful. It was a surprising and brave sortie. They killed twenty of our men and spiked 'alf a dozen cannon."

"Oh!" Savarra cried, "Who—which of our men were killed?"

"Our men? *Madame*—Justine tells me you are British—"

"I mean who was killed on either side?" Savarra flushed in the early dawn, and Verity knew she was thinking not only of her father but of McLean and his men.

"Alas, that I do not know. We killed about a dozen British and wounded a few. The man who led them was a general—a ver' brave man. He was gravely wounded. Our French surgeon is treating him."

"A general?" Verity asked quickly, "What was his name?"

Etienne Doumet shrugged, eyeing the frying meat in the skillet and sniffing the cold air. "That I do not know, madame, for which I apologize, for Justine has told me you are the American wife of a British general."

Verity's fears took an upward bound and the palms of her hands grew moist. Looking about, she saw other grimy-faced soldiers coming from the woods and other campfires being lit. There were a great number of women in this forest of tents and Verity thought humbly that she could not look down upon one of them, for she was no better than they, each following after some soldier, be he high or low.

"He was a ver' gallant general for I saw him fight to the last. It took three of our men to subdue—and wound—him."

"Did you see his hair?" Savarra asked abruptly. "Was he blond?"

Etienne smiled and shrugged again, *"Mais non, madame.* He wore a helmet and I was ver' busy myself with a mos' persisten' Englishman."

The pot containing the strong French coffee began to steam and the aroma was delicately inviting. Verity said abruptly, "I will have a cup of that before breakfast if I may, Justine?"

"But of course, madame. Wait but a moment longer for eet to reach proper flavor," and she turned to Etienne and began a steady stream of French, and Verity was able to understand how she had been able to communicate all the facts about them to Etienne in so short a time.

Etienne broke off and looked at the two girls courteously. "*Pardonnez, mesdames*, but Justine and I have not been together in many days—we 'ave much to speak of."

"Go right ahead," Savarra said moodily, sitting down on the interlaced limbs Justine had gathered to keep them and their skirts from the damp, cold earth. She looked at Verity, who sat close beside her, and said, "It does not have to be my father. There are many generals—"

"Not in Yorktown," Verity said, her voice breaking. "The only two I know of were your father and Lord Cornwallis."

Savarra said firmly, "They have received some reinforcements, I'm sure. You know they must have. There could be five generals for all we know."

"I think not," Verity said quietly.

"If 'twas my father, he is only wounded, Etienne says. Perhaps only enough to put him out of battle." Her voice rose with hope. "Perhaps we will soon be nursing him back to health."

Verity gave her a pale smile, her eyes loving. "Perhaps you are right, Savarra," but an icy kernel of doubt had taken root in her heart and a sick fear pervaded her body.

By noon, when Etienne had washed up, shaved and returned to his post at the front, Verity's limbs ached with anxiety and she had to force herself to eat the beans and rice that Justine had cooked.

"You mus' eat more, madame. You are *tres*—very thin, and there is no color in your cheeks today," she scolded. "Each of you ladies eat too small—not enough. Now Mam'selle Clarisse and Cotty—zey have zee *bon* appetite." She bent a warm glance on the two who were scraping their pewter plates, preparatory to a request for more. "Of course, you are feeding two, Clarisse," she added, her twinkling black eyes touching Verity who held her baby while Clarissa ate.

Clarissa had taken the baby back into the tent to nurse him and Savarra, Cotty and Justine were cleaning up, when there came from the woods two horsemen, one holding a drooping figure in a scarlet coat on the horse before him. The familiarity of their shapes struck Verity, who had just said, "Justine, I will take these to the creek and wash them this time—" and she broke off, plates poised in her hands.

"*Non, non, madame.* 'Tis too cold a chore on this day. I will—" She was halted by Verity's transfixed gaze. Savarra turned to look as well.

Then with a sudden violent gesture, Verity dropped the plates to the ground, picked up her heavy woolen skirts and began to run toward the riders. Savarra was close on her heels, dodging through the other campfires and their attendants. Heart pounding, breath short, Verity came up to Belion and McLean, the later holding the sagging figure of the wounded redcoated soldier. A startlingly white bandage was around his head and it was stained with blood. The hair, dark gold, gleamed in the noon sunlight. His eyes were closed, and for a moment she thought him unconscious.

"James!" she cried piercingly, "My darling—you are wounded."

The blue eyes opened slowly, focused with difficulty, and a rasping sound came from his throat as he formed the word, "Verity—"

McLean said, "The French surgeon said we might bring him to you—to nurse, Verity. He is—sorely wounded."

"His head?" she gasped.

"Nay. 'Tis but a flesh wound. 'Tis the one in his— abdomen that will—is serious."

"Get him to the tent at once. I will cleanse the wound and rebandage it."

Belion, masking his pity and love, said, "Nay, Verity, the French doctor, Hebert, has just done that. He has been given excellent care—but when we told him you and his son and daughter were waiting behind the lines, he begged to be taken to you. With Alexander Hamilton's permission, the doctor— agreed."

Verity knew a tightening of the premonition of disaster that had been with her for so many days now. It was an ache in her thighs, a congealing of blood all through her limbs. *They were not telling her the extent of James's wounds!*

"Father?" Savarra said, her voice quavering slightly, but her hand was firm as she reached for his. The clouded blue eyes swung to hers and a slight smile twitched his lips. "We will take such good care of you," she began earnestly, "you will recover in no time at all."

They had reached Justine's tent and Belion dismounted.

Putting his hands up to the drooping figure before McLean, the two men managed to get the wounded officer down. Carrying him gently between them, they entered the tent, Verity before them, and laid him on her own pallet. His fine features were almost as white beneath the tan as the bandage about his forehead.

"My darling," Verity bent over him, taking his hand in hers and putting it to her cheek where tears were wet, despite her steel will to turn them back. Again the eyes opened and this time they were a brilliant blue.

"My son," he whispered, "Captain McLean tells me you brought him with you?"

"Clarissa!" Verity rose immediately and at the tent opening called loudly, and the girl, who had been holding the child while conversing with a nearby wounded soldier, turned and hastened forward as Verity said, "Bring Lord Bainbridge's son to him!"

There were so many casualties brought in, that the many women and servants around them were inured to the sight and no one paid the slightest attention to the activity in Justine's tent. Only Cotty and Justine now came forward.

Verity took the baby in her arms, and in the gloom of the tent bent with him to the man who lay breathing heavily on the pallet. "Here he is, my love—see how much like you he is?".

It was too dark in the tent and Belion, who had followed, raised a back flap and October sunlight poured in, gilding curls on the little boy's head and those of his father as well. The sight of them together filled Verity with strange and all-encompassing joy, even as despair wrenched her, for it had come to her with unerring certainty that her beloved was a dying man.

"Ah, Verity, Verity," Lord Bainbridge murmured hoarsely. "He looks too much like me to be a handsome lad."

Verity swallowed at the thickness in her throat convulsively. "Indeed that is why he is so handsome a boy," she said, and put the small pink cheek down against the hard flat one, now bristly with beard unshaven this morning.

"But you, my dear," his voice was almost a whisper, "you are as beautiful as I remember you—how good of you to come all this way to me—so that I might see—" His breath failed and a shudder shook the broad frame.

Panic struck Verity. Holding the baby with one arm, she caught Lord Bainbridge's hand and registered the cold clamminess of it. "James, darling, we are going to nurse you back to health. You are out of this cursed war now, and Savarra and I will see to it that you get well and strong again."

He smiled faintly, "Nay, my love. I am finished—but do not grieve. Mine is a soldier's death for England. It has been inevitable and I have known for years it would be so. I am content."

Savarra knelt beside him. "Father, father! You must not talk so! You have been wounded before and you have recovered. You will live to fight again!"

He smiled at her, "My impetuous Savarra—so like your mother. Have you not learned from Lord Haverley—that all cannot be as you would will—"

"Damn him!" she burst out, confession flowing from her in a rush. "You were right all along, father, and I was a fool. I came all this way to tell you—to apologize to you for my stupidity. Can you forgive me?"

The others were standing beside the tent flap, the tall Belion and the taller McLean and the fluttering servants.

"Of course," Lord Bainbridge whispered with a fleeting smile. "It came to us by courier—the death of Peter Haverley in battle. You are well out of that liaison, my daughter." He looked from Savarra to his wife and the small perfect boy in her arms. "How good to be with those I love best at the end. I am a fortunate man."

Verity's tears flowed down her smooth cheeks, down her throat and into the small round collar of the pale blue woolen dress she wore, but her face was smooth. She would not distress him by contorting her features with the grief that was tearing her apart.

His breath became a rattle and he drew it with great difficulty. "Where is McLean?" he gasped.

"Here, sir," and McLean stepped into the tent.

"Thank you for interceding with Hamilton—now Savarra, you must give me a promise." And his daughter bent over him, her own tears falling fast. "You must promise to help Verity—to see that she and your little brother reach England and he inherits his estates. The new Lord Bainbridge," he said, the ghostly smile touching his lips. "You see, my dears, life goes on and it should not be spent in mourning—'tis better so." His breath grew rougher for he was in the final moments of his life.

Verity wanted to scream and beat her fists against the doors of heaven, rebelling against events that had blasted her dream of love, but she could only crouch there beside him, his son in her arms, her choked voice denying speech.

"I promise, father." Savarra had no handkerchief and she rubbed her eyes on the backs of her hands. Verity looked at her and recognized an agony almost as great as her own.

Lord Bainbridge rolled his head from side to side and muttered, "This war, so useless—so futile—Englishman against Englishman. God grant the wound heals in the years to come."

"It will, sir," McLean said suddenly. "We are too much alike and we are bound together by blood. In the end, our nations will be as brothers."

The breathing of the wounded man became more stertorous, more difficult, and the clouding eyes sought Verity and the baby again. "Let me hold him in my arms, Verity," he whispered, and she put the tiny bundle in the curve of his arm. He drew his son close, laying his cheek on the golden curls. "My son—my son—" he whispered, and suddenly he was gone.

Verity put her head down upon his chest, aware now of the broad bandages that covered his abdomen under the loosened breeches. She knew his life's blood had been slowly seeping out and that it was his character, his willpower that had forced him to live long enough to see his son and her—and Savarra.

For a long moment there was silence in the tent, the afternoon sunlight spilling through the back opening on the fair head of Lord Bainbridge.

Her tears ceased suddenly. She felt dry to her bones, as if there were no fluid in her body at all, only the great and desperate loss that filled her, so powerful, so all-consuming that it left nothing for tears. She wanted to lie down beside him and die herself. It was the strongest desire she had ever known, but at that moment the baby began to cry. She looked at him unseeingly for an instant, and in that instant love flooded her. She had *his* son! She must live to see Lord Bainbridge live again in that tiny morsel of humanity.

She glanced at Savarra to see that her brilliant blue eyes were dry, her mouth taut and the grief in her face too deep for tears. No one moved.

Then Savarra said harshly, "He is dead. My father is dead." But her control was astonishing. Her chin was set and courage flowed from her. Verity felt it in a wave and it lent strength to her. In her heart, she longed to burst into uncontrolled weeping, to curse the world and all wars, but Savarra, straight and strong, helped her face the moment.

McLean said low, "I'm glad we got him here in time. The doctor said we might, but he didn't guarantee it, and there were times during that last half-mile I feared we would not make it."

"You and Tyler are so good, Cutler," Verity said bravely. "I cannot thank you properly for bringing him to me."

Savarra's fathomless eyes were on McLean and she said, "We must ship him home to England for burial in the family churchyard."

Belion spoke up, "That will be hard to do. There are many Englishmen whose bones now rest in American soil." His dark eyes never left Verity's white face. "His widow will have the choice of burial places."

"He fought for England and he died for England," Savarra said stubbornly, "and he shall be buried in England. I'm sure Verity will agree."

"Yes," Verity said slowly, "he should be buried in his homeland."

Sorrow mingled with determination as Savarra continued. "As Lady Bainbridge, Verity, you must give up your American home, if you want my brother to receive his inheritance —and I must tell you it is not an inconsiderable inheritance. He will be in the House of Lords one day and his duties will be many. Father has a great staff in the London town house and at the manor houses as well who will welcome you with open arms. You will soon become part of the life in Great Britain."

At these words, Verity's heart shook. She had not thought of facing a new home in England. "Will you go with me, Savarra?"

"Of course." The beautiful features were set and the gentian eyes hard. "England is my home. There is no place for me here."

Verity was aware of McLean's stare at the girl and she thought, *Ah, but there is a place for you here—if only you could see it,* and her heart ached for these two who stood so near, yet so far apart. She had long ago decided that Savarra Bainbridge and Cutler McLean were made for each other. It sorrowed her further that misunderstanding and stiff pride in both of them was making their union impossible.

Belion said softly, "Burial is necessity, Verity—and soon." He paused tactfully and added, "Decay will set in soon."

Verity turned. "We shall have to make a coffin for him. We will seal it tightly with pitch pine—it will be air-tight. Then it will not matter how long it takes us to return him to England." She did not dare let herself think of the long voyage to England, the strangeness of those surroundings, the actual leaving of the country she loved so deeply.

"That would solve it," Belion said. "I will have some of the camp followers fashion a coffin for him, a tight one, and we shall seal him in it. There is plenty of pitch pine about. It shall be air-tight."

"Better do it now," McLean said laconically. His face was melancholy and Verity knew that he had admired and liked Lord Bainbridge, even as Lord Bainbridge had held him in high esteem.

"What of the fighting now?" Verity asked as Belion stepped out of the tent.

" 'Tis rumored that Cornwallis and his men are going to attempt an escape across the York River, along with Banastre Tarleton and all his officers," McLean said. "As for York-town, it is leveled—scarcely anyone is left alive in it."

"It looks as if we are going to win this war after all," she said bitterly, "and at what a cost!"

Tyler Belion reentered the tent as she added, "Now—I want to return to Charles Town at once."

"That you cannot do," Belion said with firm tenderness. "Verity, you know well the dangers that beset travelers at this time. You have endured some of them—you must wait until we can accompany you."

"*If* you survive," Savarra said with sudden acrimony, "for I presume you expect us to wait while you continue to slaughter my countrymen."

" 'Tis slaughter or be slaughtered, Savarra," McLean said angrily, "and you will wait until you have an escort, whether it be us or other patriots."

Verity looked into the English girl's stormy young face and saw the love hidden there, the yearning and the fear for Cutler McLean that threaded all those emotions. But then her eyes sought his and found them flat, hard, so clear and crystal a gray they mirrored only determination and anger. Did he love Savarra? She did not know. Yet there was a bond between the two. She felt it as surely as she had sensed that her beloved James was dying. It was almost tangible, hanging in the tent like invisible smoke.

As she looked back down at her husband, his face set in

the unearthly peaceful lines of death, she thought, he looks no more than twenty-four himself. She knelt beside him as the others filed out of the tent, leaving her alone with her grief.

It was late the following morning before four strong blacks, with Belion's help, had finished with a thick pine coffin. It was rough, for they had hewn the trees into boards by means of axes. It was heavily coated with pitch pine, sealed tightly against the elements. Other dead were being buried just beyond the camp in the damp, dark earth in unmarked graves. But Verity had bathed Lord Bainbridge's still, cold face under the white bandage, and as they placed his stiffened body in the coffin she stood tearless, then arranged his soiled uniform about him. Savarra's face was drawn as she bent to kiss her father's forehead before the blacks placed the shaped lid upon the open box and, with powerful strokes, hammered it down, closing it tightly, then applying the sticky pitch liberally.

"We will have to find some vehicle," Verity remarked after Belion and McLean had left to return to the American lines, "for no horse could carry that strapped to his back."

"There will be one in Williamsburg—if this battle ever ends," Savarra replied, impatience creeping into her voice. Even as she spoke, the dull boom of cannon and mortar shook the air steadily. It had been so constant, Verity felt that a sudden silence might be more nerve-wracking than restful.

Savarra made a determined effort to cheer her young step-mother that morning. As the clouds gathered and a storm appeared along the coast beyond them, she told Verity of the Bainbridge manor houses in the country, of the town house, of the stables full of beautiful, blooded horses, of the furnishings gathered from all over the world. Verity listened, but her heart was too heavy to take in the ramifications of the change that would enter her life.

As a distant roll of thunder mingled with the sound of howitzers, Savarra said, "All the servants will love you, Verity, for you are so gentle and kind," and she began reeling off their names and their duties.

Verity made a conscious effort to remember them as the sound of rain pelted the canvas tent above them. But in her mind, she still saw Lord Bainbridge in all the moods she had come to know—smiling, tender, quizzical, passionate and determined—and tears were just below the surface.

It rained all day the sixteenth of October, but the morning of the seventeenth dawned bright and clear. Justine, merry as always, had received a goodly ration of dried meats and vegetables from Etienne, who rode in with two sacks from the French commissary for her.

"We 'ave plenty rice an' shelled corn. I make a bread from ze ground corn. We will feast tonight, you shall see!" Her bucktoothed smile was endearingly warm.

"You are kind to us who are strangers," Verity said impulsively.

"*Mais non*—you are no longer strangers, but my good friends."

The ate well, but Verity forced herself to do so. The food prepared was most appetizing, but her heart was so heavy with grief that she had no desire for it.

They had not finished the meal when a rider burst from the woods into the camp shouting joyously, and immediately he was surrounded by the ragged camp followers and servants. Verity and Savarra, with the others in their tent, rushed to hear what he was bellowing.

He was very young and his uniform was tattered. He looked to be the typical American Continental, but his face was ablaze with glory.

"I tell you, people, it was the sweetest music I ever heard when that drummerboy rose to the British parapet and began his drumming. And he might have beat away until doomsday, if he hadn't been sighted by men in our front lines. But notes have been exchanged between Lord Cornwallis and General Washington already—and listen!"

The crowd fell silent and it was borne in upon them that the sound of cannon and gunfire were silent. Verity felt an eerie thrill of gooseflesh at the quietness. The fighting had stopped!

The young Continental cried, "Cornwallis is surrendering— 'tis only a matter of terms now and it will all be over. They have sent messages back and forth under a flag of truce."

Savarra turned to Verity. "If the Americans have won, our—the men will be able to take us back to Charles Town, Verity, where we will make preparations to take my father and you and little James to England."

"That is true," Verity replied, a welcome and strange relaxation creeping through her.

The next morning, the eighteenth of October, Etienne rode in on his dappled gray horse, and he had much more detailed information on the coming surrender. Over breakfast, he regaled the women.

"At first, *mes amies,* Cornwallis attempted a belated bargain—proposing that his entire army be set free under an exchange of prisoners after a ceremony of surrender. General Washington agreed to halt the bombardment while the terms of surrender were worked out, but he allowed only two hours for Cornwallis to reply after he requested that two British officers be chosen to discuss surrender terms."

He sipped the scalding French coffee with relish, his black eyes gleaming with enjoyment at the rapt attention he was receiving from all the women. "It's said that our General agreed to allow a small shipload of British and German officers and loyalist civilians to sail for New York without inspection. And among them was a Colonel Banastre Tarleton, which angered the men from Carolina greatly. But the General refused to grant immunity for most of the tories and American deserters in Yorktown. He will deal with the turncoats as he sees fit—and many a traitor will hang!"

He downed the last of the coffee and added, "Flag bearers are moving constantly between the lines, bearing messages between the headquarters—" He laughed with joyous amusement as he continued, "I must tell you Cornwallis and his officers attempted to escape over the York River, but were foiled and bottled up until this moment." He grinned with Gallic impudence. "Already two more French ships have emerged in the Chesapeake and have dropped anchor among the British hulks in the harbor. Right now, four officers are squabbling over the terms—while agreeing to unconditional surrender of the garrison, they quarrel over trifles." He shrugged. *"Alors, l'anglais!"*

"Oh, but I would like to see the surrender!" Justine said, her black eyes bright with glee.

"Bien! No reason why you should not. When all the loose ends are tied up, you ladies can ride into Yorktown—what's left of it—and witness the surrender."

Verity sipped her coffee and thought her bitter thoughts. Too late. The surrender had come too late for her and for James. Etienne went on and on interminably about the collapse of the British army. "They have wrangled over the money chest of Cornwallis, but it has been awarded to the Americans. And Cornwallis will have to look after his own sick and wounded. It is said that the British garrison will march out to surrender at two of the afternoon tomorrow. You ladies must don your best dresses to watch. They will march between the American and French soldiers." He refilled his coffee cup and continued, "They have even argued over the music to be played. Though *l'anglais* forced the Charles Town surrender to march to British tunes, they have received permission to play one of their own British tunes as they surrender their arms."

After eating an enormous breakfast and changing his uniform, Etienne rode off in the mid-October chill, leaving the women full of the events he had related.

The following morning, Verity looked out at Justine, who was stirring up the fire, placing the coffeepot on it and rustling among the pots and pans. She felt little desire to go to Yorktown, though the whole of the ragged camp about her was stirring excitedly. Even the wounded were pulling themselves up on makeshift crutches and creeping toward breakfast fires. As she looked out at the moving people, an inescapable sense of excitement communicated itself, a sense of the momentousness of the day seeped into her. She pulled her wrapper about herself and repressed a faint shiver.

At her shoulder, Savarra said grimly, "Let's get dressed. I want to see this."

"I—I had thought we might not go."

The blue eyes stared into her dark ones with a touch of defiance. "You mean miss the moment for which all the rebels have longed—the surrender of the British army?"

"With James gone, I have little interest in it." She felt the hot sting of tears.

"My father would be there, you may be sure, head high, gallant to the end—when he would hand over his sword." Savarra's own voice thickened. "He admired Cutler McLean and Tyler Belion. He thought them worthy foes—he told me so."

"You are right, of course, Savarra," she replied, and the two women moved quietly about the tent, making their toilette as silently as possible. Even so, Clarissa and Cotty roused and threw back their cloaks, and the two whispered hoarsely and excitedly together as little James slumbered undisturbed.

Justine stuck her black head in through the flap. "Breakfast's ready," she said, excitement in her quiet voice. She wore a bright red woolen dress with a small blue cape over her shoulders. There was a touch of white at the throat and she was almost handsome, her eyes gleaming and her cheeks red as apples.

Leaving the small James asleep, Clarissa and Cotty joined the other three about the fire, rubbing their hands vigorously against the morning chill. "Lord, 'tis cold enough to frost this mornin'," Clarissa said, taking up a cup for Justine to pour her coffee. The smell of frying salted pork hung about them, and the small metal oven gave forth the mouth-watering fragrance of baking bread.

"We mus' leave early, Etienne say, for all ze countryside is coming to see thees thing," she said merrily. "*Ah, Je suis heureuse!* Per'aps my Etienne an' I, we soon return to Paris together." She turned and called to the black boy who was at a campfire nearby with his mother and brothers. "Blenchie —*ici!* Please to come 'ere." And when he trotted up, she said, "Would you please to fetch our 'orses. We are going to watch the British surrender at Yorktown."

"Us, too," he grinned, and moved off to do as Justine had asked.

It was near noon and the exodus from the camp was well under way when the women mounted, with Clarissa holding the small James firmly bundled in her capable arms. They trotted leisurely through the woods and out onto the plain before the long trenches. Many others were before and after them as they neared Yorktown. When they came into view of that city, Verity drew a sharp breath, appalled at the devastation that met her eyes.

The city of Yorktown was demolished, only a few random houses left standing. The awful wreckage of war was everywhere about them. Though the dead had been hauled off and buried, both animal and human, there hung in the air the faint scent of putrefaction, and Verity swallowed down a touch of nausea. James had endured this hell for weeks and her heart ached with the knowledge.

The sunlight was very bright, revealing all the scars of battle to the civilians and camp followers who were on their way to the road outside Yorktown, down which the British must march. Verity comforted herself with the thought that when this bit of pomp and ceremony was over, McLean and the others would be ready to escort her back to Charles Town. Where were they? She looked at the horde of people milling about and could not find a familiar face.

They rode forward where most of the civilians had taken up their posts and sat waiting in the warming sunlight. The crowd was singularly quiet as if sensing the importance of the moment. The French were assembling on one side of the road, the American army on the other, and they faced each other a few yards apart. The Americans and their followers stood in two files. Continentals were in the front and militia in the rear.

Verity could see that General Washington's ragged troops had prepared for this ceremony only by washing their hands and faces and combing their untidy hair. But the French, spruce in white linen and pastel regimental silks, looked across at their tattered allies with admiration and affection. Verity knew a small surge of pride, for clad as they were in dirty and ragged uniforms, they had fought like lions and were worthy of the victory that was now theirs.

All about them were people of the countryside who had been gathering for two days, families in carriages and carts and wagons, men and women on horseback, all surrounded by throngs of Negroes. Verity eyed the carriages with silent longing. She must have one of those to carry her beloved back to Charles Town. She feared the bag of gold she had Savarra give to McLean must be nearly gone—not nearly enough left to purchase one of these precious vehicles.

She looked across the way. In the field beyond the waiting infantry where arms were to be stacked, French hussars formed a circle, a spendidly uniformed band of bemustached riders sitting restless horses whose freshly curried coats gleamed like satin in the sunlight. Hundreds of young boys and men had climbed trees all along the route, the better to see. The buzz of their voices was both subdued and triumphant.

The five women sat their horses as time slipped by, and Verity's mind, like a homesick child's, went back to Charles Town, pondered the long trip to England that faced her and her infant son. She glanced at Savarra, whose face was a mixture of emotions. The English girl's chin was high, her straight nose lifted coldly, but her eyes were like blue fire and they searched the crowd restlessly.

She is looking for McLean, Verity thought sadly, and Savarra's was not a happy face. It was a set and determined one. It was as if she had resolved some deep inner conflict and could scarcely bear to live with it.

At last—it was almost three in the afternoon—the British emerged from the village with a somber roll of drums, their column led by a guard carrying cased colors and a band playing a dirge-like march.

"They would play *that!*" Savarra said scornfully. " 'The World Turned Upside Down,' when they could have played a stirring march, to show they aren't really beaten!"

"But they are beaten," Verity said gently. "You remember Etienne said this battle will end the war—that there will be talks now between the British and Americans, but this is the end—the decisive battle."

The British soldiers looked sullen and angry as they marched down the dusty road, and Savarra said, "Perhaps you are right. God knows, 'tis a blessing to stop killing each other. But you must recall that Charles Town is still in the hands of the British, Verity. They will be a long time leaving it, I think."

"We shall be well on our way to England—perhaps there—before they leave," Verity agreed. "But I feel this is the end. America is a free nation at last."

She observed the patriots lining the road. They looked so young and so tired that her heart ached for them. They came from all the colonies, but they looked no different from the boys she had grown up with in Charles Town. The British band played the sorrowful music and, as the redcoats neared the field, they threw down their weapons with such force it was obvious they wished to break them, render them useless to the victors. Many of them were flushed and had the appearance of men who had been given a stiff ration of rum to face this moment.

Soldiers in the German ranks were even more distraught than the British, and several of them sobbed as they marched. Tears flowed down their colonel's cheeks when he ordered them to lay down their arms.

Savarra said suddenly to Verity, "I see Colonel Lee—Light Horse Harry Lee, who fought at Francis Marion's side in the swamps when I was with them."

Everyone about them seemed in the grip of a powerful emotion, and Verity felt it in the pit of her stomach as she was swept by an awful sense of the vicissitudes of human life, mingled with commiseration for the unhappy men who were laying down their arms before her. Was the newly emerging nation worth all the agony suffered by the people?

Alas, she did not know. She could only hope for a future of peace and prosperity.

"Ah, look!" Verity said quietly. "There is Colonel Coyne and his two aides, Lieutenant Keith and Sergeant Queen—they will be prisoners."

"So they will," Savarra said sorrowfully. "He loved my father well. He looks heartbroken."

But the three men did not see the women, and Verity thought it just as well, for she knew it would pain Coyne further to see Savarra witness this final humiliation.

The British were led by a brigadier general—not by Cornwallis—a man she was to learn later was Charles O'Hara, a handsome Irishman in old-fashioned military dress, whose curls hung like tiny white sausages about his dark but ruddy face. He was remarkably erect and well groomed.

The crowd was silent as he extended his sword to Rochambeau. But that worthy Frenchman gestured to General George Washington, whom Verity strained to see across the road. Smiling, O'Hara apologized for his mistake and once more offered his sword with a courtly gesture, but General Washington refused it.

Verity was fascinated by her first glimpse of the American leader. He was incredibly tall and broad-shouldered, his white wig carefully tended, his craggy face so lined with suffering, with strength and character, she felt her faith in him burst in new warmth within her breast. He left the field long before the last of the British soldiers hurled their guns onto the pile with continued violence—and many of the weapons were, as they intended, broken.

The five women and the vast number of civilians stayed to the end, and the sun was lowering when the last of the ceremonies concluded and the soldiers and civilians mingled in the milling mass. Etienne had found Justine and the others and told them he would join them in the evening with more supplies from the commissary.

They were about to leave when suddenly from the crowd Bartholomew Brim ran to them—a sadly thinner and bedraggled Brim—and his usually impassive face contorted with grief. He reached up and caught Verity's hands where she sat upon her horse. "Ah, Lady Bainbridge—his lordship is dead, they tell me—"

Verity looked down at the butler-valet from her mount. "Yes, Brim, but we have his son."

"Oh, Lady Bainbridge—I know, I know! And Mistress Savarra, thank God you are well. Will you take me back to England with you—to serve the young master? I swear you will never have cause to regret it. I will—"

"Of course, Brim," Verity said kindly. "You will be of great comfort to me, I know, for I shall need every friend I can find when I go to England to make my home there with little James."

"Thank you, Lady Bainbridge, and you, Mistress Savarra," he said, recovering some of his customary dignity. "Will it be convenient for me to accompany you back to Charles Town?"

"Yes, Brim, we will be only too glad to have you with us for it is a long and dangerous journey. Come with us now." and she spoke to Justine's lieutenant saying hopefully, "M'sieu Doumet, do you think you could secure a carriage in which we could return to Charles Town? I must have means of taking my husband's body with me."

The French soldier looked doubtful. "Madame, I will inquire, but all vehicles are at a premium now. No one has any to spare." And he wheeled his horse about to return to his regiment.

Verity thought of this on their slow trip back to camp with Brim trotting beside them, a meager pack on his back. They found the camp alive with activity when they reached it, but Verity was preoccupied with her problem. She *must* have a carriage, or at worst an open wagon. She had looked for McLean and Belion and their two companions diligently during the day, but they were lost in the great mass of humanity that crowded the scene of surrender.

Justine prepared a delicious supper, with French onion soup followed by roast fowl which she had by cajoling, coaxing and shrewd trading, secured from a neighboring camp, where there were caged chickens. Verity found that she was once more able to eat, and she did full justice to the meal. But Brim seemed to enjoy it most. His relief to be with them was touching and he was making a valiant effort to recapture his imposing dignity.

Etienne Doumet came in as they finished, and Justine served him separately with great and flattering ado. He again regaled the group with many sidelights on the surrender, one of which had created animosity among the rank and file. The opposing officers were having dinner this very evening together, and there was much anger about it among the troops. With the bloody fighting fresh in their minds, the troops resented this sudden brotherhood between former enemies.

But Savarra said, "It will be so. There is much in the American character that is admirable to us—and we are, after all, your cousins, Verity, one people with differing ideas of governments."

Verity looked at her in the waning light. Savarra's face, usually so volatile and revealing, was smooth and expressionless. Only the eyes were brilliant with life. Verity sensed once more that Savarra had this day come to grips with the unrest in her soul and made terms with it. Even so, the turmoil was still there, eager, restless, unfulfilled, full of passionate longing, for those eyes revealed it. But she had mastered it, would live with it. Yet she was so young, Verity thought with sadness, nineteen, with all life before her. Then her mind swung to Cutler McLean. She *knew* he was the source of Savarra's disquiet, the tumultuous emotions that shook her young heart. But Verity saw the cold pride, unbending, unyielding. There would be no merging of the two, for McLean, in his own male way, carried a far more unyielding pride within his own heart.

They stayed for two more days in the makeshift camp, while those about them drifted away, including Justine and her Etienne, lessening the number of people there by the hour. Brim made himself very useful, fetching wood, building fires and assisting in the preparation of food. He slept outside in the thin roll of blankets he had brought with him.

At Verity's offer to give him one of hers, he said, "Oh, no, madame. I am quite used to it, you see. Lord Bainbridge and I—" his face puckered slightly, "we have been sleeping outside the last three weeks."

On October twenty-third, McLean, Belion and their two companions, Sleep and McHorry, showed up. Verity, in the tent at the time, heard their voices and flew to the opening. Her joy was boundless when she saw that they brought a wagon, a rough-hewn vehicle with two stolid horses pulling it.

She took each man's hand warmly, holding tears of relief firmly in check. "You *have* found a wagon for us. I am so glad!"

Savarra, who had followed her out, appeared relieved as well. "Where did you get it?" she asked McLean briefly.

"From a farm family." Then as Brim came up with a load of wood, "Ah, Brim—I see you found them after all." Then turning back, he dismounted and added, "It took the last of the gold you gave me, Verity—but we've a few sovereigns left among us. Enough to get you back to Charles Town, I think. We will see you to the outskirts, then Amos and Brim can take you on into town."

McHorry, who had driven the wagon with his mare, Rosy, tied to the rear, reached down into the wagon. "Here, Brim," he said as the valet put down his wood. "Here's a British Brown Bess an' a bag o' powder an' bullets fer you."

Over Brim's thanks, McLean was adding, "Until the British leave Charles Town, Tyler and I cannot return openly —and I don't believe this time it will be necessary to risk a disguise."

The trip back to Charles Town was miserable. It seemed to Verity it rained almost all the way. The wagon was open and there was no shelter to be had. Brim rode on the hard seat beside Amos, while the others were mounted. McLean and Belion were able to gauge the miles so that each night found them at an inn of some sort where they slept, usually wretchedly damp and cold. Even Amos and Tiqua, who were so relieved to be with them and returning, complained of the weather and the long miles each day brought. There was little other conversation among them, so intent were they upon reaching their destination.

Little James, with Clarissa's rich and plentiful milk, was the only completely comfortable member of the troop for he was kept warm and dry in Clarissa's strong and protective arms. Thus the long journey was made without mishap.

When at last they reached two miles from the city of Charles Town, McLean and his three companions left them. As the four partisans rode away, Cotty wept unashamedly while Clarissa clucked over her like a mother hen. Verity knew Cotty was torn between the yearning to stay and marry one her American suitors and the desire to accompany her mistress back to England. She had overheard Savarra say she would miss her, but she left it to Cotty to decide, an impossibility for the feckless little maid.

When the four riders had disappeared in the stark, late November forest, Verity felt a leaden weight descend upon her spirits. Now she would soon leave for England, and Savarra was determined to accompany her. Yet the young girl's unhappiness was more and more apparent. The future stretched out bleak and alien before Verity. Would the English people who had been Lord Bainbridge's friends accept a common American woman as Lady Bainbridge? It seemed unlikely. Life had been gracious in Warren Pair's big house on King Street, but it was scarcely preparation for what faced her now. Oddly enough, the more she thought of it, the more concerned she became for Savarra's future happiness rather than her own.

There was cold resignation in the girl's eyes, and Verity reflected what feeble comfort there was in pride. It was a searing bedfellow, pride, leaving no warmth, no hope and comfort.

The British in charge, who stopped them as they entered Charles Town, were very kind when they discovered that she was returning with the body of her husband, Lord Bainbridge, who had died in the battle of Yorktown. Apparently the news of the defeat at Yorktown had already reached Charles Town before them, and there was great uneasiness among the commanding officers and soldiery, but there was no indication they would abandon the city.

A small troop of British soldiers insisted on escorting them to King Street, and the hubbub under the porte-cochere brought Calhoon running. When he saw Amos and Verity, he emitted a whoop, which resulted in Frances, Monique and Primrose spilling out onto the porch.

In the warmth of their greetings, Verity felt some of the load leave her heart. Yet she was still aching with the thought of the long sea voyage facing her, knowing Lord Bainbridge's big body, stilled forever, would lie in the rough sealed coffin far down in the ship's hold.

Twenty-Two

They had not been back a full eighteen hours before Bonnie Raintree was pelting through the front door, brushing past the yawning Amos in the early morning to rush upstairs, first to the sleeping Verity's bedroom, then Savarra's, where she perched excitedly on the English girl's bed.

Savarra sat up and smiled at her with a touch of weariness for she had slept but poorly, her mind struggling against the past. "Bonnie, you look wonderful," she said sincerely, for the young woman had regained her fetching plumpness and her garrulity as well.

She reached out and hugged Savarra to her full breast. "Oh, Savarra, darling—Verity was half-asleep. Surely *you* can tell me what you have seen—about the surrender at Yorktown! Dear heaven, how far you have traveled!" She held Savarra back from herself, scrutinizing her friend. "And how thin you are—not that it isn't charming, for you are so beautiful. I made Belle and Terrell stay downstairs, for I knew you wouldn't be up yet after so long a journey—oh, but you may be sure the English here have been set back—" She put a hand to her pink mouth. "I forget, you are English! You seem so much like one of *us*. Does it pain you to think of the defeat? Oh, and I am *so* sorry about your father." Her voice lowered and tears filled her eyes. She blinked them determinedly away and went on. "But they have no intention, 'tis said, of relinquishing Charles Town, but everyone knows that Benjamin Franklin will soon sail to Paris with all those other Americans to talk of terms." She paused at last and looked at Savarra expectantly.

Savarra began slowly to narrate the scenes at Yorktown while she rose and prepared to dress herself. Bonnie was rapt and silent for once under the spell of the English girl's measured voice which brought the events past to vivid brightness. Finally, brushing her long, straight black hair from her face and tying it with a pale blue velvet ribbon, she finished. "The ride home was perfectly vile. It seemed even further than it had when we set out near two months ago."

There was silence in the room behind her as she looked at her own face in the tall mirror before her. She *was* thinner, her waist narrower in the fitted bodice of the pale blue woolen dress, which accentuated the push of her pointed breasts against the lawn insert gathered across them. The planes of her face were more sharply etched, giving her a slightly feline look, but her blazing blue eyes were unquenched, looking out on the world, unreconciled and undefeated.

Bonnie said huskily, "I suppose Verity will book passage for you both in a few days—yes, my servants told me they heard it from Calhoon. Oh, but I shall miss you! It has been dreadful all these weeks with you gone—and with Anne buried—Bowman Baltazar off with General Marion in the woods and Cutler and Tyler gone until the city is free—" There were repressed tears in the words as Bonnie fell silent again.

"You and the children must have breakfast with us, Bonnie dear," Savarra said. Then, "Ah, good morning, Verity," as her young stepmother entered, fully dressed.

Bonnie leapt up in a rustle of pink taffeta petticoats, her full worsted skirts of maroon billowing about her as she caught Verity in her arms again. "You look so much stronger than when you left, Verity! I thank God for that—you were so pale the last time I saw you."

"I am stronger and you look very prosperous, my dear. You must tell us what good fortune has befallen you, for you look so much better than when last we met."

Bonnie was only too glad to respond, talking volubly all the way down the stairs and into the dining room, where Tiqua had already set places for them all and Primrose, Monique, Amos and Calhoon stood in the door to greet them.

Savarra gathered from the torrent of speech floating about them that Bonnie's parents in London had finally heard of her plight and, despite her protests, had interceded for her and sent her considerable cash money, while their influence had restored her and her children to the large and luxurious new mansion Spencer Raintree had built for his little family.

After further greetings from the children, they sat down to a sumptuous breakfast of thick pink slices of ham, hot rice, yellow and rich with butter, eggs in omelettes, smoking hot biscuits and candied peaches. The children, rosy and bright, were quiet while their mother rambled on with all the news of neighbors, both patriot and loyalist.

By the time Bonnie took a reluctant leave, Savarra felt that she and Verity had been gone no longer than a day, but for the far-reaching changes that had come into their lives over the last weeks. The chill, wet wind when the front door was closed on Bonnie and the children as Amos saw them to their carriage in the porte-cochere reminded her the last of November was upon them. The two young women stood a moment together in the great, warm hallway before turning together toward the stairs.

As they took the first step side by side, Savarra was conscious of Verity's close scrutiny, and she closed her smooth face against it. Her summer tan had faded and her skin was once more like ivory. At the top of the stairs, Verity put a warm hand on her arm.

"Savarra, it is you, now, who does not eat well and there is a look about you that worries me. Why are—you unhappy?"

Savarra was silent for a long moment, then she said, " 'Tis nothing. Only that I am no longer wholly English. Something of me is American, and I have a hard time reconciling that with my English blood."

"How are you American, Savarra?"

She shrugged. "It is an intangible—a freedom from foolish social customs, a sense of something wonderful about to happen—a kindred spirit. Ah, I've thought of the rebels—of it all, nights when I cannot sleep. I shall hate to give it up. That is all."

"That is a great deal. I have given you much thought myself and I find—I do not require you to accompany me. I have stood much and I can stand arriving in a strange country and adjusting myself. As Bonnie says, her parents will welcome me, and Brim will be with me too."

"Bonnie's father is a merchant, albeit a wealthy one, and you will be Lady Bainbridge," Savarra said, hiding her emotion. She knew what this was costing the gentle-spirited and intensely American Verity. " 'Tis one of the social customs of which I speak. Bonnie's parents will scarcely be among your close friends."

Verity's face suddenly set in lines of stubborn disbelief. "My friends will, as has always been my way, be of my own choosing. So why do you not stay in America, if that is—what you desire in your heart?"

Savarra's sudden laugh was hard and cold. "My dear Verity, where would I stay, pray, and whatever for? There is no place for a single English woman in this community. No one *needs* me. I would be an idiot to stay in Charles Town."

"You could stay here and keep the Pair house open—" Verity spoke rapidly and Savarra felt she was not saying all she was implying. "James and I would come home and visit you each year. Bonnie Raintree is so fond of you—the neighbors—" She hesitated as if she would say more.

Savarra forestalled her swiftly. "Don't be foolish, Verity. The whole idea is preposterous. You and I will book passage on the first English ship to leave for London." Her voice shook slightly. In another instant she would give away her secret! She added indifferently, "Actually, there is nothing to keep me here and I will soon forget all this idiocy about freedoms of the spirit—of custom. 'Tis a ridiculous thought. Come, let us go see my little brother."

And the two took the hall in silence. Savarra slanted a glance at Verity, but the young woman's brows were slightly drawn and there was a skepticism on the even features. Savarra's heart quailed. Had she, after all, revealed too much? She squared her shoulders. No matter, once in England, she would have her own problems, for the elderly Lady Haverley would no doubt want to welcome her as her widowed daughter-in-law and Savarra was determined to cut all ties with that family.

Yes, she would have her hands full, and forgetfulness should be easier to come by there, instead of here where everything reminded her of *him*. Before her mind could veer away, she saw him, sitting tall in his saddle, the cold gray eyes forbidding, the beautiful mouth firm, the straight nose at an arrogant angle, that dark lock of hair that was cut too short and fell over his forehead. It always filled her with a longing to brush it back, to feel its crisp dark texture. For months she had fought that desire to touch him. It was a body hunger that would not be denied.

Oh, yes, it was good that she would soon be three thousand miles from the tangled, mossy swamps of South Carolina— far from its exotic spring, filled with tropic flowers and heady fragrances.

Clarissa had just finished nursing little James and he was fast asleep when Savarra and her young stepmother entered the room. Clarissa had put him down in the crib which had, at his birth, been fetched from the attics and which had held three generations of Pairs.

Both Verity and Savarra bent over him, looking at the curved pink mouth. The golden eyebrows were drawn fiercely in some baby dream and gave him an uncanny resemblance to Lord James Bainbridge.

"How like my father he looks," Savarra whispered in a choked voice.

Verity did not answer, and when the English girl looked at her she saw two shining tears trembling on her thick lower lashes. She reached out and took Verity's slender hand, squeezing it hard and murmuring, "I'm so glad he had you, Verity. He was a lonely man, for I was little comfort to him —and I know you have happy memories."

"Yes," Verity whispered thickly. "I will have them to comfort me all of my life."

Clarissa said in her hoarse whisper, "Ma'am, could I go to the shops an' get some new dresses? I ain't got nothin' but these raggedy ol' things I wore all the way to Yorktown an' back."

"Of course, Clarissa," Verity said contritely, "and I will give you your back pay. Amos will drive you to town—"

"Oh, mistress," Cotty spoke from the door, "could I please go, too? I'm most as bad as Clarissa."

"Both of you go," Savarra said, as they all left the room together. "I will give you five pounds, Cotty." She had found that her father's solicitors had been sending her allowance steadily during her absence and she had more than a hundred pounds which had been delivered to the house for her.

Giggling delightedly, the two servants trotted off to don the best of their somewhat patchy wardrobe for a trip to the shops in downtown Charles Town.

Late that night, a bitter and vicious storm blew in from the Atlantic, with bone-chilling wind and rain lashing the house unmercifully. Verity and Savarra, who would have been going the next day to the British offices on the quay to arrange passage to London, were forced to remain inside. Neither of them regretted it overmuch, for both were still weary from their long journey and took catnaps during the day.

That night Savarra tossed and turned, listening to the howling gale. She wondered if she would ever sleep that sound slumber she had known in those long ago nights before Peter Haverley and Cutler McLean had come into her life.

The following day Bonnie Raintree and the children braved the continuing storm and spent the entire afternoon with them. The loquacious Bonnie seemed wistful and subdued. "I must see as much of you as I can, for when you leave I fear we may never meet again."

Verity assured her that she would return for visits, for her son was half-American and he would have the not-inconsiderable Pair Shipyards as his inheritance as well as his British baronetcy. But Bonnie was disconsolate, and when Savarra suggested that she take passage with them for a visit to her parents, Bonnie's face grew cold.

"I shall *never* go to England again. If I see my parents, they will have to come here. I shall *never* forgive the British for executing my Spencer—and for doing only what was his duty."

Savarra thought this singularly erratic, for Spencer Raintree had been a spy and he had been fairly caught.

She and the two children left in the downpour, swathed in heavy capes.

The storm roared on interminably for five long days. Calhoon came back from the market drenched and complaining. "I ain't never seen such a storm. Looks like it ain't never goin' to let up."

Surely, she thought on the fifth day, *I will feel normally when we are aboard ship and this preoccupation with McLean will fade.* But deep within, a still small voice replied, *You will never forget.*

That day they received a letter from Baltazar. Amos had brought it from the market place where Caleb McLean had slipped it to him as the two met. It was to both girls, and they retired to Savarra's bedroom to read it, knowing well they must destroy it immediately.

It contained news of McLean, Belion and their two compatriots, Sleep and McHorry, of Caleb and his wife, Corrie. All of them were camped in the deeps of Ox Swamp and they rode on sporadic raids to keep the last of the tories in line. There was little action and the men spent much of their time in camp, a trying occupation for restless spirits. Marion conducted a busy correspondence with Governor Rutledge regarding the civilian government he hoped to set up as soon as the terms of agreement between Britain and America were reached in faraway Paris.

His letter also revealed that the partisans had heard General Alexander Leslie had arrived in Charles Town to assume command of British operations in South Carolina, and they had laughed on hearing his boasts to put heart in the tories of the countryside.

For the partisans knew the British were sealed in Charles Town as tightly as in a corked bottle. Even the tories in the backcountry seemed to be accepting the fact that the vicious internecine wars were over.

He went on to say he missed seeing both the girls, was glad to know they had returned safely from Yorktown. He remarked, and Verity wept over his words, that he would miss Anne the rest of his life. He wished he might see Verity's baby son before she left for England, but knew it was an impossibility.

He closed, asking Savarra and Verity to write to him before they left, that Caleb would find Amos in the market place easily.

Savarra clung to the lines reading, "Cutler and Tyler are the most restless among us. It is with difficulty that we keep them from trying to ride into Charles Town secretly to see you—which would be most dangerous, for both are well known to the British now."

Did Cutler McLean really want to see *her*, Savarra wondered? Not likely, murmured her reason. His lifetime friend Verity was the source of his desire. He had been cold to Savarra since that night in the inn, when he would almost have taken her by force. She had cut him to the quick then and he had not forgiven her. Nor would he, she told herself. She was an interlude, partly pleasant but mostly irritating in his life.

She went about in downcast spirits for two days after the letter arrived and was destroyed. Verity seemed aware of this and did her best to comfort her, but with little success. Savarra was especially depressed when she went at last to the British Naval offices on the quay with Verity to arrange their passage on the H.M.S. *Richard* for England.

"The seas are very bad this time of year," the young naval officer in charge told them, "and we cannot be sure just which day we will set sail. However, I shall arrange your passage and we will send a messenger to your home, Lady Bainbridge, in sufficient time in which to ready yourselves for the voyage."

His smile at Savarra was especially winning, and she made an effort to be slightly flirtatious. Verity, when they reentered their carriage, assisted by Amos in a whipping wind off the river, said encouragingly, "He *was* a handsome man, wasn't he—and he certainly had an eye for you."

"Indeed," she replied, smiling. "I should like to know him better."

But Verity said nothing, merely staring out the window at the leaden sky reflected in the leaden river.

Finally the weather began to clear, and word came that the H.M.S. *Richard* would soon sail. When it became certain they would depart within a week, Verity asked that Savarra accompany her in one last chore, as she called the servants together in the drawing room. Her face was drawn and her dark eyes haunted.

Primrose looked excessively solemn as Amos ushered them all into the room. Monique, Tiqua and Frances appeared apprehensive. Amos and Calhoon were scowling as she began to speak.

"Amos, Calhoon—Primrose—all of you." She hesitated, her voice breaking. "I am going to close up the Pair house, but before I do, you shall each be a free person of color. I am manumitting each of you."

Primrose put her face in her apron and began to cry, and Tiqua put an arm about her as Verity said comfortingly, "Now Primrose, you know anyone in Charles Town would be only too glad to pay you for your services. There was never a better cook—"

"That ain't it, Mistress Verity," Amos put in. "We'd like to be free, but we're Pair folks an' you're Pair folks. We ain't want ter leave you."

Verity's sad face brightened, "But let me finish! I was going to tell you that you may each—if you choose—accompany me to England as free persons."

Savarra smiled at the excitement that exploded among these people she had come to know and love so well. They clustered about Verity, filled with pleasure at the prospect of the journey with her, with the knowledge they would be free and paid for jobs they knew well and enjoyed performing.

Later, Savarra spoke to Verity as they reached her bedroom. "So you shall not be leaving your beloved Charlest'n after all—you are taking most of it with you."

"The part I love best, anyway," Verity replied with a new contentment that eased Savarra as well.

That is one comfort, she thought as she went into her room. *Verity will be surrounded by people who love her.* Clarissa had long ago announced her desire to go with little James to England.

Thus, as the days passed, each of the young women, with help from Tiqua and her companions, Monique and Frances, packed her clothing carefully, leaving out one small satchel that contained the most important parts of her toilette—soap, lotions, colognes and fresh changes of chemises.

Two days before they were to depart, Savarra went to Verity's room to consult with her about sharing a small trunk and found her young stepmother writing rapidly, the quill moving with bold strokes across the paper as she sat at her secretary.

Verity looked up, startled. Savarra noted with little interest that she turned so that her hands and arms covered the paper on which she had been writing.

"You're writing a last letter to Bowman Baltazar?" 'she asked listlessly.

"Yes." There was relief in Verity's voice. "I love him dearly and I could not leave without one last letter." Then the two girls fell to discussing the small trunk, and agreed they could share it nicely as it would hold all the extras that the large portmanteaus could not carry.

Savarra saw Verity give the letter later to Amos before he went to market, admonishing him that he must seek out and tell whichever partisan he contacted that it was most important. "And hurry!" she added urgently as the slender black man left the kitchen to get his horse.

She turned to Savarra and smiled. "I want him to get it while it's still warm—Uncle Bowman is all that is left to me of the old and happy days."

The next day went by slowly, and Savarra knew the following one would be slower, for there was nothing so trying to her as having to wait. It was a sort of limbo, all chores seemed unimportant, nothing held interest, and she was growing more and more despondent.

For the last two nights, when she was safely in her bed, she had wept, something she never did and which filled her with contempt for her own weakness. Oh, God, if only she had never met the man, never known his touch and the melting desire that he evoked! She had imagined his arms about her a thousand times. She had relived the moments on the forest floor until every movement, every remembered sensation, was like a fire within her, a consuming blaze that enveloped her entire body in a kind of sweet agony.

Even the hours spent holding her dimpled brother passed all too slowly, and she could not find enough to occupy her. She quarrelled with Cotty and reduced the already miserable little maid to tears.

"You're an utter fool, Cotty," she had flared after Cotty had remarked for the hundredth time she could not choose between Gabe and Thad. "Here you are, going back to England with me, when you want to be wife to two men! I never saw such a bird-witted person in my life. If you get to England and start weeping and moaning to come back, I shall dismiss you and you will have to find another post. I've told you a hundred times you may stay here!"

Cotty's tears flowed freely. "I love you, Mistress Savarra —an' I love both Gabe an' Thad, may the good Lord forgive me. Oh, I just don't know what to do."

"Well, for heaven's sake hush, then. I suppose I can send you back, if ever you make up your mind."

Clarissa on the other hand was wildly excited. The prospect of going to England as little James's nurse made her giddy. She kept trying to comfort Cotty, reminding her that she would be her guide around London, helping her discover all the fascinating places in the great city. It did not comfort Cotty a whit. She was morose and glum and it grated on Savarra's nerves unbearably.

At last, they were to depart early the following morning. Savarra, who secretly wanted to behave much as Cotty was behaving, was rescued only by her steel pride. She held herself erect and, despite her misery, put a bold and eager face on at a cost only she could reckon. They all went to bed in a state of tension and it was two hours before Savarra fell asleep.

She was roused by a soft rap on her door, and she was wide awake instantly for her sleep had been light. She called out, "Who is it?"

" 'Tis me, Amos, Mistress Savarra."

"Just a minute," she called, rising swiftly to don her wrapper. Apprehension swarmed through her. Was the baby ill? Was Verity? Some dreadful circumstance must bring Amos to her door in the small hours of the morning! It was very dark and still, and beyond her windows she knew the December night was bitter cold. The sky was overcast and there were no stars.

She opened the door and Amos looked at her over the wavering candle. "Mistress Verity say to get your clothes on. 'Tis important."

"Are we leaving this early? Is the ship leaving so quickly?" She took his candle and lit two of her own as the big clock in the hall suddenly struck three. Returning the candle to Amos, she said brusquely, "I'll be down as soon as I can dress. Rouse Cotty—"

"I done that, mistress." He closed the door quietly.

She went to the clothing she had laid out the night before and began to dress with a speed that was increased by fear. Why would the ship leave so early? Something must be amiss. She heard no other movement in the house, but she was not listening for it. In but a few minutes she was dressed, her reticule in one hand, the small satchel in the other. Taking up a candle and snuffing the other, she left the room, her other baggage having been taken down to the quay the day before by Calhoon and Amos.

She took the stairs swiftly, and it was then she heard the dim sound of voices in the drawing room and saw the golden light from the oil lamp spilling into the hallway. She hastened to the door and froze, one hand clutching the reticule and satchel, the other holding the wildly fluttering candle.

It was as if she were spun back in time over the long months, for the sight that met her eyes was the same as when she had hastened down in her finest ball gown, expecting Peter Haverley, and found instead the grim-faced rebels who faced her now. As before, Verity was with them. Only Anne Pair was missing.

For a long moment there was a fraught silence before Savarra, looking into the somber face of Cutler McLean, asked sharply, "What is the meaning of this?"

"You will come with us immediately, Savarra," he said quietly.

Suddenly the fully dressed Cotty was at her side. "Oh, mistress, whatever is happening?"

"I don't know," Savarra said angrily, "but I shall find out."

Tyler Belion said, "We have decided to make hostages of you two, to insure that no more Charles Town citizens hang before the redcoats leave." His dark eyes were sorrowful. He looked leaner and was clean-shaven now, and there were new lines in his face. He did not look at Verity.

"Verity, this is preposterous—" Savarra began. "Can you not reason with your—your friends?"

Verity's face was white and set. "They hung Samuel Anderson and Brent Tilman yesterday, simply because they would not pledge allegiance to the crown—no other reason. They leave families with young children who must now fend for themselves."

"But the war is over to all intents and purposes," she protested to the four men. Her breath was growing short and excitement was rising in her. "You can't mean to take me off into the swamps and hold me for months!"

"You an' Miss Cotty," Thad McHorry drawled, his innocent blue eyes so guileless that they stirred her immediate suspicion. "We figger when they get word Lord Bainbirdge's daughter's a hostage, they'll tread mighty easy on killin' Americans."

"I'll not go," Savarra said flatly, but her pulse was racing in a wild tattoo as she bent her stormy gaze on McLean, clad in his leather breeches and high boots. He was standing and now he towered over her, his eyes speculative. A small flame licked up behind them, shortening her breath further.

"You will go, Savarra, if I must take you as I did the first time. It will be months before the British leave Charles Town."

Tension flowed out of her and she felt a touch giddy. Her voice was muffled. "Not like before—" and she recognized the emotion sweeping her as relief, vast and all-engulfing relief.

She would not be aboard H.M.S. *Richard* tomorrow—no, this morning. She would be in the dark tangle of woods she had come to know so well, had come to love, to feel at one with. She would be with McLean and she could not help herself. Her pride was intact and her yearning suddenly fulfilled—and she had thought never to balance the two.

Cotty giggled hysterically. "Gabe—Thad—you are beasts!"

"That's right," Gabe drawled. "An' you ladies are leavin' Charlest'n a little ahead of the good ship *Richard*."

" 'Tis late and growing later," Belion said. "We must leave between sentries and well before dawn." He turned on Verity with sudden ferocity. "Give me a final kiss, Verity—for old times' sake and for what might have been. Pretend if you must, but kiss me once as if you loved me."

Verity rose and Belion took her into a strong embrace. He kissed her slowly, lingeringly and with a depth of passion that made itself felt to everyone in the room. But Verity was serene and calm when he released her.

He said huskily, "Goodbye, my love."

"You will find another," Verity answered, but Belion's face denied it. She turned quickly and embraced Savarra briefly, and smiled sadly. "I began life as a good British subject, then I was so determined to be free of them, and now I am become British once more and will likely live my life out in England. I have come full circle."

"And I shall see you and my brother again—soon," Savarra said firmly as McLean took her arm, half pushing, half leading her to the hallway. The others trooped after them through the hall and to the kitchen as they had done on that long-ago stormy night.

In the shell courtyard were tethered six restless horses, and as the door closed behind them Savarra was struck by a glowing inner warmth, despite the icy air. She put her foot into McLean's hand and mounted a great gelding. She could hear Cotty giggling with delight as she was lifted to a saddle.

In moments they were taking the grassy sides of the shell drive and, on reaching the cobbled street, avoided it, the horses' hooves silent in the turf that ran alongside. They traveled in single file in the dark and starless night. No one spoke as they traversed the black and noiseless streets, past the square and along the narrow alley that led eventually to the edge of town. The houses passed were dark sentinels to sleeping occupants, but Savarra's heart beat fast with the knowledge of danger to the men about her.

Her eyes were sharp and her nose lifted as the scent of the river and the sea came to her. They passed a building where light shone forth dimly on the dully gleaming cobbles. A door opened and a soldier shouldering a musket stepped out.

"The sentry's changing," Belion whispered hoarsely. "We must run for it!"

The soldier's head came up as he stared before him and his voice rang out terse and strong, "Who goes there?"

Suddenly the door swung wide again and four more soldiers spilled out, two carrying lanterns, but by that time Savarra had kicked the flanks of her mount fiercely and the wind was hard against her face, blowing her hair loose when the hood of her fur-lined cape fell back and she galloped wildly beside the others.

"Mount up! Mount up!" cried one of the soldiers and there was much shouting and the noise of gunfire behind them, but already they were thundering down the narrow dirt road toward Monck's Corner, the Cooper River flowing silently beside them, the winter wind chilling and exhilarating. There were no words spoken among them and they bent low over their horses, urging them on by knee and hand.

From behind them there again came the burst of musket fire, and Savarra looked back to see the orange flashes, bright against the night.

"They're too far back to hit anything." McLean's voice came from beside her. "The Brown Bess isn't as accurate as our rifles." He sounded triumphant, elated, and Savarra's own wild spirit rushed upward to meet that triumph but she did not reply.

The wind off the river was rising, as the young naval officer had predicted when he sent word to them yesterday. In a few hours, the H.M.S. *Richard* would sail majestically forth on Charles Town Bay, the wind in her sails thrusting her forward with gathering speed. Verity and little James, with the excited Clarissa, as well as the once-again dignified Brim and all Verity's beloved servants, would be on board that ship for England. A pang struck Savarra's fast-beating heart. She would miss them!

McLean spoke again, sharp but low, "Swing off here, men —Savarra—Cotty!"

Her eyes, long ago adjusted to the pale light from the clouded sky, saw their dark shapes as they left the road and splashed across a narrow creek into the woods beyond. The brush and scrub scratched at Savarra, and instinctively she drew up one leg and flipped it neatly across the saddle, pulling her full skirts about her as she sat astride.

She hissed to Cotty, "Sit astride! 'Twill be easier to hang on in this brush," but that practical little maid had preceded her, and already her skirts were flying about her knees. Savarra laughed aloud and quelled it swiftly, whispering, "Then hold your skirts down before they're torn off you!"

She heard Gabe's low chuckle and nothing more but the sounds of the night about them, the rusty cry of a bird come south for the winter, the hushed sweep of branches that plucked at them, the far-off scream of a small animal caught in the jaws of a larger—all familiar sounds to Savarra now, familiar and stirring to her blood.

McLean reached out and caught her reins, pulled her mount to a halt. All of them halted now, the horses with heaving sides, their riders breathing hard but silently. Dimly the sound of pounding hooves came to their ears. The still-pursuing British soldiers. They were too far back from the road to see them, but their voices carried faintly on the wind as they galloped past the place where the partisans had turned off and dwindled in the distance.

"A narrow squeak," Thad murmured to Cotty.

"Oh, Thad—Gabe—" she replied in a choked voice. "I was never so glad to see anybody in my life!"

"Which one of us, Cotty?" Gabe asked softly.

"I—I—both of you."

Belion from the darkness said dryly, "You should have been an Arab potentate, Cotty. They can have as many mates as they can afford."

"Oh, Mr. Belion—what a scandalous thing to say!"

McLean said sharply, "Listen!" and they all fell silent. The horses no longer heaved. They were silent as their riders.

From the direction of the road came the dim sound of voices on the wind, wrangling, acrimonious.

McLean moved forward on his mount, parting the thick scrub which grew below the trees but which was head high. Savarra moved up beside him and together they saw two lanterns dimly. The British soldiers had carried them on their wild ride and now they were returning to Charles Town, empty-handed but for their light.

McLean laughed softly. "Why didn't you yell, Savarra? You could be safely in British hands again."

"Why didn't you gag me?" she countered, "or threaten me with a fate worse than death to keep me quiet?"

He was silent. Then, "By God, I think we *have* made a rebel out of you!" He swore quietly, his voice husky and deep with feeling.

Savarra's heart soared magically. Was there love and hope in the timbre of that voice? Surely she couldn't be mistaken! Excitement and joy were bright banners streaming through her. The rising wind in her tumbled hair heightened the intensity of her sensations. It was as if she had drunk three tumblers of champagne on an empty stomach.

"Come," McLean said abruptly and led the way back though the brush, splashing across the creek, trotting up to the road. "We'll take our old route by the river now and cross it where it narrows up ahead."

Silence was on them once more until they reached the narrowing portion of the Cooper. A false dawn was beyond the trees, and Savarra could see her companions faintly as they took the stream. It was full from the recent rains, and the lower parts of her dress and petticoats dipped into the water despite her efforts to raise them above the flood. But on the far side, she stopped and wrung the water from them.

Belion said, "We have breeches, shirts and coats for you —boots as well, hidden out in the woods where we shall stop."

"Oh," Cotty sighed with relief, "I'm glad. Dresses are no use at all in these forests."

Savarra asked suddenly, "Are we going to Dunnock's Glen?"

In the darkness beside her, McLean replied, "Yes. We'll eat—then rest there."

"Are the partisans still in Ox Swamp?"

"Nay, Savarra," he laughed. "We're in Kingstree, in respectable quarters. The British have left the backcountry cleanly. You shall have a bed and a few of the civilized niceties to which you are accustomed—until we move on."

When they reached the little dry meadow in the middle of the swamp, the sky was cerulean blue, with every cloud skimmed away by the wind. The December sun shone brightly down upon the travelers as they made camp. It felt deliciously warm across Savarra's shoulders, so much so she removed her cape and flung it over a nearby limb.

Gabe and Thad went to a fallen log and from behind it brought forth a leather bag, handing it to Cotty. " 'Tis riding clothes for you and your mistress, Cotty," Gabe said, his sleepy eyes twinkling. "We'll let you go into the woods a ways an' change."

"Lor' bless me," Cotty cried. "Mistress, let's change right now. My skirts are still wet on my ankles an' nasty cold."

While the men prepared breakfast, the two girls went into the woods. They took the short trail to what seemed to be the same stand of palmettos behind which Savarra had undressed all those months ago.

When they returned, their dresses were neatly folded in the bag, which they filled to bulging capacity. The two girls appeared neat and trim in their breeches, boots and warm woolen jackets.

Breakfast was a cheerful meal, and for the first time in weeks Savarra ate with a building appetite. Color was high in her cool cheeks. She was aware of McLean's eyes on her and once she looked up and met them, to feel her pulses quicken and her blood tingle. She longed as always to touch him, to put her hand in his big browned one, to fling herself into his arms, and she knew those longings were naked in her eyes as she looked away quickly.

"Now we'll sleep before we travel on," McLean said matter-of-factly as they concluded their repast. " 'Tis a long ride to Kingstree."

Each of the men made ready, pulling the long beards of moss from trees, throwing blankets across them and building up the fire, the warmth of which was comforting.

McLean purposefully made two beds a little apart from the others, side by side, and Savarra knew he meant to lie beside her. When she took her place there, she could look across and see his imperious profile. She lay there a long time, too filled with emotion to speak.

At last, when the others seemed to be sleeping soundly, he turned and looked into her wide eyes, his voice low and rough. "You are no hostage, Savarra. We do not hold women hostage in America. It was but a ruse to keep you here."

She sat bolt upright. "A ruse—but why?"

" 'Twas Verity's plan. She wrote to me—implying that you—were unhappy to be leaving, that your heart had become entangled with America. It was her suggestion that I —rescue you from your impending voyage."

That letter Verity had said was to Bowman Baltazar! It had been to Cutler McLean. Savarra felt color flood her face. She had indeed revealed her secret to Verity. "Did she—say anything more?"

"Yes. She said she knew you—loved me." His voice was tentative, doubt creeping in. "I can scarce believe *that*, but if you wanted to stay in America—I owe you my life, too, you know. And I took the most direct means I knew to keep you here."

Savarra was silent. Words were boiling in her, eager in their rush to be spoken, but she rode a tight rein upon them. She looked steadily at the man she had come to love so passionately that she felt herself part of his bones and blood, one with his dreams for his country. At last she said, "Verity is very wise. She knew me better than I knew myself."

"You mean she spoke the truth?"

"Insofar as she knew the truth," she replied cautiously. McLean had *not* said he loved *her*, had not touched on a *legal* relationship.

"Savarra," he said, with that faintly mocking note she knew so well, "there is a minister in Kingstree. It will be months before the British leave Charles Town and," he paused, the gray eyes suddenly hot, "I cannot wait those months to marry you. I cannot be in your presence for the coming months without taking you—by force, if I must. Can you—do you feel the same?"

She looked at him forthrightly. "Are you saying you love me, Cutler?"

"I have loved you from the first moment I held you in my arms on Jed. Nay, since you blew into my arms aboard the *Lion* on our way from England to America—for so long I have forgotten when I realized it."

"Oh, my dear," she whispered, covering the short distance between them, "I have waited so long to hear you say it!" She melted into his arms and he covered her face with kisses, growing more intense with each one.

She felt him tremble as he put her from him. "We must—I must wait. This is not the time—nor the place."

But her hand nestled in his still as she lay back upon the pungent moss beneath her blanket, her fur-lined cloak flung across both of them. Savarra sighed once before sleep took her, for on the periphery of her consciousness lay the knowledge that she was no longer British, though she loved her brave island home. She had become American and her future stretched out in this raw young land, exciting, turbulent, rich in destiny—and with this man beside her, sweet beyond measure.